M000164980

Out of Obscurity

by

Jann Rowland

One Good Sonnet Publishing

By Jann Rowland
Published by One Good Sonnet Publishing:

PRIDE AND PREJUDICE VARIATIONS

Acting on Faith
A Life from the Ashes (**Sequel to** *Acting on Faith*)
Open Your Eyes
Implacable Resentment
An Unlikely Friendship
Bound by Love
Cassandra
Obsession
Shadows Over Longbourn
The Mistress of Longbourn
My Brother's Keeper
Coincidence
The Angel of Longbourn
Chaos Comes to Kent
In the Wilds of Derbyshire
The Companion
Out of Obscurity

Co-Authored with Lelia Eye

Waiting for an Echo Volume One: Words in the Darkness
Waiting for an Echo Volume Two: Echoes at Dawn
Waiting for an Echo Two Volume Set

A Summer in Brighton
A Bevy of Suitors
Love and Laughter: A Pride and Prejudice Short Stories Anthology

THE EARTH AND SKY TRILOGY
Co-Authored with Lelia Eye

On Wings of Air
On Lonely Paths
*On Tides of Fate**

*Forthcoming

This is a work of fiction based on the works of Jane Austen. All the characters and events portrayed in this novel are products of Jane Austen's original novel or the authors' imaginations.

OUT OF OBSCURITY

Copyright © 2017 Jann Rowland

Cover Design by Marina Willis

Published by One Good Sonnet Publishing

All rights reserved.

ISBN: 1987929748
ISBN-13: 9781987929744

No part of this book may be reproduced or transmitted in any form or by any means, electronic, digital, or mechanical, including photocopying, recording, or by any information storage and retrieval system, without permission in writing from the publisher.

To my family who have, as always, shown
their unconditional love and encouragement.

PROLOGUE

Thursday, February 6, 1812
Davidson Townhouse, London

*S*ociety had never been comfortable for Fitzwilliam Darcy. Though he had often told others that he had difficulty catching the tone of conversation, of appearing interested in their concerns, the truth was that his opinion of society was poor, and he had little appetite for being agreeable to those he did not even like.

The season was, Darcy thought, a time for London society to gather and attempt to outdo one another with opulent parties and decadent balls, where propriety was often shunted aside in favor of hedonistic pleasures. Though such behavior was not confined to the highest circles, and he knew to paint all with the same brush was incorrect, it often seemed like those of high society were more prone to it. It was little wonder, in his mind, that the peasantry of France had tired of the aristocratic excesses and had risen up against them. At times, Darcy wondered why that particular cancer had not spread to England and other countries.

This harsh opinion was often decried by his friends and family. His cousin, Colonel Fitzwilliam claimed that there were relatively few who descended to such depraved depths. Darcy could not argue otherwise, for he knew his cousin was correct. But that did not eliminate his distaste for most society, for in any guest list, there was almost always someone he found objectionable. Invariably, those persons would attach themselves to his side, eager for an acquaintance with the Darcy of Pemberley or the loftier connection to his uncle, the earl.

It was in the company of good friends and acquaintances where Darcy was able to feel most at ease, and if he could not get that — which was often — Darcy usually chose to attend those events which he knew were given by those of good character. At least there he knew the entertainments would be acceptable and the general behavior would not be degenerate.

On a night in February, still early in the season, Darcy was invited to a dinner given by an acquaintance of his friend, Charles Bingley. Or perhaps his former friend — Darcy hardly knew at present. He was grateful for the fact that Bingley and his sisters — especially the younger — were absent, for if they had been in attendance, Darcy would have been obliged to decline. As it was, though Davidson was, like Bingley, a man who had risen from his family's roots in trade, Darcy knew that he was a good man and that he would only invite those of the highest character.

There were more than thirty people in attendance. Darcy thought he had been introduced to them all, but he did not have a head for remembering names, and he spent the evening speaking to several others who he knew would not become closer acquaintances. But because they were good people, he was able to tolerate the conversations, whereas he was less able to converse with most earls with any equanimity.

Throughout the evening, one young woman had caught his eye. She was pretty and petite, her long mahogany locks tied up in an elegant knot, her eyes dark and mysterious. But it was not the young lady's looks which drew his attention, nor was it her conversation, though he thought she was quite intelligent, regardless of his not having spoken with her. Rather, there was something about her which drew his notice, something he could not quite define. Was it an echo of something else, a sense of understanding or magnetism which drew him? Darcy could not be certain.

As the night continued, they sat down to dinner, and Darcy was situated several places down from her on the opposite side of the table. The young lady appeared calm and composed and comfortable in this society, suggesting she was not some new debutante or shy as a mouse like his younger sister. But there seemed to be an aura of . . . melancholy about her, which her bright responses and ready wit did not quite dispel.

After dinner, Darcy stayed in the dining room with the other men, indulging in conversation and port, but though he spoke as much as he ever did, his heart was not in what he did force himself to say, and his thoughts kept returning to the young woman he had seen. He did not wish to be perceived as overtly interested in her—at a gathering such as this, he suspected that she was of the lower gentry, at best, and it would not do to raise hopes of an alliance with one such as he. Darcy knew his duty to his family and his position in society, neither of which would be satisfied by a young woman who was not of the right standing.

But there continued to be something about her that drew his attention, and he could not quite make out what it was. Darcy found it quite maddening. Usually, a little thought on such matters would yield an answer, whatever it was. In this instance, he remained uncertain.

At length, the gentlemen rejoined the ladies, and Darcy once again found himself in the same room as the siren. Many of the gentlemen approached ladies, and Darcy thought those who were still single congregated around the young woman of the fine, dark eyes. She smiled and spoke with them all, but she still carried herself with a sense of reserve, holding back her true self from them. It was a desire Darcy could easily understand, as he had often found himself engaged in similar behavior.

A little later, the pianoforte was opened, and the mistress of the house obliged the company with a rousing song, one which was received well by all. Darcy clapped dutifully along with the rest, though he confessed to himself he had hardly heard a note. He was too occupied by wondering if the young lady who had caught his attention would take the opportunity to display her talents. That question was answered when Darcy, who was seated nearby, heard a discussion between the young woman and an older lady with whom she attended.

"Shall you not play for the company, Lizzy?"

"I think there are many who are far more skilled than I, Aunt."

"Perhaps there are. But there are few who sing as beautifully as you do. I would be very happy if you displayed your talents. It is possible one of these fine men will take a liking to you."

The words were a warning of possible mercenary tendencies, or they would have been, had the elder woman not said them in a teasing tone. The young woman turned a playful glare on the other and replied:

"Oh, Aunt, I would not wish for such a thing. I could never accept such attentions, as you well know."

"Nonsense, Lizzy. You have as much to offer a man as any woman."

But Lizzy only shook her head. "At present, I do not wish to think of it. But if you wish, I will perform, if only to make you happy."

"I do wish it."

It was decided, and after several other young ladies took their turns, the young woman rose to oblige the company.

Darcy did not consider himself to be a connoisseur of music, and he was no expert in evaluating the talents of others. But he quickly found that the older lady's assertions were no less than the truth. Perhaps this Lizzy's playing was not quite capital, for even Darcy was able to hear more than one error in her playing. But her voice was that of an angel, and she sang a song of such longing and loss as to bring a lump to one's throat and tears to one's eyes. The loud and enthusiastic applause she received when her song was finished was well earned in Darcy's estimation.

When she rose from the pianoforte, she turned to acknowledge the company, and whether it was a trick of the light or the angle to which her countenance was presented to him, Darcy felt a shock of recognition race through him. He was not certain how or why, but this young woman was familiar to him.

CHAPTER I

Tuesday, May 21, 1793
Undisclosed Location

"*S*he has done *what*?"

"It is true," said the man, unaffected by the sudden show of displeasure. "The change was filed on Wednesday last and included in the document at that time. It is now in force to the exclusion of all previous documents."

"Is *this* what I pay you for?" was the man's snarling reply. "How could you have allowed this to happen?"

A disdainful sniff preceded an arrogant reply: "You know well that I have no influence in such matters. You pay me for information only. I was fortunate to be in a position to gather as much as I was able, for she is not my client."

"Then it appears your usefulness to me is less than I had thought possible."

"Perhaps it is. In that case, I am happy to terminate our arrangement. In fact, I am sorry that I ever agreed to enter into it."

"Get out! Do not expect another payment from me."

"With pleasure, sir."

Caught up in his fuming as he was, he did not even see the other man he had hired leave. It appeared it was well that he had thought to watch her, regardless of what he had said to his informant. It appeared her words concerning the way he lived his life were more than empty admonishments if she could betray him in such a way.

The question was, what should be done about it. Though he took very little interest in matters of estates or inheritances—though he owned one himself—this could not go without response. His predilections took him down different routes, where he was the hunter of his prey, divesting them of their money with the skill of a lion bringing down its next meal. Yes, a hunter he was.

The hunter thought on the matter for some more moments. The estate fueled his needs and allowed him to live his life as he wished, but that did not mean more ready capital was not desirable. With her money, he would be allowed to join games of the highest stakes, to put his skills to the ultimate test.

It was clear this could not be allowed to stand. And so, the hunter rang the bell, calling for his man. Something must be done.

Thursday, February 6, 1812
Davidson Townhouse, London

The shock of recognition was such that Darcy was certain the entire company must have been aware of the moment it struck him. Darcy was well known for his ability to remain inscrutable, regardless of the circumstances, but his reaction had seemed open, obvious to anyone who was watching. But no one paid him any special heed, leading Darcy to believe he had managed to control his outward reaction.

If his initial surprise due to the sudden familiarity had not been obvious, Darcy thought that his increased scrutiny of the young woman surely must draw attention. Gentlemen came and went, their conversations little heard, and ladies approached him, attempting to gain his favor with fluttering eyelashes and coquettish statements. He had no attention for any of them and little for anything other than the dark-eyed beauty who had seemed familiar to him. At times, his study of her was of such intensity he thought it unlikely it could remain unnoticed. Whether it was, Darcy knew not, but he was at least happy that no one called him on it, and to the best of his knowledge, there were no rumors making their way about the room on whispered wings.

In addition to the young woman's aunt, another man was often in her company, and his age and the familiarity with her and the older woman suggested that he was an uncle, likely married to the other woman. Darcy's inspection of them revealed them to be a handsome couple, both likely no more than ten years Darcy's senior. They were fashionably dressed, though their raiment was not opulent, suggesting gentry, or perhaps a tradesman. If the man was a tradesman, he was not one who was afflicted by the need to dress in gaudy finery to try to pass himself off as a gentleman.

"Darcy," said a voice, interrupting his contemplation of the young lady. A man approached him, an acquaintance of his by the name of Grant.

Darcy greeted him, attempting to give the man more of his attention than he had to those who had approached him previously. "Grant. How are you this evening?"

"Tolerable, I suppose, but there is much to be desired in this company, though Davidson is a good sort."

Darcy smiled but did not nod. Grant was not of the first circles, but his position was higher than most in this company could boast. Though many called Darcy fastidious, it was actually Grant to whom the description could more accurately be ascribed.

"They are at least unpretentious, which must be in their favor," replied Darcy after a moment.

"I suppose you are correct." It was an irony, but Grant considered himself to be a liberal man, treating all men as equals. In truth, he was often as close-minded as anyone Darcy had ever met.

"I am surprised to see you here without that Bingley chap," said Grant, and this time the shade in his voice suggested contempt. "He is amusing enough, but it seems he has often clung to your coattails."

In fact, Darcy thought Grant liked Bingley well enough, but at the oddest times — and Grant was an odd creature, indeed — his prejudices would escape whatever control he applied to them. Now was one such time.

"I have not seen Bingley for some weeks," replied Darcy, not really wishing to speak of his friend. "I believe he is still in the north, though I expect he will return to London before the end of the season."

"Of *that*, there can be no doubt." This time the distaste in Grant's tone was beyond dispute. "That harpy of a sister of his will surely not tolerate his absence from London for the season. I expect she will be back here, spinning her webs to capture some unwary insect."

"Of that, we can agree," replied Darcy. His opinion of Miss Bingley was no higher than Grant's.

"Only ensure *you* are not the insect she catches. Most of her snares are aimed at you, old boy."

"And well I know it," replied Darcy. He did not wish to continue to discuss such an objectionable subject, so he changed it. "How is your father? I understand he was doing poorly at Christmastide."

"He is much better now, more is the pity," said Grant, his jaw working in his annoyance. "You do not know what a boon it is to possess your own estate free and clear. My father might as well be a Quaker, for he lives like one. If only he would do me the favor of joining my mother, I would be well pleased."

The question Darcy had asked Grant had been by design. Almost every time they met, Grant had some complaint to make about his father or the meddling in his life he endured. Grant could talk on the matter for hours, never requiring a response, and since he was thus engaged, Darcy could avoid the approach of anyone else and concentrate his attention on the young lady he was trying to puzzle out.

So it went throughout the evening. Darcy continued to watch her, but the reason for her familiarity remained stubbornly out of reach. The more he watched her, the more he became aware that she reminded him of someone. But who?

Late in the evening, as the party was on the verge of breaking up, Darcy happened to be standing near to "Lizzy," and he was captivated by the way her eyes danced as she smiled and bantered with a young man with whom Darcy was only a little acquainted. When she laughed out loud, the sweet, clear sound rang like a bell in Darcy's mind, clearing the detritus away and chiming together with many memories, combining with them as if they had always belonged.

And he knew. He knew of whom she reminded him and knew that the possible ramifications of such a discovery were profound. It would rock his family—and possibly society—to the core if he was correct. But could it possibly be true, and after so many years?

While Darcy was caught up in his sudden conviction of his epiphany, he almost missed the young woman's departure from the company with her uncle and aunt. Indeed, they had departed from the room to seek their outerwear while he had been distracted, and he knew he probably only had moments before they left altogether.

Quickly, Darcy surged into motion, weaving his way through those who were still present, determined to stop Lizzy and her party from departing before he could speak to them. But luck was not on his side that evening, for he was delayed by his host, who hailed him and stepped in his path.

"Darcy! I had wished to speak with you tonight."

"A moment, if you will," said Darcy, stepping around his friend and hurrying to the door.

He sped down the long hall outside the sitting-room where they were all gathered and into the entry hall. The butler, who was just entering from the coldness of the February night, was surprised to see him and was only a few hand-widths away from being bowled over. Darcy called an apology as he went to the doors and stepped outside.

The carriage was still on the drive and through a window, he could see the young woman. She met his eyes for an instant, and Darcy was more certain than ever that his supposition was correct. But then the carriage lurched into motion, and though Darcy stepped forward in an attempt to gain their attention, it soon entered the street and began to pull away from the house. Darcy stood and watched it go, looking for some identifying markings which would inform him of who rode within. But there was nothing.

"I say, Darcy, I have never seen you move so quickly as you did tonight. Why did you rush from the sitting-room to chase out here into the chill of the night?"

Darcy turned and noted his friend Davidson watching him, and another thought entered his head. As the couple and their niece had been invited to Davidson's party, he would know who they were, and even if he did not, his wife would, as she would have dispatched the invitation.

"The couple that just left — who are they?"

It was clear Davidson was taken aback by Darcy's sudden question. "You wish to know of one of my guests?"

"I do," said Darcy. "It is a private matter, but I would appreciate it if you could direct me."

Davidson looked at him as if he was uncertain of his motives, but soon he shivered and looked around, noting the night and the coldness of the air. He beckoned to Darcy, stepping back into the house.

"Let us speak of it inside, Darcy. I have no wish to remain out in the cold."

Though he had not been aware of it due to his focus on the young woman and her family, Darcy realized that clad in naught but a suit, it was, indeed, frigid, and he accepted, though not without a hint of impatience. He followed his host inside, noting the look of displeasure with which the butler regarded him as he closed the door behind them. Darcy did not pay any attention to the man — he was too interested in what Davidson would tell him.

"I might wonder why you wish for their direction, Darcy," said Davidson once they began to make their way back to the sitting-room. "You had ample enough opportunity to make their acquaintance throughout the evening. Why did you not approach me for an introduction before they departed?"

It was a fair assessment, though Darcy did not wish to speak of the matter. Thus, he only replied, saying: "At the time, I did not know I wanted an introduction. Now I would appreciate it."

Davidson frowned. "What changed to make an acquaintance so desirable?"

"I am afraid I am not at liberty to say," said Darcy, truthfully. "I noticed something about them which makes it necessary for me to be known to them. It is a matter to do with my uncle, the earl."

It was clear that Davidson did not understand. Moreover, he was skeptical of Darcy's explanation, as well he should be. Though Darcy knew it would be easier to simply state his reason, he did not wish his errand with the young lady to be known, especially in case he was wrong in his suspicions. It was fortunate that Davidson was a good man and one who knew him well.

"I will tell you, Darcy, though I believe I probably should not, and only because I know your character is beyond reproach. Please do not betray my willingness to oblige you with anything underhanded."

Had it not been for the situation and his understanding that he was making an impertinent request of his friend, Darcy might have been angry with the man for questioning his character. As it was, he knew Davidson was not questioning him, but only reminding him of the proprieties of the situation.

"Of course, my friend. My errand with them is of a delicate variety. I have no intention of making impertinent inquiries or any other such mischief."

"I know you are not, Darcy. But I should not give you this information. Instead, I should arrange to introduce you myself." Davidson waved off Darcy's protests. "I know you understand all this and it seems, as you have stated, that your errand is a sensitive one, so I will give you what you ask. The man's name is Mr. Edward Gardiner, and his address is on Gracechurch Street, not far from Cheapside."

The way Davidson watched Darcy as he imparted this information suggested he was waiting for Darcy's response and expected it to be negative. Darcy, therefore, kept his expression bland, but his manner interested. Davidson nodded once and motioned Darcy down the hall toward his study.

"Then come with me, Darcy. I have Mr. Gardiner's direction. I would be happy to write it out for you."

Grateful for his friend's willingness to assist, Darcy followed him to his study, and soon he had the directions in hand. Darcy was not familiar with that part of town, but the directions were straightforward and the location of the house should be easy to find.

"Thank you, my friend," said Darcy when he had the card in hand. "Now, if you will excuse me, I believe I will return to my home."

"But I had a matter of which I would like to speak to you."

"Is it urgent?" asked Darcy. He truly had little desire to offend his friend, but with his mind so full of what he had discovered, he did not think he would do a discussion any justice at present.

With a shaken head and a rueful smile, Davidson said: "It is clear there is little to be gained from pressing you to remain. No, it is not urgent."

"Then I hope you will forgive me if I depart. Send your card around at any time and I will be happy to receive you. Or, I could return at a later date."

"I will visit you, Darcy," replied Davidson. "I hope that someday you will be at liberty to inform me as to what the blazes your behavior tonight has been about. But for the nonce, I shall be patient."

"I appreciate that, Davidson."

Darcy shook his friend's hand and then made his way back to the front door to call for his carriage. The butler, it appeared, was still not amused by his previous venture into the dark of the night, but like a good servant, he called for Darcy's carriage and assisted him with his coat. Within a few moments, Darcy's conveyance had arrived and he was ensconced within it, on his way back toward his house. In his pocket, Darcy fancied he could feel the heat of the slip of paper, wondered if it might burn a hole through the fabric. Now that he had it, he wondered what he should do with it. There was nothing about this situation which was easy or straightforward.

Thursday, February 6, 1812
Gardiner Townhouse, London

"Uncle! That man is trying to stop the coach."

"Let him be, Elizabeth." Mr. Gardiner turned a stern eye on his niece, Elizabeth Bennet. "You are not acquainted with him, are you?"

Feeling the heat in her cheeks, Elizabeth could only shake her head.

A memory returned to her a moment later and prompted her to say: "I do recall him watching me at times during the evening."

"But he was never introduced to you?"

Elizabeth shook her head. "No, Uncle. There were times I thought he might approach, but he never did. He seemed to be a man of position in society, I thought."

"By his dress alone, he was obviously so." Mr. Gardiner paused and assumed his stern visage again. "I am not certain what a man who chases after a carriage carrying people with whom he is not acquainted can mean by it, but I doubt it can be good. You know you must take care in your situation, Lizzy—there are many men who would offer unspeakable things to you if they were aware."

"I cannot think he was that kind of man!" cried Elizabeth. "He seemed quiet and introspective, but I could detect no hint of depravity."

"That was what you thought in Meryton, did you not?" asked her uncle.

A thrill of fear and sadness passed through Elizabeth, and she hung her head, unpleasant memories flooding her consciousness.

"Lizzy," said her Aunt Gardiner, her tone softer than her husband's, "your uncle only means for you to be kept safe. He is correct: you must take great care, for your situation will make you a target."

"I understand," replied Elizabeth, though much subdued. She darted a glance at her uncle. "But I could hardly suppose that he meant to . . . *importune* me in the presence of my guardian."

Mr. Gardiner sighed. "No, Lizzy, I do not suppose you are incorrect, and I have no notion at all that your admirer is anything other than what he seems to be. But I will not take any chances with your safety, my dear. Running after our carriage when we are leaving a party, and after he could have requested an introduction at any time during the evening, is not behavior with which I am comfortable. If a man wishes to be known to you, he must ask for an introduction properly, not go haring off after a moving carriage."

"As he was at the Davidsons' party, he might still seek us out," said Aunt Gardiner.

"That is a possibility," grunted Uncle Gardiner. "I do hope Davidson has the sense to send him to *me* if that is the case, rather than to the townhouse."

"I am certain he does. If he does not, then I am certain Cecilia will set him straight."

Mr. Gardiner nodded, though distracted, and they fell silent. No one spoke again during their journey back to Gracechurch Street, and soon they had arrived and disembarked at her uncle's house. Mr. Gardiner immediately bid them good night and retired to the chambers he shared with her aunt, but before Elizabeth could likewise escape, Mrs. Gardiner shot her a meaningful glance and made her way to her own dressing room.

Sighing, and knowing her aunt would soon join her in her room, Elizabeth made her way thither, divesting herself of her dress and other accoutrements, slipping into a thick nightgown to ward off the chill of the night, and covering herself additionally with a robe. Then knowing her aunt would be with her shortly, Elizabeth sat on her bed, the light of the candle on her bedside table flickering, drawing patterns along the walls and floor. It was many minutes before her aunt joined her, and she sat almost unmoving, thinking with morose acceptance of her situation.

When her aunt entered the room, she found Elizabeth in this attitude, and she immediately came to Elizabeth's bed and put her arm around her shoulders. It was nearly enough to prompt Elizabeth to cry — her own mother had never, in her memory, acted in such a way to provide comfort. Since the events in Hertfordshire and her subsequent coming to London, she was not even certain what she could claim of those at Longbourn any longer.

"My uncle has been . . . strict since my coming to London," said Elizabeth when her aunt did not immediately speak. "I have never seen this side of him before. Is it because—"

"No!" replied her aunt, her tone gentle but unyielding. "I am surprised you would think such a thing, Lizzy."

"It is difficult not to, Aunt," replied Elizabeth, turning to meet her aunt's eyes. Within her breast, she felt a hint of her old indomitable will rise, a sensation which had been missing these past weeks. "He is not the same as he used to be."

"No, Lizzy, he is not. But you must not think that he is in any way changed toward you. He loves you as much as he ever did. But he worries for you and that causes him to be stern."

"He does not need to be," said Elizabeth, feeling a little cross. "I am well aware of my situation. He does not need to remind me."

Mrs. Gardiner sighed. "You must allow us our worries, Lizzy. Given what happened at Longbourn, it is unlikely you will return there. The question then becomes where you will go and how you will live."

"I will obtain a position if I must," averred Elizabeth. By now she was beginning to feel more than a little cross at hearing her aunt continually refer to the state of her life. She did not feel it was required. She was an intelligent woman and she well understood the ramifications of what had happened to her.

"And how will you do that?" asked her aunt, and Elizabeth could tell that she was beginning to feel vexation in return. "Lizzy, I know you are well read and intelligent, but you do not have a formal education, and that is prized by those looking for governesses or even companions."

Mrs. Gardiner held up her hand when Elizabeth began to retort angrily. "I do not say this to criticize. It is a fact. You may say that does not preclude you from finding a position, and you would be correct. But it will prevent you from applying successfully for the best positions. Furthermore, you are aware that there are *other* considerations which will make it difficult for you."

The defiance bled from Elizabeth's mind, and she turned a miserable stare on the far wall. Her aunt was not incorrect.

"Lizzy, we do not wish for you to be put in such circumstances as to require a position. You are too intelligent, too good to live such a life."

"Can I expect anything more?" asked Elizabeth, attempting to keep the bitterness from her voice.

"I believe you can." Her aunt smiled at her and laid her hand on Elizabeth's arm while rising to her feet. "There is nothing wrong with going into service, Lizzy—of course, there are drawbacks, but it is entirely respectable. But your uncle and I wish for more for you. It is possible that given enough time, we might be able to find you a man who is willing to overlook the obstacles in favor of the advantages, which, as you know, would include your person, your intelligence, and your love of life. I think you have not given up all hope of making a good marriage."

"No, I have not," replied Elizabeth. "Though I wonder at times if I am being practical."

"Hope is never lost, Lizzy, until you abandon it. You have only been with us a short time. There is no rush, for your uncle and I are quite happy to have you here with us. In time, I suspect all will be well."

Having said that, her aunt leaned over, kissed the crown of Elizabeth's head, and after bidding her a good night, left the room. Left with her own thoughts, Elizabeth hardly noted the passage of time as she considered her aunt's words. She had always had a positive outlook on life. But at present, she was finding her previous confidence to be elusive.

CHAPTER II

Wednesday, February 12, 1812
Darcy House, London

At times over the next several days, Darcy *did* have the impression the card Davidson had given him was always burning, never incinerated. The more he thought on the matter, the more he wondered if he could possibly be correct about his suspicions, and he could not determine if pursuing the young woman was the best possible course.

The matter was an old one—nearly twenty years, in fact. He had been naught but a boy when it had happened, such that his memories of that time were more than a little imprecise. What he did recall was the crying, the desolation, the desperate yearning for news—any news—which was not destined to come.

What would happen if he was incorrect? It would no doubt dredge up old memories better forgotten, reopen half-healed wounds which would bleed anew, to say nothing of the anguish of hope dashed again. It had not been spoken of in many years, and though it was not forgotten, he firmly believed those most affected preferred to remember in silence, not even speaking of the matter between themselves. Of course, if he was right in his suspicions . . .

It was that final thought which convinced Darcy he had to act, but he must do so carefully. Considering the situation, he could not speak to his aunt or uncle, and his cousins also could not be approached. The burden of the initial investigation must fall on Darcy's shoulders. Should he be completely wrong, then it would be discovered quickly, and he would only have the mortification of knowing his memories and impressions were incorrect without opening old scars and forcing them to heal again. But if he was at all correct, the happiness it would bring about was worth the possible embarrassment he might suffer himself.

In preparation, Darcy engaged an investigator to inform him of these Gardiners and their niece. The man was back with a preliminary report within two days of being retained.

"Mr. Edward Gardiner," intoned the investigator, reading his information off some sheets of paper he had brought with him. "Mr. Gardiner is seven and thirty years of age. He has been married to Madeline Gardiner for ten years — she is one and thirty. The couple has four children — two girls and two boys — aged from eight to two.

"Mr. Gardiner is a self-made man of trade whose primary business is the importing of goods from the Orient, though he has some contacts on the continent who provide him with goods as well. He is involved in several other lines of business and invests heavily in speculative stocks and bonds, and particularly in new inventions. He is well connected to certain members of the upper classes, advising them in their own investments, and though his connections do not, for the most part, extend to the nobility, he has a good reputation as being astute, intelligent, honest, and fair."

The investigator looked up at Darcy. "Of interest to you, in particular, Mr. Darcy, is that Mrs. Gardiner's maiden name is Plumber, a name with which I believe you are familiar."

Darcy frowned. "I believe Mr. Andrew Plumber was the rector of the church in Lambton until some years back."

"That is correct, sir. Mr. Plumber was the third son of a landowner, which means that Mrs. Gardiner's uncle is, himself, a gentleman. This is likely where Mr. Gardiner was able to make his initial contacts with the gentry. His own reputation has grown from there. This is only an estimate, you understand, but it is believed that Mr. Gardiner's income is in excess of five thousand per year."

Darcy nodded, though distractedly. "That is a goodly sum — more than a great many gentlemen."

"Yes, it is, sir. The address you gave me is his primary residence and is, as you say, not far from Cheapside. By all accounts, it is a fine home, well maintained and situated close to Mr. Gardiner's place of business and warehouses. Given what I was able to uncover, Mr. Gardiner could afford to live in a better neighborhood if he chose, but he finds the location convenient and the house in which he and his wife live to be comfortable.

"As for Mr. Gardiner's other connections, he has two sisters, both living in Hertfordshire, one in the village of Meryton, which is about an equal distance south between Luton and Stevenage, while the other lives just north and west of the town. His eldest sister is wife to a solicitor in Meryton by the name of Phillips—the man inherited the practice from her father when Mr. Gardiner declined to follow his father into the law. The younger sister—Mr. Gardiner is the youngest sibling—married the master of a small estate, a Mr. Henry Bennet, which yields about two thousand five hundred per annum. The elder sister is childless, but the younger has birthed five daughters. As there is no heir, the estate is entailed on a distant cousin who is, apparently, a parson in Kent."

That was promising—Lizzy would have had to have been raised as the daughter of the gentleman, as the elder sister had no children. Darcy was certain Lizzy must come from Mr. Gardiner's relations—Darcy was dimly aware of a family by the name of Plumber amongst the gentry—they had an estate in Suffolk unless he was mistaken, a property which, though not one of the great estates, still brought in a respectable income. Darcy could not remember precisely how a younger Mr. Plumber had been appointed to the living at Lambton—it was likely that Darcy's grandfather had known his father and had given the living to him as a favor.

"That is my initial report, sir," said the investigator. "If you wish me to delve into more details of the man, I can do that for you, but it will take more time. How would you like me to proceed?"

Though Darcy thought about it for a moment and was tempted to unleash the man further upon Mr. Gardiner, he knew it was now to a point where he should assume the burden of it himself. The decision made, he informed the investigator and thanked him for his diligence.

"It is no trouble, sir. If you wish me to take up the investigation again, please inform me, and I shall be happy to do so. I will keep the information I have unearthed on file."

"Thank you," said Darcy, calling for his butler to have the investigator shown out.

It was the work of a moment to decide that he would visit Mr. Gardiner the next day, and the rest of the day was spent thinking about how he would go about it, and what he would say to the man. Darcy was a private man, one who was quiet and reticent, even among his own family and friends of many years. But he was not aware he was so taciturn that night until his sister spoke to him of his distraction.

"You have been quiet of late, Brother," said Georgiana after the unusually quiet dinner, startling him out of his reverie. "I hope all is well?"

In the past, Darcy might have simply informed his sister that nothing was the matter and changed the subject. But since the previous summer, Georgiana had been at first miserable due to the actions of a certain libertine, and since her recovery, more than a little hesitant. Thus, he had learned to take a different approach with her.

"All is well, Georgiana," replied Darcy, favoring her with a smile. "I have had some matters on my mind of late, but they are simply matters of business and nothing for which you should be concerned."

Georgiana watched him for a moment, an action which broke Darcy's heart, before she responded. "That is good, then."

She had concluded that Darcy was angry and disappointed with her because of what had almost happened with the accursed Wickham, and no amount of protestations to the contrary were enough to convince her.

"Do not concern yourself, my dear. If I thought your opinion would assist, I would ask. But in this case, I am not yet at liberty to speak of it."

A hint of shock appeared on her countenance, but it was soon replaced by a—tentative—pleasure. It had been a hard road, once again attempting to build up her confidence and sense of worth. Georgiana was aware that few men would consult their young sisters on matters of business, but Darcy had made it a point in recent months.

"How are your studies?"

Georgiana blushed. "They are proceeding well. I still do not have any knack for languages, but Mrs. Annesley is happy with my other accomplishments."

And an agreeable evening was spent speaking with her about the little doings of her life of late. Darcy pushed thoughts of the young lady and her uncle to the back of his mind. At present, it was more important to give the entirety of his attention to his sister.

* * *

Thursday, February 13, 1812
Gardiner Imports, London

The residence and offices of Mr. Gardiner were, indeed, impressive. The house was clearly not immense, but it boasted a small stable around the back which housed the man's carriage and horses. The brick façade was well maintained and handsome, and the house through the windows appeared to have the touch that only a woman could provide. It was clearly the house of a man of some affluence, one who took pride in his possessions and worked hard to ensure his family was given the best possible life.

Equally impressive were Mr. Gardiner's warehouses. They were large and teemed with activity, and for a few moments Darcy sat in his carriage, watching as a shipment was efficiently unloaded from a pair of wagons and transferred into the building by a team of industrious workers who were, themselves, burly men, but clearly men of character, as evidenced by their clean clothes and groomed appearances. The man's offices were situated in a small area on the front of the building, complete with windows to allow the weak light of the February sun to flow inside.

Knowing he was only putting off the inevitable, Darcy alighted from the carriage and informed his driver to return for him in an hour before crossing the street and entering the building. The interior was, as Darcy had expected, laid out in a neat and orderly fashion, with a pair of clerks situated near the front door and several other men moving about the area in a purposeful fashion. On the far side of the room stood a door which Darcy suspected led to the warehouses, and every few moments someone walked through those doors, either to speak to the clerks or someone else in the office. And in the far corner, in an area cut off from the rest of the office by several bookcases and other necessary office furniture, sat the man he had seen at the party a few days previously.

"Can I help you, sir?" asked one of the clerks as he noted Darcy's entry.

"I am here to see Mr. Gardiner," said Darcy, producing a card from his pocket and handing it to the clerk. "My name is Fitzwilliam Darcy."

The clerk frowned. "Do you have an appointment?"

"I do not, but I hope Mr. Gardiner will consent to see me nevertheless. If it is an inconvenient time, I will return whenever convenient for Mr. Gardiner."

As if weighing the matter, the clerk looked back and forth between

Darcy and the card in his hand. In the end, Darcy thought it was his dress and bearing, which he knew marked him as a gentleman, which settled the man's mind. "If you will wait for a moment, I will see if Mr. Gardiner will see you. Might I ask you what is your business?"

"It is a private and personal matter," said Darcy.

The clerk pursed his lips as if annoyed, but he nodded and stepped away to speak to his employer. Though the offices were not especially large, Mr. Gardiner's room was closed off enough that Darcy could not hear the conversation. Nothing more than a murmur of voices reached Darcy's ears, although he did note when Mr. Gardiner looked at him as if attempting to discern his purpose from where he sat. He made a brief comment to the clerk, who then returned to where Darcy was waiting and gestured toward the office.

"Mr. Gardiner is available to see you, sir, if you will step this way."

Darcy did so gratefully and with a quietly spoken word of thanks, and in a short time, he was shown into the office. It was, like that of most men of business, a space which boasted bookcases and shelves, books of business and ledger. Additionally, there was a sturdy oak desk facing the entrance with two chairs situated in front of it. Mr. Gardiner rose as Darcy walked into the room, extending his hand, which Darcy did not hesitate to grasp.

"Welcome, Mr. Darcy." Then he turned to the clerk. "A pot of tea with two cups if you would, Travers."

The man bowed and departed, leaving Darcy alone with Mr. Gardiner. The man gestured to a chair, taking his own.

"I have wondered if you would come, sir, though I will own that I have not the slightest idea of your interest in me. Or perhaps should I say in my niece?"

"You noted my observation at Davidson's?"

"I did. Of more importance, Elizabeth did, as she did your exit from the house as my carriage was departing."

"I apologize for that, Mr. Gardiner," said Darcy. "I should have considered my actions more carefully. As it was, I was startled by what I believed I had discovered and did not stop to think of how my actions might be perceived."

Mr. Gardiner did not immediately respond—rather he inspected Darcy, his gaze steady, though it was not accusatory or negative in any way. "I believe no harm was done, sir. Perhaps you might come to the point concerning why you are here and what you believe you have discovered?"

The tea arrived at that moment, and the clerk set it upon the desk before turning to leave. As he was departing, Mr. Gardiner spoke up, saying: "Please ensure we are not disturbed for the next half hour, Travers."

Though mystified, the clerk nodded, and soon the two men were left alone. Mr. Gardiner asked after Darcy's preferences, and Darcy replied, though he was not at all certain he wished to partake. A few moments later they had their teacups in hand, and Mr. Gardiner turned an expectant look on him.

For a moment, Darcy was not certain what to say. His purpose was clear, but he had not thought about how he would present his suspicions to this man. It was quite possible he would think Darcy mad after he began, but as there was only one way to discover it, Darcy forced himself to speak.

"You have my apologies if I am in any way impertinent or if my words seem like naught but madness, but I have come to inquire after your niece. Before we get into any of the particulars, however, I should ask after the crux of the matter, for if you answer my question in the negative, there is nothing more to be said." Darcy paused for a moment and then, drawing on his courage, looked the other man in the eye. "Your niece, Miss Elizabeth—can you tell me, sir, if she is a blood relation?"

Mr. Gardiner did not react at all—rather his gaze remained steady and calm. This was the foundation of the shrewd man of business, Darcy thought; a man who could control his emotions regardless of the situation would have an advantage over other men when pursuing negotiations.

"You think she is not?" asked Mr. Gardiner quietly.

Though Darcy did not appreciate the other man's tactics, the response told him much. "I suspect she is not, sir. I watched her at Davidson's party because I believed I recognized her and could not understand why. It became apparent, later, when certain of her mannerisms told me that she is, in my opinion, likely the daughter of my aunt, sister to my close cousins."

Wednesday, June 12, 1793
Undisclosed Location

"I care not how difficult it will be. You will arrange for the girl to disappear, or I will find someone who will."

The harshness in his voice appeared to take his man by surprise. The hunter had no concern for the man's qualms. He had thought on this matter, seemingly from sunrise to sunset, every day since he had learned of it and had whipped himself into such a frenzy at times that he had thought he might go mad from the utter fury he felt. It could not be allowed!

His man, Sykes, seemed to consider it for several moments before he replied. But the hunter did not miss how closely his man watched him.

"It can be done," he finally allowed.

"How quickly?"

"It is difficult to abduct a normal child, let alone this one. If I do this, I want a sum of money paid directly to me, after which I will retire from your service."

The hunter nodded. "Very well. Plan carefully, for it will not do for you to be caught in the attempt. But do not take too long—I wish for this situation to be dealt with as soon as may be."

Thursday, February 13, 1812
Gardiner Imports, London

The inscrutability of the other man never wavered for several moments after Darcy's announcement, but he did not say anything, determined that the next move belonged to Mr. Gardiner. At length, Mr. Gardiner sighed and leaned back in his chair, his hand going to his teacup which he raised, in a distracted manner, to his lips.

"If you had come to me, Mr. Darcy, before Christmas, I would have thought you daft. Now, however, I wonder at the impossibility of this situation."

Darcy leaned forward. "Are you informing me she is not your brother's daughter?"

"It appears that she is not, though I never knew it throughout the whole course of her childhood." A ghost of a smile found Mr. Gardiner's lips. "Elizabeth has always been our favorite niece, along with her sister Jane, and she has spent at least one or two months with us every year since she turned thirteen years old. But it was not until recently we discovered that she is not my brother's true daughter. From what I understand, they never had any notion of her origins, for she came to live with them when she was naught but two years of age."

It was amazing how he had come to Mr. Gardiner, suspicion alight in his mind and heart, and yet, when the man confirmed that the woman Darcy had suspected connected to him through his uncle and aunt, he almost felt shocked in return.

"What can you tell me of her history?" asked Darcy, as much in an effort to recover from the shock as from a desire to know.

"Not much, unfortunately. My brother, when I was made aware of this, was not able to tell me from whence she had come. Henry, my brother Bennet, is actually a second son, who inherited after his brother's untimely death about fifteen years ago. At the time, he and my sister were living in Cambridge, where Bennet was a professor at the university. Their eldest daughter, Jane, is two years older than Elizabeth, and their second daughter, Mary, was a babe in arms. Their other two daughters were born while in Cambridge, though the youngest was herself, only a few months old when Bennet's brother died in a hunting accident. I was abroad much during those years, and as such, I was not aware of anything untoward, and the lack of an announcement letter from my sister concerning Elizabeth's birth was not unusual.

"As for how they found Elizabeth, I am afraid I cannot say. My brother did mention that she was found near his lodgings in Cambridge, but other than that, I am afraid I know little of the story. Elizabeth was sent to us early in January, not long after we returned from spending a week at my brother's estate in Hertfordshire. Since then I have not been at leisure to go there to demand a more accurate accounting of her history."

With a frown, Darcy said: "She was sent to you?"

It was obvious that Mr. Gardiner was uncomfortable with Darcy's question, and he shook his head and brushed the question off. "I am sorry, Mr. Darcy, but though I know the substance of what occurred in Hertfordshire, I do not know all the particulars. I would prefer that Elizabeth explain it to you when you meet her so that I do not muddy the waters with inaccurate statements."

"Of course," replied Darcy, though a part of him wished to demand as much as Mr. Gardiner knew.

"Now, what of your story, sir? You have guessed that she is not my sister's daughter by blood, but you have only stated that she is connected to you through your uncle. Shall you not be explicit?"

They spoke for some time of the particulars of Darcy's suspicions, and by the time Darcy had finished his explanation, Mr. Gardiner was wide-eyed and disbelieving. But he showed himself to be a man of good judgment, for he avoided any gauche displays and instead focused on the how of the matter.

"And she simply disappeared without a trace?"

"I was naught but ten at the time, so I remember little of it. But yes,

I remember that she suddenly disappeared. For a time, my uncle thought a ransom note would be forthcoming, but nothing was ever received, and no trace of her was ever found."

"It is difficult to fathom," said Mr. Gardiner with a shaken head.

"How do you wish to proceed, sir?" asked Darcy. It was time to move this discussion forward.

Mr. Gardiner thought about it for a moment. "I would prefer not to upset her, as she has experienced several shocks of late. As such, I will not speak of this matter to her. Perhaps, instead, we could invite you to dinner one night to meet her? There is, after all, no proof at present that she is even your cousin."

"That is true," replied Darcy, though deep down he was certain she *was*. "For similar reasons, I do not wish to inform my relations until I am as certain I can be of her identity."

"Then will you accept an invitation to dinner tomorrow night?" asked Mr. Gardiner. "I will present you as an acquaintance I have met through my business and introduce you to her. From there you may make your communication."

"I believe that would be acceptable, sir."

"Very well," replied Mr. Gardiner, rising to his feet. They shook hands and Mr. Gardiner led him from his office and to the door. "We will expect you at six o'clock, Mr. Darcy."

"Thank you, Mr. Gardiner."

And then Darcy turned and left the shop, soon to be ensconced in his carriage on its way back toward his home. Over and over in his mind, he reflected upon the surreal quality of the situation. But it was real. There was a real possibility that his cousin had been discovered after eighteen years.

Chapter III

Thursday, February 13, 1812
Gardiner Townhouse, London

*I*f Mr. Darcy thought the situation was surreal, it was nothing compared to Mr. Gardiner's surprise. He had not been dissembling when they had spoken of Elizabeth's recent past, and to have his beloved niece revealed as a foundling, and then have a man step forward to claim her as family not two months later was a strain of any credulity. Only a few short days before, Gardiner had been worried about the woman he had called niece for so many years, knowing the future for her could be bleak, indeed.

But given what Mr. Darcy had spoken of his family's situation—some of which Gardiner was aware, given his wife's connection to Derbyshire—Elizabeth's future was no longer at risk. Quite the opposite, actually. There was nothing confirmed, of course, but Gardiner was certain that his impression of Mr. Darcy was correct, and he did not think he was the sort of man to approach another in the way he had if he was not already all but certain that his supposition was true.

The question was, how to tell Elizabeth and, perhaps more

importantly, how to tell Madeline. Elizabeth, lost as she was by recent revelations, would be skeptical, but given enough proof, she would ultimately be accepting. Madeline, on the other hand, was as fierce as a lioness protecting her cubs. She would not take kindly to any upsetting of Elizabeth. Gardiner knew that he had been a little harsh on his niece since her arrival, and he knew that she was aware of the reason for it. He had endured several reprimands from his wife on the matter in recent days, and Gardiner had endeavored to bring himself under better regulation. Madeline would not be happy if the result of Mr. Darcy's visit was to leave Elizabeth's peace of mind shattered. Care would need to be taken.

As a result of his ruminations, Gardiner requested his wife's presence soon after he arrived home that evening to make the important communication. When she joined him, greeting him with affection as was her wont, she sat, and he told her about Mr. Darcy's visit and the results of it.

"I can hardly believe it!" exclaimed his wife when he had finished speaking. "Are you certain this man is to be trusted?"

Gardiner smiled at this new evidence of his wife's protective nature. "Is it not you who has often extolled the goodness of the Darcy family?" When his wife glared at him, Gardiner only put out his hands and laughed. "I have no reason to disbelieve him, Madeline."

"Could he not be dissembling? I would not wish her to be hurt if this is some kind of nefarious scheme to worm himself into her good graces."

Gardiner only shook his head. "Think of what you are saying, Madeline. Mr. Darcy is, by all accounts, a member of high society, as you have said yourself on many occasions. If his intention was to importune her in a manner which you suspect, he would have no need to invent such a story. Most men of his station are arrogant enough that they believe they can dictate and others will fall in line."

"I suppose you are correct," replied Madeline, though it was clear she was still hesitant. "So what do you intend to do about it?"

"I have invited him to dinner tomorrow. He can make his case to her at that time."

"And does he know something which will prove her identity?"

"I do not think so. That will likely need to come from his aunt and uncle—more likely his aunt."

"Then what is the purpose of inviting Mr. Darcy tomorrow night?"

"To tell her of his suspicions and hear her story for himself. The choice of whether to alert Mr. Darcy's relations to the possibility of a connection between them will be Elizabeth's."

Madeline paused and chewed her lip as she thought. "I am not sure if I wish for Elizabeth's hopes to be raised in such a way."

"If I know Elizabeth at all," replied Gardiner gently, "I would think she is more likely to deny the possibility altogether."

"You may be correct," conceded Madeline after a moment's thought. She sighed and fixed her gaze on him again. "Then what will you tell her?"

"Nothing more than that a business associate will come to dinner tomorrow. Once we sit down to dinner, Mr. Darcy can then more fully explain his presence."

Madeline laughed and reached over to pat him on the cheek, as one would a small child. "It is astonishing, Edward, that a man as intelligent and successful as you would understand a young girl like Elizabeth so little. Or perhaps it is not surprising at all."

"You think our plan is lacking?"

"I know that Elizabeth will immediately see through it. She remembers that Mr. Darcy chased after us in the carriage, and she will recognize him the moment he steps foot in the house. This talk of a 'business associate' will be seen immediately as false. It will put her on her guard."

"Then what do you suggest?"

"The truth, Edward dear." Mrs. Gardiner smiled and rose. "She is an intelligent girl. She will know that Mr. Darcy wishes to speak of something particular. But if you do not wish to speak of the matter before Mr. Darcy comes, simply tell her that he visited you at your warehouses and that he wishes to speak with her. You may then allow Mr. Darcy to make his communication, and while Elizabeth will be naturally curious, she will not resent you for attempting to obfuscate."

Gardiner smiled and nodded, catching his wife's hand in his and squeezing it with affection. "What would I do without you?"

"I know not. But I shudder to think of the mess you would make of things."

Then she turned and exited the room, Gardiner's laughter following her as she left. It was true, he thought rather ruefully. It was the lot of a man with an intelligent wife who was also his partner. Gardiner would not wish for anything less.

* * *

Friday, February 14, 1812
Gardiner Townhouse, London

"The man from Mr. Davidson's party is to come here?"

"Yes, my dear. I have invited him to dinner tonight."

Elizabeth regarded her uncle, wondering what he was about. "And what is his purpose?"

"I believe, Elizabeth, that I will allow him to relate his purpose to you directly." Her uncle must have felt her increase in displeasure, for he laughed and reached out as if to fend her off. "I am not attempting to conceal. Mr. Darcy has a matter he wishes to discuss with you, and I have given him leave. I believe, at present, it is best that he be allowed to make his own communication to you. As it is a sensitive matter, it would not do to speak out of turn."

The anger bled from Elizabeth's breast, and she nodded her understanding. There was no reason, she supposed, to castigate her Uncle Gardiner. She trusted him and knew he would not allow anything underhanded, and though her curious nature wished to be satisfied, she supposed there was no reason she could not wait until the evening meal to discover it.

"You are a good girl, Lizzy," said Uncle Gardiner, the affection she had always thought he held for her more apparent than at any time these past two months. "Do not worry. I promise you that what Mr. Darcy has to say tonight will not leave you vexed or worried. Quite the opposite, in fact."

Before Elizabeth could remark concerning his intriguing statement, he frowned and moved to another topic. "You should also know I received another letter from Longbourn this morning—a letter from my sister."

While Mrs. Gardiner rolled her eyes, an expression of utter exasperation falling over her countenance, Elizabeth only nodded. "I suppose there is no reason to guess what it contained?"

"I am certain you can well imagine," replied he. "The only reason I inform you of this now, Lizzy, is because we promised to be open. I have written back to my sister, demanding that she cease importuning me on this subject."

"I beg your pardon, Edward," said Aunt Gardiner, "but I am not certain that will be efficacious. Maggie Bennet is like a dog with a bone."

"Of this, I am well aware. I hope, however, this will be the end of her harangues on the subject, for I *may* have insinuated that if she persists in her behavior, I might withhold my support should your father pass on early."

"Oh, Uncle!" exclaimed Elizabeth, but he only grinned at her. "I will depart from your house if it will make it easier."

"Nonsense," was her uncle's firm reply. "My sister has not the right to demand *anything* of me, and I will not allow her to misbehave now." A sudden thought seemed to come to him and his grin became positively devilish. "Besides, my sister may just come to regret this unreasonable stance she has taken.

"Well, I believe I must be off to the warehouse," said Uncle Gardiner, standing and wiping his mouth on the tablecloth. Elizabeth opened her mouth to ask him about his last statement, but she decided, in the end, to allow it to pass. She knew there was little hope of his answering anyway.

"Be patient, Lizzy," said he before he left. "All will be explained this evening, and I do not think you will be disappointed with what will be revealed."

And then he was gone, leaving Elizabeth with her aunt.

"I hope this evening is not an excuse to promote me as a possible wife to this Mr. Darcy," said Elizabeth, raising her fork to her mouth in a casual manner.

Though Elizabeth had meant it partially as a tease and partially as an admonishment, her aunt only smiled and looked at her in a thoughtful manner. "He *would* make a good husband. From what I saw of him, he seemed like a handsome man, thoughtful, sober, and intelligent. From what I know of the family, he is also quite wealthy.

"In fact, the more that I think of it, the better your idea sounds. Perhaps I shall mention it to your uncle when he returns."

"Aunt!" cried Elizabeth, but her aunt only grinned. "You *know* this man?" asked she, curious about her aunt's words in spite of herself.

"I believe I have actually met him once or twice," replied Aunt Gardiner, her look one of introspection. "As you know, I was raised in the north, and his family estate is only five miles away from my father's parish, which is itself a gift of the Darcy family. He would have been quite young when I met him, however, so I doubt he would remember."

"That is a peculiar coincidence."

"It is, indeed. Now, I believe it is up to me to ensure you do not chew on this subject all day. What shall we do to occupy ourselves?"

With the help of her aunt, Elizabeth was able to put the matter from her mind for a time. She was grateful, for she knew she would have done naught but worry, had she been left to her own devices.

Friday, February 14, 1812
Gardiner Townhouse, London

When Mr. Darcy entered the house that evening, Elizabeth was forced to own that her aunt was entirely correct about him. He was tall, with dark hair which curled around his ears and on his forehead. His garb was stylish and fine, though it was sober, devoid of the embellishments that so many of the Beau Brummel set—or those that imitated them, of which there were not a few—seemed to think necessary. And he was also tall, with broad shoulders which bespoke strength and occupation. He was a man to whom every maiden's— and matron's!—eyes would be drawn the instant he walked into a room.

Mindful of her situation, Elizabeth pushed such thoughts from her mind, aware that they would do her little good. Instead, she focused on the man's bow and her responding curtsey, listening as her uncle introduced them, though not truly hearing any of the words.

"Miss Bennet," said Mr. Darcy, his voice soft and melodious. "I am honored to make your acquaintance."

How Elizabeth responded she knew not, but she must have said something acceptable, for Mr. Darcy bowed over her hand. But while she was feeling wooly-headed and distracted, Elizabeth did not miss the look of pure amusement with which her aunt regarded her. It cleared her mind and brought out her courage in a way she had not known was possible.

"Can I assume by your presence here, Mr. Darcy, that you saw so much of me at dinner that you simply had to request an introduction?"

Though Mr. Darcy appeared shocked at Elizabeth's boldness, soon his consternation was replaced by a grin, even as the soft sound of Aunt Gardiner's voice floated to her ears: "Now that is our Lizzy."

"I see that my coming does not intimidate you, Miss Bennet," said Mr. Darcy.

"Should it?"

"Definitely not," replied Mr. Darcy with a shake of his head. "In fact, I see the echoes . . ."

He trailed off and appeared a little embarrassed. For her part, Elizabeth was more intrigued at the implications of his aborted statement, but she was given no time to think on the matter or query him further, for Mrs. Gardiner invited them all to sit. Elizabeth glared at her aunt, knowing she had intervened for a purpose, but Mrs. Gardiner only smiled back, completely unrepentant.

They talked of inconsequential things for a few moments before being called into dinner, and Elizabeth did her best to watch Mr. Darcy, attempting to discover something which would inform her of the reason for his presence. Aunt Gardiner made the communication about her childhood in Derbyshire, but though Mr. Darcy responded pleasantly, and asked after her family—it seemed he remembered Reverend Plumber—Elizabeth did not think him surprised by the information. In fact, she suspected he had already known.

At length, they were called in by the housekeeper, and they sat down to dinner. From where she was, faced by Mr. Darcy on the long side of the table, Elizabeth could see that she was the focus of the man's attention. He did not seem to regard her with any admiration that she could detect. Rather, she thought him curious about her, though why that should be the case, she was not at all certain.

"If I might, Mr. Gardiner," said Mr. Darcy after the first course had been delivered and they had begun to partake, "I believe we should come to the point as to the reason for my visit tonight." He turned a wry smile on Elizabeth. "Given Miss Bennet's performance in the sitting-room, I have no doubt she has divined an ulterior motive for my presence."

"It would be difficult to miss, Mr. Darcy," replied Elizabeth.

"I am certain it would." Mr. Darcy paused for a moment, seemingly searching for the proper words to put his actions in perspective. Then he nodded once and fixed his eyes upon her. Though Elizabeth had no notion of any regard on his part, a fluttering began in her midsection.

"Though I spoke with your uncle at some length yesterday, I find myself curious about your presence here, Miss Bennet. Mr. Gardiner suggested that there is some reason for it, beyond a simple visit to beloved relations. I would like to hear more of the circumstances, if you are agreeable."

Elizabeth's hackles were instantly raised by this seemingly innocuous question. "I am sorry, sir, but I have not the slightest notion of how any of that would affect *you*."

"If you will indulge me, Miss Bennet, all will be made apparent before the dishes are cleared away."

When Elizabeth hesitated further, Mr. Darcy leaned forward and fixed her with a look of compassion. "Miss Bennet, I am aware of your history, or as much as was made known to you. I know that though you believed you were the daughter of Mr. Gardiner's sister, you have recently discovered you are not. I wish to hear more of this, not only how you discovered it, but why you are now living with your aunt and uncle."

A sudden smile settled over Mr. Darcy's face, and he continued: "I suppose I must consider it fortunate, given how I might never have been introduced to you if you were not here. But I will reserve judgment until I know the whole of the story."

"There are reasons for his questions," interjected Mr. Gardiner, when he saw that her ire was being raised again. "Answer as best you can, Lizzy, for all will be made clear shortly."

Every feeling in her rebelled against relating such matters as would sink her in Mr. Darcy's estimation—in the estimation of any man of good character—and for a moment she could not reply.

"He will not think any less of you," said her uncle. "Any more than *we* think any less of you."

"Please, Miss Bennet," added Mr. Darcy. Elizabeth turned and gazed into his eyes and she saw the compassion and worry in them, and it was these qualities which caused her defenses to collapse. She found herself speaking before she knew it.

"My father's . . ." Elizabeth trailed off, knowing she could not claim that relationship any longer. She swallowed thickly and began again.

"Mr. Bennet's estate is north of London. As he was a second son, we lived in Cambridge until I was five years of age, but I do not remember much of my time there. I was always Elizabeth Bennet, second daughter of Mr. and Mrs. Bennet of Longbourn in Hertfordshire. But that all changed soon after the New Year.

"A company of militia came to the area last autumn, and they were welcomed with open arms. Most of the men are good, kind men, but there are a few of whom I have learned to be wary. The worst of the lot of them I did not suspect of having depraved tendencies until it was almost too late."

"Did a man importune you improperly, Miss Bennet?" asked Mr. Darcy. Elizabeth's eyes darted to meet his, as his tone was as bleak as a winter wind over a blasted landscape.

"I *was* importuned, yes, but I was able to free myself from his grasp before he could do any irreparable harm to me." A harsh laugh escaped Elizabeth's mouth before she could suppress it. "Or rather, before any harm came to anything other than my reputation.

"Though I was not aware of it at the time, we were witnessed by a lady of the neighborhood who is known to be a notorious gossip, and before long, it was all over the district. Of course, it was portrayed as if I were a willing participant in the encounter, and it was soon on the tongues of everyone. None of my previous respectability, none of my fifteen years of good behavior meant anything in the face of the salacious story which was spread at my expense. Only a few of my closest friends and my dearest sister stood by my side."

"Is that the reason why you were sent to London?" asked Mr. Darcy.

"In part. My ... Mrs. Bennet, you see, is a ..." She trailed off, her eyes flicking to where her uncle sat at the head of the table.

"There is no reason to dissemble, Lizzy," said her uncle with a sigh. "I am aware of my sister's character."

Elizabeth shook her head, attempting to clear the fog she felt binding her mind. Seeing her so affected, her uncle interjected.

"My sister is not an intelligent woman, Mr. Darcy. Though she means well and does the best she can, she has always been flighty and of mean understanding. Furthermore, she has been terrified of the entail of the estate which she believes will leave her destitute when her husband passes, and that affects her judgment."

"I was never my ... Mrs. Bennet's favorite, Mr. Darcy," said Elizabeth. "For many years, I thought it was simply because I am more like Mr. Bennet in character and interests. I was always closest to my ... adopted father.

"When the situation between myself and the militiaman became known throughout the neighborhood and the Bennets began to be shunned because of it, Mrs. Bennet's fears of the hedgerows seemed to be coming true, and she demanded that my father put me out of the house. Mr. Bennet, however, was certain that the talk would die down before long, and that we would all be as we were before. I believe it was his insistence that forced Mrs. Bennet to declare that I was not her daughter.

"I was shocked," said Elizabeth, the bitter memories taking her to scenes she would prefer to forget. "When my mother first told me that I was not her daughter, I could not understand her. They have never spoken of the matter, never brought it up in my hearing, never referred to it by word or deed. I was always Elizabeth Bennet, and there was never any thought in my mind that I was not their daughter."

"That is hardly surprising," murmured Mr. Darcy. "How could you have thought such things?"

"How could I, indeed?" Elizabeth shook her head, banishing the memories and focusing again on the present. "I applied to Mr. Bennet for confirmation, and though he was loath to give it to me, he did finally confirm it. I had been found as a child and taken into the Bennets' home, raised as their daughter. As I mentioned, I was always closer to my father than my mother, but I did not feel any less loved regardless.

"In the end, however, Mrs. Bennet forced my father's hand. Unbeknownst to him, she spread the word around the neighborhood that I was not her true daughter." Elizabeth smiled thinly. "When he discovered what she had done, it provoked the worst argument between them I have ever seen. But by then the damage was irreversible. I had gone from a respectable member of society to the disgraced daughter of the Bennet family, to a fallen woman, without even a family name to my credit."

"And the neighborhood believed your mother's assertions?"

"It is easy, is it not, to believe any story, no matter how outlandish?" Elizabeth huffed. "In fact, I believe gossips are more likely to believe a story the more peculiar it becomes. It was suddenly clear to them all why I was behaving the way I was, as I was not even a Bennet. Why, who even knew if I was the daughter of a gentleman at all! I might be naught but the daughter of a whore, for all anyone knew!"

"Lizzy!" warned her uncle. "I will not have you use such words in my house, please."

"Of course, Uncle," replied Elizabeth, though she was not at all chastised by his admonishment. "At that point my situation at Longbourn became untenable, and I was forced to leave. It is only the goodness of my aunt and uncle which has allowed me to keep a roof over my head."

It was clear to Elizabeth that Mr. Darcy, rather than being disgusted as she would have thought, was rather made angry by her recitation. Elizabeth was not certain what to make of this man—would not her past with the militia officer, coupled with the uncertainty of her origins, cause him to flee without looking back?

"Has any mention of these . . . rumors followed you to London?" asked he after a moment.

"Not that I am aware," replied Elizabeth dully. Telling her story had left her feeling drained, and she wished she could go to her room, bury her head under her pillow, and wish that her life had not been destroyed these past months. "The only member of the local society who has any presence in London is Sir William Lucas, and his family has been my staunchest supporters. I cannot say how far the rumors have spread beyond Meryton's immediate environs, but I have met no censure in London."

"There is one other matter," said Mr. Gardiner. "When Elizabeth had been here for two weeks, the man who put her in this situation appeared on my doorstep with the most disgusting words of how he would provide for Elizabeth as his mistress." Mr. Gardiner's lip curled with revulsion. "I sent him away with his tail between his legs and my burliest footman's hand grasping him by the scruff of his neck. This Mr. Wickham, as he calls himself, may have spread the story further, but as he is naught but a militia officer, I cannot think he has the standing to see it spread to anyone of consequence."

If Elizabeth had thought Mr. Darcy's countenance was angry before, it now became positively forbidding. "Mr. George Wickham?" asked he of Elizabeth.

Surprised, Elizabeth nodded. "That is his name, sir. He claimed to be from Derbyshire, though he was not explicit about where."

"I am well acquainted with *that* particular libertine," said Mr. Darcy. A slow fire seemed to be burning in his eyes, though when his gaze fell upon Elizabeth, it was dimmed — but not quenched — by the expression of utmost compassion. "Mr. Wickham did not hurt you, did he, Miss Bennet?"

"Only my reputation," said Elizabeth. "I was able to fight him off before he was able to do anything other than paw at me. I gave him some scratches on his face I believe were not soon healed."

Mr. Darcy barked a laugh. "That is the least of what he deserves. He shall receive his just desserts in the future, I promise you."

"I am sorry, sir," said Elizabeth, "but I have become weary of this conversation. Might I ask you to be explicit concerning your presence here?"

"Of course, Miss Bennet," replied Mr. Darcy. "I thank you for informing me of what has happened in so precise a manner."

Mr. Darcy paused and his eyes caught Mr. Gardiner's, who nodded slightly in response.

"Miss Bennet," said Mr. Darcy, once again turning his attention to her. "The reason I wished to speak to you today, and the reason I followed you from Davidson's house, is because I have come to believe that you are, in fact, related to me. Unless I am very much mistaken, I believe you are the daughter of my uncle, Hugh Fitzwilliam, and his wife Susan. My uncle Fitzwilliam is the Earl of Matlock and my mother's brother."

CHAPTER IV

"*So this* is the daughter of an earl."

The sound of his voice caused her to stir a little, and her eyes opened, though they remained heavy-lidded. She seemed to ponder him gravely for a few moments before her eyes closed again.

"She is not impressive, is she?" asked the hunter in a conversational tone. "I had heard she is quite the little spitfire."

"She is still under the effects of the opioids," replied Sykes. The hunter did not miss the man's grimace. "She was given them to ensure she remained quiet while she was smuggled out of the house."

The hunter grunted. In truth, he did not care. "You will go east?"

"Yes," said Sykes. "I have a brother who lives in Suffolk. Once we are there I will—"

"I do not care to know," said the hunter. "Once you leave this place, I wish to have no more knowledge of the brat. Do what you will with her. Whatever it is, she must never be found."

Sykes did not say anything, but in his countenance was evidence of disgust. The hunter was amused, rather than offended, though he supposed he should not be. It was not for men such as Sykes to question *him*.

"You will need to leave immediately," said the hunter. "I have no doubt the earl's men and half of Derbyshire will be out looking for this one before long."

"Where is my money?" It was little more than a demand, spoken in a gruff voice.

The hunter produced a small purse. "Here. Take it and the girl and go. Do not contact me or try to blackmail me in the future, or it will go ill with you."

It was with a look of pure poison that Sykes picked up the small girl and left. Within moments, the hunter left as well, a spring in his step.

Friday, February 14, 1812
Gardiner Townhouse, London

Elizabeth stared at Mr. Darcy in disbelieve. "The daughter of an earl?" was all she managed to squeak in her surprise.

"Yes, Miss Bennet—or perhaps I should call you Lady Elizabeth. For I believe that is who you are."

It was beyond Elizabeth's ability to comprehend, and she could do naught but stare at Mr. Darcy for several moments. Then denial set in. She was a foundling, nothing but a girl without a home and family, erstwhile daughter of Henry and Margaret Bennet. She could not *possibly* be the daughter of an earl!

"It cannot be true, Mr. Darcy," said she out loud. "How can such a thing even be fathomed?"

"Let us speak of the facts, then, shall we?" Mr. Darcy raised his hand and began ticking points on his fingers one by one. "In the year 1793, my little cousin, Elizabeth Anne Fitzwilliam, who was two years of age at the time, went missing from my uncle's estate in Derbyshire without a trace. Nothing was ever found of her, and no ransom note was ever received. Second, you were found, in a different part of the country, yes, but as a lost child." Mr. Darcy turned to Mr. Gardiner. "The name cannot be a coincidence. Do you know how your relations came to call her by the name Elizabeth?"

"Not with any certainty, Mr. Darcy," said Mr. Gardiner. "As you recall, I was not even aware of this until two months past. To me, she has always been Elizabeth."

Mr. Darcy turned back to Elizabeth. "Then I suspect that Miss Bennet herself informed the Bennets of her name. Though she was still less than three years of age, she was still able to say an abbreviated version of her name, which sounded very much like 'Lizbeth'."

Elizabeth stared at the man shocked, and when he saw her reaction, he prompted her, saying: "Does that have any meaning to you?"

"My sister Jane used to call me Lizbeth until she was almost ten years of age. I had always thought it was a pet name for me. After that, my mother took to calling me 'Lizzy' and that name stuck."

"That is another point in favor of my theory, then," said Mr. Darcy with a nod. "Furthermore, your appearance reminds me of my aunt — it was that which caused my eyes to stray to you so often at Davidson's house. Your laugh, moreover, sounds so much like my aunt's that when I heard it for the first time, I knew who you must be. The revelations of this evening have only strengthened that belief."

"This is still all very circumstantial, Mr. Darcy," said Mrs. Gardiner. "Is there some means of identifying Elizabeth beyond all doubt?"

Mr. Darcy shook his head. "I am afraid that I know of nothing to establish her identity as fact. However, my aunt might."

"I cannot be introduced to a countess as her long-lost daughter with such thin evidence as this!" exclaimed Elizabeth. "What would she think of me? I could be anyone, a woman of base character, intent on preying upon the heartache and loss of a wealthy family."

"Do you think my word carries so little weight, Miss Bennet?" asked Mr. Darcy. Though his words were censorious, his tone was anything but. Elizabeth noted that her aunt and uncle exchanged an amused glance, and the sight made her more than a little cross.

"Even if you are proven *not* to be my cousin, Miss Bennet, my aunt and uncle will not think such ill of you, for no other reason than it was *I* who have put you forward as their daughter. You did not have any knowledge of the matter until I brought it to your attention."

"I am still not certain . . . ." said Elizabeth. "I would not wish to reopen old wounds, and I am not convinced there is any way to prove my identity. Would it not be best to simply allow this matter to rest?"

"If that is what you wish to do, then I will, of course, respect your wishes. At present, I have not informed anyone of my suspicions for precisely the reasons you have stated. But if you will allow me to inform you my opinion, I believe the possible benefits are worth the risks."

Mr. Darcy smiled at her, and she noted incongruously, given the situation, how much it transformed his countenance when he did. He was a handsome man, regardless, but when he smiled, his face was transformed to that of a veritable Adonis.

"These past months have obviously been hard for you, Miss Bennet. You have lost your family, your name, and your very identity. I would never have pursued this course if I was not convinced that you are exactly whom I believe you to be. I will not attempt to direct you and will stand down if you desire it. But knowing the happiness which would result in your being proven to be my cousin—both for you and my uncle's family—I ask you to at least consider it."

Though it seemed like an unfathomable farce, Elizabeth found herself nodding. What was the downside of agreeing to his suggestion? She might find her family, a family that, until recently, she had never even known she lost. If that was not reason enough, she did not know what was.

"I shall consider it, Mr. Darcy. Might I request that you return at a later date to further discuss the matter with me?"

"Of course, Miss Bennet," replied Mr. Darcy. "I hope I have not caused you any undue suffering because of my assertions."

"No, indeed," replied Elizabeth, feeling unaccountably shy. "But I have much on which to think."

"Then I will leave you to it. Do not hesitate to call on me should it become necessary."

"I shall," was Elizabeth's quiet reply.

Saturday, February 15, 1812
Darcy House, London

Fitzwilliam Darcy had always been a private sort of person. His public persona was one of reticence and reserve, one he cultivated assiduously as he had found that it had often spared him of the attention of those with whom he would prefer not to associate. He had also grown adept at hiding his thoughts and feelings. But as in all things, there were exceptions, and that evening at the Gardiners' house was one such.

George Wickham! How Darcy despised that name! The man was a blight upon the very world, a veritable menace to any polite society. Some of Darcy's vaunted control had slipped at Miss Bennet's mention of the despicable libertine. Even so, Darcy did not think they had realized the true measure of his disgust and anger at Wickham's actions.

For months after the Ramsgate incident, Georgiana had been uncommunicative and heartbroken. She had blamed herself for falling prey to Wickham's honeyed tongue. The reason he had not hauled

Wickham in front of a magistrate at that time was the desire to protect her reputation, as he knew Wickham was vindictive enough to attempt to ruin it, despite his deep-seated fear of Fitzwilliam.

But now, as Wickham had importuned a woman who might be Fitzwilliam's long-lost sister, Darcy knew his cousin would be out for blood, and in this instance, he was not inclined to plead for clemency. In his eagerness to protect Georgiana, Darcy had neglected to consider how Wickham would still be free to wreak his depredations upon an unsuspecting society. No longer. It was time to muzzle the mad dog and ensure he was never able to harm another.

Upon returning to his house, Darcy retired to his study to pen a missive to his steward at Pemberley, instructing that a certain package be sent to him in London posthaste. And then Darcy retired, firmly putting the matter from his mind. What he could not so easily banish were thoughts of Miss Bennet, and whether she would consent to be introduced to those, he was certain, were her true family.

The same recollections and thoughts immediately made themselves known to Darcy when he awoke the next morning, and he prepared for his day with the matter flitting about in the back of his mind. As Snell, his valet, was shaving him, Darcy's thoughts wandered back to Miss Bennet. His impression of her was nothing but positive. She was clearly an intelligent woman, poised and proper, and he suspected that she might have an outspoken streak in her the likes of which would be a pleasure to behold. It was also clear the events of the past few months had affected her in many ways, shaken her confidence and cast doubt on her own worth.

Of her reluctance to be introduced to the earl and countess, Darcy could not be anything but approving. It showed her to be a principled, upright person, not one who was grasping and artful. Many young ladies would jump at the chance to be recognized as an earl's daughter in such a circumstance, regardless of the truth of the matter. The thought of what Caroline Bingley, one of the worst leaches in society, would do if presented such an opportunity caused a shudder to run through Darcy.

"Have a care, Mr. Darcy," said Snell, his valet. "I shall cut you if you are not still."

"You have my apologies, Snell," replied Darcy, more out of habit than any real attention.

The fastidious man sniffed and returned to his work, and Darcy avoided any thoughts of Miss Bingley to avoid arousing Snell's ire. Sometimes Darcy thought that Snell cared more about his appearance than he did himself.

When he was dressed and shaved, Darcy took himself downstairs and entered the breakfast room. There he was surprised to find another was in attendance.

"Fitzwilliam!" exclaimed Darcy. "I thought you were out of town on a matter of business."

Fitzwilliam looked up from his tea and his paper and regarded Darcy, a hint of a smirk playing around the corners of his mouth. "My task was completed early, and I returned late last night. You will not need to endure my company tonight, for I am off again, and will not return until Tuesday night."

"You know that you are always welcome, Cousin."

"I do appreciate it. Father's townhouse is so dull when he and mother are not in residence. I had much rather stay here with you and Georgiana."

Setting the newspaper aside, Fitzwilliam leaned back in his chair and regarded Darcy thoughtfully. He raised his teacup to his lips, an action which gave all the appearance of absentmindedness. Darcy had seen this many times in the past and was certain his cousin was on the verge of teasing him.

"I understand that you were out last night."

"Yes," replied Darcy as he filled his plate from the sideboard. "A new acquaintance."

Fitzwilliam snorted. "Is she pretty? Otherwise, I do not think you would be so excited about meeting someone new."

Several thoughts ran through Darcy's head, and though he longed to inform Fitzwilliam of the identity of the person with whom he had dined, his promise to keep the matter of Miss Bennet from his family until she made her decision was prominent among them.

"An absolute beauty," said Darcy, deciding that two could play that game. "I have rarely met a handsomer woman, a curiosity, for, in some ways, she reminds me of *you*."

The expression on his cousin's face told Darcy that he had caught him completely by surprise. "Of me?"

"Her wit and propensity for teasing," replied Darcy, enjoying his cousin's astonishment. "But I do not hold that against her, I assure you. At least she does not *resemble* you; I would not wish that on any woman. She is as delightful a woman as I have ever met."

"Then I believe I must demand an introduction to this wondrous creature," said Fitzwilliam, ignoring Darcy's continued teasing. "Do you know if she has a substantial dowry? If she is as exquisite as you say, then perhaps I have found my heiress. You know I must marry with some attention to money."

"I am sorry, Fitzwilliam," said Darcy, feeling vastly amused, "but I do not think you would suit."

"Because you have already claimed her for yourself?"

"No, because I doubt she is what you are looking for in a wife. Besides, my understanding is that she is essentially penniless."

At present, Darcy thought to himself.

"That is a shame, indeed." Fitzwilliam watched Darcy, suspicion on his brow. "But I still would like an introduction."

"I will see what I can arrange," replied Darcy blandly. "Now, enough of that. I have recently been made privy to some information which I believe will be of great interest to you."

"Oh?"

"It concerns our old friend, George Wickham."

"Do tell," said Fitzwilliam. He leaned forward, placing his arms on the table, all pretense toward good humor absent at the mention of a man he hated more than any other. "And what has our Georgie got himself up to?"

"It appears he has joined the militia and is stationed only four hours to the north in a little town called Meryton. I also have reliable information that he has importuned at least one young woman, and I would stake my fortune that his debts in the area have already reached prodigious proportions."

Fitzwilliam snorted. "That is a fool's wager, Darcy. He cannot stay in one place for more than an hour or two without accumulating debt. The question is, what do you intend to do about it?"

"I have already sent to Pemberley for the packet containing the receipts of his prior debts."

It was clear that nothing Darcy said could have surprised his cousin more. "I might wonder what has changed to render you so determined to deal with him."

"Let us simply say that it has become clear to me that leaving George Wickham free to prey on society is not wise. It is time to do something about him."

"Past time, I should think. When do we depart?"

"It will take a few days for my letter to reach Pemberley and to receive the reply. By then, I hope to be at liberty to share some additional particulars of the situation with you. Either way, once I have his debts, I intend to see George Wickham in prison."

"Where he belongs."

"Exactly."

"I am happy you have finally come to your senses," said Fitzwilliam, rising from his chair. "I was afraid Wickham's connection to your father would forever tie your hands. I hope to learn of these other circumstances which have led to your change of heart. For the present, I must be off."

"Godspeed, Cousin," said Darcy.

Sunday, February 16, 1812
Gardiner Townhouse, London

After Elizabeth left Longbourn forever, she had no thought of ever finding her true family. Indeed, the notion seemed laughable. The fact that she might be the daughter of someone so exalted as an earl had never even entered her mind. Mr. Bennet had not been explicit and Mrs. Bennet far too flighty and angry to have mentioned much of her state when they had found her. Furthermore, Mrs. Bennet had openly speculated that her behavior rendered her more likely to be spawned from someone of common ancestry, or at the very least, someone's *natural daughter*. Though she knew her adoptive mother was prone to ridiculous behavior, it had seemed likely, if not probable.

To be suddenly confronted with the notion that she was the daughter of a peer was difficult for Elizabeth to understand, and further thought that night Sand the following morning did nothing to clarify matters in her own mind. She was grateful that her aunt had allowed her the comfort of her own thoughts—her uncle had left for his warehouses early that morning—and when Elizabeth announced her intention to walk in the nearby park, her Mrs. Gardiner had only waved her off after reaffirming her intention of taking a footman for her protection. But Elizabeth's walks, long her refuge from a house as chaotic as Longbourn, brought her no clarity either.

As astute a woman as she was, Aunt Gardiner allowed her to think on the matter for some time, choosing to share her opinion when she thought Elizabeth had exhausted her own ability to reason through the matter.

"Lizzy," called her aunt softly. Elizabeth had been sitting on the window seat by the front window, looking down on Gracechurch Street below, when her aunt's voice pulled her eyes away. "Do you wish to speak of it?"

"Will it help?" asked Elizabeth rhetorically. "I know not what can help me now."

"I believe I should be offended that you think so little of my wisdom. Here I thought you considered me to be the most rational of all your relations."

In spite of herself, Elizabeth chuckled. "Your advice has never proven to be insufficient. But this . . . situation is far beyond any such wisdom. I cannot imagine what it is I should do."

"Speaking of it will often bring clarity, even if you speak and I only listen."

So Elizabeth unburdened herself on her aunt, revealing all her thoughts, her innermost feelings, and her doubts concerning what Mr. Darcy had told her. She left nothing back, for she knew that her aunt would not judge her, and she could not give the full measure of her assistance if she did not know all of Elizabeth's hopes and worries.

"I have a question for you then, Elizabeth," said Mrs. Gardiner when Elizabeth had finished speaking. "Do your objections center around the thought that you cannot *possibly* be the daughter of an earl, or is there some other reason why you hesitate?"

With utter stupefaction, Elizabeth gaped at her aunt. "Is it really so simple?"

"That is the question I would like you to answer, Lizzy," replied Mrs. Gardiner. She reached out to grasp Elizabeth's hand and directed an earnest look in her eyes. "I would wish you to think on this carefully and come to a decision based on the facts, and if that is not enough, then base your decision on Mr. Darcy's suspicions. Do not allow feelings of inadequacy to sway you, for that path is nothing less than ridiculous."

"It sounds to me as if you wish me to agree to Mr. Darcy's request," said Elizabeth.

"I want you to have the life you deserve, Elizabeth. If that life is as the daughter of an earl, then that is what you should have."

Elizabeth considered that for a moment, knowing that on that account, her aunt was correct. She had no more notion of whether it was even possible, but if she *was* the daughter of an earl, she should have that life.

"Do you want to hear my opinion, my dear?"

Her attention brought back to her aunt, Elizabeth nodded.

"You are a strong personality, Lizzy," said Aunt Gardiner. "You are confident and poised, and you are firm in your opinions, almost to the point of obstinacy at times." Her aunt smiled, which Elizabeth returned hesitantly. "But much of your confidence has to do with the way your father raised you. It also has to do with the fact that you have always known *exactly* who you are.

"Now, however, your identity has been torn from you, leaving you adrift. For the first time in your life, you do not know exactly who you are. Are you Elizabeth Bennet? *Who* exactly *is* Elizabeth Bennet? What kind of girl is she? What should she believe, and what should her opinions be? Do her opinions have merit?

"And now there is another matter to consider—are you, in fact, Elizabeth Fitzwilliam? If so, who exactly is Elizabeth Fitzwilliam?" Her aunt's eyes bored into Elizabeth's own, and Elizabeth did not possess the power to wrench her own gaze away. "It seems to me, Elizabeth, that *if* you are Elizabeth Fitzwilliam, you would do well to discover it. Then you can, through your experiences *as* Elizabeth Fitzwilliam, determine just who that person is.

"Thus, my advice to you: take Mr. Darcy's offer to be introduced to his family. What is the most you can lose? Either they will accept you as their daughter, or they will not, based on what evidence—if any—exists."

"And what if they are so desperate to have a daughter again that they will accept me regardless? I would not wish to be accepted into their family under false pretenses."

"Elizabeth," replied Mrs. Gardiner, her tone faintly chiding, "their daughter has been gone for almost twenty years. Though I cannot imagine the wound has *ever* healed, I am certain they have reconciled themselves to your loss after all this time. I cannot imagine they would act as you describe."

With a slow nod of her head, Elizabeth acknowledged the sense in her aunt's words. "I suppose you are correct, Aunt. It all seems so clear when you speak in such a way."

"I should hope so, my dear."

Mrs. Gardiner then went away, citing the need to review her menus for the week, leaving Elizabeth to her own devices. Though she had been a bundle of contrary emotions before—most of which she had not even been able to identify—now she was calm. It was amazing how her aunt was able to focus her on the problem and help her gain perspective.

She would do as her aunt suggested. When Mr. Darcy returned, Elizabeth would inform him of her decision to meet with his relations. And if she was at all honest with herself, she could feel a measure of excitement, deep within her, at the thought of possibly having a family once again.

CHAPTER V

Monday, February 16, 1812
Gardiner Townhouse, London

*I*t was with trepidation that Darcy returned to the Gardiner house that morning to hear Miss Bennet's verdict on the matter of her introduction to the Fitzwilliams. While it was true that Darcy admired her for her uprightness and appreciated her reluctance to cause his family any further pain, he was convinced that she was a Fitzwilliam, and he longed to have it proven and acknowledged.

Darcy was uncertain why this had become so important to him. The thought of ending years of pain, of having the hole in the collective heart of his relations healed, was a powerful motivator. So too was the thought of bringing a young woman he had instantly esteemed the moment he had met her under the family's protection. But neither of these considerations was his primary motivation. As his carriage wended its way toward Gracechurch Street that morning, he attempted to decipher his feelings, while achieving little clarity. The thought that he might admire Miss Bennet was dismissed, though not completely—she was an estimable woman, he was sure, and he thought he could admire her with tolerable ease. But he had, after all, met her only once.

When Darcy entered the townhouse, only Mrs. Gardiner and her niece were there, and subsequent conversation revealed that her husband was engaged in his business. Darcy nodded thoughtfully. There was no need for Mr. Gardiner's presence, but he had struck Darcy as an admirable man, and Darcy wished to further the acquaintance.

They made the typical polite conversation for several moments, and though Darcy was impatient, he suppressed it, allowing Miss Bennet to come to the point in her own time. This was a life-changing decision for her, and Darcy would not rush her into it. In the end, however, she brought it up herself only a few moments later.

"I have given much thought to our conversation yesterday," said Miss Bennet. "I will own that I am . . . confused and unsettled, sir." Darcy thought to interject, but he sensed that she had more to say, so he held his tongue. "It has been a trying time, as I am sure you understand. I never expected to discover that I am . . . not a Bennet. Then when I knew the truth, I never expected to find my true . . . family."

She directed a helpless little smile at him, and Darcy felt his heart go out to her. "But if you are still willing, I believe I would like to be introduced to your uncle and his family." She paused and shook her head. "I still cannot imagine that I might actually be their daughter. But if I am, I feel it incumbent upon me to discover it."

"I believe you have made the correct choice, Miss Bennet," said Darcy. He attempted to bolster her courage with a smile, and she responded to it, though shyly. "And you are correct. The worst we will discover is that you are *not* my uncle's daughter, little though I think that likely at present."

"You are convinced," said Miss Bennet with something akin to wonder.

"I am," replied Darcy. "Every circumstance supports the theory, from your appearance and those mannerisms which resemble my aunt's, to the sound of your voice, to the pet name your sister called you. That does not even mention other facts surrounding your disappearance, your age, and so forth. Yes, Miss Bennet, I am convinced you are my cousin."

It appeared he had overwhelmed her again, for she fell silent.

"It appears that you have agreed to meet my family without any expectation of being proven to be their daughter."

Miss Bennet glanced at Mrs. Gardiner, and the woman shook her head with fond exasperation at her niece. "I will not say you are incorrect, sir."

"Then I will refrain from any further comments on the subject," replied Mr. Darcy. He winked at her, prompting a giggle and a smile of appreciation.

"Then what do you suggest, sir?"

"My aunt and uncle are currently not in town," replied Darcy. "I expect them to return within the next week."

It was clear he had surprised Miss Bennet. "As it is the season, I would have thought they would be in town."

"They usually are," replied Darcy. "My uncle also has his duties in the House of Lords to consider. But a matter arose at Snowlock, the family estate, and my uncle returned there to deal with it.

"In the interim, however, I suggest I introduce you to my cousin, Colonel Fitzwilliam, who is my uncle's younger son. I would also like to introduce you to my sister, Georgiana, though I believe it would be best at present to refrain from informing her of my suspicions. Might I suggest you visit her tomorrow for tea? Then I will bring Fitzwilliam around to meet you the day after—he is away from London until tomorrow evening."

Miss Bennet once again seemed ill at ease, but she gathered her courage and agreed to his plan.

"Excellent!" said Darcy. "Then I will speak to Georgiana and have her send an invitation to you for tomorrow."

"Thank you, sir," replied Miss Bennet quietly.

They conversed for some few more moments before Darcy rose to depart. But before he left, he approached Miss Bennet and grasped her hand, bowing over it.

"I know this is overwhelming for you, Miss Bennet, but for what it is worth, I believe you have made the correct choice."

"I hope so, Mr. Darcy."

Darcy squeezed her hand lightly. "It will all end well, I am sure."

Then Darcy took his leave, promising that they would meet again the next day. He returned to his home alive with purpose. He could hardly wait to introduce the family to her. In particular, he was anticipating Fitzwilliam's reaction to making her acquaintance. The man had pestered him for years with his teasing and irreverent ways— this was a golden opportunity to exact a little retribution.

* * *

Tuesday, February 18, 1812
Darcy House, London

There were times when Elizabeth wondered where the old Lizzy Bennet had gone. She had always prided herself on her fortitude, the indomitable courage which would rise at every attempt to intimidate her. Even with such changes as she had endured, should her courage not have survived, at least to some extent? Should she have been left, some quivering, timorous creature, intimidated by a visit to a young girl?

Elizabeth did not know. But she was becoming weary of being that creature, of questioning her worth and worrying for her future. The visit upon which they embarked was just another visit, the possibility of her intimate connection to the family notwithstanding. At least, she attempted to tell herself that. And she thought that she was beginning to believe it. Then the house came into sight.

"This is an affluent neighborhood," said Elizabeth quietly to her aunt as they drove through a district of massive homes and wide avenues.

"It is Mayfair," said Aunt Gardiner. "I would not have expected anything different. The Darcys, Lizzy, are an old and respected family, and their wealth is on a level far beyond anything you know."

"I can see that," replied Elizabeth.

"As an earl, I expect Mr. Darcy's uncle is also wealthy," continued Mrs. Gardiner. "Though, given the habits of some of high society that is not a guarantee. But the Earl of Matlock has a good reputation in town, and I expect that *he*, at least, has not gambled away his fortune as so many have."

"It is all so difficult to understand," replied Elizabeth.

"I would not expect any less. But I *do* expect that Lizzy Bennet will not be intimidated by a large house, furnished in the finest fashions. Mr. Darcy does not seem to be burdened by excessive pride."

Elizabeth nodded but did not respond. The house the carriage approached was not any larger or more imposing than any of the others they had seen. The façade was impressive, the driveway impeccably maintained, and the liveried servants who secured their conveyance were quick and efficient. Mr. Darcy himself was waiting on the front steps, a young woman, tall, blonde, and elegant, standing by his side. But while Mr. Darcy was watching them, his eyes alight with anticipation, the girl's countenance displayed something like anxiety.

"Welcome, Mrs. Gardiner, Miss Bennet," said Mr. Darcy when they had stepped down from the carriage. "If you would allow me to make the introductions. This is my sister, Georgiana Darcy. Georgiana, Miss Elizabeth Bennet and Mrs. Madeline Gardiner."

The ladies curtseyed to one another, but Elizabeth did not miss the glance of surprise Miss Darcy directed at her brother. Elizabeth herself had not missed the significance of the order of introductions—which would have been her due as the daughter of an earl being introduced to a gentleman's daughter. But Miss Darcy ignored it, instead greeting them in a voice which was almost audible.

Had Elizabeth any head for the details of the house into which she was led, she would have noted the wide entry hall, tiled in marble, the large curving staircase which rose to the next floor, or the elegant furnishings which proclaimed this to be the house of a man of wealth. They were led to a sitting-room not far from the entrance, a lovely room of stylish furnishings and beautiful appointments, and a long bank of windows which looked out into the street below. Georgiana Darcy exerted herself to order a tea service for their visit, and they sat. It did not miss Elizabeth's notice that Mr. Darcy encouraged his sister to sit near the two visiting ladies, and that he kept himself a little apart. When Elizabeth directed a questioning look at him, however, he only smiled, glanced at his sister, and fondly rolled his eyes.

"I thank you for receiving us today, Miss Darcy," said Elizabeth when it appeared the girl would not speak. "I understand our presence must be a surprise to you."

Miss Darcy darted another look at her brother, and his response was an encouraging smile. She visibly plucked up her courage and addressed Elizabeth.

"Have you known my brother long?"

"Only a few days," replied Elizabeth. "We were introduced at a party we were both attending and have met twice since. Your brother has told us some little about you, but I am anticipating learning more *from* you."

Nonplused by Elizabeth's assertions, Miss Darcy nevertheless attempted to smile. "Then you have me at a disadvantage, for my brother said nothing of you before informing me of your visit this morning."

Elizabeth turned her attention to Mr. Darcy and feigned a glare at him. "For shame, sir! To surprise your sister in such a way was poorly done!"

"I had much rather you form a friendship on your own, Miss

Bennet," replied Mr. Darcy. "My sister should take your likeness from her own observations, without my impressions coloring her own."

"I can see how that would be desirable, but I still think you should have given her *some* warning." Elizabeth turned a conspiratorial smile on Miss Darcy. "How shall we punish him, Miss Darcy? Surely, you, as his sister, must know some way he can be made to pay for his temerity."

A giggle, the first reaction of pleasure she had seen from the girl, escaped her lips. "I know not how it may be done, Miss Bennet. He is the perfect elder brother. It is impossible."

Elizabeth laughed and looked at Mr. Darcy. "Mr. Darcy has achieved perfection, has he? It must be quite intimidating to live with such an example every day. How will the rest of us mere mortals ever measure up?"

"You may laugh at me, Miss Bennet," replied Mr. Darcy. His manner was all ease. "But if you do so, that must render me as imperfect as anyone else. Otherwise, you would not have anything at which to laugh."

"Though I would never presume to laugh at someone unkindly," replied Elizabeth, "I am happy to hear your confession. I dearly love to laugh. I will own that I have not had much occasion to laugh of late, but I hope my good humor will soon be restored."

"I hope so too," replied Mr. Darcy.

The visit continued from there, and slowly Elizabeth drew out the quiet and shy Miss Darcy. It was a benefit to Elizabeth too, for Mr. Darcy and Aunt Gardiner appeared content to allow Elizabeth and Miss Darcy to speak. And since Miss Darcy was so reticent, Elizabeth found it necessary to carry the burden of the conversation. For the first time since that awful time in Hertfordshire she almost felt like herself again.

Soon, Elizabeth discovered that Miss Darcy was fond of music and especially of playing her pianoforte, and a new subject of conversation was born. Miss Darcy became more animated as they discussed their favorite composers and debated their merits. Elizabeth, who had some passing familiarity with the instrument, had always been drawn to the works of Mozart and Beethoven, while Miss Darcy professed an abiding love of the works of Bach.

"You seem to have a talent, Miss Bennet, of inducing my shy sister to speak," said Mr. Darcy. Georgiana was speaking to Aunt Gardiner at that moment about her aunt's knowledge of Lady Anne Darcy

"She is a sweet girl." Elizabeth turned a mischievous look on her companion. "I might have thought that she would be confident and comfortable in company, considering her elder brother, who, I am certain, does not suffer from a lack of confidence."

"We both resemble our respective parents," replied Mr. Darcy. "I am much my father's son, while my mother, though the daughter of an earl, was shy and reticent like Georgiana. She was quite different from my aunt, my mother's sister, who has, at times, been described as something akin to a force of nature."

Elizabeth laughed. "Are you at all close to your aunt, Mr. Darcy?"

"I visit her estate every spring. Though at times I will own that she is a . . . difficult woman, she is my mother's sister and deserves to be respected as such."

"Then I hope you will forgive me for hoping I am not introduced to her quickly. She sounds positively intimidating."

"I doubt she could frighten you, Miss Bennet." Mr. Darcy gave her a significant look. "In fact, I am certain you could hold your own against anyone you chose. I am surprised, however. You seem to be much more accepting than you were only yesterday."

"There is little reason to dwell on it, Mr. Darcy. I am only trying to make sense of it all and retain what reason I possess."

"Good." Mr. Darcy paused and looked at his sister, and when he spoke, his voice was once again much quieter than it had been before. "Part of the reason for my sister's shyness is that she has suffered a . . . shock of late, from which she is only just recovering. Though I would not burden you with this and have no doubt of your understanding, she was, in fact, a victim of the same reprobate who importuned you."

Elizabeth's eyes widened in shock. "Mr. Wickham attempted to assault your sister?"

"In her case, his object was Gretna Green and her dowry, so she was not subjected to that humiliation. But it affected her all the same."

Elizabeth regarded the man for a moment, wondering if she should respond. His expression invited her, so she did not scruple to do so.

"If you do not mind my saying so, Mr. Darcy, I wonder that you have allowed Mr. Wickham to continue in his ways. Might it not be better for everyone that he be brought to account for his sins?"

"At the time, I was concerned he would expose my sister," said Mr. Darcy. "But I have recently come to your way of thinking. I have already sent for the documentation which will allow me to see him punished."

"Good," said Elizabeth. "Now, if you do not mind, I believe I wish to know your sister better."

"Not at all," said Mr. Darcy.

They spent an agreeable half-hour speaking together, and at the end of it, Elizabeth rose with her aunt to return to her uncle's house. But before she left, she grasped Georgiana's hands warmly.

"I am happy to have made your acquaintance, Miss Darcy. I hope that we will have many opportunities in the future to continue it."

"So do I, Miss Bennet," replied Miss Darcy, though her words were little more than a whisper.

"Then until next time."

Elizabeth and her aunt departed, and Elizabeth's mind was full of her new friendship with the Darcys. They were certainly not what she had expected from a family of their standing. It brought her greater hope for the future.

Tuesday, February 18, 1812
Darcy House, London

As their guests left, Darcy watched as the carriage rumbled down the street until it was only a speck in the distance and then as it turned off the road onto a major thoroughfare. The visit had been a success, in Darcy's estimation—not only had Miss Bennet been at ease with his sister, but he thought she had succeeded in piercing Georgiana's veil of reticence. And Mrs. Gardiner was as proper and mannered as he had thought. No doubt his uncle and aunt would wish to maintain the connection in gratitude for returning her to them.

"I *like* Miss Bennet, Brother."

Darcy turned to his sister, who had joined him in seeing Miss Bennet to her carriage, and smiled. "I am happy to hear it, Georgiana. I believe we will be seeing much of her in the future."

They stepped back into the house and made their way back toward the sitting-room, and Darcy realized almost immediately that his sister was in a talkative mood that morning. "I was so surprised when you mentioned their call. I had not thought you had met someone you wished to introduce to me."

"There are . . . other matters of which you are not aware, Georgiana," replied Darcy. They sat down on the sofas on which they had recently entertained Miss Bennet and her aunt, and Darcy directed his full attention to his sister. "I am not yet at liberty to share them with you, but I believe the surprise you felt will more than be exceeded when you learn the full account of my acquaintance with Miss

Bennet."

Georgiana gave him a long look. "Oh? I saw you speaking closely with her, Brother. It seemed to me like you were *very* comfortable in each other's company. And so soon after making her acquaintance."

Before Darcy could regain his wits and respond, Georgiana continued, saying: "It is even more shocking when you consider that you have assiduously avoided close acquaintance with *any* young lady, with the exception of Miss Bingley, of course." Georgiana's tone suggested her opinion of the woman mirrored his own.

"You will not need to concern yourself with *that woman* any longer."

"And I appreciate that fact. Nevertheless, it is a welcome development to see you taking interest in a woman and one who is so agreeable too. Is it too early to ask when I shall have a sister?"

"You believe I *admire* Miss Bennet?" asked Darcy.

"Is that not why you wished her to meet me so quickly?"

Darcy shook his head, feeling as if it was encased in molasses. "Actually, it is another matter entirely."

The skepticism in Georgiana's face indicated that she was not convinced of the truth of his protestations, but she declined to further press him on the subject. "In that case, I apologize for my impertinence, William."

"Not at all," said Darcy. "I can see how it might seem that way."

They spent a few moments in quiet contemplation, and while Darcy was immersed in his own thoughts, he did not miss the way Georgiana watched him. He doubted he had been able to completely quell her suspicions, as her expression was calculating. Darcy did not know how else to convince her that her suppositions were mistaken, so he decided to simply remain silent. Eventually, Georgiana excused herself to go to the music room, where she stayed for the rest of the morning.

Left to his own devices, Darcy considered the matter his sister had brought up, and he began to be aware of how close his sister was to the mark. In the excitement of finding the woman and becoming more certain that she was his cousin, Darcy had not given any thought to the notion that Miss Bennet was, in her own right, a desirable woman. Yes, she was very desirable, indeed.

CHAPTER VI

As expected, Fitzwilliam returned the evening following Miss Bennet's visit, though it was late enough that Darcy had already retired. He received the intelligence of it the following morning when he arose, and he hurried Snell through his preparations that morning to attend his cousin. Fitzwilliam was a man who had become accustomed to rising early, regardless of the time he had retired the night before, and in that he matched Darcy.

His cousin was in the breakfast room when Darcy entered, and the untouched food on his plate with his tea and morning paper at hand informed Darcy that he had seated himself only a moment before. Darcy greeted him as he usually did and proceeded to gather his own breakfast and join his cousin at the table.

"Now that you have returned yet again, are you bound for another distant locale on the orders of your general?"

Fitzwilliam turned to regard him around a bite of his breakfast sausage. "In fact, I believe I am free for most of the day, though I should likely make an appearance at my barracks. My days have recently been filled with such errands, but I think I will be tied to London for the next few days at least."

"That is well, for I have someone to whom I would like to introduce you."

Surprise crossed Fitzwilliam's countenance, and he leaned back in his chair a little. "An acquaintance you met at White's?"

"No, actually. It is a young woman I met at a party given by an acquaintance of mine. She is living with her uncle and aunt on Gracechurch Street."

"That is not a fashionable address, Darcy."

"Are *you* not the one who always informs *me* that nobility is a matter of character rather than circumstance?"

"Yes, I have, and I know, given your friendship with that Bingley chap, that you are no more impressed by titles and wealth than I am myself. But Gracechurch Street is in a whole different world, Darcy. And this for people you have only just met?"

"These people are not fashionable by society's standards, Fitzwilliam," replied Darcy. "But they are good and honest, and their manners would mark them as gentlefolk if one did not already know their circumstances."

Fitzwilliam regarded him for several moments before he spoke, and when he did, it was with an uncharacteristic bluntness. "Am I about to be introduced to the future Mrs. Darcy?"

With a laugh and a shake of his head, Darcy replied: "No, Cousin. I will keep the reason for our visit to myself for the present, but I believe it will quickly become apparent why I wish you to make their acquaintance."

"Is this the young woman you mentioned the last time we spoke?"

"She is," replied Darcy, not willing to give an inch.

"You are enjoying this, are you not?" complained Fitzwilliam. "Is this in response to all the times I have tormented you in the past?"

"Actually, it is not, though you roundly deserve it." Darcy stopped and smirked at his cousin. "But you are correct that I am enjoying this. I believe I will enjoy it even more when you discover the reason for the visit."

"I have not yet agreed to it."

"You will. Your curiosity will not allow any other outcome."

In this supposition, Darcy was correct, though Fitzwilliam grumbled and groaned and attempted to use every stratagem he could muster to induce Darcy to divulge his secret. Darcy only smiled at him and shook his head. They entered the carriage and made their way through the streets of the city, and by the time they departed, Fitzwilliam had taken to watching Darcy in injured silence. That made it even more delicious, and Darcy relished it all that much more.

"I am not certain I like this person you have become this morning, Cousin," said Fitzwilliam when they had been traveling for some minutes.

"A person much more like *you*?"

Darcy almost laughed at the sour expression with which his cousin regarded him. It seemed like Fitzwilliam had emptied the juice of all the lemons in Darcy's hothouse into his teacup that morning. The fact that this was how Darcy was usually treated by his cousin was a wonderful irony to be savored.

"I can determine only two possible motivations for this morning's farce: either you are besotted by the woman, or you wish to embarrass me in front of uncouth people."

Darcy only shook his head—there was nothing to be said.

"Fine!" exclaimed Fitzwilliam. "What about Wickham? When do you anticipate cutting the head off that particular snake?"

"My timetable has not changed since the last time we spoke of it. It will take a little time to ensure all the particulars are arranged."

"We should just buy up the debts he has accumulated in whatever hole he has buried himself. That should be more than enough to see him locked up until the rest of his receipts arrive."

"There are other reasons why we should be patient."

"You know, Darcy, you are not much fun when you attempt to be me. I am much better at it than you are."

Darcy laughed. "I shall take that as a compliment."

Finally, in frustration, Fitzwilliam turned to stare moodily out the window. Though Darcy would have enjoyed his continued outbursts, he remained silent the rest of the way to their destination.

Wednesday, February 19, 1812
Gardiner Townhouse, London

It was Mrs. Gardiner's counsel to Elizabeth to simply treat Mr. Darcy and his cousin's visit as just another morning visit of new friends. To a certain extent, that assisted Elizabeth in controlling her nerves. The differences, however, were quite apparent. For one, the door knocker had been removed that morning, and the housekeeper had been instructed to allow Mr. Darcy entrance and none other. For another, Mrs. Gardiner had ensured that her children had been removed to the nursery long before the gentlemen were expected, whereas she usually allowed them a little more latitude.

It was fortunate, Elizabeth decided, that she received a letter that morning, for it allowed her to focus on another subject. "Is that letter from Jane?" asked her aunt when Elizabeth opened and began to read.

"It is," replied Elizabeth with a sigh. "As you can well imagine, Mrs. Bennet does not approve of her daughters writing to me, so Jane must take care to avoid her discovering it, and as such, her letters are much shorter than I might expect."

"Yes, I can well imagine that. What does Jane say?"

"It is largely a lament concerning the departure of Mr. Bingley from Meryton." Elizabeth sighed. "As you know, he left after the ball at Netherfield in November and has not returned since. Ma . . . Mrs. Bennet's constant bemoaning his absence has not improved Jane's mood either."

Mrs. Gardiner shook her head in exasperation. "I told Maggie she would only cause Jane greater heartache if she continued to speak of it."

"When has she ever listened to the counsel of anyone else? I am only surprised she has not found some way to blame Mr. Bingley's desertion on *me*, even though it happened more than a month before I was forced to leave.

"Though she does not state it explicitly," added Elizabeth quietly, "I believe Jane misses *my* presence too."

"You have always been her defender and her rock on which she could rely." Mrs. Gardiner sighed. "I know your mother behaved reprehensibly, and the people of Meryton, not much better, but to put it in perspective, it is not only *you* who has been affected by your trials."

"Well do I know it," replied Elizabeth.

Hurting though she was for Jane, Elizabeth did not wish to dwell on the matter of her sister's heartache, for there was truly nothing she could do about it. Thus, another distraction became necessary, and she took herself to the small pianoforte the Gardiners boasted. For a little while, she was able to immerse herself in the music and forget what was to come. The ringing of the bell, however, informed her of Mr. Darcy's imminent arrival, and her nerves returned in full force.

"Courage, Elizabeth," said Mrs. Gardiner when Elizabeth rose to stand by her side.

The gentlemen were led in, and Elizabeth caught the first glimpse of the man who might be her brother. He was tall—taller than even

Mr. Darcy, who was himself a large man—burly and broad-shouldered, and he carried himself with the precision of a man who made his life in the military. He was dressed in a suit of a gentleman, rather than his regimentals, and his dark wavy hair was combed neatly. Elizabeth could also see that he took the room in with a glance, likely a habit to one whose profession was dangerous, and where any and all information at his command might save his life.

"Mrs. Gardiner, Miss Bennet," greeted Mr. Darcy. "I thank you for receiving us today."

"Of course, Mr. Darcy," said Mrs. Gardiner. "You know that you are welcome anytime."

"If you are agreeable, I would very much like to introduce you to my cousin." He turned to the man by his side. "Fitzwilliam, this is Mrs. Madeline Gardiner and her niece, Miss Elizabeth Bennet. I made their acquaintance in the days following Davidson's dinner party. Mrs. Gardiner, Miss Bennet, please allow me to present my cousin, Colonel Anthony Fitzwilliam. Fitzwilliam is the younger son of my uncle, the Earl of Matlock."

The customary pleasantries were exchanged, and Mrs. Gardiner rang for a tea service, after which the gentlemen were invited to sit. They made easy conversation for a few moments, mostly carried by Mrs. Gardiner and Colonel Fitzwilliam, and most of which was Mrs. Gardiner asking about the colonel. But Elizabeth was perplexed by the man's behavior. Did he disapprove of Mr. Darcy's assertions concerning her identity, or was there something else at play?

"I am grateful you have agreed to be introduced to me, Colonel," said Elizabeth, attempting to cover her confusion by opening a conversation with him.

"It is no trouble, Miss Bennet," replied he. "Darcy wished me to be known to you, and I have great faith in my cousin's judge of character."

Elizabeth darted a glance at Mr. Darcy, and the man stared at her intently. She opened her mouth to speak, but Mr. Darcy only shook his head and glanced at his cousin. The significance of his action suggested to Elizabeth that he had not actually told his cousin why they were here.

The knowledge struck her as amusing, and she put her hand to her mouth, chuckling at Mr. Darcy's teasing. She would not have expected it of him, as he had always struck her as a sober sort of man.

Her motion caught Colonel Fitzwilliam's attention, and he turned to regard her, a look of puzzlement playing across his features.

Elizabeth returned his look as blandly as she could manage, which seemed to strike Mr. Darcy as diverting, for he let out a snort as he was attempting to stifle his own laughter. That, in turn, prompted the colonel's attention to shift to Mr. Darcy, who looked back at his cousin in a credible imitation of the one Elizabeth had just bestowed upon him. All the while Mrs. Gardiner—who had clearly caught on to what was happening—watched it all with amusement.

"Are you visiting town at present, Miss Bennet?" asked Colonel Fitzwilliam. Rather than shake off his confusion, Elizabeth thought the man was interrogating her, attempting to learn more."

"I am actually living here for the present, Colonel Fitzwilliam."

The colonel frowned. "Your family is not in London?"

"No," replied Elizabeth. "I was raised on a small estate not far north of London in Hertfordshire. Longbourn is situated just east of the great north road, to the south of Luton and Stevenage."

"And your father—he is a gentleman?"

"Yes, Mr. Bennet is a gentleman."

Colonel Fitzwilliam once again frowned at the way she had phrased her answers. "And Mrs. Gardiner is your aunt by marriage?"

"Yes," replied Elizabeth. "Mr. Gardiner is Mrs. Bennet's younger brother."

It was clear that the colonel was as befuddled as he had ever been. Mr. Darcy, however, interjected and began speaking of their visit to Georgiana and thanking them for their kindness to his sister, for which Elizabeth was quick to inform him such thanks were not necessary. Then talk turned to a discussion of Lambton and the locations with which both Mr. Darcy and Mrs. Gardiner were familiar. And though Elizabeth did not carry much of the conversation, she felt the weight of Colonel Fitzwilliam's gaze upon her throughout, as if she were a particularly difficult puzzle he was trying to understand.

"Excuse me, Miss Bennet," said Colonel Fitzwilliam sometime later, "but at risk of being too familiar, or possibly even sounding a little silly, it is on my mind that you remind me of someone. Or perhaps you have visited Derbyshire yourself, and we have crossed paths?"

"Finally," muttered Mr. Darcy under his breath, and when the colonel turned to stare at him, Darcy only grinned and motioned back toward Elizabeth.

"*Have* we met before?"

"No, Colonel, I believe we have not."

"Perhaps it is time you use your vaunted ability for investigation for a matter closer to home," interjected Mr. Darcy. The colonel turned and glared at him, but it affected Mr. Darcy not a jot. "*Look* at her, Fitzwilliam. Notice the shape of her jaw and her eyes. Prompt her to laugh and listen to it carefully. Can you not guess who she is?"

The colonel turned back to her, and it was clear that no understanding came, but as he inspected her as Mr. Darcy had suggested, she saw the exact moment when he stiffened and his mouth fell open. He leaned forward, and gazed at her, moving to gain another angle, his intensity easily a match for his cousin.

"You have my mother's eyes," said he softly. He seemed surprised to hear the sound of his own voice. Then he turned a severe look on his cousin.

"Are you suggesting that Miss Bennet is my lost sister?"

"It took you long enough," said Mr. Darcy, clearly enjoying his cousin's surprise.

"It took you the entirety of an evening, Mr. Darcy," admonished Mrs. Gardiner.

"Yes, but I never actually spoke to Miss Bennet." Mr. Darcy directed a sidelong look at his cousin. "Or should I call you Lady Elizabeth Fitzwilliam?"

"What makes you think she is my sister, Darcy?" Unless Elizabeth missed her guess, Colonel Fitzwilliam was beginning to become a little cross.

"Other than the physical resemblance to my aunt—or to you also, if you look closely enough? When listening to her laugh one might almost think they were listening to the countess herself. Furthermore, she is the right age, carries the right name, and has recently discovered that she was a foundling, taken in by the Bennet family when they lived in Cambridge."

"Oh, the name is a dead giveaway," scoffed Colonel Fitzwilliam. "*If* she is my sister, I am sure she would not have hesitated to inform her new family of her full name, lineage, the amount of her dowry, as well as the exact directions to return her to her home. Of course, this would all have been done in the voice of a child of two years!"

"If you recall," replied Mr. Darcy, not at all affected by his cousin's sarcasm, "your sister was able to say her name, even at her young age—or at least a form of it."

Colonel Fitzwilliam turned back to Elizabeth, an expression of incredulous eagerness demanding answers.

"I do not remember any of these events, of course," said Elizabeth, "and I do not know if I am truly your sister. But I do remember my elder sister—or the woman I knew as my sister for many years—

calling me 'Lizbeth' as a child."

The look of dubious anger instantly became one of hope long suppressed. "Lizbeth?"

"Mr. Darcy is convinced that it is so. I am not yet so persuaded, but I have allowed it to be possible."

Wonder in his eyes, Colonel Fitzwilliam rose and reached out to grasp her hand, drawing her up with him. For several moments he looked her over, as one examines a loved-one long parted for any hint of change or injury. Then he fixed his gaze upon her eyes, and he looked into their depths for several moments.

"You have my mother's eyes," whispered he. "There is no doubt at all."

And then he drew Elizabeth to him in a fierce embrace, almost rough in its neediness. Elizabeth squeaked with surprise, but the sheer want in the man's actions allowed her to accept it and melt into his arms. It felt like the embrace of a brother.

When he allowed her to separate from him, Colonel Fitzwilliam continued to look at her with admiration. "I believe I may say, Elizabeth," said he, his voice rough with emotion, "that you are the most beautiful thing I have ever seen." He paused and laughed out loud. "Indeed, I dare say you could be warty, gnarled, and your hair half fallen out and I would still consider it so."

"It is not yet confirmed, sir!" protested Elizabeth.

"No, and I shall leave the burden of proof to my mother to provide. But for myself, I have no doubts."

Colonel Fitzwilliam turned back to his cousin. "I hope you feel yourself avenged for all the times I have teased you. I cannot imagine any vengeance which would be so efficacious as this."

"Perhaps I shall give you a reprieve for now, cousin," replied Mr. Darcy. From his open smirk, he was clearly enjoying this episode. "But I will keep further vengeance in mind if you should step out of line again."

They sat once again, but this time Aunt Gardiner relinquished her seat next to Elizabeth to allow brother and sister to sit side by side. It seemed like Colonel Fitzwilliam was not about to allow any word to the contrary, so at present she was his sister.

"I do not know how I shall survive this," said Elizabeth. "This has all been so unexpected as to render me witless. How shall I ever meet your parents or be introduced to the rest of your family?"

"It *is* hard, I am sure," said Colonel Fitzwilliam. "But I have no doubt you possess the fortitude to endure it." Then he winked at her.

"If you think *our* little emotional outpouring was hard, I warn you that it will likely be nothing compared to what will ensue when my mother is introduced to you."

Colonel Fitzwilliam grinned when Elizabeth paled. "My mother, you see, has suffered from your absence more than the rest of us, especially when you consider how she has had to endure the presence of three men in her house without a woman to balance the scales."

"That is the reverse of my adoptive father's house, only to a greater degree. *He*, after all, must contend with a house of *six* ladies, and not a son with whom to commiserate."

Colonel Fitzwilliam grinned. "You must relate the circumstances of your upbringing to me, for I am quite interested to learn of it."

Then he paused and a thought seemed to cross his mind. He turned and looked at Mr. Darcy, a frown crossing his features. Mr. Darcy, however, only shook his head, a clear indication that he not only understood his cousin but that they would discuss it later.

Elizabeth was curious as to what passed between them, but her attention was deflected when the colonel demanded her story, which she did not hesitate to share. The only part of it she did not relate to him was what had happened with George Wickham and the resulting events which had led to her residence in London. Mr. Darcy's words concerning his cousin—her *brother!*—rang through her ears, and a glance at him and his minute shake of his head informed her it was best to allow him to relate the matter. At length, however, the colonel was in possession of the pertinent details of her life, and they moved to other subjects, the most important being her eventual meeting with the earl and countess.

"My most recent letter from them informed me that father and mother are enjoying a short vacation from London's season." Colonel Fitzwilliam shot a devilish glance at Darcy and added: "They are not quite like my reclusive cousin, here, but they do find the activities of the city a little much. I expect them back within a week."

"And your brother?" asked Elizabeth. "Is he also from town?"

"At present he is," replied the colonel. "*Our* brother is with his wife at a house party in Bedfordshire, and though I have no idea as to his schedule, he, too, has duties in London and must return eventually."

Elizabeth absorbed this information, wondering at the thought of having *two* brothers when she had always longed for *one*. "Will you send them word, asking them to return quickly?"

When the colonel had thought about this for a moment, he shook his head. "I do not believe there is any reason to do so. If I sent my father a letter by the usual means, he would scarcely receive it before they are to depart anyway, and I would not worry them with an express. As for my brother, I believe I will wait until my parents meet you and allow them to make the determination as to how to inform him."

"Whatever you think is best."

"In the meantime, I intend to come to know the sister I have been denied for so many years." The colonel smiled at her. "To that end, might I hope for your frequent company?"

"What if we visit the Royal Academy of the Arts?" said Mr. Darcy. "Have you ever attended, Miss Bennet?"

"I have not," replied Elizabeth, looking at her aunt. "It was, however, one of the activities we discussed when I came to London."

"Then let us go there one day this week," said Colonel Fitzwilliam. "The other days we can either find something else to amuse us or simply visit between this house and Darcy's. Of course, we would be delighted if you and your husband would attend with us, Mrs. Gardiner."

"Thank you, Colonel," replied Aunt Gardiner. "If our schedule allows, we will be happy to attend."

They spent a few more moments visiting, and then the gentlemen rose. "I would ask Mrs. Gardiner's pardon for imposing upon her home all day," said he, directing a roguish grin at them both. "But I believe I must arrange to use some of the leave I have accumulated.

"If you are agreeable," said he, speaking directly to Elizabeth, "I should like to address you by your given name, if you will do me the honor in return."

"Is that entirely advisable?" asked Elizabeth. "Nothing will be confirmed until your father comes."

"Perhaps that is true. But I am convinced you are my sister." He paused and nodded. "But yours is the prudent course. Then let us use our Christian names when we are in company with our relations or those who know the truth of your identity. We may keep to formality when among wider company, such as our visit to the academy."

"Very well," replied Elizabeth.

After a few more moments, the gentlemen took their leave, and Elizabeth saw them to the door. The colonel—Anthony—swept her up in another brief embrace before they left, and though she still felt ill at ease accepting it from a man she was not yet convinced was a close relation, it was wonderful to feel so protected. If this was what it was like having a brother, Elizabeth could not wait until it was proclaimed far and wide.

"Now, Darcy," said Fitzwilliam, as soon as the door of the coach closed behind them, "I want the full account of what has happened to Elizabeth. I did not miss the looks between you when she ended her account of her life in Hertfordshire. I suspect her presence here has something to do with your sudden desire to prosecute Wickham."

"In that, you would be correct," replied Darcy. He had known that Fitzwilliam would bring this up as soon as they left—in fact, he had been surprised when he had not insisted Elizabeth inform him of the matter himself.

"What did he do?" It was almost a snarl.

"Miss Bennet is safe, Fitzwilliam. I will require your promise that you will not head to Hertfordshire and run your sword through the reprobate. Your sister has returned after many years absence, and she does not need to witness you in a hangman's noose soon after her recovery."

"You injure me, Cousin. The likes of George Wickham do not deserve to be challenged in the manner of gentlemen—should I take action against him no one would ever find the body."

"Your promise," insisted Darcy.

"Very well," replied Fitzwilliam. "The fate you have planned for him would be far more of a punishment than simply ridding the world of his pestilence anyway."

By the time Darcy finished relating the story to his cousin, Fitzwilliam was incensed anew, and it took most of the carriage ride to calm him. As an enemy, Fitzwilliam was implacable, one whom Darcy would not wish to make. He did not *think* Fitzwilliam was capable of such actions as he intimated, but he was entirely capable of a brand of retribution in his rage which would possibly be injurious to any man who provoked him. George Wickham had made a career of provoking Anthony Fitzwilliam.

"I will have him in prison, Darcy," said Fitzwilliam, his tone merciless. "No thoughts of his being your father's favorite will buy his freedom. Given what I know of the receipts you hold, he will be an old man before he is again free. *If* he manages to avoid provoking one of his cellmates against him before."

"His offenses against Georgiana were enough to make me want to beat him within an inch of his life," said Darcy. "It was only thoughts of her which restrained me. His treatment of Miss Bennet was infinitely worse. He will receive no clemency from me."

"Good." That subject dealt with, Fitzwilliam changed to another. "I will go to my general and arrange for leave immediately."

"How long will you ask for?" asked Darcy.

"At least several weeks. In fact, I might not return to the army at all."

That surprised Darcy. "Has your sister's possible recovery worked that much of a change in you? Aunt Susan has been asking you to resign your commission for some time now, and you have always rebuffed her."

"I do not know, Cousin, which is why I will request leave first." Fitzwilliam paused and stared out the window moodily. "I have an estate, and though it is nothing to Pemberley, it is enough to keep me with food on the table and a roof over my head. Perhaps it is time to give it some of my attention.

"But of greater importance is the state of the war against the tyrant. There have been rumors that my regiment will be setting sail for the continent before long."

"Will your general give you leave if that is the case?"

"He will either approve my leave or accept my resignation," replied Fitzwilliam. "I have just regained my sister. I have no desire to end our new acquaintance by being placed inside a casket."

"I am happy to hear it," replied Darcy quietly. He had never seen his cousin in such a mood as this. The family would welcome this news, for every time he had left to go into battle, his mother had worried excessively. Darcy had no desire to lose his cousin in some meaningless skirmish against the French.

CHAPTER VII

The next few days were surreal for Elizabeth. Though Elizabeth often felt overcome, she relied on her aunt's good advice and simply accepted everything as it came. If Anthony and Mr. Darcy were correct, she would soon be openly connected to them, as strange as the notion sounded.

One other thing which changed was the manner in which Elizabeth addressed her new acquaintances. Georgiana quickly asked for the right to address her by her Christian name, which Elizabeth readily accepted. The surprise, however, was when Mr. Darcy made the same request. Though Elizabeth was just as reluctant with him as she had been with Anthony, she agreed with the same restrictions. But as Georgiana was not yet privy to the possibility of Elizabeth's hidden identity, they remained formal while in her company. But that did not prevent the girl from a certain level of confusion, as she was quick to notice the informality in their attention to Elizabeth.

"William?" asked the girl one morning while they were walking in the park near the Gardiner residence. "I am confused."

Elizabeth, who was walking behind the Darcys with Anthony, overheard and listened with interest, noting the girl did not seem to realize how her voice carried.

"Yes, Georgiana?" asked William.

"I thought you were to pay court to Elizabeth, but Anthony appears to be doing the same."

Elizabeth sucked in a breath at the girl's words, but her companion was having difficulty controlling his laughter.

"Well . . . That is to say . . ." William fell silent, clearly unaware of how to answer this unexpected question, and Elizabeth could feel Anthony quivering where her hand was resting on his arm, as he was attempting to rein in his mirth.

"I am not courting Elizabeth, Georgiana," said William at length.

Georgiana frowned. "Do you not think she is wonderful, Brother? I believe she would make an excellent sister."

Finally, Anthony was forced to stop and allow the Darcys to walk on ahead so that he could release some of the laughter which had built up in his breast. Elizabeth withdrew her hand from his arm and stood watching him, arms akimbo, as he indulged in his chuckling.

"For shame, Anthony!" exclaimed Elizabeth. "This situation is confusing dear Georgiana!"

"Actually, I think it is a delicious irony, my dear," replied Anthony, his eyes still shining. "Darcy and I have been Georgiana's joint guardians since her father passed, and she has never seen us at odds. And for her to think I am paying court to my own sister! I can barely talk for laughing so hard!"

Elizabeth regarded him with some asperity before she turned on her heel and marched away toward the Darcys, who had stopped to watch them. William appeared as if he wished to sink into the ground with embarrassment, but Georgiana was all that much more confused. Ignoring William, Elizabeth stepped toward Georgiana and, grasping her arm, pulled her away down the path, leaving the gentlemen to follow them.

"Elizabeth?" asked the girl after they had been walking a few moments.

"Yes, Georgiana?"

"Are you . . . ?" Georgiana's cheeks bloomed and she stammered to apologize, but Elizabeth only encouraged her to speak.

"I have . . . noticed that William and Anthony are both paying attention to you. I had thought William meant to court you when he insisted we be introduced."

"That is a reasonable assumption to make, Georgiana," replied Elizabeth. "But you may rest easy, for I am not being courted by either of your guardians."

"Oh," replied Georgiana, crestfallen.

"Yes, and what a relief it is." Georgiana's eyes nearly bulged out of their sockets. "They are, neither of them, serious enough for me, for they are both intent upon being amusing. I declare I do not know how you have turned out to be such a sweet girl with two such guardians attempting to corrupt you."

A soft snort reached their ears from where the gentlemen walked behind them, and Georgiana seemed to understand that Elizabeth was teasing them. She let out a nervous laugh, uncomfortable with the thought of laughing at her guardians. Elizabeth, however, encouraged her, saying:

"They are your brother and your cousin, my dear, and that is more important than being your guardians. You are allowed to laugh at them when they are being ridiculous."

The girl smiled tentatively. "I have, especially with Anthony, who has a penchant for trying to make me laugh. But I must own that I do not understand what is so amusing in this instance."

"Perhaps not," said Elizabeth with a fond smile for the girl. "But you will eventually."

Georgiana seemed to accept that, and they changed the subject. For the rest of the day, Elizabeth endeavored to avoid the sole company of either of the two gentlemen. William kept his distance, but Anthony seemed to find amusement in her behavior. Elizabeth vowed to wreak a perfect vengeance on him when the offer presented itself.

Thursday, February 27, 1812
Royal Academy of the Arts, London

A few days later Elizabeth joined the Darcys and her brother in the promised excursion to the academy. Though invited, Mr. Gardiner cited his work as a reason to decline, while Mrs. Gardiner claimed the need to care for her children. Privately, Elizabeth was certain they had declined to give her time alone with her relations, affording her the opportunity to come to know them without interference.

If Elizabeth was truthful, she was beginning to feel a little uncomfortable because of the situation. As yet, nothing had been made official—it would be up to the earl and countess to decide whether to claim her as their daughter, based—Elizabeth hoped—on further information about their daughter they might possess. But to her aunt and uncle, and William and Anthony—Georgiana still had not been told—she was a Fitzwilliam. Elizabeth knew they would not be dissuaded, for they were all convinced. Thus, she ignored their behavior.

The Royal Academy of the Arts, often called simply "the Royal Academy" or "the Academy," was a large and handsome stone building just off Piccadilly, which had been its home for the past fifty years. Though Elizabeth had never visited, she had heard much of it, and while she would not consider herself to be a connoisseur of the arts, she did have some interest.

But the first thing she noticed when she exited the carriage had nothing to do with the exhibits of art. William and Anthony—and to a lesser extent Georgiana—were obviously known in society, and their coming excited some response, mostly in the form of whispers and glances. But Elizabeth soon noted that *she* also drew some attention, because she was an unknown and had arrived with those who were *very* well known. Most just watched them and whispered between themselves, but while a few did attempt to speak to them, William and Anthony gave vague responses to those with whom they were acquainted, while the rest were sent away with little beyond a tight greeting. This circumstance persisted as long as they stayed at the academy.

Had the visit proceeded in such a fashion the entire time they were there, it would have been unremarkable. The exhibits were, as Elizabeth had expected, interesting enough, though she suspected Mary would have enjoyed it more than she herself did. There were paintings aplenty, as well as statues, busts, and other assorted works of art, all painstakingly displayed and preserved. It was a large building, and it took some time to work their way through all the halls, and even in this, she was soon to learn they would not see all of it that day.

"It is far too extensive," said Anthony when Elizabeth had inquired after their plans. "We may come again some other time if you wish to see more. But it is a large building, and the entirety of the artwork cannot be seen in the space of one afternoon. Unless one is not here for the artwork, of course."

Elizabeth instantly understood to what he referred. "I have noticed that many of those here have more interest in seeing those around them."

A snort told Elizabeth what Fitzwilliam's feelings were on the matter. "It is often thus. Members of society are much more interested in seeing and being seen than appreciating masterpieces of art. You will see this same behavior at many other venues as well. When they leave, they may comfort themselves at the thought of their being 'cultured,' though they have no recollection of what they were there to see."

It spoke to a common theme she had heard from both gentlemen several times since making their acquaintance. William was taciturn and his behavior, even at Mr. Davidson's party, informed her that his opinion of society was poor. Anthony, by contrast, was much easier in company and spoke with great animation when he met someone with whom he shared a friendly relationship. But even so, Elizabeth caught sight of him shaking his head after several encounters, displaying his opinion to be much the same as Mr. Darcy's regardless of how the application of his manners was quite different from his cousin's.

Elizabeth walked and observed and admired with the rest of her party, but there was little that caught her true fancy, and the effects of the oil lamps were more than a little unpleasant, in her opinion. Still, she quite enjoyed herself, debating the merits of this painting or that bust, or explaining what she knew of another to Georgiana. It was quite a pleasant way to spend an afternoon.

The true drama, however, was reserved for later. They had been there for some time when Elizabeth and Georgiana stopped in front of a painting and began speaking of it. How they managed to be recognized from behind, Elizabeth was not certain, but a voice she had not heard in some months interrupted their conversation.

"My dear Georgiana! How wonderful it is to see you here!"

Startled, Georgiana turned to regard the lady approaching them, drawing Elizabeth along with her. She was dressed in a pale lime gown, one constructed of obviously costly materials, which was more than a little overdone for an afternoon in an art gallery. Her turban was topped with a pair of garish ostrich feathers, dyed in the same color, and the woman, tall, bony, with spindly legs and a figure which could generously be referred to as willowy, displayed a wide smile that Elizabeth instantly determined was feigned. It was none other than Miss Caroline Bingley.

The woman opened her mouth to say something to Georgiana when she caught sight of Elizabeth and halted in her tracks, her mouth wide open. But for the moment she ignored Elizabeth and focused her considerable fawning on Georgiana.

"I had no idea you were to be here today, else I would have made certain to greet you when you arrived. How do you do, dearest Georgiana?"

That Georgiana was ill at ease Elizabeth noted almost as soon as the woman's voice pierced the bubble of their discourse. The shy Georgiana whom Elizabeth had met that first day at her brother's house once again made an appearance. She made a credible attempt at replying to Miss Bingley's greeting, but even Elizabeth, who stood by her side, could hardly hear a word she said.

"I am happy to see you too!" exclaimed Miss Bingley, as if Georgiana had just broken out into a paean at the good fortune at being accosted in such a way. "Tell me, my dear, is your brother here with you?" Miss Bingley paused and glanced about, seeming disappointed when she did not catch sight of him. "I would be happy to greet him if he is."

Georgiana responded that Mr. Darcy was, indeed, present, and Miss Bingley grasped her arm and began to steer her away from Elizabeth. "Then let us find him, shall we? I believe I must have words with him, for he is allowing you to be accosted by those with whom I am certain he would not wish for you to be acquainted."

At this blatant snub of Elizabeth, Georgiana finally showed a little fire. She removed her arm from Miss Bingley's clutches and turned back to Elizabeth, grasping her arm. Her grip was a little tight, it was true, but she glared back at Miss Bingley, attempting to assert her independence.

"Actually, Elizabeth is a member of our party today, Miss Bingley."

"Truly?" asked the woman, feigning astonishment. "I had not thought Mr. Darcy to be so negligent with your care as to allow you to associate with one who is, after all, not equal to you in society."

Elizabeth let out a breath she had not realized she had been holding. If Miss Bingley had received some information concerning the events in Hertfordshire with Mr. Wickham, her nastiness would undoubtedly approach prodigious proportions. As it was, it seemed like Miss Bingley's spite was only her usual behavior.

"*Elizabeth* is my friend, *Miss Bingley*," said Georgiana, emphasizing her level of familiarity with both ladies. "My brother is aware of Elizabeth's presence, and he is well acquainted with her himself—better than I am, in fact."

"That is astonishing, indeed," cried Miss Bingley. She turned to Elizabeth for the first time, and her tone was such that Elizabeth was surprised she could not see venom dripping from her teeth. "I know not how you managed it, Miss Eliza. The last I heard, you were still buried in that little town you call home. Has your father suddenly inherited an earldom and risen from his squalor?"

"I am happy to see you too, Miss Bingley," said Elizabeth. Georgiana giggled at the irony in her tone, while Miss Bingley's countenance darkened. "As for the manner of my introduction to Mr. Darcy and Georgiana, I am afraid that is none of your concern."

"I know what you are trying to do here, little Miss Eliza," hissed Miss Bingley. "But it will not work. I shall inform Mr. Darcy of from whence you have come and all your pretenses will be exposed. You will never again impose upon them."

"And imposition is a matter with which you are well acquainted, are you not, Miss Bingley?"

So intent had Elizabeth been on confronting Miss Bingley, even she had not noted the approach of William and Anthony. The voice, coming from behind her as it had, caused Miss Bingley to jump in surprise. She quickly recovered and soon turned her simpering upon Mr. Darcy.

"Ah, Mr. Darcy," purred she. "I have just been speaking with your delightful sister. However, I must wonder at the company you have been allowing her to keep." Miss Bingley turned a smug glance on Elizabeth. "I am certain you cannot know the details of Miss Bennet's situation, or you would not allow such an improper acquaintance."

"The matter of my sister's acquaintances is in *my* purview."

"And mine," said Anthony, stepping forward to stand beside William.

Miss Bingley appeared shocked. "But you cannot know of her situation and family. Why, we knew her in Hertfordshire when we lived there." Miss Bingley turned a withering sneer on Elizabeth. "She is naught but the daughter of a country squire, one who allows his daughters to run through the village, screeching after officers at the top of their lungs. Surely you do not wish for Georgiana to be affected by her wild ways!"

"Miss Bingley!" barked Anthony. The woman flinched in shock. "It is *you* who knows nothing, and I shall not take the time to correct you." Anthony stepped toward her, and as he was a tall and imposing man, she shrank back from him. "I would suggest, Miss Bingley, that you forget whatever it is you *thought* you knew about Miss Bennet, for your conjectures are far from correct. Let *nothing* concerning her pass your lips, for if we hear *any* rumors, we will know from whence they originated and will act accordingly. This is your only warning."

The look he threw her was one of utter contempt, before he turned, gathered Georgiana and Elizabeth to him, and led them away. Elizabeth risked a look back over her shoulder, and she noted when William stepped close to Miss Bingley and hissed something in her ear. The woman's countenance became even paler, and she looked at him with wide-eyed shock. Then he was striding quickly away from her, hurrying to catch them, while Miss Bingley watched him retreat without moving an inch.

"I was not aware you were acquainted with Miss Bingley, Elizabeth," said Georgiana after they had walked for a few moments.

"Mr. Bingley leased an estate near my father's, last autumn. I was unfortunate enough to share a neighborhood with her until the end of November when Mr. Bingley and his family suddenly returned to London."

"Then you were fortunate," said Anthony shortly. "Miss Bingley is the worst example of a fortune hunter and social climber I have ever had the misfortune to meet."

"*That* I determined from our first meeting." Elizabeth laughed. "There was no one in Meryton who met her standards of wealth or sophistication."

"You mean no one with whom she could curry favor to improve her own position," said Anthony. His tone was sour enough to turn milk.

Georgiana giggled. "She does not like Anthony," confided she.

"Oh?" asked Elizabeth, raising an eyebrow at him. "And I thought you were an amiable gentleman, beloved by all."

"Now where did you obtain *that* notion?" asked Anthony, waggling his eyebrows at her. "Darcy is the one beloved by all—I have no tolerance for many of those he calls his friends, particularly the Bingleys."

"Mr. Bingley is, at least, an amiable gentleman," protested Elizabeth.

"He is," replied Anthony. "Too amiable by half. He is so amiable that he allows his sister to rule him. She will be the ruin of him one day."

"But surely she must act as if she esteems you. You *do* inhabit the sphere to which she aspires, after all. Someone of her nature must, by her very character, give you far more deference than you would like if she is to 'curry favor,' as you call it."

Anthony smirked, one which carried particularly unpleasant overtones. "On the contrary, when I first made Miss Bingley's acquaintance, I made it *abundantly* clear that I had no intention of allowing her to simper and flutter her eyelashes at me. Consequently, she does not consider me to be worth her time." Anthony paused, and then he said in a short tone, "Darcy would have done well to have done the same."

Something about the matter struck Elizabeth as odd, but she was not quite able to puzzle it out. They continued on their way through the exhibits, but Elizabeth was not able to focus on what she was seeing like she had before. Anthony's—and, indeed, William's—antipathy for Miss Bingley she would well understand, but from their words, Elizabeth thought that William and Mr. Bingley had been friends. And then there was the matter of Anthony's final words concerning Miss Bingley, words which seemed to leave something important unsaid.

She was curious about the matter, so when the opportunity came to ask William about it, she wasted no time in doing so. Georgiana and Anthony had walked ahead, speaking of a sculpture they had seen, and Elizabeth fell back beside William.

"I was not aware that you were acquainted with Miss Bingley," said William, echoing Georgiana's earlier words.

"I did not know *you* were," rejoined Elizabeth.

William eyed her for a moment, and then he suddenly brightened, as if having solved a difficult puzzle. "You said your father's estate was near Meryton, did you not?" At Elizabeth's nod, he continued: "I feel foolish for not making the connection. Netherfield is near your father's estate, is it not?"

"It is about three miles," replied Elizabeth.

"Then that is where you met them. For myself, I have known Bingley since university, though it is only within the past three years that we have become close friends. You must not be aware, but I actually stayed at Netherfield one night in October. I *was* to stay there for two months complete."

Elizabeth's eyes widened. "I have never heard any mention of you in Meryton."

William grumbled and turned away, but Elizabeth was not about to allow him to avoid the subject. "What happened, William?"

"The blasted woman attempted to force my hand by compromising me," said he, his tone almost a snarl.

"She attempted to compromise you?" Elizabeth could hardly fathom it—she knew Miss Bingley was a proud and arrogant woman, and that she fancied herself to be of high society, but she had never thought her capable of this.

"The first night I was staying there. I had arrived a few days after

Bingley and his family. I have known that she saw herself as the perfect mistress of my estate, but it seems like more than three years of trying — and failing — to elicit a proposal from me made her desperate."

William's tone as he related his tale was devoid of any warmth or inflection — it was a harsh statement of the facts as he had lived them, and Elizabeth knew he was keeping his anger in check by only his force of will.

"She must have thought her greatest chance of success lay in catching me when I was fatigued after a day of traveling. Unfortunately, she did not count on Snell."

"Snell?" asked Elizabeth.

"Snell is my valet," replied William, and finally a gleam of something resembling warmth entered his eyes. "He is a good valet, and he cares for me like I was his child. But he is the most fastidious man I have ever met and, furthermore, has a vested interest in ensuring Miss Bingley *never* becomes the mistress of Pemberley."

"He sounds like a treasure, William."

William laughed. "I do not know that 'treasure' is precisely the word I would choose, but he has been my valet since I was a boy, and I am quite accustomed to his ways. Miss Bingley has stayed at Pemberley, and a more disagreeable stay I cannot imagine. She behaved as if she was mistress of the estate, ordering the servants with an imperiousness Queen Charlotte herself does not possess. Snell has made it his business to represent all my servants and prevent her from any machinations which would result in a woman, hated by all my servants, from becoming their mistress.

"The night we arrived at Netherfield, he requested a cot from the housekeeper and placed it no more than two feet in front of the door to my room. Miss Bingley waited for two hours after I had retired and let herself into my room with a set of keys she had . . . liberated from the housekeeper's office. But when she stepped inside, she was met by the scowling presence of Snell, who is a light sleeper. He was awake as soon as she turned the key in the lock."

"I can hardly fathom it, William. So that is why you only stayed a single night?"

William looked away, his jaw once again clenched with anger. "Snell made such a ruckus that it drew Bingley to investigate. Miss Bingley claimed that she was only attempting to ascertain whether I was comfortable in my suite of rooms. The worst betrayal, however, was when Bingley did nothing to censure her for it. He has never been able to stand up to her, and he proved it in this instance. He did nothing more than attempt to apologize to me and send her to her room, and after she left, he insinuated to me that it would be agreeable to *him* if I was to marry her. I have no doubt he only wishes someone — *anyone* — to take her off his hands. I was so angry, I called for my carriage at that moment, and I quit the house within thirty minutes. I have not spoken to Bingley since."

"Then her behavior is all that much more curious," replied Elizabeth. "For her to act like nothing happened and claim a friendship with you — the woman is positively mad!"

A snort summed up William's feelings on the subject. "She is capable of much more than that." William turned to Elizabeth and regarded her seriously. "Do not allow Miss Bingley to intimidate you, Elizabeth. She is an adder, coiled and ready to strike, and she will not hesitate to use any perceived weakness against you."

"I held my own against her in Meryton," said Elizabeth. "I have no fear of her." Elizabeth paused, thinking of the situation, and her mind wandered to Jane and her heartache in the wake of Mr. Bingley's abandonment. "I am only . . . Jane, the Bennets' eldest daughter, is one of the sweetest women I have ever met. She became quite attached to Mr. Bingley when he was in Meryton, and we all thought it was returned. When Mr. Bingley left suddenly, she was heartbroken."

William sighed. "I have not known Bingley to be callous, but he often falls in and out of love with pretty young ladies. From what you have told me, it sounds like Miss Bennet was the latest in a long line of such women."

It was difficult to hear such things, for Elizabeth had always assumed that it was Mr. Bingley's sisters who had persuaded him against Jane. To know that it was because he could not be trusted to maintain an admiration for a woman was information which would be all that much harder for Jane to hear. For a moment, Elizabeth thought it might be best to keep it from Jane, but she knew it was fruitless. She deserved to know. Though Elizabeth knew Jane would never ascribe any evil tendencies to Mr. Bingley or his sister, perhaps this knowledge would allow her to heal.

"I will tell Jane the next time I write to her. Thank you for informing me, William."

William nodded, but he did not reply. Their remaining time at the academy was not nearly so interesting as it had been prior to their meeting with Miss Bingley. To Elizabeth's relief, they left soon after. She had a letter to write, and though she was loath to do it, she knew it needed to be done.

CHAPTER VIII

Thursday, February 27, 1812
Gardiner Townhouse, London

*A*s Elizabeth had expected, writing the letter to Jane was difficult. While Jane was not deficient in understanding, she was such a trusting soul; hearing of Miss Bingley's actions and William's account of Mr. Bingley would be hard for her to credit. Elizabeth knew Jane would not doubt Elizabeth's words and would be forced to accept them, but her knowledge of Elizabeth's trustworthiness would not make it any easier.

The most difficult part of the task was attempting to determine what she should include. Any mention of Elizabeth's possible discovery of her birth family must be avoided, for there was no guarantee that Mrs. Bennet would not read it. Therefore, she must be circumspect concerning Anthony and William. In the end, she portrayed William as a new acquaintance, but one who was familiar with Mr. Bingley and his family, and could be trusted to be impartial. As well, she could not mention anything of Miss Bingley's attempted compromise for similar reasons.

When she had finally completed the letter, Elizabeth sent it, addressed to Mr. Bennet. Mrs. Bennet had decreed that no letters should be accepted from Elizabeth, and Elizabeth was certain she would destroy them if she saw any. But Mr. Bennet had a longstanding rule that his wife was not to tamper with his mail, and as a result, it was a safe way to pass letters back to her former family.

Once this was complete, Elizabeth spent the rest of the day brooding, thinking of her dear sister and wishing she could be there for Jane. Her aunt and uncle noticed her lack of spirits and attempted to cheer her, but the results were dubious at best.

"It is not that I do not think Jane will believe me," said Elizabeth, when her aunt made a comment to that effect. "The worst part is that she will have no one to turn to for help. Kitty and Lydia are, of course, a lost cause, and Mrs. Bennet is the same. Mr. Bennet will be inclined to tease Jane for being crossed in love, while Mary will turn to moralizing."

Elizabeth paused, thinking on the matter. "I hope Mary will be able to at least provide a listening ear, though I suspect she will not truly understand or sympathize with Jane's troubles. I also hope she will refrain from chastising Jane for whatever imagined faults she believes led to Jane's disappointed hopes."

"I think Mary might surprise you," said Uncle Gardiner. "A lot of her troubles are due to being ignored by both her parents. Your father has told me in his letters that Jane and Mary appear to be closer since your departure."

"I hope so," replied Elizabeth, surprised that Jane had not mentioned this in any of her infrequent letters. "Jane needs someone to support her, and Mary needs a closer relationship with her family."

"Perhaps we should invite Jane to stay here for a time," said Mrs. Gardiner,

Elizabeth looked up with hope, but her uncle's reply dashed it. "I doubt Maggie would send Jane to us now—not while we refuse to cast Elizabeth off." Mr. Gardiner tapped his lip with one finger. "If Elizabeth is proven to be the Fitzwilliams' daughter, she will likely be leaving our house to live with them. That might be a good time to ask Jane to visit, when we can truthfully say Elizabeth no longer lives with us."

"Go to live with the Fitzwilliams?" asked Elizabeth. It was very nearly a squeak.

"I have no doubt it will come to that, should your identity be proven," said Mrs. Gardiner, her tone faintly chastising. "You should expect it, Lizzy."

Elizabeth had not thought that far in advance. Now that the Gardiners had opened her eyes to the possibility, it provided one more thing for her to worry about.

Saturday, February 29, 1812
Hyde Park, London

There continued to be much congress between the Gardiner home and William's, with Elizabeth often visiting her possible relations, and the Darcys, along with Anthony, visiting Gracechurch Street on the days she did not. On a morning later that week, Elizabeth visited Mayfair in the morning, and when Georgiana was called in by her companion to her studies—Elizabeth understood they had been much disrupted of late due to her frequent presence—the gentlemen suggested a walk in nearby Hyde Park. Elizabeth, not being familiar with the area, readily agreed, curious as she was to see the wilderness in the middle of the city of which she had heard so much.

Hyde Park was, as Elizabeth had expected, delightful. She had never expected to see so much greenery in the middle of a city the size of London, but soon all her longing for nature was satisfied by the wide lanes, the tall trees swaying in a soft breeze, and the sparkling waters of the Serpentine, undulating against the banks. They wandered for some time, Elizabeth taking in the sights with interest and enthusiasm, while William and Anthony watched her, making some observations at times, or directing her toward views they thought she would appreciate.

"I have received word from my father," said Anthony after a time of wandering the park. "If all goes to schedule—and I have no doubt it will—they should be arriving within three days."

The butterflies Elizabeth always felt when considering her inevitable meeting with the earl and countess once again fluttered in her midsection, and she was forced to take a breath in to dispel them.

"You need not be anxious, Elizabeth," said Anthony when he noticed her reaction. "Even if you are *not* my sister, they will be kind."

"I am certain they will be," replied Elizabeth, with a curt hand motion, banishing any thought of unnecessary unease. "It is not every day one of my station is introduced to a member of the peerage." At Anthony's look, Elizabeth laughed and placed a hand on his arm. "Rather, at the level of society in which I was raised."

"Perhaps instead you could tell us something more about your home," suggested William. "Then we could reciprocate with some of our experiences as well. Then you might see that our situations are not so different as you think."

Elizabeth thought this was a marvelous idea. They found a bench near the path and sat to have their discussion. While there were certain things Elizabeth was not convinced she was comfortable telling these two men, at least she was able to give them a notion of what her upbringing had been like.

"If you recall, I have informed you that I have five sisters, and that my adoptive family lives on a small estate by the name of Longbourn. Mr. Bennet is an intelligent man, but of late I have realized that he is also a slothful one."

Anthony frowned. "In what way?"

"He takes almost no care for the estate." Elizabeth sighed. "It is difficult for me to criticize him. Mr. Bennet was the parent to whom I was closest when I thought I was a Bennet. We spent many hours debating points of literature, speaking of books we had read, and even discussing philosophy." Elizabeth paused and smiled. "I believe I mentioned that Mr. Bennet was an academic at Cambridge; it is a life to which he was suited.

"In some ways, it is a shame that he was forced to care for the family estate—he possesses the knowledge, but as it interests him but little, he only does what he must. Since none of his daughters will inherit and it is destined to devolve, by an entailment, to a distant cousin whom he has never met, and whose father he openly despised, he cannot be bothered with its upkeep."

"That is remarkably short-sighted if you will forgive me for saying it," said William. "While the terms of the entail mean the estate will not benefit his family after his death and might limit what he can do with it now, the income is his to do with as he wishes. His daughters' dowries should be his highest priority if he is to leave them without a home after his passing."

"It is," replied Elizabeth quietly. "When asked, however, he only says he expected to father a son and by the time they realized there would not be an heir, it was too late to begin economizing."

"It is never too late," said William, his tone curt and annoyed.

"That is where Mrs. Bennet comes in. You see, she was not born a gentlewoman—rather she is the daughter of the local attorney in Meryton."

"How did she manage to catch Mr. Bennet then?" asked Anthony. "Given what you have said, it does not sound like she had much of a dowry, and it is rare that such a marriage take place, even in a country society, when there is no significant financial benefit for the estate owner."

"You are correct—Mrs. Bennet's dowry was only five thousand pounds. To the best of my knowledge, there was never a compromise, if that is what you are suggesting, and you must remember that Mr. Bennet was a younger son, destined for a life teaching at Cambridge."

"All that much more reason for him to marry with more attention to money," replied William. "As the younger son of a minor landowner, he could not expect a wife of an exalted sphere, but surely ten thousand or even more might have been within his reach."

"I do not know. But once, when Mr. Bennet was feeling introspective, he told me that he married Mrs. Bennet in a fit of infatuation and regretted it not long after. Mrs. Bennet is . . . not the most intelligent woman."

"I assume that is a kind way of inferring her to be vapid and mean of understanding," said Anthony with a snort.

Elizabeth could only nod with unhappy agreement. "Mr. Bennet, as I said, is very intelligent, and learning he could not have a sensible conversation with his wife left him with little respect for her. They have little affection—she complains about her nerves, which are fanciful expressions of ill use, while he teases her and provokes them with his commentary." Elizabeth paused, and when she continued speaking, it was in a soft voice. "I have been witness to an unhappy union my entire life. It is for this reason that Jane and I have always determined to marry for love alone. I would not wish to be so unhappy as they."

It was clear to Elizabeth that both gentlemen disapproved of Mr. Bennet, and she could hardly censure them for it. There were so many things which could have been done—which could still be done—to improve the Bennets' situation, but neither partner had any interest or desire to expend the effort. Even now, though the Bennet daughters would never be wealthy, a campaign of economizing, insisted on by Mr. Bennet, would prevent them from being destitute when he passed on. But Elizabeth knew Mr. Bennet's study was too comfortable for him to ever put himself out to improve his daughters' situations.

"Then another kind of union you shall witness," said Anthony, breaking through Elizabeth's thoughts. "My mother and father share a kind and loving relationship."

"And you must not have been devoid of good examples," added William. "The Gardiners do not seem to be cut from the same cloth as your adoptive family."

"No, that is true," said Elizabeth. "I owe much to them. Both Jane and I have spent many months with them, and we have both greatly benefitted from their instruction."

"I do wonder about this matter of the Bennets," said Anthony, turning them back to the previous subject. "When Mrs. Bennet married Mr. Bennet, she could have had no notion that he would ever be a gentleman in his own right. As such, she must have been forced to subsist on the income of a university professor. How is it that matters have deteriorated to the point where this entailment is such a threat?"

It was something Elizabeth had considered in the past but had never had the courage to ask Mr. Bennet. "I only have suspicions. I suspect that the unexpected good fortune of becoming a gentleman's wife went to her head, and she believed it was her right to behave as a lady of means."

"And Mr. Bennet never corrected her," said William."

"Mr. Bennet has a healthy respect for his wife's ability to bring commotion and disorder to his home, and Longbourn already has enough of that, given the presence of five women and their associated concerns."

"You have not spoken much of your sisters," replied William. "Except for the eldest, of course."

"Jane," said Elizabeth, a feeling of longing for her closest friend entering her breast. "Jane and I have always shared the closest of relationships. The only word I can think of to describe her is saintly, and even that may fall short of the mark. She is calm and poised, good and caring, and cannot fathom evil tendencies in anyone."

"That seems like a recipe which would allow others to take advantage of her," said Anthony.

Elizabeth smiled at him. "I said saintly, not stupid. Jane is adept at thinking the best of others, but she also possesses a strong sense of what is right. She never questions, but she is also never induced to act against her principles." Elizabeth paused and giggled when a memory returned to her mind. "After Mr. Bingley's abandonment, Mr. Wickham attempted to charm her, and it was easy to see he was frustrated when she listened and agreed with everything he said, but would not give him any of her attention."

"And the younger Bennets?" asked William, steering the conversation away from Mr. Wickham.

"I have not much in common with any of them," said Elizabeth. "Mary is the next youngest. She is not like either of her parents or any of her siblings, and as such, she is always alone in the family. She is primarily interested in the pianoforte and reading scriptures and moralistic texts." Elizabeth paused and grimaced. "Two years ago she discovered Fordyce's sermons and since then has made a habit of quoting him when she thought she was most likely to be heard. This, obviously, has not made her a favorite with her sisters."

"I can well imagine," said Anthony, William nodding in agreement.

"Mary can be tiresome," said Elizabeth, shaking her head, "but she is, at heart, a good sort of girl. Mary requires love from her family and to be noticed by either her father or her mother. It does not help that she is the plainest of the sisters, and Mrs. Bennet is constantly bemoaning her lack of beauty where Mary can hear. In fact, Mary is not actually *plain*, though it is true she has not been blessed with as much beauty as her sisters.

"As for the youngest Bennets," said Elizabeth, hoping to move past this mortifying interview as soon as possible, "Kitty and Lydia are inseparable. Unfortunately, they are silly, idle, and vain, allowed to while their hours away in puerile pursuits. They love to dance, chase officers, and flirt. Learning anything is an anathema to them. Kitty is the elder, but she is a born follower and rides on Lydia's coattails wherever she goes. Since Lydia entered society last year, I have wondered when she would expose us all to ridicule with her wild ways."

From the sympathy in their gazes, Elizabeth was able to discern they were thinking what she was—how it had been ironic, though entirely unfair, that it was Mr. Wickham's actions toward Elizabeth which had affected the family's standing. But Elizabeth was not about to let such thoughts affect her, especially when she had done nothing wrong.

"Mrs. Bennet always favored Lydia and Jane—Lydia because she is most like Mrs. Bennet and Jane as the most beautiful of her daughters. She pins all her hopes for a good marriage on Jane, hoping she will save the family. Mr. Bennet always favored me, though again Jane is beloved of him too. The three youngest, Mr. Bennet has always referred to as the silliest girls in all England."

When she had finished her recitation, Elizabeth regarded the two men before her, daring them to say anything. They seemed disinclined to do so, and after a moment of frustration, Elizabeth continued: "There you have it—my family and upbringing. You may now despise me at your leisure."

* * *

Saturday, February 29, 1812
Hyde Park, London

"Despise you?" demanded Fitzwilliam. "Elizabeth, I worship the very ground upon which you walk!"

It was very near the same thoughts Darcy had, and he nodded vigorously to his cousin's declaration. "We might deplore the situation in which you were raised, Elizabeth, but we would never despise *you* because of it."

Elizabeth's countenance softened, and she nodded and smiled. "Thank you." The words were no less fervent for being spoken in a soft tone.

"I will say, however, that it is nothing less than amazing that you have grown to be the person you are after being raised in such an environment." Fitzwilliam paused and shook his head. "Perhaps there is something to Lady Catherine's assertions that nobility of character is a direct result of birth and lineage."

"Please do not suggest something so unnatural as Aunt Catherine being right about something!" protested Darcy.

The two men shared a laugh and Elizabeth looked on with interest, seeing an opportunity to turn the subject. "I would like to hear of some of the family. Your aunt?"

"She is sister to Darcy's mother and my father, the eldest of the three siblings" replied Fitzwilliam. "If your mother is improper and thoughtless, then Lady Catherine is improper of a purpose. She is domineering and authoritative, ruling over her estate as if it was her own little kingdom. She does not hesitate to share her opinions about anything that catches her interest, and she does not allow a lack of knowledge on a subject deter her." Fitzwilliam snorted. "Once she attempted to inform me *exactly* what was to be done to defeat the little tyrant. The laughter the account produced echoed throughout my general's office for some time."

"Surely she is not so ridiculous!" exclaimed Elizabeth.

"She is quite intelligent and manages her estate well," said Darcy. "But Fitzwilliam has the right of it. Her response to your recovery should be amusing to see, though I am not certain any of us will appreciate the humor of the situation when she is berating us all."

The portrait they had painted of their near relation brought Elizabeth to laughter. Perhaps the Bennets of Longbourn could not claim the greater part of ridiculous behavior after all.

"And the rest of your family?" asked Elizabeth.

"Lady Catherine has a daughter," said Darcy. Fitzwilliam snickered, but Darcy shot him a warning glare and he subsided, though it was clear he was still quite amused. "Anne is sickly and rarely leaves Rosings, our aunt's estate. Unfortunately, Lady Catherine's husband, Sir Lewis, passed on some years ago."

"My parents I have already spoken of," said Fitzwilliam. "I have one elder brother—James—who is the Viscount Chesterfield. James is married to Lady Constance, with whom he has two children."

"And what sort of person is my prospective brother?" asked Elizabeth with an impish smile.

Fitzwilliam laughed. "In fact, he is quite like me, in temperament, though of a slighter build. Lady Constance is the daughter of a duke, and as such you will find that she is quite impressed with her position in life. But she is a good woman and will treat you with kindness and affection. She is also a good wife and mother. She and my brother made a love match.

"Even as a child, you were a breath of fresh air upon us all, Elizabeth." Fitzwilliam directed an intense look at her, which seemed to startle her.

"In what way?"

"In your irrepressible spirits and joy of life, which were evident even as a small child. You were doted on by us all, Elizabeth. We were devastated by your loss."

It seemed like even Elizabeth's insistence that she was not yet known to be Fitzwilliam's sister could not survive the raw emotions in his voice. In the end, she only nodded and did not reply.

They fell silent and Darcy looked about, glancing about their surroundings, which had gone unnoticed while they had spoken. There were few people about, as it was still not the fashionable hour. He also knew that it would be before long, and if they remained in the park, they would draw unwanted attention. He made this observation to his companions, and they agreed to depart and return to his home. It would be time for Elizabeth to return to Gracechurch Street soon, regardless.

"If I did not already know otherwise, Mr. Darcy," said Elizabeth as they rose and began walking back toward his house, "I might assume you were embarrassed to be seen with me."

Fitzwilliam guffawed, but Darcy, being accustomed to her teasing by now, only smiled. "I might have been if I did not know who you truly are." Darcy winked at her. "I am known to be quite fastidious, you know."

"That is the truth!" exclaimed Fitzwilliam.

"Then I am happy to have escaped your contempt," said Elizabeth with a mischievous grin. "Had I known how haughty you might become, I might not have agreed to this acquaintance."

"Ah, but you have, Elizabeth," replied Darcy. "And now that we have you, I doubt we will ever allow you to simply flee."

"You are correct there," said Fitzwilliam.

For her part, Elizabeth did not respond. He thought their fervent declarations had caught her a little unaware. It was something to which she would need to become accustomed—Fitzwilliams, and those of their extended family did not do anything by half. She was already sister and cousin, and Darcy had no doubt she would remain with them, even if her identity was not proven conclusively.

CHAPTER IX

Wednesday, March 4, 1812
Fitzwilliam House, London

By the time his parents had arrived in London, the impatience
Fitzwilliam felt was nigh unbearable. Elizabeth was everything
he had always imagined his sister would be when she attained
the age of adulthood. She was confident and intelligent, mischievous,
playful, possessing an innate sense of how to behave and how to carry
herself. This, she had learned while being raised as the daughter of a
country squire and among his improper family. It was nothing less
than astonishing. The surprise his parents would feel upon learning
their lost daughter had been recovered . . . .

Inwardly Fitzwilliam chuckled. They would be shocked, no doubt,
but he thought they would handle it with the aplomb for which they
were known as one of the leading families of society. The only concern,
in Fitzwilliam's mind, was whether they could provide convincing
proof that Elizabeth was, in fact, their daughter.

They arrived the evening his father had indicated in his letter, and
Fitzwilliam greeted them, careful to keep his enthusiasm in check.
They were not to be told why they were to go to Gracechurch Street,

much as Darcy had not told him when he convinced Fitzwilliam to meet her.

"Would it not be better to inform them in advance?" Fitzwilliam had asked when Darcy cautioned him against telling them as soon as they arrived in London.

"I was not simply teasing you when I failed to inform you," had been Darcy's rejoinder. "I did not say anything because I wished you to meet her and come to your own conclusions."

"Why should it matter?"

"Because it would be better if they were to go there without any preconceived notions. The possibility remains, which you and I do not wish to acknowledge, that she is *not* your sister. Furthermore, if you tell them in advance, they will not go into the meeting with her unbiased. Let them make their own observations, Cousin, without infecting them with yours."

Though a little uneasy, Fitzwilliam had acceded to Darcy's arguments. His cousin was an astute man—as perceptive as any Fitzwilliam had ever met. He was likely correct in this matter, little though Fitzwilliam wished to remain silent.

They gathered for breakfast the next morning, his parents already much recovered from the long journey from Derbyshire. Though they were both well past fifty, his parents were healthy and full of vigor; such trifling concerns as advancing age were not at the point of affecting them just yet. Fitzwilliam waited until after they ate and were sitting at the table, their teas in hand, to inform them of the visit he had planned for that day.

"What do you know of Edward Gardiner, Father?" asked he by way of opening the conversation.

His father turned to him, curiosity in his eyes. "Gardiner . . . I believe he is an importer, is he not?"

"He is. Are you acquainted with him?"

"I am not," said the earl, shaking his head. "To be honest, I am surprised *you* are." The earl paused and regarded him, and when Fitzwilliam did not speak, he shrugged. "The Gardiners are not of our sphere, and I do not know them, though they are known to some mutual acquaintances. Mr. Gardiner, the importer, is related to them only distantly, through a branch of the family which fell from the ranks of the gentry many years ago, or so I believe. Mr. Gardiner has built his business up such that he is rather wealthy, or so I hear. His contacts among the landowner class are primarily at a level below ours. In all honesty, I would not object to an acquaintance with the man.

"Now, to what do these questions tend?"

"This morning, together with Darcy, I propose that we visit Mr. Gardiner in his townhouse on Gracechurch Street."

"Gracechurch Street is not the best area of town," said Lady Susan, Fitzwilliam's mother. "Why would you have us go there?"

"It is actually a pleasant area," said Fitzwilliam. "Darcy and I have been there a time or two in the past week."

His father's eyebrows rose at this admission. "That is interesting, especially from Darcy. He is rather fastidious."

"He is not as fussy as you think, Father. Recall his friendship with Bingley and his willingness to attend dinners at the house of Miles Davidson, both of whom are not unacquainted with trade."

"You have a point," said Matlock with a laugh. "But you still have not explained why you wish us to meet this Mr. Gardiner."

"Let us simply say that we have a matter of business with Mr. Gardiner which might interest you. To restate, I am certain it will more than interest you."

The earl eyed him for a moment, apparently taking in his mood and determination before he turned a lazy look on his wife. For her part, Lady Susan rolled her eyes.

"It seems to me that our son intends to be mysterious this morning, my dear. Shall we indulge him anyway?"

"Very well," said his mother. "I have no specific plans for today."

Though he was careful to hide it, Fitzwilliam heaved a sigh of relief. It had not been certain that his parents would agree to accompany him unless they were told the exact reason for their visit that morning. With their agreement in hand, Fitzwilliam sent a brief note to Darcy, informing him of the matter and arranging to retrieve him from Darcy house at precisely half-past ten.

At the appointed time, the carriage pulled up in front of Darcy house, and the man himself stepped into the carriage. The driver clucked the horses into motion, and they were off. The earl and countess did not waste any time in questioning them.

"Now, perhaps you boys should tell me a little more about what our purpose is this morning. Or do you feel bound by your cousin's silence too, Darcy?"

"Not bound by it," replied Darcy. "But I believe it is best that you be allowed to judge for yourself without any interference from Fitzwilliam or me."

Matlock raised an eyebrow at Darcy, but Lady Susan only shook her head. "I expect my son to tease and try to obtain his own way with frivolous nothings, but I had not expected it from you, Darcy."

"Mother!" protested Fitzwilliam. "I resent the implications in your remarks."

But Lady Susan only laughed and looked at him fondly—it was an old game they played, even as far back as when he had been a boy in school. "You are a little lacking in seriousness, Anthony. Even you must acknowledge it."

"Perhaps it is so, Mother," replied Fitzwilliam. "But in this case, I assure you that I intend no jest. The matter we are to deal with this morning is quite serious."

Her eyes darted back and forth between Fitzwilliam and Darcy, and it was clear she had sensed a shift in the mood. The earl was also aware of it, for he looked at them both as if he had never seen them before.

"This is nothing distasteful, I hope."

"No, Father. In fact, I believe you will be quite happy with what we will find at Mr. Gardiner's house. Surprised, yes, but not disappointed in any way."

A glance between husband and wife settled the matter, and though they were no less curious, they did not attempt to discover anything more. "Then you have us both intrigued, Anthony," said the earl. "Perhaps we should urge the carriage on, so we may arrive sooner."

"The situation will not change with our haste, Father. Mr. Gardiner will be there, even if we arrive five minutes later."

"I am certain he will. But I am curious, and you know I do not like to remain in that state."

Wednesday, March 4, 1812
Gardiner Townhouse, London

When Elizabeth had turned into this anxious, shivering creature she was not certain, but as she waited in the Gardiners' sitting-room for the earl and countess to make their appearance, she was as nervous as she had ever been. On some level, she knew her edginess was understandable—the results of today's interview could decide the course of the rest of her life. She could not help feeling cross with herself, however, for her cowardice.

On this occasion, at least, her aunt had little to say to her. Mrs. Gardiner undoubtedly understood Elizabeth's feelings, but it seemed like her aunt, who possessed a courage and indomitable will of her own, was also feeling the effects of the upcoming presence of a peer in her house. And perhaps even more than the earl himself, it was the thought of hosting the *countess* which disturbed her peace of mind. Only Uncle Gardiner seemed little affected. As a man who had many contacts, he was likely better positioned to retain his equilibrium.

As the door knocker echoed throughout the vestibule and from thence into the sitting-room, both Elizabeth and her aunt jumped in tandem. This, of course, led them each to gaze at the other, and from there it was hardly surprising that the laughter would flow.

"Are we not a pair of silly geese?" said Aunt Gardiner.

"I have no idea what has become of my courage, Aunt, but I shall not disagree with you."

"You *are* both silly," commented Uncle Gardiner. "You have been in company with Mr. Darcy and Colonel Fitzwilliam many times this week, and you are well acquainted with *their* characters. Their accounts of their relations in no way suggest you should be anxious at the thought of meeting them."

"Then perhaps we should show our fortitude," said Elizabeth. "I have never allowed anything to challenge my courage before—I should not start now."

"An excellent idea, my dear."

It was while Elizabeth and her aunt were smiling together that the door opened and the housekeeper led the visitors into the room, the earl and countess, by deference of their stations, leading William and Anthony. As she turned to catch her first glimpse of those who might be her parents, the smile still large upon her countenance, Elizabeth saw the countess. As such, she was witness to the exact moment the countess caught sight of her.

At first, she seemed to little comprehend what she was seeing. But after an instant, her eyes widened, and she stared at Elizabeth, hope and disbelief vying for prominence in her entire manner. Then heedless of anyone or anything else in the room, she stepped forward, her gait like that of a sleepwalker, an inexorable step, seemingly without conscious thought. Then she stopped in front of Elizabeth, gazing directly into her face. For a moment, the entire world stood still. Then, the countess's hand rose of its own accord, and she touched Elizabeth's cheek, a motion so light it was nothing more than a breath of air on an otherwise calm day.

"I think you had best tell us why we are here today, Anthony."

The countess's words seemed to break a spell cast over them all, and Elizabeth heaved a great breath of relief. But her eyes never left the countess's face—she seemed caught there, held in check, though Elizabeth could not truthfully say that it was against her will.

"Perhaps we should observe the proprieties and secure introductions to these good people first."

Hearing the voice of the earl for the first time, Elizabeth's eyes, finally freed from their prison, darted to the man, and noted that while he was no less affected by the sight of her, his eyes also roamed over her aunt and uncle. It was likely the effects of a lifetime of politics which allowed him to keep his head. Or perhaps he was not convinced or not quite understanding what his wife had seen.

"Of course," said Mr. Darcy, being the first to recover. His distance from her as a relation—and his position of knowing her the longest—worked to preserve his senses from what was happening. "Perhaps we should have planned this a little better, though I am certain we can all see that there is something significant happening here."

"That much is certain," said the countess. "I am torn between kissing you both and putting you over my knee."

The colonel laughed along with Mr. Gardiner, and it seemed a little of the tension was broken. Thus, Mr. Darcy stepped forward to do the honors.

"Uncle, Aunt, please allow me to introduce Mr. Edward Gardiner, his wife, Mrs. Madeline Gardiner, and their niece, Miss *Elizabeth* Bennet. Mr. Gardiner, Mrs. Gardiner, Miss Bennet, may I present my uncle, Hugh Fitzwilliam, the Earl of Matlock, and his wife, Lady Susan Fitzwilliam."

The emphasis on Elizabeth's first name was not missed by any of them, least of all the countess who was still inspecting Elizabeth closely. Elizabeth felt the fluttering begin again in her midsection. But the thought of her recent determination with her aunt infused Elizabeth with a sense of her old courage, which allowed her to meet Lady Susan's gaze without hesitation. After a moment, the woman nodded to her, slowly, and with approval.

"I will assume, Anthony, that given the secrecy to which you have subjected us, the manner in which you have introduced this young lady to us and the young lady's appearance—which could be a mirror for my own at her age—you are suggesting she is your sister, long lost to us."

"That is correct, Mother," replied Anthony. "Darcy and I thought it best if you came without any preconceived notions of Miss Bennet. It appears we were correct."

The countess paused for a moment, considering her words, but it was the earl—who had stepped forward and was now standing next to his wife—who answered. "Though I share your mother's inclination to turn you over my knee, I suspect you were correct."

"My lord, your ladyship," said Mrs. Gardiner, stepping into the fray, which was beginning to become fraught with emotion again, "will you not sit? I believe this interview will not be brief, nor will it be without emotion. With your permission, I will order some refreshments, and we may speak at leisure."

Lady Susan's eyes turned toward Mrs. Gardiner, and her gaze softened. "Thank you, Mrs. Gardiner. At least one of us is thinking correctly. Your suggestions are much appreciated."

They arranged themselves on the available seating, while Mrs. Gardiner rang for her housekeeper and instructed a tea service with some cakes be delivered for their consumption. Elizabeth was certain the request had been made far in advance of their guests' coming, for it was delivered almost before they were able to take their seats.

Elizabeth soon found herself seated on the Gardiners' loveseat with Lady Susan—who refused to be separated from her, even for an instant—settled in beside her. The earl, no less eager to hear the tale, was situated in a chair near the loveseat on Elizabeth's side, while the Gardiners, William, and Anthony arranged themselves on the remaining sofa and chairs. The tea service was set on the table in between, and the housekeeper soon departed, leaving them alone.

"I must own that I could never in my wildest dreams have considered *this* as the reason why you insisted on bringing us here this morning," commented the earl. "Both Susan and myself—and, I dare say, *you*, Anthony—had long given up hope Elizabeth would ever be returned to us."

"There still is no conclusive proof that I am your daughter," Elizabeth felt obliged to say.

The earl regarded her closely for several moments before he nodded slowly. "Though I would never have thought one as young as you would even have known enough to attempt to play on our old grief, that statement makes it clear to me that whatever you are, you are no fortune hunter."

"I would hope not, sir," said Elizabeth, a hint of offense rising in her breast.

Both the earl and countess seemed to catch the tone of her voice, for they smiled at her as one. "And that is the spirit I would expect to find in a daughter of mine," said Lady Susan.

"Perhaps before we go too far, you should explain what has led us to this point." The earl looked at his son and nephew, his eyebrow raised in challenge.

"It was Darcy who originally found her," replied Anthony. "Would you like the first chance of it, old man?"

Mr. Darcy readily agreed, and he began to relate how he had noticed Elizabeth at the dinner party, watched her throughout the evening, and then his moment of epiphany when he realized who she must be. He then explained the steps he had undertaken to find her, his visit to Mr. Gardiner, and the subsequent dinner at which he had learned of Elizabeth's current situation and explained his suspicions concerning her identity.

When he had finished his recitation, Lady Susan turned to Elizabeth. "Perhaps you would care to explain what has led you to this place, Elizabeth."

The countess colored, and her eyes closed for a moment in mortification. When they opened again, she looked on Elizabeth with an expression of pleading. "I hope you will forgive my lapse, my dear, but I cannot call you . . . 'Miss Bennet.' Not when I am becoming more convinced by the moment that you are *my* daughter."

Feeling suddenly short of breath, Elizabeth was nevertheless able to respond: "I am not offended, your ladyship."

Lady Susan smiled, and Elizabeth saw, in its depths, an echo of her own. It was at that moment she began to truly believe William and Anthony's suspicions might be correct. "Thank you, though we will deal with this 'your ladyship' business shortly.

"Now, am I correct in deducing that you were not aware you were not the daughter of these people who raised you?"

"No, I was not," said Elizabeth. "Not until January last."

"Then let us hear your story, my dear. I am certain it will have a great bearing on what we decide today."

And Elizabeth did, though her tale was more hesitant and less confident than Mr. Darcy's had been only moments before. She did not cover much of her upbringing, deciding that it was not relevant to the subject at hand, but she thought she saw in the countess a suggestion that she had not missed the omission. Instead, Elizabeth concentrated on the events around her departure from Hertfordshire and her coming to London. But while Elizabeth thought to exclude the matter of Mr. Wickham, Anthony stopped her and shook his head.

"No, Elizabeth, relate the entire story." He paused and smirked at William, though his expression held no mirth. "While I understand why Darcy insisted you exclude it when you were informing me of your past, neither of my parents are likely to vault onto a horse and ride to Hertfordshire in pursuit of that libertine. They need to know."

With an uncertain nod, Elizabeth indicated her understanding and told them the full story. It took no great insight to see the pinched lips of Lady Susan or the expression of the utmost fury of a peer of the realm, but Elizabeth endeavored to ignore their reactions in favor of her recitation. When she was finished, she felt drained and lightheaded.

"My dear girl," said Lady Susan, gathering her to her in a gentle embrace. "You have suffered, it seems, though not as much as I have feared, these past eighteen years. The home in which you were raised was a good one, yes?"

Elizabeth smiled, though tremulously. "Longbourn was an excellent home, your ladyship. While it was not perfect, I felt the love of parents and the bond of siblings. Knowing now that I was a foundling, I am aware that it could have been much worse."

The countess nodded and then turned to her son. "And what is your role in all of this, Anthony?"

"I was not informed of these matters until after Darcy had spoken to Elizabeth and the Gardiners." He turned an expressive look on William. "It seems he took the burden of the investigation on himself."

"It was for the best," replied William. "When I realized her resemblance to you, Aunt, I did not even know her identity or that she was a foundling. For all I knew, I might have come here and been thrown from the house by Mr. Gardiner's sizeable boot."

"If he had come only a few months before, he *would* have been," said Mr. Gardiner.

They all laughed at this observation. Lady Susan laughed along with everyone else, but her gaze fixed on her son never wavered. "But something must have convinced you of her identity."

"Darcy brought me here under the same conditions as we brought you. I will own that it took me longer to recognize the resemblance, but when I did, and when I heard her story, I became convinced." Anthony turned a smile and a wink on Elizabeth. "Since then, I have endeavored to come to know my sister better. There has not been a day since that we have not seen her, either here or at Darcy's house. We went to the Academy one day as well, in Georgiana's company."

"And does Georgiana know?"

"We have refrained from telling her," replied William. "She was born after Elizabeth's disappearance, and she has only heard a little of it. I did not wish to confuse her when we could not be certain."

The earl and countess once again shared a look. "I understand your wish to become acquainted, but you might have been better to avoid the prying eyes of society. Can I assume that no one recognized her?"

"I am hard pressed to think anyone would," replied Anthony. "There was a brief mention of Elizabeth's presence in our company in the gossip sheets, but nothing further. There are no rumors of which I am aware."

Anthony turned and lifted an eyebrow at Darcy, asking for his opinion. Darcy only shook his head. "There has been nothing in the newspapers. But as my attention has been fixed on Elizabeth, I have not been much in society."

"If there were rumors," said Lady Susan, "they would be in the papers."

"Is it possible to be certain, Mother?" asked Anthony. There was a hint of a pleading quality in his voice. "Is there some other way you can identify Elizabeth as my sister?"

The countess nodded, though slowly. "I have been thinking of that very subject since I first caught sight of Elizabeth. There were no birthmarks or other markings on your sister that I can recall. May I assume you also have no birthmarks, Elizabeth?"

Elizabeth shook her head. "No, I have no such marks."

"Then the only other thing that I can think of is a scar that my daughter had, which might persist — which I have no doubt *will* persist if you are my daughter."

Elizabeth looked at the lady, puzzled, for she could think of no scars that she possessed.

"It was on the back of your head, to the left." Lady Susan smiled at her, the vagueness of a memory recalled dimming her eyes. "You were naught but a year old, and an energetic and determined scamp you were. You learned to walk by the time you were nine months of age, and once you started to walk, there was no stopping you. One summer day, not long after your first birthday, we visited an elderly relation, and as you were running and playing, you lost your balance and fell, striking the back of your head on the corner of a table."

Lady Susan shook her head, and she focused on Elizabeth once again. "It bled profusely, and for a while, I thought we might lose you because of it." A ghost of pain crossed her features. "Like my close friend, Darcy's mother, I had struggled to carry another child after my elder children, though I was blessed with two fine sons and she only had one. But losing you in such a way would have been a devastating blow."

"Losing her in the way we did was an even greater blow," said the earl quietly.

"A scar on my head?" asked Elizabeth, feeling lightheaded.

The countess fixed her gaze upon Elizabeth again. "Yes. When it was healed, I would often touch it, massaging it as you slept or played in my arms. It was in the shape of a jagged crescent, and from the time it healed, no hair would grow upon it."

Elizabeth gasped and her hand rose to her head before she could stop it. Lady Susan watched all of this, giving no hint of her feelings. The eyes of everyone in the room were upon Elizabeth, but she could not pull her gaze away from her mother. *Her mother!*

"Do you have a scar, Elizabeth?" asked she.

"I do," said Elizabeth, her hand rising to touch the location, as familiar to her as the back of her hand.

"May I?"

With a nod, Elizabeth rose when the lady stood, allowing her to reach back and caress the back of her head. Lady Susan's hands quested through her hair, fingers finding the pins, pulling them out and depositing them on the table beside them. When the last one was removed, the wealth of Elizabeth's hair fell down her back in waves. Then with the utmost gentleness, her hands went to the place where Elizabeth's scar lay, the puckered scar rising a little above the level of her scalp, and her fingers glided along its length. Tears filled the lady's eyes.

"It seems you are who my son claims, my dear."

"Are you certain?" asked Elizabeth. "I would not wish to be acknowledged unless there was absolutely no doubt."

Lady Susan laughed at this further evidence of her stubborn nature. "I do not know what could be more certain," said she. "Beyond everything that Darcy and my son have observed about you, the scar is in the exact same location and the same shape as I remember. It is a little raised, and the size has changed, but that is unsurprising, considering you are now a woman rather than a babe. About the only thing that would convince me more is if you were to produce the dress you were wearing when you disappeared."

"We visited Longbourn many times when we were newly married, your ladyship," said Mrs. Gardiner. "Though Elizabeth was already older by then, it is possible it might have been passed down to one of her younger sisters."

It took Lady Susan a moment to visibly pull her attention from Elizabeth, but when she did, she turned to Mrs. Gardiner and attempted a smile. "It would not convince me of Elizabeth's identity any more than I already am, but I will tell you. It was a pale yellow dress with small, red roses embroidered into it. It was a gift given to Elizabeth by a distant relation, one who never had a daughter of her own, but always wished for one."

As Lady Susan was speaking, Mrs. Gardiner turned pale. "If you will give me a moment, your ladyship," said she, before she went to the door and, opening it, hurried through. Those left in the sitting-room heard a whispered conversation, but for some moments she did not return.

"Do you know what Aunt is doing, Uncle?"

For the first time since her aunt had departed, Elizabeth noticed that her uncle had turned a little pale as well. He smiled when she spoke. "I believe I do. But let us wait for your aunt to return, shall we?"

Eager though she was, Elizabeth forced herself to remain patient. Standing by her side, Lady Susan appeared no more inclined to wait, but she did not speak. Even so, Elizabeth noted that she was the focus of Lady Susan's scrutiny. It did not make her uncomfortable as she might have thought—rather, it was comforting, like the feel of wool on her skin, keeping her warm on a frigid day.

At length, there was a commotion at the door, and soon Aunt Gardiner stepped through, holding her youngest child. Elizabeth was confused until she saw what the girl wore; it was a little yellow dress, with roses embroidered upon it.

Lady Susan made a little strangled sound, and Elizabeth turned toward her, concern for her mother. She need not have worried, for her mother was merely surprised at the sight of the dress, and tears were streaming down her face.

"Can I assume this is the dress of which you spoke, your ladyship?"

"It is," managed Lady Susan.

"I have no knowledge of the origin of this dress. But Mrs. Bennet gave it to me several years ago, not long after my oldest girl was born, saying that it was too fine to be put into a trunk and left there, or to be sent to clothe the poor. I have only dressed my girls in it on special occasions, as I did this morning, thinking I might have an opportunity to introduce my children to you."

"I am glad you did, Mrs. Gardiner." Lady Susan approached Aunt Gardiner with the child in her arms. Sophie, reticent with adults she did not know, nevertheless looked up at Lady Susan, sensing this lady meant her no harm. When Mrs. Gardiner offered the child to her, Lady Susan willingly took her, cradling her in her arms, while she inspected the dress. Then she turned, her eyes finding her husband.

"There is no doubt, Hugh. The dress is an exact copy of the one

Elizabeth wore when she disappeared. She must be our daughter."

With that declaration, everything fell into place. Elizabeth was home. Only she did not understand yet exactly what home was.

CHAPTER X

Wednesday, March 4, 1812
Gardiner Townhouse, London

It was as emotional a reunion as Darcy had ever thought to witness, far surpassing what had happened when Fitzwilliam had been introduced. That was to be expected, of course, since Fitzwilliam, as a young boy, could not have had the connection to her yet that his parents had possessed.

After Lady Susan had said the words which confirmed to them all that the dress was Elizabeth's, she had almost shoved the child in her arms onto Mrs. Gardiner, and swiftly moved across the room, catching Elizabeth up in a fierce embrace. They were soon after joined by the earl, who had his arms around both, while Fitzwilliam hovered around them all, tears standing in the eyes of the career soldier.

Darcy glanced at Mrs. Gardiner, expecting her to be angry at the cavalier manner in which her youngest had been treated, but she was only smiling at the newly reunited family. She caught Darcy's eye, and the way she looked at him told him she fully understood and had expected to be required to receive her daughter with very little provocation. She clutched the child to her breast, no doubt thinking on the heartache she would experience in a similar situation. For her part, the child only watched the tearful reunion with a gravity far beyond her years, before she wriggled her way out of her mother's arms, and approached Elizabeth among the members of her family.

As one, they seemed to sense her approach and they separated— though none would retreat far from Elizabeth. She reached her arms up to Elizabeth in a silent demand to be held, and Elizabeth obliged her by stooping down and scooping the child up into her arms.

It was as the young woman brought the girl to her breast, holding her tight, the girl's hair tickling the skin of Elizabeth's cheek, that Darcy experienced a powerful sense of longing. This was a woman of rare mettle, one of courage and determination, and as she held the child to her, Darcy could well imagine her holding *their* child in such a manner. And Darcy knew that though he did not love her at present, he could easily reach that state.

"I apologize, Mrs. Gardiner," said Lady Susan, watching her daughter with fierce pride and an overwhelming sense of love. "I should not have handed your child back to you in such a manner."

"It is quite understandable, my lady," replied Mrs. Gardiner.

"Understandable, perhaps, but still unconscionable." Lady Susan turned to regard Elizabeth still cradling the child to her. "She is a lovely child."

"I shall take her upstairs and change her into another dress. I am certain you will wish to take this one with you as a memento."

"No!" exclaimed Lady Susan. She took a deep breath and forced a smile on her face. "That will not be necessary, Mrs. Gardiner, though I thank you for your considerate offer. I would be honored if your daughter would continue to wear it on such special occasions as long as it fits her. When it becomes too small, I will be happy to receive it back from you. I will then keep it for Elizabeth to clothe her own child."

Elizabeth's cheeks flushed at the mention of *her* children. For his part, Darcy was wondering if his cheeks were blooming at the same time. The image of Elizabeth—Lady Elizabeth!—with *his* child on her hip hit him so powerfully, he wondered that he had not staggered.

"Very well, my lady," said Mrs. Gardiner. "I am honored. Perhaps I should send Sophie off with the nurse again, so that we may continue our conversation."

It was unsurprising that the small child had little desire to be sent back to the nursery, and as she was naught but two years old, there was little chance of explaining the matter to her. She was eventually persuaded by Elizabeth with the promise that she would visit her upstairs once the adults were finished speaking. The girl nodded, though Darcy could see the defiance in her posture. Clearly, she could see that Elizabeth was distressed and wished to be with her. It was with an adorable little pout that she was finally able to be coaxed from the room.

"Come, let us sit and speak further," said Mrs. Gardiner. "I shall have the tea refreshed. I feel we could all use it."

Within moments a fresh pot of tea had been delivered, and they all sat down once again. Elizabeth's hair was pinned up again by her mother for the first time since she was a small child. It was not a surprise when the three Fitzwilliams congregated around their newly rediscovered member, as no one wished to be separated from her. It was a feeling Darcy could well understand—he found himself wishing to be close to her as well. But now was a time for family, and though Darcy knew that he was part of that group, he contented himself with simply sitting nearby and enjoying the reunion.

It seemed the newness of it all was difficult for them to take in, though Fitzwilliam had had time to become accustomed to the thought of his sister being returned to them. Lady Susan, in particular, was forced to prove to herself that her daughter truly was returned, as she reached out to Elizabeth several times, laying a hand on her arm, or touching her back. Elizabeth bore it all with patience and fortitude, and Darcy understood—she was not unaffected by the situation, but she also did not have eighteen years of longing with which to cope.

"Perhaps the first thing we should discuss is the matter of Elizabeth's disappearance," said Mr. Gardiner when they were all seated together again.

The earl sighed when Elizabeth nodded her head, her curiosity evident for them all to see. "Unfortunately, there is truly nothing to tell, though I understand why you might wish to know. One day after spending the morning with her mother, Elizabeth was sent back to the nursery. She disappeared from there a few hours later, and we never discovered why."

"There were no clues at all?" asked Mr. Gardiner with a frown.

"Nothing. The nurse put her down for a nap and went into an adjacent room to complete some other tasks, and when she returned, Elizabeth was gone."

"Could the nurse have been complicit in her disappearance?" asked Mrs. Gardiner.

"I doubt it," was the countess's reply. "Miss Perry was not only

Elizabeth's nurse but had been part of our household long enough to have the care of both my sons."

"Furthermore, she was so distraught at Elizabeth's disappearance, we were forced to sedate her," added the earl. "She is still part of our house, as the nurse of my eldest son's children." He smiled with fond remembrance. "She will be particularly pleased to learn of your return, Elizabeth. I believe she carries the burden of your disappearance to this day.

"Regardless," continued Lord Matlock, "we questioned the staff and sent search parties out on the grounds to discover her, but there was not a single clue to inform us of what had happened to you. For some days, we thought you had wandered out of the house and had come to some tragic end out on the estate."

"But that was not like you either," said Lady Susan. "You were a precocious and active child, but you were not intentionally disobedient, and you knew not to leave the house by yourself. Nurse Perry would have taken you outside, had you asked, and I am certain you would have known that." Lady Susan paused and smiled at Elizabeth. "You had us all wrapped around your little finger, and you knew it. That is why it seemed unlikely you would just wander off on your own."

Elizabeth returned a tentative smile to her mother, but her aunt laughed. "Then she has not changed since, your ladyship. Lizzy is well known for traipsing about the countryside by herself. Her walks are legendary in Meryton."

"I hope you are more circumspect in the city, my dear," said Lady Susan, though she appeared pleased at hearing this new intelligence of her daughter.

"I walk with a footman in attendance when in town," said Elizabeth.

"Though it was difficult for her to accept the need," interjected Mr. Gardiner. "She was only fifteen at the time, and she informed us of how she had been walking at her father's estate by herself for some months already and that she did not need a chaperone. When we explained, she *understood* the need readily enough, but that did not mean she *liked* it."

The company shared a laugh at Elizabeth's expense. She blushed and glared at them all, but her displeasure was clearly masking some other emotion, one which turned her cheeks a cherry red.

"To continue," said the earl, "when we found no trace of you on the grounds—and I believe I can safely say we searched every inch of it—

we thought you might have been taken from us. No ransom demand was ever received, and as no one at the estate had seen anything out of the ordinary, we have no way of knowing what happened to you."

"I have always thought you were alive in the world," said Lady Susan. Her voice trembled as she spoke, and the tears pooling in her eyes glittered. "But it has been many years since I dared hope that we would be reunited."

Lady Susan pulled Elizabeth to her breast again, and Elizabeth went willingly. She was healthy and hale, her character was everything any of them would have hoped and dreamed, but Darcy could not help but wonder about her interactions with her mother. She seemed almost . . . surprised to receive them. Darcy could not help but wonder about the woman who had raised her—he had heard something of her character and did not think much of the woman, but if she had been a mother to Elizabeth all those years and had not seen fit to inform her of her origins, surely she had provided the love of a mother to her?

"Then in my mind, the question is whether Elizabeth is safe, now that she has been recovered."

Fitzwilliam's blunt observation caught them all by surprise, and more than one pair of eyes turned to regard him in varying degrees of shock.

"She disappeared without a trace and has only been returned to us after eighteen years." Determined, the colonel's gaze met that of the company, distasteful though the subject was. "Given that she made her way from Derbyshire to Cambridge and was found there by the Bennets . . ." He turned to Elizabeth and the Gardiners. "Do you know when she was found?"

Thursday, September 5, 1793
The Silver Chalice Inn, Cambridge

"John!" exclaimed Hattie, entering the room with haste. "The girl—she has slipped away!"

"Slipped away? How could you be so careless?"

Hattie colored, but the look she directed at him was all defiance. "I only took my eyes from her for a moment. She is a slippery one."

Sykes scowled and looked away. There was no point arguing with Hattie over this, a point she made quite clear with her next words. "You should not have involved us in this mess. If it is ever discovered that we had the girl, it will be the gallows for us."

"I will go out and look for her," replied Sykes. He looked around the room they inhabited. "Prepare us for an immediate departure. If I can return with her, I do not wish to stay and draw any attention to us."

"It must be near dinner time," protested Hattie. "You wish to leave *now*?"

"Think of how our reception will be should we be discovered."

The woman blanched and began repacking their effects. Sykes let himself from the room and hurried down the stairs, exiting the small inn at which they had engaged a room for the night and out into the streets. The sun was still setting, bathing the city of Cambridge in the dusty rose glow of its final rays. But Sykes was a man little inclined to be moved by such displays, even if he was not preoccupied.

He searched for some moments until he was drawn by a commotion not two streets away. He took great care in edging toward it, taking in what was happening with a glance. After a moment, he made his way back to the inn and to their room where Hattie waited. After years of serving the gentleman, he had finally found a way to live his own life with his girl of many years. He would be damned if he allowed it to be taken from him now.

"Did you find her?' asked Hattie when he opened the door.

"I did, but only after some other man beat me to it."

"What will we do?"

Sykes stepped forward and caught her hands in his, attempting to calm her fretting. "There is nothing to be done. They will likely be looking for her parents. I doubt, based on what she is wearing, we could successfully claim she is ours.

"Bundle up some of our clothes and wrap it in a blanket—we need to make it look like it is the girl, for the innkeeper knows we arrived with her. I will arrange for a carriage and inform the innkeeper we have decided to press on."

"It will be easily seen that the bundle I carry is not the girl," protested Hattie.

"No one will notice if you go directly from the room to the carriage. I will distract the driver. With any luck, those who see us leave will think we have the girl with us, but the driver will not be the wiser when we are alone at the next stop. If the connection is made, we should be gone."

Though it was clear Hattie was skeptical, she did as he asked. Before long, they were in a new carriage headed east.

"I am happy to be rid of her, John," said Hattie as they settled in for another long ride. "I do not know what you were intending to do with her, but as long as she was with us, she was a danger."

Sykes did not even know himself. But he was just as grateful as Hattie that they were no longer burdened by the girl. A part of him felt a little remorse as he thought of what her life might be like in the future. She was no doubt destined for an orphanage. It was unlikely her family would ever find her so distant from her home.

Wednesday, March 4, 1812
Gardiner Townhouse, London

"I do not, and my aunt and uncle would not know," replied Elizabeth.

A nod was Fitzwilliam's response. "We have no notion as to the reason for her abduction, then, for abduction it most certainly was. If those responsible for her disappearance did not ask for a ransom, what was their purpose? Why did they leave her in Cambridge? Until we can answer these questions—if we ever can—I believe we must assume that Elizabeth's discovery will excite attention from whoever wished her harm before."

It was clear that none of them liked the portrait Fitzwilliam was drawing, but the truth of his words could not be disputed.

"I suppose then we must apply to Mr. Bennet," said Lord Matlock. "At present, he and his wife are the only links we can explore to attempt to understand this mystery." He turned his attention to Elizabeth. "If you will give me the directions to his estate, I shall write to him immediately, asking him to come to London with all expedience."

"I do not think that would be efficacious," said Elizabeth, though it was clear she was reluctant to speak. "Mr. Bennet does not like town, and he loathes traveling. I do not doubt the letter would sit on his desk for some days before he even bothered to open it."

"A letter of this much importance?" demanded the earl. It was clear he was building up an impressive measure of anger at the very thought that an earl might be ignored by a man who was nothing but a country squire.

"Unfortunately, I second Elizabeth's assessment of Mr. Bennet's likely response," said Mr. Gardiner. "It is not that he does not understand the differences in rank. He will likely either consider it a joke on Elizabeth's part or not even look at it enough to know who it is from in favor of his other pursuits. Elizabeth was not wrong when she said that Mr. Bennet is not truly suited to be the master of an estate."

"Actually, I believe it would be better if Mr. Bennet did *not* come to town," said Fitzwilliam. "I would rather go to Hertfordshire myself and question him. That way he will not have time to prepare his answers."

"Anthony!" exclaimed a shocked Elizabeth. "What are you insinuating?"

"I am insinuating nothing, dear sister," replied Fitzwilliam. For once, his tone was not teasing. "I only wish to ensure Mr. Bennet answers the questions I have for him as truthfully as possible, and without the chance to think about them in advance."

It took no great insight to see that Elizabeth was not at all mollified. Lady Susan also seemed to sense this, as she turned the subject to other matters.

"Then I will allow you to handle Mr. Bennet, Anthony," said she. "For the present, we must think of what we are to do, including how to introduce Elizabeth to society as our daughter."

"Will society remember that you *had* a daughter?" asked Darcy.

"Those of a certain age will," replied the earl. "Elizabeth's disappearance was quite the sensation; it was covered extensively by the newspapers. There were several other great families annoyed at her loss, for they had spoken to me of a possible betrothal contract with their progeny."

"My lord!" gasped Elizabeth. "Surely you do not mean to betroth me to someone I do not even know!"

"Father," corrected Lord Matlock. "I do not wish to hear any more of this 'my lord' business from my own daughter. Is that clear?"

Elizabeth nodded, albeit reluctantly, and she seemed to sense from the tenor of his reply that perhaps she had overreacted. This was confirmed by the earl's next statement.

"I refused to even consider the matter *then*, nor shall I do so now, though I know I will be inundated with such requests. I am much more concerned with your happiness, Elizabeth, than making political alliances with people for whom I have no respect."

"Surely you do not think we would barter our newly returned daughter away to some duke ancient enough to be her grandfather, Elizabeth," chided Lady Susan. Elizabeth flushed a little, but while she shook her head, a mutinous glint remained in her eye. "You must understand that this is the way of the world in which we live. Daughters are often put in arranged marriages to forge important connections between families."

"Were *you* married to my father under such a contract?" demanded Elizabeth. The strain in her jaw informed Darcy that she was truly displeased, and he was not surprised, though he was amused.

"She was not," replied the earl. "But that does not change that it is done, and as your father, I have every right to do so. But," continued he when Elizabeth tried to speak, "it has not been the practice of my family to do so for many years, and I have no intention of reviving it now. James, my eldest, made a love match with his wife, and I have no desire to interfere with you younger children doing the same."

"Elizabeth!" exclaimed Anthony. "Do you not see that we are so grateful for your recovery that we would do anything you asked? We are putty in your hands."

Elizabeth was embarrassed again, and she ducked her head as her mother and father nodded their agreement. The rest of the company watched on, amused, though Darcy was able to hear Mrs. Gardiner's softly spoken "Only you, Lizzy."

"Now," said Lady Susan, "for the moment, we should speak about what we will do in the immediate future." She turned to her son when he tried to speak. "I understand your concerns and share them, Anthony. But Elizabeth cannot live her life hiding at Snowlock, especially when it proved insufficient to protect her before."

He scowled and did not answer for a moment, but at length, Fitzwilliam nodded, though curtly.

"It is possible that the threat no longer exists," said Darcy.

"It is possible," agreed Fitzwilliam. "But we still must take every precaution."

"I agree," replied Lady Susan. "I will leave you to devise those precautions. But do not stifle Elizabeth—she is not a child of two years any longer."

Lady Susan turned back to Elizabeth and regarded her for a moment. "Anthony *is* correct, you know. The fact that you are our daughter, returned after such a long absence, will prompt the excitement of the masses, as will your eligibility as the daughter of an earl."

"And that says nothing of the interest your fortune of thirty-five thousand pounds will bring," added the earl.

Elizabeth's eyes became almost comically wide. "*Thirty-five thousand pounds?*" said she, though it came out as a squeak.

"You did not think that the daughter of an earl would not possess a dowry appropriate for her station, did you?" asked Lady Susan.

"I do not know what I thought," replied Elizabeth.

"I believe it is actually now more than fifty thousand pounds," said the earl. Elizabeth appeared like she was almost ready to faint. "Some of the interest has been reinvested, and I have added to it, here and there over the years." The earl directed a weak smile at his daughter. "I could not bear the thought of your loss, so whenever I was feeling the desolation of it, I added a little to your dowry. It helped me feel like there was a possibility of your recovery. Had you not returned, it would have been given to Anthony."

This new shock had Elizabeth darting a look at Fitzwilliam, but he forestalled any thought of her protest. "Do not say it, Elizabeth. Your return is worth far more to us all—and to *me*— than any amount of money. My parents have provided for me, so you need not worry."

A slow nod was Elizabeth's response. Darcy wondered if they should not end this discussion soon, for it was clear she was beginning to become overwhelmed.

"I think a slow introduction to society would be best," said Lady Susan, fixing a thoughtful gaze on her daughter. "The season has not yet reached its height, so there is ample time remaining for us to ensure your introduction is completed, though your curtsey before Queen Charlotte must necessarily take place next year.

"We shall start with a dinner to which we will invite only close friends and family, and then, of course, we will need to place an announcement in the newspaper."

"I assume you will tell Aunt Catherine," said Fitzwilliam. "Otherwise, I do not wish to contemplate her reaction should she not be informed."

"I do not wish to contemplate her reaction regardless," muttered Darcy.

"My sister will be difficult," said Lord Matlock. "Of that, I have no doubt."

"Of course, we will inform Catherine," said Lady Susan. "Beyond the announcement, there will be events to attend—balls, parties, the theater, and so on—and I believe we will plan a ball in your honor, where you can be introduced to the larger circle of our acquaintances."

It appeared to Darcy as if Elizabeth was about to be sick, for she seemed decidedly green. Lady Susan noted this, and she put a hand on Elizabeth's elbow. "Do not concern yourself, Elizabeth. In time you will become accustomed to it. If you perform as you have today, I have no doubt you will acquit yourself well."

"Thank you . . . Mother. I shall do my best."

"Then the only other matter is that of your living arrangements."

Elizabeth looked back warily at the countess, but her mother only looked at her with a hint of pleading in her tone. "You must understand that we have missed you for many years, Elizabeth. I understand this is all very new and overwhelming, and I would not wish to make you uncomfortable. But you are *our* daughter, and we wish to have you back in our lives."

"Perhaps easing her into her life as the daughter of an earl would be advisable," said Fitzwilliam. "I believe the Gardiners would be willing to host Elizabeth a little longer?"

"She may stay with us as long as she likes," said Mr. Gardiner.

"But I think we can both agree that her proper place is back with her family," added his wife.

"Then perhaps she could stay a few more days," said Fitzwilliam. "She can visit Darcy house again, as she has been these past days, and perhaps visit my father's house as well. Mother can show her the house she will be living in, her rooms, and so on, and once the emotion of this day has been put in the past, Elizabeth can relocate there."

"That would be acceptable," said Lady Susan. She turned to Elizabeth, and Darcy did not miss the hint of pleading in her gaze. "Elizabeth?"

It seemed like some of Elizabeth's fortitude had, indeed, returned, for she paused for a moment, took in a breath and said: "Yes, Mother, I would find that a little easier. This day has been so bewildering. A little adjustment period would be welcome."

"Thank you, my dear," said Lady Susan, enfolding her daughter again in a close embrace. "We are all so happy we have rediscovered you. I hope you will be happy with us."

Wednesday, March 4, 1812
Gardiner Townhouse, London

At present, Elizabeth was not certain of anything, for the emotions of the day, little bits of thoughts, memories of her past at Longbourn, along with concerns for the future, floated around in her mind, confusing her. She thought she would recover with enough time, to come to terms with all that had happened, but at present, she was still very much overwhelmed.

Though she had spoken and given her opinion, her mind had been preoccupied with the unlikelihood of this scene ever occurring. She was well aware that foundling children becoming separated from their families rarely found them again. What made her so special that she would deserve such happiness?

"Perhaps it would be easier to cease trying to understand it?"

Startled by the sudden words, Elizabeth turned to look at William, who was regarding her closely. Her mother and father—how strange that still seemed!—had turned their attention to the Gardiners, who were relating some anecdote, and were listening with rapt interest. Anthony was dividing his attention between the Gardiners and Elizabeth herself, curious about her past, but still obviously concerned about Elizabeth's wellbeing. Elizabeth directed a smile at him, letting him know she was well before she turned back to William.

"You think I am confused?" asked Elizabeth, a hint of a challenge in her tone.

"I think there is much about which to be bewildered," replied he. "There are many aspects of this situation we do not understand, and it is entirely possible—probable, even—that we will *never* understand them. We will seek whatever answers we can, but in the end, I think we will have to be content with the good fortune of your return."

His words were not precisely the substance of Elizabeth's worries, but she decided his advice was still sound. She turned a shy smile on him.

"Thank you, William. I will endeavor to remember that. I have no doubt in my abilities, but I do not think it is surprising that this should overpower my senses."

"It is not surprising at all. But remember you have a family who loves you and who will do anything for you. Fitzwilliam was not exaggerating when he suggested we are putty in your hands. You can turn to any of us if you feel exhausted by everything happening around you."

Elizabeth's eyes darted to where the Gardiners sat, Mrs. Gardiner still relating her tale. The Fitzwilliams were laughing at whatever she was saying, and every so often her mother would glance over at her, apparently delighted by what she was learning.

"I will be able to maintain my association with them." It was more of a question than a statement, but Elizabeth had no intention of leaving her favorite relations behind.

"Of course, you will," replied William. His tone was so firm that it pulled Elizabeth's eyes back to his. "Your parents are so grateful for your return that I almost wonder if he will push for a knighthood for your uncle."

It was with shock that Elizabeth watched William until she noticed the slight upturn at the corners of his mouth. She realized he was teasing her, and she laughed. "I do not suppose the Prince Regent would be willing to grant such a request for such a trifling matter."

"I do not know that the return of the daughter of an earl is trifling," replied William. "But you are correct that it is unlikely to occur. But my uncle is grateful for Mr. Gardiner's protection of you when you might have been alone and friendless. I am certain he already has plans for his association with Mr. Gardiner, and as you know, your uncle has many connections to the gentry already."

"I suppose he does."

Their conversation turned to other matters then, and they spent an agreeable time together. Mrs. Gardiner extended an invitation to the visitors to dine with them, but they refused, citing the shortness of the notice and the need to begin to put some of their plans in motion. But Elizabeth was treated to a fond farewell, the likes of which she would not have received at Longbourn, before they went away, amid promises of future meetings. As they went away, they invited Elizabeth and the Gardiners to dinner at the Fitzwilliams' town residence the following night. This was, of course, promptly accepted.

When they finally went away, Elizabeth kept her promise and looked in on Sophie, before taking herself to her room. She had much on which to think, and the new situation to accustom herself to.

CHAPTER XI

Wednesday, March 4, 1812
Fitzwilliam House, London

"Now, Darcy, I would hear more of this incident with the son of your father's former steward." The earl paused and looked between Darcy and Fitzwilliam, his mien demanding, exhorting them to tell him what they knew.

"I am certain that Elizabeth glossed over some of the aspects of it," continued he when they did not immediately respond. "I am pleased with her fortitude. But I am incensed at this libertine and am prepared to see him sent to Botany Bay for nothing more than laying a hand on her. If he has hurt her, I will see him in hell."

"Elizabeth did relate the gist of it to you, Uncle," said Darcy, quick to head off the earl's vengeful thoughts, though in truth he agreed with them. "He accosted her when she did not respond to his charm, and at the very least attempted liberties with her person. I do not know the extent of his intentions, and I doubt Elizabeth knew either."

"It is enough that he placed his hands on her at all! The man is an anvil around your neck, Darcy. You should have dealt with him years ago. Now he has made attempts on both Georgiana *and* Elizabeth. He cannot go unpunished."

"He will not," replied Darcy, eager to blunt his uncle's impressive anger. "I shall soon receive the debt receipts of his that I hold from both Lambton and Cambridge, and when we go to Meryton, we will buy up whatever he has there. Once I press charges against him, I doubt he will ever see outside the walls of Marshalsea again."

"I would prefer to see him swinging from the end of a rope," snarled the earl.

"Think of the benefits of permanent incarceration, Father," said Fitzwilliam. "His life—or what remains of it—will not be pleasant, and I dare say with the lack of any money he will not only never get out, but he will starve to death in only a few months." Fitzwilliam paused, and when he continued, it was in an offhand tone: "If you wish a premature end of the matter, I may simply go to Hertfordshire and call him out. The notion of Wickham moldering in a pauper's grave has an immense amount of appeal."

It was the sight of the earl's thoughtful response to his son's words that made Darcy uncomfortable. It had long been the thought of the conditions in England's prisons which had stayed Darcy's hand from accusing his childhood companion, and it still made him uncomfortable. And that was to say nothing of his disinclination to see Wickham challenged and killed in what might as well be cold blood. But the two Fitzwilliam men were in a particularly bloodthirsty mood, and George Wickham was firmly in their sights.

"While your suggestions have some appeal," said Lord Matlock at length, "I believe I would prefer a solution which prevents you from killing a man, eliminates the possibility of escape, and puts the man to some use instead of simply imprisoning him." He turned to Darcy. "I will purchase his debts from you, Darcy. Then I will see him tried and transported. Those overseeing the penal colony in Van Diemen's Land will put him to work and give his life some purpose. God knows he needs it, after his years of dissipative behavior."

"And he will survive much longer there then he might in Marshalsea." Fitzwilliam's smile was positively unpleasant.

"That *is* a side benefit," acknowledged the earl. "And without the means to gamble and wench or the society in which to affect a station he does not possess, I dare say his life will be a living hell of his own making."

The two men shared a malicious grin, and Darcy suppressed a shudder. It was a Fitzwilliam trait to be vindictive when the occasion presented itself, though they were usually affable and pleasant.

"Wickham has been a drain on me long enough that I am happy to force him to be of some use in his life," said Darcy. "But I do not understand why I would need to sell his debts to you. He can just as easily be sentenced to the penal colony while I still hold his receipts."

Lord Matlock turned and regarded Darcy. "Is there a reason why you wish to hold them?"

"He is my responsibility," replied Darcy with a shrug. "He is what his association with my family has made him, particularly because my father saw fit to educate and favor him. I would not wish another to assume that burden."

"That is nonsense, and you know it," growled Fitzwilliam. "Wickham is what his own actions have made him. *He* squandered his opportunities—not you."

"He would not have had those opportunities had my father not supported him," said Darcy stubbornly. "If he had not been given so much he might not have expected so much."

"It would not have changed him. He has always been a bad apple—you have simply had difficulty seeing that."

"That is enough, boys," said Lord Matlock, glaring at them both. "I suspect the reality is that you are both correct, and yet you are both incorrect. At this late date, however, it matters little, for Wickham is now what he is." The earl turned to Darcy. "If you wish to keep the burden of his debts, then I will not gainsay you. Regardless, the sooner he is in custody and awaiting trial, the better."

"I can certainly agree to that," said Darcy, with an accompanying grunt from Fitzwilliam.

"Which brings us to our next point," added Fitzwilliam. "We must go to this Mr. Bennet and discover what he knows about Elizabeth's disappearance. Since Wickham is in Hertfordshire, we may attend to that task at the same time."

The earl directed a long look at his son. "It seems to me you are suggesting that I allow you to handle this matter."

"I am," replied Fitzwilliam simply. "I am a colonel in the army, and I can take several men with me to apprehend Wickham and deliver him to the constabulary. There is much less chance he can slip away if we do it that way. Darcy and I will go to Hertfordshire and speak to this Mr. Bennet, and we will report back. Since I do not believe he holds any useful information, it is best if you leave this to Darcy and me."

"I am loath to agree," replied Lord Matlock, shaking his head. "I would prefer to be there, demanding the man account for how he got his hands on my little girl and why, for god's sake, he did not make any attempt to discover if she had a family."

"And those feelings are precisely why you should allow us to handle this matter." Fitzwilliam regarded his father, not a hint of their usual banter evident. "I have had longer to become accustomed to Elizabeth's return and the consequences of it. Furthermore, I have no intention of being ruled by my emotions, which you are in danger of even now."

"Fine!" exclaimed the earl, throwing his hands up in the air. "You may question this Mr. Bennet yourselves, but I warn you that I will expect a full accounting when you return. And if he is not forthcoming, I will go to Hertfordshire myself and wring the answers from him."

"Of course," replied Fitzwilliam. "I would expect nothing less."

Thursday, March 5, 1812
Fitzwilliam House, London

Later, Elizabeth would realize that it was only the frequent presence of her new family which prevented her from being completely overwhelmed by her new circumstances. The Gardiners were kind in attempting to distract her from thinking about all that had happened, but her mind would return traitorously to it whenever she was not actively engaged in some other pursuit, and this often left her feeling out of sorts and irritable.

The day after the final revelation of Elizabeth's identity, she entered the Gardiner carriage for the ride to Mayfair for the promised dinner at her father's house. And when they arrived there, though the house was similar to William's in many respects, it was more opulent, consequently making it more imposing. When they arrived, all four of her family members were present, and they greeted her with affection and welcome, and once again Elizabeth felt overcome at the changes she was undergoing. She focused on the member of the family who was not present to allow her to keep some sort of composure.

"Will Georgiana not be attending?"

"Unfortunately, no," replied William. "She is suffering from a slight indisposition tonight. The next time you visit my house we may inform her."

From the way William was speaking distantly, and the slightly uneasy cast to his countenance, Elizabeth wondered if Georgiana's indisposition was a *ladies'* issue, which men were not usually comfortable discussing. She caught her mother's eye at that moment, and Lady Susan grinned at her, confirming Elizabeth's supposition.

For a moment she thought to tease her cousin, asking for more information about Georgiana's condition, but she decided, in the end, to extend him some pity.

"That is unfortunate. But I shall anticipate meeting her again the next time. Do you think she will be well again tomorrow?"

"Ah . . . perhaps the next day might be better?"

"Very well, William, I shall be guided by your knowledge of your sister."

William watched her, clearly wondering if she was teasing him—which she *was*, despite her determination to spare him her wit. In the end, he only nodded and smiled.

"If you would visit on that day, I would be much obliged. Fitzwilliam and I are to visit Hertfordshire then, and I think Georgiana would appreciate the company."

"I would be happy to," replied Elizabeth. She had not missed the little hitch in William's voice, and she wondered what it could possibly be. But her mother called her attention at that moment, and Elizabeth was not able to consider the matter any further.

Her parents' home in London was of a different, older style than William's house which was more modern. It had all the amenities the house of an earl would be expected to have—a music room, several sitting-rooms and family rooms, a games room for the gentlemen, and a large ballroom, among a large array of bedrooms which would house many friends and acquaintances if necessary. In the ballroom, her mother was quick to point out that it was adequate—though barely so—to host Elizabeth's introduction ball, which was certain to generate the interest of society.

Elizabeth was not certain how she felt about that last point, but she allowed it to pass from her mind in favor of the tour her parents were giving them. It was a lovely house. She learned that many of the principle rooms had been updated within the past few years. She could not fault her parents' tastes in any way. The furniture they chose to adorn their house was quite obviously finely made, but it was not ostentatious or overly ornate. In that, it was a match for William's house.

"This will be your bedchamber," said Lady Susan as she opened a door not far from where they had been told the master apartments were located. "I hope you will like it, Elizabeth, but if you do not, your father and I will be happy to redecorate it in whatever way you like."

The thought of protesting against such an expense died on Elizabeth's lips as she entered and saw the room before her eyes. The door opened to a large sitting-room, with armchairs placed in front of a large, stone fireplace, an escritoire against the far wall, and a couch and several more chairs in the center of the room. There were bookshelves and tables, mostly bare of adornments, and which she realized would be hers to fill with her own personal effects. On the far wall was a bank of large windows which looked down on a garden area behind the house, and a set of stables at the corner of the lot.

Her mother then took her through a door on the right wall, which opened into her bedchamber, a similar fireplace with two more chairs across from a large bed, a pair of nightstands on either side of the bed, and another bookshelf to hold her most treasured literary works. On the far side, another door opened into a closet which was almost cavernous, boasting enough space to contain all the clothes she had ever possessed in her life. The entire suite was possibly larger than all five girls' rooms in Longbourn combined.

"Do you like it, Elizabeth?"

The tense note in her mother's voice bespoke her nervousness, and Elizabeth realized belatedly that she had been quiet for some time.

"The rooms are lovely, Mother," Elizabeth hastened to assure her. "I just . . ." Elizabeth swallowed and fixed a wry smile on both her parents. "I have not been accustomed to such . . . finery as this. Longbourn, where I was raised, is much humbler."

"We understand, Elizabeth," replied her mother, to her father's agreement. "But this is your birthright and your privilege, now that you have been recovered."

"You are now a member of the nobility, my dear," added her father. "It may take some time to become accustomed to it, but I dare say all will be well with a little familiarity."

"I am certain it shall," said Elizabeth. She smiled at her parents, noting how William and Anthony were watching her, and was heartened when they returned it. She had those to whom she was beloved to assist her transition, and though it was all so strange at present, she had no doubt her father was correct.

After a few more moments, they returned to the main floor and spent some little time speaking in a family sitting-room. Lady Susan led her to understand it was her family's favorite room in the evenings, and Elizabeth was forced to agree that it was comfortable, indeed. Uncle Gardiner stood with William, Anthony, and her father, speaking of various matters of business, while Elizabeth sat with her mother and Aunt Gardiner. It did her heart well that the Gardiners, though they were not related to her by blood, were so readily accepted by those of a more exalted station. Elizabeth did not know what she would have done had her new relations proven to be of a haughtier frame of mind.

The dinner was excellent and Elizabeth was able to see how her mother had put a lot of effort into ensuring that she was impressed with everything about the evening. Elizabeth could not imagine *not* being impressed. It was clear to her that her mother wished to make her feel welcome, that this would be a home to her. Though the circumstances were far in excess of anything Elizabeth had previously known, she thought she could be happy in this place, with such attentive parents. In that also, it was different from what she had known; Mr. Bennet could not be termed an attentive parent by any measure, and Elizabeth had often gone to great lengths to avoid Mrs. Bennet.

It was after dinner when the tone changed slightly. When they retreated to the music room after dinner, her mother played for the company and then asked Elizabeth to favor them with a song or two. She did so, though she felt a little embarrassed by her lack of ability. Her mother, however, had only listened to her and complimented her on her playing.

"You play quite well, especially since you have only had limited access to masters. If you are interested, we may bring in a master to tutor you further."

Elizabeth had always neglected her practicing in favor of many of her other interests, but she thought that she might like to practice more if she had someone to grade her endeavors. The idea appealed to her, and she agreed with alacrity.

Sometime later Elizabeth found herself speaking with William and Anthony, and for a moment it felt like it had this past week, when they had been much in one another's company. But it was not long before their conversation turned more serious in nature.

"Elizabeth," said Anthony, "as you know, we will travel to Hertfordshire in two days to speak with your father and take Wickham into custody. Before we go, I wish you to tell me something more about your adoptive father."

"I believe I have already told you of him," said Elizabeth with a frown.

"That is true. But a more in-depth character portrait would be appreciated. He is the one person who may know something of your abduction. If I am to ask him the proper questions, I must know more of his character."

"Mr. Bennet had nothing to do with my abduction!" exclaimed

Elizabeth. Her outburst drew the attention of the Gardiners and Fitzwilliams, who all turned to look at her, her parents with a concern which could not be feigned. The only reason they did not come to her, she thought, was because Anthony motioned them away for the moment.

"You cannot know that, Elizabeth," replied Anthony.

"I know my adoptive father," snapped Elizabeth. "He has his faults, but he is a good man. I will not believe he was in any way complicit. What could he possibly have to gain?"

Anthony and William shared a look, but though she thought Anthony was eager to respond, a look from William silenced him.

"I believe my cousin has overstated our suspicions, Elizabeth," said William. "I do not believe Mr. Bennet had anything to do with your disappearance. I am sure Fitzwilliam will agree with me. But it is nothing less than a fact that Mr. Bennet is the only person we know who might have some knowledge of the matter."

"And how do you mean to go about confronting him?" asked Elizabeth, feeling more than a little wary of this whole situation.

"Elizabeth, Darcy speaks the truth." Fitzwilliam looked earnestly at her. "I do not expect that we will find anything when we speak with Mr. Bennet, but the fact that he found you when you were a child is something we cannot ignore. *If* he knows something, we must discover it."

With a sigh, Elizabeth turned away and looked across the room, her eyes seeing nothing. In the back of her mind, she noted how the Gardiners and her parents watched her with seeming concern, but she had no time to spare any thought for their worries. Her years at Longbourn had at times been difficult—this she well knew—but she did not think that it had been any more difficult than the trials any other family faces. She had felt love there, from Jane and Mr. Bennet, primarily, but from them all, including Mrs. Bennet, with whom she had often shared a rocky relationship.

But Elizabeth could not believe them guilty of her disappearance. Thus, the situation demanded that she protect them as well as she was able. By giving Anthony and William whatever knowledge she possessed, she would be doing that.

"Mr. Bennet, as I have informed you, is an intelligent man, though in many ways he is not a diligent one. He is reserved and does not enjoy company, and he is often content to allow his wife and daughters to fulfill the family's requirements in society, while he remains in solitude. It is not that he does not possess the knowledge to make his estate more profitable — it is that he does not wish to take the trouble."

"I believe this much you have already told us, Elizabeth," replied Anthony. This time, Elizabeth noted that his tone was gentle and in no way demanding. "What can you tell me of his contacts, those with whom he associates, even someone from Cambridge or elsewhere with whom he corresponds?"

Elizabeth shook her head. "I do not know anything of that. His prohibition against his wife imposing upon his affairs also applies to his daughters. Even I, who helped him with his books at times, was not to snoop into the contents of his correspondence."

Elizabeth did not miss Anthony and William's shared look. "Men who involve their wives and daughters in such matters are far from uncommon," said William.

"That is true," replied Anthony. "There is nothing to assume from such information."

"What else do you wish to know?" asked Elizabeth, feeling cross with this conversation. "Perhaps you should ask, for I do not understand what you wish me to tell you."

"Very well," said Anthony.

The questions which followed concerned Mr. Bennet's habits, anything she had noticed of his comings and goings — of which there had been very little — and his general character. Elizabeth answered as well as she was able, but she could not remove the thought from her mind that her adoptive father was being investigated for some great crime. But Elizabeth held her temper in check and answered, little though she thought her words would help. Elizabeth could not believe Mr. Bennet had arranged her disappearance. It defied all logic.

Thursday, March 5, 1812
Fitzwilliam House, London

"My daughter appears to be more than a little . . . stubborn?"

Mrs. Gardiner turned and smiled. "I am surprised you have not already noticed this, your ladyship. Lizzy can be more stubborn than a mule."

Lady Susan considered this. "It is a Fitzwilliam trait, to be certain."

By her side, her husband laughed. "It is more than a Fitzwilliam trait, my dear. You were blessed with your own measure of it."

A nod was her reply, for she knew her husband only spoke the truth. His laughter was soon forgotten, and he had focused on Mr. Gardiner. "What I wish to know, Mr. Gardiner, is whether, in your experience with Mr. Bennet, she is correct." When Mr. Gardiner made to speak, her husband held a hand up. "I know I am being a little unfair in asking you this, but I believe you understand the reason for it."

"I do," was Mr. Gardiner's even reply. "Since this matter has come to light, I have searched my own memories for any suggestion that Bennet's behavior has been in any way suspicious."

"And what is your success?" Lady Susan knew her husband was more curious than demanding.

"I can remember nothing," replied Mr. Gardiner. "You must understand that my brother is a complex character, and he is an odd mix of parts, a mix my sister has never truly understood. He was committed to his career at Cambridge and had no opportunity for extended travel, at least so far as I can remember. I cannot imagine that he would have been involved in something underhanded."

Hugh considered this for a moment before he responded. "Then it seems like this journey my son and nephew are taking upon themselves is likely to reveal nothing we do not already know." He grimaced and then turned an apologetic expression on Mr. Gardiner. "I hope you understand it is a step we must take regardless."

"I do," replied Mr. Gardiner. "At the very least, you will understand how Bennet came to have custody of your daughter, even if the entire story is not his to tell."

"I also wish to thank you again, Gardiner," said her husband. "When Elizabeth was forced to leave Mr. Bennet's home, she might have been alone and friendless without you and your wife to succor her. I shudder to think of what might have happened to our daughter."

Lady Susan scowled, and she did not care to hide it. This business of Elizabeth being forced to leave the estate on which she was raised was the means whereby they had been reunited, but the lack of sympathy or concern for Elizabeth's wellbeing was something Lady Susan could not easily forgive.

"Think nothing of it," replied Mr. Gardiner. "If I had not been in a position to take Elizabeth in, she would have stayed at Longbourn—of that you may be assured. The only reason Bennet put her out of the house was to protect her against my sister's ill humors."

Not having thought of it that way before, Lady Susan felt a little better about what had happened and about this Mr. Bennet. Her opinion of Mrs. Bennet was still poor, but perhaps the gentleman had not cast Elizabeth off so callously as she had thought.

As they sat for some time after dinner, the conversation moved to other subjects, but Lady Susan's participation in it waned. Her attention was fixed on Elizabeth, often to the exclusion of all other concerns, and she watched her daughter as she spoke to the younger men. Elizabeth appeared to be agitated at times, though she always kept her composure. The girl was still struggling with the situation, but Lady Susan reaffirmed her resolution to help her accustom herself to the station which was hers by right.

CHAPTER XII

Saturday, March 7, 1812
Longbourn, Hertfordshire

They left early the morning of their sojourn into Hertfordshire, and as the carriage sped away from the city, Darcy sat back against the seats of his coach, noting the district through which they passed. As it was the beginning of March, the countryside was beginning to show some signs of awakening from its long winter rest. But the weather could still be rather fickle, with rain and sleet, and an occasional snowfall to delay the coming of warmer weather. On that day, it was blustery. The clouds were scudding across the sky in great clumps of whites and grays, but they were not the kind of clouds to threaten to release their contents against the earth below.

Across from him, seated in the rear facing bench, sat Fitzwilliam, looking out the carriage window with some interest. The great north road was a little to the west, and as it was the quickest route to Derbyshire, it was that road they usually traveled. Darcy had come this way before, of course, but much of that journey had been spent seething at the duplicity of Miss Bingley and the weakness of his friend. Thus, he had not paid much attention to his surroundings.

"You know this is likely nothing more than a wild goose chase, do you not?" said Darcy to his companion. When Fitzwilliam shot him a questioning glance, Darcy shrugged. "I agree with Elizabeth—I do not think Mr. Bennet knows anything of value."

"You may be right. It is just . . ." Fitzwilliam stopped and struggled for several moments before his temper overwhelmed his senses and he slammed a closed fist down on the seat beside him. "Damn it, man, but my sister was taken from us for almost twenty years! I wish that I had someone—anyone—to blame for my family's loss!"

"I understand, Cousin," replied Darcy. He did not attempt a soothing tone, as he knew Fitzwilliam would not appreciate it. "I think it would be best to fix your energies on being thankful that she is now returned to you, however late it may be."

Fitzwilliam grunted and turned back to the window. "You think I do not know this?"

"I *know* you know it. But it seems evident to me you are having difficulty believing it."

"Understanding *that* requires little insight."

"You never were much of a complex character, Fitzwilliam," said Darcy, grinning at his cousin. "One with such simple desires can never be a difficult study."

His jibe did the trick, as Fitzwilliam turned back to him, a gleam in his eye. "At least I am not so complex that it requires an hour in the morning to determine what I shall wear that day."

"Of course not, Cousin," replied Darcy with aplomb. "All you ever wear is scarlet and white, and as such, your suit for any day is already decided for you."

Fitzwilliam let out a great guffaw and shook his head. "I thank you for your attempts to divert my attention, Cousin. They are appreciated, regardless of how ineffectual I think they will ultimately be."

The carriage made good time on the excellent roads. As they traveled, Darcy continued to distract his cousin with observations of their path or comments designed to draw him from his morose thoughts. It was not long before they were approaching, and then traveling through, a small market town, one Darcy knew to be Meryton. There was not much to see—it was much like many other towns in many other corners of the kingdom. It was not long before they passed through and, taking a side road from the end of the town, continued toward the northwest.

"That road leads toward Netherfield," said Darcy, pointing out the right window.

Fitzwilliam snorted. "The estate at which you spent a single night?"

"Indeed," said Darcy. "Trust me, Cousin, it was one night too many."

The look Fitzwilliam bestowed on him was pointed. "You know that I have nothing against Bingley's background, do you not?" Darcy nodded. "Bingley *is* a good man, but he has allowed his harpy of a sister to rule him. She will be the ruin of him someday. I only hope it is not in front of the highest of society, for if it is, it will ruin him at *all* levels. You know how scandals often flow down through the ranks."

"I do," replied Darcy. It was difficult to hear Fitzwilliam speak of his friend in such a manner, but how many times had Darcy thought the very same himself? Far more than he wished to confess.

"That is why I feel it is best for you to make a break from him unless he learns to control his sister. Perhaps with the loss of your patronage these last months, he will grow into his responsibilities."

"I hope so," said Darcy, not at all convinced. He knew his friend far too well for that.

When he turned his attention back to his cousin, he noticed that Fitzwilliam was regarding him, a pensive expression on his face. "Elizabeth has not told me of her acquaintance with Miss Bingley, but from what I heard the woman say at the academy, it was not cordial."

"I believe it was nothing more than Miss Bingley's typical behavior," replied Darcy. "Elizabeth did not say much to me either, other than how she was able to deflect the woman. I do not know how much they were in company, but I suspect it was often. Apparently, Bingley paid a lot of attention to Jane Bennet, the eldest of the Bennet girls."

A slow nod was Fitzwilliam's response. "That is another facet of Bingley's behavior of which I do not approve. If you will pardon my saying so, I suspect the eldest Bennet might be better off without him."

Darcy nodded but kept silent; the conversation was beginning to become uncomfortable. He had spent the winter largely avoiding thinking of Bingley and the state of his friendship with the man. He did not wish to be reminded of it at present.

It was fortunate, then, that the Bennet estate drew close and they could turn their attention to the upcoming confrontation. The narrow road on which they traveled gave way to a small village consisting of nothing more than a church, a collection of houses scattered about it, and a blacksmith. On the far side of the town, they entered another road, well maintained with fresh gravel and with a modest estate at the end. It was, Darcy thought, the estate of a man of moderate means, one who would be a leader in a small society such as this, but of no true consequence outside this neighborhood. The walls of the estate were whitewashed and ivy climbed the front façade, giving it a splash of color and lending it a distinction Darcy thought it would not otherwise possess.

When the coach pulled to a stop, they alighted and approached the door. A short, staccato rap brought a middle-aged woman dressed in a simple dress and an apron, who looked on them with curiosity.

"Fitzwilliam Darcy and Anthony Fitzwilliam to see Mr. Bennet," said Darcy, handing the woman his card.

She took it and then motioned for them to enter. "If you please, sir, I will see if the master is accepting visitors."

With a bow, Darcy agreed, though by his side he heard Fitzwilliam mutter, "He had best accept us, or it will go ill with him." Although Darcy agreed, he decided it was best not to say anything. The housekeeper disappeared down a short hallway, and they could hear her knock on a door down near the end of the hall. She entered thereafter and was gone for a few moments, before reappearing.

"The master will see you," said she, motioning them forward.

The room, when they entered, was occupied by a man of approximately fifty years. He was possessed of a full head of hair, black, though giving way to the grayness of age. His face was lined, and though it showed his age, it was not so much as to make him seem ancient. The room in which he stood was dominated by an oak desk and boasted shelves along every available space on the walls. Into every available space in those shelves, books were crammed, enough that there were several piles on the floor where they would not fit into the available bookcases. A man of the written word, indeed.

"Mr. Darcy?" asked Mr. Bennet, stretching forth his hand.

Darcy accepted it and nodded. "I am Fitzwilliam Darcy, yes. This is my cousin, Colonel Anthony Fitzwilliam."

"Welcome, sir, though I will own I am surprised to see you here."

"Have you heard of me?" asked Darcy.

"I believe you have a friend by the name of Charles Bingley?" Darcy nodded, and Mr. Bennet chuckled. "It seems, sir, that your Mr. Bingley thinks quite highly of you, for his conversation is liberally sprinkled with your name, the debt he owes you, and the virtues you possess. It seems you have made quite an impression on him."

Not so much as to induce him to prevent his sister from trying to compromise me, thought Darcy, feeling the effects of his friend's betrayal all over again.

"Bingley is a man who is newly into his majority," replied Darcy, attempting diplomacy. "I have attempted to do what I can to guide his first steps so that he may thereafter stand on his own."

"Well said, sir!" replied Mr. Bennet. Then he looked at them askance. "Now that the pleasantries have been exchanged, I believe you wish something of me? I had not thought to ever make your acquaintance, especially once your friend quit the area."

"In fact, sir," interjected Fitzwilliam, "we have come to speak of Miss Elizabeth, who I believe resided in your house for more than eighteen years."

A queer look settled over Mr. Bennet's countenance, and his eyes widened in shock. "Lizzy?" His eyes darted back and forth between Darcy and Fitzwilliam. "You have come to ask about my daughter?"

"Come, Mr. Bennet," said Fitzwilliam, "we know she is not your daughter."

Mr. Bennet paused and sat back to consider them. "I do not know what you are here for, gentlemen, but I am not in the habit of speaking of my family with strangers. Shall you not come to the point?"

"What Fitzwilliam is trying to tell you, Mr. Bennet," said Darcy, "is that Miss Elizabeth is known to us. I met her some weeks ago in London when we attended the same party, and Fitzwilliam met her a few days later. Furthermore, we know she is not your true daughter and that she was a foundling you brought into your house at a very young age."

"In reality," said Fitzwilliam, "she is Lady Elizabeth Anne Fitzwilliam, daughter of Hugh Fitzwilliam, Earl of Matlock, and my sister."

The way Mr. Bennet stared at them suggested that he could not have been more surprised had they told him he was, himself, the King of Sweden. His eyes searched theirs for several moments before he made a reply, and when he did there was a note of incredulity inherent in it that Darcy immediately took as confirmation the man had not been involved in Elizabeth's abduction.

"Lizzy is the daughter of an earl?"

"To you, she is Lady Elizabeth, sir," said Fitzwilliam. His countenance was fixed and loathing, and it suggested to Darcy that he had not recognized what Darcy had.

With a start, Mr. Bennet looked at Fitzwilliam, and he frowned when he saw something in Fitzwilliam's countenance suggesting danger. Darcy intervened.

"Peace, Fitzwilliam. Give the man a chance to understand this information you have so unceremoniously dropped on him."

The sound of Darcy's voice seemed to catch both men by surprise. Mr. Bennet sat back in his chair and regarded them both warily, while Fitzwilliam glanced at Darcy, saw the minute shake of his head, and subsided, though not with any grace. He was still watchful, suspicion alive in his very posture. Darcy was confident of Mr. Bennet's innocence for himself, but he knew Fitzwilliam would not relent until it was made completely clear.

"You are attempting to tell me the woman I raised in my home is actually the daughter of an earl?" asked Mr. Bennet as soon as Darcy met his eyes again.

"Yes, Mr. Bennet, we are. Furthermore, we are here to learn something of how she came to be in your care. My uncle, the earl, was never able to find any trace of his daughter after she disappeared."

"Which leaves me as a prime suspect in her disappearance," said Mr. Bennet.

It was the speed at which the man came to an understanding of their presence which caused Fitzwilliam's glare to slip a little. Mr. Bennet's words were filled with a hint of sardonic amusement. A normal man would have been afraid unless he was skilled at concealing his emotions. Mr. Bennet, though taciturn, was not such a man.

"Rather I would say you are our only link to any sort of information which would assist us in unraveling this mystery," replied Darcy. "We now know where she has been these past eighteen years, but we do not know how she was moved from Derbyshire to Cambridge, nor how long her journey was, as neither Elizabeth nor the Gardiners had any notion of when she came to your notice. We would appreciate any information you can offer us, sir."

"Of course," replied Mr. Bennet, still shocked by what he was hearing. "I would not dream of keeping it from you. Only . . ." He paused for a moment and then looked Darcy in the eye. "Would it be possible for you to relate the story of how her identity was discovered in turn? I knew Gardiner would care for her, but I will own that I have been worried about her."

"Worried?" demanded Fitzwilliam, his voice dripping scorn. "You forced her from her home, man, left her to shift for herself in the world! And now you pretend concern? What is your game?"

"I do not know what Elizabeth has told you about this house, but I assure you I did not simply push her through the door and slam it behind her." Mr. Bennet's words were filled with the heat of his own indignation, and his eyes strove with Fitzwilliam's for supremacy. "My wife was angry with her, given what had happened, and sending Elizabeth away from this place seemed like the best solution for her. Once the rumors began—"

"Rumors started by *your* wife," accused Fitzwilliam.

"I do not deny that she renounced all association with Elizabeth. But by then the damage was already done by *Wickham.*" The loathing in the man's voice was akin to Fitzwilliam's, whenever he spoke of the man. It was another piece of evidence that Mr. Bennet was not so bad as Fitzwilliam wished to believe. "I am not asking for access to her or to be allowed to see her. I understand you will not likely allow her near us again. I merely wish to understand how you could have identified her after all these years.

"And I hope part of your purpose here is to ensure that cowardly scoundrel is made to pay for what he has done."

These last few words were spoken in a quiet voice. Darcy gazed at Mr. Bennet, and he was able to feel some compassion for him; this Mr. Bennet was not an assertive man, and he had been thrust into a role for which he was unsuited. But he was not malicious, and he had done the best he could in the situation in which he had found himself. He had not only brought Elizabeth up to be the fine woman she now was, but he had protected her when her situation in his home became untenable.

Darcy turned to Fitzwilliam, showing him a raised eyebrow. It appeared like Fitzwilliam would prefer nothing more than to continue in this combative stance, but he only returned Darcy's look and shrugged.

"Very well, Mr. Bennet. We will agree to inform you of the proof we possess of Elizabeth's identity. As for any further contact with you, that will be *her* choice, though her father will not likely allow it at present. I believe, however, if I am not very much mistaken, that you have at least one daughter from whom she will be loath to be permanently estranged."

For the first time, Mr. Bennet showed them a hint of a smile. "Yes, Jane. I can well imagine it. They have always been the closest of sisters. Jane, too, has been wild for word of Elizabeth, and I dare say the short letters she has managed to send have not assuaged Jane's concern.

"Now, gentlemen—what do you wish to know?"

"How did she come to be with your family?" asked Darcy, beginning with the obvious question.

* * *

Henry Bennet was hurrying through the streets of Cambridge when it happened. The setting sun was just descending below the tops of the houses, the air warm and dry, when he felt the impact of a small body against his legs.

Startled, Bennet looked down to see a small child clutching his legs, attempting to regain her balanced. She looked up, appearing a little dazed. Then her eyes filled with sheer terror and she poised to flee. It was only by the force of instinct that Bennet was able to reach out and grasp her arm before she darted away from him.

She was a tiny little cherub, with dark hair and eyes, wearing a pretty yellow dress which was a little smudged and dirty. Given the dress, Bennet thought she might be the daughter of a gentleman, or perhaps a wealthy merchant. But he had never seen her in the neighborhood, had no notion of from whence she might have come. It was likely she was too young to tell him.

"Wait, little one," said he to the girl in a soothing tone. He crouched down to bring his eyes to her level and put her at ease, while he continued to speak to her. "Where have you come from, and where are you going in such a hurry?"

The girl struggled to free her arm, but Bennet only gathered her in closer, speaking to her in his low tone the entire time. "Where are your parents?"

She ceased struggling, seeming to sense that she was not about to escape. Perhaps she sensed he meant her no harm. "Lock," was the single word she said.

"Lock? What does that mean?"

The little girl shook her head. "Mama. Lock."

"Perhaps I could help you find your family," replied Bennet, though he had no notion of what she was speaking.

"Mama?" asked she, looking into his eyes.

"Yes, your Mama. Shall we look for her together?"

The child seemed to think on this for a moment before she nodded. Gingerly, Bennet wrapped his arms around her and lifted her, wary of any new attempt to wriggle from his grasp. But the girl seemed to at least suffer his touch now, though he was not certain he was trusted, exactly.

Bennet caught sight of a woman approaching, one of this neighbors from a street over, Mrs. Nelson. "Who is that little child you have?"

asked she.

"I found her here," replied Bennet, noting that several others were approaching to listen to the conversation. "She ran into me only moments ago."

"She is a pretty little thing," said Mrs. Nelson, caressing the girl's cheek. The little urchin giggled a little at the touch—Mrs. Nelson had a way with Bennet's eldest daughter too.

"Her family must be nearby," said Bennet. "They must be looking for her."

"I have never seen her in these parts," replied Mrs. Nelson.

"You should ask at the local inns," added a man who was standing nearby. "Perhaps she is the daughter of someone traveling through the city."

"I will do that," replied Bennet.

The crowd began to disperse, and Bennet was soon left alone with Mrs. Nelson and the girl in his arms. "If you and Mrs. Bennet need assistance finding her family, do not hesitate to ask."

"Thank you, Mrs. Nelson. I believe all will be well."

Bennet turned and began to walk away with the child in his arms. She watched where they were going with some interest, her former fear apparently forgotten. Bennet watched her with some amusement—she seemed to be a courageous little thing.

"What is your name, my dear?"

The girl turned and regarded him, gazing at him for several moments. Finally, she responded with a single word: "Lizbeth."

Saturday, March 7, 1812
Longbourn, Hertfordshire

"This was in the city of Cambridge?" asked Fitzwilliam. During Mr. Bennet's initial recital, Fitzwilliam had leaned forward, intent upon the tale. Mr. Bennet seemed to sense that Fitzwilliam's antagonism had given away to his desperate interest in the story, and responded accordingly.

"It was. I assume you both attended there?" When Darcy and Fitzwilliam both nodded, Bennet said: "My lodgings were just on the other side of the river from the university. They were not the best for a married man with children, but they were convenient. When my younger children were born, we moved to a location a little more suitable for raising a family, with my elder brother's assistance. At that time, however, we were still in the smaller apartments."

"You say it was September?" asked Fitzwilliam as he regarded Mr. Bennet intently.

"It was," replied Mr. Bennet. "The weather was still warm, and I remember that classes had started not long before. Also . . ."

Mr. Bennet trailed off and did not speak for a moment. When he could not ignore Darcy and Fitzwilliam's scrutiny any longer, he sighed.

"In late August, my wife gave birth to my second daughter, Mary, and a stillborn son. Mary survives to this day, but my son was the only male child we managed to produce. Elizabeth came to us only about two weeks later, and though she was already more than two years of age, she immediately took the place of our lost child. In many ways, I believe we forgot at times that she was not born to us."

"Is that why you never told her of her origins?" asked Fitzwilliam.

"In part," replied Mr. Bennet. "But I also had no desire for her to believe that she was in any way inferior to my other children, especially when I inherited. Philip—my elder brother—knew Elizabeth was not our child, but at my request, he never told anyone in Meryton. When we moved to Longbourn, she moved with us, and to everyone in the neighborhood, she was Elizabeth Bennet, my second daughter."

Darcy regarded the man, attempting to make sense of what he was hearing. "What did you do to attempt to discover her origins?"

"We canvassed the neighborhood and put a notice in the local newspaper. I also checked at the local inns. Though one innkeeper told me he thought she resembled a child with a couple who had checked in earlier and suddenly checked out again, he informed me the lady was carrying their child when the left to enter the carriage which took them away."

"That seems a little suspicious," said Fitzwilliam. "Did you follow up with the driver when he returned?"

"Though I thought it was fruitless, I did," said Mr. Bennet with a nod. "The driver was surly and uncommunicative and would say no more than he knew nothing of any lost child. I discovered where he had taken them, but I lacked the resources to pursue it any further. I could never have fathomed that she had been taken away from an estate so far distant as you suggest."

"Did you not suspect she was the daughter of a gentleman, from her dress if nothing else?" asked Fitzwilliam.

"I did suspect so, but I had no way of knowing. She might have been someone's natural daughter for all I knew. She was at risk if she was taken to an orphanage, and I could not leave her on the streets, for obvious reasons. So I did the best I could—I ensured she would have the best life I could give her. Though I was naught but a professor at the time, eventually she became a gentleman's daughter."

Darcy and Fitzwilliam shared a look, and Darcy thought it likely they were thinking the same thing. Mr. Bennet *had* done much more than he might have been expected to do, to the point of giving Elizabeth a life and a home, when it could have been so much worse. Lord Matlock had investigated several orphanages in Derbyshire to see if she had been left there, but he would not have looked in one so distant from Derbyshire. They would never have found her in those circumstances, and her life would not have been pleasant.

"Then you had no notion of from whence she came?" said Fitzwilliam.

"None whatsoever. I never thought she would discover her true family. She has been my daughter since she was two years of age. In fact, in some ways, she is dearer to me than my own children. Elizabeth is more like me than any of the other girls, and at times she served as my intellectual partner. I have missed her exceedingly these past months."

It was not unexpected, but Darcy was disheartened that Mr. Bennet could not tell them anything of substance concerning Elizabeth's disappearance.

"I am sorry, Mr. Darcy, Colonel Fitzwilliam, that I have not been able to be of more assistance, but I have nothing more about the situation to relate. Will you reciprocate by informing me of how this miraculous event occurred?"

They related the story, and Mr. Bennet listened intently to their account. When it was complete, the man sat back and rubbed his chin, seeming to think of something. "That is an interesting tale, gentlemen. I do have one question, returning to our previous conversation: do you know how long it took her to travel from Derbyshire to Cambridge?"

"My father and mother would know," said Fitzwilliam. "I was at Eton when it happened, so I do not know the exact date. But depending on when you found her, I suspect it would have been no more than a day or two after her disappearance."

"Whoever took her likely traveled from Derbyshire to Cambridge," said Mr. Bennet, "though I cannot fathom what their destination might have been."

"Unless Cambridge itself was the destination," said Darcy. "It seems like she escaped her captors somehow when you found her."

"You did not see anyone loitering about when you found her?" asked Fitzwilliam.

"No one," confirmed Mr. Bennet. "And I let it be known about the neighborhood that I had found a child for several days after, and no one stepped forward to claim her."

Darcy turned and directed his gaze at Fitzwilliam once again. His cousin was thoughtful, but after a few moments, he shook his head. "It is impossible to know how she came to be there. She might have escaped earlier and wandered the streets for some time, or those who had abducted her might have fled when they noticed she was missing. I doubt a child of two could have managed to travel any distance from where she evaded her captors."

"Then it is likely we shall never know," replied Darcy.

The three men sat in that attitude for some moments, thinking about the situation. Darcy was disappointed as he knew Fitzwilliam was as well, but neither had expected this visit to give them all the answers. Unless someone stepped forward when Elizabeth's return was announced—a circumstance he considered unlikely in the extreme—this would remain a mystery.

As they sat there, Darcy began to be aware of something beyond the walls of Mr. Bennet's study. The slamming of a door caught his attention, as did the sound of feminine giggling, and a cry of anger or delight—he was not quite certain. Then the rumble of a carriage coming up the drive alerted him to the possibility that Bennet might have another visitor very soon. He caught Fitzwilliam's eye and his cousin nodded, apparently having come to the same conclusion.

"Mr. Bennet," said Darcy, "I thank you for your frankness, though it is unfortunate you do not have any more information to give us."

"It is no trouble, Mr. Darcy," replied Mr. Bennet. "I only wish I could give you more."

"I also wish to thank you on behalf of my family," said Fitzwilliam, appearing to speak with only the slightest hint of a grudge. "You were not required to take my sister into your home, but I am grateful you did. I shudder to think what might have happened to her if you had not."

"It was easy to love her as a child, Colonel Fitzwilliam," replied Mr. Bennet. "She was so bright and precocious and loving—I could no more have turned her away than I could have turned my own children away. Please, think no more on it." Mr. Bennet paused and he appeared distinctly uncomfortable. "I know these past months have been difficult for Elizabeth, but I hope you will not think poorly of us for her being in London. The continued presence of Wickham and the situation in the neighborhood made it impossible to keep her here. I could not guarantee her safety from him.

"*Wickham,*" Bennet spat the man's name like an epithet, "has attained a certain notoriety with the regiment and appears to enjoy it immensely, as it brings him the attention of many of the sillier ladies, though many of my fellow gentlemen have decreed that he is not to be allowed in their houses or associate with their daughters."

The sound of a loud giggle once again penetrated Mr. Bennet's sanctuary, as did the voice of a woman, mature, yet without any modulation of her tone. Darcy could not make out what she was saying through the heavy oak door, but it sounded like a demand of some sort.

"I am surprised, Mr. Bennet," said Fitzwilliam. "Wickham's usual habit is to run at the first sign of trouble."

"He has not this time. The people of Meryton have chosen to assign all blame for what happened to Elizabeth, and Wickham has not suffered, that I can determine, with the exception of his banishment from certain homes." It was clear from the man's tone and posture that if he were a younger man, he might have called Wickham out.

"He will not remain so for long, Mr. Bennet," replied Fitzwilliam. "We will see him pay for what he has done."

Clearly, Mr. Bennet approved of the dangerous note in Fitzwilliam's voice, and he nodded and rose to his feet. "Then I wish you every luck with the lieutenant. I am eager to hear of his upcoming troubles."

The two men shared an evil grin, a far cry from the tension which had existed between them when Darcy and Fitzwilliam had first come. But before anything else could be said, the door behind them flew open and a woman of approximately forty years entered the room in a swirl of skirts and a fluttering handkerchief. Darcy was not even able to gain an impression of her before she started to speak in a loud voice.

"Oh, Mr. Bennet, you did not inform me that you were to have visitors today." The woman sized Darcy and Fitzwilliam up with one glance, before she continued, exclaiming: "Your friends must stay for dinner, of course! I am quite eager to introduce them to the rest of the family!"

"Unfortunately, Mrs. Bennet," said Mr. Bennet, "these fine gentlemen are only here for a short time, and must depart on a matter of urgent business."

Then before Mrs. Bennet could do more than gape at him, Mr.

Bennet rounded the desk and shook Darcy and Fitzwilliam's hands in turn. "Thank you for visiting me today. Our discussion has been most enlightening. I hope that this matter will have a happy ending and that I may one day see the results of it."

"Thank you for your information, Mr. Bennet," said Darcy, eager to leave the man with his loud wife behind. "If anything more should come to light, we will send word through your brother."

Then with more eagerness than dignity, Darcy quit the room with his cousin on his heels. Throughout their short discussion with Mr. Bennet, Mrs. Bennet said not a word, though her countenance suggested astonishment. She was clearly a woman of mean intelligence, one who was not adept at understanding her husband's quickly spoken words. But when they left the room, her voice rose in consternation behind them, though Mr. Bennet quickly closed the door, muffling her cries.

"I believe I suddenly have more respect for Mr. Bennet, Cousin," said Fitzwilliam quietly in his ear. "I do not know if I could withstand such a woman for a week, let alone more than two decades."

Darcy snorted in his bid to withhold his laughter. He agreed with his cousin wholeheartedly. With such a woman as a mother, how had Elizabeth ever grown to be the woman she was?

When they exited the house, they found the carriage had been moved around beside the stables, so they waited on the front steps of the manor for it to be brought around. It was while they were waiting there that a young woman came around the corner with a book clutched in her hands. She was small of stature, with dark hair and hazel eyes, and there was a pretty sort of intelligence about her which Darcy attributed to her being one of the Bennet daughters. She also bore some resemblance to the woman they had just met.

She seemed startled to see them and for a moment seemed ready to pass them by and enter the house. At the last moment, however, she stopped and turned to them, seeming to steel her courage to address them.

"Sirs, I apologize for breaking propriety in this way, but I wished to express my pleasure that Elizabeth has found her family."

Darcy searched the girl's eyes for some hint of calculation or other motivation than what she stated, but he found only earnestness. "I am sorry Miss . . . ."

"Mary," replied the girl. "I am the Bennets' second daughter, the next youngest to Jane. For many years, Elizabeth was my elder sister, and a better one would be difficult to find. She . . ." The girl trailed off and looked out into the distance. "She was always the peacemaker in the family, and always had time for her younger sisters, though I will own that we did not always see her for the gem that she is."

"But how did you discover this? We only just came from your father's study."

The girl only smiled. "There are ways to hear what is happening in my father's study. Just now, I was sitting on a bench outside, and as he had the window ajar, I could hear some of what you were saying." Miss Mary paused and, after thinking about something for a moment, seemed to come to a resolution. "You see, I have known for several years that Elizabeth was not my sister."

Surprised, Darcy said: "Through similar means to what you overheard today?"

"Something like that," replied Mary with a smile. "I do not normally make it a habit to listen at doors, but I chanced to overhear my parents speaking when I was thirteen, and have known ever since. Elizabeth has not been any less my sister because of it. I am only happy she has found you, for these months have been difficult for her."

"They have," replied Fitzwilliam.

"You will take good care of her?" It was practically a demand.

"Indeed, we shall, Miss Mary," replied Fitzwilliam. "She will be introduced to society as my sister and will have all the rights and privileges associated with her station."

"I am happy to hear it." The girl once again stopped and considered something, before she turned her attention back to them. "I will not breathe a word of this, of course. My mother would . . . Well, she would wish to make something of the connection if she learned of it, and I do not wish Elizabeth to suffer further. But when she is settled in her new home, I hope you will allow me to correspond with her. I would not wish to lose contact."

"Miss Mary," said Fitzwilliam, bowing low, but with a smile for the young girl, "Elizabeth will decide with whom she will correspond, though I believe you are correct in that she is not likely to do so for some few months. I cannot think she would refuse to write to you."

It was clear that Miss Mary was pleased to hear it but equally clear that her courage had run its course. With a softly spoken word of thanks and a quick curtsey, the girl fairly fled into the house, leaving two bemused men behind.

* * *

Saturday, March 7, 1812
Militia Headquarters, Meryton, Hertfordshire

After the emotion of the morning with Mr. Bennet, the capture of George Wickham was anticlimactic. Fitzwilliam had arranged for four men from his regiment to enter Meryton while they were at Longbourn and detain Wickham on the authority of his general, which the man had not hesitated to give, once Fitzwilliam had explained the particulars to him. Thus, when they made their way to the headquarters of the militia in Meryton, Wickham was already shackled and guarded. His reaction to seeing them enter the building suggested sheer terror.

"Wickham," said Fitzwilliam, his voice akin to the purr of a cat, "how wonderful it is to see you again. I trust you have been well."

Wickham attempted a glare in return, but though his gaze was filled with loathing, it was also much more apprehensive in nature. Fitzwilliam only chuckled at the sight. The commander of the regiment exited his office at that moment and approached them.

"Colonel Fitzwilliam, I presume?" asked he, and when Fitzwilliam confirmed his supposition, he extended his hand. "So, you have come to relieve me of my most troublesome officer."

"Making friends already, are you Wickham?" asked Fitzwilliam, turning a lazy eye on the lieutenant. "Then again, you were always a smooth one."

"Might I know what the charges against him are?" asked Forster. "Not that it matters, of course." His eye might have flayed Wickham where he sat, had they possessed the power. "I have long been wishing Wickham gone and not only for what happened to the Bennet girl. A more slothful and indifferent officer I have never had the misfortune to meet."

"He has run up debts in several communities, which I am calling due," replied Darcy. "They are enough that a gentleman would struggle to pay them."

"Here, Darcy," attempted Wickham, "I thought we had an agreement. I was to be silent while you would not prosecute."

"That was before, Wickham," replied Fitzwilliam, his voice low and menacing. "Now *my father* has taken an interest in you, and you will not escape so lightly."

The very mention of the earl made Wickham blanch. "Yes, Georgie, you have trifled with the wrong woman."

"And part of our agreement was that you would not run up any further debts. Can I assume you have not kept your part of the bargain?"

Wickham looked away, confirming Darcy's suspicions.

"Debts in Meryton?" exclaimed Colonel Forster. "What manner of debts, and how much have you accumulated? By God, Wickham—do you not know that the regiment must cover your debts before we leave?"

"You need not worry, Colonel," said Darcy. "I shall settle Mr. Wickham's accounts before we leave today. Though I hardly need them, they will give us further leverage over this sorry excuse for a man."

Though he regarded Darcy for a moment, Colonel Forster agreed and voiced his thanks.

Fitzwilliam nodded at his men, and they hauled Wickham to his feet to guide him from the room. Fitzwilliam's mocking voice followed the man as he departed. "Be careful what you say to these fine gentlemen, Wickham. Saving your own skin was always among your greatest skills, and I know you will wish to arrive at your new home intact."

The shudder which passed through Wickham's form did not surprise Darcy, and he turned away from the man in disgust. Wickham always had been a coward.

"Can I assume the woman to whom you refer is the young Miss Bennet?"

Darcy turned back to the colonel. "It is, though I am not at liberty to speak on what has happened."

"And I will not ask further. I am only happy to be rid of the man. He is as slippery as a snake, and I have had a devil of a time controlling him these past months. I suspect he would have fled, had I not had him watched."

"Then we thank you for your diligence, Colonel," said Darcy, answering for them both. "Wickham's days in England are numbered. He will be no more trouble to any of us."

With a nod, the colonel thanked them again and they departed.

CHAPTER XIII

Saturday, March 7, 1812
Darcy House, London

While William and Anthony were in Hertfordshire speaking with Mr. Bennet about Elizabeth's past, she busied herself by visiting with Georgiana in her mother's company. Today was the day they were to tell her of Elizabeth's true identity, and Elizabeth was genuinely curious as to how the girl would receive the information.

They arrived at William's house, and once they entered, Lady Susan spoke with the housekeeper to have Georgiana summoned, and then had a word with the girl's companion, a Mrs. Annesley. When she returned to the sitting-room, Georgiana and Elizabeth were chatting about their doings in the past few days. Elizabeth's days had been quite full, of course, and while she knew it was their purpose to speak of those matters that day, Elizabeth felt strangely reluctant to do so. It was fortunate that Georgiana more than made up for Elizabeth's silence, surprising, considering how reticent she had been when Elizabeth had first met her. Then again, William had informed Elizabeth that Georgiana could be quite chatty when she was comfortable in company, so she supposed it was a good sign that she could speak with such abandon.

"It is wonderful to see you, Aunt," said Georgiana after some time of regaling them with her doings. "But I must own to a little surprise, for I never expected to receive you in Elizabeth's company. I had not known you were acquainted."

Lady Susan smiled at her niece for giving her the perfect opportunity to introduce Elizabeth as her daughter. "I made Elizabeth's acquaintance only a few days ago, Georgiana. And it is because of this that we have some momentous news with which to acquaint you."

"Oh?" asked Georgiana, her eyes swinging to Elizabeth, curiosity burning within.

"Yes. For you see, we have made a most remarkable discovery. Elizabeth is not Miss Elizabeth Bennet as you thought. In fact, she is Lady Elizabeth Anne Fitzwilliam, my daughter and your cousin."

"Cousin?" squeaked Georgiana, her eyes wide with surprise. "How could that possibly be? I do not believe I ever heard of a lost cousin."

"For obvious reasons, we did not speak much of Elizabeth, though your brother is old enough to remember her. As to how, let me explain it to you."

The tale was then told, explaining to Georgiana the revelations of the last few days, and specifically how William had recognized her and then brought the Fitzwilliam family to meet her. She also told Georgiana an abbreviated version of what they knew of Elizabeth's disappearance. By the end of it, Georgiana was a little less bewildered but no less emotional. In the middle, she had grasped Elizabeth to her and held on tightly, and Elizabeth was just as eager to keep her newly acknowledged relation close.

"I had wondered what was happening!" exclaimed she when Lady Susan had finished her explanation. "William and Anthony brought you into our lives and treated you as if you were one of the family. It turns out you were!"

Elizabeth laughed. "I suppose we shall be forced to tease the gentlemen. I am certain they thought they were clever and subtle."

"Of course, I could not know who you were," replied Georgiana. She ducked her head, displaying her shyness. "I am happy to have you as a cousin, Elizabeth. For you see, all my cousins are so much older than I. It will be delightful to have someone in the family closer to my age."

"And I am delighted to have you as a cousin, regardless of your age!" exclaimed Elizabeth.

Georgiana giggled and for some time, they were treated to a recitation of how happy Georgiana was to be introduced to her new cousin and how she was anticipating their future association. Elizabeth listened to the girl, indulging her joy, for she knew that Georgiana had, at times, lived a lonely existence. Soon, however, the subject changed to that of the extended Fitzwilliam family, and Elizabeth, having heard little of them thus far, was interested to learn more of the family she was gaining.

"I have three siblings," said Lady Susan when Elizabeth asked. "My eldest brother is an earl himself, while my younger sister is married to a Baron. My youngest brother is a captain in the navy, and as he has done well for himself in prize money, I believe he plans to retire once the troubles with France are resolved."

"Is he married?" asked Elizabeth.

"He is, but his wife does not often see him. They have two children, and they live on an estate in Bedfordshire, which he purchased with his earnings. They are not often in town, so you will not meet them this season, I suspect."

"And Father's family?"

"Your father has two sisters and two brothers," replied Lady Susan. "Lady Anne Darcy, who was William and Georgiana's mother, has passed on these last fifteen years. She was one of my closest friends as a girl and the reason I met your father, for she introduced us at a ball the season we came out. Of your father's younger brothers, one is an estate owner himself, as he inherited it from a wealthy relation, and one is a prominent judge. They are both in town, and you may be introduced to them.

"You have not mentioned Aunt Catherine," said Georgiana. The girl giggled at the mention of this other person, but there was a nervousness inherent in her voice which drew Elizabeth's attention.

"Why," said Lady Susan, "I must save the best—or the most interesting—for last!"

Lady Susan laughed and Georgiana joined her, but there was still that hint of anxiety worrying around the corners of her composure which suggested something objectionable about the woman.

"Do not allow Georgiana to alarm you, Elizabeth," said Lady Susan. "She has always felt intimidated by her aunt, but Lady Catherine's bite is much worse than her bark, though her bark *is* substantial!"

"But you must own that if anyone will object to Elizabeth's

recovery, it is my aunt," insisted Georgiana.

"In that you are correct," said Lady Susan with a sigh. "However, I do not expect any difficulty from Catherine, for she is reasonable, especially when it pertains to family. *If* she chooses to be difficult, then she will be *very* difficult!"

"Is she truly that objectionable?" asked Elizabeth with more curiosity than trepidation.

"She is authoritative and domineering," said Lady Susan. "Catherine is your father's eldest sister and quite unlike any of her siblings. She is loud, unafraid to share her opinion with any who will listen—and many who will not—and she considers herself an authority on any subject, whether she possesses any knowledge of it or not."

"Aunt Catherine quite terrifies me!" squeaked Georgiana.

Lady Susan caught her niece's gaze and watched her fondly. "Yes, Catherine can be vocal in her displeasure and determined to ensure everyone within range of her voice is aware of it, but at heart, she is a caring woman. She lives at Rosings Park in Kent with her daughter Anne, who suffers from a weak constitution. As such, they rarely come to town, even for the season."

A laugh escaped Lady Susan's mouth. "There were rumors when she was much younger that she immediately took over running Sir Lewis de Bourgh's estate when they were married. Sir Lewis was a slight and diffident man; I do not know if the rumors were true, but I would not doubt that Lady Catherine had *some* say in how her husband managed his holdings. He passed many years ago, when Anne was still a young child, and Lady Catherine has managed the estate ever since. By all accounts it is prosperous, so Catherine must have some knowledge of what is to be done."

"Then I cannot wait to meet her," said Elizabeth, vastly amused at their portrayal of Lady Catherine de Bourgh. Every family had a black sheep, she supposed, and even if this one was objectionable, Elizabeth thought she would be amusing.

"We will inform Catherine of what we have discovered after James and his family arrive in London. That will give her ample time to make her way to London so that she may inform us all of her opinion. I am certain we will not be required to wait long."

"The Viscount?" asked Elizabeth, having heard a little of him.

"Yes, my eldest son. Your father sent an express to him the morning after we learned of you, and we expect his return quickly."

"And James has two children?" asked Elizabeth.

"He does. His eldest, Cassandra, is four, and his youngest and heir, Andrew, is two years old. They are beautiful children. Given how you are with the Gardiners' children, I imagine you will enjoy meeting them."

They spent some pleasant time with Georgiana, discussing this relation or that, and Elizabeth learned that the Darcy and Fitzwilliam families had been close friends for many generations. Of Mr. Darcy's family, there were no closer relations than two generations removed — Mr. Darcy's great uncle and his family. Mr. Darcy was, of course, acquainted with them, but they were not close.

"We will not invite them to our dinner introducing you to our family," said Lady Susan. "After all, they are not truly *our* relations. I imagine you will meet them during this season, for Darcy's great uncle owns a large estate and is a member of the same circles."

After some time, they departed, allowing Georgiana to return to her studies with her companion. Elizabeth left with her mother, and they returned to the earl's house where they spent some time together, simply becoming better acquainted. It was later that afternoon when the gentlemen returned from their journey to Hertfordshire and joined Elizabeth and her mother, with the earl also in attendance.

The matter of William and Anthony's intention to speak with Mr. Bennet had not been far from Elizabeth's mind the entire day. The distractions provide by her mother and Georgiana — deliberately in the former's case — had served to prevent her from fretting about it. When the gentlemen returned, however, she found her attention once again fixed on what they had learned.

"Let us speak of Wickham first," said Anthony. "As we had planned, he was taken into custody while we were at Longbourn. After he was hauled away, we investigated his doings in Meryton."

"How much does he owe there?" asked Elizabeth's father.

"In excess of fifty pounds," replied William. He shook his head in disgust. "It amazes me that merchants will extend so much credit to men simply because they are members of the militia."

"Militia officers are much less dependable than those in the regulars," said Anthony. "But tales of unscrupulous officers can be heard from one end of the kingdom to the other."

"He owed the most at the inn," continued William. "The innkeeper was astonished when we tallied his receipts and came to a total of more than ten pounds. I dare say Wickham has been drinking himself into a stupor on a nightly basis."

"What has happened to him?" asked Elizabeth.

Anthony turned a firm look on Elizabeth, and she blushed a little. "You need not worry, dearest sister, for Wickham will never see you again. My men turned him over to the authorities in London where he will be imprisoned until called to stand trial for his misdeeds."

"And when that happens, I shall ensure he is deported to Van Diemen's Land," added the earl. "Within the week, we will be rid of George Wickham for good."

Though she took care to give nothing more than a calm response, inside Elizabeth breathed a sigh of relief. In some ways Elizabeth had been surprised he had not attempted to make her life even more uncomfortable than he had. She was also happy to know he was no longer a threat to the youngest Bennets. Kitty and Lydia, silly and thoughtless as they were, had been in danger from the man.

"That is well, then," said Lady Susan, eying Elizabeth. Elizabeth returned her look with a smile and a shrug, indicating she was well. She was not convinced her mother was at all fooled by her obfuscation, but Lady Susan relented.

"As for Mr. Bennet," continued Anthony, "it is clear the man knows nothing of Elizabeth's disappearance."

Anthony then informed them in a succinct manner the contents of their discussion with Mr. Bennet, including the details of why she had been sent to London and their brief meeting with Mrs. Bennet. Elizabeth could only cringe, knowing what she did of her adoptive mother's character. If the accounts of Lady Catherine were in any way indicative of the lady's behavior, Elizabeth thought she and Mrs. Bennet might be well matched in their ability to embarrass their families.

"Is there any chance this man was prevaricating?" asked father when Anthony had completed his recitation.

"It *is* possible, I suppose," replied Anthony. "But I hardly think it likely. I am a good judge of character, and I have been trained to spot a lie. I could not find any falsehood in Mr. Bennet's manners or his words."

"You must also remember, Uncle," said William, "that Mr. Bennet was not required to take Elizabeth into his home when he did. He could have easily turned responsibility for her over to an orphanage and washed his hands of her. Given how he was only a professor at Cambridge at the time, it would have been better financially for him if he had. I cannot imagine a scenario in which he would have stolen the daughter of an earl to raise himself."

"Might it not have been some sort of ransom scheme gone wrong?"

asked the earl. Elizabeth could see the stubbornness in his manner and knew that he was eager to find someone to blame for his family's heartache.

"If it was, I do not believe it was on Mr. Bennet's part," replied Anthony.

"You were eager to believe him the villain when we arrived there," noted William.

Anthony only shrugged. "Like my father, I wish to know why Elizabeth was taken from us, and I was not happy that she had been removed from her home because of Wickham's indiscretions."

"So your opinion has changed," said father.

"It has," replied Anthony. "I am convinced Mr. Bennet is innocent in this matter. As for Elizabeth's removal to London, while I might point out that Mr. Bennet is a weak man when it comes to his wife, and it seems he has no notion of how to control her or his daughters, I believe he did the best he could when Wickham accosted Elizabeth. He informed us it was for her protection that she was sent to Mr. Gardiner. In the end, it is for the best that Elizabeth was sent to London, as we would not have discovered her otherwise. We should be grateful for that."

Silence descended over the room. In her heart, Elizabeth was glad to hear that Mr. Bennet had been exonerated, not that she had ever had any true doubts on the matter. He was a good man, and she had been happy to call him "father" all the years of her adolescence. Her memories would not then be sullied.

"Then there are no other avenues that we may pursue to discover why she was taken from us," said the earl. The resignation in his voice was evident.

"I know not how," replied Anthony. "Elizabeth's presence in the Bennet family the past eighteen years is the only piece of information we have now that we have not known in all the years since. I doubt that any investigation in the city of Cambridge will tell us anything more."

"Then let us simply be happy that Elizabeth has been returned to us," said Lady Susan, drawing Elizabeth in for an embrace. "*That* is the most important point."

"Perhaps it is," replied Anthony. "But we must take care. I know we cannot hide Elizabeth away to protect her, but whoever took her from our home might still be lurking about somewhere."

"She was not harmed," protested Lady Susan. "If they had meant her harm, they could have done it anywhere between Derbyshire and

Cambridge."

"Mother, we do not know what happened," said Anthony. His level look informed them all how serious he was. "It is only prudent to ensure that Elizabeth is protected, no matter what may come."

With these ominous words, the discussion ended, and soon thereafter, Elizabeth boarded her father's coach for her return to Gracechurch Street. It was just as well, she decided once the carriage had lurched into motion—a pall had been cast over the company, and Elizabeth wished to return to her room at her uncle's house to mull matters over in her own mind.

Tuesday, March 10, 1812
Gardiner Townhouse, London

The next few days were filled with engagements with Elizabeth's new family. Whether they met at Gracechurch Street or Mayfair, she met her mother almost every day, and with her father, Anthony, and the Darcys almost as often. The gloom which had settled over the company upon Anthony and William's return from Hertfordshire was lifted, and though it was not forgotten by any of them, Elizabeth decided she would not worry over matters she could not control.

One of the first things her mother decided during those days was that Elizabeth's wardrobe was woefully inadequate, and as such, they needed to augment it. In this, Elizabeth could not protest, knowing that she had brought little with her from Longbourn. That did not make her any more eager to spend days shopping for clothing when she would much rather spend those hours becoming better acquainted with those from whom she had been sundered.

"Perhaps shopping with your mother and Georgiana will not be as tiresome as you believe," said Mrs. Gardiner. Lady Susan and Georgiana had come to retrieve her so they could go to Bond Street that morning, and her aunt had seen Elizabeth's look of distaste. Mrs. Gardiner was amused by it, having seen the same lack of enthusiasm from Elizabeth in the past.

"Elizabeth does not enjoy shopping?" asked her mother upon hearing this. "I have scarcely known a young lady who did not enjoy purchasing new clothes in all my life."

"I believe it stems from the fact that Mrs. Bennet was much engaged with Lizzy's clothes shopping in the past," replied Mrs. Gardiner.

"And this was a cause for concern?"

Elizabeth grimaced, but she essayed to make an answer. "The

foundation of the problem is that Mrs. Bennet and I do not share similar tastes in fashion. I prefer my clothes to be simple, yet elegant, whereas Mrs. Bennet possesses a heavy predilection for lace."

A laugh burst from her mother's mouth and she could only say: "And what would you do if *I* also possessed similar tastes as Mrs. Bennet?"

"I would likely retreat to my room and never again emerge from it," said Elizabeth, again to her mother's amusement. Georgiana was also laughing, though her laughter suggested a lack of understanding; Elizabeth suspected the girl loved few things more than shopping and could not understand how *anyone* would not enjoy it. "With Mrs. Bennet, at least I could dig in my heels and refuse to wear as much lace as she wished. I suspect if I tried to do that with you, you would simply drag me behind you, no matter how deeply I set my feet."

The two older ladies laughed while Georgiana exclaimed: "You have captured the very likeness of Aunt Susan!"

"Georgiana!" scolded Lady Susan, as if shocked. "You will have Elizabeth believe that I am no better than Catherine!"

"At times you are quite similar," said Georgiana, with a large measure of courage, Elizabeth thought. "You are nowhere near as domineering as Aunt Catherine can be, but you do enjoy having your own way."

"We *all* do, my dear," said Lady Susan, patting Georgiana's cheek with affection. "But those of us who have attained a certain maturity have not only experience to guide us, but demand the respect of the younger generations, which allows us to have our way even more often."

"I have never felt overly put upon," replied the young girl. "I have been happy that you have taken me under your wing."

"And I have been happy to have you." Lady Susan smiled at Georgiana, her lips trembling ever so slightly. "You remind me much of your mother, my dear. She was my closest friend. I have only done what I can to take her place, though I know it is not much.

"Now," said Lady Susan, shaking off the emotion of the moment, "I believe we should depart before this scene becomes positively mawkish."

Depart they did, and Elizabeth was treated to her first day shopping with her mother. Shopping with Lady Susan, as Aunt Gardiner had said, did not in any way resemble obtaining dresses in the company of Mrs. Bennet. Whenever she had visited a dressmaker with Mrs. Bennet, Elizabeth could always count on it becoming a battle for supremacy, and after she had attained a certain age, she had taken to doing her shopping when she visited the Gardiners, with Mr. Bennet's blessing. It was beneficial for him too, as listening to his wife's laments for a short time after Elizabeth returned from London was preferable to listening to her complain that Elizabeth had defied her yet again. And since London fashions were, in Mrs. Bennet's mind, superior to what could be obtained from Meryton, that fact often assuaged her displeasure.

By contrast, Lady Susan was careful to listen to Elizabeth's preference and guide her toward what she thought would suit her best given those inclinations. In this she was joined by Madam Fournier, the exclusive modiste Lady Susan and Georgiana used, a woman who displayed excellent taste and a talent for styles. Elizabeth could not say she was happy to be measured and poked and prodded and fussed over, but the experience was less frustrating than it had been in the past.

Another trait which Madam Fournier possessed was discretion, one which Elizabeth supposed was valuable for a woman in her position. When they entered the shop, Lady Susan introduced Elizabeth as her daughter, and when the woman looked at her with surprise, a quick explanation was given. Madam Fournier was profuse in her congratulations but quick to return to the business at hand and not belabor the point.

"Was that wise?" asked Elizabeth of her mother when the madam left the room to allow them to look over some fashion plates. "I had understood we were to release my identity to the public in a more formal manner."

"Madam Fournier is quite discrete, Elizabeth," said Lady Susan. "She must be, for she is in a position to learn certain secrets at times which those involved would not wish to be known. She will not speak of you to anyone."

Elizabeth nodded, but inwardly she wondered. Meryton's dressmaker was one of the most determined gossips in the neighborhood, and those who frequented her shop knew to say as little as possible in her presence. She supposed it was different in town, where the doings of the elite were greater fodder for the gossips. If Madam Fournier gained a reputation of possessing a loose tongue, her clients would likely shop elsewhere. In Meryton, there was only one dressmaker, and thus she had a much greater margin for error.

After some time with the modiste in which a great number of items, including dresses, outerwear, and assorted underclothing was ordered, they stopped by several other shops, including cobblers for sturdy boots, slippers, and shoes, a millinery, and several other locations. By the end of their travels among the shops, Elizabeth was tired but oddly exhilarated by the experience.

"We will not visit the jeweler's today," said Lady Susan as they returned to the carriage and settled in for the return to Fitzwilliam House. "Though I have it in my mind to purchase some pieces for you before your introduction to society, we do have several which were put aside for you when you were young." Lady Susan smiled softly at Elizabeth. "They have been waiting for the past eighteen years to adorn you, my lovely daughter. I could not bear to return them to the general Fitzwilliam connection."

"But—" Elizabeth stopped, and she turned a wry smile on her mother, which was returned in full.

"I know this is all unexpected, but it comes with your station, my dear. You are the daughter of an earl, and you must appear like one, lest our image suffer and we appear to be naught but paupers." Lady Susan grinned. "The Fitzwilliam family is wealthy, Elizabeth. I know you were raised on a humble estate, but now you are a member of a powerful family, with all the rights and privileges pertaining to that position."

"I know, Mother," replied Elizabeth. "It is only that I am not accustomed to it."

"You will learn, my dear. Perhaps I should not inform you of this, but I believe your father intends to surprise you with a gift of a brooch, or some other piece." Lady Susan winked and caught Georgiana's eye as well, causing the girl to let out a laugh. "But please do not mention it. He has not informed me of it himself, and I am certain he means it as a surprise."

"Then how do you know?" asked Elizabeth, curious.

"When you have been married to a man as long as I have been married to your father, you learn to understand how his mind works. You also learn to recognize when he *thinks* he is being sly."

The three ladies laughed together and continued to converse in this playful manner until they arrived back at the earl's residence. While Elizabeth still could not be easy with the thought of being showered with jewels and adorned as if she was on display, she decided it would be best to simply ignore it for the time being. She had no doubt that her mother knew her father well enough to understand his character and actions. But this gift of jewelry might never happen, so there was little reason to concern herself over it.

They arrived back at the house and entered, still speaking in animated tones. The few items that had been obtained that day—most of their purchases would be delivered at a later date—were taken to Elizabeth's room, so she would not have to move them later. They then went to the sitting-room, where they found the earl in company with a man who bore a striking resemblance to him, though of Anthony and William there was no sign. As soon as they entered, the man stood and approached the ladies, a determined air about him which bespoke confidence.

"So this is the young lady who claims to be my sister," said the man. He was tall, towering high above Elizabeth and Georgiana who, while they were not dainty, did not possess the height of the Fitzwilliam men.

"James!" scolded the countess, but he only held up a hand, looking pointedly at Elizabeth.

It seemed to be up to Elizabeth to make a response to him. "Rather, it seems like we are *all* convinced of the truth of my identity. Do you mean to dispute it?" Elizabeth arched an eyebrow at him, and she thought she saw a hint of amusement pass over his countenance, though it was gone in a moment.

"You seem to have a measure of impertinence for a young lady who has, after all, been raised as a country squire's daughter."

"And you seem to have an overinflated opinion of your own worth," replied Elizabeth. "But then again, I might have expected such from the pampered son of the nobility."

"Now that sounded suspiciously like an indictment on our class in general," said the earl as he stepped toward them.

"Not at all," replied Elizabeth, while directing a withering glare at the man she knew to be her eldest brother. "It is only a condemnation of the overly proud ones."

By this time, the viscount was grinning openly, no longer able to hide it behind his stern visage. "If I did not trust my parents to know their own daughter, I would still have been convinced by the resemblance you show to my mother." He reached forward and grasped Elizabeth's hands. "You are a sight for sore eyes, my dear sister. You have been very much missed. I hope we may become a complete family again with your return."

"I suppose that is possible," said Elizabeth with an exaggerated flippancy. "*If* you can overcome this pride, which seems to be such an integral part of your character."

The viscount guffawed. "I assure you that I have no improper pride. This is but a taste of what you will face from society. Though we will all support you, it is essential that you are able to answer the naysayers without hesitation."

"That is a discussion for another time," said the earl. "For now, we are simply happy to have Elizabeth back."

"And in that vein, I would appreciate a formal introduction to my sister."

The introductions were completed, and they sat down to visit. Elizabeth quickly discovered her eldest brother was much like her other brother in character, though he was not quite so jovial, nor did the sense of danger hover about him, though Elizabeth supposed her opinion might change should she ever witness his anger. She also learned that his wife and two children were following him and would arrive within the next two days. There was only a short time before Elizabeth was to return to Gracechurch Street, but before she left, Elizabeth came to understand that she would be able to love her eldest brother as easily as she did Anthony.

CHAPTER XIV

Thursday, March 12, 1812
Darcy House, London

With the introduction to James, Elizabeth was now known to all her immediate family, and she could not be happier. The next few days were again spent with them, and though Elizabeth often thought she was neglecting the Gardiners, they who had been the means of her salvation, they were quick to assure her they felt no such slight.

"Of course, you are often in company with your family, Elizabeth," said Uncle Gardiner when she mentioned it to him. "It is only right and expected."

"The only outcome for which we wish is for you to be happy," added Aunt Gardiner. "And, if possible, to be able to keep our connection. We would not wish to be sundered from you forever, Lizzy."

"I believe I may safely say that you will always be my uncle and aunt in my heart," replied Elizabeth. "I will not hear of anything else."

As expected, her parents were obliging when she mentioned this wish to them, her father even stating that he did not wish to give up

Mr. Gardiner's acquaintance now that he had made it. Elizabeth was content in this knowledge and happily spent her last few days living in her aunt's house.

The matter of her other relations was one which still gave Elizabeth some trouble. Jane's society she wished to retain, and she still felt the closeness to Mr. Bennet. Mary was a good girl, and though they were not much alike, Elizabeth still wished to have her for a sister, and though Kitty and Lydia were trying, she still loved them as sisters too.

Mrs. Bennet was the difficult one. Elizabeth's erstwhile mother had behaved badly after Wickham's actions, it was true, but while their relationship had been rocky at times, Elizabeth still had many fond memories of the woman. Though she was yet uncertain, Elizabeth felt unwilling to lose Mrs. Bennet's association, though it would be some time before she felt equal to meeting her again.

"You know that we are happy to indulge you in whatever you choose," said her mother, one day when they had been discussing Elizabeth's feelings. "The unfortunate fact is that your stories of Mrs. Bennet and the youngest Bennets—and perhaps even Miss Mary— dictate that you likely should not bring them to town. Their behavior will not allow it unless there is some drastic improvement. But should you wish to keep the connection, there is nothing your father or I will say to dissuade you."

"Thank you, Mother," replied Elizabeth. "I believe for the immediate future, distance would be preferable. But once I have settled into my new life, I might wish to make overtures to my previous family."

Lady Susan reaffirmed that she was happy to support Elizabeth in whatever she decided, and they allowed the matter to drop. Elizabeth was certain her mother struggled with how her daughter had called another woman mother for many years—gratitude that the Bennets had taken her in and protected her fought with the thought that *anyone* else might be considered a mother figure. Elizabeth decided it was best to simply push the matter to the side. There was no reason to dwell on it. She *was* careful, however, to avoid referring to Mrs. Bennet as her mother.

On a day when Lady Susan was occupied with some matters of the house, Elizabeth declared her intention to visit Georgiana, including her desire to walk there, as it was only two streets away. Her mother, by now accustomed to Elizabeth's ways and knowing of her proclivity for walking, only waved her away.

"Make sure you take a footman to accompany you," was her

response, followed by a softly spoken: "And make sure you are not too long. I want to speak to you regarding the dinner we are planning in your honor."

"Of course, Mother," replied Elizabeth. "I will return within the hour."

The sun was shining that morning, though the early March air ensured it was still cool. Elizabeth swung her arms as she walked, grateful to be alive and for the wonderful new turn her life had taken. As she had indicated to her mother, it only took her a few minutes to arrive at William's house, where she dismissed the footman and was taken to see Georgiana.

The girl was happy to see her. She called for tea, and they enjoyed their refreshments, eventually moving the music room to take turns playing the pianoforte. They had not been in this attitude long before they were interrupted by a visitor, one whom neither wished to see.

"Good morning, Miss Darcy," cooed Miss Bingley when she entered the room.

Then she caught sight of Elizabeth. "Miss Eliza!" said she. "My, you are a determined one, are you not?"

"It seems to me, Miss Bingley, that determination is a trait which is much in evidence of late."

It was clear from the narrowing of the woman's gaze that she understood Elizabeth's meaning. She must have decided, however, that Elizabeth was not worth her attention—at least until her claws would inevitably be unsheathed later—and she turned back to Georgiana.

"That was a lovely song you were playing, Georgiana, and I am well acquainted with it. Shall we not play together?"

Not waiting for an answer, Miss Bingley grasped Georgiana's arm and directed her back to the pianoforte, where she insisted the girl sit, then taking her place at Georgiana's side. Elizabeth watched all this with amusement mixed with exasperation, and she wondered if she should have William summoned. Given what she knew of Miss Bingley's actions in Hertfordshire, she did not think that he would be pleased with her audacity. In the end, Elizabeth settled with stepping out the door to have a quick word with the housekeeper. She was informed that Mr. Darcy was from home that morning but was expected to return shortly. Leaving instructions that he should be directed toward the music room when he arrived, Elizabeth returned, intending to rescue her cousin.

"You should take care for who you allow into your house,

Georgiana darling," said Miss Bingley, her gimlet eyes fixed on Elizabeth the moment she closed the door behind her. "Do you not know, Miss Eliza, that it is impolite to wander the halls of another's house when one is a guest?"

Elizabeth smiled at the woman's barb, even while Georgiana stopped playing and regarded her with asperity. "Elizabeth is not a guest, Miss Bingley," said Georgiana with some heat. She opened her mouth to speak again when Elizabeth shook her head, motioning for the girl to hold her tongue. Georgiana did subside, though not with much grace. Elizabeth, knowing that Miss Bingley was likely to gossip, had no wish for her new status to be bandied about town.

"You mean she has imposed herself upon you?" asked Miss Bingley, feigning shock, with a secret triumphant glare at Elizabeth. "Then you should call for your butler to evict her. I knew your brother would come to his senses and realize she is no fit companion."

"Elizabeth is welcome whenever she wishes to visit," said Georgiana, standing. Elizabeth was certain the girl was eager to separate herself from Miss Bingley. "She is . . . She has become one of my closest friends, and I am happy to have her here with me."

Georgiana then turned on her heel and strode to the sofa, sitting beside Elizabeth and directing a glare at Miss Bingley. Elizabeth watched the other woman's countenance, which quickly made its way from astonishment, to disbelief, to annoyance, and finally fury. She did her best to hide it, however, as she stood and approached the sofa.

"I understand, dear Georgiana," said she, seating herself on a nearby chair and reaching forward to put a hand on the girl's arm. Georgiana, however, flinched back, and Miss Bingley drew back. Her glance at Elizabeth, however, might have been sufficiently hot to melt steel. "It is difficult being a young girl without a woman on whom you may rely." Georgiana gasped, but Miss Bingley did not take any notice. "Anyone of more experience in the world can seem like one to emulate. But I must warn you that not everyone is as they appear."

"Indeed, they are not," said Elizabeth, while at the same time, Georgiana exclaimed: "My aunt, the Countess of Matlock, would not appreciate your suggestion I do not have someone to mentor me!"

"Of course, I do not cast any aspersions on your aunt, for I am certain she is all that is lovely. But you do not have anyone close to you in age to advise you." Miss Bingley smiled, an expression predatory and ruthless. "I would be happy to assist you wherever I can. I, like you, have been educated in the finest seminaries. I also have several years of experience in society. I would be happy to assist you in those matters which may be confusing to a young girl not yet out."

"Miss Bingley," said Elizabeth, "I hardly think you are in a position to mentor Georgiana. As she said, she has the guidance of her aunt, who is a countess. I cannot imagine what you could do for her that a countess could not."

"It would be best if you would remain silent in the face of your betters, Miss Eliza," hissed Miss Bingley.

"I assure you, Miss Bingley," said Elizabeth, "that I will be happy to do so, as soon as they arrive."

Miss Bingley sucked in an offended breath. "You are nothing but the strumpet daughter of a country squire!"

"And *you* are nothing but a social-climbing daughter of a tradesman," retorted Elizabeth. "Even worse, you are one who conspires to get what she wants at any cost, even to the point of throwing yourself on an unwilling man in an attempt to compromise him. Is *that* what you would teach Georgiana?"

Eyes as wide as saucers, Miss Bingley stared at Elizabeth, her mouth working with no sound emerging. Elizabeth wished she would stay that way forever.

Unfortunately, a woman such as Miss Bingley would not be denied. "I know not of what you speak."

"Do you not?"

"And what do you mean to obtain from Mr. Darcy, Miss Eliza?" Miss Bingley castigated Elizabeth with a sneer the likes of which Elizabeth had never seen. "I must speak with Mr. Darcy, I see. It seems he is allowing his sister to associate with ladies of questionable morals."

"Say nothing more!" exclaimed Georgiana. "You will regret it if you do!"

"Oh, Georgiana, did you not know?" The look with which Miss Bingley regarded Georgiana suggested surprise, but in reality, it was calculating and cruel. "This sort of behavior among gentlemen of a certain level of society is not unknown. I am only surprised that your brother would allow her into his house to contaminate you. But that is something we may repair if we only speak to him about it."

The depravity of which Miss Bingley was accusing her instantly fanned the flames of Elizabeth's anger to a white-hot rage. But before she was able to respond, a deep voice spoke from the entrance of the room.

*　*　*

Thursday, March 12, 1812
Darcy House, London

"That is enough, Miss Bingley!"

A gentleman did not raise his voice to a lady, but Miss Bingley had pushed him beyond all endurance. She was a succubus, preying on men with her siren call, spreading her evil and lies with the precision of a demon from hell. Darcy had no wish to ever see her again.

"Oh, Mr. Darcy—" attempted Miss Bingley, but Darcy spoke right over her.

"No, Miss Bingley, I do not wish to hear it. Come with me now; it is time for you to leave."

The woman fairly gawked at him, and Darcy was near to releasing his frustration. How could she possibly think that she was still welcome in his house?

"Now, Miss Bingley."

The woman rose, though with deliberate hesitancy, and Darcy turned and motioned for her to proceed him from the room. She shot one foul look at Elizabeth, as if *she* was to blame, before she glided toward him, looking for all the world like a queen being escorted by a courtier. She moved past him and out the door, and Darcy turned to follow. On the other side of the open door stood one of Darcy's most trusted footmen, a large and intimidating man by the name of Thompson, who fell into step behind as Darcy had instructed before he entered the room. Miss Bingley took the man's presence in with a superior huff and then ignored him.

"Mr. Darcy, I simply must speak with you. Have you no care as to the credit of your sister?"

"I have every care for her wellbeing, Miss Bingley. That is why I am ensuring that you are not in her company. I do not consider you to be a good influence on her."

"Surely you do not mean that!" cried the woman. She stopped in the middle of the hallway and put a hand to her heart as if cut to the quick. Darcy only regarded her with contempt.

"How can you expect anything else?" demanded he. "After your behavior at Netherfield, it is astounding that you possess the impudence to come here again and impose yourself upon my sister. I will not allow it. You will leave my house immediately, and you should know that the moment you have passed through the door, I will instruct my staff to deny you entrance. If you have any concern for your reputation, you will not return."

"It was all a misunderstanding, Mr. Darcy!" exclaimed Miss Bingley. "As I tried to inform you—"

"And as I informed *you*, I am not taken in by your pathetic attempts to explain your behavior away! Damnation, woman, do you think me witless?"

Miss Bingley paled at the way he swore at her, and in her shock, she said: "Where are your manners, sir? Do you often swear in the presence of a lady?"

"No, I do not," said Darcy, his voice low and menacing. "I do not consider you to be a lady! Furthermore, if you continue to approach me and mine, I will be forced to cut you in public."

Miss Bingley gasped, though Darcy could not understand why he should be surprised.

"Miss Bingley," said he again, his frustration boiling over in his voice, "I require you to leave. I have given you the option of walking from my home as if your visit has ended and you are continuing to your next call. I doubt your reputation would survive if I asked Thompson to carry you from my house and deposit you on the street."

"You would not dare!"

"Thompson!" snapped Darcy. The footman loomed behind him. "Escort Miss Bingley from the house. If she will not leave, you are given permission to evict her by whatever means necessary."

"This way, Miss Bingley," said Thompson, stepping in front of Darcy and motioning toward the door. "I will only ask once."

Miss Bingley inspected Darcy for several moments, searching for evidence of his implacable will. It appeared she did not like what she saw, for she blanched, turned on her heel, and marched away toward the door, her head held high. Darcy watched her go, hoping that this was the last time he ever saw the woman. Unfortunately, she was a leech. He doubted he could be rid of her that easily.

When the door closed behind Miss Bingley, Darcy gathered the housekeeper and butler to him, giving them instructions concerning Miss Bingley, and informing them to disseminate his words to the rest of the staff.

"What of Mrs. Hurst and Mr. Bingley?" asked Gates, his butler. "Should they be admitted if they visit?"

Darcy grimaced—he had no desire to think of Bingley. But he knew he needed to come to some decision, at least in the interim.

"If Bingley is accompanied by Miss Bingley, he is to be informed that his sister is denied entrance. If he comes alone or agrees to enter without his sister, then he may be admitted, provided I am home. In those cases, you may lead him directly to me. If Mrs. Hurst should come, the same conditions apply—under no circumstances is Miss Bingley to be allowed to enter. Mrs. Hurst may come to me, and I will hear her plea if she wishes to maintain her friendship with Georgiana. But no unsupervised visits—if I am not at home, inform her that the family is away and deny her entrance."

"Very good, sir," said Gates, his words echoed by Mrs. Mayson, the housekeeper.

The instructions having been given to the servants, Darcy returned to the music room to speak with Elizabeth and Georgiana. Given what he had overheard, he knew the confrontation had not been pleasant, and he wished to ensure that Elizabeth was not unduly upset by Miss Bingley's venom. Furthermore, he knew his aunt and uncle would take a very dim view toward *anyone* distressing their newly returned daughter, and Darcy was scarcely less tolerant of it himself.

When he arrived in the music room, he noted that Georgiana and Elizabeth were sitting on the sofa, earnest words passing between them, which Darcy expected concerned the shrew who had just been evicted from his home. They stopped when he entered and approached, and Georgiana immediately addressed him.

"The audacity of that woman! Has she no shame, Brother?"

"I believe there is little Miss Bingley might attempt which would surprise me, Georgiana. I have given the staff instructions that she is not to be allowed into the house, so you should not be required to endure her presence again."

Darcy then turned to Elizabeth. "Were you injured by her words, Elizabeth?"

While he might have expected that she would at least be angry, it seemed like Elizabeth was made of sterner stuff than that, for she only laughed. "Who could be made upset by such ridiculous suggestions, William? She is clearly blinded by jealousy and almost desperate to have you. I simply cannot understand why."

A sigh escaped Darcy's lips, and he leaned back against the chair in which he sat. The idle thought that he should have expected this reaction from Elizabeth—and the fact that he admired her all that much more because of it—hovered at the edge of his consciousness until he forced it away.

"She is desperate to marry a man of wealth and power, for the lust for such things consumes her. Unfortunately for her, though Bingley has managed to gain a certain level of acceptance, Miss Bingley has not. The ladies with whom she associates are known to be the worst gossips and shrews of society and none of the gentlemen will do anything more than dance with her. And I have it on good authority that even that well has begun to run dry, for a close friend informed me that she danced little at the last ball she attended and spent most of it on the sidelines."

"William usually dances with her when they attend the same events," added Georgiana. "But every time he does, she acts as if he has proposed to her."

Elizabeth raised an eyebrow. "I knew the woman possessed an inflated opinion of herself, but that is ridiculous. I am curious, however, why you would even pay her that much of a compliment."

"Because Bingley has been a close friend," replied Darcy with a grimace. "I felt it my duty to him to pay the appropriate attention to his sister. Toward the end of last year's season, however, a friend overheard her speaking with one of her cronies regarding her expectation that I would soon propose to her, and he informed me of the matter. For the rest of the season, I avoided attending the same events. I will not give her false hope, but I did not wish to offend Bingley. This season, as you know, I have broken all contact with her, and have not seen Bingley since I left Netherfield.

"I suppose I will be forced to call on Bingley concerning this incident. His acceptance in town is largely the result of my friendship—he must know that his sister threatens our friendship with her antics."

"Perhaps that would be best," replied Elizabeth. "Mr. Bingley's behavior informed me that he is, in essentials, a good man, though I still am not easy with his treatment of Jane. Regardless, it is past time I return home, for Mother will be wondering what has delayed me."

"I shall accompany you, Elizabeth," said Darcy. He turned to Georgiana. "I will be home in time for dinner."

"Shall I not go too?" asked Georgiana. Darcy was amused to hear a hint of a whine in her voice.

"No, dearest. I know you wish to be in Elizabeth's company, but once she is installed in Uncle's house, I doubt you will spend much time *apart* from her." Darcy directed a sly smile at her. "In fact, I believe if you apply to Aunt Susan, she will be happy to allow you to stay there when Elizabeth arrives permanently."

"Oh, that would be wonderful!" exclaimed Georgiana. She turned and caught Elizabeth up in an embrace before she retreated from the room, saying: "I shall write to my aunt directly!"

And then she was gone, leaving Darcy and Elizabeth watching her with fond amusement.

Thursday, March 12, 1812
Fitzwilliam House, London

It was no surprise to witness her mother's displeasure with a certain Miss Caroline Bingley when Elizabeth returned to her future home. William had escorted her, and they had spoken of banal subjects while walking, but his introspection suggested he knew how Lady Susan's would react and was thinking of what his own response should be. Either way, the countess's displeasure was a sight for Elizabeth to see, as she had never seen her mother in such a state before.

"You have informed me of this woman's character before, William," said she when the incident had been communicated to her, "but I had not thought her to be this senseless. To insinuate such a thing is beyond any audacity I have ever before heard. Is she quite mad?"

"Rather, I believe that she is desperate," replied William. "I am her only hope for a marriage with a member of the first circles, and it seems she has chosen to cling to that hope despite all common sense."

"She *is* senseless if she believes you will ever relent," snapped Lady Susan.

William spread his hands wide, but he did not respond. Lady Susan more than made up for his silence.

"You should speak with this Mr. Bingley and insist he exert control over his sister. She will be the ruin of him."

"I had already made that determination," replied William. "I will visit him tomorrow morning."

"Good. You had also best make the consequences of her persistence clear." Her mother's eyes burned with a cold flame. "If she does anything to affect Elizabeth's introduction to society or impede her acceptance in any way, I will ruin her forever. She should be grateful for whatever acceptance she has managed to grasp, marry some squire, and make him miserable for the rest of his life. She will not be accepted in society when I am finished with her if she pushes this doomed fantasy."

"I will do so, Lady Susan," replied William. Elizabeth watched William as he spoke, noting that he had fallen into formality because of the confrontation.

Lady Susan eyed him for a moment before her visage softened. "William, I am aware of the character of this Mr. Bingley, and I would never ask you to give up a friendship that brings you pleasure. My concern is that this man appears to allow his sister to rule him. My advice would be for him to return her to the north from whence she came, for her own actions make her nigh unmarriageable.

"Much depends on the first impression Elizabeth makes in our society—you know this. If this Miss Bingley gossips about her or defames her in any way, it will make it more difficult for Elizabeth. I will not have it!" Lady Susan's final words were spoken in a slow, determined cadence which left little room for interpretation.

A nod was William's response, followed by a softly spoken: "I have long been aware of Bingley's defects of character, but in essence, he is a good man. I would not wish to give up his friendship. But if his sister forces it, I will. I will make it abundantly clear what is expected of him.

"Now, if you will excuse me, I will be on my way."

Elizabeth and her mother stood and watched William walk from the room, and for a few long moments, Lady Susan's gaze was fixed on the door. Elizabeth simply waited, for she knew that her mother's equilibrium had been disturbed. When, at length, she turned back to Elizabeth, it was with a measure of seriousness, rather than the pleasure or love with which she was usually regarded.

"In a certain sense, James was correct. There *will* be times you will be tested by word and deed, by those who consider themselves high and mighty, or even young ladies who consider you a rival." Lady Susan grasped Elizabeth's arm and directed her back toward the sitting-room. "But most will have the sense to avoid overt insinuation of the type this Miss Bingley appears to favor. That will not make them any easier to deal with, but it will shield you from open defamation."

Her mother stopped walking and turned to Elizabeth, and something in her countenance made Elizabeth listen to her closely. "You should not be subjected to the kind of vile innuendo which Miss Bingley used. I have every confidence in your abilities, Elizabeth, but I expect that you will put anyone who attempts such tactics in their place. Your father, your brothers and cousins, and I will be there to assist, but you will not be respected unless you prove you can fend for yourself."

"I am confident I can do so, Mother," replied Elizabeth. "There may be naysayers, but they will not intimidate me. My courage always rises."

"Excellent," replied Lady Susan. "Now, let us speak of this dinner I have in mind. It will be the perfect opportunity to introduce you to the family."

Elizabeth allowed herself to be led into the sitting-room where she spoke with her mother for the rest of the time she was to be at the house that day. Her confidence she did not think was misplaced. She could handle one of much more acrimony and cleverness than Miss Bingley could boast, as anyone who challenged her would discover.

Chapter XV

Friday, March 13, 1812
Bingley Townhouse, London

*T*here was little interpretation to be attempted concerning his aunt's words. Darcy knew this, as he knew Lady Susan was implacable, especially where it concerned her family and their position in society. When one considered the newness of Elizabeth's return, coupled with the length of her absence and the heartache which had persisted for nearly two decades, Darcy was certain her viciousness would exceed that of a mother bear protecting her cubs.

The problem was that Caroline Bingley's viciousness was equal to what his aunt might display, and it was more commonly unleashed. She was a nasty woman, mean-spirited, haughty, unfeeling, and avaricious. In short, she was everything Darcy detested. If it were not for Bingley, he would simply cut her and allow her to reap what she had sown. But he did not wish to affect Bingley unless the woman's behavior demanded it. Thus, he was determined to make one last attempt to induce Bingley to see what her behavior might cost him.

Unlike the previous day's sunshine and warmth, the day he visited the Hursts' townhouse was gray and blustery, much like his own stormy mood. As he descended from his carriage outside the townhouse, Darcy huddled within his greatcoat as a defense against the chill, wishing for the warmer temperatures of summer and the ability to retreat to Pemberley. He truly was not at home in London.

He rapped sharply twice on the door knocker, and when the butler opened it, Darcy passed the man his card and requested to see Bingley. He might not have bothered, for Jeffers—the Hursts' butler—knew him well. But he wished this to be a formal visit and had no desire to endure the presence of Miss Bingley again.

The study in the house was rarely used, but it was where Hurst and Bingley entertained any gentlemen who called on them. It was a smallish room, a desk situated in the center, its top devoid of the assortment of papers, quills, ink, files, and other items which might usually adorn a gentleman's desk—the only item on its surface was an oil lamp, looking lonely and out of place on a far corner. Neither Bingley nor Hurst were diligent masters of their domains, Bingley because he was more at ease being amiable and pursuing the latest pretty face, and Hurst because his father still managed the family affairs.

When Darcy was led into the room, it was empty, as he had expected it to be, and he waited for a few moments, standing and looking out the window. The wind outside continued unabated, bowing the trees, though bare of their summer finery, and carrying bits of old, dead leaves careening down the street. In the back of his mind, he went over the arguments he was about to make to his friend, hoping that it would prompt Bingley to develop enough of a backbone to stand up to his sister.

"Darcy!" exclaimed the well-known voice of his friend, after Darcy had been waiting for some minutes. "I cannot tell you how good it is to see you. It has been far too long."

Darcy turned and looked at his friend, noting the puppyish enthusiasm with which Bingley was regarding him. There was nothing in his countenance which suggested embarrassment nor any hint of memory of the circumstances in which they had last parted. Darcy let out an inward sigh—to Bingley, nothing unpleasant had occurred and they were the closest of friends yet again. It was so very . . . juvenile and so much like Bingley.

"Please, sit down and I shall pour you a port. I am eager to hear of how you have been keeping yourself of late."

"Thank you, Bingley, but I believe I will abstain. I apologize, but I am not making a social call today—in fact, this is more of an official visit, for I have matters to discuss with you which it would behoove you to take with the seriousness with which it is intended. Might we sit?"

A frown creased Bingley's face—it seemed he was nonplused. Darcy was not surprised, for he did not think Miss Bingley would have informed him of her presence at Darcy's house the previous day or their brief meeting at the academy. She would not wish to bring Jane Bennet to his mind again, nor would she wish to confess to being thrown from Darcy's house.

"Of course, of course," replied Bingley. He gestured vaguely to one of a pair of chairs situated in front of the fireplace and took his own with an almost unseemly haste. "I must own that I have rarely seen you this grave, my friend, and that is saying something. What did you wish to discuss?"

"I wish to discuss the behavior of your sister, Bingley," replied Darcy.

"Caroline?" asked Bingley, surprised yet again. "But you have not seen her in several months, ever since . . ."

Bingley trailed off and Darcy watched him for a moment, noting how his face bloomed with embarrassment. "If you are here to discuss *that*, I wonder at how long it has taken to induce you to come to the point."

It was Darcy's turn to frown. Bingley's tone was almost petulant as if he was a child who had been caught in some misbehavior and was now resentful of the punishment imposed. It reminded him too much of *Wickham*, though a much younger Wickham. "I did not come to speak to you of that, Bingley," said Darcy. "Since you have brought it up, however, and it does fit together with the subject of my visit, allow me to tell you without prevarication that I am through with your sister. She approached Georgiana about a week ago, and she even dared visit my house yesterday. I asked her to leave and informed her she would not be welcome back. I hope you are successful convincing her I mean what I say, for I do not wish to be forced to cut her."

Bingley nodded slowly. "I cannot say I am surprised." His eyes darted up to meet Darcy's before he looked away again, his posture screaming embarrassment. "I *am* sorry for that, Darcy. I did not know she attempted to visit you and would have advised her strenuously that she not attempt it, had I known. As for what happened at Netherfield . . . Well, let us just . . . Oh, hang it all! It was such a surprise that I did not know what to do. I know she was completely in the wrong, but she *is* my sister."

"That is too often the problem, Bingley," replied Darcy, keeping his tone soft and avoiding the appearance of accusing—or at least he hoped he did. "You often do not know what to do with her. She is, if you will pardon my words, of an ungovernable temperament. She requires a firm hand. You risk your position in society if you do not act to curb her excesses.

"But, as I said, I did not come here to unearth old grievances. It was the content of those two meetings with your sister which makes me uneasy, and I have come to warn you that your sister may be on the verge of making a catastrophic error in judgment."

"Oh?" asked Bingley. He appeared to be weary. "What has she done now?"

"You lived at Netherfield for a period of more than two months, did you not?"

Bingley appeared nonplused at Darcy's seeming non-sequitur. "I did. What does that have to do with Caroline?"

"Then are you familiar with the name 'Bennet?'"

A shadow seemed to pass over Bingley's countenance. He shook his head as if to clear his thoughts. "Yes, I am familiar with them. They are a fine family, though with five daughters, if you can imagine that. Caroline did not appreciate them much, except for the eldest. As you only spent a night at Netherfield, I am surprised that you know them."

"Both times Caroline met with my sister, Georgiana was in the company of Miss Elizabeth Bennet. And both times, your sister cast aspersions on Miss Bennet's character, including some heinous comments she made only yesterday."

"Miss Bennet was with your sister?" asked Bingley. "I am sorry, my friend, but you have me completely at a loss. I was not aware that your family was acquainted with the Bennets."

"We were not until recently," replied Darcy. "I am afraid I am not at liberty to be explicit with respect to our connection with Miss Bennet. I *will* say it will soon be known to all of society.

"My reason for cautioning you today is because my aunt, Lady Matlock, has an interest in Miss Bennet, and I was subjected to a pointed discussion concerning your sister's words spoken in the presence of Miss Bennet and my sister. Lady Matlock takes a dim view of your sister's insinuations, and will not tolerate them in the future."

"Were they truly that bad?" asked Bingley, though his fretful tone suggested he believed his sister capable of anything.

"They were," said Darcy. "Furthermore, they were also insulting to *me*, as well as being well beyond anything to which I would subject

Georgiana."

It was clear that Bingley was bewildered and unable to fathom what he could do with his sister. Unfortunately, Darcy was not here to advise him on that matter. Miss Bingley was her brother's responsibility.

"I am sorry to burden you with this, Bingley, but your sister's behavior has become so objectionable that I cannot ignore it any longer. I will not, from this time forth, know Miss Bingley. If she attempts to speak to me or mine, we will cut her." Bingley gasped, but Darcy continued to speak, knowing it would do no good to extend his friend any mercy. "My friendship with you may still be salvaged—I wish it to be saved, for I have no desire to end it.

"But end it I *will* if you do nothing to control her. Please, my friend—for the sake of our friendship, rein her in. Send her to the north if you must—her dream of marrying into the first circles is doomed to failure. Perhaps she might find something there which will sustain her and bring her happiness. It is completely your discretion of how to control her, but control her you must!"

Then Darcy rose and bowed to Bingley, which his friend hardly saw, and with a few words of farewell, he let himself from the room. His words seemed like empty platitudes, for he truly did not know whether Bingley possessed the fortitude to control Miss Bingley.

When he had left the house and returned to his carriage, he allowed himself to breathe a sigh of relief. Their friendship was in Bingley's hands now. Unfortunately, Darcy could not help but suppose that Bingley would continue to be ruled by his sister.

Friday, March 13, 1812
Bingley Townhouse, London

"Yes!" said Caroline, speaking in low tones with her sister. "She was sitting in Mr. Darcy's music room with his little mouse of a sister, bold as brass, as if she was not a grasping hussy. And Georgiana, of course, looked to her with the adoration of a vacuous mind."

Caroline growled a guttural sound which she had long been unaware she made and would have vociferously denied should anyone have brought it to her attention. "The little chit even stepped out of the room for a moment, as if she was the house's mistress! It is not to be borne, Louisa! I am certain she has her eye on his fortune and becoming his wife, though I cannot fathom by what means she has managed to inveigle her way into his home, nor how she even managed to make his acquaintance."

"The fact that she is welcome in his home suggests he knows of her origins, Caroline." In Louisa's tone floated a hint of desperation, a sound which annoyed Caroline every time she heard it.

"I am convinced to the contrary," snapped Caroline. Inside she lamented—before her marriage to the drunkard, Louisa had fallen in with whatever plans Caroline made. She had grown something of a backbone since then, to the point where Caroline had not even considered trusting Louisa with her plan to attempt to compromise Mr. Darcy.

Netherfield, thought Caroline, her ire rising yet again at the backwater estate and those lowborn louts who lived nearby. Netherfield had been the location where her plans had fallen apart. If only she had insisted that odious Mr. Snell be housed with the rest of the servants where he belonged! Since Netherfield, nothing had gone the way it should, though she supposed she should be grateful that her brother had been persuaded away from that penniless, fortune-hunting Bennet girl. Caroline would not tolerate such a simpleton—a nobody!—as her future sister. Charles would be guided to a proper woman, one with fortune and connections so that their entire family's standing could be raised as a result.

As for Caroline herself, she supposed she should turn her attention to some other man of society, for surely she could find one who would prove to be more understanding of the benefits of marrying her. But the very thought caused the bile to rise in her throat. She had pursued Mr. Darcy, had thrown herself at him, had arranged the means by where he might have had his way with her without the benefit of marriage. And still, Mr. Darcy resisted! The thought of giving up her dream of marrying Mr. Darcy and surrendering him to that chit Eliza Bennet caused her jaw to ache with the clenching of her teeth.

No one must be allowed to capture Mr. Darcy—certainly no woman as lacking fashion and possessing the impertinence of the Bennet girl. No, Caroline would not give in. She had attempted to compromise him once, and she was certain if she was given the opportunity once more, she would succeed.

Perhaps the ball his aunt always gives will present the opportunity, thought she. That ball *was* still some weeks distant, which was a problem. Caroline wanted to have the man bound to her long before then. Yes, a spring wedding would do wonders for her image, and her beauty as a bride would cause every eligible woman in London to weep at the sight.

But first there was Miss Eliza Bennet to deal with, and Caroline knew just what to do about that little insect. When Caroline Bingley was finished with her, no one in England would marry the little chit. And then Mr. Darcy would come crawling to her, begging for her to accept his hand. The thrill which flowed through Caroline at the thought was almost sensual in nature. Soon, she would have what she wanted.

The opening of the sitting-room door disturbed Caroline's musings, and she looked up to see her brother enter the room, followed by Mr. Hurst. They were wearing expressions which suggested seriousness, though on Hurst it almost appeared comical. He was usually foxed by the middle of the day, and any attempt to appear sober suggested severe constipation. The man was a worthless sod, and her brother was almost as bad—he should have supported her at Netherfield, insisted that Mr. Darcy marry her. She might be Mrs. Caroline Darcy by now if he had!

"Caroline," said Charles as he stalked into the room and sat on a nearby chair. "I have a matter which I must discuss with you."

"It will need to wait," said Caroline, rising to her feet. "I have some visits I must make immediately."

"Sit down, Caroline," said Hurst, surprising her with the authority laced in his tone. His usual drunkenness was not in evidence. He almost appeared to be a man, rather than a puddle of brandy.

"As I said—"

"And as *I* said," snarled Hurst, leaning toward her and putting his face inches from her own, "your brother has something to say that you will hear. *Sit down!*"

Annoyed, Caroline looked from Hurst back to Charles, noting the glare with which Charles regarded her. He was attempting to appear authoritative, which always made it seem like he was a boy of ten. Charles was not a problem—Caroline had been ruling him for years. But Hurst was another matter, particularly when his back was up. She had no doubt he would physically restrain her, should he feel it necessary.

"Very well," snapped Caroline, sitting with a huff and crossing your arms. "You must make it quick, for I intend to be gone as soon as the carriage is called."

Hurst's eyes found Charles's, a question inherent in them. Charles grimaced, but he nodded in response to some unspoken question. They were beginning to irritate her with their looks and attitudes.

"I am afraid the carriage will not be available for your use today,

Caroline."

An angry retort sprang to Caroline's lips, but Charles only held up his hand. It was the surprise of his gesture which brought about her obedience, rather than any intention.

"When you hear what I have to say, you will understand. Hurst and I have agreed that you will stay home today to work through your anger, rather than going out immediately and saying something you should not."

"I do not know when you have become such a despot," said Caroline. "Say what you must, so that I may be about my own activities."

Charles shook his head, but he soon spoke. "I have just received a visit from Darcy."

"You have?" asked Caroline, her eyes gleaming. Perhaps the man had come to his senses. "Well, what did he say?"

"I will ask you to curb your imperious nature," growled Bingley. "Considering you have brought this family to the brink of ruin, you have nothing you may demand of any of us."

"Brink of ruin? I have no idea of what you speak."

"Charles?" asked Louisa in that tiny voice she used when she was frightened.

"Darcy is not happy with us, and he threatened not only to cut Caroline the next time he sees her but also to sever his friendship with me."

"Impossible!" cried Caroline.

"Oh, I assure you, Sister *dearest*, that it is quite possible. I am surprised he has not already done it, to tell the truth—your antics at Netherfield give him the right and the motivation to do so, even if your behavior since our return had not."

"I do not—"

"Enough!" roared Charles. Caroline was speechless—he had *never* spoken to her in such a manner before. "You *will* be silent and listen to me, Caroline, or I will put you in my coach and send you to Scarborough. Once you are there, you will never be allowed into my home again. Am I quite clear?"

Caroline felt like she was encased in molasses. She had no control over her body and even her mouth was beyond her ability to direct.

When she did not respond, Charles leaned forward, spearing her with a relentless glare. *"Do I make myself quite clear?"*

A little of Caroline's will returned, and she thought to unleash a torrent of recriminations at her brother, but given the mood he was in, she thought it best to simply allow him to have his say. Then she may be about the business of ruining Miss Eliza Bennet. Thus, she nodded once, with a poise of which she was proud. It would not do to allow Charles to think he possessed the upper hand.

"Now, apparently you have met with Miss Darcy twice in the past several weeks, including a visit to Darcy's house yesterday. Is that correct?" Caroline allowed that it was. "And both times she was in the presence of Miss Elizabeth Bennet." Caroline saw red, but she managed to control herself, again nodding, though tightly.

"How is she even acquainted with the Darcys?" asked Louisa, her tone suggesting bewilderment.

"I do not know, for Darcy would not tell me," was Charles's short reply. "But he *did* tell me that her connection with his family would soon be known. His purpose in visiting, however, was because Caroline apparently made certain disparaging remarks about Miss Bennet which Darcy did not appreciate. *Furthermore*, his aunt, Lady Matlock, also has an interest in this matter and will respond to any disparagement directed at Miss Bennet."

"Oh, Charles," exclaimed Caroline, "that is patently absurd. What could Eliza Bennet possibly have to do with the Fitzwilliams, of all people?"

"Perhaps you should take that subject up with Darcy," replied Charles, his tone positively scornful. "Of course, you cannot, for Darcy does not even wish to see you, let alone speak with you."

Caroline glared at him, promising later retribution, but her brother returned it with equal harshness.

"Darcy's decrees are not in any way ambiguous. Caroline, you are not to go to his house again. You will not speak to Darcy, and you will not approach his sister. And for heaven's sake, restrain your vitriol with respect to Miss Bennet!"

"I have no interest in that little adventuress," replied Caroline. "You need not concern yourself. Now, if you will excuse me, I will be about my business."

"As long as that business does not include leaving this house," rumbled Hurst.

"I am not a child that you may order about!"

"Right now, I consider you to be little more than a child." Caroline stared at Hurst, but he only returned it, not giving an inch. "You will stay at home today, Caroline, and as the knocker has been removed from the door, you will not have any visitors. Calm the anger that we all know is raging in your veins, and when you have calmed yourself, you may go out. But remember to keep your composure and act with restraint. I enjoy Darcy's company and his friendship. Do not do anything to jeopardize it."

"You enjoy naught but his wine cellar," sneered Caroline.

"Be that as it may, I do not wish to lose his association. Learn to behave, or you will find yourself banished from London forever."

Seeing there was no choice and no way for her to leave, Caroline stood and walked from the room, her head held high. Being confined to the house for a single day might not be such an impediment, anyway. It would give her a chance to ensure her composure was ironclad and decide what to do about Miss Elizabeth Bennet.

Saturday, March 14, 1812
Fitzwilliam House, London

Viscountess Lady Constance Fitzwilliam nee Spencer was a bright and sunny woman of perhaps five years Elizabeth's senior. She was tall, blonde, and fair of face and feature, and she was obviously delighted to make Elizabeth's acquaintance. Indeed, she reminded Elizabeth of a cross between Jane's kindness and Lydia's exuberance, though she was not nearly so reticent as Jane nor so ungovernable as Lydia.

"I have heard something of you before, you know," said Lady Constance when they sat down to speak after her arrival. "My husband, you see, has not really spoken much of you, but on certain occasions, I have managed to induce him to be open." She reached out and squeezed Elizabeth's hand. "Your return is much desired and long despaired.

"But you are now here, and I am so happy! We shall have so much fun together!"

"I am very much looking forward to it, Lady Constance," replied Elizabeth.

"None of that, now!" exclaimed she. "We are to be sisters, and I would not wish to call you 'Lady Elizabeth' all the time. It would become tiresome. We shall be on a first name basis."

There did not seem to be any stopping her, and Elizabeth did not even try, content as she was to be an intimate of this energetic young woman. But as much as Elizabeth found her new sister-in-law's exuberance to be welcome, she also found that Constance was also something of a tease, even more than Elizabeth was herself. In that way, she was much like Anthony.

Constance was also the daughter of a duke, and as such, she had a haughty streak in her manners which surpassed anything Elizabeth had ever seen. While she accepted the Gardiners for the simple fact that they had protected Elizabeth, she still reacted with distaste when she heard that Elizabeth was still staying at Gracechurch Street. Thus, on the final day she was to stay at her uncle and aunt's house, Elizabeth was surprised when Constance arrived to see her, in Lady Susan and Georgiana's company.

"I am pleased to meet you, Mrs. Gardiner," said Constance when the introductions were made. Even Elizabeth, who had been watching for it, could detect no hint of the distaste she had shown only the day before.

It helped that Aunt Gardiner's manners could be mistaken for that of a gentlewoman. She greeted the visitors with composure, deferential, but not so much that it might be considered servile. The ladies visited over tea, and soon the conversation flowed freely and with no hesitation or awkwardness.

"Are you ready for tomorrow, Elizabeth?" asked her mother when they had been sitting for some time.

"I am," replied Elizabeth. "I do not have much here which needs to be moved."

"That will change when you move into Fitzwilliam house," said Constance with a wink. "Or so I have heard. I am only disappointed that I was not present to assist you in choosing."

"Oh, Constance!" exclaimed Georgiana. "You only wish you had been here to shop yourself!"

Lady Susan and Georgiana laughed, and Constance joined them without hesitation. "Why, of course, Georgiana! You know I will never miss an opportunity!" Then Constance turned to Elizabeth. "It *will* be good to have you in the house, Elizabeth. Though my mother-in-law is all that is good, I am anticipating having another my own age with whom to talk."

"And I shall be there too!" exclaimed Georgiana. "Aunt Susan has agreed to allow me to stay for some days."

"Of course, we are happy to have you, dearest," said Lady Susan. "I believe your presence will help make Elizabeth's transition to our house easier."

When they had visited for some time, the ladies departed, Elizabeth's mother promising to return with the carriage on Monday morning, following the Sabbath, to convey Elizabeth to her new home. Though she was still feeling more than a little bemused by the suddenness at which this had all happened, Elizabeth was able to return her mother's assurances with pleasure. She *was* anticipating it, very much, indeed.

It was in this fashion that Elizabeth spent her last day in her uncle's home. The house on Gracechurch Street was not nearly as intimately known as Longbourn, nor had she spent as much time here, but in some ways, it was dearer to her. Due to recent events, it had become her haven, her protection against what must surely be a cruel world. Elizabeth spent her last day saying her farewells to all she had known, visiting with the children, and sitting with her aunt and uncle, thanking them profusely for the assistance they had been.

"We were happy to help, Elizabeth," replied her uncle. "You have always been welcome in our house. I hope you will understand that you will be welcome in the future whenever you choose to visit."

"Do not be cast down, and do not look back, Elizabeth," advised Aunt Gardiner. "You have been loved here and it was a blessing to have you with us. But you are embarking on a grand adventure. You must look toward the future, for I have no doubt you will cause a splash in town, unlike anything that has ever been seen before."

Elizabeth could not help but laugh. "I am sure I shall! Everyone will want a glimpse of the newly returned daughter of an earl and wonder where she has been these past two decades."

"The novelty will fade soon enough. But I believe you will be one of the most sought after young ladies this season." Mrs. Gardiner paused, and then she winked at Elizabeth. "Of course, if what I have seen is any indication, you already have an admirer."

Frowning, Elizabeth looked at her aunt askance. But Mrs. Gardiner, though she read the question on Elizabeth's countenance, declined to answer.

"Oh, no, Elizabeth — if you have not seen it, I would not wish to take the joy of discovery from you. I am certain you will discern it soon enough."

And thus, the countess arrived the following morning as promised, and once Elizabeth's personal effects were loaded on top of the carriage, she made her tearful farewells to the Gardiners and boarded the coach alongside her mother. She attempted to remind herself it was, indeed, an adventure, but she could not help but feel a sense of loss.

CHAPTER XVI

*P*art of Elizabeth's disquiet was relieved by the welcome she received by those who were waiting for her at her father's house. Not only were her brothers, her sister-in-law, her father, and niece and nephew present, but the Darcys were also there, and everyone present regarded her with smiles which seemed likely to split their faces in two. For the first time, Elizabeth was brought to an understanding of what her disappearance had done to these people and what her return meant to them.

There was one other in attendance who was beyond happy to see Elizabeth. Standing with Constance's children was a woman of whom she had heard, Nurse Perry, who had had the care of Elizabeth when she was naught but a child. She was a tall, severe woman, one who would command respect from her young charges. But on this occasion, tears were streaming down her face with unabashed happiness.

"I never dreamed this day would come," said the nurse to Elizabeth, enfolding her in an embrace. It may only have been a trick of the emotion of the moment, but Elizabeth thought she recognized the feel of the woman's arms around her. "I blamed myself for many days after your disappearance."

"But you did nothing wrong!" exclaimed Elizabeth.

"As I have told her many times," added Lady Susan.

"You have, your ladyship," said Nurse Perry. "But the heart is more difficult to convince than the head. I thought had I only remained with you that day as you slept, you would never have been lost."

"Did you often go into the next room while I napped?" asked Elizabeth.

Nurse Perry smiled, knowing exactly what Elizabeth was trying to say. "I did so quite often. You were a light sleeper and would often wake when I moved about the room. But I rarely leave your brother's children alone for any reason. I would not wish to lose one of them in similar circumstances."

"Then there is no blame to be apportioned. I beg you would think of it no longer."

It was clear from the way Nurse Perry's shoulders straightened that the burden had been lifted from her. The smile she bestowed on Elizabeth was tremulous with suppressed emotion.

"I would like to come to know you better," said Elizabeth. "Perhaps we could take tea together."

"I would like that very much, Lady Elizabeth."

With those words, the nurse ushered the children from the room and returned them to the nursery. Elizabeth's effects were taken to her room, and she went there for a short time to ensure her things were organized to her satisfaction. A quick look in her closet revealed that a selection of her dresses had already been delivered, as had been promised by Madam Fournier. Elizabeth smiled—it seemed a certain social stature was useful in ensuring good service. Though still uncomfortable with the level of deference she knew she could expect in the future, in this instance she decided she was happy to be the recipient of it.

When Elizabeth had refreshed herself, she returned to the sitting-room where she found the rest of her family gathered. When she entered the room, she thought she had interrupted a discussion between the occupants, and when he saw her confusion, her father spoke.

"Come, Elizabeth, sit among us." He rose and led her to the sofa, ensuring she was seated next to her mother in what appeared to be a position of honor. "As I promised, I dispatched a letter to your Aunt Catherine this morning, informing her of your recovery."

"And this was the reason for such interest for all my family?"

"Aunt Catherine is . . ." began William, only to be interrupted by Anthony's snort.

"Aunt Catherine is a meddling, self-centered, ambitious woman, who is insistent on ordering the world to her desires."

"Anthony!" barked the earl. "You should not speak of your aunt in such a fashion!"

"Have I misrepresented her in any way?" Anthony's manner was all insolence, a fact which had not missed the notice of any of the family in the slightest, given the smirks which were directed at him.

"It is not that you have misrepresented her," said James. "It is merely the fact that Lady Catherine demands respect."

"You should respect *all* of your elders," added Lord Matlock. Though his countenance suggested severity, he winked at Elizabeth outrageously, showing that he was enjoying the banter as much as his sons were. "Even if some *are* objectionable."

"I am afraid that in this instance I have already been jaded against this unknown aunt," said Elizabeth. "Anthony, William, and Georgiana have all had some choice words to say about Lady Catherine. Had Georgiana not echoed Anthony and William's words, I might have thought they were exaggerating."

"Unfortunately, I suspect they did not embellish the matter much," replied Lord Matlock with a sigh. "My sister is . . . difficult at the best of times, and I do not believe this will be the best of times. Catherine will almost certainly have her say, regardless of how much I attempt to silence her."

"The question is, will she be induced to be reasonable?" said Anthony. "Previous experience suggests she will subside and accept, but only after she realizes further protestation will be fruitless."

"I believe you do Catherine a disservice," said Lady Susan. "She will inspect Elizabeth to ensure there is nothing the matter with her, but in the end, I believe she will capitulate without much trouble."

It was not difficult to see the skepticism in most of her family's faces, though Georgiana was notable in the same look of trepidation Elizabeth had previously seen when this Lady Catherine had been mentioned. William and Anthony shared a look, and they both shook their heads, Anthony going so far as to mouth something at William, which produced a grimace from her cousin. At the same time, however, they both noticed Lady Susan looking at them through narrowed eyes. They directed such expressions of innocence at her that Elizabeth was forced to bring a hand to her face to cover a laugh.

"Come now," said Lady Susan, "let us leave this subject for the present. Catherine should receive the letter today. You did send it express, did you not?"

This last was directed at her husband, who nodded, though not without a twist of his mouth in response. Lady Susan continued: "Then the earliest Catherine will arrive will be tomorrow, though I suspect she may delay another day in deference to Anne's health. Either way, what will be, will be. In the meantime, we should begin to plan the family dinner, for that is the greater issue at present."

"Yes, let us!" exclaimed Constance. "Most of the family is amiable, Elizabeth, and I believe you will like them very well." Constance turned to Georgiana. "You should join us too, my dear. It would do you good to have some experience in planning a dinner, as you will come out before long."

"I believe this is our cue to depart," said the earl, rising to his feet. "We will leave you ladies to it, while we discuss other aspects of Elizabeth's return."

Elizabeth eyed her father as he departed with the other gentleman. Though he had not been explicit, she was certain he was referring to the still unknown reason for her disappearance. Elizabeth did not think she was in any danger, but she knew her family would fret.

Besides, she knew the days of her freedom as a country miss were now over, for the daughter of an earl must be protected, lest an unscrupulous person take advantage of her for gain. Elizabeth was not yet easy with the notion, but she understood its necessity.

Tuesday, March 17, 1812
Fitzwilliam House, London

The adjustment Elizabeth was forced to make when removing to her father's house was, at times, difficult. But Elizabeth knew that had she moved directly from Longbourn it would have been an even greater shock. The Gardiners' home was, at least, a calm and quiet place, though any house with children living within could not be quiet at *all* times. Calm and quiet were terms which could not be used to describe Longbourn—not with Lydia and Kitty Bennet in residence.

But the differences between the house on Gracechurch Street and her father's home *were* striking. For one, an earl's house was much larger than anything to which Elizabeth had been accustomed before. Longbourn was a humble estate, and while there were enough rooms for each daughter to have her own, that left only the guest bedroom—

which was rather small—and the nursery, which was typically not in use unless the Gardiners were visiting. Similarly, the house on Gracechurch Street, though comfortable for a man of business with four children, could not be compared to a house in Mayfair. The residence of the Earl of Matlock in London was three stories, boasted a family wing—in which *all* the residents present were able to comfortably stay—a guest wing, many common rooms for the family's comfort, and a large ballroom Elizabeth knew would be in use within the next few weeks.

Elizabeth quickly discovered that navigating the house was a skill which must be learned with experience. There was an occasion or two that first day where she opened a door, only to find it was not the room she had been expecting. She quickly learned to rely on the servants, who seemed eager to help.

The other large change in Elizabeth's mind was the assignment of a young woman to be her personal maid. A maid assigned to care for her alone was a luxury her adoptive father had not been able to afford—he had several servants, but only one was a maid to be shared among six women, though one of the upstairs maids often assisted in that capacity. While she felt uncomfortable, Elizabeth did not make any mention of it, for she knew it was one of those things with which she would need to become accustomed.

There were other items which were different from what she had known all her life, but they were often that which passed fleetingly and accepted without effort. Of more immediate concern was the close proximity of the new members of her family and the fact that she now lived with them, whereas in the past she had been a visitor in their home. This changed circumstance made the situation real in her mind like she had merely been pretending before.

The night of Elizabeth's arrival, William stayed with them for dinner until he was required to return to his own house for the night. He came again the next morning, and Elizabeth was grateful for the constancy of his presence. That afternoon, the gentlemen were to attend the court-martial and trial of the former Lieutenant Wickham. By the following day, the man would be on a ship bound for the penal colony in Van Diemen's Land. Elizabeth had not thought of Mr. Wickham much since he had been incarcerated, but she was glad he would be gone and no longer a threat to society.

Much of that first day was spent with the ladies of the company planning for the introductory meal to be held a few days hence. Since Elizabeth did not know any of the people they discussed, she did not attempt to insert her opinion, but she did take the opportunity to listen and learn as much about the new relations she was gaining as possible. She was certain her attention now would serve her in good stead when it came time for her to make their acquaintances.

"These are all close family members, are they not?" asked Elizabeth of Constance during a brief period when her mother left the room to speak with the housekeeper.

"Yes, most of them are," replied Constance. "I am not as well acquainted with your mother's relations, though I am not unknown to them. Your father's family are much closer, and I know them quite well."

"Your father and mother will also be in attendance?"

"They will." Constance seemed to sense the measure of apprehension Elizabeth was feeling, for she reached out a hand and patted Elizabeth's knee. "Do not concern yourself, Elizabeth. Our fathers are close friends, and he and my mother will accept you on your parents' recommendation alone."

"I am grateful to hear it," replied Elizabeth, still feeling a little overwhelmed at the thought of meeting a duke and duchess. "Are there any others of lofty station of whom I should be aware?"

Constance laughed at Elizabeth's attempt to lighten the atmosphere. "No, I believe my father is the most illustrious personage you are likely to meet at dinner."

"Are there any other cousins of whom I should be aware?"

"James could inform you more of that." Constance shrugged. "I do not know of any. There are, like in any family, some who are not completely well thought of, and I know there are a few with whom your parents do not wish to associate.

"Do not concern yourself, Elizabeth," continued Constance. "You will win them all over within moments of being introduced."

Elizabeth nodded, and they turned back to the plans, the menu, and certain other assorted items which went into planning for an event of this sort. Elizabeth continued to give her input whenever she was asked, but she still tended toward silence. If a dinner was this complex, she shuddered to think of what effort must go into the preparation of a ball, such as the one which was to be held in her honor. She was not anticipating planning for *that* function in the slightest!

The disturbance in the hall began as a low, understated noise akin to the rumbling of thunder in the distance—Elizabeth could hear it, but at first, she did not take any heed. As Elizabeth continued to speak with Constance and Georgiana, however, the noise became more pronounced and began to intrude upon her notice. It was the sound of a voice—or perhaps voices, though one rose above the rest—which caught her attention. Elizabeth looked up, wondering what would be able to penetrate the thick door which blocked the room in which they sat from the rest of the house. It soon became evident that her companions heard it too, though their responses were different. Constance looked up and attempted to shake her head and put the matter from her mind, but Georgiana's countenance suddenly turned white, as if the girl had taken ill.

"What is it, Georgiana?" asked Elizabeth, distracted away from the noise in the hall.

But before Georgiana could answer, the commotion in the hall suddenly grew much louder, and one voice rose above the rest, saying: "Where is she? I shall not wait. Take me to her at once!"

Awe at the power of the loud female voice caused Elizabeth's eyes to dart back to the door, and as such, she was witness to the exact moment when it swung open and a woman stood framed within. She was large in scale, tall, but slender under all her finery. As she stepped into the room, Elizabeth's senses were assaulted by the sight of costly materials in muted colors, but the woman's eyes caught her attention and held them. They were dark, almost black, complemented by the woman's dark hair which, though she was obviously of age with Elizabeth's father, was tainted with only a hint of grey about her temples. The moment she walked into the room, the woman's eyes were fixed on her, and Elizabeth could not help but imagine that she was being weighed by some imaginary scale. No doubt she was found wanting by those judgmental eyes.

As one, the three younger ladies rose to their feet at the sight of the fearsome monster, and Elizabeth could almost feel Georgiana's quaking as she stood beside her. With an absence of thought, Elizabeth reached to her cousin and grasped her hand. Georgiana returned the gesture, squeezing painfully, her fear evident through the tightness of her grip. For a moment silence reigned in the room.

"Constance, Georgiana," said the woman as she advanced into the room. Elizabeth noted that while she had spoken to the other two ladies, her eyes never left Elizabeth herself. Behind her, through the open door, another woman entered and sat in a chair, small and drowning in her own silks, which were a match for the first woman's. Though Elizabeth could not see her well due to the dominating and large presence, she thought the second woman appeared frail, her countenance almost gray.

"I assume you must be this *Elizabeth Fitzwilliam*, whom I have been informed has recently returned after so many years." The woman looked at her, an imperious question in her gaze, and when Elizabeth did not immediately respond, she barked: "Will you not answer me, child? I asked you a simple question!"

"I believe, Aunt," said Constance, "that Elizabeth is waiting for an introduction, as is proper."

In reality, Elizabeth was still only astonished by this woman's forceful nature and had not mustered the words to respond. But she was grateful to Constance for her intervention nevertheless.

"Then introduce her, girl!" snapped Lady Catherine—for this was who Elizabeth knew the woman must be.

"I believe *I* shall claim the privilege of introducing her, Catherine."

As one the company looked to the door to see Lady Susan standing there, regarding Lady Catherine as if she was an enemy combatant on a field of battle. Lady Susan entered the room, but she stopped by the younger woman, leaning down to say a few words to her and take her hand. The younger woman responded with a few words of her own and a wan smile, before dropping her hand and allowing Lady Susan to continue into the room.

"Catherine," said Lady Susan. "I am surprised by your presence. We had thought you might delay an extra day before coming to London."

"Considering the news I received from my brother, I thought it prudent to come directly." Lady Catherine huffed in annoyance. "Now, shall you provide the introductions so that I may be known to this young lady?"

"Of course," replied Lady Susan. She turned to Elizabeth and stretched out her hand, which Elizabeth readily took, allowing herself to be drawn to her mother's side. It was clear her mother wished to protect her from whatever response this imperious lady might wish to make, and given the lady's tight lips and narrowed eyes, she had not missed it either.

"Catherine, it is my distinct pleasure to introduce you to Lady Elizabeth Anne Fitzwilliam, my newly recovered daughter. Elizabeth, this is your father's sister, Lady Catherine de Bourgh of Rosings Park in Kent. In addition," said Lady Susan, turning to the younger lady who had stood and approached them while they were speaking, "this is Miss Anne de Bourgh, Lady Catherine's daughter and my niece. Anne, my daughter, Elizabeth."

Elizabeth curtseyed deeply to her newly introduced relations, an action which Miss de Bourgh returned, though Lady Catherine did not. The lady's eyes never left her, and that sensation of being judged only intensified.

"Shall we sit, Catherine?" asked Lady Susan. "I could send for some tea. Or perhaps you and Anne would prefer to be shown to your rooms to refresh yourself?"

Though appearing reluctant to discontinue her study of Elizabeth, Lady Catherine turned and looked at her daughter. An understanding seemed to pass between them.

"Perhaps that would be for the best in Anne's case," said Lady Catherine at length. "For myself, I am eager to learn of my new niece, if she will oblige me."

It was a request, which surprised Elizabeth—she thought the lady would simply have demanded her attention and compliance. Lady Susan readily agreed, and seeing that Georgiana was still watching Lady Catherine with a gaze akin to a mouse watching a snake, she drafted the girl to assist Anne to her room. Georgiana accepted with alacrity, almost wilting with relief at the ability to escape her overbearing aunt. Lady Susan then called for tea and the four remaining women took their seats. It soon became clear to Elizabeth that Lady Catherine was not the sort of woman to allow uncomfortable silences to develop. She was more apt to fill any silence with the sound of her own voice.

"I will own that I am curious, Susan," said Lady Catherine the moment she was seated in her chair. "For you and Hugh to have claimed the girl in such a manner, you must have been convinced by her story. Might I inquire as to the proof which has led you to this conclusion?"

"Of course, Catherine," replied Lady Susan. "I would be happy to oblige. The first clue is, of course, the resemblance between us. I assume you can see it?"

Lady Catherine snorted. "Oh, the resemblance is there. But that is not evidence enough by itself. What else have you discovered?"

"The scar on the back of her head, as well as the dress she was wearing the day she disappeared. You might remember—it was the yellow frock with the embroidered red flowers."

Eyes wide, Lady Catherine said: "That dress survives?"

"It does, though I do not have it at present. The woman with whom Elizabeth was staying when we discovered her dresses her youngest in it. When the girl outgrows the dress, she has promised to return it."

"I see," replied Lady Catherine. For a moment her gaze was

introspective, but then she turned her attention back to Elizabeth. "There will be time for an accounting later, but I would inquire as to how this all came about and where you have been these eighteen years. How can it be possible that you are recovered after all this time? I never thought we should see you again."

There was a quality in Lady Catherine's voice which approached pleading, though it was not without the imperious quality Elizabeth already connected with the lady's manners. Lady Susan seemed to hear it too, as she smiled at Lady Catherine for the first time since her coming.

"It has only happened by the strangest of chance, Catherine. But we will be happy to share the story with you if you would hear it."

And so the tale was told, and Lady Catherine listened intently, interrupting here and there to ask a question or to clarify some point. But the communication was made more expeditiously than Elizabeth would have thought possible.

When they had related the pertinent part of the past several weeks to Lady Catherine's satisfaction, the lady sat back, her expression thoughtful. "Though it seems like another implausible coincidence, I am not unfamiliar with the name Bennet."

"Oh?" asked Elizabeth, speaking for the first time since her mother began to relate her story. "Have you been to Meryton?"

"No, but there is a living in Kent which is in my power to grant, and in it, I have installed a man by the name of William Collins. I assume that name is not unknown to you?"

"I believe a Mr. Collins is a cousin of my adoptive father, and is also his heir," said Elizabeth, her brow creased in thought. "There was a disagreement between the elder Mr. Collins and Mr. Bennet, the genesis of which I am not familiar. But they did not speak for many years, and I am certain the present Mr. Collins has never met Mr. Bennet."

"Yes, that is much the same story he gave me," said Lady Catherine, "and I can assure you that he was eager to give it." The lady paused and she shook her head, as if in disgust. "My parson is not the most . . . intelligent specimen, but he is obedient and determined to do the best he can. But he is also stubborn. I attempted to convince him to reach out to Mr. Bennet and bridge the impasse between them, for there is nothing worse than discord between family members. But he refused my instruction, convinced that *his* father had been wronged by Mr. Bennet, and as such, it was Mr. Bennet's responsibility to apologize first." Lady Catherine huffed. "It is the only matter on which the man has ever dared contradict me."

"Mr. Bennet has, at times, spoken of the elder Mr. Collins as an odious, obstinate man," replied Elizabeth. "But your portrayal of his son suggests a measure of sycophancy which is surprising."

"It is not surprising if you consider Mr. Collins's history," replied Lady Catherine. "I suspect that his father ruled him with an iron fist, for he looks to others to direct him. It is one of the reasons why I offered him the living — I doubt he would be able to obtain another otherwise."

Lady Catherine paused in thought, but her eyes darted to Elizabeth's a few times before she sighed. "You may wish to write to Mr. Bennet and inform him that if he has not planned for his family's support after his demise, he had best do so immediately. Though I have tried to counsel Mr. Collins, he has a curious propensity to promote a strict interpretation of Christian behavior, while rationalizing that it does not apply to himself. I doubt there will be much charity in his heart when he eventually inherits."

"Thank you, Lady Catherine," replied Elizabeth, her own thoughts going to her former family, and how she doubted Mr. Bennet would be induced to act, regardless of what she informed him.

"Mr. Collins has recently married a young lady of the parish," continued Lady Catherine. "She is a sensible girl, and I hope to have success teaching her the proper way to act. But if I know Mr. Collins, I do not think he will listen to a mere wife. His mixture of pomposity and servility is truly a sight to be seen, but they each extend in different directions. Servility he shows to me, but pomposity to all those he deems below his exalted position as a parson."

There was nothing to say to that, so Elizabeth did not respond. It seemed to her that Lady Catherine had softened her stance toward Elizabeth, a fact her mother seemed to see as well, for Elizabeth thought her more relaxed than she had been before. Constance, by contrast, was watching them all, a grin affixed to her face. She caught Elizabeth watching her and winked, before fixing her eyes on Lady Catherine and rolling them. Elizabeth stifled a chuckle of her own. So far she could not state that her cousins' words concerning Lady Catherine were in any way incorrect. But at the same time, Lady Catherine had not acted as Elizabeth might have thought she would.

At length, the lady paused, and she made a show of inspecting every inch of Elizabeth's person. Elizabeth bore it with patience, for if this lady's scrutiny must be borne to ensure her good opinion, then Elizabeth was willing.

"You seem to be a pretty sort of girl," said Lady Catherine, more speaking to herself than the others in the room. "You are obviously intelligent, you speak well and articulate your opinions clearly. Though I detect a hint of impertinence in your manner, it is nothing which cannot be repaired by the proper instruction."

Lady Catherine turned to Elizabeth's mother. "This Mr. Bennet— you did not say as much, but considering you did not speak of it, might I assume he was not responsible for Elizabeth's disappearance?"

"Anthony and William questioned him, and they believe he is not," replied Lady Susan. "There is still much I do not think we will ever know, but that is not important now."

"Then I suppose we must simply be grateful for your return," said Lady Catherine. Her voice was infused with a confidence and surety of purpose. "You *will*, of course, be required to grow into your new role as the daughter of an earl, but I believe you will learn what you must know with a little effort on your part."

"Of course," replied Elizabeth. "I have already determined to look to my family to become accustomed to my new situation."

"Very well," said Lady Catherine, standing and turning her attention to Lady Susan. "I believe I will go to my own room to refresh before I join you again."

"I shall call the housekeeper," said Lady Susan.

But Lady Catherine only waved her off. "I am quite familiar with the house, Susan, and may find my own way. Can I assume you have placed both Anne and I in our usual rooms?"

"I did," replied Lady Susan.

"Then I shall go to them and return later."

With those final words, Lady Catherine inclined her head and let herself from the room, leaving three bemused ladies behind.

"Was that truly Lady Catherine?" asked Constance. Her manner suggested a knowing sort of amusement.

"It was," replied Lady Susan.

"She is not nearly so fearsome as Anthony and William would have me believe." Elizabeth paused for a moment, thinking on what she had just witnessed, before correcting herself. "Or perhaps she *is* fearsome, and did not show it in this instance."

"You have the right of it, Elizabeth," said her mother. "I knew she would be accepting when the particulars were explained to her. Catherine is excessively jealous of the family's position in society, and by extension, proud of her own position in it. Once she had confirmed your suitability and could find no obvious flaws in our reasoning, her acceptance was a fait accompli."

"It appears you were correct," replied Constance, her face still split by a smirk. "I expect the coming days will be interesting. Lady Catherine de Bourgh will bring any naysayers in line and allow no dissent. She will be Elizabeth's most enthusiastic advocate."

"I know," replied Lady Susan. Her manner was positively overflowing with self-satisfaction.

CHAPTER XVII

Tuesday, March 17, 1812
Fitzwilliam House, London

The reason for her mother's smug demeanor was soon to become evident to Elizabeth, though she already had a notion of what it was about. The earl and his sons, in William's company, had been away from the house that afternoon at Mr. Wickham's trial, and their trepidation upon learning that Lady Catherine had arrived, was more than a little amusing.

"I am surprised that we did not hear her voice all the way across town," groused the earl. "I should have thought her complaints would have echoed all throughout London."

"You do your sister a disservice, Hugh," replied Lady Susan. "In fact, Catherine was accommodating toward our daughter and has expressed a wish to become better acquainted with her."

The skepticism in his look was easy to see, and it almost set the ladies to laughter. William and Anthony looked on, their own expressions suggesting they could not quite believe what Lady Susan was telling them, and even James was looking at Constance askance. Constance only shook her head and gave her husband a mysterious smile, one which he did not appear to understand. The earl essayed to ignore the situation for a moment, and he made a quiet communication to Elizabeth and the other ladies. As had been expected, Mr. Wickham had been found guilty and been sentenced to twenty years of hard labor in Van Diemen's Land. He would not be returning.

When Lady Catherine joined them in the company of her daughter, all four men eyed her with suspicion, though they kept their own counsel. She greeted them all with what Elizabeth was coming to expect was her usual imperious manner, but then she settled down next to Elizabeth—displacing William with a short command, and proceeded to monopolize the general conversation and Elizabeth's in particular. It was much the same when they were called to dinner, for Lady Catherine caught Elizabeth's arm and directed her toward the dining room.

"You may accompany me, Elizabeth, for there is still much for us to discuss." Lady Catherine waved her hand in a perfunctory manner at William. "Darcy, you will escort Anne."

There seemed to be a measure of some emotion that passed through the rest of the family, though Elizabeth could not quite understand it. For her part, Lady Catherine either did not notice or ignored it altogether. William did not respond; instead, he turned to Miss de Bourgh and offered her his arm, which she accepted, though without visible emotion.

They sat at the dinner table as the first course was served, and when Lady Catherine turned and spoke to her, Elizabeth noted that she did so in the same tone in which she usually spoke—in other words, loud and authoritative, and not caring if she was interrupting others' conversations in the process.

"I understand there is to be a dinner to introduce you to the family. Given the circumstances in which you were raised, I can imagine you are nervous at the prospect."

Elizabeth's eyes darted to the other members of the family, particularly her mother and father and Anthony, who seemed the most protective of her. She was a little surprised when none of them essayed to respond to Lady Catherine's words. Her mother only nodded her encouragement, and Elizabeth turned back to Lady Catherine.

"I will own to a little anxiety at the prospect of meeting so many people I do not know. But I am convinced that they will be won over and accept me for who I am."

"Your convictions do you credit," replied Lady Catherine. "All of society will be watching you for the rest of the season, and from what I have seen, I believe you will do well. The opinion of the family is the most important. No one else will dare question your position once the family approves, though I do not doubt there will be some who will resent you."

"Resentment I can withstand," replied Elizabeth. "The opinions of those with whom I am in no way connected do not concern me."

"Perhaps," replied Lady Catherine in a noncommittal tone. "But you must never allow anyone to see weakness. You are inviting unkindness and censure if you do."

Elizabeth smiled at the woman with amusement. "Did you not just inform me that no one will dare question my position?"

A snort sounded from further down the table, and though he looked at Elizabeth with innocence written on his brow, Elizabeth was certain it was Anthony. Lady Catherine seemed to agree with Elizabeth if her glare was any indication. In the end, she only sniffed and turned her attention back to Elizabeth.

"No one will question you openly. But that does not mean you will not face resentment, envy, contempt for your upbringing, and a desire to see you humbled as many will think you should be." Lady Catherine's gaze softened. "But you have the fortitude to withstand such things—I can sense this.

"Now come, I would know more of this family with whom you were raised, so we may plan the appropriate steps to ensure you are trained to do the family credit."

Again, Elizabeth thought someone might speak up—her mother, if no one else. But Lady Susan seemed to sense that there was nothing to be done except allow Lady Catherine to have her say, so she only rolled her eyes and turned her attention to Georgiana who was sitting nearby.

What followed was an interrogation akin to what the questioners of the Spanish Inquisition might have conducted. Lady Catherine inquired into every aspect of her life, no matter how minute or inconsequential. She was shocked and appalled to learn that Elizabeth had never had a governess, and then dismayed to discover that Mr. Bennet had not even been a gentleman when Elizabeth had come to live with him. However, she was pleased with Elizabeth's words concerning her education which she had directed herself, including her admission of her abilities on the pianoforte, abjuring her to practice, for she would be expected to entertain when in company.

She was not pleased to hear of Mrs. Bennet and the younger daughters—though Elizabeth attempted to blunt her explanation of their character defects—but she was happy to hear of her friendship with Jane and Elizabeth's special bond with Mr. Bennet. The society of Meryton was glossed over with very little explanation from Elizabeth, and Lady Catherine declared it did not signify.

"I am familiar with small societies such as the one you describe, so there is no need to be explicit. London and the season is quite different from what you will have known in Hertfordshire, but I am certain my sister has begun to instruct you on what you might expect."

"I have," confirmed Lady Susan without delay. "The differences are superficial. I have every confidence in Elizabeth's abilities."

"Very well, then," replied Lady Catherine, and on they went. By the time dinner ended, Elizabeth was feeling drained from the constant probing questions. The woman was indefatigable!

After dinner, Elizabeth was allowed a little respite, for Lady Catherine walked with Elizabeth back to the music room and then went to sit beside Elizabeth's mother. For a time, they sat with their heads together talking earnestly. Elizabeth was certain they were planning out the rest of her new life in minute detail. While it would have irritated her under other circumstances, she decided that her mother would not allow any of Lady Catherine's more outlandish ideas, and she turned her attention to other matters.

When she looked about, Elizabeth discovered that she was situated nearby her cousin, and as she was the only one to whom she was not yet known, she essayed to make some conversation with Miss Anne de Bourgh.

"Do you come to London often, Miss de Bourgh?"

"Please, just call me Anne," said the other woman. Her manner suggested fatigue and she fairly drooped where she sat on the sofa next to Elizabeth. "We are cousins; I do not think we need to cling to formality."

"Of course," replied Elizabeth.

"As for your question, I rarely come to town." Anne smiled, though wanly. "This is an unusual circumstance, indeed. But I am thankful for it. Rosings is my home and I love it prodigiously, but it *is* tiresome to be there at all times."

At Elizabeth's uncomprehending gaze, Anne colored a little and looked down. The blush on her skin was like the sight of a blood red rose laying upon a blanket of newly fallen snow.

"You must have understood the fact that I am not healthy, Cousin."

"I have," said Elizabeth, though carefully, not wishing to offend Anne. "But I would not have thought ill health would have prevented your presence in town or kept you from enjoying your life as much as you are able."

"You may be correct," replied Anne. "But what you have not considered is my mother. She is not only forceful and demanding, but she is also quite protective of me. Anything that she deems a possible detriment to my health must be avoided at all costs."

"Thus, you are kept at Rosings."

Anne shrugged. "I have nothing against Rosings; it is a beautiful estate. I will own that there are times when I wish for more freedom — to be allowed to do as other young ladies do. But I am not unhappy."

Carefully, still wary of causing offense, Elizabeth essayed to ask: "What about society and creating friendships, acquaintances, and connections? What of marriage?"

With a shaken head, Anne said: "I do not think of marriage, for I do not wish to be married, though my mother's opinion is different. As for friendships and the like, I am friendly with my cousins and some other ladies of the district in which we live. I am content with that."

"Then I am happy to give you another familiar face," replied Elizabeth. "I hope we shall be good friends."

"I am certain we shall."

Their hesitant conversation continued for some time after, and Elizabeth learned that while Anne's body was not possessed of much strength, there was nothing affecting her mind. Anne was, in fact, quite observant, and she was also intelligent, though Elizabeth found her knowledge of certain subjects to be lacking. Of course, with Lady Catherine de Bourgh as a mother, there would be subjects which were approved for Anne to study, while others — those Lady Catherine deemed irrelevant or improper — would be forbidden. If Elizabeth was honest with herself, she found Lady Catherine's methods to be approaching draconian, though Anne did not seem to mind them herself. It was how she had been raised, so she knew no other way. Elizabeth would have found the restrictions chafing, indeed.

After Lady Catherine had sat with Elizabeth's mother for some time, discussing what she assumed was Elizabeth's introduction to society, she returned to the general conversation of the room. It was not long after that, however, that she began speaking of a subject which was, quite obviously, dear to her heart. It was equally obvious that it was *not* dear to the heart of anyone else in the room.

"It has come to my mind," said Lady Catherine, in her usual loud and authoritative voice, "that our coming to London at this time is most especially auspicious. We are all happy for Elizabeth's recovery," Lady Catherine nodded at Elizabeth, "but the time appears ripe to ensure the happiness of another kind."

Though Elizabeth was not certain of what her aunt was speaking, it appeared no one else in the room was similarly afflicted. There were several instances of rolled eyes, shaken heads, and Elizabeth thought some even suppressed groans.

"A spring wedding would be lovely," said Lady Catherine, continuing to pontificate while remaining oblivious to the reaction of the rest of the family. "And of course, Darcy, as you are already eight and twenty, it is high time you took a wife and went about the business of begetting an heir. And Anne is particularly suited to be your wife, for I have trained her to know everything she must to be an excellent mistress of both Pemberley and Rosings."

William made some noncommittal comment under his breath which Lady Catherine appeared to take as an agreement, for she continued to speak without ceasing for some time. And while several other members of the family attempted to have their own quiet conversations, the loudness of the lady's voice and force of her pronouncements rendered it difficult.

The principles themselves were listening to Lady Catherine's words, but Elizabeth could not see in them any eagerness to comply. On the contrary, William's mouth was a tight line and his glare at Lady Catherine suggested he would have muzzled her, had the opportunity presented itself. For her part, Anne shook her head slightly every so often, though her eyes were alight with more amusement than anger. The rest of the family was watching the spectacle with equal parts exasperation and resignation.

When she saw Elizabeth watching her, Anne leaned closer to Elizabeth and said: "Would you like to help me plan for the wedding?"

Elizabeth glanced at William, who had noted their proximity and directed a pointed look at Anne as if exhorting her to turn to her cousin for an explanation. For her part, Elizabeth could not quite understand what she felt at Anne's evident jest. Something in her rebelled at the very notion of William marrying Anne, though she was not quite certain why that should be so.

"Should I congratulate you?" asked Elizabeth, still uncertain. "William has not mentioned the fact that he was engaged."

"That is because he is not," replied Anne, her eyes still dancing with amusement.

"Then your mother . . ."

"Is determined, but I believe William and I are equally so."

"Why is she so determined?"

"She claims it came about because of an arrangement she made with her sister — William's mother." Anne's snort told Elizabeth what her cousin thought of that. "In fact, the family suspects that Lady Anne

Darcy *might* have discussed the matter with her, but as she was a reticent woman not in the habit of defying an older and more forceful sibling, we think she agreed to anything my mother said to avoid an argument.

"When my mother approached Darcy's father about formalizing the arrangement, his father categorically refused to do so and would not hear any of my mother's repeated attempts to solicit an agreement. As there was nothing she could do, my mother waited and planned. When Darcy's father passed away, she began to make the claim that her sister agreed to the betrothal. Everyone in the family knows differently, but no one wishes to provoke an argument by disagreeing with her."

Elizabeth digested this bit of information, thanking Anne for clarifying it for her, but still wondering about it. Clearly, Lady Catherine meant to be obeyed, while it was equally clear her daughter and nephew had no intention of being compelled. But the lady continued to wax poetic on the matter, and the rest of the family listened in silence. Elizabeth found she could endure the lack of the others' conversation cheerfully—it allowed her to think without interruption and nothing more than the droning of Lady Catherine's voice buzzing in the back of her mind.

Friday, March 20, 1812
Fitzwilliam House, London

It was curious, but the matter of William's supposed engagement to Anne was not canvassed after that night. Lady Catherine did not seem inclined to push it further, and the rest of the family was eager to allow it to rest. Elizabeth might have stayed in the dark concerning the matter, had Constance not endeavored to help her understand.

"It is ever thus when the family is gathered together. It seems Lady Catherine is determined that no one should forget about it, but after making her sentiments known, she concentrates on other matters."

"Does she not understand that Anne and William do not appear to be interested in bending to her will?"

"Perhaps she does," replied Constance with a grin. "It is what leads me to suspect that she does not expect to realize her dream. But she is not able to simply allow it to rest. She *is* a forceful woman, you understand, unaccustomed to being disobeyed. If she maintains her stance, it allows her to keep the fantasy that she will eventually have her own way."

"At least until William actually marries."

Constance's grin only widened. "That *does* appear to be a problem, does it not?"

The ladies laughed together and allowed the subject to drop. Elizabeth suspected Constance had the right of it.

A new event soon dominated the daily life of the family, for the dinner at which she would be introduced was quickly approaching. Elizabeth did not know what to think. On the one hand, she found herself wishing she could return to her life in obscurity, to remain naught but a country girl. At other times, however, she was curious about those she would meet and the events of society of which she had often heard but never experienced.

When the day arrived, Elizabeth rose like it was any other day, only to find that it was not. For one difference, her mother had definite ideas on how Elizabeth should prepare, in dress, hairstyle, and even the amount of jewelry she would wear.

"It is important to make the best impression, my dearest daughter," said her mother, caressing her cheek with affection when she noticed Elizabeth's displeasure. "It is all so very superficial, but much of what others think of you is based on what they can see, usually before any words are exchanged. If you appear looking like nothing but a country miss, they will treat you as one, regardless of what we tell them. If you emerge looking every inch an earl's daughter—looking like Lady Elizabeth Fitzwilliam—they will behave as if that is what you are."

"Is this really necessary, even with family?" demanded Elizabeth.

"I believe you will find it is," said Lady Susan, though her manner was apologetic. "Come, let us dress you for the evening. I am certain you will cut quite a swath through all our relations."

Lady Susan's prediction of her husband's intentions was proven correct. As they were preparing to depart for the family sitting-room, a knock was heard on Elizabeth's door, and when it was opened, it was revealed to be the earl. In his hand, he held a small box.

"Your mother has likely already divined my purpose, Elizabeth."

"I have," was her mother's amused response.

The earl grinned at her. "I have purchased a piece of jewelry I would like you to wear for the evening. He opened the box, and inside was revealed to be a delicate necklace, fashioned of gold, bearing a small locket. The earl took it in his hand and, almost reverently, depressed a catch, revealing a miniature portrait inside, showing a child with dark brown locks and a mischievous glint in her eye.

"Is that me?" asked Elizabeth hesitantly, reaching out and touching the portrait. The canvas was rough under her finger, the ridges of paint rising along the lines of her face and hair.

"It is," replied her father. "Your mother had a devil of a time holding you still enough to have it painted, and several times we thought the master would run screaming from the house." He chuckled. "The original is hanging at Snowlock. When you went missing, I had the artist create that miniature, which your mother and I have kept with us always. Your recovery suggested it was time to let go, so I had the locket created and the portrait enclosed within."

At a motion from her father, Elizabeth turned and allowed him to fasten it around her neck. When he spoke again, his voice was rough with emotion. "This symbolizes the child you were, and the woman you have become, and forever binds you, our daughter returned, to us."

"Thank you, Father," said Elizabeth, holding the tears in check.

"It looks lovely on you, my darling daughter," said Lady Susan. "I have no doubt you will wear it with distinction."

And so it was that Elizabeth made her way down to the main rooms of her family's house, feeling hundreds of nervous butterflies hovering in her midsection. William and Anthony had been deputized to stand beside her and shield her from the curious gazes of the family, for she would be introduced when everyone was present. It also gave Elizabeth the added benefit of hearing their commentary on each of the new arrivals as they entered the room.

"Do not be nervous," said Anthony when he had joined her in their appointed place. "You will be fine. Everyone who is present tonight is a relation of some sort. There should not be any objectionable characters."

Elizabeth thought it was easy for him to *say* that she should not be anxious, but at that moment William approached with a glass of wine in his hand, which he handed to her. "Sip this, Elizabeth," instructed he. "It will help calm your nerves."

Whether it did or not, Elizabeth was not entirely certain, but she dutifully tasted the wine every few moments, and if nothing else, it gave her something on which to focus her attention. The banter between her cousin and brother also assisted Elizabeth to maintain her composure, and though most of their observations informed her of who the attendees were, she would not remember most after even five minutes. But there were a few who stood out.

"That is father's cousin and his wife," said William after the first couple was led into the room. "Baron and Baroness Longfellow."

"And the pimply young man behind them is their son, Farnsworth," added Anthony.

Elizabeth raised her glass to her lips to stifle a laugh. In fact, Anthony was correct—the young man seemed to have a rash of pimples on each cheek, and his thin, stick-like body, long neck and head, covered by a shock of messy black hair, did not help his appearance. William shot a glare at Anthony, but her brother did not even seem like he noticed it.

"The dignified-looking couple are the Spencers, Duke and Duchess of Cheshire," added Anthony a few moments later.

"And behind them is their heir, the Marquess of Didsbury, and his wife."

"Constance's elder brother?" asked Elizabeth.

"Yes," replied Anthony. "They are good people and have been allies of the Fitzwilliams since time out of mind. Constance's marriage into the Fitzwilliam family is the latest of several over the centuries."

A great many more people followed. The list of those invited also included her mother's brother, her uncle having inherited his own earldom some years previously. There were also several more cousins, one uncle of William's, who, Elizabeth understood, was a prominent judge, as well as a few other assorted relations of a slightly more distant nature. In all, by the time they had all entered the room, there were slightly more than thirty people present.

As the room filled, Elizabeth noted that she soon became an object of curiosity, for she was the only one in the room not known to any of the others. Several members of the family came to greet Anthony and William, and while several asked to be introduced to her, Anthony obliged by doing so with only her Christian name and refusing to divulge anything further. This garnered them more than one peculiar look, but those attending that evening were, in general, too well-mannered to make an issue of it.

It continued in this manner until the last members of the dinner party arrived. When William named the family who had entered as her mother's younger sister and her husband, as well as their elder children, Elizabeth happened to be watching the woman who greeted her mother with a smile and an embrace. She turned a moment later and surveyed the room, and the moment her eyes settled on Elizabeth, they widened. The woman then abandoned her sister and made her way directly to Elizabeth and her two escorts, her gaze never leaving Elizabeth's face.

"Anthony," said the woman in a low tone, "I would ask you to

introduce this young lady to me if I did not already know who she is."
She stepped forward and grasped Elizabeth's hands, holding them
tightly as if she expected Elizabeth to disappear in a puff of smoke.
"You *are* Elizabeth Anne, are you not?"

Though surprised, Elizabeth retained the use of her faculties, but
she did not quite know what to say.

"Come, my dear, it is obvious that my sister has called us all
together tonight to announce your return. I had thought she was acting
strangely of late. Now tell me — are you her daughter?"

"I am," was all Elizabeth could say.

"Then I am so pleased to make your acquaintance," said the
woman, drawing Elizabeth into a fierce embrace. After a moment, she
released Elizabeth, though she kept hold of her hands. She looked
Elizabeth in the eye, and Elizabeth noted that her gaze had become
more than a little watery. "I am Althea Prescott, your mother's
youngest sister and your aunt. I am so very happy to see you, my
dear."

Her aunt Althea paused for a moment, her mind seeming far away.
"I remember well the time you were lost and the devastating effect it
had on my sister. I hope that with your return, the healing can begin."

"I hope so too," said Elizabeth, feeling so overwhelmed that it was
difficult to form a response.

"It seems you have let the cat out of the bag, Sister."

Elizabeth and her aunt turned as one to regard her mother, who
was watching them with fond affection. For the first time since Lady
Althea had approached her, Elizabeth noted how everyone in the room
was watching them, some with surprise and puzzlement, though the
nearer ones were whispering to each other from behind hands or
staring at her, comprehension beginning to dawn. From across the
room, her father was approaching, pride for her evident in his smile
and his nod.

Sensing the mood had changed and the moment of truth was at
hand, Elizabeth gathered the tatters of her composure in with her
courage and accepted the hands her father and mother extended to
her. And with her aunt on the other side of her mother, and William
and Anthony standing by her father, she turned and faced the
gathering.

"As many of you have guessed," began Lord Matlock, "there are
significant events afoot tonight, and this is no mere dinner party. Some
of you may know of the tragedy which befell us many years ago, and
some will remember that time as I do — as if it happened only

yesterday.

"It is my distinct pleasure to announce to you all, my closest friends and family, that the young lady on my arm is none other than my daughter, Elizabeth Anne Fitzwilliam, who has been returned to us after a long absence."

Friday, March 20, 1812
Fitzwilliam House, London

The rest of the evening passed as a blur for Elizabeth. She was introduced personally to everyone present, and she made some observations regarding the characters in the room. By and large, however, the exact events of that evening did not remain in her memory long after, and what she did remember was a long line of introductions.

Most of those in attendance, as she had observed on seeing them enter, appeared to be borne out in their manners when speaking with her. They were, she thought, a rather proud lot, perhaps unsurprising considering the least exalted among them were members of the gentry possessing old and prominent names. Those with whom she spoke were kind, asking after her and commenting on how she seemed overwhelmed, and only a few sought to ask questions which might be deemed impertinent or intrusive. And those that did were quickly redirected by her father, who escorted her and stayed by her side as she circled the room.

She was given a place of honor by her father's side at the dinner table, a position rightly belonging to the Duchess of Cheshire as the highest-ranking woman present. It was clear that the friendship between these people was long and enduring, for the duchess, when she saw her father's intent to escort her into the dining room, only laughed and encouraged them to go to it.

"I cannot think we should stick to stuffy rules on such a momentous occasion," said she, directing a bright smile at Elizabeth. "I do hope, my dear, that you will sit with me later, for I should like to become better acquainted with the daughter of my dear friends."

Elizabeth could only agree, and she felt like the duchess would be well worth knowing, for she was quite like her daughter in many respects, and with Constance, Elizabeth had already formed a close and enduring friendship.

After dinner, when they once again retired to the other rooms for coffee and cakes, Elizabeth was prevailed upon to display her talents on the pianoforte. While she could not call her efforts capital, she thought she acquitted herself well. She could not determine whether the enthusiastic applause of the assembled was due to her talent or the wonder of her sudden return, but she remembered William's approving expression in particular.

Two other incidents that evening were firmly etched upon her memory, and Elizabeth would remember them better than anything else that happened. The first she happened to overhear as she was speaking to another in the long list of relations, though she would not remember who.

"I will own to some surprise, Catherine," said a voice, "I had thought that if anyone would object to this sudden return of Susan's child it would be you."

While still appearing to attend to her conversation partner, Elizabeth turned her head slightly to the side and noted that the speaker was her Aunt Althea, and she was speaking to none other than Aunt Catherine.

"Why would you assume such a thing, Althea?" asked Lady Catherine.

"No reason," replied Lady Althea, though mirth shone in her eyes.

"You may put away your humor, Althea. I am well aware of what is often said of me, and it concerns me not a jot."

"The proof your brother has offered you is sufficient then?"

"That my brother and sister are certain is enough for me," replied Lady Catherine. "There is nothing more important than family, and as Hugh is convinced, so must I be. I offer my unreserved support."

Lady Catherine paused for a moment, seeming caught in the throes of some deep thought. "You have hit on the matter admirably, Althea, loath though I am to confess it. Proving her identity is difficult, indeed, and there will be some who will be unconvinced, regardless of whatever proof they are given. Then there are those who will use her naïveté in society to attempt to exploit her, especially once the details of her dowry become known to the public. As I recall, it was substantial; you know to what lengths impoverished nobility will go to revive their fortunes.

"As for the girl herself . . ." Lady Catherine paused, and a half smile appeared on her face, accompanying her far-off look. "She is a little unpolished, unsurprising considering her upbringing in a family who, while they might be all that is good, are still naught but minor gentry. But Elizabeth is delightful. She is intelligent and forthright, and though these events have naturally made her more cautious, I am sure with more confidence she will be a force in our society."

Elizabeth was shocked, for she thought she saw a hint of a tear glistening in the corner of Lady Catherine's eye. "She reminds me very much of my dear sister Anne, though she certainly possesses much more boldness than Anne did. But Anne was also witty and intelligent, and so very beautiful that many young men of her day were half in love with her from nothing more than the force of her smile. Elizabeth will be the same way."

"Then we shall be required to protect her from those who will seek to do her harm."

With Aunt Althea's declaration, Lady Catherine looked back at her, and an expression of such determination appeared on her countenance as to leave no one who saw it any doubt as to this woman's formidable nature. "Of course, we shall. Under our tutelage, Elizabeth will become the most potent force this city has ever seen!"

The exchange left Elizabeth with far warmer feelings for her irascible aunt than she had ever expected to have. It also allowed her a little more insight into the workings of her family, and specifically how important her return was to them.

The second incident which left a lasting impression upon her occurred as the evening was coming to a close. Elizabeth had noted throughout the evening that she was an object of much interest in particular to her father's cousin, the Baron Longfellow. He was an expansive and jovial man, as wide around the middle as his son was thin. He was also blessed — or cursed — with a loud, deep voice, his face was covered with a shortly cropped beard which seemed mostly gray, and he appeared insistent upon pushing his son toward Elizabeth. What the son — Farnsworth — thought of this was not readily apparent, though it was true that the tall, gangly youth had trouble looking Elizabeth in the eye.

Near the end of the evening, the baron, with his son standing just behind, cornered her and began to speak of his lands and his estate, which he claimed was quite extensive. He even went so far as to ask his son for a description of the district, which the young man gave, though in a voice as soft as his father's was loud. Elizabeth had quickly come to the conclusion that the man was a bore and his son only barely tolerable, and it was not long before she was searching for a way to escape. Her means soon arrived in the person of her father, who no doubt noticed how uncomfortable she was becoming.

"Longfellow," said her father by way of greeting as he joined them. Then he turned to Elizabeth, his expression softening. "My dear

Elizabeth. How are you getting on tonight?"

"Very well, Papa," said Elizabeth. She accepted his offered hand, grateful he had seen fit to rescue her. "I was just speaking with the baron and his son about their estate. It is in Cumbria, is it not?"

"It is," replied the baron, apparently pleased that she had remembered. "We would be happy to have you visit us at any time convenient." Baron Longfellow turned to Lord Matlock. "Perhaps we should have you all visit us. After the season? The Northlands are beautiful in the summer and not nearly so stifling as the south."

"Yes, they are," agreed Lord Matlock, "though I will contend that Derbyshire is equally beautiful and also benefits from a slightly cooler climate. I believe, however, that we are for Snowlock when we leave London, for I would like to show Elizabeth her ancestral home."

"Of course," replied the baron, though his manner appeared a little disappointed. "Then perhaps we may visit you. I was just noting how well Farnsworth and Elizabeth were getting on together. If we encourage their friendship, perhaps more will develop between them, eh?"

This last was said with a smile and a wink, but Elizabeth thought that Farnsworth's opinion of his father's assertion was as indifferent as Elizabeth's own. The boy looked at Elizabeth and quickly turned away as if embarrassed. For her part, Elizabeth turned to look at her father, remembering his promise that he would allow her to choose her own way in life. The grin her father shot at her confirmed that he remembered it himself.

"There may be an opportunity to have you stay with us," said Lord Matlock. "But as for the other, Elizabeth is newly returned to us, and I would not wish to give her up again so soon."

"Of course!" replied Baron Longfellow expansively. "But you cannot leave these things to chance, and Lady Elizabeth will be a person of such interest this season. You know the attention she will receive. Why do we not come to an agreement now? There is no need for a marriage to take place immediately, but having Elizabeth protected from the rakes of society can only be beneficial."

"She has enough protection with myself, her brothers, and Darcy looking after her." When the baron made to reply, the earl held up his hand. "I know you mean well, Longfellow, but I will not be entering Elizabeth into a contracted marriage. Her return means too much to me to barter her off in such a manner. If Farnsworth has an interest in her, then he may attempt to woo her. But he will not have any assistance from me."

Apparently, the baron realized that his pleas were not about to move her father, so he subsided. "Then that is the way it must be. I am certain Farnsworth can be as persuasive as any other man, eh, boy?"

The expression which appeared on Farnsworth's face was sickly in nature, but his eyes rested on Lord Matlock in what Elizabeth took to be gratitude. Lord Matlock only smiled and nodded, and soon they excused themselves, leaving Elizabeth with her father.

"Thank you, Papa," said she once they were beyond hearing. "I expected to hear such comments, but I had not thought it would be so soon."

"I am at your service, my dear." Then the earl paused and laughed. "If it is any consolation, I do not believe Longfellow is interested in having *you* as a daughter in particular. Farnsworth is naught but one and twenty and does not need to marry for some time yet, but I have heard that he has become enamored of a young lady in the neighborhood of his father's estate."

"And this is something to concern his father?" asked Elizabeth with a raised eyebrow.

"It is when the girl is the daughter of a minor country squire with an estate much smaller even than that of Mr. Bennet's. Longfellow has had his heart set on a much more exalted match for his son, one which would bring a more substantial dowry. He has been throwing Farnsworth at every available young lady all season. I dare say he remembers the amount of your dowry and thinks it would be a perfect solution."

"Then I hope he is discouraged by what you told him," said Elizabeth. "I have no interest in marrying Farnsworth."

The earl laughed with amusement. "No, my dear. I had not thought you would."

CHAPTER XVIII

Monday, March 23, 1812
White's, London

A nother late night led to a later morning. Brandy and port had rendered his head weak against the midday sun. But such it always was. It was a small price to pay for the lifestyle to which he had grown so accustomed. Many thought to attempt to lead him away from it, to *restore his honor* and make him more *respectable*.

Fools! There is nothing wrong with the way I conduct my affairs.

Perhaps it was not perfect, but no life was. There were times when his head pounded, and he regretted how much he imbibed or wondered if his tender belly would survive the revelries planned for the coming evening. But in the end, his lifestyle was his own, and it hurt no one. He was a bachelor and content to be one, free from the restraints of a wife and children, who would inevitably pull him from his activities. He was the hunter.

A laugh almost escaped. The silly little nickname he had given himself nearly twenty years before had stuck, at least in the contents of his own mind. He often thought of himself as the hunter, hunter of fortune, of games of subtle skill and a little luck, where fortunes could be made or lost in an instant. And he prided himself on winning far more often than he lost. The lure of gaming tables was far more seductive than any female could ever be. And if he required comfort of *another* kind, why, any willing wench would do.

The hunter laughed—in fact, he did not require them to be *completely* willing. Warm, well-rounded, and available was all he required. After all, he was a member of a privileged set—few women would dare refuse him.

The mirror in front of him showed him a man who, though beginning to advance in years, still maintained an impressive figure in his tailored trousers and jacket. He still possessed a full head of hair, and though it was beginning to be streaked by gray, he thought it distinguished him even further. Even the lines on his face, which, of late, had proliferated in earnest, did nothing to detract from his attractions.

The hunter's fingers twitched, and he looked down at them, noting their slender lengths. He could hold a hand of cards without a hint of a tremble, and his ability to bluff had always been second to none. And today more revelries were planned. The hunter could hardly wait.

When he left his sanctuary, the hunter spent his day much as he ever would. Much of society avoided him, and he was content to be shunned. Those with whom he associated provided all he needed— companionship, camaraderie, and a healthy sum of money waiting for a skillful man to relieve them of it at the card tables.

His club was a haven for the stodgy members of society, and the only reason he visited was to partake of a bite of supper and gain a bit of news. And if there was a card game or two in progress, why, the hunter was happy to join in, though most of his gambling was conducted in a location which was not nearly so pretty.

The hunter had been sitting with his dinner for some little time when an acquaintance strolled up to his table and sat with nary a by your leave. He greeted the man with perfunctory disinterest and continued to eat his dinner. Tonight there was to be a large game of chance down by the waterfront, and he meant to be there early to obtain an optimum location from which to place his wagers. It was all part of the game, and he was a master at it.

So intent was he on the evening ahead that he almost missed what his unwanted companion was saying, unsurprising, since the hunter considered him a bore and usually did not listen to one word in five.

"I beg your pardon, but what did you just say?"

The other man regarded him with a smirk, suggesting he was not so oblivious of being ignored as the hunter had thought. "Only that it was amazing that she should reappear after so many years of being lost. I cannot imagine how they managed to identify her or what proof they have that she is, in fact, their daughter, but I suppose it does not matter. The house of Fitzwilliam, backed by the Duke of Cheshire and all their other sundry connections, will have no trouble with naysayers."

"Fitzwilliam?" asked the hunter with a sinking feeling in the bottom of his stomach.

"Yes," replied the other man. "Did you not hear a word I said? News of Lady Elizabeth Fitzwilliam's return is spreading through our set like wildfire. I cannot but imagine that an announcement is forthcoming before long, for the earl would likely have insisted upon silence if they were not to announce it."

The other man looked at him, but he was unable to respond due to his shock. The girl had returned? How had this happened?

"Oh, that is correct—you are related to his lordship, are you not?"

"I am, though the connection is somewhat distant," the hunter was finally able to say. Then he directed a piercing look at his acquaintance. "Are you certain it is Lady Elizabeth who has returned?"

"Yes, I am." The man laughed. "I heard it from Longfellow if you must know. I find it most amusing, as he is determined to tie that unimpressive son of his to the young heiress. But if his reports of her beauty are any indication, I cannot imagine she would wish to be saddled with him."

The man trailed off in thought. "Perhaps it is fortuitous for me. As you know, my wife passed some years ago—it would be a great comfort to have a pretty young thing in my bed every night in the years of my dotage."

"You think she would look at a man twice her age?"

"I am wealthy and connected enough that I believe I would be appealing to her." The man shrugged. "If not, then no loss. My mistress still has enough charms to appeal to me, and if I tire of her, I may always procure another.

"Well, well," said the man, rising to his feet. "I believe I must return home to plan my conquest. A good day to you."

And then he sauntered away and left the club. The one who remained behind, however, did not take any notice of him when he walked away, for he was focused on his own thoughts and his rapidly rising ire.

She was back.

That blasted girl was back!

Tuesday, March 24, 1812
Fitzwilliam House, London

There was to be no rest for Elizabeth after the dinner party concluded. As it was now nearing the end of March, the season was in full flight, and that meant she would be partaking as a member of one of the most prominent families in the kingdom. While Elizabeth had always been at home in society, that of the first circles was another matter entirely. She wondered if she would be able to leave a good impression on them.

Her father had not asked for his family to keep her recovery a secret, and because of it, Elizabeth thought news of her recovery must be making its way through town. Add to that the fact that several ladies—including the Duchess of Cheshire and Lady Althea—were often to be found at Fitzwilliam house, and Elizabeth thought rumors must be making their way through town. Finally, only two nights after the dinner party, the whole family was to attend the theater together, and a statement was being prepared for the newspapers, announcing her return.

Elizabeth's salvation those days was the presence of those younger members of her family, particularly those who had known her the longest. Georgiana was a dear girl and was staying with them, so she was a constant comforting presence, and Elizabeth had always enjoyed Constance's company. But Anthony and William were perhaps more important to Elizabeth's peace of mind. William, in particular, seemed to be adept at knowing when Elizabeth was becoming tired of all the attention and inventing some reason for her to gain a respite.

On one such occasion, the day before they were to go to the theater, he proposed that they walk in the nearby park, and Elizabeth accepted. Georgiana was away from the house in the company of Constance, shopping on Bond Street, and Anthony was occupied with some other business, leaving Elizabeth to walk alone with her cousin.

They had gone out with her mother's blessing, though they were admonished not be out too long. Elizabeth, curious as she was about his seeming insight, made it a point of asking her cousin to account for his understanding of her character.

"Your character is much different from mine," said William, smiling as he replied to her query. "But as I am not comfortable in company, I suppose it gives me an understanding of when others experience similar feelings."

"I have always been quite comfortable in company," muttered Elizabeth.

William laughed. "I am not surprised. And I think you will be again, once you become accustomed to your new situation. At present, however, I can see when your expression becomes hunted, as I imagine it is similar to what I often feel when I am in company. That informs me when it is time to intervene."

"Then I am grateful for it. I must own, however, that I wonder how a man as intelligent and confident as you could be so ill at ease in society."

"It is a family trait, I suppose," replied William. "My father was much the same, though my mother tended toward more shyness. My sister and I are a close facsimile of our parents. Fitzwilliam revels in what attention he receives, but I have always felt like a horse at the auction. It is one of the reasons I am not yet married—I have not found a woman yet who is interested in me rather than what my money and connections can do for them."

"I suppose I must become accustomed to it, then." Elizabeth sighed. "I imagine much of the attention I shall receive will be for similar reasons."

"Of that, you may be certain."

"But how shall I ever discern who is genuine and who is false?"

"If I was not concerned about the possibility of angering your mother, I might suggest that just about *everyone* you meet will have an ulterior motive."

The twinkling in his eyes suggested he was, at least in part, jesting, though Elizabeth knew he was also serious. She laughed along with him, however, finding the mirth soothing.

"Mama might not appreciate your humor, but I doubt she would disagree much. For that matter, Anthony would agree wholeheartedly."

"That he would." William paused, and then shot her a smile which suggested a hint of embarrassment. "Anthony has always been my closest friend, even closer than his brother. James is a good man and has always been a confidante, but Anthony and I are closer in age and we think alike."

Elizabeth nodded and they continued to walk. When she thought back on their conversation, she realized it gave her a greater insight into her cousin. She could see where some might call him proud and aloof, but in reality, he was just a man who was not comfortable as the center of attention. She could not blame him.

When they returned to the house, they were met by Georgiana and Constance, whose carriage had just stopped there. They had relatively few packages, for their errands had been small in nature, and these they consigned to the care of the servants. As soon as they espied Elizabeth and William, however, they greeted them with pleasure, though Georgiana's eyes suggested more than a hint of worry.

"We have some news for you," said Constance, claiming Elizabeth's arm. "Let us go in to see your mother, for I have no doubt she will wish to hear it as well.

Though concerned, Elizabeth did not press her. They entered the house and divested their outerwear, making their way to the sitting-room in which her mother was closeted with Lady Catherine, Lady Althea, and the duchess. The greetings were completed in short order, during which Anthony wandered in, greeting Elizabeth with a smile and kiss on the cheek. Then they all sat down when Constance requested their attention.

"Georgiana happened to come across an acquaintance of William's by chance while we were shopping."

"It was Miss Bingley," said Georgiana, her lip curled with distaste.

Lady Susan, who had not released her resentment of the woman's insinuations the last time they had seen her, looked sharply at the two younger ladies. "Dare I hope that she behaved better this time?"

"She should not even have approached you," said William. "I made it clear that she would not be known to the Darcys any longer."

"Then she did not hear you," replied Constance, "for she greeted Georgiana as if they were the greatest of friends, and all but demanded an introduction to me."

"I attempted to ignore her, but she was most persistent," said Georgiana, her distress leading her to worry at a handkerchief she held in her hands.

"I beg your pardon," said the Duchess of Cheshire, "but who is Miss Bingley?"

"Her brother is a friend of mine from university," replied William. "Bingley is a jovial fellow, and I have always valued his company, for he is able to lighten the mood wherever he goes. But his sister . . ."

"Let us simply say she is a leech," interjected Lady Susan. It was clear she was not amused. "She attempts to reach high above her. William has been her target."

"Little I say has had any effect in deterring her." William paused and snuck a glance at Lady Catherine. The lady was watching him intently, clearly suspecting what he was about to say. Elizabeth knew she would not be happy. "I agreed to stay with Bingley after Michaelmas last year, to assist him in learning to manage the estate he was leasing. This estate is coincidentally near to Longbourn, Elizabeth's adoptive father's estate. On the first night at Bingley's estate, she attempted to compromise me and force a marriage between us."

"That trollop!" exclaimed Lady Catherine, her furious response everything Elizabeth would have expected. "How dare she? That is the result of befriending people who are so wholly unsuitable, Darcy. I have told you again and again."

"There is little of Bingley which is objectionable," replied Darcy, ignoring her outburst. "Unfortunately, his temperament is easy, and he does not excel when it comes to controlling his sister. She visited last week and made some truly deplorable insinuations regarding Elizabeth. After, I visited Bingley and made sure he understood in no uncertain terms that I would not know his sister any longer and that she risked his acceptance in town if he did not check her behavior."

"Do Mr. or Miss Bingley know of Elizabeth's true identity?" asked Constance.

"No," replied William. "The last time I met with Bingley, it was still considered a secret. I ensured that Bingley knew that his sister was not to speak of Elizabeth as Lady Susan had a *particular interest* in her. But I did not inform them of the truth."

Constance pursed her lips. "It may have been better if you informed them of it. Though this Miss Bingley did not even say Elizabeth's name, she did allude to her in connection to you, William."

"If I had informed them, Elizabeth's identity would be on the tongues of everyone in London by now," replied William.

"Do you suspect she has spoken of these insinuations she made of Elizabeth to others?" Lady Catherine, who had asked the question, was obviously furious, but her very being radiated purpose, which Elizabeth was certain was not to Caroline Bingley's benefit.

"It is difficult to say," replied Constance. "I do have some acquaintances from the lower circles, but I have not heard anything about Elizabeth." Constance turned to William. "Might I assume her insinuations were concerning your relationship with Elizabeth?"

"Yes, though I will not repeat them," replied William. He sighed and passed a hand over his brow. "I suppose I will need to go and visit Bingley again. I had hoped he would take my words with the gravity I intended and do something, but it seems I was overly optimistic."

"I think it best that you do not visit him, William," said the duchess. At William's questioning glance, she continued: "If this Miss Bingley has already gossiped of Elizabeth in such a manner, then her fate is already sealed. If she has not, the knowledge of Elizabeth's identity will surely prompt her to relinquish her resentment and cease her objectionable words. Either way, the next time you see her, she will reveal her true colors."

"I believe Sarah is correct, William," said Lady Susan. "Allow Miss Bingley to indict herself if that is her purpose. We are announcing Elizabeth's identity soon. If Miss Bingley has not gossiped, then we will simply respond to any ill behavior. If she has, her own words will convict her, as no one will believe them over the words of an earl."

William's discomfort was evident, but he allowed their arguments were sensible. "I do not know if we will meet them in society. I am Bingley's patron, and since I have distanced myself from his family, we usually do not attend the same events."

"What about the theater tomorrow?" asked Elizabeth.

There was a rumbling of approval for Elizabeth's insight, and several of her family nodded their heads. William looked at Elizabeth, his expression unreadable, before he sighed and nodded.

"Yes, it is quite possible they will be present tomorrow. Miss Bingley enjoys attending the theater, though I am certain it is not for any enjoyment in the arts. Bingley will often rent a box when his sister cannot engineer their presence in my box when I am there. I cannot speak to their plans, but it would not surprise me if they attended."

Lady Susan nodded. "Then perhaps tomorrow will reveal this woman's actions."

"If she makes any comment which might be deemed objectionable, I will ruin her," promised Lady Catherine. "I will not allow my family's name—and Elizabeth's in particular—to be sullied by such a base woman."

"And in this, you will be joined by us all," said Constance, to Lady Susan and Lady Althea's vigorous agreement. "No one can make statements about Elizabeth without a response."

Elizabeth was grateful for her family's protectiveness, but at the same time, she was concerned for William. He did nothing more than nod his head at Constance's declaration, though his expression was unreadable. Elizabeth watched him as the conversation turned to other matters, wishing to speak to him and thank him personally for his support. She also did not wish him to think he was alone when it came to the Bingley family—Elizabeth herself considered Bingley to be a good man, though his sisters and brother-in-law were of a different sort. Even so, the only objectionable character belonged to Miss Bingley, and Elizabeth did not wish to forget that.

The opportunity to talk to him came a short time later when he excused himself to return home. Though Elizabeth had no real reason to walk out with him, she invented an excuse to leave the room and hurried to the front door, hoping to catch him before he left. Fortune smiled on her, for he was just shrugging his coat onto his shoulders with the help of the butler when she arrived.

"William," said Elizabeth, "I wished to thank you for your support and apologize for this difficulty with Mr. Bingley. He is a good man, and I would not wish your friendship with him to be ruined because of me."

"I thank you for the sentiment," said William with a soft smile for her. "But it can hardly be deemed your fault. I made certain Miss Bingley understood the consequences of speaking of you and warned Bingley to control her. If he has not, then the results of this inability to act will be on his head."

"But it is sad that such a close friendship will be forfeit."

"It is, but it is not unexpected." William shook his head. "I have known since November that his friendship might not be salvaged. I hope her behavior has altered, but I do not blame you, of all people, if it has not."

William reached out and grasped Elizabeth's hand, and he squeezed it lightly. "Do not think on it any longer, Elizabeth. What will be, will be. Your recovery is much more important than my friendship with Bingley. Do not ever allow yourself to think otherwise."

Then releasing her hand, William bowed and departed, leaving Elizabeth watching him as he left. She stood there for some time, even though the door was closed, her hand feeling the warmth where he had held it. Within her breast, a powerful feeling of affection had welled up, leaving her grateful that she had met Fitzwilliam Darcy.

Tuesday, March 24, 1812
Fitzwilliam House, London

Later that same afternoon, Elizabeth received a visit which filled her with joy, though the news she heard caused consternation. It was not long after William left when she was led into the room where the ladies were still congregated, and Elizabeth—having missed her aunt— jumped up and embraced her happily.

"Aunt Gardiner! I had no notion you were to come today, but I am glad you did. How are the children?"

"They are well and asking for you constantly, Lady Elizabeth. I hope you will have time to visit them, for I am having difficulty explaining to Sophie why you are no longer with us."

Mrs. Gardiner paused and looked out over the ladies who had risen when she had entered the room. "But where are our manners, Lady Elizabeth? We should not be standing here speaking while these fine ladies wait on us."

"You are always welcome, Mrs. Gardiner," said Lady Susan. She approached and startled Mrs. Gardiner by pulling her into an embrace. "Come, let me introduce you to everyone."

Elizabeth had always been impressed by her aunt's manners, her poise, and her ability to fit into any society, but being introduced to another wife of an earl as well as a duchess induced an air of astonishment which Elizabeth could not fault. She still had trouble believing she kept such company herself. The appropriate comments were made, the pleasure of being introduced and the ladies' thanks to her for protecting Elizabeth when she had found herself in need. And through it, Elizabeth felt herself a little puzzled, for her aunt kept referring to her as 'Lady Elizabeth,' rather than the more familiar terms she had used as long as Elizabeth could remember. Elizabeth found she did not like it—she wished to remain this woman's relation, not allow the needs of rank to intrude.

"Shall you not call me 'Lizzy' again, Aunt?" blurted Elizabeth at the first available opportunity.

"But you are no longer merely 'Lizzy,'" replied Aunt Gardiner. "You are now Lady Elizabeth Fitzwilliam, the daughter of an earl. It would be unseemly to use so familiar a moniker."

"You are still my aunt, and I wish to keep your connection. What could be unseemly about it?"

"Mrs. Gardiner is correct, Elizabeth," interjected Lady Susan. "Should Mrs. Gardiner be observed in company referring to you so familiarly, she would be thought of as pretentious at best."

"But we are not in such company," said Elizabeth, frustrated at her mother's apparent pride.

"No, we are not," was her mother's gentle response. "But Mrs. Gardiner did not know this upon entering the room, and as a result, she fell back on formality, which, though it is sometimes distasteful, is *always* safe."

Elizabeth blushed, noting the other ladies were watching her with various degrees of amused tolerance. "Of course. But I believe that you may refer to me as you desire in *this* company, Aunt Gardiner. In fact, I believe I might insist upon it."

"Well then, *Lizzy*, I would not dream of disobeying such an instruction."

The heat of Elizabeth's cheeks threatened to outshine the light of the sun through the windows. The other ladies laughed at her embarrassment, and several looked at Mrs. Gardiner with interest. Mrs. Gardiner, however, had eyes only for Elizabeth—she laughed and pressed a hand to Elizabeth's arm, and assured her that she was happy to maintain their connection and pleased to refer to her however she wished, as long as they were not in company.

For several moments after the conversation continued in a light fashion, and Elizabeth could see that many of her new family and friends were quite interested in hearing of Mrs. Gardiner. And her aunt acquitted herself well, even in the face of so many formidable ladies. It was not long, however, before she turned her attention to the reason for her coming.

"I come bearing news of the Bennets," said Mrs. Gardiner, "along with a letter from Jane." Mrs. Gardiner produced a thick missive from her reticule and handed it to Elizabeth. "Though it is not a matter which is *too* distressing, I thought that I should come and inform you of it. You see, it appears Mrs. Bennet has discovered your identity."

Friday, March 20, 1812
Longbourn, Hertfordshire

Mr. Henry Bennet was a man who possessed a healthy respect for his wife's ability to disrupt his house. She was a loud woman at the best of times, one who could never speak when shrieking was possible. That her two youngest daughters were much like her in temperament—though Bennet knew that Kitty, at least, only behaved that way because Lydia did—meant the noise levels in the house were almost always prodigious. Jane and Mary were quiet, of course, but their other, more voluble relations more than made up for their lack.

Since Elizabeth's departure, unfortunately, the situation in the house had become that much more unbearable. Bennet had taken to staying in his bookroom much more than was his previous custom, but the noise of the house still intruded. But that was nothing compared to the furor which had persisted since the visit and subsequent departure of the two gentlemen who claimed to be Elizabeth's relations.

"Mr. Bennet!" his wife had exclaimed when Mr. Darcy and Colonel Fitzwilliam fled the room. "What do you mean by ushering those fine gentlemen from the room in such haste? Did you not think how their association may improve our family's position?"

"How can you know that, Mrs. Bennet?" he had responded. "You know not who they are, after all."

"I know they are gentlemen of some standing."

"Oh? And how did you come to that conclusion?"

"By their dress and their bearing. Such fine clothes as they wore, so well-tailored. They cannot be anything but gentlemen of means and wealth!"

Once again, Bennet was forced to acknowledge that his wife was observant, even if she was not clever. She could sniff out a rich man from one hundred paces!

"Even if they are, I cannot imagine why you would harbor such expectations for them so soon."

"Because Jane is so beautiful and is able to catch the eye of any man!" exclaimed Mrs. Bennet.

"And yet she remains unmarried," muttered Bennet. Jane was a good girl, sweet and beautiful, but Bennet understood that was often not enough. It worried him, as her tender heart had recently been hurt.

Mrs. Bennet, however, did not even hear his words. "And my Lydia is so lively and gay. I am certain that had you only invited them to dinner, my daughters would have caught their eye."

"They were not inclined to stay, for they had business in town, necessitating their immediate return."

"Then you must invite them back."

With a sigh, Mr. Bennet turned away and seated himself again at his desk. "I met those two men over a small matter of business, Mrs. Bennet. They shall not be returning.

"Now," said he, raising his voice over his wife's continued protests, "I should like the use of my bookroom returned to me. Please close the door after you leave."

With a deliberate motion, Bennet picked up the book he had been reading when the two gentlemen had arrived and fixed his gaze upon the pages. Mrs. Bennet regarded him with suspicion for several moments before she finally huffed and left the room. It was a testament to her restraint—what there was of it—that she did not slam the door behind her.

If Bennet thought that was to be the end of the matter, he was sorely mistaken. He was not surprised, of course—ever since Mr. Bingley had departed, leaving Jane behind with nary a backward glance, Mrs. Bennet had become that much more desperate. There were few suitable men in the area, and none of them looked upon her daughters as potential partners in marriage, partially because the youngest were silly and ignorant, and the rest because their dowry was small. As such, the possibility of two wealthy gentlemen was not an opportunity she was ready to relinquish without a fight.

At first, Bennet found his wife's antics to be amusing, but so it always was when she got a bee in her bonnet. She attempted every stratagem to learn the identities of the two men. She asked, she pleaded, she introduced them in conversation, hoping he would slip and let something loose. And through all of this, Bennet parried her attempts with the ability born of many years of practice.

But then it became tiresome when she would not relent, and Bennet began to avoid her even more than before. He even took the expedient of locking the door to his bookroom to prevent her from entering. It was unfortunate that the doors were not so thick as to prevent the sound of her screeching from reaching his ears.

In other circumstances, he might have simply told her to buy himself a little peace. In this instance, however, he resisted. It was not his place to tell her the story, as it was Elizabeth's life and her privilege to acquaint whomever she would with the true details of her parentage. Furthermore, he expected an announcement to appear in the newspapers before long, and as his wife was an avid reader of the society pages, she would learn the truth at that time.

More importantly for his family, however, Bennet was certain that his wife would make a fool of herself when she learned of it, and he wished to put her raptures off as long as he possibly could. Her badgering of him would be nothing compared to the effusions to which he would be subjected when she learned the truth. And he would not put it past her to journey to London to see Elizabeth, conveniently forgetting that it was by her insistence the girl had been put out of their home in the first place. Given the way Colonel Fitzwilliam had behaved, Bennet had no illusions as to the rest of his family's opinions about the Bennets.

Unfortunately for Bennet, Mrs. Bennet had a way of wearing him down, of eventually, through sheer tenacity and the volume of her strident voice, bending him to her will. It was on a lovely day in spring when she finally broke through his defenses.

"Enough, woman!" roared he. She had followed him into his study, managing to slip through the door before he closed it. Then she proceeded to continue to attempt to wheedle the story from him, snapping his temper in the end.

"The business those two men came to conduct had nothing to do with your daughters. They had no intention of ever asking for an introduction. In fact, I doubt they ever wish to so much as lay eyes on any of us again!"

"Then why were they here?" demanded Mrs. Bennet, her countenance alive with her offense.

"They came to ask about Elizabeth!"

For a moment, there was blessed silence, for Mrs. Bennet was so shocked she could not respond. It was truly unfortunate that state of affairs could not continue.

"To ask about Lizzy? What has that girl done now? Did you tell them she is not even our daughter? I will not have her ruining my daughters when she has already ruined her own prospects."

"They already knew she was not our daughter, Mrs. Bennet," said Mr. Bennet, sinking down into his chair and feeling unaccountably weary.

"I suppose the rumors have reached town, then." Mrs. Bennet sat primly on a chair in front of Bennet's desk, the sneer for Elizabeth looming unpleasant on her face. "Then I suppose it is well you sent them away, for they cannot be true gentlemen if they were interested in *her*. I suppose they want her for whatever disgusting habits she gets up to now."

"Mrs. Bennet," said Bennet, shaking from rage by the time she had finished her sickening soliloquy, "I have often thought you senseless, but your words are even more abhorrent than I had thought possible. I have half a mind to take you over my knee for spewing such putrid drivel about a woman we called our daughter for eighteen years."

By the end, Mr. Bennet was yelling, and he cared not for his ungentlemanly behavior. His wife attempted to speak, but he would not allow it.

"No! Not another word, lest you push me beyond all endurance. If you say another word about Elizabeth, I shall hold your pin money for the next year!"

Mrs. Bennet's mouth closed with an audible clack, though her glare impaled him. Bennet cared not—he had never been more disgusted with the woman, and though he had never, in all his life, raised his hand to a woman, if she said another word he would not be responsible for his actions!

"Papa?"

A small voice caught his attention and Bennet looked up at the door, noting it had been left ajar. Jane now stood in the frame, watching them with wild eyes. She had heard the entire argument. Her look at her mother was disbelieving, though colored with a hint of resentment, such as he would never have expected to see from her. Jane looked at *him* with confusion.

"You have heard from Lizzy? I have been worried, for I have not received word from her in some time."

"You have had letters from Elizabeth?" demanded Mrs. Bennet. "I told you—"

"Enough, Mrs. Bennet!" His wife glared mutinously at him, but Bennet only scowled back. "I will remind you that *I* am master of Longbourn, and as such, I may correspond with whomever I please. And Jane may write to Lizzy if she desires. Do not attempt to gainsay me, or it will go ill with you."

At Mrs. Bennet's angered glare, Bennet decided there was no choice but to inform them of the truth of Elizabeth's situation. Any other action could be disastrous if the daft woman should press her dislike and do something to truly offend the Fitzwilliam family.

"Yes, I have news of Elizabeth. Jane, come in and close the door, for you have as much right to hear this as your mother." Bennet glared at Mrs. Bennet when she opened her mouth, and she closed it once again. "In fact, in light of recent events, I dare say you have *more* right to it."

Though confused, Jane did as she was bid. She took a seat next to her mother, though Bennet noted that she leaned away from Mrs. Bennet, her anger for her mother's words still present. Bennet ignored the interplay between them—he was attempting to decide how much to reveal and how he could prevent his wife from making a fool of herself. Unfortunately, there was little chance of that.

"You have heard of the two men who visited here?" asked Bennet of Jane, knowing her answer.

Her eyes darted to her mother. "The ones that Mama speaks of?"

"Yes, indeed. She has been plaguing me to reveal their identities ever since they departed. Until this moment, I have resisted, as I do not believe this is my tale to tell. However, your mother's words have the potential to truly harm our family if she does not control herself."

"How could it affect us?" asked Mrs. Bennet with a disdainful sniff, her tone harsh and sarcastic. "Elizabeth is nothing but a—"

Bennet rose swiftly from his chair, putting his hands on his desk and leaning over it, looking directly at his wife. Mrs. Bennet, seeming to understand for the first time that he was seriously displeased, shrank back from him, fear turning her complexion white.

"Turning you over my knee is still an option, Mrs. Bennet. Do not say another word about Elizabeth!"

A jerky nod met his command. Bennet glared at her a little longer before sinking back into his seat. "You do not know how close you come to ruining us forever with this petulant grudge you have against Elizabeth. Let go of your resentment! Elizabeth was not at fault for what happened—it was all the work of that libertine, Wickham."

The thought of the man brought another matter to Bennet's mind and he changed tack slightly. "You are aware of Wickham's arrest and incarceration, are you not?"

Mrs. Bennet nodded, though hesitantly.

"He found himself in such a situation, because of his past behavior, but also in particular because of how he importuned Elizabeth. It appears he fixed his attention upon the wrong woman. And it was done at the behest of the two men you found in my study."

Apparently, that connection had never been made by the gossips of the town, as Mrs. Bennet started in surprise. "Those men had Mr. Wickham taken away?"

"They did," confirmed Bennet. "By now he will have been tried and sent to Van Diemen's Land if they did not simply have him hanged. Such is the price for crossing powerful men."

"Oh, I knew it!" exclaimed Mrs. Bennet. "They are wealthy and connected. You *must* invite them back here, Mr. Bennet. They may be our family's salvation."

"I assure you, Mrs. Bennet, they have no wish to have anything to do with our family."

"How can you know?" demanded Mrs. Bennet. "I am sure my girls can charm them if only given a chance!"

"That is because you do not know them." Bennet glared at his wife, silencing her for the moment, though he knew it would not last long. "The two men in my study that day, Mrs. Bennet, were Mr. Fitzwilliam Darcy, and his cousin, Colonel Anthony Fitzwilliam, the younger son of the Earl of Matlock. They visited that day to ask after the young woman we called our daughter for eighteen years, Miss Elizabeth Bennet.

"But an amazing discovery has been made, for Elizabeth's identity is far more prestigious than we ever would have imagined. She is Lady Elizabeth Fitzwilliam, daughter of that same earl, and brother to one of the men who graced my bookroom that day."

An expression of utter stupefaction came over Mrs. Bennet. Jane, who had been watching her parents argue through wide eyes, was no less shocked. But she was quicker to overcome it.

"Lizzy is the daughter of an earl?"

"She is, Jane." Bennet sat back wearily, feeling spent by the argument, wondering if he had made the correct choice. "Her identity was first suspected by Mr. Darcy and Colonel Fitzwilliam, and then confirmed by her mother and father."

"How is it possible?"

"I do not know. I have no knowledge of her before I found her in Cambridge, and the Fitzwilliams do not know how she came to be there. She disappeared from their estate in Derbyshire, and they never saw her again.

"But it has now been proven. Among other things, including a striking resemblance to her mother, it is my understanding that the little dress she was wearing — the pale yellow dress with roses — was positively identified by Lady Matlock. By now she will be living with them, and I do not doubt there will be an announcement before long."

"The dress?" Mrs. Bennet had finally found her tongue, though her shock still made her hesitant.

"Yes, Mrs. Bennet. As you recall, you gave it to your sister Gardiner, and she dresses Sophie in it. From what I understand, Sophie was wearing it the day the Fitzwilliams met Elizabeth."

"Oh dear, oh dear," chanted Mrs. Bennet, her hands fluttering while she shook her head. "We are saved. Oh, heavens be praised, we are saved."

"Are you daft, woman?" demanded Bennet. "What can Elizabeth's recovery possibly have to do with us?"

"We kept her all those years, clothed her, fed her," replied Mrs. Bennet. He could tell she was still lost in her own thoughts. "Of course, she will wish to assist us. She will not wish for us to be homeless when you pass on."

"Once again, Mrs. Bennet, I thank you for your confidence in my imminent mortality." Bennet's sardonic tone was wasted on the woman, for he did not think she heard two words he said. "Be that as it may, how can you possibly think that Elizabeth will wish to maintain a connection with us after you forced her from this house to fend for herself? Are you completely mad?"

"She will understand!" snapped Mrs. Bennet. "Lizzy is an intelligent girl — she knows that I needed to protect the other girls. I am her mother. She will not forget that."

"You should recall, Mrs. Bennet, that you are *not* her mother." Mrs.

Bennet turned to him, a retort on her lips, but Bennet did not wish to hear it. "Lady Matlock is her mother, and I believe she would take a dim view of you attempting to assert your relationship after your behavior to her."

"Oh, I must call for the carriage and go to Meryton!" exclaimed Mrs. Bennet, proving she still possessed the ability to lie to herself. "Mrs. Phillips will be so surprised! And I must arrange to go to town to see her! She must not be allowed to forget us."

With the spryness of a woman half her age, Mrs. Bennet jumped to her feet and dashed from the room. Bennet could only shake his head. It was clear there was nothing he could say to dissuade her. He would need to ensure the horses were not available for her use.

"Papa?" asked the meek voice of Jane.

Bennet had almost forgotten her presence, but he smiled at the girl, thinking to himself that she was the most exceptional of his children. "Yes, Jane, it is true. Lizzy is actually the daughter of an earl."

"I do not doubt you, Papa. It is only . . ." Jane paused and wrung her hands in her agitation. "I wondered if it would be proper for me to write to Lizzy. I know that she may not wish to receive anything from me, but . . ."

Bennet rose and walked around the desk, sitting in the chair vacated by his wife, and catching Jane's hands up in his own. "You are the only member of the family with whom she may wish to keep a connection, Jane. If you write to your Aunt Gardiner and enclose a letter to Elizabeth, I am sure your aunt will ensure it is placed in Elizabeth's hands."

"Do you think she will be happy to receive it?"

"You were always the closest of sisters. I cannot think she has changed her feelings toward you. Write to her—I am certain you will not be disappointed."

With a hesitant smile, Jane nodded and rose to leave the room. Bennet was left by himself, wondering how he was to manage the situation to ensure his family was not ruined. It may have been best to maintain his silence. But the secret would have come out eventually. Perhaps it was best that it did so now so that he could manage the consequences and check his wife. It may have been, had he any confidence he could control her.

*   *   *

Tuesday, March 24, 1812
Fitzwilliam House, London

"Here is a letter from Jane which Mr. Bennet enclosed in his missive to Mr. Gardiner," said Mrs. Gardiner. She produced a few sheets of paper, folded and addressed in Jane's handwriting. Elizabeth accepted it, weighing it, wondering at Jane's reaction to her new identity.

"Had I considered it, I would have known Mrs. Bennet would attempt to re-establish our relationship," said Elizabeth, putting the letter aside to read later. It was just like Mrs. Bennet, she knew. The woman would not consider how they parted of any importance. What would matter is that Elizabeth was now connected and accepted in town. Mrs. Bennet would naturally expect her to invite her daughters to town and introduce them to wealthy men.

"Elizabeth," said her mother gently, drawing her attention, "we have not spoken much of your adoptive family. But you know we cannot allow them to impose upon you in this manner."

"I know," replied Elizabeth simply. "It is just . . ." Elizabeth swallowed and determined her own feelings on the subject. "I do not think I would wish to be separated from them forever, but it is hard. I was always close to Mr. Bennet, and Jane is the best friend I have ever had. Mary, too, is not objectionable, though her tendency to moralize can be tiresome.

"But the younger Bennets are wild, and my relationship with Mrs. Bennet has always been . . . trying. Regardless, she does not have the manners to move among society successfully, and the youngest girls would embarrass me within minutes."

"Much as I wish I could disagree, what you have said is entirely accurate." Mrs. Gardiner sighed. "My brother Bennet informed us he will attempt to prevent his wife from doing something foolish, but I have every confidence in Mrs. Bennet's ability to wear him down."

"You think she will come to London?" asked Elizabeth. Then she grimaced and answered her own question. "Of course, she will. She will see me as the means whereby she can obtain security despite the entail."

"I will do my best to waylay her, Elizabeth," said Aunt Gardiner. "And I will attempt to get word to you if she does come."

"Thank you," replied Elizabeth.

Mrs. Gardiner stayed for some time after, and Elizabeth was given all the pleasure of seeing one she truly esteemed accepted by her new family. It was true that Lady Catherine was a little aloof and the duchess, a little haughty, but by and large, they behaved well. When Mrs. Gardiner went away, Elizabeth farewelled her, hoping to see her again soon. But not in the company of Mrs. Bennet. It would be better if she attained more distance before she was once again faced with the presence of her erstwhile mother. Her feelings were still too complex for her to understand them.

CHAPTER XIX

Wednesday, March 25, 1812
Fitzwilliam House, London

*T*he next morning was the day they were to attend the theater, and Elizabeth awoke, once again caught in the nervous excitement the day would bring. It was a day when things would change for her dramatically. Her mother had timed it so that the notices would appear in the paper the following morning, but she knew the news of her return had already spread. She would appear tonight at the theater as an object of interest for many. It would be different from the family dinner, where those in attendance were disposed to accept her at her parents' recommendation. Tonight, for the first time, she would truly face the ton.

"It is an auspicious day, my dear," said her mother when they met for the morning meal. The rest of her immediate family in residence looked on with amusement.

"I suppose it remains to be seen exactly what sort of day it will be," replied Elizabeth.

"We will all be with you, Elizabeth," said Constance. "There is nothing to fear."

Grateful as she was for the support, Elizabeth nodded and attempted a smile. But for most of the rest of the day, she attempted to treat it like any other. She walked in Hyde Park with Anthony, laughing at his stories and appreciating his ability to distract her. She played pianoforte with Georgiana and bantered with her eldest brother and his wife. And for a time, it worked, as she did not think about the coming evening.

Later in the day, the family partook of a light dinner—very light, as they were all to gather at the duke's house for dinner after the performance. After they had eaten, Elizabeth followed her mother upstairs to ready herself. Lady Susan entrusted her to the care of her maid while she attended her own preparations, but she returned far sooner than Elizabeth might have expected.

"I rushed my preparations," said she to Elizabeth's questioning look. "It is not every day a woman is able to help her daughter prepare for her effective debut in society. You will understand when you have a daughter of your own."

While the maid fussed with Elizabeth's hair, her mother engaged herself in preparing Elizabeth's dress for the evening. It was the most beautiful gown that had been purchased for her, a light pink confection with a wrap of a darker color and, to Elizabeth's satisfaction, only a little lace around the sleeves and bodice. While she busied herself with her tasks, Lady Susan reminisced.

"You know, my own coming out was undertaken at an even younger age than yours, for I was naught but eighteen years of age." Lady Susan paused and laughed. "Of course, I will own that I was eager for it. A close cousin was newly married, and I had heard all her stories of the events she had attended. I was a little jealous of her good fortune. My mother had a difficult time holding me back.

"But it was a magical time. My first ball was where I met your father, and though I will own that he did not impress me at the time, I was soon drawn to his character. It did not hurt that he is a very handsome man too."

Elizabeth could not help but laugh. "So yours was not an arranged marriage?"

"The Fitzwilliam family has not typically engaged in such practices. Your father and I met and became acquainted through the usual means of courtship. I will not say that our families were not eager for the match when they learned of our growing attachment, but that did not make it any less our decision.

"If there is one bit of advice I could give you, Elizabeth, it is to make sure of your affections before you marry." Lady Susan smiled at Elizabeth and caressed her cheek. "Though I do have friends who have agreeable marriages with their husbands and do not love them, there are many examples of the opposite, where the husband and wife hardly know each other. I cannot help but suppose that my marriage, which is founded on affection, is not more agreeable still. Loving your husband does not guarantee there will not be arguments or disagreements, but it provides an extra impetus for you to resolve your differences."

"I believe you have little to worry on that score, Mama," replied Elizabeth. At her mother's questioning glance, Elizabeth was induced to say: "Mr. and Mrs. Bennet do not share an agreeable marriage. He is an intelligent man, and she . . . well, she is not a gifted intellectual. She complains of her nerves, and he avoids her, while he teases and vexes her, and she makes his life miserable.

"As I have had the example of the loving relationship shared by the Gardiners, I have always been determined that I would not marry unless it was for the deepest love. Jane and I were united in this resolve."

Lady Susan sighed. "Though it seems silly, I sometimes forget you were brought up in a house completely different from what you would have experienced with us." She fixed a gaze on Elizabeth. "You *were* happy there, were you not?"

"I was." Elizabeth shook her head and smiled. "One cannot be happy at all times. There were challenges at Longbourn and vexations aplenty. But I was given a wonderful sister and a father with whom I shared a close relationship. Given what we know of my history, it could have been much worse."

"It could have, indeed," replied her mother. Her voice was almost a whisper.

The maid pronounced her hair finished at that moment, and Elizabeth stood to be helped into her clothes. Lady Susan produced a small pair of diamond earrings and fastened them to Elizabeth's ears.

As she worked, Elizabeth could see a frown on her mother's face, which suggested deep concentration.

"Your life has been different from what I anticipated for you, Elizabeth," said Lady Susan at length. "As such, so will your coming out be. In fact, you will not even have your curtsey before the queen until next year."

Elizabeth smiled shyly at her mother's words, not at all displeased she would be able to avoid that trial for another year. But her mother continued to speak.

"I want you to know, my dearest daughter, that I love you, and not only because you have been proven to be my daughter. You have also demonstrated that you are intelligent, poised, accomplished, and a true delight to know. Even though I have had very little to do with your upbringing, I cannot imagine you as a better person if you had been raised with us. For that, I will always be thankful to your adoptive family.

"What I am attempting to say is that you will do well. I know you are beset with nerves, and that is not unexpected. But trust yourself, trust your abilities. I have no doubt you will be one of the most sought-after ladies of the season, for reasons far beyond the sensation of your sudden return."

"Thank you, Mother," replied Elizabeth, feeling the hints of happy tears pooling in the corners of her eyes. "I will do my best to make you proud."

"That is all anyone could ask. But no tears!" Lady Susan laughed and drew Elizabeth in for an embrace. She reveled in the feelings elicited by the simple gesture, love and gratitude welling up within her for this woman. "We would not wish to undo all the work which has been done to render you irresistible to the masses of jealous suitors!"

The laugh with which Elizabeth responded was a little forced, but her mother only grinned.

Wednesday, March 25, 1812
Bingley townhouse, London

In another part of town, a very different scene was taking place. Caroline Bingley was anticipating the night at the theater, and not only for her usual reasons. The excitement had always been there—the ability to see and be seen, to mingle with the best society had to offer. But more than that, she suspected that Mr. Darcy might be there that evening, and she suspected that he would be in the company of the detestable Miss Eliza Bennet.

The thought of that *woman* caused Caroline to clench her hands. How she hated Eliza Bennet, had hated her from the first moment of their acquaintance. Well, Caroline would see her brought low, see her cast out for the improper, insolent girl she was. It was nothing of any consequence—a few words here and there in the ears of those who would spread the story wide and far, and never enough to link it back to Caroline herself. Gossip had a way of spreading in London, and even if those with whom she had shared her knowledge were not of the first circles themselves, Caroline had no doubt it would spread to them just as easily. Eliza would be ruined in Mr. Darcy's circle, as well as every other. Caroline could hardly wait.

The damage with respect to Mr. Darcy, however, appeared to have been done, much though Caroline was loath to confess it. It was time to allow Mr. Darcy to wallow in the squalor of his own ignorance, for it seemed he was not as discerning as Caroline had hoped. She would find some other man who appreciated what she could bring to them as a marriage partner, one of greater consequence and standing than Mr. Darcy. Perhaps she could even aspire to a peer!

When Caroline descended for the evening, she was met by her family. Louisa, who had descended to treachery in her refusal to support Caroline against Miss Eliza, was already waiting for her as was Hurst. Caroline ignored the man, knowing he was likely already in his cups. Only Charles had yet to arrive, though his absence was no loss. All her family were complicit in this failure to support her, and Caroline was not about to forgive them soon. Once she saw Charles married to an heiress to raise their consequence, she would use it to make herself an even more attractive marriage partner. When she was married, however, she would see her brother and sister as little as possible. Let *them* become supplicants to *her*.

Charles appeared soon after, and he nodded to Hurst and cast a severe look upon Caroline. Or what passed for a severe look on the silly man's face—he was about as frightening as a mouse. Caroline would not be intimidated.

"Remember, Caroline, I do not know if Darcy is to be at the theater tonight, but you are to remain strictly apart from him and his family." Charles paused, seeming to make certain she was listening to him, and then spoke again. "As for Miss Elizabeth Bennet, please remember to avoid speaking of her, for he warned me against it specifically."

"Really, Charles," said Caroline in an airy tone of unconcern, "I do not know where you arrived at this delusion. What could Miss Eliza be to Mr. Darcy? What could she possibly be to someone as exalted at Lady Matlock?"

"I do not know," replied Charles. "Darcy would not tell me."

"Then you must have misunderstood."

"'Lady Matlock has taken an interest in Miss Bennet,'" replied Charles. "That is what Darcy said. Please, Caroline, tell me how I may have misunderstood Darcy's meaning."

"You did not, Charles," said Louisa.

Traitor. Caroline attempted to glare at her sister, but Louisa did not pay her any attention.

"Thank you, Louisa." Charles's eyes swung back to Caroline. "Caroline, we have already had this discussion. I will say no more, except to remind you of your situation. If you breach any of the conditions we have set for you, I will send you back to Scarborough to live with our family there."

"I have no intention of approaching Mr. Darcy," said Caroline, and she surprised herself by meaning it. There was nothing left for her with the man, so there was little to be gained by pressing him.

"And Miss Bennet?"

"I have no interest in *her*," replied Caroline. *Once she has been disgraced forever.*

"Very well. Then we should depart."

Caroline rose with the rest of her family, and they made their way to the entrance, where they donned their outerwear and removed themselves to the waiting carriage. Hurst, in particular, watched her as if he did not trust her, but Caroline ignored him. She was anticipating this evening more than she had any event in some time. It was a new start for her. Caroline could hardly wait.

Wednesday, March 25, 1812
Covent Gardens, London

For a moment, all noise in the foyer ceased. The more curious among them, expecting something momentous, had chosen to stand near the door, and when a certain party arrived, their eyes immediately sought the newcomers, taking in the sight among whispers and gestures, wide eyes and narrow glares. Those further away, who either claimed less interest or had possessed lesser foresight, attempted to strain to see above or around those between them and the doors. And for the moment after their entrance, the new party was the absolute focus of everyone present.

It was nothing less than Elizabeth had expected, though the fact that such a large room with so many people had become so quiet at her entrance was a little unnerving. Elizabeth did her best to ignore them, settling on speaking quietly with her mother and Lady Catherine, and accepting Anthony's help in divesting herself of her outer garments.

By the time they had completed these simple tasks, the noise in the hall had started again and those standing within had renewed their previous conversations. But Elizabeth could still feel the eyes of the curious full upon her, and she found the attention disconcerting.

"Are you ready to do battle, my lady?"

The words were spoken with volumes of irony, and Elizabeth turned and looked at William, noting that he was watching her with interest.

"I think I might actually feel safer if I was wearing a breastplate," confided she.

William laughed and Elizabeth noted that several of those in close proximity seemed surprised at it. Could he possibly have such a reputation that people would think him incapable of laughing?

"I doubt the knives will be unsheathed tonight," replied he. "Those in attendance—specifically the ladies who will be your rivals—will wish to gain some insight into your weaknesses before they resort to such tactics."

"But I sense your inference that the knives *will* eventually leave their coverings."

"I think that is unavoidable. But I am convinced you possess more than enough skill to parry their attacks."

"Oh, Elizabeth, do not allow William to color your impression of society." Her mother, who had approached Elizabeth from the side, fixed William with a mock glare, which he returned with a show of innocence. "There *are* objectionable elements of society, but not everyone is as he describes. I suspect you will find many agreeable young ladies with whom you will become friendly."

"Of course, she will," replied William. Then he winked at her. "But always remember to wear your breastplate, for you never know when a close friend will become a hated enemy."

Then with a bow, William turned away and joined James and the earl, where they were speaking together. Elizabeth and her mother shared a look before they broke into laughter.

"There is some time before the performance is to start," said Lady Susan. "Let us introduce you to some friends."

What followed was another dizzying array of acquaintances, and Elizabeth thought she should have a book in which to write names, so she could remember them later. Not everyone was known to her mother by any means, but she met more people than she had thought possible in the crowds assembled for the theater that night. Most were quite friendly, and Elizabeth thought she would like to deepen the acquaintance with several.

She was also introduced to friends of James or Anthony, and she thought she detected a hint of interest lurking in more than one pair of eyes. Her brother stayed nearby to offer his support and assistance and even sent a few young men scurrying by the force of his glare alone. But even so, Elizabeth missed the solid presence of her cousin, as William stayed on the fringes of the group watching, but never interfering. For the first time, Elizabeth began to obtain some hint of his infamous disinclination for company.

Elizabeth felt fortunate when the first act of the play was about to start and the crowd began to make their way toward their seats, leaving her free to do likewise. They were to use her father and William's boxes that evening, which were near each other, and Elizabeth eventually settled into her father's box with Anthony, Lady Catherine, and her parents close by, while Georgiana, William, and James and Constance went to the other box. Althea and her husband were also in attendance, though they were situated in their own box with some of her husband's family attending them.

Elizabeth was relieved—the night had started out well. She only needed to endure the intermission.

Wednesday, March 25, 1812
Covent Gardens, London

Arriving late as was fashionable, the Bingley party made their way into the foyer of Covent Gardens to find that most of those in attendance were already making their way to their seats. The crowd seemed to be especially abuzz about something that evening, but Caroline could not make out anything that was being said. While she was helped out of her pelisse, she saw Charles speaking with an acquaintance, but though she cast about for an acquaintance to speak to, she could not see anyone she knew. Vexed, Caroline waited impatiently while he finished his conversation, and then returned to them.

"Let us find our seats," said he, taking Caroline's arm and guiding her toward the entrance to the theater.

"What is happening, Charles?" asked Caroline. "Is there something of special interest happening tonight?"

"There is some new heiress present tonight," rumbled Hurst.

"Who?" asked Caroline, challenging him with her eyes.

"I know not," replied her sister's husband. "I was only able to have a quick word with Travers. There was no time for explanations."

Caroline's gaze swung to Charles, but he did no more than shrug.

"Hurst knows more than I do myself. I was speaking about a different matter entirely."

Trust Charles to ignore what was important. A new heiress! Caroline could not fathom what it possibly meant, for new heiresses were usually introduced to society at the beginning of the season, not the middle of March. But there was nothing to be done, so she allowed herself to be led away by her brother, her sister and brother-in-law following behind. Then Caroline noticed to where Charles was escorting them.

"Charles!" hissed she. "What is the meaning of this? These doors lead to the gallery."

"I am aware of that Caroline," said Charles. "Unfortunately, it seems like tonight's performance was highly anticipated, and there were no boxes to be had."

"What of Mr. Darcy's?"

"It is being used tonight by Darcy himself, from what I understand," replied Charles. "And no, Caroline, I would not even endeavor to ask him if he will allow us to join him, for I know what his answer would be."

The glare which accompanied Charles's words was pointed, and Caroline felt a blush climbing her cheeks. The reminder of what had happened at Netherfield made her feel more than a little cross, but Caroline pushed her thoughts away as one would wave at an annoying gnat. She had done what she had done, and no amount of wishing could change the past. It seemed it had been her only chance to gain him for a husband, and she could only regret she had not been successful.

For seats in the gallery, they were actually quite good. Situated no more than ten rows back and next to the aisle, Caroline had a good view of the stage, and though the vantage seemed strange, there was nothing Caroline could not see. Of course, Caroline was not one who enjoyed the performance on stage with anything resembling pleasure; the theater was a place to gather with the best of society—nothing more.

One of the first things Caroline did was to raise her eyes up to the box she knew was Mr. Darcy's—it was one she knew intimately, given the number of times she had been inside. The angle was such that it was difficult to see inside to any great degree, but Caroline was certain she could see Mr. Darcy's head of wavy hair seated within, with Georgiana situated at his side. There were others in the box, but she could not quite make out who they were.

The important point, to Caroline's mind, was the absence of Miss Elizabeth Bennet in Mr. Darcy's box. Or at least Caroline could not make out any hint of the woman.

At least he has not brought his doxy to the theater, thought she with a hint of satisfaction. Given the manner in which the woman had seemed at home in his house with his sister, Caroline would not have been surprised if she had been present.

While the final few stragglers found their seats, Caroline looked absently at the boxes situated around the gallery below. There were many prominent personages in attendance tonight, including several dukes, and many earls. There even appeared to be several people in the Fitzwilliam box, only a few boxes away from Mr. Darcy's on the same level. Caroline could see Lady Susan Fitzwilliam, seated beside her husband, Lord Matlock, and she noted as the woman turned to her husband and said something to him, prompting a smile and a comment in return.

Caroline had dreamed of making the Fitzwilliams' acquaintance, and the sight of them made the loss of Mr. Darcy all that much more unbearable. Then Caroline's eyes followed Lady Matlock when the lady leaned to the side and made some comment to the woman in the seat next to her.

At that moment Caroline's heart almost stopped in her breast. The woman at Lady Matlock's side, with whom she had just spoken so familiarly, was none other than Miss Eliza Bennet! Caroline's eyes narrowed, watching as the little chit laughed and said something in return.

What was happening here? Could Charles have been correct? The way they were acting together suggested a familiarity which Caroline had always dreamed of between herself and the lady. How had such a dowdy country miss managed such a feat?

"Do you believe me now, Caroline?"

Distracted from her thoughts, Caroline turned back to her brother. Charles was watching her intently, and then—quite deliberately—his gaze rose to the box above them. Caroline's eyes followed his, and she saw that Lord Matlock had leaned across his wife to Miss Eliza and said something to her. The tinkling sound of Miss Bennet's laughter reached Caroline's ears below, and it seemed like the noise in the theater suddenly lessened in response.

"It appears Darcy was speaking the truth, does it not?"

"How could she possibly be so familiar with them?" asked Caroline.

"It must be something momentous, do you not agree?" Charles's voice pulled Caroline's attention back to him. "I am as much at sea as you are, Caroline. The last I knew of Miss Bennet she was still in Hertfordshire. This development is as confusing to me as it is to you."

Bile rose in the back of Caroline's throat. "It seems as if they have known each other for some time. Might Miss Bennet have been keeping her connections secret? But why would she? And why is the rest of the family not present?"

"I cannot answer your questions. But I hope you now understand it is best to avoid provoking the Fitzwilliams' displeasure with respect to Miss Bennet."

"Of course," replied Caroline.

In truth, she did not know what to think. There was something at play here, something of which Caroline had no knowledge. But she was suddenly glad she had not begun to spread the rumors she meant to spread.

But whatever was happening, Caroline was determined not to remain in the dark. She meant to understand it. Perhaps she would obtain clarity during the intermission.

The curtain soon went up and the lights dimmed, but when the actors appeared on the stage, Caroline could spare no more than cursory attention for them. She spent most of the first act with her eyes on the Fitzwilliam box as surreptitiously as she was able to manage. Miss Elizabeth Bennet, she noted, seemed to have more interest in the production than Caroline did herself, for her eyes rarely left the stage. But Caroline was witness to more than one instance where her interactions with Lord and Lady Matlock showed the same ease and familiarity as before. And the colonel was seated by her side, along with an older lady.

She had been accepted by these people. Caroline did not know how. Thus, whatever she attempted would need to be taken with great care.

Wednesday, March 25, 1812
Covent Gardens, London

"Has something caught your attention, Elizabeth?"

Elizabeth turned to her mother and smiled at her. "It seems like Miss Bingley *has* attended tonight."

"Where?" asked Lady Susan, leaning out over the edge of the box into the gallery below.

"Right along the aisle about ten rows back," said Elizabeth, attempting to draw her mother's attention to the woman without pointing. "She is wearing a burnt umber dress with the lace fichu over the top. Next to her, with the shock of red hair, is her brother, Mr. Charles Bingley, while on his other side sit the Hursts, their sister and brother-in-law."

"She is dressed well, though I am not certain I approve of the color choice with her complexion." She turned back to Elizabeth. "She is a handsome woman, and with what I have heard of her dowry, I cannot imagine she would find it impossible to make a good match. Of course, she may be required to lower her sights a little."

Elizabeth rolled her eyes. "That seems unlikely. She is as proud as anyone I have ever met."

"Then I suspect she shall be disappointed." Her mother leaned in close and said in a quiet voice. "Of course, she does not hold a candle to you, my dear. I can quite confidently state that you outshine every other young lady here."

Nervous laughter erupted from Elizabeth's breast. "That is only because you see me with the eyes of a mother."

"Perhaps that is so. But I am also acknowledged as a woman of discerning taste."

"You should listen to her, Elizabeth," said her father, leaning close to them to inject his opinion. "Never let it be said that my daughter is not the belle of the ball."

Elizabeth could not help but laugh at the absurdity of it all. "I beg you, do not flatter me so excessively! I am certain I shall turn into that which I detest if you do!"

"There is no need to fear of that, my dear," replied her mother. "But the play is about to start, so we should return our attention to the stage, lest we offend our neighbors."

A quick glance around revealed less interest in the play than Elizabeth might have thought, and an inordinate amount of attention on her father's box. "If only it were so," murmured she.

"Do not let it affect you, Elizabeth. It will not be long before they will become accustomed to your return."

"I do not think that will lessen the scrutiny."

"No, I dare say it will not. But then again, you will become accustomed to it yourself."

The glare Elizabeth shot at her mother was ineffectual, for the woman was laughing at her. Lady Susan reached over and grasped Elizabeth's hand and held it to her side, a wonderful physical gesture displaying the happiness she felt at Elizabeth's return. Elizabeth continued to hold her mother's hand as the curtain rose before she lost herself in the events which unfolded before her eyes.

Wednesday, March 25, 1812
Covent Gardens, London

"What?" demanded Caroline, shocked at the intelligence she had just received from her friend.

"Lady Elizabeth Fitzwilliam, or so I have heard," replied Rachel Parker, a longstanding friend. "The news has been making its way through the city like wildfire. I am told there will be an announcement in tomorrow's newspapers."

"But how can that be?" asked Caroline, thinking furiously. "I knew her in Hertfordshire, for her father owned a small estate not far from the one my brother was leasing. She is one of five daughters. How can she now be connected to the Earl of Matlock?"

"I do not know the entire story," replied Rachel, speaking slowly as if attempting to remember. "It is said that she did not know who she was until recently when the Fitzwilliam family discovered her."

"And what is the proof?" asked Caroline.

Rachel shot her a hard glance. Caroline was forced to concede that it had been more than a little petulant. But she was caught off guard by this new intelligence and had not the means to make any sense of it.

"You well know that no proof is required," scolded Rachel. "If the earl claims her as his daughter, then his daughter she is, and only the Prince Regent himself can gainsay him." Rachel's gaze softened. "However, though I am not privy to the details, it is my understanding that the evidence is compelling and was confirmed by Lady Matlock herself. Whatever it is, it matched what they knew of their daughter, who disappeared eighteen years ago."

"I was not even aware they had lost a daughter."

"It is not much spoken of," replied Rachel. "But I hear it was quite well known when it happened. I hope to receive an introduction to her, though I am certain it will not be tonight. She is quite stunning in that dress; do you not think? And the resemblance to the countess is quite unmistakable."

Though she had no wish to do so, Caroline was forced to agree that there was some slight resemblance between them. Rachel continued to prattle away as Caroline thought of the situation. She was Caroline's most highly placed friend, daughter, as she was, to a gentleman of means, and a cousin—albeit distantly—to an earl. Many times Caroline had lamented that she was not a relation of the Earl of Matlock, for Caroline might have been able to secure an introduction to Mr. Darcy's aunt and uncle if she had been.

Not that Mr. Darcy had ever seen fit to introduce her. Caroline suppressed a scowl. In hindsight, it was clear that the man had never truly esteemed her as much as she had always thought. If it had been Rachel, her closest friend from their school days, she would have secured the introduction. But Mr. Darcy's reserve, to which she had always attributed his hesitance, was now revealed as indifference, much though Caroline did not wish to acknowledge it.

"Perhaps you could secure an introduction for me."

Rachel's statement brought Caroline's attention back to her friend, but there was little she could say that brought her pleasure.

"I do not truly know her well, and it has been some months since I was in Hertfordshire. I do not think a slight acquaintance with the daughter of a minor country squire translates to an acquaintance of the daughter of an earl."

"I suppose not, though it *is* unfortunate."

Caroline could only agree with her.

"Then perhaps *I* shall secure an introduction for *you*." Rachel laughed. "Assuming I can procure one for myself, of course. Regardless, I should find my mother."

"Thank you for this intelligence, Rachel."

"You are welcome. I shall visit you soon, so we can speak of this matter further."

Then Rachel excused herself, leaving Caroline alone with her thoughts. A glance about revealed that her brother was standing not far away, speaking with an acquaintance, while the Hursts stood close to him, speaking to each other. It did not escape Caroline's attention that they were both watching her, likely attempting to ensure she did not do something to ruin their standing in society.

A hot wave of disappointment flowed through Caroline's veins. If she had only known the true identity of the woman in Hertfordshire, she might be able to claim a member of the nobility as a close acquaintance! How could this have come about? It was all ruined, from her expectations concerning Mr. Darcy, her lost opportunity with Miss Bennet, the possibility of moving ever higher in society. All gone. And Caroline felt the loss hit her right where it hurt the most—her vanity.

The loss of what might have been excellent prospects caused Caroline to hang her head. At least she thought there would be no one who would know the details of the missed opportunity. Her behavior toward Miss Bennet would affect her reputation if it were known. One did not insult a member of a family so highly placed in society and emerge unscathed.

Unless . . . Unless the woman had informed others of it in revenge for how she had been treated. Caroline grimaced—it was what she herself might have done. Would Miss Bennet have acted any differently?

The very notion gave Caroline the sensation that everyone in the foyer was watching her, condemnation in their eyes. Unable to help herself, she glanced around—

And came face to face with Miss Elizabeth Bennet. Caroline held back a gasp at the sight, for the woman was walking toward her, though she did not appear to be aware of Caroline's presence. The instant Miss Bennet saw her, she came to an abrupt halt, her eyes widening in surprise.

It was with a critical gaze that Caroline inspected Miss Bennet. She had always considered Miss Bennet to be a woman of overly simple tastes, and that was reflected in the styles of dress she wore, though the availability of funds for the purchase of more fashionable clothes was certainly an inhibiting factor. But there was nothing simple about the dress she was wearing that day, though Caroline might have commissioned something even more stunning, had she had the opportunity to do so. It was finely made, and obviously of beautiful material, likely created by one of the premiere modistes in London.

And Miss Bennet wore it well. Caroline was loath to confess it, loath to assign anything good to this woman. But there was no mistaking it, and Caroline could not think anything else and say that she was in any way truthful. Miss Bennet's stature was somehow subtly changed as well. She had always carried herself with confidence, little though Caroline had thought her confidence was deserved. Now, however, she looked like she belonged in the dress, belonged with the exalted company she now kept. It was difficult, but Caroline had to confess that the other woman was looking as elegant as Caroline had ever seen her, and she was forced to accept that what she had been told was the truth.

"Miss Bingley," said Miss Bennet at that moment. "How do you do?"

Startled by the sound of the other woman's voice, many thoughts rolled through her mind simultaneously. She thought to push this woman away, to accuse her of using some stratagem to obtain her current position. She thought to remind her of her common origins, to bring to her remembrance the behavior of the youngest Bennets. The insults were on the tip of her tongue, needing only Caroline's will to unleash them, to bring the upstart to her knees and humble her like she had never been humbled before.

But none of them issued forth from her mouth. At that moment, the flash of insight hit her, and she knew instinctively what would happen should she yield to that temptation. A life away from London, separate from that for which she had wished all her life. Now more than ever, Caroline understood that one did not insult an earl's daughter and escape unscathed. Lady Matlock obviously considered this woman to be her daughter. She had the power to ruin Caroline forever if she paid anything less than the utmost deference.

"Mi—" Caroline swallowed and amended her words. "Lady Elizabeth. I do very well, thank you. Might you allow me to offer my congratulations for reuniting with your family?"

It was clear that Caroline had surprised her, but Lady Elizabeth quickly masked her surprise and smiled. "Thank you, Miss Bingley. You may not credit it, but I had no notion until recently that I was not Miss Elizabeth Bennet. This has all been so sudden."

"I can imagine," said Caroline. The woman was even more gracious than Caroline could have been in her place. Now she wished for nothing more than to be out of her presence, preferably away from Covent Gardens.

But Caroline Bingley would not be intimidated in such a way. She would not run with her tail between her legs.

"If you will excuse me, Lady Elizabeth, I believe I should return to my family." Caroline curtseyed and turned away.

"Of course," she heard the other woman say. "Please give my regards to your brother."

And then she was gone. Her mind full of what had just happened, Caroline walked toward her brother. But she had not gone five steps before Charles hurried to her and hissed:

"What did you say to Lady Elizabeth, Caroline?"

Caroline looked up at her brother and noted the wildness in his eyes. Charles clearly expected the worst.

"I only congratulated her on finding her family." Caroline paused, and a nervous laugh bubbled up from her midsection. It sounded manic to Caroline's own ears. "She told me that she was shocked herself, for it has all come on so suddenly."

When Caroline looked up again and saw her brother, she could read his suspicion and confusion. In truth, Caroline was not certain she believed herself. Her feelings upon entering the theater were so different now from what they had been before. The events of the past few minutes were nothing like she had expected when she had arrived.

"Nothing . . . untoward occurred?"

A little of the old Caroline returned, and she shook her head, even as her eyes sought out her former rival. "Does it appear to you like she is disturbed by anything untoward?"

Charles glanced in the direction Caroline had, and he noted that Lady Elizabeth was standing beside Mr. Darcy, speaking and laughing with him, as if she had not a care in the world. It was not the visage of a woman who had just had an objectionable encounter. Idly, Caroline wondered if their laughter was at her expense. Then she decided it did not signify.

"Come, Charles," said Caroline, feeling unaccountably weary. "I wish to return to my seat."

"Of course," said Charles.

He turned and allowed her to take his arm, guiding her back into the theater, the Hursts following close behind. Caroline walked with her head held high. She had acquitted herself well, she decided. Her future had been balanced upon the razor's edge, and she had emerged unscathed. But it had been close. So very close.

Wednesday, March 25, 1812
Covent Gardens, London

"Elizabeth, was that Miss Bingley with whom I saw you speaking?"

"It was, Mother," said Elizabeth, her eyes meeting Lady Susan's worried gaze.

"By Elizabeth's account, their exchange was civil," said William by her side. "To own the truth, I am shocked. I could not have imagined that my counsel to Bingley would work such a change. I did not think he had it in him to check her."

A glance back at the woman revealed that she had returned to the company of Mr. Bingley and the Hursts and was now making her way back into the theater. If Elizabeth was honest with herself, she had been expecting at least something in the way of vitriol, and for a moment she had thought Miss Bingley was on the verge of unleashing it.

But then something had changed as if she had suddenly recognized the truth of Elizabeth's parentage. Or perhaps it was nothing more than a recognition of the social power which could be brought to bear against her. Regardless, whatever she had thought to say had gone unsaid. With all that had happened between William and Miss Bingley, Elizabeth doubted the woman would ever be anything more than a persona non grata to the Fitzwilliam clan. But Elizabeth was glad that she had, at least, been able to speak without the venom which Elizabeth knew the woman had in her power to unleash.

"Then let us return to our seats," said her mother, starting Elizabeth from her thoughts. "I believe the second act is about to start."

With one final look at the retreating form of Miss Bingley, Elizabeth allowed herself to be led away.

Chapter XX

Thursday, March 26, 1812
Undisclosed Location

"So, she attended the theater."

Sitting back in the chair in his study, the hunter took a long pull of his cigar and blew the smoke up into the air, watching as it eddied and swirled in the currents, tiny motes of burnt tobacco shining in the light of the sun flowing in through the windows. The situation with the newly returned Lady Elizabeth Fitzwilliam had vexed him since he had learned of it, such that it had taken him most of a day to control his temper and consider the matter rationally. He had lost a substantial amount of money that day, which had made his temper worse. The wench he had used later had paid the price for his ill temper.

But now he was calm and logical, and the hunter knew there were several ways he could deal with this interloper. His distant cousin would no doubt be watching the girl closely, given what had happened to her in the past. Once a length of time passed, they would grow complacent, which would allow him to strike. He did not know what went wrong last time, but *this* time he would ensure there were no mistakes.

Or perhaps he could simply marry the chit. That angle had a certain amount of appeal, he was forced to own, as he raised the cigar to his lips again. The hunter had never married and, as such, had fathered no children, meaning he had no heir. That fact did not mean much to him, but he supposed it would be desirable to leave his possessions to an heir, rather than some distant relation. He did not even know who would be in line to inherit. The most appealing part of that option was the thought that he would have her under his control and could administer retribution for intruding on his designs.

Then again, having a wife would be such a bother, and he did not think a child would be any better. Perhaps there was a way to discredit her? If there was anything objectionable in her past, perhaps his cousin would see the need of casting her off again. He might even be able to prove that she was not his daughter.

He did not think it likely, but it *was* possible. This whole situation was a bother, and he wished he did not have to deal with it.

If wishes were horses, beggars would ride.

It was trite but so very true. Thus, the situation demanded action.

With a pull of the bell, he summoned his butler and instructed that his man be sent to him. When he arrived, his man—Cooper—was revealed to be a heavyset, solid man of about thirty, though his stature was that of muscle and sinew.

"I need you to find out everything you can about Lady Elizabeth Fitzwilliam," said the hunter without preamble. He never did like to waste words.

"The daughter of an earl will be difficult to approach," replied his man.

The hunter shook his head. "You do not need to approach her. I want to know of her past, specifically where she lived before she was recognized by my cousin, anything of her background which might be useful, and anything of her character which I may be able to use against her."

Cooper sat back in thought for a moment. "It is said she was raised on an estate in Hertfordshire."

"Then you may start there." The hunter looked at his man pointedly. "There is no need to rush. Take care and do not be caught."

"I understand," said Cooper.

Dismissed, his man left the room, leaving him to his thoughts and his cigar. Having a man who was loyal and ruthless was a boon. He would find out what was needed, and then he would be able to act against the so-called Lady Elizabeth. This time, there would be no mistakes.

Thursday, March 26, 1812
Darcy House, London

As Bingley entered his study, Darcy studied him, thinking he had been given the perfect opportunity to question him on certain circumstances of his visit in Hertfordshire. Normally, Darcy would not even think to raise such a subject. Bingley was his own man with his own fortune, well able to direct his own life, his lack of drive and shrewish sister notwithstanding. But Elizabeth had asked him to do so. Darcy was amused to note that she had the entire family wrapped around her little finger. There was nothing any of them would not do for her, Darcy no less than the rest. So here he was.

"You know of my adoptive family, of course." They had been speaking the previous evening during the second intermission when the subject of Bingley and his sister had been raised.

Darcy had nodded. "I met Mr. Bennet, of course, and his wife, albeit briefly."

"I am more concerned about Mr. Bingley and his actions toward Jane. I . . ." Elizabeth paused, exerting control over her emotions if Darcy was not mistaken. "I am concerned for her, William. I received a letter from her yesterday. She attempts to convey the same measure of cheer as always, but I am certain she still pines after Mr. Bingley."

Darcy was certain he could see what Elizabeth wished from him. "To clarify, you wish me to ask Bingley about his connection with her, but you are not asking me to urge him to return. Is that correct?"

"Yes." Elizabeth's manner was filled with determination. "It will do neither of them any good if Mr. Bingley returns to Hertfordshire unwillingly. He may direct his own affairs. I simply wish to inform Jane as to the state of his intentions, for she still hopes for his return. If he does not intend it, I believe it will assist Jane in overcoming the feelings she harbors for him."

"I have already informed her of Miss Bingley and my encounters with her, though not what happened tonight, of course." A wry smile settled over Elizabeth's countenance. "Jane has difficulty believing in the deceit of anyone, but I could not allow her to persist in the impression that Miss Bingley was her friend. Even after informing her, I have doubts about whether she truly believes me."

"Then if the opportunity presents itself, I will ask Bingley. But I will not seek him out for such a purpose."

"That is all I ask."

Thus, Darcy could not consider Bingley's visit the very next day to be anything less than providential. He did not anticipate inquiring into the minute details of Bingley's life, but he had promised, and therefore he would act. Darcy invited his friend, who appeared quite subdued, to sit and share tea with him.

"I apologize for imposing upon you, my friend," said Bingley, his tone clearly stating that he was not certain he could still claim that title. "But I wished to speak with you about what happened last night at the theater. You are aware that your cousin and my sister exchanged words—are you not?"

"I am," replied Darcy.

"Lady Elizabeth is not . . . upset in any way by anything my sister said. Is she?"

Darcy had seen Bingley unsure of himself more times than he could count, but even so, he had rarely seen Bingley so reticent.

"My understanding is that their exchange was quite civil. Elizabeth was not in any way distressed."

Relief bled through Bingley, and he slumped in his chair. "Thank you for that confirmation. Caroline's account was similar, but I . . . Well, there have been times in the past when she twisted the truth. I could tell she was not happy when we left the house last night and thought she might be plotting something, but when she saw . . ."

"She saw Elizabeth with my aunt, perhaps?" prompted Darcy when Bingley trailed off.

"We both did before the curtain rose," replied Bingley. "Their manner together was so familiar that I believe it was that, in part, which convinced her. She was quite forceful in her opinion before we departed yesterday evening that I had somehow mistaken what you told me."

That was unsurprising to Darcy. "It seems like she came to the correct conclusion."

"And I am grateful she did. She seems resigned now. I do not think you will have any more difficulty with her."

"Then I thank you, Bingley. I did not wish your sister to come between us, but I hope you can understand that her actions have made any rapprochement between her and myself unlikely."

"Yes, I do understand." Bingley paused, again seeming distinctly uncertain of himself. "I hope that *our* friendship will not be affected as a result."

Darcy took a moment to consider the matter. It was true that there were certain things about Bingley which frustrated him. The man was lacking a backbone, though his actions concerning his sister were a positive sign. He was also cavalier in his attentions to the fairer sex and possessed little drive to fulfill his father's desire and settle down attending to an estate. He seemed content to drift through his life being civil and attentive and paying attention to the next pretty face while living on the four percents his father had left to him.

But then again, there was something in *everyone*, even those to whom Darcy was closest, which was objectionable. There were parts of Darcy's character which were not laudable, and one of the reasons he had always enjoyed Bingley's society so much was how Bingley affected his own demeanor. He was a loyal friend who could always be counted on to lighten the mood. No, Darcy had no desire to lose Bingley's society.

"I would be happy to keep your friendship, Bingley," replied Darcy. Though he had only taken an instant to consider his response, Bingley still appeared as if a great weight had been removed from his shoulders. He had obviously doubted Darcy's answer, and Darcy could understand his trepidation. They had never had any major disagreements before; this was the first real test of their friendship.

"Thank you, my friend. I am happy to hear it."

"There is something about which I have been charged to ask you," said Darcy, deciding that enough had been said about Miss Bingley.

"Of course," replied Bingley with his typical grin. "How may I help you?"

"My cousin, Lady Elizabeth, is, of course, known to you." Bingley cheerfully agreed that it was so. "She has asked me about your intentions toward one Miss Jane Bennet." The light of Bingley's smile dimmed. "I understand you paid her some attention this past autumn and that an expectation arose of an eventual announcement between you?"

Bingley's smile was gone, replaced with a frown. "The people of Meryton thought I intended to propose to her?"

"You must remember Meryton is a small town," replied Darcy. "There are likely few eligible men in residence, and when one arrives, conclusions are drawn with little provocation. Of more concern, however, is that Miss Bennet became attached to you and has wished for your return."

The surprise with which Bingley reacted to that bit of news could not be feigned. Darcy had known that his friend was not callous, but the confirmation was welcome nonetheless.

"I will own I had considered deepening our acquaintance. But when I returned to London, Caroline and Louisa returned after me, and they raised some valid objections to the match. We were only in Hertfordshire for two months—I had not thought enough time had passed for her to become attached to me."

It was not a surprise to hear Bingley say that his sisters had talked him out of returning to Hertfordshire. It was not the sort of place where they would be happy, and in their defense, it was not the sort of match they would hope for their brother. Though Darcy had never met the girl, he had every confidence in Elizabeth's opinion, and if she said Jane Bennet was an estimable girl, he had no choice but to assume she was. But Bingley did not sound like *he* had become attached to the girl, at least nothing more than his usual infatuation. Perhaps his sisters were correct in this instance.

"Does Lady Elizabeth wish me to return to Hertfordshire and pay my addresses?" asked Bingley. The consternation in his tone told Darcy that Bingley had no business paying any further attention to the girl.

"Of course not, Bingley." Again, a sense of relief fell over his friend. "She merely wished to be of use to her adoptive sister, to inform her if she was holding onto a vain hope."

"I *am* sorry for causing distress to Miss Bennet," replied Bingley slowly. "I never meant it that way. In reality, Darcy, she is an angel—one of the best women I have ever met. But there are clear . . . drawbacks in any offer for her, which may not be overcome easily."

"Do not concern yourself with offending me, Bingley," said Darcy, putting his hand up to forestall a lengthy apology. "I am aware of the Bennets' situation, and I know something of the family. Mrs. Bennet, from what little I have seen of her, would be a detriment to any sort of alliance, and the younger girls are not much better. I also understand that she must not have much in the way of dowry and her connections are almost nonexistent."

At this last statement, Bingley perked up a little. "Do you know if Lady Elizabeth means to keep up the connection? Though they are not truly related, that would go at least some way in making Miss Bennet more acceptable."

"I am not privy to Lady Elizabeth's feelings, though I suspect she will maintain her connection with Miss Bennet." Darcy paused, looking at his friend, wondering if he should further advise him. In the end, he felt he had no choice. "I do not think this should be a factor in determining whether you will pursue Miss Bennet, Bingley. The other drawbacks still exist and will not be mitigated. I would not advise you to return to Meryton for anything other than unalloyed inclination."

"You are correct, of course," replied Bingley. "She is a wonderful woman, it is true. But I do not believe I should pursue her. I do feel for her, though. It was certainly not my intention to raise any expectations or dash any hopes."

"I know, Bingley," replied Darcy, suppressing a sigh. "Perhaps in the future, it would be best to practice circumspection."

Bingley nodded. "I agree."

They spent some few more minutes speaking before Bingley left after they had agreed to meet again at their club later in the week. Whether his friend would truly act on his decision to exercise more care in his attention to young ladies, Darcy could not say. But Bingley was his own man. He could act as he chose.

Thursday, March 26, 1812
Fitzwilliam House, London

"And that is the extent to which I will meddle in this affair."

Elizabeth digested what William had informed her of Mr. Bingley, and she directed a smile at her cousin. "Thank you, William. I would not wish you to direct your friend."

"In the end, I believe this is for the best," said Lady Catherine. The lady had listened carefully as William had detailed his encounter with Mr. Bingley, and she now spoke her opinion in a no-nonsense tone. "This Jane Bennet of whom you speak sounds like an estimable girl. You would not wish her to settle in marriage to a man who seems to lack fortitude. His sister would rule them and make their lives miserable."

Though William appeared to take a little umbrage at Lady Catherine's blunt assessment, Elizabeth could not find it in her to disagree. She had suspected this would be the result of her request, and the fact that the sisters had persuaded Mr. Bingley against Jane suggested an attachment which was superficial at best. Jane was such a good-hearted and loving soul — she would be devastated if she were to marry a man who was not devoted to her.

"I agree, and I thank you, William, for speaking with your friend." Elizabeth smiled at him. "I am also happy that your friendship with Mr. Bingley has not ended. I still think highly of him, despite what has happened with respect to Jane."

Lady Catherine released a not so subtle huff, but then again, with her rigid ideas of the classes, she could hardly be expected to agree with William's friendship with a man who was, after all, descended from a line of tradesmen. Darcy, however, smiled at Elizabeth.

"I am grateful too. Bingley is a good man. He has flaws, the same as anyone else, but his presence often lightens my mood."

"Then you will write to Miss Bennet with this information?" asked Elizabeth's mother.

"Yes, I will do so this morning," replied Elizabeth. She sighed. "It will be hard, for I know what I must tell her will cause her much heartache. But it must be done."

"It is why you asked William to speak with Mr. Bingley," said Lady Susan. "For what it is worth, I believe you are doing right by your adoptive sister. If Miss Bennet is suffering from Mr. Bingley's defection, it is a kindness to inform her of the truth." She paused for a moment, and then fixed her attention back on Elizabeth. "If you like, perhaps when the situation has settled, we might have Miss Bennet stay with us for a time."

"I would like that very much," replied Elizabeth.

"*If* she can comport herself in a way that upholds the honor of the family," said Lady Catherine. Elizabeth frowned, but Lady Catherine was not about to yield. "Elizabeth, you have conducted yourself in a manner which has exceeded my expectations. If everything you have informed us of is true, then this Miss Bennet will have no trouble behaving properly.

"But in London, as I am sure you already know, it is imperative for our reputation as a family that anyone we sponsor is a credit to us."

"We may discuss it later," said Lady Susan, shooting a glance at her sister.

"Of course," replied Elizabeth. There was no reason to argue the point at present, for Elizabeth knew her mother would not consider inviting Jane until Elizabeth had been established in society. It was possible Jane's introduction to a much better level of society would result in her finding someone who was willing to overlook her lack of dowry and make her an offer. It was the least Elizabeth thought she could do for a sweet young woman who had been her salvation through many years in her adoptive family's home.

"Now, I would like to turn the conversation to our upcoming ball to be held in your honor," said Lady Susan.

"Yes, Mother," said Elizabeth. She had little desire to be so occupied that morning, but she supposed it was important for her ultimate acceptance. It would also be an opportunity for her to learn what was necessary to host a ball, for Elizabeth expected she would be required to do so at some point.

"Then that would be my cue to leave," said William in an amused tone.

"Oh?" asked Elizabeth, arching an eyebrow at him. "The prospect of planning a ball does not appeal to you?"

William returned her grin. "Not even as much as the thought of *attending* one."

The ladies laughed at William's words, Lady Susan shaking her head and saying: "You can be quite predictable, William. Society is not nearly as bad as you seem to think."

"Parts of it are not," agreed William affably. "But other parts are, indeed, much worse. I will be quite happy to attend the ball, but I have no desire to assist in planning one.

"However," continued he, turning to Elizabeth and smiling at her, "I would like to take this opportunity to request your supper set the night of the ball."

Elizabeth was nonplused. "Why the *supper* set, William? Why not the first, if you are so interested in tweaking my brothers' noses?"

The smile the William sported transformed into a positively smug grin. "Because I know the earl will insist upon your first dance, and I have no desire to trespass upon his right as your father."

"But Anthony and James will both wish for Elizabeth's supper dance," observed Lady Susan.

"I know," replied William. "Though I would not challenge the earl's right to claim the first dance with his daughter, I have no qualms about stepping on my cousins' toes."

Once again, the ladies laughed, though this time their amusement was punctuated by Lady Catherine's loudly stated: "Oh, Darcy!" Furthermore, Elizabeth noted a queer look on her countenance as she glared at the man, but William only returned their grins with one of his own.

"I should have known," said Lady Susan. "Your rivalry with Anthony I have long known of, but I thought you had given it up with James."

"That is only because I do not see James as much," said William with a shrug. "I am certain they will both badger me to give up my dance, but now that I have secured it, I shall not be induced to part with it."

"You forget that I have yet made no answer," said Elizabeth. "And behavior such as this is not likely to induce me to be agreeable."

Elizabeth's declaration brought on such a look of feigned dejection that she could do nothing but laugh and immediately agree to accede to his request. No sooner had she done so than William's smugness made a return.

"I thank you, Elizabeth," said he. "But I believe it is time that I departed."

William rose to leave, but before he could move, his departure was forestalled by the sound of voices on the other side of the door, which soon opened, allowing several people to enter. Among their number were James and Constance, as well as Anthony, and an older man whom Elizabeth had never met. The behaviors of those of her immediate family informed her that something was amiss, for Anthony was regarding the newcomer with unconcealed distaste, while Constance was watching him warily. James was engaged in conversation with the man, but her eldest brother's visage was carefully blank, leading Elizabeth to believe he enjoyed this man's presence no more than his wife or brother.

"Mother," said Anthony as they proceeded into the room. "We happened across Standish when he arrived to call on us."

Both Lady Catherine and Lady Susan rose with Elizabeth following their lead. But Elizabeth happened to glance at William, and she noted that he was watching this man—Standish—with as little warmth as any of his relations. For that matter, neither her mother nor her aunt appeared happy to see him.

"Lady Susan," said the man with a bow. "Lady Catherine, Mr. Darcy. I am fortunate to have found you at home today." His eyes turned on Elizabeth, and she was startled to see the calculation with which he regarded her. "I heard of your daughter's return and determined that I should come and pay my respects if you would do the honors."

"Of course," replied Lady Susan, her tone giving no hint as to her thoughts. "Elizabeth, this is my distant cousin, Mr. Victor Standish. Mr. Standish, my newly recovered daughter, Lady Elizabeth Fitzwilliam."

Mr. Standish bowed to Elizabeth's curtsey, and when he rose, Elizabeth attempted to take his measure. He was not a tall man, but he was not lacking in height either, standing perhaps a hand shorter than Anthony, who was a large man. He was perhaps fifty years of age or a little less, his hair dark speckled gray, and his face, while it was generally smooth, was lined on his forehead and under his eyes. He was slender, though not athletic, except for a pronounced paunch which his clothes did little to cover. In short, Elizabeth thought there was little remarkable about his appearance. Appearances could be deceiving, however, and her family's reaction to the man taught her that care would need to be taken in his company.

"I am happy to make your acquaintance. In fact, I am a little surprised that I was not invited to the family dinner I understand took place." His eyes moved to Lady Susan, a question inherent in them.

"You have my apologies, Mr. Standish, but the dinner was reserved for only very close relations. Ours is more distant."

"And yet the Duke of Cheshire was in attendance."

"You may have forgotten, sir," said Constance, "but the duke is my father."

"Ah, yes, of course," replied Standish, though Elizabeth thought he was not at all appeased. "That explains it, then." He paused, and a winsome smile appeared on his countenance. "I did not come to protest that exclusion, for I quite understand. But I wished to meet the daughter long sundered."

"And now you have," said Anthony. His tone was not at all friendly.

"Yes, indeed."

It was clear that most of those in the room wished Mr. Standish gone, but equally evident he had no desire to depart. Lady Susan, showing her gentility, invited him to sit, but when she offered to send for refreshments, he declined.

"In fact, I will not be afforded the opportunity to stay long, for I have another appointment. I hope there will be other occasions to more fully come known to your daughter. The ball you are planning, for example? I hear many invitations have already been dispatched. Dare I hope that I have been included?"

"You have," said Lady Susan. "The invitations were all delivered yesterday. Your butler has likely already placed it on your desk."

"Excellent!" Then for the first time since he had arrived, Mr. Standish turned the full brunt of his attention on Elizabeth, and she was made to feel a little disquiet by it. "Your recovery is a matter of interest to society. I can only assume some extraordinary circumstances have led to it."

"Nothing more than the recognition of the possibility and then a confirmation based on certain facts known to the earl and countess," replied Mr. Darcy.

Mr. Standish arched an eyebrow at William. "From your words, might I be given to understand that you were instrumental in this event?"

"I did have some small part in it, sir," replied William.

It seemed that Mr. Standish was not insensible to the fact that William did not wish to discuss it, and as the rest of her family were no more eager, he allowed the topic to rest. They spent several minutes speaking, the conversation mostly consisting of Mr. Standish inquiring after her opinions and how she was settling into her new life.

At length, however, he declared his need to depart and quit the room. It was telling that no one in the family—not even Anthony, who had watched him with suspicion the entire time he had been there—escorted him from the house. When the door closed behind him, silence reigned for a few moments. Elizabeth watched her family, curious as to the hostility in the air, wondering if any would explain it.

Finally, her mother sighed and turned to Elizabeth, her expression faintly apologetic. "What did you think of your distant cousin, Elizabeth?"

"I hardly know what to think," replied she. "It was obvious the moment he entered the room that he is held in little esteem."

"That would be an understatement," muttered Anthony.

"Standish has a certain . . . reputation, Elizabeth." William, who had spoken, grimaced and shook his head. "Many of his vices are not fit for a lady's ears. He is not what any of us would call a good man."

"Nonsense," said Lady Catherine. "You cannot tell Elizabeth that the man is depraved and not explain the circumstances to her. Elizabeth is an intelligent, rational girl. I cannot imagine she is ignorant about the ways of the world."

Lady Catherine turned to Elizabeth, who was grateful to her aunt for speaking up. "Standish has quite a number of disgusting habits. He games and gambles at all hours of the day and night, is a known womanizer, and has little respect for anyone or anything. The most important thing in his life is his vices. It is best to stay clear of him, Elizabeth."

"We attempt to avoid speaking of him," said Lady Susan. "And he is usually content to hold us at arms' length." Her mother's smile lightened Elizabeth's mood. "You must be aware that every family has at least one objectionable member. Standish is ours, though he is not truly a close relation."

"I am surprised he means to attend the ball," said Anthony. "Usually he is content to avoid the events of higher society in favor of his gaming hells."

"That is not precisely fair," interjected James. "Standish *does* attend events at times."

"I think he does it to ensure we do not forget about him," added William.

"Regardless," said Lady Susan, "he is a disagreeable subject. I prefer not to speak of him. We should return to the topic at hand."

"I believe it is time to depart," said William. As he rose, he turned to his cousins, and Elizabeth could easily make out his mouthed "Ball preparations" as he caught their eyes. When they understood the significance, James and Anthony were eager themselves to be absent from the room, much to Elizabeth's amusement and that of the other ladies.

The rest of the afternoon was spent in conversation and planning. Elizabeth found herself most agreeably engaged the entire time.

CHAPTER XXI

Friday, March 27, 1812
Fitzwilliam House, London

As the date of the ball drew closer, Elizabeth found that William's prediction of how Anthony and James would react to his request for the supper dance to be absolutely correct. Elizabeth had seen the cousins at odds but rarely, and though it was obvious they were close to each other, she attributed it to the newness of her recovery. In those days, it soon became clear that though they were great friends and confidants, it did not stop them from vying for supremacy over each other.

"I suppose I must take this opportunity to solicit a dance for the ball, Elizabeth," said Anthony. "If I do not, I am certain my brother will swoop in and secure it for himself. I would like the supper dance if you please."

It was the day after William had already asked her, and Anthony's smug glance at his brother suggested he thought himself quite clever for thinking of it first. William, who had stayed to eat dinner with them that night, raised his hand to his mouth to suppress a grin, and Lady Susan smiled knowingly at them. For her part, Lady Catherine only muttered something about the childishness of her nephews and turned to say something to Anne, who was sitting beside her.

"It is quite sensible of you to ask for the supper dance," said Elizabeth's father, winking at her with amusement. "I must have the first for myself. A father's pride at seeing his daughter admired by hordes of gentlemen must be assuaged, you know."

"Unfortunately for Anthony, he shall not have the supper set either," said Elizabeth.

The confused look with which Anthony regarded Elizabeth almost set her to giggling. He obviously noted her reaction, for the look he directed at her was pointed.

"And might I ask why I am denied with nary an explanation?"

"I am happy to explain, Brother," replied Elizabeth, still attempting to stifle her laughter. "I am unable to give you the supper dance because it has already been claimed."

Anthony turned an accusing glance on his elder brother, but James only shook his head. "It was not me, Brother. But now that I know Elizabeth's supper set has been taken, I will solicit your hand for the last, my dearest sister."

"Of course, James," replied Elizabeth. She supposed she should not be enjoying this so much, but Anthony's amazement was quickly turning to annoyance as all the significant sets of her evening were snapped up. Elizabeth was reminded of the look a stray dog had once given Lydia when she had kicked at it, sending it scuttling away with a reproachful growl.

"Might I ask who has claimed your supper dance, Elizabeth?" asked Anthony. He was watching her with some suspicion like he thought she was attempting to tease him.

Elizabeth was far too diverted to deflect his question. "Why, it is William who has acted first, Anthony. He secured it yesterday."

With amazement, Anthony turned to William, whose smugness of the day before had returned. Then Anthony tried to do exactly what William said he would.

"But I am Elizabeth's closest brother. I believe the set should belong to me, by right."

The viscount smiled and the earl guffawed, but William was entirely unmoved by Anthony's statement. "I do not know how that would be, and I think James would dispute the title of 'closest brother.' Regardless, I believe a lady's dances are claimed by those who act first, and as I spoke first, I will not relinquish that which I have gained."

And firm to his purpose William was, though Anthony was not of a mind to allow the subject to rest. Several times in the ensuing days, he pressed William for the sets, using every tactic he could devise to induce him to capitulate. When that did not work, he tried to persuade Elizabeth that he should have the dances instead of his cousin. In the end, he became quite surly about the entire matter, though he did act to secure Elizabeth's second sets when William suggested he might lose even those if he did not cease his grumbling.

When the evening of the ball arrived, Elizabeth could not feel that she was truly ready to face society. However, she also possessed the knowledge that she would never feel like she was ready, and that allowed her the courage to lift her head high and meet those whose society she was joining with fortitude. She was clothed in one of her new gowns, a concoction her mother informed her quite became her. Inherent in this observation was the suggestion that she thought Elizabeth would be the belle of the ball, a circumstance Elizabeth thought was inevitable, given the sensational nature of her return to society.

The family gathered together and formed a line to greet their guests, Elizabeth standing next to her mother, who performed the honors for those she had not yet met. The line seemed endless, and Elizabeth was certain that there must be ten times the number of people in attendance that night as there had been the night of the dinner. And then Elizabeth found herself face to face with a man she had thought might join the receiving line with them.

Tuesday, March 31, 1812
Fitzwilliam House, London

It was all Darcy could do to avoid staring as he was confronted by the sight of Lady Elizabeth Fitzwilliam that night. Since first seeing her in Davidson's sitting-room, Darcy had thought she was a handsome woman. But the admiration which had been growing as she was accepted by the family and had begun to settle into her new role was now bursting into an all-consuming passion for this woman. What a bright light she was, and how much brighter she would be when she became comfortable in the company of the society to which she had been born!

"Lady Elizabeth," said Darcy, as he stepped forward and greeted her. "You are lovely tonight."

Unable to help himself, Darcy reached out and grasped her hand, bowing over it and bestowing a kiss on its back. His words were nothing less than the truth. The wealth of her deep mahogany hair had been bound and tied back into an elegant knot, her eyes were bright with curiosity and intelligence, and the light of her spirit lay within. Her dress was a soft green, with a wrap of a darker shade, and he could not imagine how every man in the room would not be in love with her by the end of the first dance.

"Thank you, William," said she, the lightest dusting of color staining her cheeks. "You are very handsome yourself."

With a smile, Darcy stepped closer, still grasping her hand. "Are you well? This has not been too tiresome, has it?"

Elizabeth laughed, a sound he had grown to treasure. "It is not. I cannot hope to remember everyone I have met tonight, but though I have been subject to many gawkers, I cannot say I have been made uncomfortable."

"That is well then." Darcy bowed and made to withdraw, but Elizabeth's softly spoken words halted his retreat.

"I had thought you would join the line with us."

"I felt no need to do so," replied he. Darcy favored her with a mischievous smile. "It is one of the benefits of my continued residence at my own home. I can claim that I, too, am a guest. As you know I am not at my best in society, so I am more than happy to take that opportunity to avoid a receiving line."

"Well played, sir," said Elizabeth, her eyes alight with amusement. "It seems you have given this matter much thought."

"It takes no real thought." He paused and then continued: "I see your mother's eyes upbraiding me for taking too long with you, so I shall depart. I am anticipating our dance keenly."

Then with another bow at Elizabeth and a wink for her mother— Lady Susan had been watching him with a little impatience—Darcy took himself away from her and made his way to the ballroom.

The room was, as he had suspected, filled to overflowing with members of society. It seemed like she had invited everyone who could possibly fit into the room and many more who could not. Lady Susan was usually more selective about whom she invited to events she hosted, but in this instance, Darcy knew it was imperative for Elizabeth to be introduced to as many people as possible. Thus, the larger than usual guest list.

There was a reason why Darcy did not like the ballroom much. Most of those with whom he associated were at least tolerable, but he possessed only a small circle of those he would truly call his friends. Others he would speak with, endure their conversation and their impertinence which manifest itself at times. Those who were truly objectionable, he attempted to hold at arms' length.

Unfortunately, it was much more difficult to do that in a ballroom where those in attendance were in much closer quarters. The main topic of conversation that night was, of course, Lady Elizabeth Fitzwilliam and her sudden reappearance. In another venue, he might have been able to avoid impertinent questions. In the ballroom, however, escape options were much more limited.

"I was not even aware that the Fitzwilliams *had* a daughter, much less that they have discovered her again. How much are you a part of their counsels?"

Darcy eyed the man who had questioned him with distaste. His name was Alistair Trenton, Earl of Winchester, a man who claimed a distant relationship with the Fitzwilliam family, though Darcy was not certain of the exact connection. He was also an objectionable man, both being too fond of his mistresses—of which it was said he kept at least two—and too fond of all manner of wagering, specifically with respect to horses. Winchester was also of a proud, haughty character and was not much liked in town. He was said to be quite wealthy, though Darcy was not certain if the man's habits had affected his finances.

"I have always known of their missing daughter," replied Darcy. He did not even wish to speak with Trenton, let alone answer any of his questions. "I remember when it happened, though I, too, was still quite young."

Trenton shook his head. "Then I am curious, for I remember nothing of it, and I am some years older than you." He shrugged. "I suppose I must attribute it to being far from your uncle's home. News must not have reached Kent."

The only answer Darcy permitted himself was a grunt—news of the matter had been all over the kingdom, for it was not every day that an earl's daughter disappeared without a trace. Trenton must have been, even then, absorbed in his vices to have missed such a sensational event.

"Surely you must know of her. What can you tell me?"

Darcy turned and regarded the man, noting his intensity and the way his countenance demanded Darcy tell him all he knew. Could the return of the lost daughter be of such importance?

"I believe it might be best for you to become acquainted and form your own opinions, my lord," replied Darcy. "I am certain I would not do Lady Elizabeth justice, should I try to portray her."

Though uncertain what he had expected, Darcy was not sure it would have been the earl's laughing agreement. "Spoken truly, to be certain. Thank you, Darcy — I believe I shall do just that."

The earl slapped him on the back and turned to make his way to the entrance to the ballroom, where Elizabeth had appeared on her father's arm only a moment before. The man bowed and shared a few words with her, and Darcy felt a moment of triumph when Elizabeth shook her head several times, no doubt in response to sets which had already been claimed. Trenton showed a little frustration, but after a moment he seemed to come to some agreement, and he bowed and went away. Darcy did not miss the way he had attempted to capture Elizabeth's hand, only for her to refuse to give it to him.

Darcy's glaring eyes followed Winchester as he moved through the room and took up a seat which would allow him an unimpeded view of the dance floor. The likes of Alistair Trenton were certainly not good enough for Elizabeth. Darcy's mood was not made any better when Winchester noticed him watching, and he nodded, his laughter seeming to ring mockingly through Darcy's mind. Darcy turned away from him — there were much more agreeable subjects to consider, not the least of which was the sight of his cousin settling across from her father where the dancers were assembling.

Though Darcy had known Elizabeth for some weeks now, he had never seen her dancing — this was the first time they had attended a ball together. She was light on her feet, gliding smoothly and without hesitation, seeming to float above the floor on wings of angels. As they danced, she carried on a conversation with her father, laughed when he plied her with jests and observations. Darcy was grateful to the earl — he was giving her something to think about other than her nervousness.

It was the third dance of the evening — the set the detestable Trenton had managed to secure with her — that Darcy realized the downside of claiming Elizabeth's supper sets for himself. He had not danced at all that evening, though his aunt had already teased him once for his reticence. Though he might have thought Fitzwilliam would be equally amused, it appeared Fitzwilliam only had eyes for one other person in the room.

"I would prefer she did not dance with men such as Winchester," said Fitzwilliam as he joined Darcy where he was standing beside the dance floor. Darcy had a strange sense of their roles being reversed.

"You can hardly prevent it, Fitzwilliam. You know that a woman must sit out if she refuses a dance. Given what I have seen, your sister enjoys the activity very much."

Fitzwilliam grunted. "I believe she does, and she dances well. But she is yet a newcomer, and these waters are filled with sharks. The man with whom she dances at present is not the least of them."

"I do not think you need to worry." Darcy gestured at Elizabeth, who was smiling at something the earl said, but she still regarded him through lidded eyes, a wariness which only someone familiar with her would recognize. "She is not taken in."

"No, in that, at least, you are correct."

"Fitzwilliam," said Darcy, feeling it incumbent upon himself to speak on his cousin's behalf. "You may be as protective as you like, and I am certain Elizabeth will be appreciative of your concern. But take care not to smother her. She has impressed me as an independent lady. I doubt she would appreciate an overbearing protector."

"But—" attempted Fitzwilliam before he paused, shooting a glance at Darcy.

"She is not witless. Allow her enough respect that she will understand a man of Winchester's ilk. She is not taken in by him."

His eyes darting back to Elizabeth, Darcy saw the exact moment when his cousin capitulated, though it was not with any grace. Darcy's gaze had followed his cousin's, and he noted Elizabeth's fixed smile and the lack of any true humor in her countenance. No, she was not fooled by the earl, and only ten minutes in his company seemed to have her wishing she could quit it.

"You are correct, of course," said Fitzwilliam. "But she is my sister, and I wish the best for her. Winchester is certainly *not* the best."

"I understand what you mean," replied Darcy. "At least you have already had your dance."

Fitzwilliam's brow rose at Darcy's statement. For himself, Darcy was concentrating on the form of Elizabeth, hardly noticing that his words had been spoken aloud. All he knew was he was to be forced to watch as Elizabeth danced with every man in the room while he stood on the side watching. Was there another torture as exquisite as this?

Tuesday, March 31, 1812
Fitzwilliam House, London

Though she had known she was not likely to sit all evening, Elizabeth could not have imagined the true drudgery of a ballroom in London. As a vibrant young woman, Elizabeth had always prided herself on her abilities in society, for she had always been much sought after as a partner, even in the small neighborhood of Meryton. She had rarely been required to sit out, and she fancied that she provided more than just someone to partner for a few steps in a dance. Her wit and ability to converse made a dance with her more than what silly, empty-headed, and giggling Lydia could provide.

But though her aforementioned sister would have been thrilled to receive the attention Elizabeth did that night, Elizabeth found herself more disquieted than pleased. It must be stated that Elizabeth did enjoy some of the dances, and several of her partners were agreeable men. But it seemed like the majority watched her with lascivious thoughts or hinted openly, attempting to discover the size of her dowry. Thoughts of courtship or marriage were far from Elizabeth's mind, having only just entered this society. But it seemed many men were determined not to lose any time. That Elizabeth ignored their insinuations did nothing to deter them, it seemed.

Then, of course, she was forced to endure the presence of Farnsworth Longfellow and his overbearing father. The boy had approached her not long after the ball had started and secured one of her sets, but it was clear from the way he had looked sullenly at his father that he had little desire to do so. The elder man watched them while they danced, an air of satisfaction hovering about him, and while the son was gangly and a little clumsy, he was not *too* inept on the dance floor.

It was with a profound sense of relief that the supper sets finally arrived, and William approached her to claim her hand. She noted more than one look of disgruntlement he received, and in a moment of pique, Elizabeth decided to exaggerate her pleasure at seeing him.

"Thank you, William," said Elizabeth as they walked toward the line to take their places. Her hand was situated on his arm, and she brought her other hand up to clasp it close to her side, her eyes darting back toward her legion of admirers. Several watched, their countenances falling in disappointment, or directed dark looks at William. Lord Winchester, however, only looked on with amusement, though what he could find diverting Elizabeth had little notion.

"Are you attempting to make others jealous?" asked William.

Elizabeth should have known he was perceptive enough to see through her actions, and she felt the embarrassment settle over her. But she did not back down.

"I only wish them to understand that I am not interested in gaining a betrothed by this time next week."

A chuckle met her words. "Now you see why I am reticent in society. I have been subjected to overt attentions from the fairer sex since I inherited, and even though he is not yet an earl, James has had it even worse."

"I can certainly see that. But the lack of tact is stunning. Do you know I heard several people discussing the size of my dowry?"

Elizabeth shook her head, the disgust for their avaricious natures washing over her again. They took their places on the dance floor and soon they began to move in the steps. Elizabeth's thoughts were far from focused on the demands of the dance, and had she thought of how little attention she was paying to it, she would have been thankful she knew them so well.

"Several of the men with whom I spoke made it clear that it was agreeable to *them* if we were to become *much* closer," said she at the first opportunity, not quite feeling ready to release her frustration.

"And Winchester?" asked William. Elizabeth shot him a look, noting his curiosity in addition to . . . some other quality. Elizabeth could not quite make it out.

"*He* was the worst," growled Elizabeth. "It seems he has already decided the date of our wedding, the exact composition of the guest list, and what shall be served at our wedding breakfast."

William chuckled and Elizabeth glared at him, annoyed that he was apparently enjoying her pique.

"In the end, I believe that Winchester is harmless, though he may *think* he is able to woo you successfully. Given enough time, I believe he will fall back to his original pursuits. I doubt he has any true interest in marrying."

"Then he is certain the consummate actor," muttered Elizabeth.

"Do not concern yourself with it. If he becomes too aggressive, then speak with your father or brothers. I am certain they would be happy to intimidate him for you. They would be happy to do it for any of your suitors."

Though William's tone was light, Elizabeth thought she detected a hint of some other feeling when he used the word "suitor." She gazed at him, wondering if she had imagined it, but he had looked away at that moment. The dance took them apart, and then close again, but this time William did not open his mouth, and they continued in silence, leaving Elizabeth to contemplate him.

She had been completely sincere in her earlier assessment of his appearance that night. His dark suit over a white shirt, with his blue cravat tied expertly by his valet was only the physical covering of his form, and as it was his usual mode of dress—though finer—she did not think much of it. However, it covered a body which was athletic and lithe, and his unruly hair, with several strands hanging over his forehead only accentuated his strong jaw and high cheekbones. He was, indeed, a handsome man—perhaps the most handsome man she had ever seen. And his upright and moral character was also appealing, as was his diligence and responsibility, evidenced by the care he took for his sister—the care he exercised with Elizabeth herself. There were few better men than Fitzwilliam Darcy.

"Elizabeth," said he when they came close again. "You . . . Well, you *will* take care, will you not?"

The silence between them had been of such duration that Elizabeth was almost surprised when he spoke. She was filled with the warmth of his concern and interest in her wellbeing.

"I will," replied she simply. "None of these coxcombs have impressed me tonight. Besides, I have only just entered society, and I have no interest in jumping into a courtship with a man I hardly know. I am not yet one and twenty, so there is plenty of time."

"But some men . . ." William trailed off and he swallowed. "Some men may not be content with such an answer. We are all . . . worried for you, Elizabeth. Please understand that we all wish the best for you. I do not wish to see you hurt."

"I do appreciate it," replied Elizabeth. "I have not the least intention of allowing one of these," Elizabeth waved her hand at the room, "to get the best of me. I will stay close to Anthony and James. I will stay close to you, William."

A brilliant smile settled over his countenance, and Elizabeth was captivated by how it transformed his face. Fitzwilliam Darcy was, indeed, a handsome man, but his countenance when he smiled was sufficient to make maidens swoon.

"Thank you, Elizabeth. Trust in us. We will not fail you."

It was the conviction with which he spoke that told Elizabeth he was entirely sincere. With this man in attendance, no one could possibly hurt her—all the Winchesters in the world would dash themselves against the wall of his fortitude and not cause it to yield an inch. Never had Elizabeth felt so safe and protected.

They finished the rest of the dance in silence, William seemingly content to watch her and the rest of the room, scanning it for threats, unless she missed her guess. For Elizabeth, she was simply happy to be in his presence, glad to have known William and Anthony, and all her family. They were exalted of station and great of wealth, but they were humble and had been transformed by her return. How she knew that Elizabeth could not say, but she knew it to be true.

After the dance, William escorted her into the dining room and sat her beside him, insisting upon fixing her a plate. On her other side sat Lady Catherine, whom Elizabeth had noticed had stayed nearby most of the night when Elizabeth was not on the dance floor. All about her the buzz of conversation played in her ears, a comforting counterpoint to the clatter of utensils on plates. It was quite a contrast to the last ball she had attended. At the ball at Netherfield, Mrs. Bennet had crowed about Jane and Bingley's future felicity to all within hearing, Mary had performed for the company and would not relinquish the pianoforte until her father told her, quite loudly, to allow other ladies to play, and Kitty and Lydia had run among the officers, laughing and giggling and bringing their respectability into question.

"Why the sigh, Elizabeth?"

Elizabeth directed a wan smile at her aunt. "I was just remembering the last time I attended a ball. It was . . . well, it was akin to a disaster for my adoptive family."

"Oh?" asked Lady Catherine.

The one word conveyed a wealth of meaning, and Elizabeth felt obliged to explain, in brief terms, just what had happened. Lady Catherine listened attentively, saying nothing, and when Elizabeth had finished her explanation, Lady Catherine shook her head.

"Being raised in such an environment, it is a wonder that you are the person you are."

"I must attribute it to Mrs. Gardiner's influence," replied Elizabeth. "Though I will own that I never found the activities of the youngest Bennets to be appealing."

"Yes, Mrs. Gardiner impressed me as a genteel sort of woman, though she is naught but the wife of a tradesman." Lady Catherine's words were spoken without any hint of rancor, though Elizabeth was still annoyed for Mrs. Gardiner's sake. "But I must also attribute it to the benefits of superior breeding. It is further proof that breeding wins out in such situations."

It was all Elizabeth could do not to roll her eyes. Though Lady Catherine was certain of her convictions, Elizabeth thought it overly haughty of her. The previous thought of her family's humility entered Elizabeth's mind, and she almost giggled—Lady Catherine could *not*, under any circumstances, be deemed *humble*. But Elizabeth would not dispute the matter—Lady Catherine de Bourgh was not the type of woman who would accept being contradicted with any equanimity.

"Ah, Lady Elizabeth, I have been searching for you."

The narrowing of Lady Catherine's eyes past her told Elizabeth that the chair next to her had been occupied, and not by anyone welcome. Certain who it was who had dared to sit, Elizabeth turned and looked into the smirking countenance of Lord Winchester.

"Lady Elizabeth," said he, nodding his head. "I cannot imagine what might have happened for your companion to abandon you during supper. But I suppose I must count myself fortunate, for it has allowed me to once again be in your company."

"She has not been abandoned." Elizabeth looked up to see William standing above them, looking down on the earl with some distaste. "I was merely fixing her a plate. If you would kindly vacate that chair, I would be much obliged, for I believe it is mine."

"Ah, Darcy," said the earl, though he made no move to stand. "I suppose I should have expected it, though I do not know that you could be accused of the ability to appreciate a beautiful woman."

"In fact, I have appreciated her for some weeks. Now, if you please?"

The earl rose, though in an unhurried fashion which reeked of insolence. "Of course, old man. I had just approached for an entirely different purpose when I noticed the empty chair."

Lord Winchester turned to Elizabeth. "Lady Elizabeth, I have found myself sufficiently enchanted by you that I desire a second set. Will you oblige me with another—the last, perhaps?"

The grinding of William's teeth was almost audible from where Elizabeth sat, and the huff she heard from Lady Catherine told her the lady was no more pleased with the earl's behavior than he.

"Unfortunately, all my remaining sets are spoken for," said Elizabeth. Though she had earlier lamented the hordes of admirers which beset her, Elizabeth could now only be grateful that she had not another dance to give this man.

"That is, indeed, unfortunate." Elizabeth suspected he knew she was disinclined to his company, and it did not matter to him a jot. "Then perhaps it would be best for me to obtain an advantage over the competition. Would you do me the honor of reserving the supper set at the next ball at which we both attend?"

His tone suggested that he would be careful to attend every ball she did, and Elizabeth was annoyed all over again by the man's presumption.

"I do not believe that would be appropriate, sir." While she might have hoped he would be offended by her chilly tone, Lord Winchester only grinned. "I do not even know when that might be, and I shall certainly not agree to such an unreasonable request."

"Then I suppose I must be quicker than all your other admirers. Until then, my lady."

He bowed and attempted to capture her hand, but Elizabeth pulled it back before he could. Even this did not deter him, for his expression was all insolence, suggesting he had no doubt as to her eventual capitulation to his charms.

As he turned and walked away, Elizabeth watched him go. Beyond him and to the right, she caught sight of the other objectionable man she had met recently—Victor Standish. He was sitting next to some acquaintance or another, but Elizabeth could see his calculating gaze upon her, and she wondered what he was about. He did not nod or make any other gesture when he noticed her eyes upon him—he watched her for a moment longer before he turned away. In that moment, Elizabeth felt a hint of a shiver pass through her. Though not all gentlemen she had met that evening were objectionable, enough of them were that she wondered how she would endure this society.

"That man is nothing less than a wolf."

Lady Catherine's voice brought Elizabeth's thoughts back to her companions, and she turned and shared a commiserating nod with her aunt. For his part, Darcy roused himself from his glare at the earl, seating himself beside Elizabeth and putting her plate before her.

"I hope this meets with your approval, Elizabeth."

"It does." Elizabeth smiled. "Thank you, William, both for the meal, and for your protection from certain unendurable gentlemen."

"Think nothing of it."

They sat and ate their dinner and conversed, and Elizabeth was made to forget Lord Winchester and others of his ilk. Lady Catherine, of course, had her own part of the conversation, but she seemed distracted, so she was quieter than her wont.

Chapter XXII

Wednesday, April 1, 1812
Undisclosed Location

The girl's first few nights in society had been a success, it seemed. While the mere sight of her was enough to cause him to clench his fists in anger, he had controlled himself, watching her closely to see how she would conduct herself and made some attempts to pay her attention and learn of her.

Thus far, the hunter was forced to acknowledge that the chit knew how to act, though he could not imagine how it could be so, considering her upbringing. She had been perfectly calm and poised at the Fitzwilliam ball, and from what he had heard, she had been equally impressive at the theater. No doubt the family would continue to attend the events of the season with her, though he very much doubted her father would force her into a marriage.

With a sigh, the hunter sat back in his chair, tilting the glass of port which he held in one hand this way and that, watching as the liquid within sloshed from one side to the other. Wooing her would be difficult, though not impossible. Though she conducted herself with the grace of a daughter of the nobility, he thought she still possessed enough naïveté to allow him to swoop in and claim her hand—he was not foolish enough to think that he could command her heart with little difficulty. It was not her heart he wished for, regardless—it was the money he knew she was destined to receive.

He could . . . Well, there were several ways he could handle the situation. Marrying her would, of course, bring the money to him, but the problem of the Fitzwilliam men, all with their chests puffed out, standing over her like a pride of lions protecting their young, was problematic. And that did not even consider that prig Darcy and his obvious intentions toward the girl. It would be much simpler to kill the wench and be done with it. That solution posed its own problems. Either way, he would need to wait until they let their guards down before he made his move.

Thus, he would continue to play the friend, the suitor. Perhaps she was ingenuous under her intelligent façade. Perhaps he could woo her. Only time would tell.

Wednesday, April 1, 1812
Longbourn, Hertfordshire

Jane Bennet sat on a bench in Longbourn's back lawn, a letter held loosely in one hand. On her cheek, one single tear trickled down her face, touching the edge of her mouth and continuing its way down to her chin. There it stayed, not large enough to detach and splash down on her dress, and a moment later, annoyed by the sensation of the small drop poised on her jaw, she raised a hand and dashed it away.

She could never be annoyed with Lizzy—for eighteen years, Lizzy had been the best friend and sister she could ever have wanted. In fact, she was grateful to Lizzy for discovering Mr. Bingley's intentions and warning her of them. Jane had been holding onto hope for his return for far too long. It was time to let go.

But a part of her also wished she could continue to be blissfully unaware of the man's lack of fortitude. Lizzy had not come out and stated it openly, but Jane could read between the lines of her sister's missive. It seemed Mr. Bingley was adept at falling in love with young ladies and equally capable of falling out of love with them just as quickly. The duplicity hurt, though Jane knew that he was not precisely being deceitful. That did not apply to his sister, of course, who was now revealed as a social climbing shrew.

The worst part of it was the necessity of informing her mother. She could well imagine how Mrs. Bennet would take the news, the lamentations of the loss of Mr. Bingley, the constant complaints about what would happen to them when Mr. Bennet died. Her mother had been focused on Elizabeth's new situation and how they might exploit it, but Jane suspected that would all be forgotten with the news of Mr. Bingley's defection.

There was nothing to be done. She would simply have to inform her mother of it and bear what came with whatever fortitude she possessed. So, Jane rose from the bench and made her way around the house, entering through the front door. She paused in the foyer, ensuring her appearance showed no signs of the single tear she had shed. Then she entered the sitting-room to confront her mother.

Kitty and Lydia were both there, though Mary was absent, and as she entered, Jane looked at them through eyes more critical than was her custom. Though Jane always attempted to see the best of any situation, she was aware that her mother and sisters were serious impediments against her ever marrying advantageously. They had taken to doing this much more of late—ever since Mrs. Bennet had discovered the truth of Elizabeth's identity, they had planned and schemed, thinking up means by which they could ingratiate themselves to her notice. Jane found it all very pathetic and not a little silly.

"Jane!" exclaimed her mother. "Come and sit with us. We have been devising a means by which we may persuade your father to take us all to town. Any suggestions you have would be welcome."

"Papa will not be moved, Mama," said Jane. Before her mother could rebut her words, however, Jane spoke again. "I have received a letter from Lizzy."

"And what does she say, girl?" demanded Mrs. Bennet. "Never mind, I shall read it myself."

Mrs. Bennet rose to snatch the letter from Jane's hand, but Jane only pulled it away. "No, Mama, this is my private correspondence from Lizzy. You shall not read it."

Though her mouth opened, no doubt to exclaim her displeasure, Mrs. Bennet must have seen something in Jane's countenance, for she sank back down on the chair with a disgruntled huff.

"I do not know what she has to say that I cannot see, but it shall be as you like. Has she invited us to stay with her family?"

"No, Mama, and I do not expect she will. In fact, she has written to put me on my guard."

"Put you on your guard?" Suspicion was alight in her eyes along with an almost manic demand for Jane to state her meaning. "If that girl thinks to shunt us aside because she is now *high and mighty*, she will think again. Otherwise, she will pay for her intractability—of that you may be certain."

Though Jane was afraid of what her mother might be contemplating, she pushed it to the side for the moment. "She spoke of nothing of that sort, Mother. She wrote only to put me on my guard with respect to Mr. Bingley. It seems she has confirmed that he has no intention of pursuing me. He will not return to Netherfield."

Of all the responses Jane might have expected from her mother, a sniff of disdain was not among them. "And what, pray, do we care for Mr. Bingley?"

Jane gaped at Mrs. Bennet, but her mother kept speaking. "I am sure Mr. Bingley is nothing to us. No, Jane, it is all clear to me now. You can do better than Mr. Bingley, as your sister is now daughter to an earl. When Lizzy introduces you to all her new friends, why, I am certain you will catch the eye of no less than a peer!"

"Lizzy is not my sister," said Jane, the words hurting her more than she thought possible.

"She was raised as your sister!" There was a note of desperate defiance in Mrs. Bennet's tone. "She will be made to remember it!"

Then Mrs. Bennet calmed herself with an effort and turned a smile on Jane. "Do not be cast down, Jane. Mr. Bingley is not worth your concern."

"But I esteem Mr. Bingley greatly, Mama," replied Jane.

"I dare say you do. But it is clear his affections for you are not the equal of yours." It hurt for it to be openly stated in such a way, but it was nothing less than the truth. "Come, let us speak and make our plans. You have always been so close to Lizzy—I am certain she will not turn you out. And through your acceptance, the other girls will also be introduced to London society. I am certain you shall all do very well."

It was clear her mother would not be gainsaid, so Jane decided to hold her tongue. But she did not have as much confidence in her mother's words, especially considering the way Elizabeth had been forced from Longbourn. Perhaps Lizzy herself would hold no grudges, but Jane was not certain her new family would be so forgiving.

She would listen and inform her father if there was anything concerning in what her mother planned. It was the least she could do for Elizabeth. And for a time, focusing on her mother's machinations allowed Jane to shunt her own heartbreak to the side. It was not forgotten, but in time, perhaps it would be.

Due to the ball ending in the wee hours of the morning, the knocker stayed off the door of the Fitzwilliam townhouse, and for that Elizabeth found herself grateful. Even more than the night of the theater, the ball had proven to her that there were some facets of being part of the first circles which would not agree with her. The late night also ensured that she did not arise as early as was her wont, though she awoke far earlier than she wished.

When she finally did arise, Elizabeth found that she was not the only one. It seemed her new family was not prone to sleeping late, regardless of the hour in which they sought their beds. Her father had already partaken of his breakfast and retired to his study to see to some correspondence, and Anthony and James were about, though James had departed some time earlier. Her mother and Constance greeted her with a fond welcome, Anne, with her usual reticence, and Lady Catherine greeted her as well, though with a sense of reserve Elizabeth had noticed from the lady of late. But there was one present who had been in her bed much earlier the previous evening, and she was impatient for details of the previous night and not at all shy about demanding them.

"Well, Elizabeth?" demanded Georgiana as soon as she entered the room. "What was last night like for you?" Georgiana scowled at Lady Susan. "My aunt even made certain I could not spy on you all last night, so I was forced to listen to the sounds of the ballroom without the ability to partake in the fun."

"Would you prefer we had ordered you back to your brother's house?" asked Lady Catherine in a pointed fashion.

"Of course not, Aunt," said Georgiana, though her eagerness had retreated a little in the face of Lady Catherine's belligerence.

"I *am* surprised, Georgiana," said Lady Susan as she buttered some toast. "Only a few months ago, did you not declare that you had no desire to come out?"

"The thought *does* still cause me concern," confessed Georgiana. "But with Elizabeth next to me, I think I might be able to withstand it. And the curiosity of what I was able to hear last night has almost overwhelmed me."

Elizabeth smiled at the girl. "It was different from what I experienced in Hertfordshire in some ways, but not in all, and I did not like all the attention I received. But I do enjoy dancing, and there were many people I met last night whom I believe I will esteem very well."

"Elizabeth has the right of it," said Lady Catherine. "While society can provide much enjoyment, there will always be objectionable people and activities in which we would rather not participate. Your own coming out will be neither so delightful nor so frightening as you fear."

"I understand, Aunt," said Georgiana. "Can you tell me a little of what you experienced?"

The pleading tone the girl used tugged at Elizabeth's sense of humor, and she raised a cup to her mouth to avoid smiling. She was not in any way opposed to informing Georgiana of the evening, so she proceeded to tell her a little of her doings last night, though she avoided mention of the objectionable actions of Lord Winchester. The girl was enthralled, asking questions of this or that of her partners, and more particularly about her dance with William. In the end, Elizabeth found that she was able to satisfy Georgiana's curiosity, such that when Mrs. Annesley, her companion, informed her of the need to see to her morning studies, she complied without complaint.

After breakfast, the ladies went their separate ways for a time. Her mother, Elizabeth thought, was basking in the warmth of a successful ball and debut for her daughter, and announced her intention to retire to her rooms to read and rest after the exertions of the previous days. Constance took herself back to her own rooms, declaring she would rest until luncheon, while Lady Catherine and Anne removed themselves to some other part of the house. Left at loose ends, and grateful for the solitude, Elizabeth took herself to the library to find a book.

The library at the Fitzwilliam townhouse was an impressive room. It was comfortable and cozy, not too large, but with several bookshelves which provided enough delights to satisfy even Elizabeth's desire for the written word. It was not nearly so large as the one at William's house—nor was the one at Snowlock anything to the library at Pemberley, William had informed her with obvious smugness. But the warm and cheery fireplace and the book of poetry made her feel quite comfortable, and after reading for a time, Elizabeth began to feel drowsy. It was the sound of the door opening which startled her to full wakefulness, and the angle of the light of the sun through the windows informed Elizabeth that she had, in fact, dozed for a time.

"I suppose I should have looked here first," said a voice. Elizabeth looked up and saw Anthony striding toward her. "Of your penchant for books I have heard, but it has not been in evidence since you joined us here."

"That is because there have been so many other things to do," replied Elizabeth.

Anthony grinned at her and sat on a nearby chair. "You and William make a good pair. He, too, always has his nose buried in the pages of a book."

Surprised, Elizabeth shot a look at him, wondering if he was insinuating anything. Anthony's returning gaze was placid—almost too much so. But it did not reveal anything, so she ignored it.

"Then you do not appreciate books as much?"

"It is not that," replied Anthony with a shrug. "I like to read as much as the next man, I dare say. But I am also a man of action." He grinned. "That is why I preferred the army to the church, though mother protested my choice vehemently. But I do not regret it."

Elizabeth paused, her brother's words having brought another matter to her mind. "You have not been on duty lately, Anthony. Can I assume you will be returning to your regiment soon?"

"Why? Do you wish me gone already?"

Though Elizabeth glared at him, Anthony only laughed at his own jest. "The fact is that I have taken very little leave in the past. I am currently on leave, and with Father's influence, it can be extended for some more weeks. That is all I am willing to say on the subject at present."

"Very well," replied Elizabeth.

"I have something in particular about which I wished to speak with you, Elizabeth. I am glad I found you alone?"

"Oh?" asked Elizabeth. "What you have to say cannot be overheard by the rest of the family?"

"No, it is not that. But I am certain that my mother especially is concerned for you, so I have taken it upon myself to offer my assistance to you whenever required. And I am concerned about some of the men with whom you danced last night."

The insinuation made Elizabeth more than a little cross. "About what do you have to concern yourself? If you recall, I am at the mercy of those men in attendance. If I am asked to dance, I must accept or forego the activity for the evening."

"I am aware of that," replied Anthony. "I am not calling into question *your* behavior. But as you are still lacking in experience, I wish to advise you as much as I can. Specifically, I noticed you dancing with

Lord Winchester last night, and I wish to inform you not to be taken in by his smooth manners."

"And what do you have to say against him?" asked Elizabeth. Her frustration had all but evaporated, given what William had already said about Lord Winchester the previous evening.

"Only that he is a libertine and not a suitable partner for a young woman. He is also sly, and known to be careless with the reputations of young gentlewomen."

"Surely he would not try anything with me. My father would not stand for it."

Anthony shook his head. "I quite agree. But it is not beyond his capacity to attempt to woo you. I understand some women find his roguish manners to be strangely compelling."

A laugh escaped Elizabeth's lips, but Anthony appeared serious. "I am happy you can find the ridiculous in this conversation, Elizabeth. But I wish you would take the matter with the gravity it deserves. At the very least, should you marry the man, he would not remain faithful to you."

"I cannot believe we are having this conversation!" exclaimed Elizabeth. "I only met Lord Winchester last night. Whatever *he* believes, I am certainly not ready to throw myself into his arms and be swept off my feet!"

"What he believes?" Anthony pressed.

Elizabeth shook her head, still astonished that he was pressing forward with this discussion. "I dare say he believes he may charm me at his leisure."

"Darcy mentioned that he was already planning your nuptials?"

"It was an exaggeration," said Elizabeth. "I thought William understood that. Yes, he was more forward than I might have expected, but I did not like him at all. In fact, I believe I would be happy to never dance with him again. Unfortunately, he has made it clear that he will seek me out. He even asked for the supper set at the next ball we both attend."

Anthony appeared relieved. Elizabeth, though she knew her family was just protective of her—no one more than Anthony—was a little peeved that he seemed to think so little of her sensibility.

"That is well, Elizabeth. I did not think you were taken in by him, but I wished to be certain. I hope you are not offended."

"No, I am not," replied Elizabeth, resisting the urge to tease him. "I am grateful for your care. But I will remind you that I am not helpless or witless. I am able to handle the dear earl, should he become unruly."

"Good," said Anthony. Then he paused, and his look was inward for a few moments before a devilish grin appeared on his face. "So, our dear earl means to attempt to gain your supper set, does he?"

"Or the first or last sets," replied Elizabeth with distaste unfeigned. "Any of the important sets will serve his designs, though the supper would allow him more time in my company."

"Then we shall simply need to ensure those dances are *always* taken."

Elizabeth quickly understood what he was saying and her grin matched his. "I *do* have four close relations. If you, William, James, and Father always have those sets . . ."

"Then our dear earl will no doubt become frustrated over time. Perhaps he will even understand the hint."

They shared an evil grin for a few moments before they burst into laughter. "I believe you give him too much credit, Brother, but I am quite happy to arrange matters in that fashion. It will also protect me from Farnsworth, another man I have no desire to show any favor. But the earl may retaliate by asking for two dances."

"Then simply have Father forbid you from dancing more than once with any man," replied Anthony as if it was not at all important. He paused and smiled. "I am glad you are not in any hurry to attach yourself to a man. I just recovered my sister — I am loath to lose you to some unworthy cretin anytime soon."

"I am not interested in leaving my home for another," replied Elizabeth. "I am quite happy with you all here."

Their banter continued for some time. Anthony found himself a book from one of the shelves, and he stayed with her for the rest of the morning, discussing what they read and debating some of the finer points. Elizabeth was happy to sit with him. She had always thought it would be a fine thing to have a brother. Now she had two, and she could not be happier.

Wednesday, April 1, 1812
Fitzwilliam House, London

Though Fitzwilliam had told Elizabeth he was not eager to see her married in the near future, the truth was he did not wish to see her married to the wrong man. Should she be wedded to a man he felt deserving of her, who would treat her like the treasure she was, Fitzwilliam would not object. And he was certain he knew exactly who that man should be, given his suspicions of what he was seeing.

After spending a lively morning in Elizabeth's company, Fitzwilliam escorted her to the dining room where they partook of a light luncheon, and thither they also found Darcy. Their cousin had joined them often of late, spending almost as much time at Fitzwilliam house as he did at his own. They were a small party — his mother and father were not in evidence, James had not returned, and Constance was still resting. Thus, only the Darcy siblings, Fitzwilliam, Elizabeth, Anne, and Lady Catherine were present. But that suited Fitzwilliam's purposes, as he was interested in observing Darcy and Elizabeth together.

Soon his sister's attention was diverted away from him and toward Darcy and Georgiana, and they spent some time in happy banter. Just about any conversation which included Elizabeth devolved into happy banter, which was one of the reasons he had grown to love his sister with ease. The only one who did not seem to be happy was Lady Catherine, who watched them as an owl watches a fat mouse. But at least her ladyship stayed silent, though Fitzwilliam thought she suspected as much as he did himself.

After luncheon, James returned, and Fitzwilliam caught his eye and nodded his head slightly. His brother understood the gesture, as they had previously discussed the matter. It was time to talk to Darcy.

The desired meeting was easy to bring about. It seemed Elizabeth was finally fatigued from her own late night and early rise, and she retired to her room to nap. And with Georgiana back in her lessons and Lady Catherine with Anne, the brothers had no difficulty cornering Darcy.

"What is this all about?" asked Darcy when they were alone in a smaller drawing room. Fitzwilliam nodded — he had not thought his cousin would misunderstand their desire to speak to him.

"Let us simply say that we have noticed your regard for our sister, Darcy. We would like to know what you mean by it."

It was clear that Darcy was flustered for a moment. Fitzwilliam owned to a little surprise — he thought Darcy would have understood of what they wished to speak.

"I mean to come to know my cousin better," said Darcy, his tone defensive. "Do you accuse me of something more?"

Fitzwilliam shared a look with his brother, but it was James who responded. "Of course, we do not, Darcy. We both know you are upright of character and would never attempt anything underhanded."

"But it also has not escaped our attention that you admire her," added Fitzwilliam.

Darcy was as self-possessed a man as Fitzwilliam had ever met, but he positively started in surprise.

"Come, Darcy," said James, "your growing regard for her has not been hidden. Though you take delight in your inscrutability and your facility for confounding members of society, you must remember that we know you much better than they."

"Even Lady Catherine has noted it, though I am not certain Georgiana has," added Fitzwilliam.

Darcy groaned and shook his head. "If that is so, I wonder why Lady Catherine has not mentioned it."

"That is simple to explain," replied James. "Lady Catherine, you must see, is in a difficult position. If she protests your interest in Elizabeth, she must explain to mother and father why *her* daughter is a better match for you than *theirs*."

A snort was Darcy's response. "It matters little, regardless, as I have no intention of marrying Anne. And you both know *her* feelings on the subject."

"We do," confirmed Fitzwilliam. "But at present, we are much more interested in your feelings for our sister."

This time Darcy appeared a little defensive. "Of course, I admire Elizabeth. Who would not? But I fully understand the situation. Elizabeth's return is still new, and I understand your mother and father do not wish to give her up so soon. I have no intention of taking her away from your family so soon after her recovery."

Fitzwilliam shared a glance with his brother. "Perhaps it would be best not to be so hasty."

"I beg your pardon?" demanded Darcy. "I have not the pleasure of understanding you."

"Darcy," said Fitzwilliam, as he sighed and leaned back in his chair, "my brother and I both appreciate your consideration for the family. But I believe you may not be considering this correctly. James and I did not approach you to warn you away from her. In fact, we wished to speak to discover if your admiration prompted any intentions."

"I cannot believe what I am hearing." Darcy grimaced and shook his head. "Surely you do not wish to give her up only months after finding her."

"Would we truly be giving her up?" asked James. "If she were to marry you, she would still be close to us all, for your house is only a few streets over, and Pemberley is not far distant from Snowlock. And what better man for our sister than one with whom we have always been like brothers, who will treat her as she should be treated?"

"Of course, I would," replied Darcy. "But that is not the point. Elizabeth has only just come out in society. Surely she will wish to experience what it has to offer. Your mother must wish to keep her close by as long as she possibly can."

"She has been to one ball, one family dinner, and one night at the theater, and already I can tell you she is not enamored with it. Though she carries herself as if she were a duchess, she is not one who cares for high society, and she does not relish the attention."

"What are you suggesting?" asked Darcy, eying them both with faint suspicion.

"Nothing in particular," replied James. "I merely wish to inform you that I do not believe Mother and Father would be as opposed to Elizabeth marrying as you seem to think. Above all, they wish to see her protected. What better protection for her than to be married to a man we all trust and respect?"

Darcy seemed to think on this for several moments, and as the silence stretched on, Fitzwilliam felt it incumbent upon himself to add: "There is also the matter of her disappearance."

"Her disappearance?" asked Darcy, his gaze once again keen on Fitzwilliam. "Is there some threat against her of which I am not aware?"

"Nothing at present," replied Fitzwilliam. "But we still no know more about what happened to her between her disappearance from Snowlock to Mr. Bennet finding her in Cambridge. There may be nothing with which to concern ourselves, but we would be foolish if we did not assume there is someone out there who means her harm."

With a quick nod, Darcy indicated his understanding. "Whether you approve of any attentions to her, I am not ready to take such a step as a proposal. Furthermore, she is not ready to hear one."

"You are correct," replied James. "But we," he indicated both Fitzwilliam and himself, "do not want you to hesitate to proceed for fear that the family will not approve."

"With the exception of Lady Catherine," said Fitzwilliam.

James grinned at him and then turned back to Darcy. "*Most* of the family will approve. We know you are a cautious man, Darcy, and it does you credit. You seem to be proceeding apace with her—already she is comfortable with you and esteems you. Proceed as you wish. But if you find you are in a position to propose to her, do not hesitate because of her recent return to the family. Mother would much prefer her daughter under your protection at Pemberley than have someone else importuning her."

"And perhaps her marriage would remove whatever target has been painted on her back," said Fitzwilliam.

"I cannot imagine how that would matter," replied Darcy.

Fitzwilliam only shrugged. "I will own that I do not know either. But a married woman is easier to protect than a maiden in society."

When Darcy nodded, Fitzwilliam could easily see his distraction, and he decided they had spoken enough on the subject. The brothers excused themselves from the room, but Darcy did not even seem to notice when they departed, so deep in thought was he.

"Do you think he will pursue her?" asked James.

"It is always difficult with Darcy. He admires her—of that I am certain. We will simply need to wait and see."

CHAPTER XXIII

April 1 to May 4, 1812
Fitzwilliam House, London

*I*n the days and weeks that followed, society and the season were an ever-present entity, a constant trial to be endured, and a treat to be enjoyed. It was a curious juxtaposition, Elizabeth knew, but it summed up her feelings with exactness.

The attention she had initially received waned a little as time wore on, but Elizabeth's celebrity status never diminished. She was still sought after by young gentlemen, young ladies approached to become friendly, matrons simpered and gossiped, and rakes congregated and strutted, like peacocks searching for a mate. But Elizabeth endured, and soon she began to see that not all was objectionable. In fact, there were some parts of the season which were pleasant.

It was not long after her introduction that she began to make friends with those young ladies in similar circumstances. It was true that she tended to avoid those who seemed to hold an elevated opinion of themselves, but there were enough lively and witty ladies that she never wanted for companionship.

Of the gentlemen, she found there were many who were amiable and kind, with whom it was not a punishment to associate. Unfortunately, there were enough of the other kind that her enjoyment was often ruined by them.

The chief among these, of course, was Lord Winchester, he of the towering conceit and narcissistic self-absorption. The very first day he could manage it—which was the second day after the Fitzwilliam ball—he had come to visit her, and thereafter he came most days and could not be dissuaded from it. All of Elizabeth's pointed remarks and disavowals of her interest in him were met with nothing more than a shrug and an entirely unwarranted level of confidence.

"You will soon come to appreciate me, my dear Lady Elizabeth. I have no doubt my attentions will become welcome in the end."

"My father will not force me into marriage, sir, and I have no intention of allowing you to pay your addresses. Can you not simply focus your attention on some other, more willing woman?"

"But the perfect woman is before me. I have no need to look elsewhere."

It was all Elizabeth could do not to grind her teeth in frustration. She was grateful for the vigilance of her closest relations, and especially Anthony, who seemed to have appointed himself her protector. When Lord Winchester came to visit, Anthony would watch him as the fox watches another who has trespassed on his territory. Lord Winchester did not miss this behavior, but he did a credible job of ignoring it.

"If you would like, I can bar Winchester from our house," said her father one day when she complained about the earl's continued interest. "I cannot prevent him from approaching you at a ball without inciting gossip, but here at the house is another matter. If I refuse him entrance, perhaps he will get the point."

Though it was tempting, Elizabeth decided against it. "Thank you, Father, but I do not believe it is necessary. He *is* odious, but I will be required to withstand odious people."

"Very well, Elizabeth. But if he makes you uncomfortable, please let me know, and I will take steps against him."

Elizabeth decided against mentioning that the man already made her uncomfortable. In some ways, he reminded her of Samuel Lucas, who, though he had never pursued Elizabeth, was still oily and objectionable, oozing insincere charm. Elizabeth decided if she was able to deal with Mr. Lucas, she could very well deal with Lord Winchester.

The other objectionable presence was that of Victor Standish, though Elizabeth was at least able to state that Mr. Standish did not intrude upon her notice nearly so much as Lord Winchester did. Mr. Standish made it a habit of watching her closely, though whether he thought she would fail and he waited impatiently for it or if he intended to vie with Lord Winchester for her hand, she could not be certain. He was always friendly and polite, but Elizabeth always sensed something underneath this, and though she did not know what it was, it disquieted her. She could not make the man out at all.

These two were by no means the only objectionable presences, but they were the most overt, the most determined to pursue her. There were others, but she noticed that several of them shared their favors indiscriminately or paid their attentions to several women at once, though whether this was to ensure they were to be a consideration for as many wealthy women as possible or because they were naturally incapable of behaving properly, Elizabeth could not determine.

One objectionable presence who was soon resolved was that of Farnsworth Longfellow. While his father was clearly intent upon brokering a match between them, Elizabeth chanced to have a conversation with the son soon after that first ball which clarified matters between them.

It was at Elizabeth's second ball when Farnsworth reluctantly approached her to ask for a set, and as Elizabeth still had one available, she was forced to promise it to the youth. When they had met on the dance floor later that evening, the young man had seemed unwilling to speak, and Elizabeth, not wishing to give him any encouragement, had taken it as a sign she could refrain from speaking herself. Thus, when he finally opened his mouth near the end of their time together, he caught Elizabeth by surprise.

"I hope you understand that I approach you by my father's command, Lady Elizabeth."

A glance around the room showed the elder Longfellow standing by the side of the dance floor watching them intently. From the grimace which he sported, Elizabeth thought it likely he was looking for any hint of a connection between them.

"That would have been difficult to misunderstand, Mr. Longfellow," replied Elizabeth. "What I did not understand quite as well was the state of your own wishes."

"I do not wish to appear rude," replied Mr. Longfellow after a short pause, "but I have no intention of paying you my addresses."

Elizabeth carefully suppressed a sigh of relief. Though Elizabeth still thought him a callow youth with little of the social graces, he was a good sort of man, and she did not wish to offend him.

"Then I am grateful, for I do not mean to marry this season. I have found this all . . . overwhelming, to say the least."

"It can be a little much." Mr. Longfellow paused and then spoke slowly. "My father enjoys the season and always stays for as much of it as he can. For myself, I am much more partial to our estate, though it is far from London."

"I can understand it, sir." It was Elizabeth's turn to hesitate, for she was not certain she had any business asking her next question. But it was begged to be asked, so she screwed up her courage. "I have heard reports that you admire a young lady of the neighborhood in which you reside."

Elizabeth was about to ask after the truth of that rumor, but as soon as she mentioned it, the young man colored in embarrassment and looked away. They separated for a time due to the steps of the dance, and Elizabeth wondered if he would possess the capacity to speak of it when they drew closer once again.

When they finally did come together, it seemed like he had regained a measure of his composure, though he still appeared embarrassed. "My father has, perhaps, misspoken. There *is* a young lady near my home whom I find agreeable, but she is yet but seventeen. And as I am only two and twenty, I do not feel any need to marry at present.

"In the future, should the opportunity present itself, I might enjoy paying her my attentions. But I have no intention of doing so now."

"Then why is your father so insistent?" asked Elizabeth.

Again, it took a moment for Mr. Longfellow to muster the wherewithal to respond. "When you were born, it seems he spoke to your father about betrothing us. Now that you have returned . . ."

Elizabeth could only gape at him. "Your father wished to make an arrangement between us? At such a young age?"

"It is not entirely unheard of. You must understand, Lady Elizabeth, that my father wishes for a rise in our family's fortunes."

"But he already has a connection with my family!"

"Yes, but a marriage would be a much closer connection, and your dowry would significantly enhance our coffers."

Elizabeth shook her head, feeling unaccountably weary. "I am not accustomed to this way of life. I feel there should be something more between a man and a woman than a desire to improve a position in society."

"I feel the same way," replied Mr. Longfellow with a nod. "I hope you will not be offended should I continue to pay attention to you, if only to satisfy my father. But I would have you know that I have no intentions whatsoever."

For a moment Elizabeth did not know whether to be relieved or insulted at the way he phrased his declaration. It was what she wished, so she assured him that she fully understood, and they finished the dance in silence. After he left, Elizabeth noticed him approach his father and his father's close query after. Whatever he said must have satisfied the elder man, for he smiled and patted his son on the back. Thereafter, while the son's overt attentions did not cease, Elizabeth found them less frustrating.

And so matters continued through the remainder of April and into May, and as the month turned, so did the weather, continuing on its inevitable cycle toward the warmth and beauty of summer, which Elizabeth had always loved. The events of the season did not slacken — in fact, they seemed to become busier and more intense the later in the season it became. It was fortunate, indeed, that the Fitzwilliam family seemed little inclined to display themselves at every event to which they were invited, allowing Elizabeth the occasional break from all the activity.

On a bright and clear day in May, Elizabeth found herself sitting at home in the morning with Constance keeping her company. Lady Catherine and her mother had gone out that morning to meet with a friend who was ailing, and as a result, Elizabeth and her cousin by marriage were the only two ladies in the sitting-room that morning when the expected callers arrived. The first was a welcome sight, for he was a man she esteemed as much as she did her brothers and who had been successful in assisting her to avoid those she found objectionable.

"How are you this morning, Elizabeth?" asked William when he stepped into the room.

"Very well, William," replied Elizabeth. "Have you left Georgiana at home this morning?"

William smiled — Georgiana had returned home some days before, quite against her own wishes, but at William's insistence. She had imposed quite long enough, he stated when he informed her that she would be moving back into his house, and all her pleading had served her little. Elizabeth had visited several times to ease the girl's anguish, and Georgiana still spent almost as much time at Fitzwilliam house as she did at her brother's. But it was still a continuing sense of amusement for them all, as every time she was forced to leave to return to her home, the girl acted as if she was being sentenced to prison.

"Not today. She is studying German with Mrs. Annesley this morning."

"Ah, then I feel for her," said Elizabeth. "I always found German to be quite incomprehensible."

They sat and visited for some time, as William usually arrived before true visiting hours. Elizabeth thought Anthony might have requested it of him, particularly since both Anthony and James were away that morning. If Anthony was not present, Elizabeth could count on being attended by either her elder brother or the cousin who had first recognized her.

It was within a half hour of William's arrival that other visitors began to arrive at Fitzwilliam house. Among these were a few young ladies with whom Elizabeth had become friendly these past weeks. Of course, no party could possibly be complete without several admirers also present. Most of those were not any true difficulty, for Elizabeth had become accustomed to the attention to a certain extent. That Baron Longfellow, in the company of Farnsworth, was among the company was only a minor annoyance, considering Elizabeth's understanding with the younger man. Lord Winchester's arrival soon after, however, was not equally tolerable.

"Ah, Lady Elizabeth!" said he expansively when he entered the room. "How is the fairest flower in all London today?"

"I know not, Lord Winchester," replied Elizabeth, replying in a teasing tone she often used when she was made to feel uncomfortable. "Perhaps if you asked her she would tell you."

Lord Winchester laughed, far louder and longer than Elizabeth thought warranted from such a trite quip, but then again his reactions with her were always exaggerated. Why he would think her affected by such silliness, Elizabeth could not say.

"We shall do well together, my dear, for I do so love your ability to make me laugh."

"Moderate your language, Winchester," interjected William. "Do not claim a connection which is not warranted."

"Why? So *you* can?" Lord Winchester's words were filled with scorn. "I might wonder why you are here at all, Darcy. Do you doubt Lady Elizabeth's safety in the confines of her own home?"

"I am here to keep the likes of you in check," replied William. Elizabeth was impressed with the manner in which he held his own temper, not giving any hint of annoyance with the earl. "As you know, there are difficulties in Elizabeth's past. It is only prudent that she has someone here to protect her."

"Here, here," said Baron Longfellow. "I, for one, applaud you, Darcy. But where are your cousins this morning?"

"Chesterfield had an appointment in the company of the earl with the family solicitor, and Fitzwilliam is at his barracks, dealing with a matter which has arisen."

"I must say," said Lord Winchester in an insolent tone, "I have rarely seen Fitzwilliam in his regimentals of late, and it seems his duties in the army have suffered. Perhaps he has been called in to account for his lack of diligence?"

"On the contrary, Lord Winchester," said Elizabeth, speaking an instant before William did himself, "my brother has taken a leave of absence due to my recent recovery. In fact, I understand that he is not required to serve his country at all, as he possesses his own estate. It is his sense of duty which has compelled him to do so."

"A meager estate which is barely deserving of the title." Lord Winchester's tone was all insolence and dismissal.

"I would not call Thorndell a 'meager estate,'" said William. "It is not Pemberley, but then again it is not a mere farmer's plot either. With a little work and the purchase of a few more fields, I dare say my cousin will do quite well, indeed."

It seemed like Lord Winchester became belatedly aware that insulting Elizabeth's brother was not the way to her heart. He bestowed a long look at her, which Elizabeth returned with a placidity she did not feel before he turned abruptly and sat down on a chair nearby. Several times he attempted to speak to draw Elizabeth's attention solely to him, but in that he was unsuccessful. The rest of the company seemed determined to thwart him, even Farnsworth, who was intent upon paying her as little attention as possible.

"I must say, Lady Elizabeth," said Lord Winchester, speaking to the entire room when he realized he could not speak to her alone, "I have had some difficulty in securing the sets I want at the balls we both attend. I do not suppose you would accept my solicitation of your hand for the first at the next ball we jointly attend?"

Though Elizabeth noticed a smirk pass between William and Constance—the former being a conspirator in the matter, while the latter was aware of it—she avoided looking at them for fear she would laugh. "I apologize, sir, but as I stated before, I will not agree to any dances in advance of any event."

Lord Winchester regarded her, and while his countenance was impassive, she could detect a hint of simmering discontent under his placid façade. Elizabeth knew the earl was understood the subterfuge, but he could do nothing about it. Elizabeth did not care for his opinion—she had done almost everything but hit the man over the head with her lack of interest in him. If he could not see it, she would not concern herself for his feelings.

"No, I suppose you will not," said he. And he fell silent.

The ensuing few moments were the pleasantest Elizabeth had ever spent in the company of the Earl of Winchester, for he said not a word. The conversation was carried on in a general fashion by the rest of those in the room, and the subject matter was nothing of any great significance. But it was made all that much more interesting because Elizabeth was not forced to listen to the man's attempts at wooing or his smug pronouncements. Within a few moments, Elizabeth was engrossed in a conversation with William in which he was describing his estate. Elizabeth, who had never been north of Luton, was interested to hear of his observations of the Peak District and hoped that she would be able to visit one day. It was during this conversation that she completely lost track of anything Lord Winchester said and was brought back to a remembrance of his presence by his again objectionable assertions.

"Of course, we do not visit Lady Elizabeth for my own benefit," Baron Longfellow was saying when Elizabeth became aware of the conversation. "But I have some hope that she and my Farnsworth are getting on well. He is full young, but I think they might do well together."

"You think that, do you?" asked the earl, his tone filled with scorn. "Lady Elizabeth strikes me as a worldly young woman. You think a callow youth such as your son could possibly catch her eye?"

The baron sputtered, offense written all over his countenance. "My son is a good lad. He *is* yet young, but he is good at heart and diligent on the estate. I could not be prouder of him!"

"He is not nearly man enough to attract a woman of any worth. As I have informed you, my good baron, I am determined to make Lady Elizabeth mine. Your son would be better to mature for a few years before attempting to find a wife."

Though Elizabeth might have thought the baron would become offended at Lord Winchester's characterization of his only son, he only responded with a faint smile. "You are, indeed, a charming conversationalist, my lord. My observations of you in the company of Lady Elizabeth leave me with the impression that you will be disappointed. I am certain she is not the type of woman to favor a coxcomb."

Then the baron turned to Elizabeth and smiled. "If you will excuse us, my lady, I believe it is time Farnsworth and I departed. Please give my regards to your father when he returns home."

"Thank you, Lord Longfellow," said Elizabeth, refraining from speaking of how they were much more welcome to her than Lord Winchester. "I will be certain to do so." Then she smiled at Farnsworth, ensuring the earl would see it. "Thank you for visiting me. You are welcome here at any time."

"Thank you, Lady Elizabeth."

The two men bowed and then let themselves from the room, leaving Elizabeth in the company of William, Constance, and the ever-detestable Lord Winchester. The moment they were out of hearing, Lord Winchester let out an exaggerated sigh.

"I thought they would never leave! Longfellow is a bore and his son is no better. It would be best if they would simply remain at his dreary estate in the hinterlands of the kingdom and not impose themselves on polite society."

"On the contrary, Lord Winchester," said Elizabeth, her anger burning within her, "I find them perfectly polite and unassuming. In fact, they are much more welcome here than certain others I can mention."

While it was clear that the earl understood her meaning with exactness, he only regarded her for a moment before turning to William. "It seems like you have recently lost your shadow, Darcy. I have rarely seen you without that Gimbley chap, and yet, of late, you seem to have distanced yourself from him. I can only applaud your sensibility, for though you are naught but a gentleman, still you must guard against infection from those of such an objectionable background."

Elizabeth could not determine if the earl meant to anger William, but if he had, then he failed spectacularly, for William only favored him with a faint smile. "My friendship with *Bingley* is still in place, Winchester. I highly value his friendship, for he is a good man, regardless of his background."

"I am also acquainted with Mr. Bingley," declared Elizabeth. "I find him as engaging as Mr. Darcy does."

"Yes, your upbringing rearing its unfortunate head once again." Lord Winchester shook his head and rose. "I will trespass on your time no longer. But if I might make a suggestion, Lady Elizabeth . . ."

Elizabeth turned her head away, not interested in hearing anything he had to say. Unfortunately, it did not deter the earl in the slightest.

"If you wish anyone in town to accept you, you should leave the past where it belongs. You are now a member of a privileged set and must behave accordingly. Any man who shows interest in you will wish to confirm you will not allow such a base upbringing to follow you through the days of your life."

"Then it is quite fortunate, my lord, that I do not intend to marry any man who cannot accept me for who I am, regardless of my past. In fact, as I have informed you several times already, I do not mean to marry in the near future, so it is of little matter."

With this final declaration, Elizabeth turned to look the earl full in the eye. He watched her for several moments, appearing to attempt to determine whether she was being open in her declaration. Elizabeth did not know what his final judgment was, for he allowed little to be seen on his face.

"Then I bid you a good day."

And with that, he was gone, leaving a fuming Elizabeth behind. The door closed behind him, and only then did Elizabeth heave a sigh of relief. It seemed she was not the only one.

"He is as odious a man as I have ever met," said Constance.

"Even more so than Standish?" asked William.

"At least Mr. Standish is not nearly so . . . explicit," said Elizabeth. "I find him more than a little disquieting as well, but he keeps his distance."

"All that is required is to inform your father, and he will prevent the earl from visiting." Constance gave Elizabeth a true smile of amusement. "But I am certain you will demur, for I know you are far too polite."

"It is not politeness which stays my hand," replied Elizabeth. "If he were denied entrance into the house, I have no doubt he would become even more insufferable in society."

"I do not know why you should be concerned about that," said William. "If he is angry and throws a tantrum, what is it to you? He cannot do anything with others about."

Though Elizabeth could not explain precisely why, she worried that Lord Winchester could, in fact, do something, and as he was already an irritant, she did not wish for him to further curtail her activities. And even if his presence in her father's home was a trial at times, Elizabeth was confident in her ability to handle the man.

"There is no need," said Elizabeth. "He feigns confidence and acts as if he is Adonis, capable of wooing any maiden he chooses, but I think he is toothless in the end. I am quite able to deal with him."

Constance nodded, though she appeared troubled. William only regarded her with his usual placidity. The events of the day would no doubt make their way to Anthony and James's ears, and their vigilance would increase as a result. It might have aggravated Elizabeth's nerves in another situation, but she could only be thankful for the care and attention of her new family.

CHAPTER XXIV

Wednesday, May 6, 1812
Undisclosed Location

"So, there is nothing in her past which can be used against her?"

"No, sir. Though she was raised in less than exalted circumstances, she was well respected and considered to be a level-headed girl."

The hunter sat back in his chair, looking over the report Cooper had compiled, thanking his foresight to ensure his servant was literate before hiring him. It had taken some time and several journeys to Hertfordshire to investigate the matter, and though it appeared as if nothing would come of it, he could not call it a wasted effort. He was gleaning new information about the girl from it, and he had no doubt it would assist him in the future.

As he was looking over the papers, a note caught his eye, and when he had read through it, his eyes rose to regard his man.

"What of this incident with the militia officer?"

"There is little to be said," replied Cooper with a shrug. "Apparently he imposed himself on her and was disabused of her willingness to be importuned. It is my conjecture that initially those of local society were inclined to blame her for the matter, regardless of how it all came about. Now, however, it seems they have remembered the esteem in which she had been held previously, as no one will say a word against her. The town is positively agog with news of the daughter of an earl who had lived unknowingly among them for so many years. That avenue is all but closed."

"And the officer?" asked the hunter, wondering if he could use the man for his own ends.

"Not long before her return was announced, Mr. Darcy and Colonel Fitzwilliam paid a visit to Hertfordshire. The militia officer, who was apparently connected to Mr. Darcy in the past, was arrested and transported to Van Diemen's Land."

"No doubt by the earl's hand."

Deep in thought, the hunter leaned back in his chair and considered the matter. Though he wanted to believe that this was the answer to his dilemma, he was forced to believe that his man was correct. Moreover, as the girl's father was already aware of the incident, and had acted to protect her, bringing it again to his attention would do nothing. He could, he supposed, spread rumors in society concerning her disgrace, but he doubted it would be likely that she would be disowned. And even if he did attempt to ruin her reputation, the circumstances were such that the gossip would be a minor annoyance rather than a catastrophic blow to her standing. It seemed like no matter what he considered, he was always led back to the inescapable fact that he was left with two options: ensure she was dealt with *permanently*, or marry her and gain her money by more legitimate means.

In reality, he found that he was rather amused by what he was seeing of the girl in society. There were many who had attempted to become close to her—rakes, young boys who had no excuse for being out of the schoolroom, and even a few older men seeking a young wife. And yet she parried them all with an expertise he would not have expected from so young a woman.

He had no doubt of his own eventual success, should he truly press his suit. She was intelligent, it seemed, but in the end, she was still naught but a country girl, unskilled and inexperienced with the intricacies of town. But he was still uncertain as to whether he wished to attempt marriage—toying with her was diverting, but marriage was another matter, and he was not certain he wished to have the trouble of a wife, even to gain an heir. This would require more thought

"Thank you for your work," said the hunter to his man,

remembering Cooper had been sitting and waiting for a response for some time. "I will have other tasks for you to complete when the time is right. For now, you may return to your usual duties."

"Very good, sir," replied the man before he rose and left the room.

After sitting in that attitude for some few moments, the hunter rose and quit the room himself. It was late and he was tired. He would need a clear mind to plot his next move.

Thursday, May 7, 1812
Fitzwilliam House, London

"Father, Mother, may I speak with you for a moment?"

"Of course, Anthony," said his mother, gesturing for him to enter their private sitting-room. "How may we help you?"

Fitzwilliam stepped into the room, taking the measure of his parents. His mother was openly curious, likely because he rarely approached them when they were alone in their rooms together. His father, however, looked at him with shrewd understanding. Fitzwilliam knew he had been more vocal about certain subjects as the days passed, and his father likely had a notion of what he wished to speak.

"There are a few subjects of which I wish to acquaint you. First, though I know Father is at least somewhat aware of my intentions, I wanted to inform you, Mother, of my plan to sell my commission at the earliest opportunity."

"That is excellent news, Anthony!" exclaimed his mother, as she stood and enveloped him in an embrace. "I am happy you have finally come to your senses."

"I think we owe this to Elizabeth," said Lord Matlock. "It seems her recovery has prompted you to think about your future."

"It has," confessed Fitzwilliam. "I also have news that the regiment is to enter intense training for the purpose of being dispatched to Spain, likely early in the New Year. As we have just been reunited with Elizabeth, I find I have little desire to be separated from her again so soon. Darcy has been excellent in managing my estate when I have been unable to take a direct hand, but I think it is time I became actively involved myself."

"An excellent decision," replied his father. "As we discussed previously, I am more than happy to assist with improving the estate. There are several plots of land adjacent to Thorndell with which we should be able to persuade the owners to part."

"Thank you, Father, I appreciate the assistance." Fitzwilliam took a deep breath, which both his parents saw, and when his mother shot him a look askance, he chuckled and turned his attention to the other matter he wished to discuss. "I also wished to speak to you both about Elizabeth."

"Oh?" asked his mother. "What of her?"

"I am . . . concerned for her, Mother."

"As are we all," replied his father. "Is there something in particular which concerns you?"

"This attention she has been receiving, and especially that libertine, Winchester." Both his parents grimaced at the mention of the man's name, but Fitzwilliam pressed on. "I am assuming you know about his behavior the day only William was here to attend her?"

The darkening of his father's countenance and his mother's pursed lips told Fitzwilliam all he needed to know. His father had, he knew, had words with Winchester to warn him away from her, but Fitzwilliam knew they had ultimately had little effect.

"He appears to have redoubled his efforts since that day, and I know he makes Elizabeth uncomfortable. Standish also seems to be appearing more than she would wish, and that does not mention all the other men who seem to believe she would be the perfect mistress of their estates. I have every confidence in my sister's abilities, but I do not trust either of those men to respect her wishes."

"Has Winchester spoken of such matters aloud again?" demanded the earl. "I will have his hide if he has."

"No, but that does not make him any less determined to court your daughter, sir. Other than calling him out and keeping Elizabeth by our side constantly, I am not certain what else we can do. But there is something brewing, and since I believe you have noted it, I thought I would mention it."

Lady Susan looked at him, her eyes demanding that he inform her directly of his meaning. For his part, the earl again appeared to have some inclination of what Fitzwilliam was about to say.

"I speak of Darcy."

Neither of his parents responded immediately. His father appeared thoughtful, while his mother was disgruntled.

"I have noticed some partiality from Darcy's side, I will own," said his mother at length. "Are you suggesting something more?"

"You have been so focused on your daughter that you have missed the obvious," replied Lord Matlock, clearly enjoying the fact that he had seen something his wife had not. "The boy is as adept at hiding his feelings as anyone I have ever met, but if you know what to look for, it is obvious. He is besotted with your daughter."

It was clear her husband had caught her by surprise, for Lady Susan searched his eyes before turning to Fitzwilliam and watching him as closely. "Are you suggesting he is on the verge of proposing to her?"

"Not yet," replied Fitzwilliam. "But I do not think it will be long before he feels ready to do so."

"He will need to restrain himself, then," said Lady Susan. Her tone was firm and even a little icy. "I am not ready to part with her yet."

"Perhaps it is best not to be hasty," replied Lord Matlock, which earned him a hard glance from his wife. "Our son has a reason for speaking of this with us. Do you care to elaborate, Son?"

"Other than the fact that she returns his regard?" asked Fitzwilliam rhetorically.

Lady Susan gasped, but the earl only nodded slowly.

"Oh, I do not think she is as aware of her regard as he is, but it is there nonetheless. *Darcy* is at liberty to focus his attention on her, while *Elizabeth* has been required to accustom herself to a new situation, a new family, not to mention the pressure society puts on her. Thus, her feelings, while present, are yet a mystery to her."

The look Lady Susan bestowed upon him was still colored with a hint of defiance, but it was also uncertain. His father merely looked thoughtful.

"If she returns his regard," said Lady Susan, though with hesitation, "I would not stand in her way. But is it not understandable that I do not wish to give her up so quickly? I would think that Darcy knows this."

"He does," replied Fitzwilliam. "James and I spoke with him of it, and he was as surprised as you. He attempted to deny it, but we already knew."

"You spoke with Darcy?" asked the earl.

"We did. In all honesty, we were not certain that Darcy even understood his feelings or that he would act on them." Fitzwilliam proceeded to relay the particulars of their discussion, including his reasons for considering such a step as this for his dear sister.

"I do not think our protection is lacking," replied his father. "Surely we can protect her from the objectionable elements of society such as Winchester."

"But would she not be better protected in marriage?" asked Fitzwilliam. "At least then, those who are merely sniffing about for a wealthy *unmarried* woman will leave her alone. Then *if* there is anyone out there who still means her harm, I believe we will be better able to spot them."

"And what of Elizabeth's choice?" demanded Lady Susan. She turned an accusing glare on her husband. "Did you not promise Elizabeth you would not force her into marriage?"

"I did, and I will keep my promise," replied her husband.

"Mother, I am not suggesting that we push her into marriage with William, or any other man. I merely wished to bring this to your attention, for I believe an attachment between them is being formed. We all wish for nothing more than Elizabeth to be happy, and a marriage to a man she esteems is the best way to bring that about. And remember—Pemberley is not far distant from Snowlock. I dare say Darcy would be happy to host you for a year if it means he could have Elizabeth as a wife."

The earl nodded and spoke, preempting whatever his wife was about to say. "That is a good point, Fitzwilliam. We will take your advice under consideration. Should Darcy propose, I will not refuse him out of hand."

"Good," said Fitzwilliam. He rose to depart, but before he did, he turned and addressed his mother again. "I know you wish to keep Elizabeth with you forever, Mother. But think of her happiness. I am not suggesting we should see them married tomorrow. I *am* suggesting that any attachment between them be allowed to form naturally. I believe they would do well together."

Fitzwilliam let himself out of the room. The conversation had proceeded much the way he had expected. Now it was left to Darcy and Elizabeth to resolve—should they do so in the manner Fitzwilliam suspected, his parents would be prepared. At present, however, Fitzwilliam had other matters to attend to, the primary one being the sale of his commission. Though he would not have been able to fathom leaving the army only a few short months ago, now he was feeling positively buoyant.

Thursday, May 7, 1812
Fitzwilliam House, London

Lady Susan had never felt so selfish. At the same time, she wondered if she did not have a right to feel that way. Was it not understandable that after missing her daughter for almost two decades she would wish to keep her for a little longer? Lady Susan did not think so, which made the sensation of discomfort when she considered her own desires all that much more curious.

In hindsight, it was all so clear. She *had* noticed Darcy's interest in Elizabeth, almost from the first moment she had been introduced to her daughter. But the novelty of meeting Elizabeth, of coming to know her, and all the pageantry which had accompanied her introduction to society, had quite driven such thoughts from her mind. Now that Anthony had pointed it out to her so forcefully, it was easy to see that Anthony had been completely correct. She wondered that she had not seen it herself.

Her disinclination for handing her daughter's care to another — even one as fine and upright as William — still did not sit well with her. It did not matter how much she tried to remind herself of her desire for Elizabeth's happiness, or any of the other points Anthony had made. She still wished to keep her daughter close to her.

It was these feelings which prompted her to seek Elizabeth out that afternoon. She was not certain quite what she hoped to accomplish — perhaps a vindication of her stance, or maybe it was to confirm for herself that Elizabeth was not yet at the point of wishing to accept Darcy's overtures. Whatever it was, she was certain she would find some peace in speaking with her daughter.

Elizabeth was soon found in the music room practicing the pianoforte, the sounds of her efforts guiding Lady Susan to her like a lighthouse guides a ship to a safe haven. She stood in the doorway, watching as her daughter played her way through scales and exercises, and eventually on to some pieces of music Lady Susan had learned she was particularly fond of. When Elizabeth finished playing a song Lady Susan thought she had played quite well, she announced her presence and approached her daughter.

"I have noticed of late that when I wish to find you, I merely have to listen for the sound of the pianoforte."

Elizabeth smiled and looked down, seeming embarrassed. "I have not often practiced as I should, and it shows in my playing. I have no wish to embarrass my family when I am asked to perform."

"And you think your playing will embarrass us?" asked Lady Susan. "Elizabeth, you could not shame us if you tried, for we are far too proud of you. Considering you have not had the advantage of masters, I declare you do remarkably well."

"I have not always lacked masters," replied Elizabeth. "Though our educations were not structured, whenever we wished for masters, they would be engaged for us. I *have* had instruction, though it was several years ago."

"Then let us say you have had *little* access to masters," said Lady Susan.

"My disinclination for practice is just as much to blame."

"Then you are rectifying that at present." Lady Susan smiled at her daughter and gestured toward a nearby sofa. "But I did not come to speak of such things. Will you join me?"

Though Elizabeth appeared curious, she willingly allowed herself to be led to the sofa, where Lady Susan sat by her side.

"I . . ."

Lady Susan realized she was not even certain what to say. She could not come out and forbid Elizabeth from accepting Darcy's advances, nor would she wish to do so, regardless of her own feelings. But how could she possibly discover what she wished without arousing Elizabeth's suspicions? Did she even know what she wished to discover?

"I apologize, Elizabeth," said Lady Susan at length, noting Elizabeth's tentative amusement at her inability to speak. "I wished to speak to you today, but I find I am having difficulty knowing what words to use."

"You are not alone in that state, Mother," said Elizabeth. "I have often felt the same."

Lady Susan shot Elizabeth a searching look. "Does the discomfort of being with us still haunt you?"

"No, quite the opposite, in fact." Elizabeth smiled, that beautiful gesture which Lady Susan thought enhanced every facet of her appearance and made her seem almost ethereal. "You are all more than I would ever have imagined gaining as a family, and I am grateful for your kindness in taking me into your hearts. It is just . . ." Elizabeth paused and showed a grimacing sort of grin. "There is so much happening that at times I wonder if it is naught but a dream."

With a slow nod, Lady Susan used the opportunity to move the conversation in the direction she had initially intended. "I know you find society challenging at times."

"It is not society, so much." Elizabeth paused, struggling to voice her feelings. "It is only . . ." She sighed. "I suppose if I was not the focus of every man in need of a wife it would be easier."

"Surely there were men like that in Meryton."

A firm shake of her head was Elizabeth's answer. "Unmarried men there were, though few of them. Most were searching for a woman who could raise their fortunes, which, as Miss Elizabeth Bennet, I had no power to do. There is a large difference between interaction with a man with no real purpose and the courtship rituals in which men engage when they are interested in furthering a relationship with a woman."

"You speak of Lord Winchester."

"He *is* the most determined, yes." A ghost of an amused smile appeared on Elizabeth's face. "But he is not the only one. I . . . I suppose part of my disquiet is accustoming myself to a very different society, while at the same time trying to fend off every man in need of a wife. I have never . . . It was always Jane who received most of the attention—not me. She is the beautiful daughter. I was the intelligent and playful daughter."

And there it was, and a much easier explanation than Lady Susan had thought possible. She wondered why she had not thought of it herself. Lady Susan, when she had appeared in society for the first time, had held all the same fears and nervousness of any young woman attaining maturity in a society such as theirs. But she had been raised all her life for it, trained by those who raised her and supported by a loving mother who ensured her every need was met. Elizabeth carried herself with poise and confidence, but it was not to be wondered that she found it overwhelming at times.

"Though I have never met Jane, I cannot imagine she could be more beautiful than you, my dearest daughter." Elizabeth blushed at the praise, but she did not speak. "Thank you for explaining it. You have done well, I think, but I had never considered the additional pressures you must be feeling when compared with my own coming out."

"I do not wish to disappoint you." Elizabeth's words were spoken with quiet conviction, and Lady Susan, who had not thought she could love her daughter more, felt her heart swell ever larger.

"Do not even consider such things, Elizabeth. You could *never* disappoint us."

The look Elizabeth bestowed on her was filled with gratitude, but also a measure of uncertainty. Lady Susan forced herself to see it from Elizabeth's perspective, and she knew that even though they all professed their approbation, Elizabeth would still worry she would make some faux pas which would embarrass the family. Lady Susan decided not to press her daughter—experience would give her further confidence, and when she attained a full measure of it, she would become a force in society. Of that, Lady Susan had little doubt.

"Elizabeth, what say you to an early departure to our estate?"

A frown settled over her face. "Will society not gossip if we retire early?"

"I care little what society thinks." Elizabeth's eyes shot to meet Lady Susan's, the questions evident in their depths. "You have just been recovered, Elizabeth, and it is understandable we would wish to show you your home. And I do. Even as a child of two, you loved to run in the gardens behind the estate. I believe you would love the wildness of nature in that part of the kingdom, especially with what you have told me of your habits in Hertfordshire.

"But of more importance, I wish you to be happy. There is no need to push yourself in society when you have already acquitted yourself very well. When we return for the little season, you will be much more comfortable here, and by next season, you will truly be the most formidable young lady in London. The novelty will have worn off, the shine of newness removed in favor of the shine of *you* and your character bursting forth. For now, there is no shame in leaving it all behind in favor of more comfortable surroundings."

Elizabeth considered the matter for a few moments, and when she responded, Lady Susan thought she was happier than she had been only moments before. "I would like to see the estate of my birth, Mother. I do not wish to flee London, but if you think it would be acceptable to depart early, then I have no objection."

"Excellent! I will speak with your father, and we will make plans. I suspect we will stay until at least the end of the month, but after that we will take you to the north."

Rising, Lady Susan pressed a kiss to her daughter's forehead and turned to leave the room. But then another thought occurred to her — the subject she had come to discuss with her daughter — and she turned back to Elizabeth, who was watching her with something akin to wonder.

"I am curious, though. I know you cannot abide Winchester, and I know of your agreement with Farnsworth. Is there any man you favor?"

There was a hint of . . . something in Elizabeth's countenance, which informed Lady Susan that she was not indifferent to *everyone* she had met. But Elizabeth blushed and shook her head, looking down at her hands folded neatly in her lap. Lady Susan nodded to herself — based on Anthony's words and her own observations, which she could now acknowledge, Elizabeth *was* forming an attachment with Darcy. But Lady Susan thought it would not be swift in forming into a bond which would lead to marriage. She would have her daughter for a little longer.

* * *

Thursday, May 7, 1812
Hyde Park, London

A walk was the very thing to allow her to put things in perspective, Elizabeth decided. After the surprising conversation with her mother, she needed some time to allow her to think, and in the past, her solitary walks had always provided her that opportunity, and an escape from a house where the atmosphere was rarely restful.

Thus, Elizabeth informed her father of her intention to walk to Hyde Park, and though he looked on her with some concern, in the end, he allowed it. "As long as you take a footman, Elizabeth. But please do not stay out long, or your mother will worry."

"I will return before long," replied Elizabeth.

It was with a hint of childlike enthusiasm that Elizabeth prepared herself to go out as she had rarely done in recent months. The warmth of May was in evidence that day, which allowed her to depart with nothing more encumbering her than a light spenser and the bonnet protecting her head from the sun. Her father's house was only a little distance from the famous park, and thus it was only moments before Elizabeth was wandering its paths.

At her back walked the footman, Thompson. He was a tall and burly man, as tall as Anthony, but much heavier, a man of raw physical strength, bearing himself with the barely checked threat of violence of a champion pugilist. He was employed in William's house but had been loaned to the Fitzwilliam household specifically for the purpose of protecting Elizabeth. His solid presence was comforting, but he stayed far enough away that Elizabeth was given the illusion of privacy.

As she wandered, many thoughts crossed her mind. She thought of her mother and the conversation they had just had, her father and the love and acceptance she had found from him, similar, yet different, from the previous man she had called father. She thought of her brothers and Georgiana, a sister in all but name. Even Lady Catherine and Anne had found a place in her life, along with Constance, and her other relations whom she saw often. And she thought of William, his handsome countenance and his goodness and attentiveness. For a moment Elizabeth wondered if her mother had been referring to her burgeoning feelings for her cousin when she had asked if a man had caught her eye. Then Elizabeth decided it did not matter, for surely her mother would not object to an attachment with such a beloved relation.

Elizabeth had not walked long before she met by chance an acquaintance she had not seen in some time. Though she could not claim to be friendly with this person, at least the last time they had spoken there had been nothing but pleasant words between them.

"Lady Elizabeth," said Miss Bingley with a curtsey when their paths intersected. "How do you do today?"

"Very well, I thank you," said Elizabeth. She was surprised to see Miss Bingley at that time, for it was not yet the fashionable hour to walk. There was a footman following Miss Bingley, much as one trailed Elizabeth herself. Miss Bingley seemed introspective.

"Do you often walk in Hyde Park?" asked Elizabeth, more for the desire to avoid descending into an awkward silence.

"At times," said Miss Bingley. "It is a little distant from my brother's house, but I come here when I can."

"I hope your family is all well?"

"They are." Miss Bingley paused, and her gaze met the ground, in a fashion most unlike her. "You probably do not know, but I have recently been receiving the . . . attentions of a man of society."

"That is excellent news, Miss Bingley! I hope you understand that I wish for whatever result will make you happy."

"Thank you," whispered the woman. She spoke again, her voice a little stronger. "I . . . Well, this man approached me after the night at the theater. I . . . I think he has some esteem for me, but I have the sense he sought me out after seeing me speaking with you." A sickly sort of smile came over her countenance. "I will own I have not disabused him of the notion that we are friends, though he has not asked after you."

"Miss Bingley," said Elizabeth, "though I do not think we can be considered precisely friends, I see no reason why we cannot meet in a friendly manner. There is nothing I can say with respect to your relationship with this gentleman, but if you expect me to cut you in public, please release that notion at once, for I have no intention of it."

Wonder spread over the woman's countenance. Elizabeth understood immediately—Miss Bingley, no doubt, would not have hesitated to do exactly that, had their situations been reversed. There was some great change in her. Elizabeth did not know if it was all because of whatever humbling she had endured by witnessing Elizabeth's elevation, but whatever it was, she decided it made Miss Bingley much more tolerable.

"You are too good, Lady Elizabeth," said Miss Bingley. "But I thank you for your words. I, too, hope we can be friendly when we meet."

"I am sure we shall. Now, if you will excuse me, I believe I will continue my walk, for the time of my return swiftly approaches."

Miss Bingley agreed and curtseyed, allowing Elizabeth to continue down the path. But before she proceeded very far, the woman's voice interrupted her again.

"Lady Elizabeth, please accept my apologies for my previous behavior. It was very wrong of me. I am grateful for your forbearance. I am grateful that my actions did not ruin my friendship between my brother and Mr. Darcy."

"It is all forgotten," said Elizabeth. "Please understand that I wish you every happiness and hold you no ill will."

It seemed Miss Bingley was much relieved after Elizabeth's declaration, for she smiled, curtseyed yet again, and moved on. For a few moments, Elizabeth watched her walk away, wondering at the changes in the previously objectionable woman. It seemed Miss Bingley had been properly humbled.

"Lady Elizabeth Fitzwilliam."

The voice nearby startled Elizabeth, and she turned and saw a grinning Victor Standish approaching her, his hat raised from his head in greeting.

"I see I am quite fortunate to come across you today. Shall we walk together for a time?"

Elizabeth looked longingly at the path down which she had been walking before she had come upon Miss Bingley. It was, unfortunately, near the time she should be returning to her father's house, and she knew they would worry excessively if she did not return on time.

"It seems I have walked as far as I can today, Mr. Standish. I believe it would be best to turn my steps back toward my father's house."

"Then I shall escort you, for I am walking in that direction anyway."

There was nothing to be done, so Elizabeth allowed herself to fall in beside him, and they walked back in the direction of the house. It may have been a trick of her imagination, but she thought the trailing footman stayed closer, his eyes watchful on the person of her companion. Whether he had received some specific instructions concerning Mr. Standish or it was just the presence of a man, Elizabeth was uncertain.

"Do you walk out often, Lady Elizabeth?"

"Not so often as I would like," replied Elizabeth. "When I lived in Hertfordshire, I could often be found walking the paths near my adoptive father's estate. But there are too many activities in London for me to indulge as often as I did previously."

"And London is not as safe," replied Mr. Standish. His reply seemed more an absence of mind than anything else, for Elizabeth could see his eyes were far away.

There was something about this man which was ... In fact, Elizabeth could not say exactly what it was. He had a calculating gleam in his eye, similar to what she often saw from Lord Winchester, but different at the same time. She could not quite explain it, but she felt wary in his presence, like he was a horse not fully broken, which might rear at any moment.

It seemed Mr. Standish had no compunction whatsoever against speaking, and he did so without cessation after his momentary distraction passed. Elizabeth wished to be out of his company as soon as she could arrange, and thus, the only benefit of his constant words was that it relieved the necessity of her response.

When they reached the end of the park, Elizabeth felt obliged to invite him into the house, but he declined it, much to Elizabeth's surprise.

"I have business elsewhere," said he. "I will visit at another time. Thank you for a pleasant few moments, Lady Elizabeth."

And with that, he walked away, leaving Elizabeth watching after him. His manners, she decided, had been all ease and friendliness, and nothing like the overt stalking with which Lord Winchester pursued her. But she could not feel anything but disquiet when confronted by the man. She could not fathom what he was about.

CHAPTER XXV

Thursday, May 7, 1812
Fitzwilliam House, London

"*P*ersonally, I suggest we pay a visit to our excellent Mr. Standish and determine what he is about."

It was the implied threat of violence in Anthony's tone which startled Elizabeth. Her family was overly protective of her—that she knew. But she did not think that whatever Mr. Standish intended warranted such a response. As yet, he had been one of the less objectionable men she had met, regardless of her instinctive distrust of him.

"I hardly think that is necessary, Anthony," said Lady Susan.

"We only met by chance in the park," added Elizabeth. "I do not like him, but a man cannot be blamed for greeting an acquaintance in a public space."

Anthony grunted and James said: "I have never known Standish to walk any further than the distance from his carriage into his favorite gaming hell."

"Might he have planned to meet you there?" asked Lady Catherine. The light of suspicion was shining in her eyes.

"I cannot imagine how," replied Elizabeth. "Unless he has someone watching the house to inform him when I depart. He has enough opportunity at various events to approach me, so I am not certain why he would think it necessary to meet by chance."

"To avoid other potential suitors, perhaps?" said Lady Catherine. When Elizabeth rolled her eyes, Lady Catherine's gaze softened. "I will not openly support the idea of a conspiracy, Elizabeth. But the man makes me more than a little uneasy, and I am not easily intimidated."

"Standish is an annoyance," said Lady Susan, "but I am more interested in this meeting of yours with Miss Bingley. You said that she was not at all what you remembered in Hertfordshire?"

"No, she was almost . . . humble," said Elizabeth. "I have never seen her behave in such a fashion."

"She could use a little humility," muttered William.

"I dare say she can," replied Elizabeth, amused at his obvious distaste for her. "I know what you hold against her, William, and I sympathize with your feelings. But I have no overt injuries to resent and, therefore, have no intention of treating her as anything other than an acquaintance."

"You are far too good, Elizabeth," replied he. "If she were in your position, she would lose no time venting her vitriol for all to hear."

"I am sure you are correct. But it would not make *me* any more estimable to behave in a manner in which I *imagine* she would conduct herself. I am happy that someone is paying attention to her, and I hope it will turn out well. But I have no intention of ever becoming an intimate friend, and I do not believe she expects it either."

William only grunted, and the discussion turned to other matters. Elizabeth watched her cousin, knowing that he had suffered from Miss Bingley's overt pursuit of him over the years of their acquaintance. He was not a vindictive man, but she sensed that it was not easy for him to forget slights against him perpetrated by others. It was not an attractive trait, but it was understandable.

The discussion centered on Mr. Standish and his actions that day, but Elizabeth was tired of hearing of it. Nothing had happened, and she did not think that the conversation of an entire evening should be wasted on such subjects. When, a little later, they began discussing other matters, she allowed herself to sigh in relief.

*　　*　　*

Jealousy. It was jealousy, pure and simple, a primal sort of emotion which invaded the mind, affected the senses, beat against the wall of consciousness and held a man in its grip. It was not laudable. But it was there, nonetheless, an ever-present anger against those foolish enough to press their suits for the most beautiful woman in the room.

Fitzwilliam Darcy had always been one who attempted to regulate his baser impulses, to strive to improve himself, to be a better man. Never before, however, had he felt the urge to throw all caution to the wind as now when he found his attachment to Lady Elizabeth Fitzwilliam growing ever stronger. Though he wished her attention on him always, he knew how silly such a desire was. But there it was all the same.

Though Darcy could endure the attention paid to her by most members of society there were a few, especially the detestable Lord Winchester and the less explicit, but still present, Victor Standish, whose actions caused Darcy to grind his teeth with anger. It was well, Darcy decided, that they had concocted their scheme to ensure Elizabeth was never forced to dance a significant set with anyone she did not wish, for the earl appeared incapable of taking a hint.

They were to attend a ball at the home of friends of his aunt and uncle, the man the same rank of nobility, and part of his uncle's faction in parliament. Though Darcy had never found balls to be of any interest, of late the presence of Lady Elizabeth meant he almost anticipated them, if only to be in her company, to speak with her, to take her to the dance floor himself. He endured her dances with other men by the simple expedient of focusing on her, watching her smile and laugh, watch the way in which she floated about, a literal fairy in the world of men.

That night, however, they had only just entered the room when Winchester approached them, his eyes predatory and hungry on Elizabeth.

"Lady Elizabeth, I would like to take this opportunity to solicit your hand for the first dance. Since you have only just entered the room, I am confident no one has yet secured it."

Elizabeth stiffened at the man's approach, which she always did, though he had not the wit to recognize it. Then she smiled that guarded expression and turned to William. "I am sorry, sir, but Mr. Darcy has already claimed that dance."

In fact, though their agreement was still in force, they had not yet spoken that evening concerning who would dance which sets with her. Darcy knew that it was natural she would turn to him, as it happened to be on his arm she had entered the ballroom, but he still felt a fierce measure of self-satisfaction that it was to Darcy himself she had turned. But the earl was not amused.

"It seems you have broken your own rule. How else could you have already promised those dances unless you did it before coming?"

"You truly are bacon brained, Winchester." Mr. Standish approached them and smiled at Elizabeth, before turning a scathing glance back on the earl. "It is quite clear Lady Elizabeth has no desire to dance with you. Unfortunately, you are the only man in London who cannot see it."

The earl's mien reddened in fury, but Standish had already returned his attention to Elizabeth, restrained laughter on his lips. "Since I suspect that one of your father or brothers has the supper, last, and second sets, might I petition you for the third?"

Though the earl gasped in outrage, Darcy was amused at the way Mr. Standish was baiting him. It seemed like Elizabeth recognized it herself, for her expression was warmer than it had ever been in his presence. "Of course, sir. I have those sets free and would be happy to cede them to you."

Mr. Standish bowed, and after a short greeting with the entire company turned his attention back to the seething earl. "Unlike you, Winchester, I have no illusions about the state of my friendship with Lady Elizabeth. But that does not prevent me from behaving properly and sharing a pleasant time with her. Perhaps you should take such a strategy under advisement."

Then he left, with Winchester's eyes impaling his back as he walked away. Before they could move away from him, however, he turned back to them and fixed Elizabeth with an imperious glare. "I suppose Standish has the right of it? The sets he mentioned have all been claimed?"

"They have, your lordship," replied Elizabeth, with nary a hint of embarrassment.

"Then I suppose I must claim your fourth sets if you will oblige me."

"Of course, my lord," replied Elizabeth. "They are yours."

Darcy decided that enough was enough, and he began to guide Elizabeth away from the earl. The man, however, was not finished with them.

"You should consider, Lady Elizabeth, that Darcy here is naught but a gentleman. Though you may retain the title 'Lady' if you marry him, in reality, you will be lowering yourself. I can make you a countess."

"If that was all that concerned me, I might give your argument some weight, sir," said Elizabeth. Darcy noted that she did not deny any attachment between them, and though he knew there was nothing yet, it gave him hope for the future. "As it is, I have nothing but contempt for those who consider such things to the exclusion of all else. You should judge your approach better, sir, for I find it wanting."

Lord Matlock approached at that moment, his annoyance for Winchester clear for all to see. He nodded at Darcy, which Darcy took as permission to lead Elizabeth away from the objectionable man. As they walked, Darcy could hear the earl berating his peer.

"I have warned you before, Winchester, not to impose on my daughter. If you persist in this behavior, I will forbid all contact with her."

The rest of the earl's words were lost in the murmur of conversation rising in the ballroom. They situated themselves on a side of the room, with several others of their party in attendance, but while Aunt Susan questioned Elizabeth to assure herself of her daughter's wellbeing, Darcy felt a fierce pride well up in his heart for this woman. She handled herself as if she were a queen and Winchester, nothing more than a peasant. It was clear she could not be intimidated by anyone.

The dance with her was sublime, but then it always was. The feelings Darcy felt when her laughing eyes were upon him, the warmth of her hand in his as they moved through the steps, thrilled Darcy and filled him with contentment. Her observations were witty and her comments intelligent, but Darcy thought there was something special in the way she looked at him. He was so lost in her that half the time he was not aware of their topic of conversation, though it appeared he made the appropriate responses. She did not state it outright, but Darcy was certain she was warming to him. These other pretenders who thought they could capture her heart were destined to be disappointed.

But then the dance ended and she was consigned to the arms of other men, and again, Darcy knew the exquisite torture of being in her presence but having her focus on someone else. She danced the next with her father, but the one after was the dance she had promised to Standish. Darcy had not seen the man dance for some time, but it seemed he still knew the steps. He watched for any hint of Elizabeth's discomfort, but he saw only friendly ease. On Standish's part, he did not seem intent upon pressing his attentions on her.

Winchester was another story. From the moment their dance began, Darcy could see the man looming over her, how he held her hand during the passes of the dance long after it was deemed polite to release her, and the defensive way in which she parried his advances. And Darcy was not the only one. Anthony appeared ready to strangle the earl with his own cravat, and he caught James cracking his knuckles on more than one occasion.

When the dance ended, Winchester caught hold of her hand and attempted to lead her away from their company. Incensed by this treatment, Darcy was already moving before he was even aware, his cousins by his side. But they were not the first to reach them, as Elizabeth attempted to free her hand.

"Unhand my niece, cur!"

The voice of Lady Catherine, so often raised in strident tones of anger, was low and menacing, only barely audible to Darcy, who approached from a short distance away. Winchester started in surprise, and Elizabeth used the opportunity to whip her hand from his grasp.

"How dare you take such liberties? Do you not see that she detests the very sight of you?"

"It was nothing, madam," said Winchester, haughtily drawing himself up to his full height. "I merely thought to obtain some refreshments for Lady Elizabeth."

"And as I told you," replied Elizabeth, her eyes flashing with anger, "I have no need of anything at present."

"You are a mewling puppy, Winchester," said Lady Catherine. "My niece is not a plaything for your amusement. Go find yourself another woman to torment."

"I am only acting as a man interested in a woman would usually act—nothing more."

"Then let me take this opportunity to inform you your attentions are not welcome," said Elizabeth.

While Darcy might have expected him to react with anger, Winchester only smiled at her, a particularly oily sight. "You protest now, Lady Elizabeth. But I know how it will be. For now, I wish you a pleasant evening with all the *boys* who attempt to make love to you."

Then, with a glare at Darcy, he bowed low and disappeared from the ballroom.

"I have it in mind to exact some payment on his hide," growled

Anthony as he watched the man retreat.

"There is nothing to be done in the middle of a ballroom," said Lady Catherine. "Or at least nothing which would not result in rumors and innuendo. I think Winchester is not nearly the wolf he believes himself to be, though I do wonder at his persistence. There are no rumors in Kent of any financial difficulties with his estate. I have known few men who would pursue so long and fervently for anything less when they understood the woman was so set against them."

"Perhaps now is not the time," said Anthony. "But I will not always be required to be so circumspect."

He turned to Elizabeth. "You are well?"

"It takes more than Lord Winchester to intimidate me, Brother."

"Excellent!" Anthony extended his arm, which Elizabeth took. "Let us forget about Winchester for the evening and enjoy ourselves. I believe *I* have the supper set tonight."

James groaned, but Elizabeth only laughed. "I suppose you must have it. James may dance with his wife, for it would not do for her to think he is neglecting her."

They all laughed and moved back to their previous position on the side of the dance floor. And then it began all over again. And the torment was so very intense. But Darcy would not have it any other way.

Saturday, May 16, 1812
Fitzwilliam House, London

It was the very next morning when the peace of the house was shattered by the arrival of an objectionable presence. The first hint Elizabeth had of any intrusion was the sound of a loud voice penetrating the door of the sitting-room where she was speaking with her mother, Constance, and Lady Catherine. Lady Althea had also visited that morning, and Elizabeth, who had come to esteem the woman greatly, was enjoying their visit.

She knew that voice. She knew it almost as well as she knew her own, for had she not often heard it raised in anger, or screeching out her lamentations of this matter or that, or tittering over some piece of juicy gossip? The heat of embarrassment settled over Elizabeth's face as she rose without thought, knowing the true measure of her upbringing was about to be revealed to those whose opinions she had come to value.

When the footman opened the door, the situation was revealed to be even worse than Elizabeth had imagined, for Mrs. Margaret Bennet was not the only person to enter the room. Immediately behind her walked Kitty and Lydia, their eyes wide as they gazed around, astonished by what they were seeing. But that did not halt their excessive giggling and loud exclamations which mingled with Mrs. Bennet's. Dear, sweet Jane was also there, watching her mother through frightened eyes, with Mary following behind. Aunt Gardiner was also present, and she walked alongside Maggie Bennet, attempting to settle her, though her words were having little effect.

"Lizzy!" squealed Mrs. Bennet when she caught sight of her former least favorite daughter. "How happy we are all to see you! And in such fine surroundings! I dare say I have never seen such happy appointments as I see before me. The lady of the house must possess great taste and discernment, for even great wealth cannot account for the beauty of this house."

Elizabeth's eyes closed in mortification, and when she opened them, she was almost afraid of what she would see. Her mother was watching the approaching ladies with a countenance devoid of all emotion, but Constance was amused, while Lady Althea shocked. Lady Catherine, who could never be accused of hiding her opinions, was watching Mrs. Bennet as if she was a particularly virulent form of the plague in human form.

"I apologize that we did not attend you earlier," said Mrs. Bennet, completely unaware of anything other than ingratiating herself with Elizabeth. "But had Mr. Bennet . . . Well, that is not important, though I will say that your father was most disobliging for keeping the truth of the situation from us. But I am so happy to be here now. We are staying with my brother, but I am sure you will wish to welcome us with open arms. I can hardly wait for you to take your sisters into your bosom and introduce them to the many rich men with whom you now associate."

"Maggie, that is enough!" hissed Mrs. Gardiner. "Can you not see you are making Elizabeth uncomfortable?"

"Why should that be?" demanded Maggie Bennet. "She was raised as my daughter for eighteen years. Should she not be grateful? Should she not be happy to see her sisters and allow them to partake in her good fortune?"

"For heaven's sake, woman!" exclaimed Lady Catherine when she could no longer hold her temper. "I have never seen such a disgusting display of avarice and ill manners in my life. Do you have no sense at all?"

"And who are you?" sneered Mrs. Bennet. "By what right do you speak to me in such a way?"

"I am Lady Catherine de Bourgh, sister to the Earl of Matlock, and aunt to Lady Elizabeth Fitzwilliam. *Who* are *you*, madam?"

It was the titles as much as the haughty way in which Lady Catherine spoke which silenced Mrs. Bennet, Elizabeth thought. Mrs. Bennet had always had the ability to display her own brand of haughtiness when she deemed necessary, but it had always been tempered by the woman's silliness, which hovered about her like a miasma. It seemed for the first time she realized with *whom* she was speaking, for she gaped at Lady Catherine, and when her eyes turned to Lady Susan, they became even wider.

"Elizabeth," said Lady Susan, "this is Mrs. Bennet, I presume?"

"It is," replied Elizabeth, though she wished the ground would open and swallow her. "And these are her daughters, Jane, Mary, Catherine, and Lydia."

Lady Susan's gaze swept over them all, and though they softened a little when she looked at Jane, it was clear she did not think much of the rest of them. Jane appeared as embarrassed as Elizabeth herself, and Mary was gazing about in awe, though her cheeks were a little pink as well. Only Kitty and Lydia appeared unaffected, as they giggled and whispered back and forth.

"Mrs. Bennet, though I am grateful to your family for providing a home to my daughter, I do not appreciate your barging into my home and speaking in such a manner. It is the height of rudeness to say such things in a loud voice for all to hear."

"Lizzy!" exclaimed Lydia as if she had not heard Lady Susan's admonishments. "I can hardly believe you live in such a place. But I cannot imagine the gentlemen here are more pleasant than the officers."

"But they must be wealthier!" exclaimed Kitty, and the girls collapsed into giggles. "I cannot wait until you introduce us to them."

"As I was saying," said Lady Susan, her glare flaying the two girls where they stood, "this invasion into our home is not appreciated. You will all leave, at once. When Elizabeth is ready, she will initiate contact with you, but not until then."

It was apparent that this rebuke did not sit well with Mrs. Bennet. The woman had never been able to read the moods of others, and she was senseless enough that she did not realize that an angry countess was not one with whom she should trifle.

"Elizabeth was *my* daughter for many years. Did we not take her in and clothe her for years without recompense?"

"You have the audacity to say this considering how Elizabeth was forced to leave your house?" demanded Lady Catherine.

"Elizabeth knows why that was necessary," said Mrs. Bennet, her impatience showing through. "My daughters are her sisters, and we are her family. Now her family needs her. If she does not agree to sponsor my daughters and introduce them to society as her sisters, I will let it be known far and wide that she cannot be your daughter — that I birthed her."

If Elizabeth thought her mother and aunt were furious before, it was nothing compared to their reaction to Mrs. Bennet's inane statement. At once, Mrs. Bennet seemed to realize her mistake, for she grew pale in the face of their forbidding countenances. Mrs. Gardiner, who understood exactly what difficulties could come her way if she persisted, grasped Mrs. Bennet's arm in a tight grip.

"Maggie, unless you wish to ruin your family forever, you will not say another word." She turned to Lady Susan and curtseyed deep in apology, pulling a clearly reluctant Mrs. Bennet down with her. "Lady Susan, you have my deepest apologies. It is clear I did not do enough to prevent this incident from occurring, and I deeply regret the disturbance of your home. We shall leave immediately."

Though Elizabeth's mother appeared as if she wished to humiliate Mrs. Bennet where she stood, it was clear her esteem for Mrs. Gardiner tempered her response.

"Mrs. Gardiner, I appreciate your efforts, but it is clear your sister does whatever she pleases, in defiance of all sense."

Mrs. Bennet's mouth tightened in a firm line, but she had the sense to keep her peace. Mrs. Gardiner's hand tightening on her arm might have had something to do with it.

"As for you, Mrs. Bennet, you should know that we have proof that Elizabeth is my daughter, and your husband has already confessed to finding her in Cambridge. If you say *anything* to cast aspersions on Elizabeth's right to be recognized as my daughter, it will go ill with you. Do you understand?"

Lady Susan's last words were spoken in a slow and deliberate pace, and her eyes bored into Mrs. Bennet's. The woman grimaced, but she nodded. It was clear her thoughts were centered on the shattering of her dreams of insinuating her daughters into the highest of society.

"Now," continued Lady Susan, "if Elizabeth wishes to retain her connection to your family, she will do so, but it will be *her* choice. You and your daughters may write to her if she wishes it, but you *will not* importune her again. Have I made myself quite clear?"

"Yes, your ladyship," said Mrs. Bennet, a sullenness underlying her words.

"Good. Then you may depart. But before you do, you should know that you will never be welcome in London society with such behavior as you have shown here today. You would be ridiculed, and Elizabeth along with you. If you wish to see Elizabeth in society, you should learn how to restrain yourself." Lady Susan's eyes flicked to Kitty and Lydia, who were watching them with mouths wide open. "And your youngest daughters had best learn some manners too, else they will not be welcome here."

"I am fifteen and have been in society this past year," said an affronted Lydia.

Lady Susan's glare silenced her immediately. "You are a silly and ignorant child. Even if you learn how to behave, you would not be eligible to be introduced to society until you are eighteen."

Lydia glared mutinously at Lady Susan, but she refrained from speaking again. Mrs. Gardiner took the opportunity to herd her family from the room.

"My apologies, Lady Susan. It is time for us to depart."

And with Lydia and Kitty in tow, Mrs. Gardiner guided Mrs. Bennet from the room, leaving Mary and Jane behind. Though Jane was quite obviously mortified due to her mother's behavior, she pushed it aside and approached Elizabeth, seeming unsure of herself. Elizabeth was having nothing of any form of deference from her dearest sister and threw her arms around Jane.

"I *am* happy to see you again, Jane." She disengaged from Jane and smiled at Mary, drawing her in for another embrace. "And you, Mary."

"We will trespass on your kindness no longer," said Jane. "But I hope you will think kindly of us once the shock has dissipated."

"Of course, I do," replied Elizabeth. "My life is unsettled at present, but I have no intention of losing my connection with you both."

Jane appeared to wilt with relief. "Thank you, Lizzy." Then her hand flew to her mouth and she looked wildly at Lady Susan. "I am sorry! Lady Elizabeth, of course!"

"Miss Bennet," said Lady Susan, smiling at Jane, "you have known my daughter as 'Lizzy' for many years now. If Elizabeth has no objections, I do not mind if you continue to do so."

"Thank you," replied Jane with a deep curtsey.

"I hope that we will see you in Meryton when matters settle," said Mary. "Until then, we will do our best to keep Mama away."

Elizabeth laughed, and her sisters laughed with her. "She has a will of iron. Perhaps it would be best to help her understand, for I believe understanding has eluded her."

"You are correct, of course," replied Mary.

Then, sensitive to the fact that Mrs. Gardiner was likely waiting for them and eager to avoid their mother's entrance yet again, Jane and Mary departed, amid wishes for Elizabeth's happiness and hopes of meeting again soon. Elizabeth was already missing her sisters, and she promised she would not become a stranger to them. And then they were gone.

"If I had not met her, I could scarce have believed it," said Lady Catherine into the silence.

"Mrs. Bennet is difficult," said Elizabeth, "but she is rarely this . . . agitated. I dare say she saw the opportunity to save her family and was desperate to bring it about."

"I have sympathy for her situation," replied Lady Susan. "But her behavior was abhorrent. She must improve, or she will not be welcome in society."

"Indeed, she must," said Elizabeth.

CHAPTER XXVI

Sunday, May 24, 1812
Fitzwilliam House, London

While Elizabeth felt all the mortification of her adoptive mother's coming, she found great comfort in the assurances of all who were witness to the spectacle. They were effuse in assuring her they did not think any less of her because of it.

"You can no more influence the behavior of the woman who raised you than you could avoid being taken away as a child," said Lady Catherine, stating the matter with a succinctness which was her custom. "Do not think further on the subject. That you have acquitted yourself well is a testament to your own abilities."

"It seems she had some little influence on you," said Constance *sotto voce.*

They all laughed, and the matter was dropped. Later, when the matter was explained to the gentlemen, they all shook their heads and openly wondered how Mrs. Bennet could be so completely senseless. Anthony, being the only man who had seen her (William and Georgiana had not eaten dinner with them that night) only smiled, a mysterious sort of amusement evident in his manner.

The other fact that Elizabeth noticed in the ensuing days was the behavior of Lord Winchester. He had not, by any means, given up in his pursuit of her. He still approached her on any occasion in which they were together at an event, which was not at all infrequent. But his blatant interest in her was now tempered, and his actions were more reserved. Where he had advanced openly and aggressively in the past, he now watched and waited. Elizabeth supposed she should be wary of him and wonder what he planned, but she could only be grateful for the cessation of his onerous attentions. And though Mr. Standish filled that void, his own attentions growing to a certain extent, even the two men together did not match Lord Winchester's previous ardor, so Elizabeth found herself well pleased.

What she was not pleased about was the fact that two men, both many years her senior, were showing interest in her to such a great degree.

"Am I doomed to attract only men who are old enough to be my father?" complained she one day to her mother. "I would have thought there are good men of an age with me who would pursue me, but even Farnsworth Longfellow has no real interest."

"Do you truly want more attention?" Lady Susan's smile shone with suppressed mirth. "I thought you were quite willing to forgo *all* attention."

While Elizabeth understood her mother's amusement, at that moment she was able to see nothing more than her own pique. "It would be gratifying to know that *someone* close to my age considers me handsome enough to tempt them."

Constance, who was sitting close by, burst into laughter, seeming unable to hold it in. Elizabeth glared at her, but it only made Constance laugh harder. The affront caused in Elizabeth a reaction which might have been attributed to Lydia—she crossed her arms and let out a loud huff.

"I find this conversation quite interesting, my dearest daughter," said Lady Susan. "Though I thought I had found in you a young woman who was unflappable, it seems like you are capable of silliness on occasion."

"She appears much like the youngest Bennet, does she not?" asked Constance in between peals of laughter.

Elizabeth had the grace to feel embarrassed, but that did not diminish her annoyance, as much with Constance's observation as her own disgust for the situation.

"What I believe you have neglected to notice, Elizabeth," said Lady

Susan, "is that there are many men who have shown interest in you. But you have been so set on ensuring you do not give encouragement that they have largely stepped back. Assuming you do not make a match this year, I believe you will have more young men vying for your hand than you wish when we return next year."

"Or perhaps even during the little season," added Lady Catherine.

"Only Standish and Winchester have pressed their suits, though with Standish I cannot even accuse him of that much." Lady Susan patted Elizabeth's hand. "Now, has your little bout of peevishness passed?"

"It has," said Elizabeth, feeling a hint of embarrassment pass over her. "I only hope something presents itself before that happens. The attention of Lord Winchester alone has left me with a sour taste for *any* courtship."

"That is only because you have not yet been courted by a good man," said Constance. "When you are, you will find it is well worth it."

Elizabeth nodded, but she was distracted by the thought of a tall man, with wavy hair and blue eyes, paying her exquisite attentions. Any woman could not help but wish for the devotion of such a man. Could he possibly favor her with them? Elizabeth could not state for certain, but if she *was* the recipient, she could not imagine refusing. But she said nothing and attempted to return her thoughts to the conversation—Constance, in particular, would see it as an opportunity to tease her, should she learn of Elizabeth's reflections.

As the days slipped by, Elizabeth enjoyed as much of society as she could, and as she did, she watched, trying to see the truth of her mother's assertions for herself. There were, of course, those who were objectionable, aside from the two whose actions formed the basis for her discontent. But there were also many of whom she thought fondly, and while she was not certain, she thought her mother's opinions had some basis in fact. At any ball, her sets were almost always taken quickly, and though some voiced displeasure that she was never available for the most important sets, the majority seemed to understand, and eventually ceased importuning her for them.

One of those Elizabeth had not thought to feel exactly friendly for was Farnsworth, but she was quickly forced to reevaluate his character. Though he was still the same gangly youth who did not stimulate her mind much, she came to understand that he was a kind-hearted young man. He also exerted himself in her protection, often claiming a dance or her attention to ensure others could not. Her feelings warmed toward him considerably given his actions, and before long, Elizabeth knew she could count on him to assist where needed if her other protectors were not available.

On a certain day late in May, Elizabeth happened to be in the library, perusing the collection of books, when her father came upon her. Elizabeth was not certain if he had been looking for her, or if their meeting was accidental, but he took the opportunity to stop and speak. Of all those of her new family, Elizabeth thought that coming to know the earl had been the most difficult. He was an affable man, but one who was a little intimidating, and though Elizabeth knew he was happy with her and pleased at her return, she still found it difficult to speak with him at times.

"You mother has mentioned our thoughts about returning early to our estate, has she not?"

"Yes," replied Elizabeth, recalling that conversation had taken place almost two weeks before. "I am happy to endure the season as long as you wish, but I am curious to see Snowlock."

The earl laughed. "I find your choice of words to be revealing, Elizabeth."

Coloring, Elizabeth returning his smile tentatively. "Perhaps they are. You will find I am more comfortable in the country. Town has its benefits, but I have lived all my life on an estate, and that is what I love best."

"I understand," replied Lord Matlock. "You fit well among the rest of us, for we are all the same." He grinned. "No doubt Catherine will claim comfort in any kind of society and berate us all for suggesting we are anything but one of England's leading families, but she, herself, has but rarely left Rosings in recent years."

"I had understood part of that was because of Anne's health." The state of Anne's wellbeing was a matter which confused Elizabeth. The woman was not robust—this was true. But Elizabeth wondered how much of her infirmity was physical limitation and how much was the coddling she endured from her mother.

"It undoubtedly is," said the earl, blithely unaware of the direction of Elizabeth's thoughts. "But Catherine's only interest in London society is the necessity of maintaining the family's standing, and that she is content to leave to others."

Elizabeth saw the truth in what her father was saying and she nodded.

"Regardless," continued the earl, "I have been making arrangements for our departure and wished to inform you of them. If you are agreeable, I believe we may depart by next week."

"That is quite agreeable to me. I only worry about how our departure will be seen by society."

"How we are seen by others has never been of concern to the Fitzwilliam family, beyond the general desire to be regarded well. If the gossips wish to speak of our early departure, let them do so, for it will not affect us.

"It will not cause any great excitement anyway. The greater part of the season ends at the end of May, though there are always events in June. But by the third or fourth week of June, most families will have retreated to their country estates. We are only leaving a little early, and we have done it enough in the past that it will not excite much commentary."

"I am happy to hear it," replied Elizabeth. Then she turned her attention to her future home—the home of her distant past. "I understand Snowlock is a large estate. Can you tell me something of it?"

They had a pleasant conversation for some time on the topic of the estate, and she found that her father was even a greater source of information than her mother had been. Lady Susan cared for the house and the tenants, but it was by the earl's management that the estate was made prosperous. It was that management which rendered him familiar with seemingly every inch of his lands. Of the most interest to Elizabeth was the extent of the park—which she already knew was large—and the paths which would lead her to hidden delights in the woods and fields, the rivers which meandered through the estate.

"It is not so close to the Peak District," said her father in describing it to her. "As such, though there are some sections which are rugged, it is not so much so as Darcy's estate, which is far closer to the peaks. Darcy will tell you that *his* estate is much more beautiful."

Elizabeth smiled, certain that William was, indeed, proud of his home. "Then you dispute his assertion?"

"I did not say that." The earl's eyes twinkled in mirth. "Darcy's pride is well founded. But Snowlock is not devoid of beauty either. The land rises to the north, and there is an extensive range of woods there through which a picturesque river runs. What I know of your habits suggests that I may have difficulty keeping you from them."

"I will attempt to avoid being *too* much trouble," said Elizabeth with a straight face.

The earl chuckled, but before long his mirth was gone, replaced by a sort of seriousness which suggested to Elizabeth he had something of import he wished to discuss. Once again that sense of awe for the man and his position settled over her. Though she attempted to remain as easy as their previous conversation had been, she understood a man of his perception might easily be able to detect her façade.

"Elizabeth, I sense that it has been difficult at times for you to come to know me."

A feeling of mortification swept over Elizabeth, and she closed her eyes. She opened them again when she felt the earl's hand close about her own. When he looked at her, she could see no censure—nothing but concern for her radiated from him, and Elizabeth felt comforted by it.

"I am not censuring you, my dear," said he, his voice quiet. "Nothing could be further from the truth. I understand it, you see. Your stories of Mr. and Mrs. Bennet have painted a clear picture of your life with them. It is only natural that a closeness with your mother would develop quickly, given how you view Mrs. Bennet. By the same token, I understand your closeness with Mr. Bennet has inhibited our connection."

Elizabeth had not thought of it in that manner before, but she knew he was likely correct. In some ways, becoming close to her real father had almost seemed like a . . . betrayal, though she was not certain she could use that word. When she understood, a hot wave of shame came over her. But before she could consider it any further, the hand still holding hers squeezed, and she looked up at him, afraid of the censure which might be there.

Instead, there was nothing but understanding. "Do not concern yourself, Elizabeth. As I said, I have recognized what is holding you in check. Dare I hope that such limitations may be overcome?"

"I hope so, Father," said Elizabeth, realizing it was true. This man had suffered as much as had her mother—did she not owe him as much of her affection as possible?

Then Elizabeth paused when she realized that he would not wish for obligation. And she did not wish it either. He was her *father* and one who had loved her and taken her into his home without hesitation. Elizabeth very much wished to know him intimately as father, protector, and the man who had a part in bringing her into being.

"In fact, I would like that very much," Elizabeth was able to say, with complete conviction.

He must have recognized it, for he showed her a heartfelt smile which seemed to bare his very soul to her. Elizabeth could not be more touched.

"Then what shall we discuss?" asked he. His eyes roamed around the room before coming to rest again upon her, one eyebrow raised. "Books, perhaps? It seems appropriate, considering where we are."

Elizabeth laughed. "I might have expected such an approach from William. But I am completely happy to discuss books. They are, as you know, one of my favorite topics."

And so they did, staying in the room together for most of the morning and into the afternoon. Elizabeth found that her father was as well read as her adoptive father, though his opinions of what he read were quite different from Mr. Bennet's. He was obviously a master debater, a skill which came in handy when he was arguing his opinions in the House of Lords.

He was also much less cynical than Mr. Bennet, and he looked at the world through eyes less sardonic, and ultimately less judgmental. Though it would take time, Elizabeth thought they were well on their way to a true meeting of minds. And she could not be happier.

Friday, May 29, 1812
Cheshire House, London

It was early the next week when Elizabeth and her family were invited to a dinner at the house of the Duke of Cheshire. Though she had not known at the time, the Duchess's traditional ball had been held at the beginning of the season, before Elizabeth had become known to her family. The dinner, of course, would be a much more intimate event, though still attended by many more people than could be accommodated in Mrs. Bennet's dining room.

The duke and duchess were not well known to Elizabeth. They were friendly and affable when Elizabeth had an opportunity to speak with them, but those opportunities had been sparse. Elizabeth might have thought they did not approve of her, for whatever reason, had Constance not chanced to make a comment to Elizabeth which changed her perspective.

"My mother is very impressed with you. She has told me she was not certain what to expect when you were introduced. But you have exceeded all her expectations."

Elizabeth was surprised, but she endeavored to hide it. "Your mother is too kind. I do not think we have been much in company."

"That is because Mother knew it would be overwhelming for you, my dear," replied Constance. "She has kept her distance in order to avoid increasing your distress. But I think you can expect her to be much more amiable tonight."

And Constance's words were borne out when they arrived. The duchess was on hand to greet them, and after embracing her daughter and greeting her close friends, it was to Elizabeth she turned.

"Lady Elizabeth, I am happy to finally have you visit my home."

"Perhaps I should have had Constance bring me by for tea," said Elizabeth, shooting an amused grin at her sister by marriage. "I did not know you were so eager to have me here."

Constance returned her look with a waggle of her eyebrows before she allowed James to escort her away to speak with some other friends. It was clear the sharp-eyed duchess had not missed their exchange.

"I see you have become excellent friends with my daughter. I know you have had a trying time of it, my dear. I am only happy you are here now."

"Thank you, Your Grace. I find that I am growing more comfortable as I gain more experience."

"Of course, you are. Now, let us make our way inside. I hope you will agree to perform for us tonight, for your mother informs me that you play very well."

As they entered, the duchess continued to speak, and Elizabeth attended to her conversation as much as she could. She was distracted by thoughts of possibly obliging the company with a song later, and she was grateful now that she had followed her inclination to practice. Though she had performed several times, she had not done so in a location so fine as the house of a duke.

In time, the duchess was obliged to leave her to attend to her other guests, but by this time Elizabeth was comfortable with those in attendance. She mingled among them, speaking with several whom she found interesting, but she was ever aware of the members of her family watching her with care. Though she might have wondered if they were afraid of her making some social gaffe, instead she knew they were just concerned for her. Both Lord Winchester and Mr. Standish were present, though Elizabeth did not know what connection either had with the duke.

For a time, they did not approach—Mr. Standish was engaged in conversation with someone with whom Elizabeth was only little acquainted, while the earl seemed content to simply watch her from afar. The time before dinner was spent with pleasant company, and when the entered the dining room, Elizabeth was situated at a distance from her tormentors, and in a small breach of etiquette, in a place of honor next to the duchess. The dinner hour passed in a pleasant manner, indeed.

Of course, the objectionable members of the company were not to be held at bay for the entire evening, as Elizabeth had known they would not. The first to approach was Mr. Standish. He was pleasant and made every attempt at being amiable, and though Elizabeth was still wary of the man, she found her feelings a little more ambiguous than they had been before. The way he had outmaneuvered Lord Winchester at the ball was still a matter of amusement for her, and she was forced to confess that he had been nothing but pleasant. She was still not certain what a man saw in a girl less than half his age, but she supposed that was how things were done in high society, so she pushed it to the back of her mind.

They spoke of inconsequential matters for some moments, and while Elizabeth might have preferred to give her attention to others who interested her more, her conversation with Mr. Standish was acceptable. But the other man—one who made her even more uncomfortable—appeared unwilling to allow another to monopolize her attention.

"Lady Elizabeth," said Lord Winchester as he stepped to her and bowed. "I hope you are having a pleasant evening."

"Quite pleasant, thank you," replied Elizabeth. Her blithe tone insinuated that it had been acceptable until then, due in large part to the fact that she had not been required to speak to him. Mr. Standish obviously understood her meaning, as did the earl, little though the latter appreciated it.

"We have had an interesting conversation, old boy," said Mr. Standish, an insolent grin descending on Lord Winchester. "I must say that I find Lady Elizabeth to be both intelligent and witty."

"Yes, I dare say she is." The earl's gaze lingered on Elizabeth, attempting to pierce into the depths of her mind, seeking to understand. "Perhaps Lady Elizabeth would prefer my company for a time? I doubt you have the capacity to speak to her of anything other than your recent winning wagers."

"No more than you, Winchester," replied Mr. Standish. "I seem to remember seeing you at many of the same events I have recently attended myself."

Lord Winchester only sneered at Mr. Standish. "I doubt it, sir. I do not frequent the dens of the common folk." His eyes flicked to Elizabeth. "Though I suppose you can hardly be blamed for giving consequence to men related to you, there are few who can aspire to the nobility. You had best think about what you wish in your life, Lady

Elizabeth, for there are *some* who are unable to give you that respectability you deserve."

A cold fury erupted in Elizabeth's heart at the man's words. "It seems to me, Lord Winchester, that you—none of you—understand my wishes. I have respectability aplenty, I thank you very much. It is no wonder that you are unmarried at your age, for surely there is no woman who can withstand the towering monument to your conceit."

Elizabeth turned and left the two men behind, feeling nothing but offense at the audacity of the earl. As she stalked away, she heard a chuckle, and the sound of Mr. Standish saying: "I believe she has you there, Winchester. By all means, continue to importune her—I dare say the sight of your humiliation is amusing for all to see."

"What is it, Elizabeth?" asked her mother as Elizabeth approached her. "Were those two libertines making you uneasy?"

A glance back in the direction of the two men revealed that Mr. Standish had left the earl standing there by himself. He watched her through narrow eyes, his stance screaming his affront, the hot fire of his temper burning. Elizabeth caught his eye and as his jaw tightened, she turned away with a superior glare and a haughty sniff. He was not worth her time, either to converse, to consider, or even to think about in passing.

"It is surprising, but Mr. Standish is not intolerable," replied Elizabeth to her mother's query. "Lord Winchester, however, is beyond all endurance. I dare say I have never met such an objectionable man."

A movement out of the corner of her eye caught Elizabeth's attention, and she turned to see the earl march from the room, his posture rigid in his fury. "With any luck, he will not return for the rest of the evening."

Lady Susan regarded her for a moment before she nodded and smiled. "It is well that we are leaving town soon. Lord Winchester gives the appearance of a man who does not mean to be thwarted."

"He is nothing," declared Elizabeth. "He has moved from lofty self-assurance to petulant insistence, and I have half a mind to cut him the next time I see him."

"My fiery daughter," said her mother, obviously delighted. "It is a dangerous game to cut an earl when you are only the daughter of one. But let us see if we can avoid such a drastic statement, shall we not?"

Elizabeth smiled and agreed, and soon she was in a better frame of mind, speaking with some acquaintances which included Anthony and William. And for the rest of the evening, she did not see Lord Winchester, and Mr. Standish kept his distance. And that was agreeable to Elizabeth.

Chapter XXVII

Friday, May 29, 1812
The Streets of London

*R*egardless of anything else, the girl was certainly a spitfire;
though the hunter could feel offense when her flashing eyes and
sharp tongue were fixed upon him, it never lasted long. And she
was becoming more comfortable in society as time wore on, as her
performance at the duchess's dinner party showed. He doubted she
would have had the courage to behave in such a manner when she had
first been introduced—familiarity and confidence were a contagious
sort of disease, it seemed, and she was not devoid of either.

The carriage moved through the streets of London, the slow,
cadence of the horses' hooves on the street providing a steady
backdrop to his thoughts. Tonight, he was headed for one of his
favorite gaming halls after leaving the duke's residence. It was,
perhaps, an activity which he should avoid until the problem of Lady
Elizabeth Fitzwilliam had been resolved. But he had put much of his
usual activities on hold of late, and he was becoming increasingly loath
to continue to do so. Soon the season would be over, and the games
would largely dry up as well. The amusements at his estate were not

nearly so interesting as those he could find during the season. Thus, he had succumbed to the temptation.

As the carriage rumbled on, he turned his attention again to the girl. She was, he could readily confess, a pretty girl, well-formed and womanly. The more he came to know her, paid her his civility, the more he realized that he could move forward and claim her without sullying his hands by seeing that she never inherited. It was a relief— he would do it if necessary, but gaining the funds *through* her would be the same as gaining them *instead* of her.

When he arrived at his destination, however, all thoughts of Lady Elizabeth Fitzwilliam left his mind. There were other matters to consider, and he would work this one out when the time came. Everything in its place and season, he decided.

And with these thoughts, the hunter alighted from his carriage and strode into the building.

Saturday, May 30, 1812
Fitzwilliam House, London

Had Elizabeth felt anything for Lord Winchester other than anger, she might have been wary of the possibility of retaliation. As it was, she was disposed to think of nothing but how the man continued to offend her with his advances and disgust her with his pride and conceit. Though he was not in evidence for the rest of the evening, she continued to seethe in discontented fury, and it faded but little, even after she returned to her home and sought her bed.

It is an understood fact that a cornered animal becomes all that much more dangerous, as it will fight for its life. Or perhaps more appropriate to the situation, a man scorned was likely to behave in a manner which was even more objectionable than he had before. So it was with Lord Winchester, as Elizabeth was to discover.

The morning after the dinner party was spent in leisurely pursuits. The door knocker was left up, but they had only a few visitors, none of whom stayed long or had much, in Elizabeth's opinion, to say. The family party was fractured that morning, all involved in their own activities, and since Elizabeth showed no inclination to go out, her usual protectors seemed to have decided that she was safe enough in the house.

Though Elizabeth did not often feel the need to be apart from others, on that morning she had felt disinclined for their company and had spent much of the morning in her own room, descending for a short time to greet those few who had visited. After the visits, Elizabeth retreated to the library and spent the rest of the morning there, a book open on her lap. But while she made some progress reading it, she spent much more time looking down at her book while seeing nothing on the pages.

When the door opened behind her, Elizabeth thought nothing of it—it was undoubtedly Anthony, coming to confirm for himself that she was safe and unbothered. Or perhaps William had visited. The thought of William come to see her, his eyes alight with interest in whatever she said, produced a wave of happiness, and her lips curved in response.

"Had I known of your desire to see me, I would have come sooner, Lady Elizabeth."

Startled, Elizabeth scrambled to her feet, only to see the smirking visage of Lord Winchester facing her. The man stood in the doorway watching her, the leer with which he regarded her making her feel instantly uncomfortable. Of the butler or any other servant, there was no sign. Elizabeth could not fathom how he had come to be in this part of the house.

"Lord Winchester," said Elizabeth, quickly recovering her wits. "What a singularly unpleasant surprise to see you here. Why have you come?"

His grin faltered a little at Elizabeth's words, but he soon recovered and sauntered further into the room. Elizabeth, not wishing to be in his company, looked toward the door and was relieved to see Thompson poking his head through, catching her eye, a question in his expression. Elizabeth motioned him to take up position on the inside of the door.

"I suppose I should not be surprised to find you in the library," said Lord Winchester, looking about the room with interest. "You seem to be the bluestocking type, with your impertinent opinions and tendency to amaze the room with witty comments. It is less surprising to know that your father indulges you in this, though you would be better served learning your place in society."

"My place in society is no mystery to me, sir," replied Elizabeth. "What I do with my time is not your concern."

"It is the concern of every man who witnesses a woman attempting to be more than she ought. I doubt you would draw much interest, if not for me, despite a connection to a noble family and a handsome dowry. No man appreciates a wife who tries to show herself to be more intelligent than he."

"Then I wonder why you pursue me so diligently, Lord Winchester," said Elizabeth. Her voice was dripping with sarcasm of a purpose, to see if she could offend him. "If men such as you prefer a stupid wife, then they should look for one. If you do not wish a wife who *tries* to show she is more intelligent than you, why would you pursue one who *is*?"

The retort pierced Lord Winchester's barrier of haughtiness and for the briefest of instants, he looked at her with blazing affront. Soon, however, he mastered his pique and it was hidden behind his veneer of sardonic boredom.

"It seems like you still have not learned your lesson. I pursue you because it is what I want. I am not accustomed to being denied anything I wish to possess."

"I am not chattel. I am not a possession for which to be bartered. Your expectations shall be denied. While it may be pitiable for *you*, it will have no effect on *me*."

"Be silent!" snarled the earl. Where before he had kept his careful countenance, now the veil had been removed, and the true measure of the man was revealed. "You will not interrupt me. While you have been raised to this estate by the dubious claims of the obviously addled Earl of Matlock, you are naught but a commoner, a country miss with more cleverness than sense."

"Then why would you wish to continue to importune me?" cried Elizabeth. "Surely I do not measure up to your sense of an exalted female. Why should you debase yourself with such an obviously inferior female?"

"My reasons are my own, and not open to discussion with you. It is enough to know that I mean to have you as my wife."

"No, you will not. I would not marry you if you were the Prince Regent himself."

Lord Winchester scowled at her. "You will not speak to me in such a manner. I am an earl, and you will respect me as such."

"It appears you required a reminder, sir," said Elizabeth. "My father is also an earl, and he will take a dim view of how you are importuning me *again*."

"He will be reasonable when our engagement is presented as a fait accompli. I have much to offer him. He knows this."

Elizabeth laughed, a harsh, contemptuous gesture. "You know nothing. My father loves me. He wishes me to be happy. I could no more be happy with *you* for a husband than I could be if I married a toad."

"I said you will not speak to me in such a way!" The earl stepped forward, but Elizabeth, expecting such intimidation, managed to sidestep him and put the sofa between them.

"If you behaved like a gentleman, I would not speak to you so," said Elizabeth. Her eyes darted to the footman still standing uncertainly by the door. He seemed to catch her message, for he moved into the room, ready to restrain the earl should he make a violent move.

"You have pluck—I will give you that." Lord Winchester sneered at her. "I will enjoy taming that wild spirit of yours."

"My lord," said Thompson, interrupting the earl's objectionable words, "Lady Elizabeth has requested you leave."

"Begone!" growled the earl. "I will not be denied by a mere servant."

"I have already warned you once, your lordship," persisted Thompson.

"Do you wish to lose your position?" asked the earl, as he turned and glared at the man. "One more word from you and I will make it impossible for you to be employed again."

"My master has given us all leave to deal with any threats to Lady Elizabeth by any means necessary."

"I am to be her future husband. I am no threat!"

"Lady Elizabeth does not wish for your attentions. She has already made it clear. Now, I will escort you from the house. You may take up the matter with Lord Matlock at another time."

The situation was escalating, and Elizabeth could see the pulsing veins on Lord Winchester's temples, and the clenching of his hands into tight fists. He was clearly on the verge of physically attacking the footman.

Though she did not fear his ability to deal with the younger man and make a move against her, Elizabeth determined that it was time to get help from others in the house. She turned and made her way around the couch in the direction of the footman, and when she did so, Lord Winchester tried to follow her. But Thompson, seeing her move, intercepted him, and held him back so that Elizabeth could escape.

"Unhand me!" demanded the earl.

He raised his hand to strike Thompson, but the man caught his hand in one meaty fist, halting the earl's attack without batting an eye. He moved away a little, releasing Lord Winchester's arm, though keeping his position between Elizabeth and the now enraged earl.

"I will see you hang for this!" screamed Lord Winchester, and he stepped forward to cut Elizabeth off from the door, only to be intercepted once again.

By this time, Elizabeth had already reached the open portal, and she used the opportunity to move through it and escape from the odious man. But before she could, she was confronted with the sight of her father, Anthony, and William, in the company of the butler, with Mr. Standish trailing along behind. They entered the room quickly in response to the still screaming Lord Winchester, William pausing to look in Elizabeth's eyes, concern written upon his brow.

"I am well, William. Thompson protected me."

William nodded, but his fury did not abate. He turned back to the scene unfolding in the library, and Elizabeth followed his gaze. The entrance of the five men had silenced Lord Winchester's tirade, but he did not appear any less determined to have his way. He glared at Elizabeth from across the room, and in response, William stepped forward, putting himself between them in an obvious gesture of protection. Lord Winchester did not miss the meaning of his movement, and he directed a look of pure poison at William.

But soon he was confronted by other problems. Anthony, who was as tall as the footman Thompson, though not so burly, rushed to place himself in front of the man, and her father was only a step behind. Lord Winchester was not a diminutive man, but the sight of three larger men regarding him with murder in their eyes was enough to intimidate many a brave man, and he retreated a step.

"What is the meaning of this, Winchester?" asked her father. His voice was low and foreboding, and Elizabeth knew he was about to lose his composure.

Though Lord Winchester appeared unwilling to answer, he drew himself up to his full height. "I have come to petition you for the hand of your daughter, Lady Elizabeth Fitzwilliam, in marriage."

"And you do this by importuning her in private?" asked an incensed Lord Matlock. "Have you taken leave of your senses, man?"

"It is customary," replied Lord Winchester through clenched teeth, "to ask the young lady for her hand before approaching the father."

"It is customary," echoed her father, "to request a formal courtship, is it not?"

"Courtship may be dispensed with in the right circumstances."

"And what possible reasoning could you use to think this is the right circumstances? Are you completely witless? My daughter despises the very sight of you. How can you think she would accept your advances and that I would agree to it, even if she were coerced?"

"I cannot believe she is indifferent to me," said Lord Winchester. He puffed his chest out in a manner which reminded Elizabeth of a peacock. It was unfortunate for the earl, but Elizabeth considered the peacock to be far more appealing.

A soft snort caught Elizabeth's attention, and she turned her head to the side to see Mr. Standish regarding Lord Winchester with an expression of utter contempt. When he noted Elizabeth watching him, he shot her a sardonic smile and said but one word: "Idiot."

It was incongruous to the situation, but Elizabeth felt a hint of hysterical laughter push against her composure. It was all she could do to limit it to a chuckle. Mr. Standish's voice, while soft, was still heard throughout the room. Lord Winchester purpled in rage, but the other men only continued to watch him, though she was certain they agreed with Mr. Standish's assessment.

"You believe she is not indifferent to you," repeated her father. He turned and looked over his shoulder at Elizabeth, showing her an arched eyebrow.

"The earl is delusional," said Elizabeth, directing a frown of utter scorn at the man. "I would rather marry an asp than such an objectionable man. I have no doubt the asp would be pleasanter."

It was at this moment that Elizabeth began to worry for Lord Winchester's health, though she supposed she should not be concerned for such a cretin. His purple countenance was so dark that she wondered if he was about to suffer apoplexy.

"There you have it, Winchester," said Lord Matlock, turning back to him. "My daughter has no interest in you, and I have no interest in directing her heart. I expect you will turn your attention to some other woman from this moment forward."

It was with an effort that Lord Winchester mastered his fury and addressed Lord Matlock, his voice raspy with suppressed emotion. "Be reasonable, Matlock. You know what I can offer her. She will be a countess in her own right, quite apart from the benefit you will gain from an alliance with my family. Are the romantic wishes of a young woman who has, after all, been raised in most unsuitable circumstances, to thwart what would be beneficial for all?"

"Lord Winchester," said her father, "you seem to forget that my daughter has been returned to us only recently, and as such, we are not prepared to part with her."

"Then it may be a long engagement."

"You misunderstand me. I have no need of an alliance with you, and no interest in bartering my daughter to obtain it. My primary concern is Elizabeth's happiness. It is clear to me she could not be happy with you, so I will never consent to such a match, regardless of whatever arguments you use to convince yourself of your worthiness. You are a stain upon the nobility. My daughter will not marry you."

His face ablaze with anger, Lord Winchester turned to Elizabeth. "Is this how it will be? Will you throw away all that I could give you?"

"You could give me nothing more than misery, Lord Winchester. You must know that I have no need to marry if I do not wish it. Why, then, would I would I marry an objectionable man? I will marry for love or not marry at all."

The way Lord Winchester watched her told Elizabeth that he was attempting to discern the strength of her resolve. It seemed he did not like what he saw, as a sneer soon came over his countenance.

"Very well, then," said he. "It is clear that your years in objectionable circumstances have done away with the balance of your sense."

He moved to depart from the room, Thompson and Anthony watching closely for any moves against Elizabeth. There were none, though he glanced at her more than once, his disdain clear for all to see. But before he left, her father spoke once more.

"Do not approach my daughter again, Winchester. She will not be available to dance with you at any events we attend as long as we are here for the season. And next year she will not even acknowledge you."

"You are set to leave already?" asked Lord Winchester. "Typical that you would wish to hide away your disappointment of a daughter. If, indeed, she is simply not some manner of wishful thinking on your part."

"She is not being hidden away and will return when the time comes. Either way, it is none of your concern."

Lord Winchester only shook his head and departed, Mr. Thompson following him to see to it that he left. In the wake of his going, silence reigned in the room.

"Well, who would have thought Winchester could be so foolish?"

Elizabeth turned to Mr. Standish and stared at him. But he only chuckled and shook his head.

"I am aware that I am only tolerated, as you do not appreciate my habits. But at least I am fully aware of my standing. Lord Winchester seems to think he may charm you and win the fair Lady Elizabeth with nothing more than his insistence. I knew he was self-centered, but I never thought him capable of lying to himself so completely."

"You have my apologies, Mr. Standish," said Elizabeth, not of a mind to be importuned any further, "but I had not expected to see you today."

Mr. Standish's grin never wavered. "No, I suppose you would not have expected it. But I found I had business with your father."

"You are well, Elizabeth?" asked her father, grasping her hands.

"I am," replied Elizabeth, still regarding the visitor with more than a hint of suspicion.

"That is well, then." He glanced at Mr. Standish before turning his attention once again on Elizabeth. "As for Standish, he was the one who warned us of Winchester's coming. Perhaps a little politeness would be proper?"

"It is no trouble," replied Mr. Standish, waving her father's concern away before Elizabeth could reply. "You daughter has had a trying morning. I do not begrudge her wariness. It has done her good, after all."

"My father is correct, Mr. Standish," replied Elizabeth, curtseying to him. "I apologize for my rudeness."

"I thank you," replied Mr. Standish. He bowed, but Elizabeth thought there was a mocking quality in his tone and actions. But she knew no ill of him, and it was perhaps only his character to seem that way to her. Elizabeth knew she would need to be politer to him, if only in gratitude for his actions.

"How did you know of Winchester's coming?" asked Anthony.

"I happened to come to the door just after he had entered. Though I would cast no aspersions on the diligence of your butler, it appeared like no one was present at the door, and Winchester came inside and began his search without anyone being the wiser. When I knocked and was let in by your man, I was surprised not to see Winchester and reacted accordingly."

"Well. it is good you did, though Thompson seemed to have everything in hand." The earl grunted. "I do not suppose you will release that mountain of a man to work for me, will you, Darcy? He is so large that I have no doubt anyone would think twice about attempting something with her, as long as he looms over her."

"His family has lived on my estate for generations," replied William. "He is happy, I think, to assist in Elizabeth's care, but I do not wish to release him from my service."

The earl grunted and the matter was dropped. Mr. Standish spoke into the silence.

"Excuse me, Lord Matlock, but I should depart. I am curious, however—am I to understand that you mean to retire to your estate early?"

"We do, though we have not made it widely known," replied Lord Matlock. "We will leave by the end of the week."

Mr. Standish's eyes found Elizabeth. "Might I assume it is because your daughter is desirous of departing town?"

"I *have* had enough of society for the present, Mr. Standish," replied Elizabeth icily. "My family is indulging my wish of seeing the home I have not seen in many years."

"Of course," was Mr. Standish's easy reply. "I apologize if I have caused offense. I had no intention of casting aspersions on you." He paused and chuckled. "London society can be a trial. Being thrown in, even with your family's assistance, cannot but be exhausting. You will likely see me there, then, for my estate abuts your father's to the west."

"You are to return too?" Elizabeth could not help but be suspicious.

"I will, though not immediately. I will likely stay at least another two weeks, perhaps longer. But I will be in residence at my estate for the summer."

With a bow over her reluctant hand, Mr. Standish excused himself and left the room.

"Does anyone else feel like the world has turned on its head when Standish is not behaving like an arrogant bastard?" asked Anthony of no one.

Her father shot Anthony a quelling look, but William only nodded in agreement. When he noticed Elizabeth looking at him with evident curiosity, he endeavored to explain.

"Standish is a good name for him, as he has always been rather standoffish. He has never truly given much attention to the family, and when he encountered us, he has never shown us much more than cold politeness."

"Darcy is not truly related to Standish," added Anthony. "He is a distant cousin on mother's side."

"I have often felt uncomfortable with him," replied Elizabeth. "But he has always been at least pleasant."

"That is more than *we* have ever had from him," said Anthony.

"I think that is enough, Son," said Lord Matlock firmly, though Elizabeth could easily see that he was not displeased. "He *is* family, as you have pointed out, and much of the distance between us is *our* fault."

"That is only because we do not find his habits agreeable." Anthony held up his hands in surrender when his father scowled at him. "They are his own words, Father. And they are nothing less than the truth."

"I know. But I am still grateful to him for making us aware of the situation here today." Lord Matlock approached Elizabeth and took her hand, putting it into the crook of his arm and leading her from the room. "It appears Darcy and Anthony are intent upon maligning the name of our relation. Perhaps we should retire to the sitting-room so your mother may fuss over you."

Elizabeth laughed and directed a mischievous look at the other two men. "Perhaps you are correct, Father. I am well, but Mother will wish to confirm it with her own eyes."

With a nod, the earl led her from the room, the other two men following. With any luck, the days of Lord Winchester pressing her with his attentions were now over. The event had been unhappy, but the result should be anything but.

Chapter XXVIII

*T*he following days were, indeed, witness to a cessation of Lord Winchester's attention to Elizabeth. He did not come to the house, which was a relief, and the one time they saw him in company, he did not approach. He sneered at her when he saw her, but then turned back to the conversation in which he was engaged. It did excite some commentary from the gossips, but as they were only in London for a few days after, they would soon be leaving the city and its intrigues behind. The matter would undoubtedly be forgotten by the time they returned.

As Elizabeth had expected, her mother was not pleased to hear about Lord Winchester's actions and eager to assure herself of Elizabeth's safety. Elizabeth submitted to it, knowing her mother was still concerned for her, a worry which would not subside with time.

"It seems you have done well in standing up to the man," said Lady Susan when they sat down for dinner that evening. "I declare, I can see no ill effects of his attempts to importune you."

"In all honesty," replied Elizabeth, "Thompson was with me the whole time. He acted to put himself in the earl's path, so I could escape."

"Still, you have shown fortitude," said Lady Catherine. "That is something of which to be proud."

It struck Elizabeth that Lady Catherine had been much quieter of late, though she could not fathom the reason for it. She was simply not the sort of person to avoid inserting her opinions or giving instructions for any length of time. Whenever Elizabeth was in company with her, Lady Catherine had been quiet and watchful, but other than a few pronouncements—even a greater quietude would not silence her entirely—she had kept herself reserved.

"Thompson *has* been a great asset in Elizabeth's protection," said Lady Susan, interrupting Elizabeth's thoughts. "If you would release him, William, I would like to hire him to take on her care on a more permanent basis."

"I have already had this conversation with Darcy," said Lord Matlock with a bark of laughter. "Thus far he is being stubborn."

"It is not stubbornness," replied William. "Thompson's family have been our retainers for generations, and he has a wife at Pemberley."

"Then she can come to Snowlock too," insisted Lady Susan.

It was clear that Lady Susan was determined, and William, apparently understanding it, did not demur. "You are welcome to speak to him. While I am certain he will be happy to assist with Elizabeth's protection for the present, he will not wish to move to a new estate."

The look with which Lady Susan regarded William was suspicious, but in the end, she seemed to understand there was little need to press him. Thus, she dropped the subject and it was forgotten.

As they were to leave on Thursday, so they could arrive by Saturday, the final days were those of leave-taking. Elizabeth had not become close to many in society, but there were a few with whom she was friendly. On impulse, she even visited the Bingley family, astonishing Miss Bingley exceedingly. But she was welcomed and made to feel like the daughter of an earl due to their excessive deference when she would have wished them to be friendly, rather than subservient. Miss Bingley's suitor—a Mr. Powell—was also present when she visited, and she found him a pleasant man who seemed to truly care for Miss Bingley.

At length, Elizabeth took her leave and was escorted to the door by Miss Bingley, who was effusive in her thanks for Elizabeth's visit. It appeared Miss Bingley was getting on quite well with her suitor, and

Elizabeth did not think that her visit had made a marriage any likelier than it was before. But it made her feel good that she had been able to put the past behind her and treat the woman as an acquaintance.

"I wish you the best of luck with Mr. Powell, Miss Bingley," said Elizabeth as she was exiting the house to her carriage. "He appears to be quite attentive to you."

Miss Bingley blushed, but she maintained her composure. "Thank you, Lady Elizabeth. I find . . . I find I am quite pleased with his devotion."

"I believe you will do well together.'

The two ladies curtseyed to each other, and Elizabeth stepped up into her carriage. She was not insensible to the fact that Miss Bingley watched her carriage as she departed. Elizabeth did not know what the woman was thinking, but she hoped that at least she was thought of in a positive manner.

The final visit Elizabeth made was to her aunt and uncle's house. It was strange, Elizabeth decided, as the carriage clattered on the cobblestones before coming to a stop at the house on Gracechurch Street, that she was still most comfortable considering them her blood relations, when those she had formerly referred to as her mother and father were now firmly Mr. and Mrs. Bennet. Perhaps it was the way she had left Longbourn or the unstinting support and succor given to her by the Gardiners. Either way, she was more interested in keeping her connection with them than she was to the Bennets, with the exception of dear Jane, and possibly Mary, of course.

The visit was not long, for Elizabeth was to return to her home to complete the final preparations for the following day's departure. But the short length was more than made up for in the number of tears shed by both ladies. Even her uncle, who was present due to the note Elizabeth had sent ahead to let them know she was to visit, did not escape unscathed.

"You depart tomorrow?" asked Mrs. Gardiner. She made a credible attempt to hide how distressed she was by the coming separation, but Elizabeth knew her aunt well and knew that she would miss Elizabeth as much as the reverse.

"We do." Elizabeth laughed. "My father is adamant that we must start out early so that we can make the estate on Saturday. He has no love of inns and does not wish to be delayed, as it would necessitate two extra nights due to the Sabbath.

"But then William told him not to be foolish. Pemberley is further than Snowlock, and he says he has no difficulty making the journey in three days."

They all laughed at Elizabeth's words, and Mrs. Gardiner said: "Mr. Darcy is correct. Since I was raised in Lambton, which is very near Pemberley, I know the journey, as we have been back a time or two. Three days should more than suffice, especially if your father's estate is much closer."

"But the earl is also correct to ensure you depart at the time intended," added Mr. Gardiner. "There may be unforeseen delays, after all."

"They wished to come today," said Elizabeth, feeling the need to inform her relations why her family had not accompanied her. "But I wished to say my farewells in private, and they respected my wishes."

"You do not need to explain, Elizabeth," replied Mrs. Gardiner. "We are happy if your family wishes to maintain the connection. If they do not, we fully understand."

"They do. And I would not give you up. Even though we are not . . . not family, I consider you to be the family of my heart."

"What is family but a group of people who share affection and interest in one another's welfare?" was Mr. Gardiner's rhetorical question. "Yes, blood ties play an important part, but they are not the only consideration."

"No, they are not," said Elizabeth. Her voice was so quiet, she hardly heard the words issue from her own lips.

After a few more moments of conversation, Elizabeth excused herself, promising to return to visit them as soon as she returned to town. There would be many more chances to see them, she told herself. But at that moment, she could almost fancy that she was leaving for the other side of the world and would never see them again. The thought unsettled her.

Thursday, June 4, 1812
The Bell Inn, Broughton

As the family departed the next morning, Elizabeth's mood seemed complicated. It was easy to see her excitement for the upcoming journey, for by the afternoon of that day, they would be entering previously unknown territory, as she had never journeyed to the north. On the other hand, however, some matter seemed to be weighing down on her mind, affecting her spirits. The family was quick to engage her, to draw her thoughts away from whatever had her under its thrall, and it seemed to be successful, as she was soon chatting and laughing, asking questions about their destination and the sights she would see along the way.

Ah, for the resilience and optimism of youth! Would that the stories of previously unseen vistas could remove the cares of life so easily, so seamlessly direct one's concentration to the joys of life, rather than the hardships. But those things were not so easily forgotten, especially when the dreams of a lifetime seemed about to be dashed upon the rocks of indifference, as another possibility blossomed right before their eyes.

It was with an effort that Catherine turned her thoughts away from such melancholy subjects. They were traveling north from London in a cavalcade of three main carriages, and Catherine along with Anne were situated in the first, with Elizabeth and Susan rounding out their party. The earl and his sons, his daughter-in-law, and the Darcys were all strung along in the other carriages, and though Catherine thought they would change places at certain times, she owned the privilege of her niece and sister's company for the present.

Outside, the sun shone, and though it was not truly warm, the bright light gave the appearance of a beautiful summer day. A bird flew past the window where the curtains had been drawn back to let in the light, followed closely by three others in succession. Their warbling filled the air and lent a beauty to the scene which complemented rolling hills and trees waving in the breeze, showing their new summer greenery.

As the day progressed and Catherine watched her niece, she was moved by the excitement and joy with which Elizabeth greeted every experience, every explanation, every view of new sights. It was impossible to find oneself unmoved by such simple joy in life, such honest appreciation of every moment. Given the woman who had raised her, it would not be surprising should Elizabeth have turned out to be a hoyden, one who would need much guidance in their world. But that had been furthest from the truth.

Her thoughts kept her occupied for most of the day, and that evening after they had arrived at the inn, Catherine found herself wandering aimlessly into her daughter's rooms. She did not know what she intended. Perhaps it was nothing more than a desire to see her child, a desperate wish for encouragement that all her dreams were not for naught.

"Something is bothering you, Mother," said Anne when Catherine had entered the room. "Do you wish to speak of it?"

Catherine directed a curious look at her only child; Anne had never been precisely observant. She had usually been content to allow the world to pass her by without her direct involvement. In fact, Catherine was certain that had Anne only exerted herself, she might have been married to Darcy some time ago.

"I hardly know," said Catherine after a few moments' thought. "I *should* be angry, but I find myself wondering if I have the right."

"You are speaking of Darcy's feelings for Elizabeth."

Catherine regarded Anne, shocked that her daughter had been attentive enough to notice it. "You know?"

"Of course, I know, Mother," replied Anne as if it was the most obvious thing in the world. "Just because I make no comment does not mean that I do not notice. I like to consider myself rather observant if you must know."

"Then . . ." Catherine swallowed and wondered how she, of all people, could be made to feel off balance. She was Lady Catherine de Bourgh! It was *she* who made *others* uncomfortable.

"What do you intend to do about it?"

It was Anne's amusement which gave her a hint of what her daughter would say before she opened her mouth. "Nothing."

"Nothing?"

"Mother, I am aware that you have always intended that I marry Darcy. But neither of us will obey your edict."

Catherine was beginning to feel a little vexed. "When did you intend to inform *me* of your decision? Have you no sense of duty? What of the agreement I made with Darcy's mother all those years ago? Is that of no importance to you?"

"We intended to inform you when it became necessary, Mother." The accompanying pointed look brought Catherine up short. "We knew you would not accept the matter without a fight, and we did not wish to bring any discord into the family before it became necessary."

A frown descended over Catherine's face. "Would it have been that bad?"

Anne looked at her as if she thought her lacking intelligence. "You *do* like to have your own way, Mother. You like to have it very much, indeed. We knew you would not relinquish your obsession without a fight."

Feeling unaccountably weary, Catherine sank into a chair. "Am I truly that difficult?"

"You have your moments, Mother."

Catherine looked up to see Anne grinning at her. Grinning! As if they were sharing tea and a juicy piece of gossip.

"It is not every day that one is told she is a virago by her own daughter, who is smiling like she is imparting some great joke."

If anything, Anne's smile widened. "I would not call you a virago, Mother, though there are undoubtedly those who would."

"Thank you," replied Catherine in a dry tone.

"You are welcome," said Anne, with a primness Catherine did not think she had ever seen from her daughter. "But let us be serious. I was not being flippant when I said you like to have your own way, for you do. You tend to speak and direct people with authority, even when there is no reason for you to do so. And, you can be downright stubborn, as no one I have ever known.

"However, you are loyal, both to me and the family, with an unshakable conviction. You manage Rosings well and care for everyone within the range of your influence, and you care for me as if I was a treasure to be guarded and protected. You are not perfect. But none of us are."

"Well, then I thank you for that . . . interesting bit of praise," said Catherine, not quite knowing what to think.

Anne, seeing her discomfort, smiled and leaned forward to place a hand on Catherine's arm. "Do you not see that Darcy and I do not suit? Not only is he a great, tall fellow while I am rather diminutive, but we are both of a taciturn disposition. I dare say that should we marry, we may not exchange one word a week!"

For the first time in her life, Catherine wondered if she knew her daughter at all. While she had always assumed that Anne possessed an understated enthusiasm for Darcy, or at the very least a quiet acceptance, she could not remember a single time when Anne had reacted positively to the suggestion that she and Darcy would marry. In fact, when they were alone, Anne would often listen and then change the subject. The question which begged to be asked, then, was if Anne did not wish to marry her cousin, what *did* she want?

Catherine's uncertainty screamed at her from the depths of her surety that she had always known how it would be, and she posed the question of her daughter. To her utter shock, Anne only smiled with amusement.

"I do not know, Mother," replied she. "As you know, my health is not the best, and I do not know if I could withstand the rigors of childbearing. On the other hand, I have seen firsthand these past weeks the beauty of the affection which has grown between William and Elizabeth, and I find myself wanting the same. I *may* be induced to chance it if I were to meet with a man who looks on me the way

William looks on Elizabeth, but if I cannot find him, I am perfectly content to remain unmarried."

"And Rosings?" asked Catherine.

It was an unsubtle final desperate ploy to induce her daughter to fall in with her plans. It was also evident that her daughter saw through it, for she shook her head in apparent amusement.

"Rosings may be left to whomever I please, Mother—I am the heir, as you know, and there is no restriction on the disposition of the estate, should I pass on without issue. I may leave it to Cousin Anthony, or allow one of my de Bourgh cousins to inherit if it comes to that."

Catherine sniffed with distaste—Lewis's cousins were dissipative and objectionable, and she rarely deigned to see them. One of them had thought her an easy mark after Lewis's death, arriving within days, insisting she pass the estate to him, as she was obviously incapable of managing it. More than fifteen years of prosperity had proven her capabilities, and this was no less satisfying than the lecture she had given the man, causing him to slink away with his tail between his legs.

"Or perhaps not one of the de Bourghs," said Anne, reading Catherine's expression correctly. "There will be options, however. James or even William might have multiple sons for whom to provide."

Catherine snorted. "Darcy owns multiple estates. He likely has the means to provide for five sons, should he choose to do so. And the Fitzwilliams are very wealthy."

"I am aware of that," replied Anne. "But my point is it would not be difficult to find someone to provide for. But that is a discussion to have later. Have I answered all your questions?"

"All except for one," said Catherine. "How long have you known of William's admiration for Elizabeth?"

"Since soon after we came to London. I know not how anyone who sees them cannot understand it. It is as plain as day."

A sigh escaped her lips. It seemed like there was nothing she could do. Not only could she not object to Hugh's daughter marrying Darcy, but her own had made it clear she did not wish for the match. Dearest Anne, her beloved sister, with whom she had planned a union, both young mothers, unaware of the frailty of life, not knowing that Catherine would survive her beloved younger sister, would be the only one of the four parents to live to see the children old enough to marry. She, alone, would bear witness to the death of that dream, the scheme into which they had put so much energy, all the while expecting they would both be there to witness it.

But even as the thought of her long-lost sister came into Catherine's mind, she knew that Anne would have wanted her son to be happy. Perhaps had she survived Georgiana's birth, she might, with Catherine's aid, have been able to push her son toward Anne, assisting Catherine in advising them. But had Darcy balked even with that guidance, Anne would never have insisted, would never have stripped from him the freedom of his choice. Of Elizabeth, Anne would have had no objections at all. She would have welcomed her return to the family. She would have been the greatest champion of a match between Elizabeth and Darcy.

It was time the dream was put to rest. There was no way for it to be realized. Catherine knew it would be difficult, for she loved her daughter and wished her to be happy with Darcy. But it was not to be.

"Then I will not create a scene," said Catherine at length, when she realized she had been lost in her thoughts for some time. "But do not expect me to be sanguine about the matter. I will need to adjust. It will not be easy."

"Thank you, Mother. I believe I know something of what this will cost you."

Catherine nodded, not trusting herself to speak. At length she excused herself to return to her room, welcoming the solitude in which to organize her own thoughts. She would need to prepare herself, to firmly ingrain her acceptance of the situation in the confines of her own mind. If she was again in their company without it, she may very well say something she should not, as she almost had these past few weeks.

Thursday, June 4, 1812
Longbourn, Hertfordshire

At the very moment Lady Catherine de Bourgh was coming to terms with the death of her long-held dream, Mrs. Margaret Bennet was attempting to understand. Had it not been such a spectacle of moaning about her nerves, or screeching about Elizabeth's betrayal, Bennet might have almost enjoyed the opening of his wife's eyes. The problem was, of course, that her eyes had not been opened in any way.

It was the fate of a rational man who knew his shortcomings to understand exactly where he had failed. Bennet knew himself, was intelligent enough to see those things he should do better but had never taken the time — had never had the conviction — to change in his character. He should have provided better for his family. He should have reined in his youngest daughters. He should have attempted to explain to his wife, to bring her to a greater understanding, and if that was not possible, to at least ensure that her behavior improved as much as possible. Perhaps he should have listened to his elder brother, seen what an unsuitable woman she was and refrained from proposing to her.

There was no excuse, and he would not attempt to make one, especially to himself, and especially when the woman could not avoid what she was. The fact of the matter was that Mrs. Bennet's shortcomings were at least partially his fault. Now, more than ever, he felt his failures keenly, when his family might have benefitted from the fortuitous circumstance of having cared for the daughter of an earl all those years.

But Bennet thought it was not all ruined. There was still time to fix his mistakes, and he was determined to do so. So Bennet sat watching his wife that evening, noting her ever-present histrionics, how she wailed and cried, bemoaning the fate which had been assigned to them. Along with her, her youngest daughters moaned their own fates, certain they would not be invited to partake in imagined delights of the season.

"It is not fair, Mama!" exclaimed Lydia as the evening grew late. "Why could I not have been the daughter of an earl? I am sure I would dance with many more gentleman than Lizzy."

"I would too," declared Kitty. "Lizzy likely does nothing but speak of books."

"How bored they must be with her." Lydia's tone was all spite. "They must be longing for a real vivacious woman to attend to."

"Oh, do not say such things!" wailed Mrs. Bennet. "It would be too cruel if I was forced to give my dear Lydia up to such circumstances."

"At least you would know *I* would not betray you."

And on and on they went, alternately castigating Elizabeth for her unfeeling and irrational actions, and wishing they were in her place. Bennet was amused—his wife did not quite know what to think of Lydia's professed desire to be the daughter of an earl. On the one hand, even the fancy of riches and her eventual security was a powerful lure, but she seemed, on the other hand, more than a little betrayed that her favorite would want to be anything other than her daughter.

At length Bennet tired of waiting for them to cease their lamentations. "Kitty, Lydia," said he, interrupting Lydia mid-wail, "it is time for you to go to your rooms for the night. Off you go now."

"But Papa, it is not nearly the time I would usually seek my bed," protested Lydia.

"I did not ask for your opinion or a reminder of the time. Get along with you.

"Now!" said Bennet when she protested again. He did not raise his voice, but he injected a hint of steel in it that his daughters knew well. He did not use it often, but the girls were well enough accustomed to it to obey, though they could not be counted on to do so without protest.

"Mary and I will accompany them, Papa," said Jane.

Bennet smiled at her. Jane seemed to understand that something was afoot, though he did not think she knew why he wished her sisters to retire. But Jane was a dutiful girl and would do as asked without question.

The two younger girls were escorted from the room, their protests all but silenced in the face of Bennet's resolve and Jane's quiet fortitude. Bennet waited until the door closed behind them and the sounds of their footsteps on the stairs had faded away before he turned to his wife.

The suspicion with which Mrs. Bennet regarded him struck Bennet as diverting, and he almost laughed, wondering what she might be thinking. But he attempted to sober himself, for the matter was too important to be lost to his sense of the humorous.

"I might wonder why you have sent my daughters to bed," said Mrs. Bennet. Bennet was surprised to hear the note of resentment in her voice. "Am I to be sent to my room as well?"

"No, Mrs. Bennet," replied Bennet, wondering at his wife's odd statement. "In fact, I thought we should take the time to discuss the particulars of that matter which has occupied you of late."

Mrs. Bennet snorted. "Why would I wish to speak of that ungrateful girl?"

"Why, indeed? I am afraid I do not know, Mrs. Bennet. But as you have talked of little else of late, it seems like you are determined."

It seemed Mrs. Bennet was not at all impressed with his response, for she rolled her eyes, thinking that he only meant to tease her as he had so many times in the past. Perhaps his words had been overly mocking, but in this instance, he did not mean to provoke.

"You have asked a question repeatedly these past days, Mrs. Bennet," said he. "Ever since your return from London, where I expressly informed you that you were not to go, this question has consumed you. I merely thought I should explain a few matters to you so that you will no longer misunderstand."

Mrs. Bennet did not even have the grace to blush at his pointed reminder. But instead of grasping at the offer for an explanation, she moaned again and threw her head back against the chair, once again descending into dramatics.

"She has betrayed me—that is all. Ungrateful, unfeeling girl! We should never have taken her in."

"That is enough, Mrs. Bennet!" His wife gasped and looked at him, an outraged retort on her lips. But she did not release it. For once she seemed to understand he was not to be interrupted.

"I will not have you say such things, for it might ruin any possibility of reconciliation between Lady Elizabeth and *any* of us. It would behoove you to listen carefully to what I say, for if you truly do not understand why you were sent away so unceremoniously, I will explain it so we may attempt to overcome the damage your impromptu visit has wrought."

Once again, she seemed about to reply with a caustic comment, but it again remained unspoken. Though Bennet thought she wished for nothing more than to return to her lamentations, he had piqued her curiosity.

"Mrs. Bennet, London society is quite different from what we see in the small neighborhood of Meryton. There is a certain level of sophistication and good behavior which is expected in those who are part of it. I regret to inform you that neither you nor your daughters possess the manners which would enable you to move in society in London. *That* is why you have been sent away from the earl's house so unceremoniously. You would be an embarrassment to Lizzy there, one from which she might not recover."

"But you have always lamented the behavior of those in town," protested Mrs. Bennet. "Which is it to be, Mr. Bennet? You cannot have it both ways."

"Yes, in fact, I can," replied Bennet. "Those people who do not behave, yet are still accepted, have several advantages we lack, Mrs. Bennet. Primary among those advantages are money and standing. Many an objectionable trait will be forgiven if the recipient possesses the wealth to smooth over any memory of misbehavior and the standing to explain it all away.

"Even more importantly, when one is new to society, those who are more established often look on them with suspicion and jealousy, as if those newly arrived are trying to usurp their position. All newcomers must be in complete control of themselves, for any opportunity to criticize will be used against them. Many a reputation has been destroyed by the slightest of transgressions, Mrs. Bennet."

His wife watched him, aghast at what she was hearing. "For what purpose?"

"For what purpose can a reputation be destroyed in Meryton?" asked Mr. Bennet pointedly. This time Margaret had the grace to blush. "I see you are beginning to understand. Often there is no purpose. Tales begin, are spread and embellished, and soon the victim is shunned. It does not take much as we all have seen.

"London is much like this. But there is also another element which shows the worst of human behavior, for jealousy and hate can be powerful motivators. There are times when victims are attacked unfairly because others are jealous of them. Tell me, Mrs. Bennet— what do you think other young ladies feel about Lady Elizabeth's sudden elevation as the daughter of an earl?"

"I would hope she is accepted."

"Why?"

Margaret was flustered. "Because she is the daughter of an earl, is she not?"

"Have they been given proof? Or are they simply told that is the case and are forced to accept it?" It was clear she had no answer for that. "In fact, exalted personages such as the nobility have great power in our society. If the Earl of Matlock is satisfied that Elizabeth is who he thinks she is, he may acknowledge her as his daughter, and none may gainsay him.

"Now, how do you think the young daughter of a baron would feel if she was the center of attention when Elizabeth's recovery is announced, and she is suddenly ignored?"

"I suppose they might be jealous," replied Margaret. "Are you saying society is full of such girls?"

"There are doubtlessly many fine young ladies who would not hold a grudge. But there must be those who do. Thus, Elizabeth is held to a higher standard of behavior. Any hint of weakness is exploited, and Elizabeth's standing is reduced because of it."

"But you said that the importance of her father would prevent it!"

Bennet shook his head. "It does, to a certain extent. But there are many ways to show disdain or disfavor without overt unkindness. I have no doubt that Elizabeth's behavior is impeccable. She would not do anything which would allow others to criticize her.

"But what if it was known that her adoptive mother entered her father's house without an invitation, screeching at the top of her lungs how much she was anticipating the delights to come, of gentlemen and dancing, not to mention the fine appointments of a large house?" Finally, Mrs. Bennet seemed to understand where she had erred, and she went white. But Bennet was not about to let up just yet. "What if it was known that her family is loud and boisterous, that she has sisters who flirt with every man in a red coat? What if they knew what circumstances in which she was raised? Do you not think the shrews of society would use those circumstances to attack her, to make her feel inferior?"

By this time Margaret was distressed, wringing her hands and moaning. It was a pitiful sight, and one Mr. Bennet knew might have been lessened if he had taken her in hand previously. But now was not the time to dwell on such things.

"I do not mean to be unkind, Mrs. Bennet. I merely wish you to understand how your actions may be perceived by others. I dare say that Elizabeth's new family is protective of her and will do nothing to jeopardize her standing in society. Thus, I cannot imagine your designs of being introduced will come to fruition if matters do not change."

"But I do not understand," said Margaret. "Lydia is energetic and handsome. How can her manners be reproached?"

Sighing, and wishing this conversation would end, so he could go drown his sorrows in his bookroom, Mr. Bennet essayed to respond. "Mrs. Bennet, if you would understand, simply compare the behavior of your eldest to that of your youngest. And then compare how they are perceived in society. You say Jane is admired wherever she goes. Is that not correct?"

Mrs. Bennet allowed it to be so. "She is so admired because she is reserved and well-behaved, not because of her beauty." Bennet held up a hand when his wife tried to speak. "Yes, it is, in part, due to her beauty. But all the beauty in the world is not enough for most men. Beauty fades, and when it is gone, what is left behind? Some men are shallow and care for nothing but a pretty face. But I would not wish your daughter to be married to such a man. I dare say Mr. Bingley is such a man, for he proved it when he did not return for her."

Again, Mrs. Bennet had nothing to say in response. In truth, Bennet suspected there were other considerations which prevented Mr. Bingley from returning. But the quickness with which he had turned his attention on Jane suggested a temperament which was quickly enamored, and such temperaments did not often belong to men of sense and purpose.

"Now, Mrs. Bennet, you should contrast that with your youngest daughter's behavior. Lydia is exuberant to the point of being improper. She carries on, laughing louder than she ought, displaying a lack of restraint which suggests a lack of delicacy. The officers, which you laud from sunrise to sunset, clearly consider her to be nothing but a bit of muslin, a girl with nothing but fluff between her ears. I would hope that she has enough sense to refrain from losing her virtue to such a man, but I suspect she has, at least, shared some of her favors. And such men will not stop her — they will encourage her."

Aghast, Margaret stared at him. "Surely not!"

"I do not think she has done anything irreversible. But I suspect she is not lily white, either. Do you see the difference between them?"

Margaret nodded, although hesitantly.

"Then the rest is simple. Jane, as her manners are constituted at present, would do well in society, simply due to her angelic character and her mild behavior. But Lydia, unless she learns to restrain herself, will never be accepted in the circle Elizabeth now inhabits."

"What is to be done?" wailed Mrs. Bennet.

"Schooling?" Margaret stopped short and stared at him. She did not seem to like the notion. "A school will teach a girl how to behave, and some specialize in taking in girls who are ungovernable and imbuing them with better manners. Lydia will never be as Jane is, but if she can be taught moderation, to think before she speaks and laugh softly, to speak with intelligence and avoid overt flirtations, she might be acceptable. Kitty, I think, would benefit even more than Lydia. Kitty follows wherever Lydia leads. If Kitty were to gain a little independence and confidence of her own, I believe she would do well."

"Do you truly think it is necessary?" asked Margaret. "And what of the expense?"

"I do believe it is necessary," replied Bennet. "It is if you wish to see your daughters invited to spend time with Lady Elizabeth in London. As for the expense, not only are we feeding one less than we were before, but Lydia's and Kitty's portions would be reduced due to their residence in school. We shall manage, Mrs. Bennet.

"As for Mary, I believe she would welcome the opportunity to receive the instruction of some masters. Perhaps the Gardiners would take her for some time to assist."

"And Jane?"

"As I said, Jane is ready now to move in those circles, but perhaps a few more accomplishments would not go amiss. I believe it may be best to speak with her and ask her what she wishes. She will be invited to attend Lady Elizabeth before any of the rest of us. Should that happen, we would wish to ensure she is displayed to her best advantage."

Margaret nodded slowly. Bennet was relieved—it seemed he had been successful in persuading her. It had never been certain, as his wife was as stubborn as the day was long when she felt she was right.

"I shall give some thought to this," said she after a moment's thought. "May I do so before we inform the girls?"

"Of course, Mrs. Bennet. But we should not wait too long to make our decisions. It would be best to act swiftly."

Though distracted, Margaret agreed and rose. She walked to the door and opened it to leave the room. But a sudden thought stopped her, and she turned to regard him.

"Might I assume that my own behavior must also be amended?"

"Though it may pain you to hear it, yes, it must. I would recommend thinking before you speak and attempting a quieter, more demure posture. We may discuss further later. For now, I wish for you to simply think on what I have said."

With a distracted nod, Mrs. Bennet exited the room. Bennet heaved a sigh of relief. It had been an utterly uncomfortable conversation, but he knew it had been required. Too often in the past he had ridiculed where he should have guided, and he had been afraid she would assume he was doing nothing more than the same now.

But she was thinking, truly considering what he had told her. Perhaps there was some hope yet for them.

CHAPTER **XXIX**

Saturday, June 6, 1812
Snowlock, Derbyshire

*I*n a light afternoon breeze, the company made the final way toward the Fitzwilliam estate at Snowlock. It had been three long days of travel, and having never undertaken such a journey before, Elizabeth was ready for it to be completed. The sighs and expectation of impending relief from her companions told Elizabeth that they were as ready as she to find the end of the road. But they said nothing; instead, she found the attention strangely on her, as if they were seeing her for the first time.

It *was* strange, she decided. There had been much talk upon their leaving their last rest stop, and though nothing more than murmurs reached Elizabeth's ears, she had the distinct impression that the positions next to her in the carriage had been in high demand. In the end, it had been her mother and father and Anthony who had secured them, though that had not been without disagreement. What or why she could not say, but she was grateful for their presence nonetheless.

As they traveled, she could see that Derbyshire was, indeed, a different land from Hertfordshire. Whereas Hertfordshire had been a flat land with the occasional rolling hills, Derbyshire was much more angular, the hills steeper, with occasional rocks and large lines of stony cliffs to break up the monotony. In the distance, Elizabeth wondered if she could just make out the lines of great peaks, though she knew from what her family had told her that Snowlock was not near enough to see them. It must be her imagination, as active as ever, fooling her eyes and betraying her senses.

"It seems you are ready to arrive," observed Lady Susan when Elizabeth shifted slightly in her seat. The discomfort of a stitch in her back, which she had hardly noticed, announced itself in a most insistent way, and Elizabeth reached back and massaged it, smiling ruefully at her mother.

"This land is beautiful, but could you not move it closer to London? What a tiresome journey this has been!"

Her three companions chuckled, but it was her brother who responded. "Of course, we can. While we are thus engaged, is there anything else you would like? Perhaps the moon should be closer, or mayhap we could bring a bit of the sea in to abut the estate?"

"That would be lovely, Anthony," replied Elizabeth. "I have seen the sea once, many years ago, but its song has never quite left me."

"Had you been a man, you likely would have been a sailor. I am told that for some men, the lure of the sea is an irresistible pull."

"Perhaps not," replied Elizabeth. "I did enjoy watching the pounding of the waves on the shore, but I felt no call to travel upon its surface."

"I, for one, am grateful," said Lady Susan. "I would not wish for my only daughter to be constantly beset by wanderlust."

They all laughed at that before the earl inserted: "I believe we will come in sight of the house soon. I am anticipating the sight of Elizabeth's first view of her new home."

Elizabeth regarded her father curiously. "Is that why there was so much discussion about who would ride with me in the carriage?"

"And also why you were steered toward the lead carriage," said Lord Matlock. "We have been speaking since we left, and there are those among us who wonder if any hint of a memory will surface when you see it."

"I was two years of age, Father," protested Elizabeth. "I can hardly be expected to remember."

"Perhaps not, my dear," said Lady Susan. "But it *is* possible a little sliver of familiarity might make an appearance."

Not certain what to think, Elizabeth spread her hands wide and turned to look out the window yet again. They were passing through a low valley, not much more than a slight depression in the land, with strands of tall trees and fields of green stretched out before her. The carriage clattered along the road for several more moments until, after they had rounded a bend which took them adjacent to a small wood, the sight of a large house came into view.

It was a handsome stone building, standing three stories tall with long lines of windows looking down on the drive on which they approached. To one side Elizabeth saw a series of lower buildings, which she thought must be the stables and other support structures, and she thought she caught a glimpse of a horse or two grazing in the distance. There was a break in the wings of building in the exact center, where the building fell away into a large courtyard, cobbled with a lighter colored stone than the house. It was for this courtyard that they were making.

"Snowlock?" asked she, though she thought it was rather obvious.

"Indeed, my daughter," replied her mother. "Welcome back to your home. It has been far too long since you were here."

Elizabeth nodded, feeling too moved to make any other response. She turned back to the approaching house, watching it critically for any hint of recognition. The sunlight gleamed off the windows as the carriage entered the drive, sending the bright light of the sun flashing across her eyes, leaving her with images seared onto her vision, which slid this way and that as she studied the house. But there was nothing which jogged any memory, nothing to suggest she had ever seen these halls before.

"Do not be cast down, Elizabeth," said her mother, drawing Elizabeth's attention back to her. She must have seen the welling of Elizabeth's disappointment. "None of us expected you to remember. You *were* naught but two years of age, as you pointed out."

"Let us make new memories," added Anthony. "I have no doubt you will know the paths and woods of the estate better than any of us within a week."

"And how would you know that?" asked Elizabeth. "You have never seen me in the country."

"From your own mouth, dear sister. I am anticipating the sight of you traipsing all over the estate. The gardens were your favorite place as a child."

"But let us not forget your safety," interjected her father. "You may have the run of the estate, of course. But you have disappeared from Snowlock once—I would not have it happen again. I think a footman for your protection at a minimum."

Elizabeth was not one to have company on her walks, for she enjoyed the solitude she would obtain when out in the bosom of nature. But she knew her family was concerned with her wellbeing, and she knew this was a sacrifice she would need to make.

Nothing else was said as the conveyance rolled toward the end of their long journey. At length, the driver pulled it to a stop in the wide drive before the courtyard, and there the door was opened by the footman, and Elizabeth was helped to the ground by the hand of her father.

The house was even more impressive when one was standing below it, for it towered above her, a great stone edifice which seemed as permanent as the mountains. The sounds of the other coaches and their rolling wheels echoed off the house, sounding like a veritable army returning instead of three lone carriages of travelers and their associated servants.

The remaining members of the party alighted from their own carriages, their groans of discomfort filling the air and telling Elizabeth that they were just as happy to have finally arrived as she was herself. They gathered in front of the building, exchanging a few words of appreciation, and her brother and his wife extended to her a welcome to her new and old home. But the most animation was reserved for William, who when hearing her state her appreciation for what she was seeing, was quick to fan the flames.

"It is nothing to Pemberley, of course," said he, showing a wide grin for all to see.

A chorus of groans told Elizabeth that this was a commonly discussed topic.

"This is my daughter's first view of her home, William," said Lady Susan, wagging a finger at him. "Do not bring up that old debate here, young man."

Rather than be chastened, William only laughed. "But it is the truth, is it not? Snowlock is a fine estate, but you must all own that Pemberley is the more beautiful."

The responses to William's words consisted of nothing more than exaggerated sighs and shaken heads. William only grinned, showing a glee Elizabeth had not often seen in his manners.

As they entered the house, Elizabeth considered what she had seen and heard. Though William had made the claim about Pemberley, she had not missed the fact that no one had seen fit to disagree with him. If, indeed, Pemberley was so much grander than Snowlock, Elizabeth could not imagine how it would be, for Snowlock was everything beautiful. Finding herself at William's side, Elizabeth regarded him curiously before asking him to account for his surety.

"One day you will see Pemberley and will judge for yourself," replied he, his words completely unhelpful. "But I am confident that you, of all people, will agree with me."

William fell silent, and nothing Elizabeth said could induce him to elaborate on the subject. Elizabeth did not know whether to feel vexed with him or diverted, and she wondered why she should find his estate superior to her ancestral home. The other members of the party only looked on, amused. Deciding that to dwell on the matter would end with her caught in the grip of annoyance, she decided to relegate it to the back of her mind.

Inside the house, a man and woman, both approximately her parents' age, were waiting for the party. Her mother, grasping her arm, led Elizabeth forward and introduced them as Mr. Granger, the butler, and Mrs. Hanson, the housekeeper.

"We did not wish you to be overwhelmed, so we did not gather the staff together to meet you," said Mrs. Hanson, her eyes shining with delight at the sight of Elizabeth. "But we are all so happy you have been returned, Lady Elizabeth. Welcome to your home."

"Mrs. Hanson has been with us since before we lost you, Elizabeth," said her mother. "She was one of the maids, and if I am not mistaken, she was often called on to assist in your care when you were a child."

"That I was," agreed the housekeeper with an amused smile. "You reminded me of my youngest daughter, you did. She, too, was a precocious scamp, always running from one place to the other. Your nurse, Miss Perry, despaired of you, for she could never keep you in one place long."

At that moment there was a commotion, and a voice rang out, saying: "Attila!"

From the corner of her eye, Elizabeth saw a large dog running down the hall toward them, and she reflexively took a step back in alarm. The dog, however, seeing her, skidded to a halt, its eyes wide as it looked at her. Then it stepped forward cautiously and put a wet and velvety nose to her hand, snuffling about as if attempting to determine who she was.

"Oh, Attila," said her father, shaking his head. "You *are* trained, even if you do not always show it."

"But he is exuberant and will often forget his training," said Anthony.

They were both watching the dog, who was still busily inspecting Elizabeth, snuffling about her this way and that, his shoulder reaching almost to Elizabeth's waist.

"I do not think I have ever seen a dog this large," said Elizabeth. "What is he?"

"This is an English Mastiff," said Anthony. "We have three others, but none of them are as protective of the family as Attila."

"He seems to believe he *must* greet us whenever we return home," added Lady Susan.

At that moment the dog finished his inspection and sat on the ground in front of Elizabeth, his tongue hanging out the side of his mouth as he panted. When she did nothing in response, Attila pushed her hand with his head, a clear demand to scratch his ears. Elizabeth did so willingly, and the dog closed his eyes and leaned into her hand, pleased with the attention.

"He seems to have accepted you, Elizabeth," said James. Elizabeth looked up to see him grinning at her. "Attila is very loyal and considers the family to be his own. Now you will have to put up with his constant demands for attention, his desire to play, and his protective nature."

"How old is he?" asked Elizabeth. "I mean, he cannot be old enough to remember me."

"No, but he is intelligent and can sense that you are part of the family," said her father. "Your scent will also be similar to ours."

"He is four years of age," said Anthony. "He is the largest of his litter, standing almost four and thirty inches tall, and he weighs more than sixteen stone."

Elizabeth's eyes widened, and she gaped at her brother. Anthony only waggled his eyebrows. "Yes, he is heavier than most full-grown men. But as father said, he is loyal and an excellent protector. We, none of us, missed your disinclination to accept the company of a footman when you walk the countryside. Perhaps Attila would be an acceptable compromise."

This last was directed at her father. Elizabeth, though she had never walked with a dog before, had often played with the dogs at Longbourn and was quite fond of them. The more she thought about it, the more it appealed to her—she would be given a companion and protector, yet have the privacy she desired.

Her father frowned, looking between them. "Perhaps it might be acceptable. But for the next several days, let us stick with the original plan, at least until you become familiar with the estate. And perhaps when you intend to walk further."

"Yes, Father," said Elizabeth. He obviously did not know how far she had often ranged at Longbourn, and Elizabeth was not eager to inform him at this time for fear her habits would be curtailed. It was, perhaps, not the wisest course of action, but since there had been no hint of danger to her since her recovery, Elizabeth decided there was unlikely to be any risk.

"Come, Attila," said a man Elizabeth thought was one of the dog handlers, but the dog only looked back at him and shifted his great bulk until he was seated in front of Elizabeth, looking for all intents and purposes like a guardian. The family laughed at his antics, and Elizabeth wondered if it was not this, in part, which drove his disobedience.

"He is welcome to come upstairs with me if he likes," said Elizabeth.

Her father seemed to think about it before he shook his head. "Perhaps it would be best not to. He is already indulged more than he should. He can see you again tonight if you wish to go outside and visit."

"Of course," said Elizabeth. She leaned down and once again scratched his ears, prompting a look of what she took to be utter adoration. "Go now, Attila. I will visit you."

The dog seemed to consider that, but it did not hesitate when the man called him again. He padded obediently away, though he did look back in Elizabeth's direction several times as if wishing to confirm she was well without him. Elizabeth only shooed him away, and before long he broke into a trot, disappearing through the door at the end of the long hall, out to the kennels, Elizabeth presumed.

"Well, my dear," said Lady Susan, "it seems you have charmed at least one of the residents. Come, let us get you settled in your room."

Sunday, June 7, 1812
Snowlock, Derbyshire

It was the next day when Elizabeth learned that one of the company was to decamp from Snowlock, at least for a short time. There was some discussion of the estate between the gentlemen after they arrived back, primarily between her father and eldest brother, though Anthony also showed some interest. For his part, William stayed silent, though he contributed a few words when asked. Elizabeth found out, however, that his own estate, some thirty miles distant, had been without his attention for some time.

"I rarely spend the entire season in London," said William when he spoke with her about his intentions. "I almost always journey to Pemberley for a few weeks to oversee the planting, and I will usually spend a few weeks at Lady Catherine's estate in Kent."

"Might I assume you remained in London this year due to my recovery?" When he confirmed her supposition, Elizabeth said: "Then I apologize for pulling you from your responsibilities. You must have been wishing to be away, though I must own I am surprised that anyone would wish to make a three-day journey to the north simply to avoid the season."

William grinned, correctly interpreting her manner as teasing. "It was no trouble, I assure you, Lady Elizabeth. In fact, your influence has been such that I have not repined my time in London this year as I usually do."

Not quite knowing what to say about that, Elizabeth changed the subject. "You leave tomorrow then? And Georgiana will not go with you?"

"No. I believe she will be happier here with you. I will not be gone long—perhaps a week. But I have been away long enough and have some tasks which await me there."

"Then we will anticipate your return," said Elizabeth.

A pause ensued, one where William looked at Elizabeth, attempting to find the words he wished to say. "I wish . . . No, I hope that you, in particular, will anticipate my coming Elizabeth. I have grown to appreciate your company. I hope we can continue to become closer when I return."

Understanding washed over Elizabeth in an instant, but instead of embarrassment at such a blatant statement of regard, Elizabeth could only feel a sense of happiness. "I hope we can too, William."

And thus, he went away, on horseback the next morning, claiming that he was happy to ride for the exercise and the ability to complete the day's journey in a more expeditious manner than the carriage might have allowed. Her heart told Elizabeth that he wished to complete it quickly, so he could return to *her*. But she did not say anything—what had happened between them was private, and she did not wish to share it.

Those days of William's absence, Elizabeth became accustomed to the home she had known as a child. The house was large, but the layout being predictable and logical, she did not find it difficult to make her way within it. The principal rooms were soon known to her, as were the gardens, where her mother loved to walk in the mornings. For Elizabeth herself, though the gardens were a delightful riot of colors and scents, the longer paths around the estate beckoned, and it was only a day or two later that she indulged in that call, walking out in the woods to the north of the house.

In her ramblings, she was accompanied by Attila, who it seemed had adopted her readily as one of the family. The dog was eager to be out, to run without fetters, and though he was rambunctious and playful, he was also obedient when Elizabeth would call him. They often made a game of it, the dog running ahead of her until she could hardly see him, and then bounding back with some stick to induce her to throw it for him. But he never wandered out of sight, seeming to possess some uncanny knack for always knowing where she was and whether she was about to lose sight of him.

"That dog obeys you better than he does me," said Mr. Mills, one of the men in charge of the dogs one morning when she was about to set out. "He is a good boy, but he is also a free spirit."

"That perfectly describes our Elizabeth," said Anthony with a laugh. Elizabeth turned to glare at him, but he only gave her a cheeky grin.

"He tends to wander off too," said her father, scratching his chin as he regarded Elizabeth's antics with the dog.

"No, he never does," asserted Elizabeth, informing her father of what she had noticed during those few days they had ranged out together. "He always knows where I am, and he always comes back."

The earl thought on the matter for a few moments before he turned back to Elizabeth. "Thompson has told me the same," said he, speaking of the footman who was tasked with Elizabeth's safety. "Perhaps it is possible that you may walk out by yourself. But at present, please take Thompson until we know Attila is reliable."

Though Elizabeth felt a little affronted on Attila's behalf, she remained silent and bowed to her father's decree. And so the game went on, and she ranged a little further every day with her faithful companion and the ever-attentive Thompson following behind. In time Elizabeth began to be familiar with many of the paths, feeling confident enough to walk them by herself, though she knew her father would not yet allow it—perhaps he never would.

*　　*　　*

About a week after William's departure, and only a day before his scheduled return, Elizabeth's mother spoke to her after breakfast. "Today I would like to visit a relation who lives in our dower house."

"A relation?" asked Elizabeth.

"Yes. Her name is Emma Seward, and she is my grandmother's youngest sister." Lady Susan paused and smiled. "Actually, she is grandmother's half-sister, my grandfather having remarried late in his life and producing her and another sister. Aunt Emma was the youngest by some years. Though she was not full sister to my grandmother and she is really my great aunt, I have always referred to her as my aunt."

"She must be quite elderly if she is your grandmother's sister," observed Elizabeth.

"Yes, she is," agreed her mother. "Aunt Emma is five and eighty years of age. She is still in health and is spry for her age, though she is mostly confined to the house. She was also enamored of you when you were a child and will, I have no doubt, be happy to see you."

"I am happy to visit her," said Elizabeth.

They finished their breakfast, and then Elizabeth and her mother entered the carriage which would convey them on the short journey to the dower house. When the carriage lurched into motion, Elizabeth noticed they were following a road which wended its way around the side of the house to the north, through several copses of trees of ash, oak, and birch. In one location, Elizabeth thought she saw a deer off in the trees some distance away, but she was not certain.

"There are some deer in the area," said her mother when she asked. "We do not see them near the house, of course, but there are some in the woods occasionally."

Elizabeth nodded. "This kinswoman we are going to see—has she lived in the dower house for long?"

"Since before you were born," said Lady Susan. "Your grandmother died before your grandfather, and never used the house. It was empty for some years before my aunt took up residence."

"She is a spinster?"

"No, a widow." Lady Susan fell silent, obviously deep in thought. "Though I do not remember the particulars, her husband died not long after their marriage. Aunt Emma declared there would be no other for her and never remarried. She has lived for many years by herself. If asked, she will claim that she has had a good life, though she has lived most of it alone.

"She is also very wealthy, for not only did she possess a handsome dowry, but her husband left her with a large fortune in her marriage settlement. She lives frugally, with only a few servants for company, and she has not left the estate in many years. I expect that money has grown greatly in the years since she lost her husband."

For the rest of the short journey, Elizabeth was silent, thinking of a woman whom she could never remember meeting. From what her mother had told her, Mrs. Seward had been alone for sixty years or more — or at least she had been without a husband that long. What great love must have existed between them for her to eschew establishing another relationship, knowing that she must have several decades alone if she did not!

The image of William rose within her mind as she thought of the love this woman must have for another, and Elizabeth felt her cheeks heating in response. It was fortunate her mother was looking out the window on the other side, for Elizabeth was certain she would have asked had she seen it. The thought warmed her, however. William was a good man, and Elizabeth had been feeling closer to him these past weeks. Was it love? She did not know. But the thought of it prompted a warmth in her breast at his upcoming return. Perhaps she would discover it in the coming days.

It was not long after when the coach drew to a halt in front of a building. The dower house at Snowlock was a large, handsome building which, though it was not the size of the manor house, was still larger than Longbourn. It might even rival Netherfield in size, Elizabeth thought, though she was not quite certain. It was built in the same stone which graced Snowlock's walls, and as Elizabeth and her mother passed through the door, which was opened by the butler, she noted that it was as finely constructed as her father's home.

They were led up the large staircase to the second floor and the apartments beyond, Elizabeth looking around with interest. It was, on second thought, not as large as Netherfield, though it was constructed in the same manner with high ceilings, beautiful marble stonework, and details wrought in fine English oak.

"Aunt Emma does not come below stairs much any longer," said Lady Susan as they walked. "Though she is still able to move about, albeit slowly, she finds the stairs difficult to navigate."

"I would find that hard, indeed," said Elizabeth. "I love the outdoors so much it would be a trial to be denied it."

Lady Susan smile at her. "That is quite evident, my dear. But she has a balcony attached to her bedchamber from which she may partake of nature any time she desires. And on the occasions which she wishes to be in the garden, she has a chair which the footmen may lift down the stairs. She is not completely denied."

"Perhaps it would simply be easier to convert a room on the lower floor to a bedchamber," said Elizabeth. "Then she may find it easier to exit the house."

"That is a radical idea, indeed," replied Lady Susan with a laugh. "I suppose I should not be surprised that *you* would think of it."

"It simply makes sense," said Elizabeth. "We need not care for convention in such a location as this."

"I believe Aunt Emma would agree with you."

The housekeeper approached a door near the end of the stairs and opened it, allowing them to pass through to the room beyond. It was a sitting-room, wide and spacious, with a large fireplace on one end and a set of two chairs and one sofa in front of it. At various positions around the room, there were also an escritoire and a pianoforte, which was a curious affectation in a private sitting-room. There was also a chaise lounge nearby, on which rested a lady—presumably the very Aunt Emma they had come to visit.

She was diminutive, though as she was resting across the chaise, it was difficult to know how tall she was. Her face was weathered and lined, but in its depths, Elizabeth thought she could see traces remaining of what would have been a handsome countenance in her youth. Her hair was still thick and wavy, fully white and gathered behind her head in a knot. Her eyes were bright blue, and there was no hint of any dimness or lack of recognition in them.

"Susan," said she, as she pushed herself off the edge of the chaise with some effort. "This, I suppose is the woman you believe to be your daughter?"

"She *is* my daughter, Aunt Emma," said Elizabeth's mother evenly. "She even has the scar on the back of her head."

Elizabeth approached along with her mother, and when they reached the elderly woman, they assisted her to rise at her imperious command. When she rose, Elizabeth could see that though she wavered a little, once she stood, she did so with very little stoop in her posture. Then, having attained her feet, Aunt Emma gazed deeply into Elizabeth's eyes. For a long moment she did not speak—Elizabeth and her mother remained silent, awaiting her verdict.

"It *is* you, Elizabeth," said she at length, tears suddenly springing up in her eyes.

With deliberate care, Aunt Emma reached out and put her arms around Elizabeth, and drew her close. Having become used to this sort of reaction by now, Elizabeth allowed herself to be embraced, returning the woman's obvious happiness with her own arms.

"I had given up hope of your return, my dear," said Aunt Emma after a moment, drawing back to look into Elizabeth's face yet again.

"How is it that you are convinced without any other explanation?" asked her mother.

"It is in her eyes," said Aunt Emma. "She bears the eyes of you and your grandmother—it was one of the first things I noticed about her when she was a child."

"You know of my scar as well?" asked Elizabeth.

"Indeed, I do, young lady," said Aunt Emma, the lines of her mouth crinkling in her laughter. "You received that scar in my sitting-room below stairs. I thought your mother would expire from her fright for you. But I knew you were strong and would not succumb to such a trifling injury."

"What trifling injury do you call it?" exclaimed Lady Susan. "When she fell, I thought every bit of blood in her body had exited through that small wound!"

The two older ladies bantered back and forth, and for a moment Elizabeth wondered what they were about. Then the light of understanding came to her, and she realized that they had long suppressed any talk of her due to the pain of her absence. It was as if all those years were falling away, taking away all the hurt and anguish with them.

"Now," said Aunt Emma with a welcoming gesture toward the nearby sofas, "come, Lizzy. Let us sit and have tea, for I am eager to hear of the adventures of the past years when you were not with your family. I am certain you have much to tell."

"Lizzy?" asked Elizabeth curiously. "My adoptive family called me Lizzy for years, though my friends often used Eliza too."

"It was my pet name for you," said Aunt Emma. "I am glad it has survived to this day. While your family called you Lizbeth—though your brother Anthony took to calling you Bessie for a while—to me you were always Lizzy."

"Then I am happy to respond to it, for I have been doing it for years."

They sat down to tea, which was delivered directly, and Elizabeth found herself the recipient of all her elderly relation's attention. There was no detail too small to excite Aunt Emma's interest, and she listened to everything Elizabeth had to tell her with rapt attention. Elizabeth covered her childhood and her experiences as an adolescent and then an adult, detailed her coming out, and spoke of those she had called family. All of this she did with Aunt Emma pulling little details out with the skill of a weaver plucking threads.

When they arrived at Elizabeth's departure from Hertfordshire and the subsequent events which had led to her residence in London and her discovery there, Aunt Emma was astounded at the chance which had led to her discovery. She felt close to this woman as if she had not been missing for the better part of two decades. Her character was the highest, her good humor was infectious, and Elizabeth no longer wondered why she was held in such high esteem by her family.

"I always knew that boy had a good head on his shoulders," said Aunt Emma of William when Elizabeth's story wound down to its conclusion. "And we must all be grateful that he is so observant, for we owe him your return."

"You are acquainted with William?" asked Elizabeth. To the best of her knowledge, the Darcy family was not related—Aunt Emma was a relation of Elizabeth's mother, after all.

"Of course, I am," replied Aunt Emma. "He is kind enough to visit whenever he is staying at Snowlock, though of late it has not been often. I seem to remember that he was particularly enamored of *you* when you were naught but a babe."

"It seems like little has changed," was her mother's dry observation.

"Mother!" exclaimed Elizabeth, mortified.

But Aunt Emma only cackled and patted Elizabeth on her knee. "A young woman could do much worse than Fitzwilliam Darcy for a husband, my dear. Not only is he a handsome man, but he will never have difficulty supporting you and any children you might have.

"Then again, you are wealthy enough that you do not require a wealthy husband to live comfortably." Again, Aunt Emma patted Elizabeth's hands. "But you should remember that a marriage of affection to a man is a wonderful blessing. Search for the right man, Lizzy. Do not allow life to pass you by without knowing this beautiful gift. I still remember my Edgar, how I loved him when we married. Our time was short, but there was no happier time in my life than those few short years."

As she spoke, Aunt Emma's eyes were far away, filled with visions no one else could see. Lady Susan watched her elderly relation for some minutes with fondness, and before long, Elizabeth noticed that she had begun to nod off, peacefully dreaming those memories which had, moments before, beset her. Elizabeth rose at her mother's silent gesture, and they made their way from the room, careful to step softly and close the door with a gentle hand to avoid waking her.

"It is often thus," said Lady Susan as they made their way back through the house to the carriage awaiting them. "She is still in control of her wits, but she tires easily and will often sleep without much provocation."

"She must have loved her husband very much," said Elizabeth, feeling unaccountably solemn.

"I believe she did," replied her mother. "She does not talk of him. I believe we have been quite privileged today."

Elizabeth nodded but did not speak. In her heart she was considering the words Aunt Emma had said to her, thinking of William and the role he had played in her recovery. Aunt Emma's exhortations concerning finding a husband had found fertile ground in Elizabeth's heart, and while she had always wanted to marry for love, she now was convinced she could never do anything else. But was William the man?

As for Aunt Emma, Elizabeth was determined to visit her frequently. She had already missed so much time to come to know her due to her disappearance. She would not miss any opportunity for further intimacy in the future.

CHAPTER XXX

June 8 to June 16, 1812
Pemberley to Snowlock, Derbyshire

*P*emberley was a vast estate, one which had been possessed by the Darcy family for many generations. While the manor house was not nearly that old—it had been built in the time of Darcy's grandfather—it still seemed part of the permanence of the estate, the bastion of the Darcy family, which was as immovable as England itself. And in a sense it was—to Darcy, who had never known the land without the stately manor presiding over it, it *was* an enduring symbol of his family's legacy.

The grand estate had always been a home to Darcy, a place where he could retreat when the trials of the world became too much for him to bear. But those few days he spent there alone were nothing less than an ordeal, a cross to be born. Pemberley, while it was lovely, was *not* where he wished to be at that moment, little experience though he had with that sentiment.

Thus, Darcy found himself hurrying through work he would have taken his time with, in an effort to return to Snowlock as soon as he could. Furthermore, he found himself losing focus, required to ask his steward to repeat himself more than once, where he might have chided others for their inability to concentrate. His steward—a good man who had been with him since his father's death five years before—bore it all with patience. But Darcy did not miss the curious looks, of which he was the recipient, on those many occasions where he was forced to ask the poor man to repeat himself.

It fell to Mrs. Reynolds, his housekeeper and confidante, to make the connection between Darcy's inattention and the reason for it.

"If I did not know you better, Master Darcy," said the elderly lady several days after his return, "I might think some young miss has caught your eye."

The raising of her eyebrow was enough to make Darcy blush, and he turned away from her. Most housekeepers in England could not imagine taking such liberties with her employer, but Mrs. Reynolds had long been more friend than employee. His reaction was all that the woman needed, she knew him so well.

"You have!" cried she, clapping her hands with delight. "Might we be hearing wedding bells soon, followed by the laughter of children running through the halls of Pemberley?"

It was all Darcy could do not to lose himself in the thought of children, with Elizabeth as their mother, filling the rooms of his estate.

"Come, Master Fitzwilliam," said she when he did not immediately speak. "Might I know who she is?"

"I am not courting any young woman," said Darcy at length. "But I do find the recently recovered Lady Elizabeth Fitzwilliam to be enchanting."

Mrs. Reynolds's eyes widened in surprise, then she laughed and pressed her fingers to his hand. "What an excellent notion! Then there will be two Fitzwilliam brides in successive generations. Are we to meet this delightful creature?"

"Perhaps she might come to Pemberley in the next few months," replied Darcy. "For the present, I believe her mother wishes to have her close at home."

"As is proper." Mrs. Reynolds smiled, a countenance positively shining with the prospect of the next generation of Darcys making Pemberley their home. "But you should invite them all to Pemberley. We can, as you know, host any of your family you see fit to invite. When she was a child she loved the gardens of Pemberley as much as she loved her home. I am certain she must love them as much now."

Darcy grinned. "There is also the matter of which is the more beautiful estate to consider."

Laughter rang out from his housekeeper. "I am sure there is! If you bring her here, she is sure to agree that Pemberley is the superior. I can hardly wait to meet her."

Soon Mrs. Reynolds went away, her mind aflame with thoughts and plans, stratagems she could use to persuade Lady Elizabeth to stay here forever. Darcy watched her with an indulgent smile—though she would strive to show Pemberley off to its best advantage, Mrs. Reynolds would never stray into territory improper or beyond her purview. She would not attempt to court Lady Elizabeth in Darcy's stead. But Mrs. Reynolds was the best person to display the qualities of his estate—in many ways she was better positioned than he was himself. She was part of the permanence of the estate, though Darcy knew he would need to pension her to a comfortable home before too many more years had passed.

As soon as Darcy had completed the work he had come to Pemberley to do, he prepared for his departure again, saddling his horse early one morning and hastening to return to Snowlock. The miles flew by as he urged his horse into a ground-eating canter, stopping only once to give the beast a rest while he drank some water from a nearby brook and splashed it on his face.

He made such good time that it was still before luncheon when he arrived, and he vaulted from his steed, eager to once again be in Elizabeth's presence. When he entered the hall, he was met by the butler who showed him to his room where he changed and washed the dust of the road from his face and hair. Within a few moments, he was once again on the move, striding down the stairs and toward the family sitting-room, where he hoped he might meet his quarry.

When he entered, however, he was greeted by the sight of Lady Catherine and Anne, sitting together. Of Lady Susan or her daughter, there was no sign. Though Lady Catherine was one of the last people he wished to be in company with, he knew it would appear churlish if he departed from the room again without so much as a word.

"Darcy," said Lady Catherine, her countenance revealing nothing of her feelings. "It is well that you have returned, for I believe there is a matter of which we must speak. You will attend me now."

Inside Darcy indulged in a groan. Though Lady Catherine had been mercifully silent since she had come to London and thence to Snowlock, there was but one subject on which she would wish to speak. It was the one which Darcy would wish to never speak of again. Then again, perhaps now was a propitious time to settle the issue once and for all.

"Oh, do not be tiresome, Darcy," said Lady Catherine when Darcy hesitated. "It is nothing which should cause you such consternation. Sit down, and we shall discuss it in a rational fashion."

There was no other choice to be had, so Darcy did as he was bid, though he settled himself on a chair across from her, unwilling to give her any perceived control by sitting nearby. If Lady Catherine noticed his choice, she did not mention it. She regarded him, and though Darcy was still fearful of what she wished to say, he was forced to acknowledge she did not loom over him and display her indomitable will for all to see.

"As you know," said Lady Catherine, "it has long been known to the family that my sister—your mother—and I came to an agreement to bind our children together in matrimony. This agreement served the purpose to bind our family's wealth together to forward our position in society. Since we were so close, we desired to see our children wed, to bring us ever closer to each other.

"My sister, God rest her soul, did not live to see the fulfillment of our agreement, and likewise, your father and my husband have passed on to their eternal rewards. As the sole remaining survivor of my generation, it has always been my intention to see the wishes of my sister carried out to their conclusion. I have long trusted in the honor and integrity of our children to abide by the decision made so long ago."

Lady Catherine paused and Darcy, aware of where this discussion was tending, thought to interrupt her, so as to bring about the final dissolution of Lady Catherine's plans in a more expedient fashion. But when he opened his mouth to speak, he happened to catch sight of Anne, and what he saw shocked him. Anne was laughing at him. Laughing at him! He knew she had as little intention as he to be forced into a marriage which neither wanted, but he did not think her mother's insistence would incite hilarity. It was more likely to provoke indigestion!

"It seems, however," continued Lady Catherine while Darcy was distracted, "that the wishes of our children are incompatible with our desires, and as such, I have no choice but to allow this dream to die."

Shocked, Darcy gaped at Lady Catherine, wondering if he had heard her correctly. At the same time, Anne's laughter got the best of her, and he heard an unladylike snort escape from her lips. Lady Catherine did not miss it, for she turned to her daughter and glared at her.

"I hardly think that is necessary, Anne. It was *you* who persuaded me to surrender the dream I have held for many years. The very least you can do is respect the sacrifice I am making for your happiness."

"And a great sacrifice it is, Mother," said Anne. Once again, Darcy was shocked, this time because of the sardonic note in his cousin's words toward her mother. Lady Catherine did not miss it either.

"There is no need to be snide, Anne," said she with a sniff. "Though I know you and Darcy have been skeptical of the matter for years, my sister and I truly *did* discuss the matter when you were both children. Anne, for all her shyness and tendency to allow others their opinions without comment, was not a woman to sit idly by if she did not agree. Had she not wished for it herself, she would have disabused me of the notion without delay."

"Why then are you giving this dream up now?" asked Darcy.

"Because I have little choice," said Lady Catherine. She massaged her temples, a calming motion, Darcy thought, before she looked him in the eye. "Our plans were always dependent upon you and Anne agreeing and choosing to bind yourselves to the other. Your fathers, though they were supportive of the notion, refused to finalize it legally, as they both wished for you to have your choice."

"And the years you have spent attempting to force us into this match?" asked Darcy. "'The favorite wish of our mothers?' It often seemed more of a demand than a matter which was left to our choice."

Lady Catherine had the grace to appear a little abashed, an odd affectation in such a self-possessed woman. "Yes, indeed. I suppose you may convict me of overzealousness in that respect, Darcy. When first my husband passed away and then my sister, your marriage became a way I could bind more of my family to me. You have my apologies if it is necessary. It appears that I was more . . . insistent than the agreement between sisters would call for."

It was the sight of Anne, sitting by her mother's side, which prevented Darcy from reacting with annoyance. This cradle betrothal had been the source of much grief, not only for Darcy himself, but even more so for Anne, who was forced to live with the woman.

"I suppose it is understandable," replied Darcy, the harsh feelings toward this woman draining out of him. "I am happy the matter has at last been put to rest."

Darcy injected a questioning quality into his tone, and he regarded Lady Catherine for several moments, wondering how she would respond. She only favored Darcy with a sniff and a stiff nod.

"Good," replied Darcy.

"Indeed," added Anne. "Now you may turn to your courting

without any fear of mother interfering."

Once again Darcy felt his jaw drop in shock. Never had he known Anne to behave in such a manner, and her giggles at his response, coupled with Lady Catherine's accompanying chuckles, made him wonder if the entire world had turned upside-down.

"I do not believe . . ." said Darcy, attempting to find something he could say in response.

"It is clear to just about anyone who has seen you together," said Anne.

"It was that as much as anything which prompted me to relent," added Lady Catherine.

"I would say the field is clear, Darcy." Anne smiled and rose to her feet. "You have her here alone at Snowlock where there are no others to come in your way, and everyone in the family is supportive. I would say 'go to it' but I am certain you have already begun!"

While Darcy was once again at a loss for words, the door opened to allow Lady Susan and Elizabeth to step into the room. Elizabeth immediately noted that something important had happened, and the way her mother looked at him, she too was not ignorant of it.

"I see you have returned, William," said Lady Susan. "I had thought your return was scheduled for tomorrow."

"I finished my business early," Darcy heard himself say. As he looked around the room, he was struck but the thought that the ladies of his family were all laughing at him. But then he caught sight of Elizabeth, noted the slight tilt of her head as if she was trying to understand some puzzle, and all thoughts of teasing or the amusement of the rest of the family were taken from his mind. For nothing mattered but her.

Friday, June 19, 1812
Snowlock, Derbyshire

In the ensuing days and weeks, Fitzwilliam Darcy was a constant presence in Elizabeth's life. The days were idyllic as late spring made way for summer. Whether it was because of the freedom to roam afforded her by the warm weather or her favorite scenes full of greenery or life, summer had always been Elizabeth's favorite season. And while Hertfordshire had been her home for many years, being in Derbyshire, knowing it had been the home of her earliest childhood, meant something special to her. She had somehow returned home in a real sense, in a way that was more profound than simply hearing the stories of her childhood antics from her family.

Through all of these days, William was her companion, the one with whom she spent even more time than she did with her mother. Lady Susan had rapidly become Elizabeth's confidante, her happiness, and her love all in one. But William was somehow becoming her very soul, her hope for the future, her trust and an extension to her happiness all in one. He seemed to understand her, the confusion which still sometimes beset her, the uncertainty with which she viewed the world, insecurities she never even allowed her mother to see.

Together with the ever-faithful Attila, they walked the estate, seeing much of her father's lands, and Elizabeth quickly understood that William knew Snowlock almost as well as he knew Pemberley.

"I spent much time here as a boy, you understand," said he. "I was always close with James and, more particularly, with Anthony. I have no other cousins who are so close, and thus the three of us were inseparable."

"Do my brothers know Pemberley as well as you know Snowlock?" asked Elizabeth curiously.

William scratched his chin in thought. "Anthony is quite familiar with it, but though James is as well, he is several years older than I and was in school by the time I was about six years of age. After that, except for summers, it was usually Anthony and me."

Some days after William returned, Elizabeth's father turned his attention to Elizabeth's education in an area in which she had little experience, as she confessed herself. "I have never ridden much," said she when the subject was broached. "Jane is the rider in the Bennet family. Mr. Bennet only owns one mare, and as Jane enjoyed riding, Nelly became hers. For myself, I have always trusted my own two feet to take me to where I wished to go."

"But you have no fear of horses, correct?" pressed her father.

"No. But I have never had any great desire to ride either."

"I think you have not considered the matter properly," said William. He regarded her with a look which spoke amusement and anticipation. "After all, if you love nature so very much, think of how much more you would be able to see if you were atop a beast which could convey you to much more distant locales."

"William!" admonished Lady Susan. "I lose Elizabeth enough to nature already—do not give her ideas."

They all laughed, and Elizabeth exclaimed: "That is an inducement, indeed, William. But perhaps I would not be a good student."

"I doubt that, Elizabeth," said her father. "Unless you object, we will begin tomorrow. There is no reason why you should not ride."

As it turned out, Elizabeth was not at all against learning, and thus the next day she allowed herself to be led to the paddock. Her father had purchased a mare for her use, a beautiful chestnut she soon christened Hera, and Elizabeth fell in love with the gentle animal the first time they met. Thereafter, she received lessons, not only from her father but also from her brothers and cousin. Elizabeth might not have been able to credit how sore she would feel after a few lessons, but soon the pain receded, and she found that she was at least competent quickly, though she could not call herself an expert.

In this manner, she found herself often astride with her brothers on short journeys around the property, and she was also afforded the opportunity to accompany her mother often, as Lady Susan was an avid and expert horsewoman. They ranged about the estate many times, showing Elizabeth the beauties contained therein or visiting tenants.

But Elizabeth still loved her walks, and on those, she was most often accompanied by William when she was not alone with Attila. It was during these walks that Elizabeth learned much she had not previously known of her cousin, for they spoke of seemingly every subject she could imagine. In particular, one conversation with him stood out and would be remembered for the rest of her life as the moment in which she learned of the true nature of his regard for her.

It was not long after William's return to Snowlock, when Elizabeth had, with Attila in her company, set out to walk out to the woods for a time. As she had been able to convince her father that she did not require the presence of Thompson, she was intending to walk out on her own. But William had come upon her as she was leaving the house and after he had inquired as to her plans, requested permission to accompany her. Though Elizabeth had been anticipating some time to herself, she agreed and they set off. She did not miss the look of satisfaction her father gave her as they passed, leading her to divine that William's request was at least in part at her father's instigation. The show of love and concern for her disarmed any annoyance she might have felt, though she felt it appropriate to show her father an arched eyebrow. He only smiled at her knowingly and disappeared.

The pair chose a particularly beloved path through the gardens, and when they came to the edge, it was only a short distance to the woods. The sounds of a busy estate—the barking of dogs, the occasional rumble of a wagon, or the shouts of men at work—fell away, leaving them to the tranquility of the woods. Elizabeth sighed in contentment; she was a social woman and enjoyed company, but the quietude of the woods would always draw her back into their embrace.

"If I had any doubt as to your love of nature, the sight I see before me would convince me."

Elizabeth turned to see William regarding her. He wore the hint of a smile, no more than the upturn of the corner of his mouth. The intensity with which he regarded her, something she had come to associate as pure William, was present, and though Elizabeth could not determine its meaning, she sensed a measure of admiration and looked away, lest he witness her blush. At that moment, Attila, who had ranged far ahead, came bounding back with a stick in his mouth and, surrendering it to Elizabeth, hopped around with eager anticipation, waiting for Elizabeth to throw it. She did so readily, grateful for the distraction, and the large dog raced off after it.

"I did not think that love of nature was ever in doubt."

"No, it was not. But seeing it and hearing of it are two different matters entirely. It is one of the reasons I believe you would be as enamored of Pemberley as am I."

"Oh?" asked Elizabeth, her eyes once again seeking his. "Is this the reason why you believe I will support your claim of Pemberley being the superior estate?"

This was not the first time Elizabeth had tried to induce William to confess to his reasons for wishing her at his estate, but he was as evasive as ever. He only smiled and said: "Perhaps I merely think you will enjoy the lovely pianoforte I have just purchased for Georgiana."

Elizabeth shook her head. "What silliness."

With a grin, William said: "Please do not inform Georgiana. It is to be a surprise when she returns home."

Attila approached at a gallop with his prize, and Elizabeth turned her attention away from William to send him flying off after the stick once again. As the great dog sped away, Elizabeth watched him with an indulgent smile; he was a great baby, but she had grown fond of him.

"I trust everything was well at the estate when you left," said Elizabeth.

"Of course," replied William. "You can hardly suppose I would leave Pemberley if all was *not* well, can you? Or do you think so little of my dedication to duty?"

His tone told Elizabeth that William was amused. When she turned to regard him, she noticed that he was watching the approaching Attila once again. William beckoned to the dog, holding out his hand to accept the stick. But Attila, other than a glance in his direction, ignored him and made directly for Elizabeth, depositing the stick in her hand. Elizabeth could not resist favoring William with a superior smile.

"That dog is not only a menace," said William agreeably. "He is also a traitor."

"A traitor? How so?"

"A few winsome smiles and he has given his allegiance over to you. He has always been friendly with all the family, but now he ignores everyone else in favor of his new mistress."

"Perhaps he has now discerned true nobility and seeks to show his appreciation."

Elizabeth exchanged a look with William and soon they both broke into laughter. "I am happy you have taken to your new life so easily, Lady Elizabeth." William's tone was dry, mixed with a hint of teasing. "The family had worried for your ability to adapt."

"They did?" asked Elizabeth, curiosity coloring her tone. "Mother and Father only showed confidence in my abilities, and my brothers have always assured me that they expected me to take London by storm."

"And so they did. You would not expect them to speak of their concerns to you."

Elizabeth considered that for a moment. "No, I suppose not. I am torn between appreciating their concern and offense that they thought so little of my capabilities."

"No one doubted your abilities, Elizabeth." The sound of his voice, slightly rough with emotion, but completely confident, caught Elizabeth's attention. She regarded him, noting the sincerity radiating from his very being. "But it *was* a monumental transformation, do you not agree?"

"I suppose," replied Elizabeth, feeling a little flustered at his praise. "But I do not consider it any great accomplishment."

"And I assure you, it was," replied William. "I understand that your upbringing consisted of little nurturing from your adoptive mother, and left you uncomfortable with praise as a result. But Elizabeth, you must understand that young ladies of your station are prepared to assume their place in society from their early childhood. That you were able to step into your position without pause is no less than astonishing."

"It has not seemed much different from what I experienced in

Hertfordshire," said Elizabeth, trying to calm the thrills of pleasure his compliments engendered.

"And that is part of the wonder of your abilities. Can you imagine Miss Lydia Bennet adapting with as much composure as you have?"

"Lydia Bennet is naught but a silly young girl," said Elizabeth. "I do not consider her to be a suitable comparison."

"Perhaps she is not. But choose the best young ladies of your acquaintance. Can you imagine any of them faring as well as you did?"

Immediately thoughts of Jane and Charlotte sprung to Elizabeth's mind. Jane was angelic, but she was also too reticent to put herself forward. Elizabeth thought she might do well, but she would likely leave society wondering who exactly she was, as she would not stand out in a crowd. As for Charlotte, while she was an amiable friend, Elizabeth could not imagine her cynical friend immersed in the first circles. Charlotte's capabilities were such that she could do it if she wished, but she would always assume that others were laughing at her behind her back. Of course, that was not necessarily untrue in the sometimes vicious waters of London, but the ability to look for the good in others was also to be prized. If Jane had a little more Charlotte, and Charlotte had a little more Jane in their characters, they would both do better.

"I know not," said Elizabeth at length. "There are a few who would likely not wilt under the pressure."

"But you have thrived under it," said William quietly. "I know I may be overstating it, Elizabeth, but I have been impressed by your demeanor, and I know all of your family feels likewise. Lady Catherine is nothing less than astonished at how well you have held yourself. You have much of which to be proud."

Not knowing what to say, Elizabeth continued to walk, playing with Attila, at times wrestling with the dog when he brought back the stick and refused to surrender it to her, and at others, accepting it and throwing it for him to chase. Through all of this, William walked alongside her, and she felt his eyes upon her constantly. But rather than confuse or unnerve her, she found it comforting, like a blanket on her bed that she drew about her for warmth on a cold winter night.

"I believe I *would* like to see Pemberley, William," said Elizabeth after some time had passed without words between them. "Perhaps we could all go there?"

"I would like that very much," replied William softly. "There are some places on Pemberley's grounds I would like to show you, and now that you ride, we may see them all if we like."

There was something more in William's statement than Elizabeth could immediately catch. After a moment's thought, she decided that he had spoken of more than a single summer. Instead, his words evoked a future of laughter and love, of exploration and discovery, of the passing of the seasons noticed, but only in the manner in which one marks the passing of time. Of home and happiness.

And Elizabeth wanted that, she decided. William could give it to her—this she knew. But she needed to be cautious, for there were considerations to contemplate other than the contents of her heart.

CHAPTER XXXI

Monday, June 22, 1812
Undisclosed Location

Perhaps he should not have stayed in London. There was no telling what the woman had been up to since the last time he had seen her. But her absence from town removed the problem of her presence in society. And there was not an abundance of men in the neighborhood in which Snowlock was situated who would command her attention as the daughter of an earl. The hunter had felt safe in leaving her to her own devices for a few weeks while he remained in the city.

But he should not have stayed after the end of the season, for the longer he was away from her, the longer that puppy Darcy possessed to shower her with his attentions. The hunter snorted at the thought—she was the kind of romantic woman who would no doubt swoon at the pretty attentions paid to her by a man as tight as a miser's generosity.

The lure of the tables, however, proved too great, and he had spent the last month making up for the time he had lost pursuing the silly woman. He had allowed himself to become distracted by his activities and had ended staying in London until the last possible moment. Had he stayed longer, he would have been playing against those who lived in London the whole year and had no ability to play for the stakes he preferred, for all the rich men would have departed. It was then the hunter finally came to his senses and hurried back to his estate.

Cooper had been sent on ahead when the Fitzwilliams had decamped. Thus, when the hunter retired to his study after cleaning himself from his journey, he sent for a bite of supper and his man. The food arrived first, and he set to it with a will, having eaten little in his hurry to return. It was some moments before his man arrived. Cooper sat in the chair indicated and waited patiently for the hunter to finish eating, and when he did, he sat back with a glass of wine and considered the servant in front of him.

"What have you to report?"

"Very little," replied Cooper in his typical gruff manner. "I watched the girl when I could, but I could not approach."

The hunter grunted; the earl guarded his privacy, which would be enhanced with his long-lost daughter in residence for the first time in many years.

"I understand. What have you been able to observe?"

"The girl loves nature. She is always walking on the grounds, usually with one of the earl's dogs. When she does not walk, she is with her mother, either on horseback or in the house. They visit occasionally, though most families are only just returning to the area. And they have visited the dower house."

The hunter scowled at the mention of the dower house and its inhabitant, but he forced those thoughts away. There was no reason to consider the old bat. The path to what he deserved went through the girl, not the woman.

"Continue to observe her whenever the opportunity presents itself," instructed the hunter. "But do not take any chances. I do not wish to attempt to explain to the earl why one of my men is trespassing on his estate."

"Of course," replied his man.

The servant rose and excused himself, leaving the hunter to ruminate on the situation. It was clear the Darcy was trying to woo the girl, but regardless, he did not think Darcy would be successful so quickly. That gave him a reprieve.

It would be enough. The hunter did not mean to allow anything to deter him, or anything to stand his way. He would have what was his at long last.

Thursday, June 25, 1812
Snowlock, Derbyshire

It was a pleasant time spent in Derbyshire at her father's house, and the longer Elizabeth stayed in residence at Snowlock, the more she came to love it. There was something about the land, something undefinable, which had not been present in Hertfordshire. Whether it was because of her latent connection to it, she could not be certain. But she was pleased nonetheless.

For a time, she spent her days riding with her mother, walking the estate, interspersed with visits in the neighborhood, and even an assembly where she danced the first with her cousin William. Elizabeth could not remember a happier time. It was in these circumstances, far from the pressure of society in London, that in later years she determined that she finally came into her own as the daughter of an earl.

It was also during those days that one of the gentlemen who had paid her attention in London returned to her notice. After the morning in her father's music room, Elizabeth had seen Lord Winchester only once, and she had heard nothing from the man thereafter. One day while they had been speaking of inconsequential matters, James had made mention that Lord Winchester owned a small estate in Leicestershire which was not at all distant from Snowlock, but though Elizabeth half expected the man to come smirking into her father's sitting-room, he did not appear.

The same could not be said of Mr. Standish. For a month after the family had left London she was free of his presence, but whereas the earl did not appear, one morning Mr. Standish arrived to call on the family.

"Good morning, Cousin," said he to the earl, though Elizabeth knew by now that he was actually related to her mother, though distantly. "Lady Elizabeth. I see you have made your escape from town. I hope reacquainting yourself with your father's estate has been agreeable?"

"It has," replied Elizabeth. "I could hardly imagine a more beautiful place than Snowlock."

Mr. Standish laughed. "I doubt Darcy here would agree with you." He turned a grin on Elizabeth's cousin. "He is well-known for touting his estate's superiority to all who will listen."

"Perhaps I am," replied William. "But I believe I have a good reason."

"I do not deny that," agreed Mr. Standish. "But it is true all the same."

In the ensuing moments, Elizabeth watched Mr. Standish as he spoke, primarily with her brothers, and she was struck by the difference in their behavior toward him as opposed to what it had been when he had first been introduced to her. While it was clear there was some residual reserve for him, their manner was distinctly warmer than it had been. Whether it was because the man had assisted in protecting her from Lord Winchester's machinations or because he had proven himself to be more than they had expected, Elizabeth could not be certain.

He was, she thought, not the best of men — her brothers and William held that distinction in Elizabeth's estimation. She knew little of his habits aside from what her family had told her and was ready to concede there were objectionable aspects of his character of which she was unaware. But he had been nothing but kind to Elizabeth, and as such, it was not a facet of her character to behave to him as if he had committed some great offense. Thus, though she still, at times, found herself disquieted by him, she exerted herself to speak kindly with him, though she could never summon the animation which William commanded from her.

For some time, the conversation wound on, centering on Elizabeth's impressions of Derbyshire and her doings since she had come to the area. The previous month had been one of tranquil pursuits, and Elizabeth did not think it was all that interesting. But Mr. Standish listened to everything she said with an intentness unfeigned. There was an eagerness in his manner which Elizabeth did not think she had seen previously and which she could not explain.

Elizabeth was recounting some of the people she had met in Derbyshire when a thought struck her, and she said: "I also met my mother's Aunt Emma. Are you acquainted with her? Since you are a relation of my mother's I suppose you must be a relation of Aunt Emma's too?"

For a moment, all expression fled Mr. Standish's countenance, and Elizabeth had the distinct impression that he was mastering some great emotion. But the moment passed, and Mr. Standish nodded.

"Yes, I am acquainted with Mrs. Seward. How did you find her?"

"I like her very much," replied Elizabeth. "Mama and I visit her every few days. She was quite gratified at my return, and I was happy to make her acquaintance."

"I am certain she was," replied Mr. Standish. He paused and

directed an odd look at her. "I seem to recall she was enamored with you as a child. I suppose she has regaled you with tales of your antics as a toddler?"

"To a certain extent, yes," said Elizabeth. "The scar on my head which identifies me was apparently obtained during a visit there."

"Indeed?" Mr. Standish looked about the room with interest. "I have never heard tell of *how* you determined Lady Elizabeth was your daughter. This scar was the final proof?"

"There were a number of factors," replied the earl. A quick look at him revealed that he was not happy with the question. "We did not feel it was necessary to make the exact circumstances or identifying characteristics fodder for the gossips of society."

"Prudent," replied Mr. Standish. "Too many details would allow others to attempt to cast aspersions on her identity. It was undoubtedly for the best that you did not publish these matters."

While her father seemed somewhat mollified at Mr. Standish's response, he continued to watch the man for the rest of the visit, and if Elizabeth's observation was any indication, his scrutiny was less than friendly, distinctly at odds with what Elizabeth had witnessed from her brothers earlier. For Elizabeth's part, though she had owned to herself that Mr. Standish did seem to be at least an agreeable man, this visual response to him from her father once again put her on her guard. It was strange and not a little frustrating to continually have her opinion swing from one extreme to the other. But there seemed little she could do about it.

When Mr. Standish excused himself and departed, Elizabeth watched him go with mixed feelings. Kinsman he might be, but Elizabeth decided she could cheerfully give up his society.

Thursday, June 25, 1812
Snowlock, Derbyshire

There was one in the room who was not amused by Mr. Standish's coming and was not happy with his attentions toward Elizabeth. Lord Matlock watched him, noted his interest in Elizabeth, the way he spoke to her and the lengths to which he went to hide his true self from her.

Matlock was not deceived. Standish had long been an acquaintance, not only by virtue of his connection with Susan but also due to the proximity of his estate, which bordered Snowlock to the west. In the past, they had often gone months without contact with him, as he was entirely devoted to his vices. Now, suddenly, they saw him frequently, and though he hid it, Matlock was certain he looked on Elizabeth through calculating eyes. Matlock was grateful the man had assisted in the matter of Lord Winchester, but he still did not trust him.

When Standish rose to depart, Matlock also rose, offering to accompany him back to his coach. When Standish's expression became sardonic, Matlock was certain the man knew what he was about. But Matlock was not accustomed to allowing mere gentlemen to behave in such a careless manner, and so confronted him in the entrance hall before he could make his escape.

"Just what are your intentions, Standish?"

"Must I have any intentions?" the man rejoined. "Perhaps I am only wishing to strengthen my bonds with my family."

Matlock regarded him with open skepticism. "When you have never cared for your family — or anything beyond your vices and immediate gratification? You will forgive my disbelief."

Though he had hoped to provoke Standish into revealing something, the other man only shrugged. "I suppose I can hardly blame you for that, Matlock. I have given you little reason to believe me, I suppose."

Standish stopped walking and turned to Matlock. "There is nothing sinister in my actions. Your daughter interests me, as she does so many others. How could she not? Disappeared for many years, only to return to the bosom of her family without warning? It sounds like Radcliff at her most imaginative, you must agree."

"And to what does this interest tend?" asked Matlock. While Standish's explanation sounded reasonable, he could not silence the voice in the back of his head which told him there must be more to it. He could not imagine the man cared for the return of a young woman so long lost, regardless of his connection to her. He had shown years of dissipative behavior without any hint of interest in anything else. Why now?

"If you are asking if I wish her for a wife, I had not thought of it," replied Standish, surprising Matlock by speaking of it openly. "But now that you mention it, I *am* getting on in years. Perhaps it is time to marry.

"What think you?" asked he before Matlock could respond. "She is pretty and her connections are excellent. And if I was to marry her, you would benefit from having her nearby. She may visit you whenever she likes. And I would finally have an heir."

"Have you forgotten what I told Winchester?" growled Matlock. "I have no intention of bartering my daughter to a man who can give her a home nearby. If she marries, it will be her choice, and that of none other."

With a shaken head and a chuckle, Standish began walking toward the door again. Matlock did not care for the way he was acting—*this* was more the Standish of old than he had been these previous months of attempting to make love to them all.

"You need not concern yourself, Matlock. I know what you told Winchester. You must own that Lady Elizabeth is now one of the most eligible women in society, and you will shortly be inundated with young bloodhounds sniffing about her. If I am interested in her for that purpose, can you be surprised? There are certain advantages to such a match. I am certain I do not have to explain them to you.

"But I have also seen Darcy hovering around her like a puppy, and as you have not warned *him* away, I must assume you favor a match with him. Pity. I suppose it is her tender heart and romantic sensibilities which lead you to accept him. Or perhaps it is his uprightness and stiff-necked adherence to duty which appeals to you. Regardless, you need have no fear from me."

"As I said to Winchester," replied Matlock from between clenched teeth, "if Darcy is favored, it is because he makes her happy. I will not force her hand in this. Elizabeth will marry where she likes, and I can guarantee that she does *not* like you."

"Then you have even less reason to concern yourself."

The insolent tone in which Standish spoke infuriated Matlock, but as they had reached the door and his carriage waited in front of them, he decided there was little reason to argue with him. With nary a gesture or another word, Standish climbed aboard the coach and rapped on the roof. Matlock watched it as the carriage lurched into motion.

When it was gone, Matlock turned away and slowly made his way back into the house, unsettled by the confrontation. He had never had a good opinion of Standish, so he supposed his annoyance was nothing out of the ordinary.

Thursday, June 25, 1812
Snowlock, Derbyshire

By that evening, Elizabeth had forgotten all about Mr. Standish and her ever-changing feelings about the man, as there were much more interesting subjects on which to think. Her father, however, approached her, his mien troubled—or at least that was what she thought, for he appeared to be doing his best to present a complaisant image before the company.

"Our relation has once again made an appearance it seems," said he.

"Mr. Standish," said Elizabeth, grasping the subject of her father's comment. "It seems he has. I do wonder about him, for you have all told me he is not sociable."

"That is why I am curious about your impressions of the man, Elizabeth. You have informed me in the past you did not care for him—has that opinion changed?"

Elizabeth frowned, not certain to what her father was referring. "I find that my feelings for Mr. Standish change rather rapidly. He seems to be making an effort to be agreeable, and for a man who has lived his life in search of selfish gratification, I suppose it must speak well to him."

"Then you favor him."

Her frown deepening, Elizabeth was quick to say: "I am not certain where you might have obtained that impression, Father. I am polite to Mr. Standish, as I would be to anyone. There is still something about him which disquiets me. I expect it is the knowledge of his proclivities. But I do not favor him, especially not as a potential suitor."

It seemed her father was relieved at Elizabeth's declaration. "That is well, my daughter. I had thought that Darcy was rising in your esteem, but with Standish's actions whenever he is in company, I wished to be certain."

Elizabeth flushed at the mention of William, but her father did not seem to notice. "Then you may put your concerns to rest. Even if Mr. Standish should attempt to pay me such attention, I would remain unmoved."

Saturday, June 27, 1812
Snowlock, Derbyshire

Unfortunately, Elizabeth's newfound freedom to walk the estate as she chose was not to last. Mr. Standish was one reason, of course, for it was not the last time they saw him at Snowlock. In fact, though her father watched him whenever he came, Mr. Standish seemed to take great pleasure in imposing his presence upon Elizabeth and monopolizing her attention at every opportunity. Between Mr. Standish and the rest of the company, Elizabeth gradually saw a degradation in their relationships, until he was viewed by them all with barely concealed hostility. But he seemed not to care—he came to speak to Elizabeth, and he did so, bold as brass, to the exclusion of all others.

The other matter which led to the curtailing of her freedom was an event which occurred a few days after Mr. Standish's first visit to Snowlock. Anthony had gone to Derby for the day on an errand, and when he returned, he did so with a troubled countenance and an agitation which bespoke anger.

"I came across Lord Winchester when I was in Derby," announced he to the room without even a greeting.

"Winchester?" asked Lord Matlock, his voice low and dangerous. "What was he doing there?"

"He would not say," said Anthony. "I confronted him, but he was his usual pleasant self. I was able to wring from him that he was staying at his estate in Leicestershire and that he intends to be there all summer."

This news was not received well by anyone in the room. Elizabeth's mother, aunt, and cousins scowled, but from the expressions on the faces of the gentlemen, she thought they might sortie at dawn to do battle with the Earl of Winchester. Thus, she felt it incumbent upon herself to inject a little levity into the situation.

"Heaven forbid a man visit an estate which he lawfully owns or walks a public street in a large city."

Perhaps she should have predicted it, but no one in the room thought her jest amusing.

"Have you already forgotten what he tried to do when we were in London?" demanded Anthony.

"No, I have not," replied Elizabeth. "But I cannot imagine he would skulk about the estate of another peer, waiting for a chance to throw me over his horse and make for the blacksmith in Gretna Green."

"Oh, Elizabeth," said Lady Susan. "Do not even suggest such a thing."

While a chorus of voices rose to support her mother's words, Lord Matlock looked at her, apparently deep in thought. Elizabeth was quite certain she did not like the direction his deliberations were tending, and when he spoke, that supposition was borne out.

"While I agree with Elizabeth's assertion, I am still wary of what he may try. And with Standish also in the area, I believe caution is warranted."

Elizabeth sighed. "I suppose my days of walking with no one more than Attila for company are over?"

She was slightly mollified by her father's apologetic gaze. "I know you prefer your freedom, Elizabeth, but while the chances of either gentleman attempting something are small, I do not wish to test the theory. It would bring us all peace of mind if you were to accept it with whatever grace you can muster."

"Then I have little choice." Elizabeth smiled. "I hope the grace I am currently displaying is enough, for I cannot summon more."

"It will do," said her mother, fixing Elizabeth with a fond smile.

Monday, June 29, 1812
Snowlock, Derbyshire

Thus, Elizabeth was again attended by Thompson whenever she went out on the estate. The man was quiet and watchful, and he followed at a distance sufficient to afford her enough privacy, but the restriction still chafed, especially as Elizabeth did not view either Mr. Standish or Lord Winchester as a threat. Therefore, she grew to resent them both simply because they were the cause of the constraints under which she was forced to submit. Or perhaps it was more accurate to say she grew to resent them more — she had never liked *either* man.

"Pardon me for saying it, Lady Elizabeth, but it seems that your mood is not the best today."

"I am sorry, William," replied Elizabeth, realizing she had been silent for several moments. Again, they were walking the paths of her father's estate with the faithful Attila in attendance. "I am simply ruminating on the unfairness of my situation."

"Oh?" asked William. "I was not aware the lot of the daughter of an earl was so onerous."

It was his amused tone which told Elizabeth she was acting silly, but she was not prepared to simply allow the matter to rest. "I am referring to this situation with Mr. Standish," replied she. Elizabeth could well acknowledge she was feeling more than a little peevish. "Mr. Standish has never been threatening, and yet I must endure the limitations my father has decreed because of his continued presence."

"Standish is *not* a good man, Elizabeth," admonished William. "And you did not even mention Lord Winchester."

"I have not so much as laid eyes on Lord Winchester since London. I do not doubt your good information concerning Mr. Standish, but I cannot see that he is a threat either. I think he comes to vex you all."

William grinned. "You may very well be correct. But I find I must apologize, Lady Elizabeth. If I had known my company was so objectionable I would not have imposed upon you."

A sharp glance at William informed Elizabeth that the man was laughing at her. Elizabeth decided this would not be allowed to stand.

"Then next time you will be in a position to judge better."

They shared a long look before bursting into laughter. Elizabeth felt lighter as the pique of the moment departed, better able to think rationally. And what she found when she considered it did not please her.

"I suppose I may have been a little silly," said she, feeling abashed.

"It is understandable. You have long been accustomed to having as much freedom as you like, going where you will, walking as long as you wish. There *are* certain limitations imposed upon the daughter of an earl that a simple country miss might not experience. Only remember that your family loves you and wishes to keep you safe."

"I know that, William."

"Good. Then your sometimes fractious behavior is endurable."

Elizabeth turned to regard him. "Have I truly been that difficult?"

"Only this morning," replied he with no hint of a grin.

Elizabeth more than made up for it with her responding laughter. "Then I will strive to improve myself."

With the annoyance of the moment dispelled, they turned and walked on for some time, a comfortable silence descending between them. She had, Elizabeth reflected, always felt comfortable in his company, especially after the initial surprise and confusion of their original introduction had dissipated. Now that she was close to all her family, she found she preferred William's company to any other, though she loved all her family. Part of her whispered that it was due to her ever-growing feelings, the kind a woman has for a good man of her acquaintance. The thought warmed her. Who would have thought such a fate awaited her when she left Longbourn?

For some moments, Elizabeth lost herself in thoughts of what she found agreeable in her companion. He was stalwart and dependable, always carrying through with whatever he promised. He was honest and good, as upright a man as she had ever met. He was fair and rational. And it did not hurt that he was as handsome a man as Elizabeth had ever met. He was a veritable God of Olympus sent down to mortal realms, to dazzle all the maidens with his beauty and goodness.

A giggle escaped Elizabeth's lips at the silly thoughts passing through her mind. It did not go unnoticed by William.

"Perhaps you might share the reason for your laughter?"

Sharing her thoughts was naturally the last thing Elizabeth wanted to do. "It was nothing more than a random thought," said she, when no other better explanation came to mind. When he appeared like he wished to pursue it further, she was quick to say: "We have wandered far. Perhaps it is time to turn back?"

William glanced about, and Elizabeth noted that he was not unaware of their location. It was a direction she had never walked by herself and further than she usually ranged. They walked alongside thicker woods than she had seen in most parts of the estate, the thick underbrush beneath rendering it passable only with difficulty. In the distance across an open field on the other side of the path there was a fence marking the boundary with the next estate.

"In a moment," said William.

His gaze turned to Elizabeth, and she felt a painful fluttering in her midsection, which worsened as he approached her, his eyes upon her like the heat of a thousand suns. Elizabeth, who had been standing close to a tree, leaned back against it, and he stepped close, leaning an arm up against the tree and looked down at her. He was close, the scent of his cologne hovering about her like that of a flower garden, sweet and musky all at once. When she looked up into his eyes, she was caught, unable to move or even to breathe.

"I will not ask what you thought, for I suspect it embarrassed you."

He nodded when Elizabeth flushed and looked down, but he was not about to allow her to avoid his gaze, for he used one finger to tilt her head back so she was once again facing him.

"I believe I have promised to show Pemberley to you. And yet we are still here at Snowlock. Would it please you if I extended an invitation to you and all your family to join me at Pemberley for a few weeks?"

"Of course," was Elizabeth's quiet reply. "You and Georgiana have both spoken of it in glowing terms. I would be happy to visit."

William's eyes bored into hers. "Though the prospect of you 'visiting for a time' has a certain appeal, I am more interested to know if you would consider it a home of a longer duration."

When Elizabeth gasped, William chuckled and shook his head. "I apologize for stating it in such a bald fashion, but I am certain you must know by now that my interest in you is not merely that of a cousin. While I do not wish to confuse or push you more than you are prepared, I also wish to know that you consider me a more welcome presence than that of Mr. Standish. Or Lord Winchester, for that matter."

Laughter bubbled up in Elizabeth's chest, and she let it loose, pleased when William began laughing along with her. "I do not know why you would wish to be compared to those two gentlemen. Even if you *are* more welcome, that is hardly a ringing endorsement."

"I suppose not," replied William. "But you did not answer the question."

Elizabeth could be nothing but honest. "Then I shall answer: yes, William, you are much more welcome than the likes of either of the two gentlemen you named. But you already knew that. Furthermore, I would be happy to visit Pemberley and pleased to consider if it might suit as a home of longer duration."

"Thank you," said William. He said nothing further, his response thereafter consisting of him reaching down to grasp her hand and raise it to his lips. His kiss lingered on the back of her hand, the warmth of his breath causing shivers to travel up her arm, and tickling where it flowed against the fine hairs. It was the most perfect moment Elizabeth had ever experienced.

It was interrupted by the sound of a voice, one which Elizabeth had tolerated, but now detested for its unwitting interruption.

"Darcy! Lady Elizabeth!"

William dropped Elizabeth's hand and he turned, allowing her to see past him. There, striding through the field, a grin plastered on his face, was Mr. Standish, looking for all the world like he had not seen either of them in weeks. Elizabeth watched him approach, wishing for the first time since she had met him that he would leave her be. A glance at William showed him to be watching the man with barely concealed suspicion.

Before Mr. Standish could approach them, however, Attila, who had been gamboling about while they spoke, raced forward and skidded to a halt in front of Elizabeth. The dog deliberately sat in front of her and bared his teeth in a low growl.

"Your dog?" asked Mr. Standish, motioning to the beast.

"Attila, heel," said William. Attila stopped growling, but his vigilance never ceased, and he would not be moved from where he sat.

"What a fortunate happenstance this is," said Mr. Standish, apparently deciding it was best to simply ignore Elizabeth's protector. "I have rarely seen anyone from Snowlock walking this part of the estate. You are far from home, are you not?"

The last remark was directed at Elizabeth—it was all she could do not to scowl. "I am sorry, sir," said she, ignoring his question. "I had not thought to see you in such a place. Why are you here?"

The raised eyebrow showed Mr. Standish was not put off by her incivility, and the slight smirk further informed her that he was diverted by it.

"I might ask the same of you," said he. Mr. Standish turned and pointed across the field. "Beyond that fence lies my estate. My house is closer than yours."

If he meant to soothe her, it must have been a vast disappointment. Elizabeth's pique only rose at his tone rather than the reverse, and she found herself snapping a response.

"Then I must point out that we have not trespassed on your property, sir. Where I walk on my father's estate is none of your concern."

Mr. Standish regarded her, his amusement never dwindling. "It seems you are not in a mood for my company today, Lady Elizabeth. It is a great pity. I will leave you to your faithful followers."

With a significant glance at both William and Attila, the man turned and began to saunter away without a further glance. Attila rose and followed him for a short distance, but when he understood that Mr. Standish was departing and would not return, he turned and made his way to Elizabeth's side. He accepted her scratching of his ears as nothing more than his due, and sat on his haunches, still watching the retreating back of her tormentor.

"I believe Standish is correct about one thing," said William. "We have walked far enough today. It is time to return to the house."

Elizabeth acquiesced, and with her hand on his arm, they began walking back in the direction of the manor. As they walked, she thought of the puzzle of Mr. Standish, wondering what the man was about. He displayed the fervency of a suitor at times, but at others, he seemed to view her as a joke to which only he was privy. She was now more uncomfortable around him than ever, though she did not know why she felt that way.

"Were you aware we were so close to his estate?" asked Elizabeth of William when they had walked for several moments.

"I was," said William. "But he has long had little interest in it, and I had not thought we would see him."

For a moment Elizabeth considered this. "I believe I will be glad to go to Pemberley. He will not visit so easily if we are there."

"Then I will issue the invitation to your father as soon as we return. Perhaps another month away from his company will persuade Standish to return to his vices."

While Elizabeth hoped that was so, doubt gnawed at her heart. Mr. Standish wanted something from her—but she could not determine what it was.

CHAPTER XXXII

Monday, June 29, 1812
Snowlock, Derbyshire

*T*heir arrival back at the estate was met with some measure of disquiet. Consumed as she was by William's presence, Elizabeth had not realized that they had been gone for longer than she usually spent on her walks.

"It was only because William accompanied you that prevented me from mounting a search party," said her father when they had been led to the rest of the family.

"Even then we had to restrain Anthony," added James, grinning at his brother. "He was certain that Winchester had descended with a large force of men to carry you off to Kent. Or perhaps Gretna Green."

"I did not," replied Anthony. "I would be subjected to the sharp side of my sister's tongue if I presumed to be so protective."

"I am well," Elizabeth was quick to assure them. "Attila will not allow anyone near."

"Though we did happen across Standish again."

"Oh?" asked her father, a dangerous light entering his eyes. "What was he doing on my estate?"

"We had wandered quite near to his lands," said Elizabeth, eager to avoid any unpleasantness.

The story of their encounter with their neighbor was disseminated, and though it mollified them all, her father still appeared unhappy with Standish. Elizabeth wondered at his seeming change of heart. His suspicion seemed to have grown much more quickly than that of her brothers. It was odd, considering their protective nature.

"I have spoken with Elizabeth today about visiting Pemberley," said William, before anyone could say anything further about her ardent admirers. "She has never been to my home and has expressed a desire to see it. And there is still the question of which estate is the more beautiful."

Though his purpose was to induce a little levity into the situation, it appeared to fall flat. A groan swept through the company, and Lady Susan could be heard to mutter: "Oh, William!"

"Perhaps my humor was ill-judged," said he, "but the invitation stands. Of further benefit, it would remove Elizabeth from the immediate notice of the area. The distance would mean that Standish would not easily impose upon her every day as he does now. Furthermore, Lord Winchester's estate in Leicestershire would be even further distant"

"There is some merit to that suggestion," said Lady Catherine. "If you are truly concerned about them, then she will be beyond their reach at Pemberley for a time."

Elizabeth noted that her mother and father, in the manner of couples long married, looked at one another, seeming to be able to communicate without words. When her mother gave a minute nod of approval, Lord Matlock turned back to William.

"Thank you, William, we accept. I propose that we prepare quickly and be gone. Let us leave Standish without any indication we have decamped. Perhaps he will get the point. If we leave immediately, it might also pull Winchester out from wherever he is lurking."

"While I would never accuse your lordship of wishful thinking, I agree. Georgiana and I will depart tomorrow to prepare for your arrival."

Wednesday, July 1, 1812
Snowlock, Derbyshire

Thus decided, the preparations began and were hurried to completion. William and Georgiana left the following morning as was his design, and though Elizabeth and her family were only to stay at Snowlock for another three days, Elizabeth found herself missing him. It was a longing for an old friend, a new love, and it consumed her days, even as she went about cheerfully, showing her family nothing but complaisance and happiness. And happy she was, for she would finally see the place of which she had long been told.

But this feeling of longing for William worried Elizabeth, coupled with the obvious concern her family had displayed when they had returned from their walk. Elizabeth felt she was experiencing the high waves and low troughs of a ship on a stormy sea. She had become much closer to William, to the extent that she wished for his courtship, felt she was on the cusp of wishing for a proposal from him. And then she remembered that she was only just returned to her family after a long absence. They cared for her, feared for her. How would she be repaying them if she accepted a proposal from William so soon after her recovery?

Once again it was left to the blunt forthrightness of Lady Catherine to calm Elizabeth's fears. Though they did not disappear with her aunt's words, the lady managed to impart some measure of understanding which Elizabeth thought she sorely needed.

"Elizabeth," said the lady, entering Elizabeth's sitting-room attached to her bedchamber the day before they were to depart. "I would like to speak to you for a moment if you will oblige me."

While she had noted that Lady Catherine often couched such statements as questions, refusal was not an option. Or perhaps it was more accurate to state that refusal would only be allowed with much difficulty. As it was, Elizabeth had little reason to object.

"It seems to me," said Lady Catherine in her usually imperious tone, "that you have been laboring under some difficulty. Though I would allow you to come to terms with your concerns without interference, your distraction is causing your mother grief. Thus, I have determined to intervene."

"Mother?" asked Elizabeth. "I have noticed nothing to suggest concern."

"That is because she takes pains to hide it from you, not wishing to add to your burdens. But I, who have known Susan for many years, am not so easily fooled. Now, will you not share your worries with me?"

Lady Catherine was not the sort of person to be a sympathetic listener. In fact, Elizabeth thought the lady was much more likely to browbeat and force concerns away with her indomitable will.

Harmony, in Lady Catherine's world, would be bought at the expense of freedom. Elizabeth was also wary of saying anything concerning William, knowing the hopes Lady Catherine espoused with respect to her daughter.

"Then perhaps I should inform you of my observations, and you may tell me if I am correct," said Lady Catherine, when Elizabeth did not immediately speak. "You lament Darcy's departure and wish to be reunited again. Furthermore, you wish for a union with him, but you worry that your family will not wish to give you up so quickly."

Elizabeth gaped at the woman—what she had always taken for haughty indifference and a tendency to believe what she wished to believe had, in this instance, been shown to be a keen understanding of the situation.

"I am not a foolish old woman, blind to those about her," snapped Lady Catherine. "Nor do I watch the world through lenses colored by wishful thinking and a determination to have my own way. I knew of Darcy's interest in you from almost the very moment I arrived in London."

"Then you do not wish for a marriage between William and Anne?"

"I *did* wish for it. But it appears *they* do not. As the completion of the plans I designed with my sister depended upon *them*, and they do not wish to oblige me, I had no choice but to accept their decision with whatever grace I could muster.

"But we have departed from the subject. It is good that you now know of this, as it will prevent any altruistic nonsense later. Are my suppositions accurate?"

Something in Elizabeth's manner must have told Lady Catherine the truth, for she nodded slowly. "I thought as much. I will not attribute your disquiet to any hesitation regarding Darcy. He is the best of men. Thus, I must assume you are anxious about your family's imagined reaction to the knowledge you wish to leave them so soon after your recovery.

"Now, if my suppositions are correct, I would ask you to consider one simple question: what do you suppose your family wishes for you, other than your happiness?"

The blunt question startled Elizabeth, and for a moment she was unable to respond, her mind a whirling mixture of confused thoughts.

"My safety, perhaps?" said she at length. Already she was beginning to feel a little foolish.

"Of course," replied Lady Catherine. "That is so obvious it does not even bear repeating. But along with that, I assure you your family wants your happiness. Consider this: your safety Darcy can ensure, and it seems to me that your happiness would also be secure. I know not what else a mother may wish for her daughter."

With an effort, Elizabeth turned her attention away from that, as she had caught some deeper meaning in Lady Catherine's words. "It was hard, was it not? Giving up your dream of William and Anne's marriage?"

Lady Catherine blinked, surprised by the sudden change in subject. But she did not demur.

"It was. It was possibly the most difficult thing I have ever done, perhaps even as difficult as enduring the loss of my beloved sister and husband. I do not . . . I am unsure I have come to terms with it even now. But I have been forced to think of my child's happiness. Of Darcy's happiness. Your mother and father — all of us — will think of your happiness too. Do not think Susan would begrudge you the love of a good man, even if it will take you from her home."

"But I am not sure I am even ready," replied Elizabeth.

"I believe you are more ready than you think," was Lady Catherine's quick reply. "But if you are not, long engagements are not unknown, nor are long courtships. But do not ever think that your mother would hold you back from living your life."

Lady Catherine's words rang in Elizabeth's ears for the rest of the day, and she remained introspective. The more she thought about it, the more she knew that the lady was correct. It did not do away with her worries — some were ingrained in her, and she did not think they would be dispelled until events had progressed to the point where they were not relevant any longer. But she found a certain calmness within herself that all the previous assurances had not quite managed.

Wednesday, July 1, 1812
Snowlock, Derbyshire

But there was one further step involved, and that was for Elizabeth to speak to her mother on the subject. And she determined to do just that before they left for Pemberley the next morning. Her mother had been supervising the preparation of the personal effects the family would be carrying to Pemberley, and in so doing, she had been busy most of the day. That evening, however, Elizabeth was able to speak with her, and she made a discovery at the same time which gave her much pleasure.

"I have noticed that your hopeful suitor has not been present the past few days," observed Lady Susan. "I hope you are not repining the loss of his society."

Though Elizabeth had been occupied thinking on William and her situation, Mr. Standish's failure to appear since William's departure had not escaped her notice. "I was a little . . . rude to him when William and I met him near his estate. Maybe he has thought better of his actions."

Amid the murmur of amusement, Constance laughed out loud, saying: "If only you had known rudeness was the key to being free of him. You might have done it much sooner and spared yourself his odious company!"

General laughter erupted at her cousin's words, and Elizabeth laughed the loudest. "I do not condone it on a normal basis, but in this instance, I believe I will make an exception." Elizabeth paused and looked at Constance curiously. "I have wondered, Cousin—I have not seen much of your preparations to go to Pemberley. Have you completed them?"

James and Constance exchanged a glance before she returned her gaze to Elizabeth. "That is because we shall not accompany you. For you see, though it is not yet confirmed, I believe I am with child."

It appeared Elizabeth was not the only one who had not known of this development, for several of the company exclaimed their surprise, and congratulations were shared among them. For her part, Elizabeth, mindful of Constance's condition, went to her and enveloped her in a fervent embrace.

"I am very happy for you, Cousin. But how do you know? Have you felt the quickening?"

"No," replied Constance. "But I have had trouble with illness in the morning, much the same as I had with my other children. I expect I should feel the quickening in another month, and the child will be born after the New Year."

"Then congratulations are in order. But we shall miss you at Pemberley."

Constance's responding smile was filled with mischief. "With the beauties of Pemberley and its master at your disposal, I doubt you will pine for my presence."

The teasing jest was so like her cousin that Elizabeth could only smile and embrace her once again. They spoke for some time of Constance's condition, though with circumspection, respecting Elizabeth's status as a maiden. James, Elizabeth noted, was very much the proud expectant papa, accepting the congratulations of the men as if it was his due as a virile male. Elizabeth could not help but laugh at his antics.

Later, after Constance and James had retired early, Elizabeth found herself seated next to her mother, speaking of the evening's events.

"You were already aware of Constance's condition, were you not?"

"I was," replied her mother. "Not only did I bear three children myself and understand the signs, but she told me in confidence when she first suspected. I am happy I will have another grandchild to spoil, though I will own to wondering when my *younger* children will provide me with more."

Elizabeth flushed at her mother's arched eyebrow but took it as a perfect opportunity to speak of her concerns. "Perhaps that day is not as distant as you thought."

"Why? Have you become engaged without my knowing?"

Her mother's frank question was spoken with an air of levity, but Elizabeth could detect a probing undertone.

"I have not," replied Elizabeth. "But I wished . . ." She paused, not quite knowing what to say. "I have wondered what you think about the possibility of marriage. I am, as you know, now one and twenty, and can be expected to receive even more attention from prospective suitors when we return to town."

"And you are not receiving such devotion even now?"

"I am, though nothing formal, of course," replied Elizabeth. "I am merely wishing to ascertain how you feel about it, given my recent return."

Lady Susan watched Elizabeth for a few moments before she spoke. "Catherine told me of your conversation, Elizabeth." Elizabeth's eyes darted to where Lady Catherine was watching them. When she saw Elizabeth's glance, her demeanor became positively smug. "I already knew something of your worries, of course, but I thought to allow you to work your way through them yourself. Catherine blocked that strategy."

"Then you will not object should I choose to accept a proposal from William?"

"Silly goose," said Lady Susan, though with evident fondness. "Why would I oppose your happiness? I will own I would prefer it delayed a little, but if you and William both wished to be married before the end of summer, I would not object."

"Thank you, Mother," said Elizabeth quietly. "But I do not think we shall be that precipitous. Perhaps a spring wedding next year might be lovely?"

Lady Susan laughed and drew Elizabeth close. "I am sure it would be. And I cannot imagine a more beautiful bride."

Thursday, July 2, 1812
Snowlock, Derbyshire

The night before their departure for Pemberley, it was also revealed that Anthony would not be accompanying them — or at least not for a few days.

"Since I have now officially retired from active duty," said he, "William has returned control of my estate to me." He regarded her with a devilish grin. "He seems to think I need to be more responsible, though I have no idea why he would entertain such a notion."

Elizabeth laughed. "Why, indeed? Is your estate that far distant?"

"Not at all. It is west of here. Pemberley, Thorndell, and Snowlock form a triangle, though Thorndell is closer to Snowlock than Pemberley. Since our cousin has seen fit to burden me, I suppose I must return there. I have a few matters which must be seen to, and when they are complete, I will join you at Pemberley."

Though Elizabeth knew his responsibilities must take precedence, she was disquieted by his impending absence. When she thought on the matter as she readied herself to retire that night, she determined that it was due, in large part, to the constancy of his presence in her life. Other than William's short sojourn at Pemberley after their arrival at Snowlock, both her cousin and her brother had been by her side without fail. Now with William at his estate and Anthony bound for his own, the short distance between Snowlock and Pemberley would be the first time she had been without both since that spring.

Furthermore, Anthony was a large man and an intimidating presence, and the nearness of his person had often filled her with a sense of invincibility, the notion that nothing could touch her while she was under his watchful eye. And his irrepressible good humor had never failed to raise Elizabeth's spirits. He would be very much missed.

The following morning, they were gathered together on the front drive awaiting the loading of the luggage. Servants moved this way and that, lugging the heavy trunks which were then secured to the tops of the carriages with thick ropes. The drivers and footmen were speaking with Lord Matlock, receiving their final instructions, their livery pristine in the light of the morning sun. Near the door, her mother was having a final word with the housekeeper.

A moment of confusion occurred when Attila appeared at a dead run and approached Elizabeth, whining and pawing at her dress.

"Down, Attila," said Elizabeth, grateful it had not rained. "You will be well here at Snowlock until I return."

The dog only whined, seeming to understand that she meant to leave him behind. He pawed at her again, then circled her several times, barking and whining, pulling all eyes to him.

"It appears your faithful servant does not mean to leave you behind," commented Constance with a laugh.

"Sometimes I wonder if he *is* my servant. I think he considers me to be little more than his possession."

"He is disobedient," said her father as he approached them. "Heel, Attila!"

The dog's rump immediately hit the ground, but his whining only increased. Lord Matlock regarded the recalcitrant canine with more than a hint of exasperation.

"Perhaps we should simply allow him to go," said Lady Susan. "He has been an excellent protector for our daughter."

"He is naught but a puppy," grumbled Lord Matlock, "though he has been trained to be an adult." He paused and then shrugged. "Perhaps it is best that he goes at that. He may ride in the third carriage, for there will be room for him there. I wonder what Darcy will say."

They all chuckled at that, knowing that William might be a little annoyed with the presence of the large dog. With permission given, Elizabeth guided Attila to the third carriage, where he bounded in, seeming to understand he had gotten his way. As soon as he was within, he stretched across the front seat and promptly went to sleep.

"That dog is a menace," said Anthony, though his tone was good-natured.

"He is a good boy. He has become my protector these past weeks."

"I suppose we must allow him that," said her brother.

"How long do you think you will be at Thorndell?" asked Elizabeth.

"Perhaps a week," replied Anthony. "Do not worry, sister dearest—I will be along before you know it. Just do not allow Darcy to propose before I am able to protect you from him."

"Do I *need* protection from William?"

"Of course." Anthony winked outrageously. "He *is* a man sniffing about my sister like a bloodhound. I do not trust him any more than any other man."

"Even Mr. Standish?" asked Constance, seeming thoroughly amused.

Anthony made a great show of thinking about it. "Well, perhaps he is a *little* more trustworthy."

They shared a laugh, and Elizabeth followed it up with a mock glare. "It seems to me, Brother, that you require a wife to keep you in line."

An exaggerated shudder was Anthony's response. "Please do not say such things. I have no wish to give up my freedom to a woman as William is on the verge of ceding his to you."

"He is not nearly so objectionable as he would have you believe," said Constance *sotto voce*.

"Yes, I am."

While Constance laughed again, Elizabeth only looked at her brother, feigning deep thought. "Perhaps Jane would do. Yes, perhaps I shall introduce Jane to your acquaintance when the opportunity presents itself."

"No matchmaking, Elizabeth. I beg you."

"Oh, I will do nothing of the sort," said Elizabeth, giving him a mysterious smile. "I will simply ensure she is introduced to you. Jane's sweetness will do the rest."

Anthony eyed her, but he was able to say nothing more as the time to depart was upon them. Soon he was mounted on his charger, waving farewell and galloping off down the road toward his estate. Elizabeth shared a tearful farewell with Constance, and she realized how much she had come to rely on the woman's irrepressible good humor.

"This is such a poor time to be with child!" said she, embracing Elizabeth as if she would never let go. "I hope we can join you as soon as may be, for you have become as dear to me as my own sister."

"I feel the same way," whispered Elizabeth. Then she pulled away and said in her sternest tone: "You take care of your health, Constance. Remember the child and do not overexert yourself."

"I *have* been with child before, Elizabeth. I know what is to be done."

"Good. Then I shall see you in a month or so at the very latest."

The two women separated, and Elizabeth's father handed her mother and then herself into the carriage. And soon they pulled away from her new home. Elizabeth felt sorrow at leaving James and Constance behind and sadness to see Snowlock recede into the distance. But she was filled with excitement at the prospect of seeing William's home. In the back of her mind, she wondered if it might soon be *her* home.

CHAPTER XXXIII

Thursday, July 2, 1812
Pemberley, Derbyshire

*S*ince the Darcy siblings' return three days earlier, Pemberley had been a hive of activity, as the housekeeper directed all within her domain on a frenetic bid to render the stately mansion pristine. Every surface glowed. If there was a speck of dust in the entire building, Darcy was certain it was hidden well for fear of being discovered and eradicated. Darcy watched it all with bemused gratitude—nothing more than the word that Lady Elizabeth Fitzwilliam and her family would be arriving within three days had been said to prompt Mrs. Reynolds to begin her crusade of cleaning. Visions of a future Mrs. Darcy no doubt danced in her head as she strode through the halls, admonishing, exhorting, and assisting where required. She might be more excited about Elizabeth's arrival than Darcy was himself.

When the party from Snowlock appeared that day, not long after luncheon, Darcy only had eyes for one of the party. The carriages made their way down the drive, pulling to a stop in front of them, and Darcy made his way down the steps to where the footmen were disembarking and preparing to assist the passengers. Impatient from the wait of the past three days, Darcy stepped forward and opened the coach door himself, though he did allow one of the footmen to place a step beneath the door.

"Welcome to Pemberley," said he, attempting to speak to them all, rather than directly to Elizabeth.

It turned out there were five passengers in the first coach, which comprised the whole of his guests. Lady Catherine and Lord Matlock sat in the rear-facing seat, while Lady Susan, Elizabeth, and Anne sat in the other, no doubt due to the three ladies' dainty sizes. Darcy stepped aside while his uncle made his way down from the carriage, stretching to work out the kinks which he had endured while traveling in the cramped space and then stepping back to hand his wife from the carriage. Then he winked at Darcy and turned away, no doubt knowing that Darcy wished to assist at least *one* of the remaining passengers.

Darcy did so, first assisting Lady Catherine, then Elizabeth and finally Anne from the coach. When they were on firm ground, the footmen swarmed over the coach, unloading the trunks and preparing the vehicle to be removed to the stables for storage. Darcy turned to Elizabeth and Anne, offering his arms to both.

"I am happy to have all of you here," said he. "I hope your journey was quite comfortable.

Lord Matlock snorted. "I believe I begin to understand what Elizabeth's adoptive father, Mr. Bennet, endured all those years in a house full of females. I thought the subjects of choice might drive me mad if we had continued on much longer."

There were several protests from the ladies, though Elizabeth's was nothing more than a raised eyebrow and a chuckle.

"I think you have a long way to go before you approach Mr. Bennet's feelings on such subjects, Father," said Elizabeth. "You must remember that in his own words, he is father to 'three of the silliest girls in all England.' Excepting Mary, who is a good girl, despite a tendency to moralize at times, I do not think I can dispute what he says!"

"Well, at least I do not need to deal with silliness," said Lord Matlock. "Though I do sometimes wonder about Catherine."

This last was said with a wink at his sister. Lady Catherine said nothing, contenting herself with a disdainful sniff. Thereafter she ignored him completely.

The party entered the house, and Darcy introduced Mrs. Reynolds, watching the woman's understated pleasure when Elizabeth complimented her on the beauty of the house. As they spoke, Darcy watched Elizabeth carefully, interested to see her reaction to his home. She was, he knew, calm and collected, and would not praise it with a Mrs. Bennet-like awe or vulgar avarice. But he expected to see at least some interest in the sight of Pemberley which was, he knew, a fine estate.

While Elizabeth looked about, her response was muted. As the trip from Snowlock was not a long one, the company was shown to the sitting-room by his sister, who was showing a childlike enthusiasm, where tea and other refreshments awaited them. When they were seated and served, Elizabeth still made little comment. Eager for her opinion, Darcy decided he would wait no longer.

"Well, Elizabeth? What say you?"

"Concerning what?" asked Elizabeth as she sipped her tea.

Astonished and unable to account for this indifferent behavior, Darcy gaped at her. It was then that he noticed the slight upturn in the corners of her lips and the way the amusement shone from her eyes. Then he viewed her with suspicion, and she could not quite stifle a giggle. Anne, who was sitting next to her, soon caught on, and a moment later they were giggling together, while the earl and countess looked on with glee.

"It seems that I must remind myself of your teasing nature," said Darcy, prompting further laughter from the younger ladies, in which Georgiana also joined.

"It serves you right, William," said Lady Susan. "We have not been here ten minutes, and already you are speaking of that silly disagreement. Can you not simply accept that both Pemberley and Snowlock are fine estates and have done?"

"You mistake me, Lady Susan," said Darcy, affecting an uncaring attitude. "I was merely asking for Elizabeth's opinion without any reference whatsoever to Snowlock. You see, there truly is no comparison, so I did not think I needed to comment on it."

"Oh, Darcy," said Lady Catherine, while Lady Susan only laughed.

"But now that you mention it . . ." Darcy looked over at Elizabeth and waited for her to respond.

"I have seen so little of Pemberley that I am sure I could not say anything now," replied Elizabeth. It seemed she was determined to confound him.

"Then we must ensure you have ample opportunity to make a judgment. There are many paths you may walk, and I would be happy to personally show them to you."

"I believe I would like that, William," said Elizabeth, filling Darcy with a swell of happiness. "What I have seen of the grounds is delightful. I will own that I have not noticed anything about the house which suggests superiority, for I have grown to love my father's house. The true difference may be the location, though again I will stress that I need more time to make an accurate judgment."

"That was poorly done, Elizabeth," said Lord Matlock. "Now Darcy will crow from sunup to sundown that you have judged Pemberley to be superior."

"I have made no such determination, Father," said Elizabeth, completely unconcerned. "I have only asked for more time."

"Ah, but you have confessed that Pemberley is in a superior locale, Elizabeth," said Darcy. "That is quite enough for me."

Elizabeth only smiled at him. "If you will recall my words, I only said that the locales were *different*, not that Pemberley was superior. You really must listen better, William, for it seems to me that you have some trouble in that regard."

Her father laughed, and Lady Susan looked on them with exasperation. Much though he was enjoying the banter, Darcy knew it was time to end it.

"Then I will allow you to go to it, Cousin. I am sure you will have much enjoyment in the discovery."

"Indeed, I will, William," replied Elizabeth. Then she turned to Georgiana and began to speak with her.

They sat together for some time until his aunt and uncle excused themselves to go to their rooms to rest, as did Lady Catherine and Anne. It appeared Elizabeth had no desire or need to retire to her rooms, for she seemed eager to speak with Georgiana. While Darcy might have wished for her attention to be fixed on him alone, he derived much enjoyment from watching her speak with his shy sister.

"Do you like your new pianoforte?" asked she after some time. She looked at Darcy and added: "I had understood from your brother that he was to purchase one for you."

"Oh, yes, it is lovely!" said Georgiana. Then she colored, and her eyes found the floor below her feet. "I do not deserve it. But William is the best of brothers."

"I am certain you *do* deserve it," replied Elizabeth, drawing Georgiana's eyes to her once again. "I have a firm opinion of your goodness, my dear cousin, and if your brother—who you know is rarely wrong—deems you worthy of it, then deserving you must be!"

"Oh, Elizabeth," said Georgiana. "You should not say such things. It is already difficult living with such a paragon as William without you stating it. Now that you have said it openly, I am certain he will be all that much more demanding."

"I might wonder where you have learned to speak such nonsense," said Darcy, feeling compelled to return the teasing Elizabeth always heaped upon him. "I do try to avoid those weaknesses which blatantly force the viewer to acknowledge them, but I am no more perfect than the next man."

The amused look Elizabeth bestowed upon him was one he had seen many times, and he knew it would result in her saying something witty. He was not disappointed.

"It takes a wise man to know he is lacking in some areas, but the true test of wisdom is to know where and to make the effort to improve. In your case, William, to a much younger sister, everything you do must be perfection. Take care, lest you cause your sister to knock the pedestal from under you."

William returned her grin. "I am sure Georgiana knows I have faults. I have never striven to hide my lack of perfection."

"Faults, perhaps. But I do not believe she finds you silly. Then again, with your performance every time the subject of your estate is raised, it is not surprising she does not worship the very ground upon which you walk."

"He is an excellent brother," said Georgiana. "I am afraid I know no harm of him. Save for, perhaps, one matter."

"Oh?" asked Elizabeth, turning back to Georgiana. "And what might that be?"

"That he has not yet given me a sister," replied Georgiana with nary a hint of a smile. "Do you know anyone who might be interested in the position?"

Elizabeth gaped at Georgiana for a moment, surprised, and then she shook her head in mock severity. For his part, Darcy was having difficulty holding in his own mirth. While he would not have made such a blatant statement as Georgiana had just made, he appreciated his sister's support.

"I believe, William," said Elizabeth, "that your sister has become quite outspoken. Perhaps you should do something to correct this grievous character defect."

"I am quite certain, Lady Elizabeth," replied Darcy, "that if she *has*, it must be because of her recent association with a certain young lady of our acquaintance. To correct *that* lady's impertinence, you would need to apply to her father."

Elizabeth looked at him for a moment before they all erupted in laughter. "Perhaps we should not be so hasty then," said Elizabeth. "We would not wish to crush Georgiana's spirit."

"No, indeed," replied Darcy. "That would be a shame."

Monday, July 6, 1812
Snowlock, Derbyshire

No more than a week after the last visit of Mr. Standish to Snowlock, the estate saw a pair of visitors, neither of whom were welcome. The first was the aforementioned Mr. Standish, and though James had been surprised the man had not appeared sooner, he supposed the tenor of his last meeting with Elizabeth, by all accounts, had been enough for him to allow a little time to pass in the hope her disposition toward him would be improved.

"Mr. Standish," said James, when the man was led into the room. "How good of you to call today."

When Standish glanced around, apparently searching for Elizabeth, James could not quite stifle a grin. The man was destined to be disappointed today, and James had not a hint of sympathy for him.

"My lord," said Standish. "I am sorry, but your housekeeper appears to have made a mistake. I have come to visit your sister."

"Ah, then there has been no mistake, though I suppose it must be unfortunate for you."

Standish frowned. "What do you mean? Has your father decided to hide Lady Elizabeth away, or has he decided that *I*, in particular, am to be denied her company?"

"Neither, I assure you," replied James. He was well able to own that he was enjoying this immensely. "Simply put, my sister is not at Snowlock at present. Thus, you were led to me when you asked for her. It is no mystery, and there is nothing being done to keep Elizabeth from society."

James watched closely as Standish listened to his explanation. He managed to control his reaction credibly, but his annoyance at being thwarted was clear. "She is not at Snowlock? She has gone to visit some ladies of the neighborhood, perhaps? Or have your parents decided to take her into Derby for the day?"

"She has gone to stay at my cousin's estate for some few weeks, as has been planned since we quit London. I myself would be with them even now, had my wife not been indisposed."

"And might I ask the identity of this cousin?"

The question was largely rhetorical in nature, for James was aware that Standish knew well to which cousin he was referring.

"Why, Darcy, of course. I am surprised you would ask. He has been with us constantly these past months since Elizabeth's recovery—in fact, it was he who originally suspected her identity. Or perhaps you were not aware?"

"I believe I had heard something of it."

James paused for several moments, giving the impression of deep thought. "Darcy's estate is, you see, quite picturesque, and as Elizabeth is fond of nature, it was only a matter of time before an invitation was extended. It is quite apparent to us all that they are quite close, and Georgiana already considers Elizabeth to be a sister. I am certain she will be comfortable at Pemberley—they will likely stay for several weeks."

The inference in his words was quite clear, and James added a smirk to reinforce what he was saying. Unfortunately, it did not provoke the reaction he wanted, for Standish appeared quite at ease with the news.

"Then I hope she enjoys Darcy's estate," was all he said. "I have heard that Darcy is quite proud of his little parcel of land."

"What 'little parcel' do you call it?" asked James with a chuckle. "The park alone is ten miles around, and the estate produces enough to ensure that Darcy's income rivals my father's. As it is close to the peak district, it is quite beautiful. A woman like Elizabeth, who has such an affinity for nature, can hardly be unmoved by such sights."

"I have every confidence in Lady Elizabeth's ability to be impressed by trees and hills," said Standish. "I will own to some curiosity, though; I was not aware of any impending departure the last time I visited."

"The exact timing was a sudden decision, but we all knew at least part of the summer would be spent at Pemberley."

"Thank you for your good information, Lord Chesterfield." Standish rose to take his leave. "I shall not take up any more of your time. Please pass my regards to your excellent wife. I suppose I shall be required to search for your sister at Darcy's estate since she is not here."

James pursed his lips, and Standish appeared pleased to have prompted a response. James watched him go, wondering at Standish's game. At least he would be thwarted for the present, though James was aware his next destination would likely be Pemberley.

"He is gone?" the voice of his wife interrupted his musings.

"He is," replied James to his wife. "And he was none too pleased to learn that Elizabeth is not here."

Constance sighed with exasperation. "Elizabeth does not appreciate his fervency. It would be best if your father were to simply bar him from seeing her."

"I do not disagree. But father does not wish there to be an open rift in the family."

"*He* is not family." His wife's tone was brimming with contempt. James could hardly disagree with her. None of them wished to have Standish in their lives, and he knew Elizabeth wished heartily that he would return to his vices.

"I suppose I should write to father and let him know Standish visited," said James. "He will no doubt go to Pemberley to importune her again, though if he means to go often he will need to take a room at the inn in Lambton."

Constance made no objection, and James took up a sheet of paper. He was unable to write, however, as the door opened again that moment, allowing entrance to another who was, if it was even possible, less welcome than Standish had been.

"Lord Winchester," growled James, coming to his feet. "What a singularly unpleasant surprise. I suppose we should have judged better and informed the butler not to allow you entrance. To what do I owe the displeasure of your visit?"

"I wished to see your sister," was Winchester's even response.

James directed a harsh, derisive laugh at the earl, even while Constance impaled the man with the spear-like sharpness of her glare. "Do you actually think I would allow my sister to be in the same room with the likes of you? Your audacity knows no bounds!"

"You have no reason to trust me—this I know." James was surprised at how even the man's voice was. "I have only come to tender my apologies to her for my behavior."

"Apologies? From you? You must forgive me, but I find that difficult to credit."

Lord Winchester shrugged. "I do not blame you."

There was no reason to believe the man and every reason to suspect his supposed apology was being rendered for some purpose of his own. But James was not certain what it was, and a glance shared with his wife told him she was no more trusting than he.

"Then you have made your journey here in vain, Winchester. My sister is not at Snowlock at present, and she has not been here since last week."

"She is at Pemberley?" James's countenance must have betrayed the truth, though he had not intended to inform Winchester of the whereabouts of his sister. "I might have expected it. Darcy was . . . Well, let us simply say that his attentions toward her were no less fervent than my own, though perhaps better judged."

"Do not importune her, Winchester. I suggest you do not go to Pemberley, lest you be run off by Darcy's men with torches and pitchforks."

The earl sighed. "I have no intention of going to Pemberley. You have nothing to fear from me. When I reflected on my behavior this spring I . . ." The man looked away in seeming embarrassment. "What I found was not to my satisfaction.

"But I agree with your assessment, and I will not presume to impose my presence upon your family at Pemberley. I will seek some other occasion to tender my apologies."

And with those words, Winchester turned on his heel and quit the room in a few short strides. James watched him go, suspicion flowing through him in waves. Constance approached him as he was deep in thought and placed her hand on his arm, drawing his attention to her.

"Do you think he is in earnest?"

James shook his head. "I have never known Winchester to be anything other than arrogant and unpleasant. I am afraid I cannot trust his sincerity."

"If he was not sincere, he is skilled in the art of subterfuge. I could see nothing in his manner or words which suggested duplicity."

"Neither can I. *That* is what worries me."

When James sat down to pen his missive, he had much more to say than he had expected. Both objectionable gentlemen now knew the location of Elizabeth's residence. His father needed to be made aware of the situation.

Tuesday, July 7, 1812
Pemberley, Derbyshire

It seemed it was too much to ask that Elizabeth be spared the presence of those objectionable men of her acquaintance for more than a few days. She supposed, however, that the last time she saw Mr. Standish was three days before coming to Pemberley and five days had passed before the man showed his face at William's estate. She had not seen Lord Winchester since that objectionable scene in her father's library.

Even so, neither was in any way sufficient.

They had been forewarned of the arrival of at least one of the gentlemen. The previous day, one of Snowlock's footmen had ridden up the drive to Pemberley with a letter addressed to her father. Lord Matlock had glanced at the missive, frowned, and then looked up at the family.

"It seems Standish has made an appearance at Snowlock. And perhaps of more concern, Winchester arrived soon after."

"Winchester?" demanded Lady Susan. Her tone was particularly vicious, such that had Winchester been present, Elizabeth thought she might attack him with her claws. "What could he possibly mean by showing his face there?"

"According to James, he claimed to wish to apologize."

That brought Lady Susan up short. "Apologize? And he thinks we will believe him?"

"James, at least, does not," replied her husband. "He writes to warn us. Standish, he believes, will likely come to Pemberley before long. As for Winchester, he promised not to come here, but James's skepticism practically bleeds through the paper."

Elizabeth sighed with resignation and nodded, but her mother was not happy. "I believe I have had just about enough of the likes of both." She turned to William. "Would you object to denying them access to Pemberley?"

"Not at all, Aunt," replied William. "I have no desire to speak with either, and it is clear Elizabeth wishes to see them even less."

"I am not certain it will deter them," said Lady Catherine. "They seem desperate to be in her company."

The earl sighed. "It seems likely that the one we must concern ourselves with is Standish. If Winchester comes here, it will be as a thief in the night."

"If Standish comes, perhaps, a subtler course may be pursued?"

Everyone looked at the speaker, surprised that Anne had spoken. She rarely interjected her opinions into group discussions.

"What did you have in mind, Anne?" asked Lady Susan.

"If he is desperate to visit, why not show him how little we all wish for his presence? Might he not understand and cease to importune us?"

"I think you attribute too much sense to the man," said William.

"That is possible," said Lady Susan. "But if we couple our indifference to his presence to a very . . . visible show of attachment between Elizabeth and William, it might be enough to show that he has no chance to obtain his desire. For a man as self-centered as

Standish, I suspect he will decide that he does not wish to be humiliated and move on."

"It seems we think alike, Aunt," said Anne, shooting Lady Susan a mischievous grin. "It is not kind, but kindness does not seem to have worked with that particular gentleman."

"Thus, more active measures must be pursued," said Lord Matlock. "I like it."

"But . . ." said Elizabeth, her cheeks flaming with the heat of her blush. "William and I . . . We have not . . ."

"We know, Elizabeth," said her mother. "But you—neither of you—can deny that something is brewing between you. I am certain you have it within you to play up whatever feelings you currently possess for Mr. Standish's benefit. And it may just buy you a cessation of his notice for a time."

Still feeling the weight of embarrassment, Elizabeth chanced a look at William. The man's eyes positively shone with the notion which had just been raised—he was eager to be about it! All Elizabeth's inhibitions fell away, and she realized she did not need to hide her burgeoning feelings for this man, certainly not in front of her family, among whom it was already a poorly kept secret.

"Then let us give Mr. Standish something to consider. But what if the earl comes?"

"As I said," replied her father, "he will not come to the sitting-room to beg an audience. If he does, he should be allowed to say what he wishes and then ushered from the estate. If he appears on the grounds, I will remind him that it is a poor decision to anger an earl, even if one is of the same level of society."

As the letter had arrived late in the afternoon, they were convinced Mr. Standish would not come that day, so they planned for him to impose upon them the next. As the work of the estate had largely been completed on William's earlier visit, not to mention the three days before Elizabeth's arrival, he was at leisure to spend his days with her. In the early morning Elizabeth still walked out, in the company of both William and Attila, but once they had returned and had refreshed themselves, they repaired to the sitting-room with the rest of the company, where William sat close by Elizabeth, engaging her in conversation.

It was lighthearted, even with the slight sense of anxiety which wended its way through Elizabeth's mind. She often found herself distracted, not giving as much of her attention to William as she ought.

"Are you well, Elizabeth?" asked William. Blinking, Elizabeth thought back to the past few moments and realized she had been lost in her thoughts.

"I apologize, William," said she, turning a smile on him. "I believe I must have become distracted." She paused for a moment, grateful that he was willing to allow her to collect her thoughts. "Does this whole situation not seem . . . feigned to you? We are usually able to speak with no awkwardness. But this morning I feel as if I am on stage, playing before an audience."

Elizabeth noted William's surreptitious look around the room, and she followed it reflexively. The others, though they were engaged in their own pursuits, seemed to be watching Elizabeth and William more than they normally would, some with interest or protectiveness, though Lady Catherine's glances were still melancholy in nature.

"Then perhaps we should simply fall back into what is easy between us," suggested William. "Books, for example."

Elizabeth laughed. "Have we not already discussed every volume in your library?"

"Oh, I think there may be one or two yet to which we have not turned our attention."

A laugh escaped Elizabeth's lips, and the tension she had not even known existed was broken. It almost seemed like a sigh passed through the company. Out of the corner of her eye, she saw her mother smile at her before she turned to Lady Catherine and began speaking of some matter or another, in which Anne was soon included. Lord Matlock, the only other man in the room, nodded once to himself, though he did not release the paper he had been reading. The only member of their immediate party who was not present was Georgiana—it had been decided that her lessons were more important. They did not know what Mr. Standish's reaction would be, so she was sent to her room to remove her from any possible unpleasantness.

It was in this attitude that Mr. Standish found them when he appeared, as they had expected, some half an hour later. When he entered the room, his eyes immediately settled upon Elizabeth herself, and his sardonic grin of amusement suggested he had foiled her plans to avoid him. The sight angered Elizabeth and firmed her resolve to avoid giving him any hint of her notice.

"Lord Matlock," said Mr. Standish, greeting her father first. "How pleased I am to see you."

"Standish," said her father, though he made an overt and significant glance at William. "What a surprise it is to see you here. It must have taken you some time to make the journey."

"The same amount of tie your journey consumed, I presume," said Mr. Standish. "How surprised I was that you decamped to Pemberley with nary a word of your going."

"My sons knew, of course," replied Lord Matlock. "I do not believe I am beholden to anyone else such that I must inform them of my movements."

"Quite," replied Mr. Standish. He turned to Elizabeth and made a florid bow. "Lady Elizabeth. I am quite enraptured to see you again. I trust you are well?"

Elizabeth was becoming quite annoyed with the man's continued snub of William, which she knew was not accidental. "Indeed, I am, Mr. Standish. William's estate is quite beautiful, do you not agree? I am certain I could stay here the rest of my life and never repine my situation."

A faint smile came over the man's face, but he seemed to take the hint. "Darcy. It seems you have a pretty little estate here."

"It has been in my family for generations," replied Darcy. He seemed amused by Mr. Standish's characterization of his beloved home, rather than offended as was the man's intent. "And it is agreeable to have beloved family members share in the tranquility which exists here."

"I am sure it must."

Mr. Standish then glanced about, looking for a place where he could sit, but this, too, had been deliberately orchestrated in advance. Elizabeth was seated beside William on a small sofa, leaving no room on either side, while to their left, Lady Catherine, Lady Susan, and Anne sat on the large sofa. To their right, Lord Matlock was seated in the nearer chair, leaving only another pair of chairs on his far side, and the far end of the configuration of the sitting-room in which Mr. Standish might sit. There would be no easy way for him to dominate Elizabeth's attention that morning.

When he had considered it for a moment, Mr. Standish chose the chair at the far end of the sofa. This was largely, Elizabeth thought, so that he could face them directly, rather than on an angle, which the chair next to her father would have necessitated.

As had been previously planned, as soon as Standish took his seat, Elizabeth turned back to William, and they resumed the conversation which had been interrupted by the objectionable man's arrival. Though Mr. Standish was separated from her father by an empty chair, the earl attempted to make slight conversation. The three ladies on the sofa ignored him.

But regardless of Lord Matlock's attempts to engage him, Mr. Standish seemed little inclined to respond. He watched Elizabeth and Darcy as they spoke, and though Elizabeth was aware of his scrutiny, she took comfort in the ease of conversation and kept her attention away from the objectionable interloper.

"I am curious about your opinions of Mr. Darcy's estate, Lady Elizabeth," said Mr. Standish. The words were spoken suddenly and after her father had spoken, meaning they could be construed as quite rude. Lord Matlock watched Standish without expression, though Elizabeth thought he was amused.

"I cannot think of anyone who would not approve," said Elizabeth. "Pemberley is a jewel among estates." Elizabeth turned a smile on her father. "I hope you will not be offended to hear me speak thus. Snowlock, too, is very beautiful."

"Of course not," said the earl, a grin appearing for her reintroduction of the subject. "I am well able to confess to Pemberley's beauties, though I am partial to my own home."

"You should visit Kent when next we are in town," added Lady Catherine. "Kent is not called the Garden of England for no reason. I feel you would grow to love the woods there as much as anything Derbyshire has to offer."

"I am hurt by your insinuations, Lady Catherine," said William, looking at her with mock affront. "Kent is far too tame—there is nothing to compare with the open wildness of Derbyshire." William turned to Elizabeth. "Do you not agree?"

"I love to see the countryside as nature intended it. But there is much charm to be had in formal gardens, and I am certain not all of Lady Catherine's estate has been forced into preconceived notions of beauty."

"Of course not," replied Lady Catherine. "The woods are pristine and have been left untouched. My late husband used to hunt there frequently. You do not have *all* the beauty in Derbyshire, Darcy, though I will grant you it is very pretty here."

As they continued to banter back and forth, Elizabeth noted that Mr. Standish watched them, his eyes darting around the room. A frown creased his forehead, and though his eyes flitted between them all, they kept darting back to Elizabeth. There was a certain amount of consideration in that gaze, not, she thought, that he was attempting to understand her. She was certain he must know of her disinclination for his company by now. Rather it was something more . . . elusive.

"Is this your first time in the north, Lady Elizabeth?" asked he at the first lull in the conversation.

"It is," replied she. "My adoptive father's estate is in Hertfordshire, and he loathes travel. The only place we ever went was London, where Mrs. Bennet's brother resides."

"Ah, yes," said Mr. Standish, his face lighting up with an unpleasant smile. "I believe I know something of a man in trade connected to the family that raised you. Does he reside in a fashionable neighborhood? I suspect not, otherwise, you might have been discovered earlier."

"Mr. Gardiner lives in Cheapside," said William. "But that is entirely by choice, and due to the proximity of his business."

"Excellent people, the Gardiners," added Lady Susan. "Even if Elizabeth was not determined to keep up the connection, I believe we would wish to remain known to them. They display not a hint of pretension. Though Mrs. Gardiner might prefer a more fashionable house in a better neighborhood, she is more concerned for the comfort of her husband. If she wished for advancement in society, no doubt her opinion would be different."

"And she has taken great care of our Elizabeth," added William. He reached for her hand and grasped it tenderly, a motion no less thrilling for the fact that it was entirely premeditated. "She is quite devoted to them."

"I am," replied Elizabeth. "I would not give up their society for anything."

Mr. Standish watched them, seemingly unable to believe what he was hearing. He was an odd man, she decided. He focused most of his attention on his questionable activities—when he was not importuning Elizabeth—but he seemed to cling to notions of class.

"It speaks well of you, to be certain," said he. "Once you are married, however, I believe you may judge differently. Perhaps your husband would not wish to keep such connections."

Elizabeth turned a cold glare on Mr. Standish, and he started at the sight of it. "If a man cannot respect my wishes and that I know my own mind regarding my connections, then I would not accept a proposal from him."

"Would it be in your best interests to reject a proposal?" asked Mr. Standish. The question saw the return of his smug indifference, which Elizabeth thought curious. "Forgive me, Lady Elizabeth, but your return to society is quite new, and though you are the daughter of an earl, your own position is far from assured. You would not, I think, wish for any greater attention than that which you must already endure."

"I care not for the opinion of society," replied Elizabeth. "Whether *they* accept me is irrelevant next to the love of my family."

"And I do not know by what scale you measure such things," said Lady Catherine, her eyes raking over Mr. Standish as if she found him foul, "but Elizabeth's acceptance was easily obtained. Yes, the support of the family has eased her way, but she, herself, has done far more to gain it by simply being an intelligent, estimable woman. You would do well to remember that."

Mr. Standish returned Lady Catherine's glare with seeming unconcern, and then he turned back to Elizabeth. "You have my apologies, Lady Elizabeth. I can assure you I meant no slight."

"None was taken, sir," replied Elizabeth. She hesitated, wondering if she should push further. Then she decided he deserved whatever disappointment he received. "In fact, I have reason to believe that the Gardiners will not be as objectionable to my future husband as you believe." Elizabeth turned quite deliberately to look at William. "All my family like and respect them. I am sure there can be no impediment."

Her gesture was not lost on Mr. Standish, but again the man remained difficult to read. She thought she had raised his ire, but the hoped-for bleakness of his suit did not register on his countenance. He only eyed her, considering, but with no evident disappointment.

"Perhaps you are correct," said he at length. Then he rose. "It appears, Lady Elizabeth, that you have found ample means to amuse yourself and that your family is as protective as they ever were. Regardless, I believe I have found less welcome here than I hoped, so I will depart. I hope to see you returned to your father's estate before the end of summer."

"I do not know," replied Elizabeth with a shrug. "For the present, I believe we are firmly fixed at Pemberley. It is possible we will return to Snowlock before the end of August."

"Then until we meet again."

And with a short bow, Mr. Standish departed the room. In his wake, he left silence behind, as those remaining looked at each other, questions written on every brow.

"He seems to understand that we do not wish him back," said Lord Matlock.

"I doubt the message we sent was misunderstood," replied Lady Catherine. "The question is whether he will heed it."

"I hope so," said Elizabeth. "I am coming to detest the very sight of the man."

No one objected to that statement, for they all felt the same. Now she would only be required to endure Lord Winchester if he should come. Elizabeth hoped fervently that he would not.

Chapter XXXIV

*I*t appeared Standish had given up for the time being, for none of the inhabitants of Pemberley or Snowlock saw him again for the rest of the week. Likewise, Lord Winchester was absent, though James at Snowlock had heard that he was still in residence at his Leicestershire estate. And the peace of both estates was assured with their absence, particularly, it was to be presumed, for those at Pemberley. Darcy would now have free rein to court Elizabeth whenever he liked, and Elizabeth would not be subjected to such objectionable gentlemen.

At first, when he heard of their plan, James wondered if it would be enough to dissuade Standish from continuing to plague her. Nothing he had done thus far seemed to suggest a particular motive. Standish did not woo as a suitor might have, but there definitely seemed to be an element of courtship in his actions. His motive must not be, though he had said as much, to simply come to know her better, for his prior actions gave the lie to that assertion. James could not quite make him out.

But the ensuing letters spoke to the man's absence, a circumstance for which he could only be grateful. Mayhap his attentions were not at an end, but while Elizabeth stayed at Pemberley, it was possible he would stay away. Once they returned to Snowlock, he would no doubt return, but perhaps by then, they would have an announcement of an engagement, which would end his hopes forever—if that truly was his intention. Constance seemed to think an engagement was in the offing, and in matters such as this, James did not doubt his wife's instincts.

The days passed and with them the next week came, and James settled into the management of the estate in his father's stead. But with the new week, a most curious summons arrived from an entirely unexpected corner.

"What is it?" asked Constance when the footman handed him a note. They had just sat down to breakfast, James noting that his wife's color was good and the illness which had plagued her in the mornings seemed to be easing. No doubt she would demand that they go to Pemberley before much longer—she and Elizabeth had become close in a shorter period than he might have imagined.

"It is from Aunt Emma," said James after he had opened it and scanned the short missive. "She asks that I attend her as soon as may be arranged."

"You were there only last week," said his wife. "What could she possibly want?"

"I am sure I do not know," replied James. "But she asks me to go on a matter of the utmost urgency." James sighed and put the letter down on the table. "I suppose there is little choice, though I do not know what she might consider so important."

"Do you mean to go this morning?"

"I suppose I should. I have other things to accomplish today. If I attend her this morning, I may attend to those items thereafter."

"Then I shall accompany you." James gave his wife a steady look, but she only shook her head and focused her attention back on her meal. "I am feeling much better these past days. There is no danger to my health."

Well did James know his wife's determination. It was one of the reasons he suspected she got on with Elizabeth so well, for in that regard they were a matched pair. Thus, he did not protest her going or attempt to insist she stay behind.

The dower house was an easy distance from the manor, and usually, James would have either ridden his horse or simply walked there. In deference to Constance's condition, however, he ordered an open carriage to convey them. She undoubtedly realized why he had done so, but she decided not to raise the subject. Instead, she turned to him and wrapped her hands around his arm, leaning against him and sighing.

"It has been too long since we have done this. It reminds me of the days when we were courting."

"Perhaps we should make the time to do so, especially while you are in the early stages of your confinement when you are not able to ride as much as you might like."

"I believe I would like that a great deal."

They spent the short journey speaking of nothing in particular, though they both enjoyed themselves. Much of their time was spent with family, and as such, there often seemed to be little time to focus on each other.

They were led into the house as soon as the carriage stopped, and they were met by the butler at the front door. James immediately noted the man's relief when he saw them. His words were unsettling.

"Thank you for coming, my lord. Mrs. Seward has been agitated all morning, waiting for your arrival."

"Do you know what has unsettled her?"

"No, my lord. She requested that you be sent for with all possible haste, but she did not explain her concerns."

James glanced at his wife and then motioned the butler to lead them to the house's mistress. He had been there many times, and the way was familiar to him, but he welcomed the chance to follow the butler, as it allowed him to bring his perturbation under good regulation. He still could not imagine what had caused this odd request, but if she was distressed, he did not wish to increase it needlessly.

When visiting her in the past, she had usually been reclining, especially in recent years. But that morning, Aunt Emma was sitting on the sofa, her hands gathered in her lap where she was fidgeting with a handkerchief. James could not help but notice that there was a tear in the fabric, a testament to her disturbance of mind.

"Aunt Emma," said he, stepping forward and greeting her. He sat quickly by her side, to avoid requiring her to look up at him. Constance sat at her other side. "Whatever is the matter?"

"Have you heard from your father?" asked Aunt Emma. "Is Elizabeth well?"

Perplexed at the sudden odd question, James hastened to reassure her. "Elizabeth was quite well when I heard from my father last. The distance is not great, and we have been exchanging letters almost daily."

Aunt Emma closed her eyes as if in relief, and when she opened them again, James could see that the immediate anxiety had disappeared, but the concern remained. He attempted to see if her abilities were dulled by age, but she appeared to be as sound and focused as he had ever seen.

"You must think me a silly old woman."

Again, James found himself surprised. "Indeed, I do not. But I *am* confused. Why are you fearful for Elizabeth?"

"Because I believe I may have unwittingly set in motion the events of twenty years ago, which resulted in her removal from your family."

Had she told him she was the long-lost daughter of the king, James could not have been more surprised. "You had something to do with Elizabeth's disappearance?"

"No, but something has occurred to me in recent days which makes me think it happened due to my actions. I understand that Mr. Standish visited the manor looking for Elizabeth, and it prompted me to think of certain events in the past. Did he also appear at Pemberley?"

"He did," said James. "What do you know of Standish?"

Aunt Emma took a deep breath and she closed her eyes for a moment. When she opened them again they were brimming with purpose.

"How much do you know of my history, James?"

"What is commonly known," replied he. "You married and your husband passed away not long after, leaving you a widow. You decided you would not marry again when you lost him."

"Yes, that is correct," said Aunt Emma. "But it is not the whole story. For you see, Edgar was my dearest friend in the world. We were neighbors, and as he was only a year older than I, we were often playmates before he was old enough to go to Eton. I was a bit of a wild child, you see, and would often play with the boys in their games. Even then he was a special lad, for he championed my participation when the other boys would wish me gone. When he returned from University, he was an excellent man, one with whom any young maiden might fall in love.

"But he was also very ill." Aunt Emma smiled, though it contained the tremulous quality of suppressed emotion. "His heart, you see, was weak, likely from an illness he had suffered as a child. To most observers, he was the very picture of health. But when a fit came upon him, he would clutch at his chest and gasp for breath, at times his lips turning blue.

"I knew nothing of this until after we were married. When the first fit came over him a month later, he confessed all to me. We hoped we would have many years together, though he would always take great care for his health. Alas, it was not to be, for his heart stopped one morning a year after we were married, and he passed away in my arms."

James did not know what to say. He had never heard the particulars of her loss, and what he saw before him suggested that her pain persisted. But he was not certain how her history related to Elizabeth. She must have seen his confusion in his eyes, for she chuckled.

"No, James, I have not lost my faculties yet. I thank you for indulging in the reminiscences of an old woman—I have not spoken of these events in many years, and it lightens my heart to unburden myself again.

"When my husband married me, he wished to ensure that I would be protected should the worst come to pass. Furthermore, should we have only girl children, his estate was entailed upon a distant relation, meaning I would lose my home should he pass without an heir. I was . . . with child when he passed, but my darling boy was stillborn. My husband's foresight was then proven prophetic, for his heir turned me out of the home almost as soon as I was up out of my bed.

"As he wished to provide for me and hoped I would have at least some children to support, he ensured my jointure was substantial. When added to my dowry, which was also healthy, I emerged from my marriage a very wealthy woman. My money has only grown since then, as I have used very little for my support."

"How much?" asked James.

"More than three hundred thousand pounds, though I have paid my bank statements very little attention in recent years."

James looked at the woman as if she had sprouted horns. "Three hundred thousand pounds? That is a huge sum of money, Aunt Emma. I dare say had it been known, you would have been inundated with suitors of all stripes, even now."

"Why do you think I kept it secret? It was not nearly so much when I was young, but still a handsome sum. But after my Edgar was taken from me, I had no desire to remarry. As such, I kept the matter quiet."

"Aunt Emma," interjected Constance, "who is your heir?"

With a start, James looked at his wife. Then he realized what she had said, and an awful premonition came over him. He turned back to the elderly woman, and all his suspicions seemed to be confirmed in the pain-filled depths of her eyes.

"My primary heir, since soon after her first birthday, is your sister, Elizabeth."

The words hovered between them like a dark miasma. That sum of money was enough to make anyone desperate to receive it, but it was clear that there was still a missing piece. James turned back to her and said to her in a gentle tone:

"How does this relate to Standish?"

"I am not absolutely certain it relates at all. I have only suspicion."

"Please, what makes you suspect him?"

Aunt Emma sighed and closed her eyes again. "Beatrice was my favorite sister. Though we were close to our half-siblings as well, Beatrice was my only full sibling, though she was six years older than I. When she married, it was to a man of property, and she gave birth to one daughter. That daughter, when she was grown, married a man by the name of Standish."

The name hung in the air between them until James ventured to say: "I am aware of the family connection. Are you saying that Victor Standish was your heir until after Elizabeth was born?"

"I am." Aunt Emma looked at him intently. "When my sister passed away, I made her daughter my heir, and when she passed away, her son. I had thought to honor my sister's memory and the love we had shared by making her progeny my heirs. But to be brutally frank, Victor Standish is a disappointment in many ways, and my sister would have felt the same. I comforted myself that I was living long enough that his lifestyle would kill him before he was able to dissipate my fortune, and my money would go to his children, who would hopefully be of better character."

"Even twenty years ago it seemed evident that he had no intention of marrying," said James.

"I thought the same. When your sister was born, I became quickly enamored of her. She was such a bright, beautiful child, precocious and intelligent, and I noticed immediately that she inherited her great grandmother's eyes. Though I was much younger than your mother's grandmother, I was still close to her. I thought I could leave my wealth to someone I could watch grow, have a hand in raising to be a credit to society. Though I have not had a hand in her upbringing, I am confident that she is a beautiful soul. Some of the money has been set aside for your brother, but the bulk is to go to Elizabeth."

"You told Standish about this?"

"I did not," replied Aunt Emma. "I made the change in my will quietly, as I had done before. No one was to know. When your sister disappeared, eighteen months later, I did not even consider the change in my will. All my focus was on her recovery. In the years since, I could not bear to change it again, for to do so would be to somehow acknowledge that she would not return. It was in my mind, however, that I would make one more change should my health deteriorate, and I sent a request to my solicitor. In it, I instructed him to add an addendum to my will that would leave my estate divided between you and your brother should I pass before Elizabeth was found."

"But what makes you believe that Standish discovered this?" asked James. "I knew nothing of it, and I am certain father is not aware of it either. How could Standish have known?"

"I do not know. He visited me about two years ago, and he was solicitous of my health and kindly listened to me for some time. Before he left, however, he was insistent in reminding me of our kinship, and though I thought nothing of it at the time, I believe he was attempting to ensure that I remembered our connection and that he had been destined to inherit.

"I am afraid for Elizabeth, James!" Aunt Emma clutched his hand. "I would never forgive myself if something happened to that dear girl. Standish may think that if she is no longer able to inherit it might default to him. At the time he visited me, I had already made the changes leaving Anthony the bulk of my estate. It is possible he knows nothing of it."

"It is also possible he means to marry her to obtain your money."

James turned to his wife, noting her grim visage. "He has not been acting like a suitor."

"No, but that is only if you consider how a true suitor behaves. If anything, he acts like a man who considers her to be rightfully his."

Unable to bear the tension, James rose and began to pace the room, clenching his fists in his agitation.

"The picture you pain is worrisome, Constance. Darcy has been rising in Elizabeth's esteem — I dare say the entire family considers an engagement between them to be nothing more than a matter of time."

"I doubt Standish would care even if they did come to an agreement," said Aunt Emma. "He likely thinks that he can simply whisk her off to Gretna Green, marry her and be assured of inheriting the bulk of my fortune."

"Then he does not know Anthony — or William and me — if he believes we would roll over and accept such a heinous act."

"A man who believes he has been wrongly passed over for another might not think clearly, Husband," said Constance. "Standish has always struck me as a man who believes the world is there for his taking. It is the habit of men to believe what they wish. Standish obviously believes Elizabeth is his."

"You must go to Pemberley, James," pleaded Aunt Emma. "I believe Elizabeth is in danger. Her father must know of this."

"Of course," replied James. "I will leave directly when we return."

"I wish to go to Pemberley too," said Constance.

"In your condition, I do not believe it would be advisable," replied James.

"I will not be left behind," said Constance. The fire in her eyes was a counterpoint to the steel in her tone, a quality which both entranced James at times and utterly infuriated him at others. "You will need to travel swiftly by horseback—I understand this. I will follow in the carriage. I will be well, husband. But if Standish does make an attempt on Elizabeth, I wish to be there for her."

"Please send word to me as soon as may be," begged Aunt Emma. "I cannot bear to wait without knowing."

"I will be certain to," replied James. He strode to her and knelt by her side. "Thank you for bringing this to me. We may now take action to protect Elizabeth from him."

"I only regret the years of sorrow my actions have wrought."

"Nonsense." James regarded this beloved relation, hoping she took his words as the kindness they were. "You could not have foreseen such consequences to your actions. You have a right to distribute your wealth in any manner you see fit. *If* Standish was behind Elizabeth's disappearance, then *he* is to blame for it. You are blameless."

"Thank you, dear boy. Now go. There is no time to be lost."

Monday, July 13, 1812
Pemberley, Derbyshire

The days at Pemberley had given Elizabeth a confidence in the paths of the estate. While she had not explored everything it had to offer, she thought William had shown her most of the principal paths. They were delightful, as was everything about the park. Elizabeth refrained from saying that to him—her father was correct in that William was puffed up with pride concerning his estate. It was impossible to blame him, for he was correct.

While he most often accompanied her willingly, he still had an estate to manage, and there were times when he was pulled from her side by those concerns. Elizabeth, though she enjoyed his company, knew he was a diligent man, and she did not begrudge him the time he spent looking after his affairs. She admired him for it, for she had not been raised with such an example of industry.

But when he was not available, Elizabeth would often walk without him; Pemberley was so fine that on many days she walked out more than once. If William was not available, Thompson would trail behind her, and she was always with Attila. On a certain day, she departed the manor after luncheon, intending to walk through the woods to a certain brook she had seen in William's company a few days earlier. Her family, by now quite familiar with her habits, only bid her a pleasant walk.

"If Thompson is with you, you may walk as much as you like," said her mother. "But do not stay out long."

"I will not, Mother," replied Elizabeth dutifully. "I shall be back before tea time."

And she left, with Attila bounding after her as was his wont. The back gardens were as lovely as ever, but Elizabeth walked through them quickly, and soon she had passed the border of the woods. The sounds of insects and the wind blowing in the trees settled over her, tranquil and pleasing, and the light of the sun became dappled where it made its way through the forest. More than once Elizabeth saw squirrels chittering in the trees, hopping from one branch to the other on nimble paws, working industriously to lay up their hoard for the coming winter.

As she walked, Elizabeth watched Attila as he bounded this way and that. Several times he brought her sticks and she was obliged to play with him, but for the most part, he seemed content to run back and forth, always carefully keeping her in sight. They walked uphill for a time, and the path, though it was a well-marked trail of packed earth, was narrow, and the ever-present tree roots protruding through the soil necessitated Elizabeth's care.

After some time, she came to the brook, happily bubbling over a bed of small, smooth stones, and she paused there while Attila drank his fill. The wood was peaceful and calm, and Elizabeth basked in the warmth of a patch of sun shining down through the foliage.

It was at that moment she noticed that Thompson had not followed her to the river. Frowning, Elizabeth looked about, wondering if perhaps he had stepped away to watch through the trees, but she could not catch any glimpse of him. It was strange, for she did not think the man had ever let her out of his sight before.

Elizabeth considered the matter—she was with Attila, so she did not think any danger could come to her. But Thompson's disappearance was decidedly odd, and though she could not imagine anything had happened, it seemed best to see if she could locate him.

Spying a low slope back through the trees, Elizabeth turned and started toward it, thinking it might give her a vantage from which to see the missing footman. The path she had trod had led her just below the small hill, and she could see as she approached it and climbed, that the foliage at the crown was thinner than it was in the valley. When she reached it, she began to climb, taking care for her footing, as she did not wish to fall.

When she reached the top, she found that it truly was not much of a vantage. It stood perhaps no more than triple her height, and as the trees still crowded around its base, there was little to be seen. What she could see gave her no hint of the missing footman.

Elizabeth let loose a sigh. "I suppose we shall have to return to the house," said Elizabeth to the canine standing by her side. "I hope Thompson is not injured somewhere."

The dog, however, surprised her by turning and barking, jumping up and down where he stood. Wondering what had agitated him, Elizabeth turned.

CHAPTER XXXV

Monday, July 13, 1812
Snowlock, Derbyshire

After a week at Thorndell, Fitzwilliam was ready to return to his family. Though he would never say anything to Darcy, he wondered how his cousin could withstand so sedentary a life managing an estate. It seemed to Fitzwilliam that a gentleman's lot, though it provided him with wealth far above what most other men would expect, was nothing but a long list of tenants' concerns, problems, and time-consuming minutia. It was enough to drive a man to Bedlam!

While the army had its drawbacks—the French shooting at him was one which readily came to mind—it was rarely dull. Or at least it was rarely dull until one was slated for a posting behind a desk. Such a position would be infinitely safer, but provide little in the way of distraction. It was what he had become accustomed to, and while he knew his parents appreciated the safety his resignation had bought, he knew it would be some time before his new life took hold of him.

So eager was Fitzwilliam to depart from his estate that he had his horse saddled as soon as he awoke, and taking the light breakfast provided by his cook, he departed for Snowlock. He would spend a day or two with his brother and sister-in-law before pressing on to Pemberley and his sister, who he already missed. His horse, a well-trained beast with stamina to spare, made short work of the distance between the two estates, and as such, he found himself riding up the drive to his father's house before visiting hours had even begun. He was surprised by what he found there.

"James!" called he when he saw his brother step from the house clad in riding leathers. Waiting on the drive was a saddled horse. To the other side of the horse, it appeared a carriage was being made ready for departure. "Where are you bound?"

"Anthony," replied his brother. "I am happy to see you."

Seeing the concern etched into his brother's forehead, Fitzwilliam vaulted down from his horse and caught James's shoulders. "What has happened?"

"There is no time," said James. "I am bound for Pemberley this very instant. If you can accompany me, I would appreciate your assistance."

"Of course," replied Fitzwilliam.

"You there!" exclaimed Fitzwilliam at one of the nearby stable hands. "Water my horse at once! Not too much, mind you—just enough to slake his immediate thirst."

As Fitzwilliam's instructions were being carried out, Constance emerged from the house and approached them. Fitzwilliam noted that her pace was not a leisurely walk—she was hurrying and possessed no less concern than his brother.

"I shall depart immediately, James," said she, greeting Fitzwilliam with nothing more than a brief—though not quite curt—nod. "You will no doubt pass me on the road, but the sooner I arrive there, the sooner I can be of use."

"What in the blazes has happened?" demanded Fitzwilliam. "Has someone at Pemberley been injured?"

"I will tell you once we are on the road," said James.

He turned to assist his wife into the carriage, and with a softly spoken word with the driver, he stepped back and watched it roll from the yard, the dust of its passage eddying in the slight breeze. With his wife departed, he turned back to Fitzwilliam and looked critically at his mount.

"I assume you have traveled from Thorndell this morning?" When Fitzwilliam nodded, he said: "Will you be able to keep up on that nag of yours, or will you exchange him for one of Father's horses?"

Fitzwilliam grinned—his brother was attempting to make light sport with him, which was a good sign. "Jupiter will ride that prancing enthusiast of yours into the ground, old man."

They laughed together and stepped to their horses—Fitzwilliam's well-trained war horse silent and still as he waited for instructions, while his brother's horse, as Fitzwilliam had noted, was quivering with eagerness. The water pail had been taken from his mount's nose, and though he gave no visible sign of it, Fitzwilliam knew that Jupiter was eager to be off himself. He had not had as much exercise himself since Fitzwilliam had given up his commission, and a short three-hour journey from Thorndell had not daunted him in the slightest.

"Come, Brother," said James as they heeled their mounts out onto the road, following the rapidly retreating carriage. "Let us run a little and put some distance behind us, and I will tell you what we have learned. I will warn you, however, that we *know* nothing at this point."

With those cryptic words, he dug his heels into his horse and it took off at a gallop, Fitzwilliam urging Jupiter to follow close behind. They quickly overtook the carriage, the driver slowing and guiding the conveyance to the side of the road to allow them to pass, and they continued to gallop for another fifteen minutes or so. The secret to gaining the most distance from a mount, while keeping it fresh, was to vary the speed of travel, and they slowed to a trot soon after. It was then that James essayed to explain what he had heard that morning from Aunt Emma.

"That is quite the story, Brother," said Fitzwilliam when James had relayed what he knew. "Are you certain it is not the ramblings of an elderly woman?"

"I never would have taken you for a skeptic, Anthony."

"It is just that it seems so sudden for her to have connected such a disjointed series of clues."

"*That*, I believe, we may at least partially attribute to advancing age. But the facts seem to fit together quite well. Constance believes that Standish means to have her by whatever means necessary."

"Then he better have a good doctor if he tries anything," muttered Fitzwilliam. "I cannot imagine how he could think that we would endure his interference with Elizabeth without response."

"He is so self-centered, he may not even understand the ties which bind us."

Fitzwilliam grunted. "Well, I do not mean to allow him to have his way. Let us move on quickly."

"Hold, Brother," said James, putting out a hand and pulling his mount to a halt. In the distance, they could hear the sound of a horse's hooves pounding against the gravel road, echoing through the surrounding woods like hammer blows on an anvil. "I sent a footman to Harringward to ascertain if he is home."

"Standish's estate," grunted Fitzwilliam.

They waited for a moment as the hoof beats grew louder, and soon a man in Snowlock livery came into sight. Following his brother, Fitzwilliam spurred his horse forward to meet the man.

"My lord," said the footman without waiting to be addressed. "The butler informed me that Mr. Standish departed the estate early this morning. He was not told where Mr. Standish was bound, nor when he was expected to return."

James swore and his mount danced to the side at his rider's agitation, but James only pulled on the reins, quieting him. "Thank you. You may return to Snowlock — we will press on."

Then without waiting for a response, he urged his horse onward in a ground-eating canter. Fitzwilliam matched him stride for stride, but now Fitzwilliam knew he was sporting a frown which was the mirror image of his brother's.

"It might still be nothing," said he, though he lacked conviction.

"It might not," was James's reply.

To that, Fitzwilliam had no answer. Thus, they pressed on, determined to reach Pemberley as soon as possible. Once his sister's protection was secured, Fitzwilliam aimed to find Standish and discover the truth of the matter. He would have it, even if he had to beat it from the man.

Monday, July 13, 1812
Pemberley, Derbyshire

When his business was finished, Darcy walked the halls of Pemberley, looking for Elizabeth. The matter he had been required to resolve had been a dispute between two of his tenants, men who had long been rivals for the favor of the Darcy family. Though such matters were not pleasant to mediate at the best of times, that day was not the best of times in any way, and Darcy had found himself snapping at them for their stupidity. He would not normally behave in such a way, but his short-temper carried the benefit of ending in a quick resolution.

As the matter was dealt with, Darcy was free to once again seek Elizabeth out. He thought she would not object to a turn through the gardens, though they had already walked out that morning. A smile settled over Darcy's face as he thought of her, remembered the wonder he had seen on her countenance many times as she enjoyed nature to its fullest. A man would do much to be the recipient of such appreciation all the days of his life.

"Elizabeth is already out walking the estate," said Lady Susan when Darcy found her sitting with Anne in her private sitting-room attached to the suite she shared with her husband. Of Lady Catherine, there was no sign. "You did not think she would be kept inside on such a fine day, do you?"

"I suppose not," allowed Darcy. "She did not go out alone, did she?"

"Attila is with her, along with that mountain of a footman."

Darcy nodded. "Very well. I shall search for her, I think."

"Do not stay out too late," cautioned Lady Susan. "I have already extracted a promise from Elizabeth to return by tea. When you are out together, you often lose track of time."

Anne giggled at their aunt's words, but Darcy only shook his head. "I will remember."

Though he had thought to set out on foot to search for her, Darcy decided in the end to ride. Lady Susan, who was not a great walker, did not know it, but Elizabeth was a *prodigious* walker. Had she not promised to return by tea time, Darcy would not have been surprised to learn that she had attempted to walk the full ten miles around the park. As it was, she had likely walked quickly and with purpose, and he was certain he would find her some distance from the house.

A few moments later, he was astride his horse and riding out into the woods. Inside he was afire with anticipation. Perhaps today would be the day their closer relationship was formalized.

Monday, July 13, 1812
Pemberley, Derbyshire

At the crest of the slight rise in the road to Pemberley, the Fitzwilliam brothers reined in their horses. Though neither mentioned it, they were both relieved to see the manor in the distance.

"Shall we press on?" asked Fitzwilliam of his brother.

"We are not here for the view, though Darcy *is* inordinately proud of this prospect," replied James.

They spurred on their horses, though Fitzwilliam did so gingerly. Jupiter had developed a hesitation in his gait which may presage a hint of lameness, but as the horse had pressed on and not complained, Fitzwilliam had not stopped, except for a short rest to check for a rock in his shoe. Even the eagerness of James's mount was muted, and the horse's head hung in fatigue. The journey had only been a matter of a few hours, but they had pushed the horses on. They would need a rest of several days before they were once again fit to be ridden.

"Hopefully Elizabeth will be in the house," said James as they continued.

"You know Elizabeth," replied Fitzwilliam. "Any opportunity she can find she will be out of doors."

James only grunted and pushed his horse a little faster. They pulled up in front of the house and dismounted, making their way to the front door, where they were met by an obviously surprised Mrs. Reynolds.

"My apologies, Lord Chesterfield, Colonel Fitzwilliam, but we had no notice of your coming."

"It is no trouble. But if you would, please have my suite prepared for occupation. Lady Chesterfield is behind me on the road in our carriage."

Though Mrs. Reynolds was shocked at the sudden command, she was not able to respond, for Fitzwilliam was impatiently waiting to speak. "Is my sister within?"

"Lady Elizabeth left for a walk some time ago," replied Mrs. Reynolds, apparently even more confused. "I believe Mr. Darcy left some time after to find her."

The brothers exchanged a glance. "Where are our father and mother?"

"I believe they are in Lady Susan's sitting-room."

"You go speak with our parents," said Fitzwilliam. "I will have horses saddled for our immediate departure."

With a nod, James bounded away into the house. Fitzwilliam was about to turn away toward the stables when the housekeeper's voice arrested his departure. "Is there something wrong, Colonel Fitzwilliam?"

"I am not certain," said Fitzwilliam. "Mrs. Reynolds, has Mr. Standish been seen in the area recently?"

Taken aback, Mrs. Reynolds still responded. "Not since he visited last week."

"Have some men search the borders of the estate to make sure he is not skulking about. James and I will go after Darcy and Elizabeth as soon as James returns."

The ever-efficient housekeeper clearly understood there was no time for further questions, and she turned and departed to relay Fitzwilliam's instructions. Outside, a pair of stable hands were leading the two tired mounts which had carried them to Pemberley away. Fitzwilliam bounded down the stairs and approached them at a trot.

"Where is the lead stable hand?"

The man he addressed turned to him, startled at his abrupt tone, but he pointed toward the stables and led Fitzwilliam there. As they walked, his eyes took in the state of the two horses they were leading, and he ventured to say:

"These horses have been ridden hard, sir. It seems your errand was an urgent one."

"It was," replied Fitzwilliam shortly. "See they are given the best care. Jupiter seemed to be slightly favoring his right foreleg—please ensure he is looked over carefully."

"Yes, sir."

When they entered the low building, Fitzwilliam lost no time in issuing instructions. "Have several mounts saddled and ready to depart immediately. My brother and I will be riding into the estate, and we will need an escort of some of your stouter lads."

"Of course," replied the lead stable hand.

Within moments, the mounts were being led around. Though Fitzwilliam chafed at the delay, he knew no good would come of one of them falling from a horse because of an improperly cinched strap. With any luck, Darcy would already have found her, and she should be accompanied by Thompson and Attila too.

When James appeared a few moments later, he was accompanied by their father. The greetings exchanged were gruff in nature and completed quickly. Then the earl looked at them both gravely.

"If I am honest with you, I consider this story of Standish to be a little peculiar. The man is unpleasant, but would he stoop to stealing my daughter away for monetary gain? Gain that he may not even realize? He could hardly influence Aunt Emma without exerting the sort of pressure which would alert us."

"I do not know, Father," said Fitzwilliam. "But it seems prudent to ensure Elizabeth's protection until we have confirmed the situation."

"I cannot argue with that, I suppose."

Within moments the horses were saddled, and they began to make their way out through the fields. Four horses had been saddled, but since the earl had insisted on accompanying them, they were only escorted by a single stable hand. The man directed them across a large field toward the forest beyond as the last direction in which Elizabeth had been seen. It was not long before they entered the woods.

As Fitzwilliam was familiar with the estate, he directed them with the hand's assistance, and they made good time through the trees. But they rode on for about fifteen minutes and saw no sign of either Elizabeth or Darcy. Fitzwilliam was beginning to become concerned, when a motion behind one of the trees caught his attention and he pulled his horse to a halt, vaulting down and starting toward the motion.

Out from behind a tree staggered a large man. He was dressed in Pemberley's livery and was groaning, one hand held to the back of his head. He looked up and saw Fitzwilliam approaching, and took his hand away from his head. It was bloodied. The man was Thompson.

"Thompson!" exclaimed Fitzwilliam, hurrying forward to support the footman where he was swaying. "What happened, man?"

"I know not," replied Thompson. He groaned, and Fitzwilliam caught his arm and helped him to sit on the turf, while his father and brother crowded around. "I was following Lady Elizabeth on her walk when I noticed movement in the brush. I went to investigate and blacked out. I must have been struck in the back of the head."

"Standish!" growled Fitzwilliam. Even his father, who had been openly skeptical, was now looking about with anger and fear warring in his countenance.

"Go find Lady Elizabeth," said Thompson. "I will be well waiting here."

Fitzwilliam looked at the man, and though he still did not look well, Thompson appeared to be regaining a hint of his color. Fitzwilliam strode to his horse and removed a water skin which had been placed there, and he took it and handed it to the unfortunate footman.

"Drink this. We will return for you, or send someone to assist."

"Do not concern yourself for me, Colonel. Just find the bastard who did this and make sure he does not hurt Lady Elizabeth."

"With pleasure," answered James.

Soon they were mounted again and riding down the path at a quicker pace. They had no way to determine how far down the path Elizabeth had walked without Thompson, or how long it had been since he had been attacked, but Fitzwilliam felt she was not far distant.

Monday, July 13, 1812
Pemberley, Derbyshire

Though Elizabeth was surprised at Mr. Standish's sudden appearance, she was not alarmed. She was more curious, wondering what he could be doing here, on an isolated path in the heart of William's estate.

Attila, however, was not pleased to see him, and he continued to bark, regardless of Elizabeth's attempts to calm him.

"It appears your friend is a menace," said Mr. Standish when Attila had calmed sufficiently for him to be heard.

"There is nothing the matter with Attila," said Elizabeth. "He is only protective of me. I wonder at your presence here, Mr. Standish. You do not seem the kind of man to walk the paths of estates, especially one which is so far from your own."

For a man who had always attempted to be agreeable, Elizabeth instantly noticed that he apparently felt no need to do so at present. His response to her words was an unpleasant sneer and a sardonic:

"Your family praises you for your intelligence, but it is evident to me that you are naught but a silly child. I have dispatched your guard and have now found you alone. Are you not yet frightened?"

The first sense of unease came over Elizabeth, but she was determined not to show it to this man. "You have me at a disadvantage, sir. Of what have I to be frightened?"

Mr. Standish shook his head and he halted his climb a few feet from where Elizabeth stood. "I have seen recently that you have become rather close to Darcy." A snort indicated his thoughts concerning the subject. "Trust a Fitzwilliam to show interest in a stiff prude such as Darcy."

"I do not know how it is any of your concern, sir," said Elizabeth, anger replacing the unease in her breast.

"It is my concern when you will possess something of mine in the future. I will not allow the likes of Fitzwilliam Darcy to take what is mine. If I must take the woman he wishes to have in the bargain, then that is what must be."

Elizabeth searched his eyes, not understanding to what he was referring. She had never seen anything in the man but lazy amiability or, at times, sardonic amusement—it was disquieting to see him focused and intent.

"What will I possess?" asked Elizabeth. "I do not understand you."

His eyebrow rose at her pronouncement. "She has not told you?"

"Who?" demanded Elizabeth in her irritation. "I know nothing of what you speak."

A chuckle and a shake of the head met her declaration. "I suppose it is not surprising. She has not spoken of it all these years—why should she speak of it now?"

"I do not know," said Elizabeth, her tone testy. "Perhaps if you would explain it to me?"

"I think not. Eventually, you will discover it, though it will be too late then. At present, you will come with me. We have a pair of horses to make our way to a carriage I have waiting outside Pemberley's boundaries. Our next stop will be Gretna Green."

"Gretna Green?" echoed Elizabeth. "I am not going to Scotland."

"In fact, you are. Send that beast away and come with me now."

He reached for her, but Elizabeth stepped back, even as Attila snapped at his arm. He stood between them and snarled, hackles raised. Mr. Standish had jerked his arm back and was now staring at the dog, enraged at being thwarted.

"Cooper!" snarled he, and from the trees down on the path, Elizabeth saw a rough-looking man leading a pair of horses step forward. "If this mongrel does not move out of the way, you will shoot it."

Nodding, the man produced a rifle from one of the saddles and held it in his hands negligently, as if he knew how to use it. Standish turned back to Elizabeth and smirked, raising an eyebrow at her as if they were playing chess and he was acknowledging the next move was hers. Elizabeth thought furiously. She had to delay—despite what Mr. Standish said, Mr. Thompson must be along soon, or perhaps William would find her.

"Do you truly think you shall be successful?" asked she, reaching out and grasping the scruff of Attila's neck to prevent him from attacking. "Do you think my father and brothers will allow this contemptible action to go unchallenged? Do you think William will simply allow you to steal away with me in the night?"

"They will have no choice once you are mine by law. If they do not withdraw then they will not like what I do to their precious girl." The sneer was now truly dreadful, and Elizabeth believed the man capable of anything.

"I think you misjudge them, sir. Anthony, in particular, does not seem the kind of man to simply allow you to have your way."

"Then that is something *I* shall be required to worry about. You're only concern is coming along now without being forced to do so."

When Elizabeth hesitated, he flicked a finger at his man, causing Cooper to raise the rifle he was carrying. "Now, Lady Elizabeth. Send the dog away."

"Attila!" commanded Elizabeth, seeing she had no choice in the matter. "Heel, Attila." Attila looked back at her, seeming to ask the question with his eyes. "Go back to Pemberley, boy. Go get William and Anthony."

With one last growl at Standish, the dog rose and padded a few steps away. Mr. Standish only laughed.

"Do you truly think that dog will bring your rescuers back to prevent me?"

That was when Elizabeth saw a movement out of the corner of her eye and heard a shout from behind her. All hell broke loose.

Monday, July 13, 1812
Pemberley, Derbyshire

It was some time after Darcy entered the woods that he began to be concerned. Elizabeth had walked further that day than he might have expected, especially considering their sojourn that morning. There was no sign of her in the mottled light of the sun filtering down through the trees. All was silent.

It was too silent, thought Darcy as he looked about. It was nothing more than his imagination, he knew, but the sense of disquiet looming over the wood unsettled him. Darcy reined his horse in and looked about into the foliage on either side of the path. Nothing seemed to be out of place. If he recalled correctly, there was a stream Elizabeth had exclaimed over when they had come upon it late the previous week. Perhaps she had gone there.

Darcy had only just clucked his horse into motion once again when he heard barking echoing through the woods. Stopping once again, he realized the sound was echoing from further down the path, and he kicked his horse into motion. As he did so, he had the impression he had been joined by another horse—or more—but there was no time to stop, and he urged the beast forward.

The ride was chaotic. He weaved down the narrow path, ducking to avoid long branches of the surrounding trees as they reached out to grasp and tear him from his mount. He avoided them as best he could, feeling the sting several times as branches scratched his hands or face as he rode by. All the while, he prayed that his horse would not stumble on the uneven ground.

When Darcy rounded a corner, he could see Elizabeth standing on a small rise up the path, with one man confronting her, while another stood at the foot with a pair of horses. The man held a long rifle.

At that moment, several things happened at once. Elizabeth turned and spoke to the dog, commanding it back to the estate with a pointed finger, all this while the man at the foot of the rise lifted his rifle and pointed it at her. At the same time, a group of horsemen pulled up behind him, and Darcy heard his cousin's voice raised in anger.

"Standish! You will not harm a hair on her head!"

Needing no more urging, Darcy goaded his mount into motion. At that precise moment, Attila used the distraction and abruptly reversed course, leaping at Standish with a vicious snarl. The man at the foot of the hill fired a shot, and Elizabeth ducked away—at least Darcy hoped she had only ducked. The dog and man disappeared down the far side of the rise, tumbling together, Attila snapping at Standish's face as they fell. Then the horsemen were upon them.

"Drop your weapon!" the commanding voice of his cousin once again rang out, and the man holding the rifle grimaced and complied.

Darcy did not hesitate—he spared not a second glance for the man, instead, vaulting from his saddle and surging up the side of the hill toward Elizabeth.

Chapter XXXVI

Monday, July 13, 1812
Pemberley, Derbyshire

*T*he first thing Elizabeth noticed after she fell was the pain in her ankle. The second was the sound of William calling out to her. Oh, the sweet sound of his voice!

"Elizabeth!" exclaimed he as he rushed up to her.

Elizabeth rolled and came to a sitting position, holding her injured leg out in front of her. William slid to a stop in front of her, heedless of the turf beneath his knees. Then in an action so beyond propriety that Elizabeth could not even properly respond, he gathered her into his arms, cradling her head against his shoulder.

"You are not injured?"

"Only a slight twist of my ankle," said Elizabeth.

He pulled away from her, holding her at arms' length, his eyes searching her face, before continuing down her body, searching for evidence of any further damage. "You were not hit?"

"No," replied she. "It is only my foot from where I turned away to avoid Attila."

"What are we to do with you, Elizabeth?"

A glance up revealed her father, and Elizabeth willingly went to his strong arms. "I am sure I do not know," said she around the tears pooling at the corners of her eyes. "I certainly did not invite Mr. Standish to accost me in the middle of Pemberley's woods."

"I am only glad we have not lost you again, dear girl. I do not think I could have withstood it, to say nothing of what your mother might have felt."

With the two men cooperating, her father and William soon had her standing between them. With an experimental step, Elizabeth soon discovered that her ankle was not nearly so bad as she had feared. She would not be capable of walking back to Pemberley, but she was not an invalid either. She could put weight on it, though gingerly.

"Attila!" exclaimed Elizabeth when the dog trotted up to her, seeming none the worse for wear after his adventure. Elizabeth sank to her knees again and threw her arms around her savior. "You have been a bad boy, not obeying. But I am very glad you did not, and happier you were not injured."

The dog seemed to understand, and he puffed out his chest as if with pride, as he met Elizabeth's gaze and panted at her. The two men standing behind her broke out into chuckles, and Elizabeth joined them.

When Elizabeth rose once again, she noted that Anthony had taken the rifle belonging to Mr. Standish's man and was holding it in one hand, pointed in the general direction of his captive. For his part, the man—Elizabeth thought she remembered Mr. Standish calling him Cooper—was sitting on the forest floor, glaring at the colonel sullenly. From the other side of the mound behind them, Elizabeth saw James appear with one of Pemberley's footmen.

"Standish?" asked her father when he caught sight of them.

James shook his head. "He broke his neck during his tumble down the hill. He is dead."

The shock at learning that a man had died in front of her caused Elizabeth to gasp, and she would have sunk to the ground had William not held her up.

"It is time to return Elizabeth to Pemberley," said her father, taking charge of the situation. "We can return later for Standish's body and question his man when we arrive at Pemberley." He turned to William. "William, see to Elizabeth, please."

Though still beyond the ability to speak, Elizabeth did not need to look at William to know that he was more than willing to help her. She went along docilely where he led, understanding everything that was happening around her but lost in a fog. A man had died confronting her. How was such a thing possible?

Monday, July 13, 1812
Pemberley, Derbyshire

In the end, Darcy chose the simple expedient of lifting Elizabeth onto his horse and scrambling up behind her. Her lack of response was worrying, but she did not seem to be hurt, other than her ankle. He knew she would laugh that minor hurt away and be walking the grounds of Pemberley before her family was ready to let her out of their sight. But this silence was troubling.

Not wishing to become separated from the rest of the party, Darcy waited on his horse while they prepared to depart. Cooper was put on a horse, but the footman held the reins while Fitzwilliam rode behind him, the rifle in his hands a pointed reminder of what would happen to him if he made a bid for freedom. After the others had mounted up—the rider-less horse bringing up the rear—they began to make their way back toward the estate.

"What the blazes has happened here today, Cousin?" asked Darcy. "And why are you here?"

"We will explain it when we return to the house," replied James. "But it seems we finally have some indication of why Elizabeth was taken from us, though I doubt we will ever know the entire truth of the matter."

"Standish was behind it?"

"It seems so," replied James.

"Tell me?" In response, both men looked at the small form of Elizabeth in Darcy's arms, Darcy looking down at the crown of her head while James looked at her with love and compassion.

"Perhaps it would be best to wait until later, Elizabeth. You have had a bad fright today."

"I am well," said she, rousing a little of her indomitable will and glaring at him in defiance. "I wish to know what has happened, why he acted the way he did today. He claimed that I had taken something from him. I wish to know why."

Though it was clear James would have preferred to demur, he apparently saw what Darcy did—that Elizabeth was not about to be denied. Darcy caught his eye and gave him a slight nod. Whatever brought Elizabeth back to her previous self quickly should be allowed.

James seemed to understand Darcy's gesture, for he shrugged and proceeded to relate what he knew of the tale. Elizabeth listened carefully and seemed to regain more of herself the longer her brother spoke. When the tale had been told, she sighed and — unconsciously, Darcy thought — nestled closer to him.

"All the hardship and sorrow for nothing more than avarice. How is such disgusting greed to be fathomed?"

"I know not, Elizabeth. But it is now at an end, for Standish is no more."

Elizabeth fell silent once again and did not speak the rest of the trip back to Pemberley. On the way there, they came across Thompson who was struggling to return to the estate. He gratefully accepted the horse trailing behind them and sat upon it, slumped over. Darcy watched him, worried at his apparent lethargy — they must have hit him with great force. The doctor would need to be summoned as soon as they arrived at Pemberley, for both Elizabeth and Thompson would need his services.

At length, they came to the edge of the woods, and Pemberley rose in the distance. They were spied as they approached the house, and a veritable army of footmen, stable hands and maids exited the house to assist them. In the midst of them all stood Lady Susan and Lady Catherine, directing the activity. Lady Susan's eyes narrowed at Darcy riding toward her with his precious burden. When he stopped in front of her, he slid from the horse and then pulled an unresisting Elizabeth from the top of the beast.

"Are you hurt, Elizabeth?" asked Lady Susan.

When Elizabeth did not respond, Darcy felt obliged to say: "She said her ankle was sprained, but other than that, I know of no harm. She has not spoken much, however."

"It *was* Standish," said the earl. "He is dead now, which seems to have affected our Elizabeth."

"Then let us return her to the house." Lady Susan stood in front of her daughter and coaxed her to look up. "Can you walk into the house, Elizabeth?"

"I can," was the only reply she made.

Lady Susan nodded and took charge of her unresponsive daughter. As they walked, she turned and looked back at her husband and Darcy. "We will set Elizabeth to rights. When you have finished, perhaps you should bring what you learn to us. I would like to speak of it once and leave it forever in the past."

"That is likely for the best, my dear," agreed the earl.

He turned away and began issuing orders. Darcy went with him, though he had little desire to leave Elizabeth. His heart was entering the house, and more than anything he longed to be with her.

Monday, July 13, 1812
Pemberley, Derbyshire

"I do not need to be fussed over," said Elizabeth with some asperity. "I have injured my foot. I am not an invalid."

"Elizabeth," came the stern voice of her aunt, "you have given your mother a fright. Our fussing, if that is how you must refer to it, is as much for *our* benefit as it is for *yours*."

Embarrassed, Elizabeth ducked her head. The time since the confrontation in the forest had been a fog of activity, and though she was aware of what was happening around her, it seemed beyond her to affect the world herself. It was like she was caught in the prison of her own mind.

As she had been guided into the house and taken up the stairs—they had drafted a footman to carry her, rather than chance a further injury to her ankle—where her mother had begun to work on her. First, she had been divested of her dress and undergarments and submerged in a tub of hot water, bathed and washed, and then put into a clean dress. The physician had then been by and had pronounced her injury to be naught but a slight sprain. He had bound it and informed her that she could walk if she felt comfortable, but to avoid long walks for the next two weeks.

As Elizabeth sat in front of her vanity after her bath, her mother sat behind her, arranging her hair into a simple style while Lady Catherine looked on and made comments at irregular intervals. The feeling of being smothered had come upon Elizabeth suddenly, and she had spoken without thinking.

"My independent daughter," said Lady Susan, fondness infusing her voice. "You are so fierce and determined, Elizabeth. I could not have imagined a better woman had I raised you myself."

"But she is also impatient and headstrong," grumbled Lady Catherine.

Elizabeth flushed, especially as her mother was watching her now with a knowing smile. In the end, she decided there was no reason to respond to their teasing, so she subsided. For quite some time, she allowed the soporific effect of the strokes of her mother's brush through her hair lull her into a trance-like state.

It was some time later—Elizabeth did not know how long it had been—when there was a knock on the door. The maid went to answer it and, after speaking with the person out in the hallway for a few moments, closed the door and returned to address Lady Susan.

"Lord Matlock wishes to inform you that the gentlemen are waiting in the sitting-room for your attendance."

Lady Susan nodded and turned to Elizabeth. "Are you able to join the rest of the company?"

Though Elizabeth wished to see William, she could not help but hesitate. How did she feel? Was it possible she could face the rest of the company with what she had seen hovering before her eyes?

"Oh, Elizabeth!" said Lady Catherine, causing Elizabeth's eyes to find the lady, surprised at her outburst. "You blame yourself in some way for Standish's death. Am I correct?"

Elizabeth gaped at Lady Catherine, wondering if that was correct. Could she possibly be having difficulty due to a belief that she had somehow been complicit in the man's death?

"Perhaps not exactly," said her mother, a shrewd look at Elizabeth seeming to bare her soul for Lady Susan to see. "Is it more the fact of seeing a man die before you that has you so quiet?"

"I hardly know," replied Elizabeth. "I . . . I think there was little I could have done differently, but I wonder . . ."

Lady Catherine opened her mouth to say something, but Lady Susan motioned her to silence. Lady Catherine subsided, and Elizabeth felt the faint wisp of a smile lifting the corners of her lips—one did not see the great Lady Catherine silenced often, even by a woman who was her superior in society.

"Can you tell us of it, Elizabeth? My understanding is he confronted you and demanded you send Attila away, on the pain of shooting your protector. What could you have done differently?"

The redness of a flush came over Elizabeth, and she wondered at the heat in her cheeks. "When you put it in that fashion . . ."

"I do." Lady Susan grasped Elizabeth's hands and held them tight, her gaze capturing Elizabeth's and not allowing her to retreat. "A man died today, Elizabeth, and that is always difficult. But you must understand that he wrought his own ruin. Not only did he attempt to spirit you away from us *again*, but he threatened you with a rifle! If I am honest with you, I am happy Attila disobeyed the way he did. I much rather we are required to bury Victor Standish, and not my only daughter, returned to us after so long."

"You are correct, of course," replied Elizabeth. "It *is* hard. Everything happened so quickly that I could hardly comprehend it."

"It is understandable, my dear," said Lady Susan. "But as much as you can, remember that the events of the day—and everything we have endured in our lives since you were taken from us—were the work of Mr. Standish. Spare your pity for those who deserve to receive it, and your guilt for those times when it is actually deserved."

Elizabeth agreed, and her mother turned her attention back to her hair. A few moments later when it had been tied up in a simple knot, they rose to leave the room and attend the gentlemen. Elizabeth hobbled down the hall from her room, and though she felt her foot was strong and able to bear her weight down the stairs, her mother would have none of it, insisting that a nearby footman carry her down the stairs.

A few moments later they entered the sitting-room, and Elizabeth immediately felt the weight of everyone's eyes on her. She looked down in self-consciousness, a feeling swelling in her breast that they were all regarding her with judgment in their eyes. But her feeling was soon revealed to be the silliness it was and dispelled.

"Elizabeth, are you well?" asked her eldest brother as he stepped forward and grasped her shoulders.

"I am," replied she. "Thank you, James." Elizabeth smiled at Anthony and William, who had also crowded around her. Then Georgiana came forward and engulfed her in a gentle embrace while her father patted her on the back. When Georgiana stepped back, another made herself known to Elizabeth, and with a laugh, Elizabeth stepped into Constance's embrace.

"I thought you were to stay at Pemberley."

"Do you think I could stay away when my new favorite sister was revealed to be in such danger?"

It seemed to Elizabeth that she had done nothing but blush the entire day. But she was grateful to Constance, even while she was concerned for her.

"You have no need to concern yourself," said she, guessing Elizabeth's thoughts. "I have been much recovered these past days."

"I am happy to hear it," replied Elizabeth quietly.

Soon Elizabeth was led to a sofa where she settled in, Constance by her side holding her hands tightly. William claimed the seat on her other side when Elizabeth might have expected her mother to step forward. But Lady Susan only looked on them both with amusement and sat nearby. Though Elizabeth's attention was primarily on Constance, she caught a glimpse of William's eyes, his heart contained within the look he gave her. Elizabeth had rarely felt so loved during her entire life.

"Perhaps we should start with explanations of what led to today's excitement," said her father. "James, since you made the first discovery, perhaps you would go first?"

The explanations were not completed quickly, for there was much to be said. James had informed them of what he had learned from Aunt Emma and recited his actions after. Anthony mentioned how he had come to Snowlock as James was about to depart and accompanied him on to Pemberley. Then William informed them of his own actions that day, how he had gone out to find Elizabeth when he finished with his business, and how he had heard Attila barking and gone to investigate. Then Elizabeth responded and informed them of seeing Mr. Standish, what he had said, and how he had demanded she go with him. When they had put all the pieces together, the puzzle was still incomplete, though Elizabeth was relieved that they knew more of it than they had before.

"Did the servant say anything of his master's actions when you questioned him?" asked Lady Susan.

"Little of use," replied Anthony. "The man has been in service to Standish for several years, and Standish has used him to accomplish certain distasteful tasks. He was instructed to investigate Elizabeth's background to see if there was anything he could use to discredit her. But anything beyond that, he does not know. He certainly has no knowledge of events from eighteen years ago."

"Would he know of any other servants who would have more information?" asked Constance.

"It does not appear so," replied Anthony. "Standish appears to have had difficulty keeping others in his employ. Whoever orchestrated Elizabeth's disappearance has not been in Standish's service for many years. This Cooper would have been trusted with it, but he has not been in his position long enough."

"He might be attempting to save himself," said Lord Matlock.

"It is possible," replied Anthony. "I will go to Harringward and bear the news of Standish's demise. I will also attempt to discover who Cooper replaced, and see if I can find a direction to him. Standish might also have left some records, for which I will conduct a search." He paused and directed a questioning glance at his father. "Do you know who the heir of the estate will be?"

"Not exactly," said the earl, stroking his chin in thought. "It must be a distant cousin, as I do not believe he had any living relatives from his father's generation."

"Then I suppose we shall never know what happened when I disappeared," said Elizabeth into the silence which ensued.

"Not the exact events," said her father. "But I believe we may safely say that your initial disappearance was the work of Victor Standish. Though we are still missing information, he has all but confessed to it. That and the testimony of Aunt Emma means he had the motive. I simply wonder why he did not simply have you murdered, my dear. He had the opportunity, with you being so young."

"He may simply not have had the stomach for it," said Anthony.

"The important point is that he did not," said Lady Susan, her tone leaving no room for any other comments. "Regardless, we now have you back, and it seems there is little reason to think that you are still in danger. Perhaps we may all relax now."

"What will happen to the servant?" asked Elizabeth.

"I will have him transported," replied her father. "Though we know nothing of his crimes, he was obviously willing to do whatever he was told, including acting against the daughter of an earl. It is best that he be sent to a location where he is no longer a threat."

Elizabeth agreed that it was likely for the best and said nothing. The conversation soon turned to other matters, and the ensuing time was spent in the company of beloved family members. Elizabeth did not say much, as she was consumed with thoughts of what had happened, intermixed with feelings of these people she now called her family.

It was beyond comprehension, she thought, how close she had come to them in such a short time. Only half a year before, Elizabeth had not known anyone in the room. But now she loved them—loved them as if she had been known to them all her life. And it had all been so easy. Perhaps it was the way *she* had been allowed into *their* hearts which had prompted her to respond. They had certainly been desperate to accept her based on the possibility that she might be their daughter.

"You seem lost in your thoughts," said a voice, and Elizabeth turned to see William watching her carefully. A quick glance around the room showed her that the others were involved in their own discussions. A closer look, however, revealed that they were all vigilant toward Elizabeth herself, for she noticed several glances in her direction. A feeling of love once again filled her at their acceptance and concern for her.

"Or am I mistaken?"

Elizabeth turned back to her cousin. "I was only thinking about the first days of my acquaintance with everyone in the room. It seemed you were all most anxious to accept me as a Fitzwilliam."

The brief pause before William's response told Elizabeth that he was considering her words. Elizabeth waited patiently, curious about the perspective of one who, by her estimation, had been eager to accept her.

"Perhaps that is true to a certain extent, from your mother especially," said William at length. "But I was afflicted by no such feelings. I saw in your face the echo of my aunt, and that led me to contact Mr. Gardiner. But though I remember the time of your disappearance and had loved you as a young cousin, I do not believe I was motivated by anything other than trying to determine if you *were* my cousin.

"And even your mother would not have accepted you, had you not been conclusively proven to be her daughter." William smiled at her and nodded. "We are, I believe, a passionate bunch. But we are also rational. We would not have wished to find *anyone* to take the place of our beloved relation. We wished to have *you* returned to us."

Elizabeth looked down, moved by his impassioned statement. "You make me feel inadequate, William."

"Why?"

The question was unexpected, though Elizabeth knew it should not have been.

"I . . ."

The words would not come. Perhaps they did not exist. Elizabeth hardly knew what she felt, and giving words to feelings she did not understand seemed about as possible as walking to the moon. William—bless him—did not say anything. Instead, he waited with patience for her to articulate her thoughts. Elizabeth was grateful for the reprieve.

"I . . ." Elizabeth tried again. "I have been given so much by you all: a family I never thought to have again; love and devotion, though I have not always thought myself deserving of it; protection from the world and those who would cause me harm; and perhaps most of all, your *belief* in me. Your conviction that I *am* Elizabeth Fitzwilliam, rather than merely the lost girl who did not know who she was when she left Hertfordshire."

"You doubted your identity? Even after all that was said and done to prove who you are?"

"Not precisely doubted," replied Elizabeth, still struggling to convey what she wished. "I believe I accepted your conviction in my identity. But I . . . well, perhaps I doubted *myself*. I doubted my own merit—my *worthiness* to be your relation.

"I am not saying this well." Elizabeth paused and let out a chuckle, one which sounded almost hysterical. "It may be that I doubted that one such as I could be a proper member of the family of a peer."

"And yet you have handled it with the aplomb of a woman who had trained all her life for the role."

"So you all have told me," murmured Elizabeth.

William looked at her with frank appraisal, making Elizabeth more than a little uncomfortable. "It seems to me you have not believed us."

Though she opened her mouth to reply, Elizabeth found she could not. There was nothing she could say to that, for she thought he was right, though, in her defense, Elizabeth decided she had not even understood her own feelings.

"Elizabeth." Her name on his lips, softly spoken and full of *meaning*, pulled Elizabeth's attention back to him. He was regarding her with a tender expression which spoke volumes, confirmed every emotion of Elizabeth's heart, everything she had suspected of his feelings toward her. "We have not spoken of your ease in society to make you feel better, nor have we done it idly. You *have* acquitted yourself better in society than any of us might have expected.

"But if I am honest with you, I suspected from the very beginning that you would not falter. That night at Davidson's house, I saw a young woman who seemed uncertain of her place, and yet, held her chin up high and conducted herself with the grace of a queen. I believe it was that very night that I began to see you as a woman I could view with the highest regard."

Elizabeth smiled at him. "Are you speaking of love at first sight? It is a pretty notion, is it not? But it does not seem to work in the world of real people and hearts, though the poets would have us believe differently."

"*You* are the one who raised the subject of love," said he, causing Elizabeth to blush. A snort brought her attention to a nearby chair, and she noted Anthony looking at them with evident mirth. He did not speak, merely contenting himself with a grin at William and a circular motion with his hand, a clear demand that they get on with their conversation. She directed a glare at him, promising future vengeance, but his grin only broadened.

"But now that you have mentioned it," continued William, bringing Elizabeth's gaze streaking back to him, "I would have you know the day's adventure interfered with my intention for the day."

"Intention?" echoed Elizabeth.

"Yes. You see, it was in my mind that I should discover whether you might have been amenable to a more . . . permanent relationship with me."

"And being cousins is not permanent enough for you?" Elizabeth arched an eyebrow at him which prompted a laugh.

"Being a cousin to you is wonderful, but it is far from what I want. I would love you, as a man loves a woman. I would give you everything that is mine, share it with you for a lifetime. I would give you the one thing I would never be able to give to another woman— my heart. If you would have it."

It was not a proposal, but it was tantamount to one. He was baring his heart to her, and Elizabeth could not imagine a more wonderful prospect than being loved by Fitzwilliam Darcy. But the day had also seen horrors. It had seen the revealing of the culprit who had caused her family grief for so many years. It had seen the death of that malefactor within her sight, and though he had been a reprehensible man, one did not recover from such an event quickly. As much as she wished to accept William's assurances at that moment, she thought she would be doing no one a favor by being so precipitous in the wake of such events.

"I accept your feelings with gratitude, William," replied Elizabeth. "But as your proposal has been interrupted by these events, I think it would be best to come to terms with them and allow the day to fade a little before we take such a step."

"And I agree." William paused. "I do not mean to make a proposal. I would rather make a much greater impression than to do so with a hurried proposal now only hours after you had such a traumatic experience. I merely wished to inform you of my feelings and determine if yours are a match for mine."

"They are," said Elizabeth, "as I am sure you have already suspected."

"Then let us allow some time before we formalize matters between us. I am quite happy to continue to pay court to you. But I warn you, Elizabeth."

"Of what do you warn me?" queried she. Elizabeth attempted to suppress a smile, amused as she was by their banter.

"I will not wait forever," said he. "Before we enter London society again, I will have at the very least a courtship from you. I will not sit idly by again while the rakes of society ply the woman I intend to marry with pretty words and flattery. I want it known to all that we are meant to be together."

Elizabeth paused, drawing in a great breath, which she then let out slowly. "I believe, William, I can promise I will not refuse you. Let us take matters as they come. I have no desire to return to London to be the focus of every man on the prowl for a woman of fortune."

"Then we have come to an agreement," said William. "Or at least it is a promise of an agreement. I will hold you to it, Elizabeth."

"I anticipate it very much," replied Elizabeth.

Their hands joined as they turned to others to speak and laugh, for Elizabeth to obtain the first hints of healing. Though the others of the family obviously noticed what had passed between them, they said nothing. Even Anthony, who grinned in a knowing fashion, did not make any overt mention of it, though his innuendo was a little thick. But he was clearly happy for them, as all the rest of the family was as well.

Somehow amid all that had happened, Elizabeth had found her home. She had found her heart. And she knew herself to be blessed because of it.

EPILOGUE

Wednesday, July 21, 1813
Pemberley, Derbyshire

" *I* beg you, Elizabeth—do not tease me!"

"Pray, why would I spare you my wit?" asked Elizabeth, vainly attempting to hold in her laughter. "I seem to remember my own courtship being fraught with clever comments of all kinds, and nothing we said diminished them in any way."

"He just does not wish to receive a taste of his own medicine," said William. It was clear he was enjoying himself immensely, and well he should. From what Elizabeth knew, the teasing she had endured had been nothing compared to what William had received from Anthony when the gentlemen were together.

"You would not treat Jane in such a way," exclaimed Anthony.

"Oh, Jane has been subjected to teasing, indeed," said Elizabeth. "But I will own it is gentler. But she is not a tease herself, so it is only fair. Would you not agree?"

Anthony looked at them helplessly for a moment, then threw up his hands and stalked away, muttering under his breath. Elizabeth followed him with her eyes, immensely diverted. At her side, she felt

William move a little closer, his hand going to the small of her back.

"I know I should not take such enjoyment in his discomfort," said William, "but revenge is sweet, indeed."

"I dare say it is, William. I would take pity on him, but for the fact that he had none for me."

"That boy has always been thus," said Lady Susan. She had entered the room while they were speaking. She watched her son as he sat on a nearby chair, continuing to speak to himself. "He was much like his father at that age."

"Some things never change," said Elizabeth, smiling at her father, who had entered behind her mother. "I seem to remember a few choice observations when William was courting me that did not originate from Anthony."

"Perhaps that is correct," replied Lord Matlock "But I like to think that my humor contains less bite than Anthony's. I am also able to see the signs which point to a person reaching their limit and can determine when it is best to cease."

"That, indeed, is Anthony's greatest failing," said Lady Susan. She turned and looked at her son, catching Anthony's eyes and prompting a scowl. Anthony then turned away and resolutely determined not to look at them, much to their general amusement.

"If he cannot endure a little teasing, then I must think much less of him than I did before," said William. "It is not as if our outing ended with comments and invective hurled from all sides."

"No, but you must own that you and I were not kind."

William turned to see James regarding him, his unrepentant gaze at odds with his words. "I will confess to nothing," replied William airily. "Nothing that he did not deserve, in any case."

Their conversation was interrupted at that moment by one of the subjects of what they were saying. Jane Bennet had been invited to Pemberley for the summer, included in a gathering with the Fitzwilliam and Darcy families, the first one of the Bennet family with whom Elizabeth had regained her previous connection. Elizabeth had attempted to reconnect with her earlier, but Jane had demurred when she had been invited for the season, stating she would not feel comfortable joining Elizabeth with all the attention of society on her. Thus, the invitation had been modified for the summer.

"Jane!" said Elizabeth with delight, going to the woman she had called her closest sister for many years, and drawing her into the room with the rest of the family. "Are you refreshed after our outing?"

"I am," replied Jane quietly. "Pemberley is very lovely, Mr. Darcy.

I can see how Elizabeth became enraptured with it so quickly."

Initially, Jane had insisted on referring to Elizabeth with the "Lady" appellation applied, but Elizabeth had quickly convinced her she did not need to do so.

"Thank you, Jane," said William. "I will own that I am inordinately proud of it."

"That is an understatement," said Anthony *sotto voce*.

Elizabeth turned, noting that Anthony had risen in response to Jane's entrance. She covered her mouth to hide a smile at the enraptured light in his eyes at the sight of the eldest Bennet daughter. The rest of the family were in similar straits, and William even snorted at the sight. Jane blushed at the scrutiny, but it was clear that she was not averse to it. In fact, since Jane had arrived two weeks before, it had been clear to them all that there was something in the air. And Elizabeth could not be happier, not to mention a little smug—she had thought they would be compatible if she could get them together. The only issue might be the problem of Anthony having the Bennets for relations, though that was also fixing itself little by little as time went on.

"Come, Jane," said Elizabeth, pulling her to a nearby sofa. "Let us sit and call for tea. We are to attend an assembly tonight, as you know. I am certain you will be the most popular girl in attendance tonight."

Constance snickered, and she caught Jane's other arm and accompanied them to the furniture. Elizabeth did not miss the asperity which crossed Anthony's countenance and noted the pleading look he sent her. But it was all part of her plan. Far from matchmaking, they were all doing their part to force Anthony to work for Jane's attention—not only did Jane deserve proof of his devotion, but it would do him no harm to be forced from her company from time to time. And there was his usual insouciance, which Elizabeth thought would cause Jane some difficulty.

"I do not know anyone in the neighborhood," said Jane hesitantly. "Surely there will be other ladies there who will command more attention than I will myself."

"Nonsense," said Constance. "You will be the most beautiful girl present. Besides, your newness will surely intrigue those in attendance. You should not lack partners for the evening."

"In fact," said Elizabeth with a sly look at her brother, "I have in mind one of the young men of the neighboring estates, a kind and attentive young man who would be the perfect one to ask you for the first dance."

As Elizabeth had expected—and intended—Anthony had enough of her teasing at that point. He approached, pushing his way through the barrier his cousin and brother had formed around the ladies and bowed gallantly to Jane.

"I believe that will not be necessary. In fact, Miss Bennet, I would be honored if you would accept my hand for the first dance of the evening."

Jane, who had been looking back and forth between Elizabeth and Constance with alarm, turned her startled gaze upon Anthony when he spoke. Far from being averse to the notion, however, she quickly averted her eyes and said:

"Thank you, Colonel Fitzwilliam, I would be honored."

"And your supper set," said Anthony, causing her eyes to fly back to him. It was clear she was shocked that he had not only asked for a second dance with such alacrity but had also not even thanked her for accepting his hand for the first. But her surprise did not last long, for her consternation melted in an instant.

"I would like that, Colonel Fitzwilliam. You may have those two dances."

"Thank you, Miss Bennet. Now, if you will, I believe I would like some private conversation with you. Shall we?"

Jane shot an apologetic look at Elizabeth, but she did not object, instead taking his hand and allowing him to pull her to her feet. Soon they were ensconced in a two-seat sofa, speaking together in low voices. Elizabeth was delighted; it reminded her of Jane's behavior when Mr. Bingley had commanded her attention almost two years before. But it was at the same time more meaningful, more like a courtship than Mr. Bingley's puppy-like attentions. Anthony could never be called a puppy—a wolf, perhaps, when he was in a mood.

"You are positively devious, Elizabeth," said Constance. "Had you not pushed him, he would not have acted so swiftly."

"I hope we have not pushed too much," said William. "I would not wish either of them to hurry into marriage."

"Do not worry, William," said Elizabeth. "Anthony is a gentleman and will not act precipitously, and Jane has obtained a modicum of caution since the debacle with Mr. Bingley. They will come to an agreement in their own time if that is what they desire."

"I still cannot fathom the rest of the Bennet family as you have described them, Elizabeth," said Constance.

"You were not there when Mrs. Bennet paid us a visit in London?" asked Elizabeth with feigned astonishment.

"Well, perhaps aside from Mrs. Bennet," amended Constance with a laugh. "It is only strange that the daughters are so different. When one meets Jane Bennet, it is easy to assume her sisters are also sweet and angelic."

"Angelic is not a term one may use when describing Lydia Bennet," replied Elizabeth. "Fortunately, I hear from Jane—and the infrequent letters I have received from Mr. Bennet—that she is much improved due to the school she attends. Kitty is too. I only wish Mary would have accepted my invitation."

"It makes sense from her point of view," said William. "She knows how close you and Jane are. I am certain we will succeed in persuading her next time."

"I was quite surprised to learn what she said about me when you visited Longbourn," said Elizabeth. "I never had any notion she viewed me with such esteem. But she is still young. There is still time, even if she does not visit us this year."

Constance laughed. "Do you mean to see *all* your adoptive sisters married?"

"It is the least I can do," said Elizabeth with a straight face. "It has been Mrs. Bennet's ambition all these years. If I can assist by introducing them to 'rich men,' as she would say, then I am happy to do it."

Lady Susan shook her head. "Unfortunately, I suspect there is little hope for Mrs. Bennet. She is too set in her ways."

"For that, you should be grateful," said a new voice. Lady Catherine had just entered the room with Anne, and she took the opportunity to state her opinion for all to hear. Elizabeth snuck a look at Jane but was relieved to see that Jane's attention was solely on Anthony. Jane was aware of her mother's character, but her feelings would be bruised to hear Mrs. Bennet spoken of in such a way.

"She *is* set in her ways," said Elizabeth, hoping to put the matter to rest. "She will be content with her gossip and friends in Meryton. Mr. Bennet informs me that she was quite intimidated by all the 'fine ladies' she met at my father's house. Or at least she was when the reality of *who* they were set in."

The earl snorted at Elizabeth's characterization of his family, but his wife and Lady Catherine regarded him, the expressions daring him to say anything more. In that moment he proved the Fitzwilliam men were blessed with intelligence and discretion; he held his tongue.

"But it *is* well that you will have a relationship with the rest of the family who raised you," said Lady Catherine. "We are much in their debt for their care of you."

"I shall have a relationship with Mrs. Bennet too," said Elizabeth. She smiled warmly at William. "After all, my dear husband has purchased a wonderful gift for me, which means we may stay in the neighborhood whenever we please."

The earl looked at William askance. "My beloved wife is correct. Bingley gave up the lease on Netherfield in September last year, and it has sat empty since."

"It has been thus for many years now," said Elizabeth.

"As it is a good estate, we decided it would be a good investment, and allow us to visit the neighborhood whenever we like. So we purchased it."

"Should Anthony propose to Jane, we may all stay at Netherfield for the wedding," added Elizabeth.

"And your friend Bingley?" asked Lord Matlock, turning to William. "Is he recovered from his infatuation with Miss Bennet?"

A shaken head was William's response. "Bingley's infatuations never last long. When I saw him this spring, he waxed poetic about how he found her to be an angel on one occasion, but he did not seem interested in returning to Hertfordshire and pursuing her." William turned to look at Elizabeth. "Did Miss Bingley not say that she had some hope for her brother and a young lady of her acquaintance?"

"She did," replied Elizabeth. "I know not how much of that is wishful thinking and how much is fact."

"I am surprised you still speak with that woman," said Constance with a sniff.

"Now that she has been humbled, I have found her to be almost tolerable," said Elizabeth. "And her marriage has improved her further. We shall never be great friends, but I do not mind speaking with her as indifferent acquaintances."

"I believe Darcy was speaking of his friend," said Lord Matlock.

"There is little more to say," replied William, "I do not believe that Bingley will be an impediment to a marriage between Fitzwilliam and Miss Bennet. He will, no doubt, succumb to the charms of a woman one day, but I cannot say when that will be. Until then, he is content to move from one pretty lady to the next, enjoying their smiles until he tires of them."

"It is unseemly," muttered Lady Catherine.

"In some ways, it is," replied William. "But Bingley is a friend of longstanding, and as his sister is no longer an impediment to our friendship, I am loath to lose it."

"He is a good man," added Elizabeth. "But I would not call him the most constant of men."

"How do you find the new master of Harringward?" asked William. Elizabeth looked at him and noted he was eager to speak of something else. Few in the family approved of his friendship with Mr. Bingley, and as such he usually wished to avoid the subject.

"I find him much better than the old master," replied Lord Matlock. "A distant cousin, several times removed, as I recall. That side of the family had fallen from the ranks of gentlemen, and as I understand it, he had been working as the clerk of a country solicitor. But he is bright and eager to learn, and though he is inexperienced, I have no doubt that young Mr. Tisdale will be an admirable master of his estate."

"He could hardly be worse than the last," muttered James.

But Elizabeth hardly heard him, surprised as she was by her father's words. "Mr. Tisdale?" she asked, a hint of incredulity in her voice. "The new master of Harringward is Mr. Jonathan Tisdale?"

"I believe that is his name," said her father. "Are you acquainted with him?"

"I am sure that I am," said Elizabeth. "What a strange coincidence this is."

"How are you acquainted with our new neighbor, Elizabeth?" asked Lady Susan.

"He is—or was—employed by the Bennets' relation, Mr. Phillips. Mrs. Phillips is Mrs. Bennet's sister. He is the solicitor in Meryton, near Longbourn."

"Are you certain this is the same man?" asked William.

"I would have to meet him to be sure," said Elizabeth. "But I think it must be. The name is the same, and he was a clerk at a country solicitor." Her father nodded. "Then I hardly think there can be *two* men with the same name in similar employment circumstances. And the Mr. Tisdale that I knew was quite young. Perhaps no more than six or seven and twenty?"

This last was said to her father, who agreed. "Then it must be the same man. In fact . . ."

Elizabeth allowed a slow smile to spread over her countenance at the thought that had just occurred to her. "Well, well. How fortunate this is!"

"How so?" asked her mother curiously.

"We have long known that Mr. Tisdale admires Mary," replied Elizabeth, still smiling widely. "Mr. Phillips has no heir, as he had no children of his own, and Mr. Gardiner's children are much too young at present to be groomed as his successors. There has been talk that Mr. Phillips would make Mr. Tisdale the heir to his business, thereby allowing him to propose to Mary. Mrs. Bennet did not like the idea, as it would be a clear step down in status. But she is also pragmatic concerning the matter, as she has long considered Mary to be the most problematic in her ambition to marry all her daughters to eligible men."

"Harringward has suffered a little under Standish's ownership," said her father. "But once Mr. Tisdale learns what he must and returns it to full prosperity, she will not object any further. The estate should clear a good six thousand pounds if it is managed properly. Perhaps more."

"Well, well," repeated Elizabeth. "That is quite interesting, indeed. Mary informed me, through a letter Jane carried with her, that Mr. Tisdale had been obliged to leave Meryton due to a family matter, but I had never imagined the true reason for his departure."

"I do not wish to cast aspersions on the young man," said James, "but might it not be prudent to warn Miss Mary to temper her expectations? Many a young man has raised their sights when they come into good fortune."

"I believe all will be well," replied Elizabeth. "Though we never made much of it due to his situation, he has admired her from almost the time he arrived in the neighborhood. My father has the right of it— he is quite conscientious and sober, a perfect match for Mary. Once he feels he can manage the estate properly, I suspect he will return to Meryton for her. Or perhaps we could arrange a meeting between them. I wonder if I could persuade Mary to come later this year."

"It would be best to allow them to come to a resolution on their own," said William. "You, my beloved wife, seem to have developed a propensity for matchmaking since you were able to persuade Miss Bennet to come to us."

"I am no matchmaker, William," sniffed Elizabeth, feigning disdain. "I merely allow lovers to meet and have the opportunity to create an attachment."

The rest of the family looked at one another, and soon laughter was heard from among them. Elizabeth laughed along with them— William's jest had become a familiar one, and Elizabeth took every opportunity to use it to provoke further laughter. It was an activity she dearly loved, after all.

"Well, I am certain it shall all turn out as it should," said Elizabeth at length. "Mr. Tisdale can see to his own wooing—I doubt he will delay long."

"I am sure it will," said Lady Susan. "There is nothing wrong with giving a couple a little nudge every now and then, Elizabeth."

"The problem," interjected William drolly, "is when that nudge becomes a battering ram."

They all laughed again. "I am happy you have such a high opinion of my abilities, Husband!" cried Elizabeth. "You must think me clumsy in the application of my persuasion."

"I have nothing but confidence in your abilities, my dear," said William. "But I also have every confidence in your desire to do well by the people you called family for many years. It is commendable, but there is also danger of reaching too far."

Elizabeth reached to her husband and squeezed his hand fondly. "With you here to provide a check on my exuberance, I have no doubt all will be well."

For that moment, there seemed to be no one present but Elizabeth and Darcy. She smiled. Her life was now the way it was meant to be.

The End

PLEASE ENJOY THE FOLLOWING EXCERPT FROM THE UPCOMING NOVEL ON TIDES OF FATE, BOOK THREE OF THE EARTH AND SKY TRILOGY.

Wisteria was much as Terrace remembered. She was heavyset, though not quite overweight, with the brown hair and eyes of her people, and though her younger sister was delicate and slender, Wisteria was rather like a battering ram in comparison. She was not unattractive, but Terrace knew many men would be put off by her plainer features and the contemptuous curl of her lips. If, indeed, they had not already been put off by her domineering manner and poisonous tongue. With some interest, Terrace noted a few pockmarked scars on Wisteria's face, including one — quite deep — just under her left eye. Terrace wondered whether she had been in a battle of some kind.

There were a number of noble men and women standing by in the room, gazing on Terrace, as though wondering what she would do. Wisteria held her hand out to a nearby servant, who placed a goblet in her hand, backing away deferentially, almost genuflecting before the woman.

Terrace watched this scene with shock. Groundbreathers had never required such strong obeisance from their subjects. Most of those who lived in the castle were Groundbreathers themselves, descended from the same people who had originally been blessed by Terrain. Tillman's requirements for respect had been almost perfunctory in nature, though Sequoia had always been more stringent. But even *that* imperious woman, who Terrace knew to be a good person at heart, had not acted the way her oldest daughter did. The girl almost seemed to think that she was Terrain himself.

"Welcome, Aunt," Wisteria said, her contemptuous amusement not hidden when she paused to drink deeply from the goblet that had been provided to her. "To what do I owe the honor of this unannounced visit?"

"I am sure you understand exactly why I am here, Wisteria. I wish to know what happened to my brother, and I want to know what you have done with River."

Wisteria cocked her head to the side. "You were informed, were you not?"

"I was. But I would hear it from you nonetheless."

Wisteria shrugged. "It is as you were told. There was an attempt to take over the castle, and my father was an unfortunate casualty."

"You speak of him as if he was nothing more than a Groundwalker," Terrace spat. "He was *king* of our people!"

"You had best moderate your tone," the chamberlain said. "Your niece is to be addressed with the respect she deserves and referred to as 'Your Majesty.'"

"I changed her soiled linens when she was a child and swatted her bottom when she misbehaved," Terrace snapped. "You had best mind your manners, or my niece will need a new toady to do her bidding."

The man stiffened at the insult, but Terrace's glare must have been fierce enough that he knew better than to speak any further. The sullen glare he directed at her, however, informed Terrace that she had made an enemy. But she did not fear what a man who kissed her niece's feet could do, and she turned her stony gaze back on Wisteria.

"Well, Wisteria?" Terrace prompted. "I am waiting for your answer."

"I do not make light of my father's death," Wisteria responded. "I mourn his passing as much as anyone, but as *I* am the eldest and the leadership of our people must be maintained, I have put my personal feelings aside for the good of the people and so that I might act in obedience to Terrain."

Terrace glared at her niece. Wisteria had rarely been obedient to anyone, and Terrace had always thought her devotion to the earth god to be little more than superficial.

"Where is River?" Terrace asked, deciding a different tack was required. "Where are Sequoia and Tierra?"

Watching for Wisteria's reaction as she was, Terrace was not surprised when an expression of almost insane revulsion crossed the young woman's face. Wisteria had always hated Tierra with an antipathy so deep that Terrace suspected Wisteria would not shed a tear if Tierra fell over dead.

"My mother disappeared in the chaos," Wisteria replied, though her short tone indicated her patience was being exhausted. "As for River and *Tierra*, they are safe at present. That is all you need to know."

"River is my daughter, and I demand — "

"You are in a position to demand nothing!"

Aunt and niece glared at each other, neither giving an inch. Wisteria stared with cold eyes, her gaze almost seeming to bore through Terrace as though she were not even there. Belatedly, Terrace realized that this woman now held absolute power over the castle and its surrounding environs. These strange Iron Swords guaranteed that.

Wisteria would not be loved by her people. She did not have the ability to inspire such loyalty. Rather, she would rule by fear and her implacable will. Judging by the atmosphere in the throne room, she had already made a start down that path.

It was time to take greater care. Terrace could not do anything from the inside of a cell, and Wisteria would have no compunction about incarcerating her own aunt if her displeasure grew too great.

"I am merely concerned over my daughter," Terrace said. Her attempt at a conciliatory tone was likely an abject failure, but Terrace thought Wisteria would care more about outward respect than inner feelings.

"I know you are concerned," Wisteria replied, her grating attempt at a soothing tone nearly causing Terrace to grimace, "but at present, you must trust me. River will be returned to you, and I promise you she has not been harmed."

Terrace did not miss how Wisteria did not even attempt to mollify her concerning the fate of Tierra. "And when will that be?"

Again, Wisteria's composure cracked, though she controlled her tone. "That is yet to be determined. I will keep you informed of her status. At present, I believe it would be best to return to your home."

Though it galled Terrace to be forced to retreat in such a manner, there was nothing more to be done. "Very well. But I must insist you inform me the moment there is any news."

Terrace inclined her head in farewell and turned to leave, but she was arrested by the sound of Wisteria's voice.

"Aunt, I am afraid I must ask you to remember that my father is dead . . . and *I* am now the queen. My father's reign was marred by laxness, not only in the manner in which his subjects were allowed to behave, but also in . . . other matters that he championed before his death. I have restored the order of our kingdom now. I require all my subjects to behave properly, as our god would require it. I will not hesitate to enforce my dictates. Am I understood?"

Once again, Wisteria and Terrace stared at each other, Terrace searching for any hint of weakness. If there was any, it was well-hidden, for Wisteria's expression was unreadable. It appeared Tillman was correct after all. He had often mentioned his concerns over the fitness of his daughter to rule when he passed away, and Terrace could see nothing before her but the realization of those fears. Wisteria was not to be trifled with, and if she were not stopped, then she had the potential to become the worst despot in the history of their people.

"Perfectly," Terrace replied.

"Excellent! Then we shall see each other anon. Changes are coming,

Aunt, and we must do our part to bring about our god's designs."

Terrace nodded and turned to leave the room, her retinue trailing behind her. She did not understand what Wisteria meant concerning Terrain, but she feared it nonetheless. It was at times like this that she wished Heath was still with her. He had always known what to do, and he had possessed an instinctual ability to read others and determine their motivations with a single glance. Terrace missed him; she had loved and cherished him, and theirs had been a marriage of the hearts.

But there was no point in dwelling on her loss. Terrace had to take action. First, Terrace needed to try to find Sequoia. She was the key. If Terrace could find Sequoia, then Tierra and River could be located afterward.

But first, Terrace needed to involve Basil. As it was his fiancée who was missing, Basil had a direct interest in the matter, and Terrace would not leave him out of it.

And so Terrace departed the castle. But it would not be for the last time. She was now convinced that Wisteria had played a part in Tillman's demise. Terrace meant to find out what had happened to her brother. Wisteria would be held responsible, even if she had only failed to act to save him.

FROM ONE GOOD SONNET PUBLISHING

http://onegoodsonnet.com/

FOR READERS WHO LIKED
OUT OF OBSCURITY

Chaos Comes to Kent
Mr. Collins invites his cousin to stay at his parsonage and the Bennets go to Kent and are introduced to an amiable Lady Catherine de Bourgh. When Mr. Darcy and his cousin, Colonel Fitzwilliam, visit Lady Catherine at the same time, they each begin to focus on a Bennet sister, prodded by well-meaning relations, but spurred on by their own feelings.

Coincidence
Fitzwilliam Darcy finds Miss Elizabeth Bennet visiting her friend, Mrs. Collins, in Kent, only to realize that she detests him. It is not long before he is bewitched by her all over again, and he resolves to change her opinion of him and win her at all costs. Though she only wishes to visit her friend, Elizabeth Bennet is soon made uncomfortable by the presence of Mr. Darcy, who always seems to be near. As their acquaintance deepens, them much learn more about each other in order to find their happiness.

In the Wilds of Derbyshire
Elizabeth Bennet goes to her uncle's estate in Derbyshire after Jane's marriage to Mr. Bingley, feeling there is nothing left for her in Meryton. She quickly becomes close to her young cousin and uncle, though her aunt seems to hold a grudge against her. She also meets the handsome Mr. Fitzwilliam Darcy, and she realizes that she can still have everything she has ever wished to have. But there are obstacles she must overcome . . .

Netherfield's Secret
Elizabeth soon determines that her brother's friend, Fitzwilliam Darcy, suffers from an excess of pride, and it comes as a shock when the man reveals himself to be in love with her. But even that revelation is not as surprising as the secret Netherfield has borne witness to. Netherfield's secret shatters Elizabeth's perception of herself and the world around her, and Mr. Darcy is the only one capable of picking up the pieces. But will Elizabeth allow him to do so?

The Angel of Longbourn
When Elizabeth Bennet finds Fitzwilliam Darcy unconscious and suffering from a serious illness, the Bennets quickly return him to their house, where they care for him like he is one of their own. Mr. Darcy soon forms an attachment with the young woman he comes to view as his personal angel. But the course of true love cannot proceed smoothly, for others have an interest in Darcy for their own selfish reasons...

The Companion
A sudden tragedy during Elizabeth's visit to Kent leaves her directly in Lady Catherine de Bourgh's sights. With Elizabeth's help, a woman long-oppressed has begun to spread her wings. What comes after is a whirlwind of events in which Elizabeth discovers that her carefully held opinions are not infallible. Furthermore, a certain gentleman of her acquaintance might be the key to Elizabeth's happiness.

For more details, visit
http://www.onegoodsonnet.com/genres/pride-and-prejudice-variations

ALSO BY ONE GOOD SONNET PUBLISHING

THE SMOTHERED ROSE TRILOGY

BOOK 1: THORNY

In this retelling of "Beauty and the Beast," a spoiled boy who is forced to watch over a flock of sheep finds himself more interested in catching the eye of a girl with lovely ground-trailing tresses than he is in protecting his charges. But when he cries "wolf" twice, a determined fairy decides to teach him a lesson once and for all.

BOOK 2: UNSOILED

When Elle finds herself practically enslaved by her stepmother, she scarcely has time to even clean the soot off her hands before she collapses in exhaustion. So when Thorny tries to convince her to go on a quest and leave her identity as Cinderbella behind her, she consents. Little does she know that she will face challenges such as a determined huntsman, hungry dwarves, and powerful curses . . . .

BOOK 3: ROSEBLOOD

Both Elle and Thorny are unhappy with the way their lives are going, and the revelations they have had about each other have only served to drive them apart. What is a mother to do? Reunite them, of course. Unfortunately, things are not quite so simple when a magical lettuce called "rapunzel" is involved.

If you're a fan of thieves with a heart of gold, then you don't want to Miss . . .

The Princes and the Peas
A Tale of Robin Hood

A Novel of Thieves, Royalty, and Irrepressible Legumes

by Lelia Eye

An infamous thief faces his greatest challenge yet when he is pitted against forty-nine princes and the queen of a kingdom with an unnatural obsession with legumes. Sleeping on top of a pea hidden beneath a pile of mattresses? Easy. Faking a singing contest? He could do that in his sleep. But stealing something precious out from under "Old Maid" Marian's nose . . . now that is a challenge that even the great Robin Hood might not be able to surmount.

When Robin Hood comes up with a scheme that involves disguising himself as a prince and participating in a series of contests for a queen's hand, his Merry Men provide him their support. Unfortunately, however, Prince John attends the contests with the Sheriff of Nottingham in tow, and as all of the Merry Men know, Robin Hood's pride will never let him remain inconspicuous. From sneaking peas onto his neighbors' plates to tweaking the noses of prideful men like the queen's chamberlain, Robin Hood is certain to make an impression on everyone attending the contests. But whether he can escape from the kingdom of Clorinda with his prize in hand before his true identity comes to light is another matter entirely.

About the Author

Jann Rowland is a Canadian, born and bred. Other than a two-year span in which he lived in Japan, he has been a resident of the Great White North his entire life, though he professes to still hate the winters.

Though Jann did not start writing until his mid-twenties, writing has grown from a hobby to an all-consuming passion. His interests as a child were almost exclusively centered on the exotic fantasy worlds of Tolkien and Eddings, among a host of others. As an adult, his interests have grown to include historical fiction and romance, with a particular focus on the works of Jane Austen.

When Jann is not writing, he enjoys rooting for his favorite sports teams. He is also a master musician (in his own mind) who enjoys playing piano and singing as well as moonlighting as the choir director in his church's congregation.

Jann lives in Alberta with his wife of more than twenty years, two grown sons, and one young daughter. He is convinced that whatever hair he has left will be entirely gone by the time his little girl hits her teenage years. Sadly, though he has told his daughter repeatedly that she is not allowed to grow up, she continues to ignore him.

For more information on Jann Rowland, please visit:
http://onegoodsonnet.com.

67206334R00272

Made in the USA
Middletown, DE
19 March 2018